ANAM CARA

anam cara

ᘓ ᙠ

MARY T. KREMER

AONIAN PRESS
JAMES A. ROCK & COMPANY, PUBLISHERS
FLORENCE • SOUTH CAROLINA

Anam Cara by Mary T. Kremer

is an imprint of JAMES A. ROCK & CO., PUBLISHERS

Anam Cara copyright ©2009 by Mary T. Kremer

Special contents of this edition copyright ©2009
by James A. Rock & Co., Publishers

Address comments and inquiries to:

AONIAN PRESS
James A. Rock & Company, Publishers
900 South Irby Street, #508
Florence, South Carolina 29501

E-mail:
jrock@rockpublishing.com   lrock@rockpublishing.com
Internet URL: www.rockpublishing.com

ISBN-13/EAN: 978-1-59663-672-9

Library of Congress Control Number: 2008925485

Printed in the United States of America

First Edition: 2009

For

my Irish mother

the kindest, wisest

strongest

woman

You

are the

finite mentor

ACKNOWLEDGMENTS

A heartfelt appreciation to James A. Rock and Lynne Rock of Rock Publishing for taking a chance on a novice author. With experienced hands, professionalism, confidence and encouragement, they walked me through the baby-steps of my first published manuscript. Whatever success this novel enjoys, found its roots in their dedicated editing and publishing efforts.

New Orleans

The city was reluctant to wake. The early morning hours of Ash Wednesday had put an end to the weeklong celebration and New Orleans was nursing a monumental hangover. If abstinence didn't sober them up, Lent would.

The streets were nearly vacant. A mere handful of people with too little sense or too much guilt had dared to crawl from their nests and venture out. Only the street cleaners appeared to have any purposeful motivation as the machines swept last night's debris from the pavement and down the gutters.

The drone of the engines and whirr of the brushes wafted upwards and penetrated the slatted shutters of the buildings. Room 512 of the Beaumont Hotel was dark as a cave, the heavy drapes drawn to smother the morning sunlight. A ceiling fan slowly turned in an effort to circulate the muggy, stagnant air so familiar to New Orleans. Even in February.

Though the room was lightless, the woman snoring in the bed had a black sleep mask over her eyes. On any normal day, she rarely rose before noon and during Mardi Gras, she wouldn't stir before four. It had been a long week and even longer night. Partying and self-indulgence could be exhausting and she slept soundly, oblivious to the noisy street sweepers or any other sound that found its way into her room.

Chicago

Biting winds howled off Lake Michigan, the sun non-existent behind a curtain of clouds. Traffic moved steadily as people began their day of work or shopping or merely trying to survive another icy northern winter. Three-foot-high piles of packed snow clung to the curbs and buildings. Only two days before, Chicago had dug itself out from the fourth blizzard of the season. Everyone wondered when spring would arrive even the man huddled in the marina, trying not to freeze. Cloudy puffs of air condensed as he blew into his gloved hands. He felt no particular animosity toward winter, per se. It wasn't personal. It was simply that winter stood between him and the warm winds of summer.

In spite of the freezing temperature in the boathouse, his eyes sparkled as he looked upward studying the sailboat that hung from the hoist. God, she was magnificent. A thirty-two-foot sleek beauty of brass, teak and nautical engineering. He had ordered the boat last spring and she was every bit as gorgeous

1

as he had imagined. He was so close, now. A month, maybe less, and she would be on her way home and the snug slip that waited patiently. It would be an unnatural journey for her, across land, but necessary. Eden Lake, Michigan was land-locked and there was no way to sail her home.

He stomped his feet to coax some circulation into his extremities. But neither the wait nor the temperature could dampen his mood. A broad smile, a mixture of admiration and pleasure, spread across his face. He was reluctant to leave her, like a lover that willed the night to never end.

Eden Croft

Even though ice cycles hung from the eaves like Yeti's teeth and a gentle and a silent snow was falling, it was warm and sultry as the tropics inside the solarium.

The man rose slowly. His legs felt older than their years and were cramped from tending the bed of staghorn ferns that he had just finished thinning. Turning a critical eye toward the ferns, he critiqued his morning's task. The exercise was unnecessary. His handiwork was always meticulous.

He was totally unaware of the particulars on the outside or the days on the calendar, only that they marked one of the four seasons. Soon, winter would evaporate into spring. With the arrival of the warmer months, he would be able to lift the great walls of glass and open the solarium to the fresh air so long denied.

He looked about his quiet world of plants, trees and flowers. He could almost imagine the homogenous sound of respiration coming from the plants, but there was no sound save the soft rush of air of his own breath. He preferred it that way. Human voice and activity were not welcome and he would have considered them intrusive. The vegetation was company enough.

There were no classes scheduled on Wednesdays. Stacks of uncorrected tests and thesis presentations littered his office. But those could wait. That day, he had no desire for paperwork or responsibility. He needed the therapy of the gardens to replenish his soul. He would finish pruning in time to make the afternoon department meeting.

℃₈ ℞

Whether the woman, or the man, or the professor believed in fate, kismet, destiny, the synchronic laws of Nature or the hand of God didn't matter. The precise set of events that would forever change their lives was already in motion. Their three individual paths were about to converge. Like three meteors on pre-destined courses, their worlds were about to collide. And none of them would ever be the same again.

2

chapter one

St. Christopher was really getting on her nerves and was dangerously close to being banished to the dark recesses of the glove compartment. See how well he would fare confined in tight quarters with a boisterous youngster.

For three days he had stood there on the dashboard of the De Soto calm, cool and annoyingly smug, as though he had cornered the market on unflappable composure while being cooped up, mile after endless mile, for three days with four noisy boys.

She resisted the knee-jerk reaction to toss him into the glove compartment or stick her tongue out at him. It bordered on sacrilege and would have been childish and exactly the sort of thing one of the twins would have done. Besides, he had answered her prayers and brought them this far safely and incident free; no flat tires, no collisions, no breakdowns. The trailer hadn't come unhitched and careened off into a ditch spilling all their worldly possessions like discarded rubbish. At the very least, she should be grateful for that and not sentence him to exile. Instead, she released the death grip she had on the steering wheel and gently turned him to face the highway.

Come on, Chris, she mentally cheered him on. *This is the last day. Don't let me down now.*

The steady motion of the car and the warm mid-morning sun transformed the car into a snug cocoon and had lulled Tommy and the twins to sleep in the back seat. The last thing she wanted was to stop the car and risk disturbing them. Her patience had been completely exhausted. And that was saying something because her ma always said she had the patience of a saint.

Yet, even she had reached the point where she could not bear to hear one more "he's touching me" or "he's crossed over the line into my space" or one more, "are we almost there?" But, she desperately needed to find a restroom and stretch her cramped, tensed muscles. Besides, the mayonnaise jars were nearly full and needed to be emptied.

Katie's tension had increased gradually during the past three days as she and her little brood came closer to the strange, the alien and unknown. *What ifs* and *maybes* had become as repetitious to her as the endless white line of the highway. *What if the move was a huge mistake? What if Brendan never forgave her? What if she could never forgive herself? Maybe her expectations had been too high. Maybe she had committed them to a foolish scheme that was doomed to fail. What then?*

The three days of driving had left her with far too much time to think. She realized that sometimes thinking could be dangerous and could go on for too long. Sometimes it could carry a person to dark and scary places.

Like the tumblers in a lock, silent but precise, the memories of the past year and a half whirled through her mind. Danny's death and the long months since had stripped her of passion and purpose. The end result was a harsh reality and the facts hit her in the face like a wave of icy water. It was painfully clear that somewhere in those months she had lost her way. More frightening than that, she had lost herself.

That loss, perhaps more than any other, had caused her, the greatest regret. The agonizing truth was Mary Katherine O'Neill did not like the person she had become. She tried to avoid the eyes of the stranger who stared back at her in the rear view mirror and her stomach pitched every time she caught a glimpse of her panicked reflection.

A deep sigh escaped her as her thoughts drifted back to the war years and swirled through her mind like confetti of photographs tossed in the wind. As a new bride and an even newer mother, she had dealt with the anxiety, worry and realization that Danny might never come home. She had witnessed first hand the devastation of loss as friends, neighbors and even family had their hearts rent with the death of a husband, a father, a brother or son. No one had been immune. The war had touched everyone and every part of their lives.

Each day that ended without the arrival of the dreaded telegram confirmed that Danny was still alive. As she traced his steps through Europe with pins on the map that had hung on the kitchen wall, each *X*, each pin marked his steady progress home. There was a purpose and meaning to the wait as days turned into weeks, into months, into years. Then she had hope and promise, now, only a biting, raw reality.

Katie shook her head trying to dismiss the recreant thoughts. She loathed self-pity in others and found it even more unattractive in herself. It was self-defeating and all consuming until it choked out any room for renascence. Yet, all too often, in the past months, she had found herself wallowing in it—another foreign, despicable characteristic she had adopted. It was another personal demon with which she had to struggle.

As she chased away the scary realities of the present, Katie let her mind seek the more comforting memories of the past. A hint of a smile coaxed her lips as she recalled those warm memories. She relived the immense elation of 1945 when her prayers had been answered. After four long years, Danny did come home from the war, safe and whole. And with his homecoming, they resumed their lives dismissing the past four years as nothing more than an unpleasant dream. They had again found paradise.

The loneliness and worries of the war years dissolved quickly replaced by the challenges and rewards of family life. Danny and Brendan, separated when Brendan was not yet one, were reintroduced and the delayed bond between father and son formed and flourished. She and Danny became reacquainted; their love story reaffirmed and resumed. Their little family grew quickly and within a year Tommy came. Two weeks after the doctor gave her the nod to resume sexual relations she was pregnant with the twins.

For Katie, it was a storybook life. She was content and happy.

Then, her entire universe was smashed to pieces. Only six years after the war ended, Danny was killed in a car accident coming home from work. In a single instant, Katie's world collapsed, leaving her a widow of thirty-one and her four young sons fatherless.

She could still recall the policeman's words as he recounted the accident that had ripped Danny away from them and tearing away a part of her. Like the precise, sterile incision of a surgeon's scalpel, that vital part of her being had been cleanly excised and in its place, remained a deep, raw, aching gash.

She had burned that memory into her mind, punishing herself by reliving it over and over again. She pictured the young policeman in his crisp navy blue uniform with brass buttons that glinted in the sunlight when he moved in just the right way. The spit polished black boots that he focused on when he lowered his eyes, unable to find the mettle to look her in the eyes. She could still see his curly, short cropped hair when he politely removed his hat. The way he played continuously with the hat, turning it around and around, nervously in his hands as he perched precariously on the edge of the sofa, like a frightened bird anxious to take flight.

He had seemed so young, no more than a mere lad himself, less like a police*man*, more of a police*boy*, with smooth, freckled skin. He had fumbled and stammered nervously trying to find the right words, too naive and inexperienced to know that there were no right words. She remembered how strange and inexplicable it was, that she actually felt as though he needed consolation more than she.

Katie squinted her eyes, trying to shut out the memory of devastation of that day and the beginning of a terrifying nightmare, a nightmare that didn't end with the promise of morning.

She had stumbled through the aftermath with bared emotions and raw senses. At times it seemed to go on forever, and yet, she could not discern one specific day from another, as loss, anguish and heartache melded together as one. It was as though a cyclone had swooped down, spun her world upside down and spat her out, all in a matter of a few, horrifying moments.

Her personal heartache and grief hadn't had the chance to run its curative course. The immediate needs and demands of the boys pushed aside her needs. She had four sons to raise, expenses to deal with and all with absolutely no idea how she was going to do it. She had barely enough money coming in and even less emotional support. Katie finally managed to throw off the shroud of grief that was strangling her to focus on the present. The ever-present, desperate need for money replaced her grief and nagged at her with the urgency of a hungry child.

Katie had been an only child and the war had left Danny an only child, too, claiming his two older brothers. Both of their parents had passed away and, excluding a handful of neighbors and friends, Katie was alone.

With the exception of Dee and Moira.

The thought of her two closest friends brought a smile to her face.

What a crazy threesome they had been. Friends since kindergarten, Dee and Moira had become her surrogate sisters. Though the three were as different as lava and ice, they were inseparable. Like the random pieces of a jigsaw puzzle that fit together perfectly to complete the picture.

Moira was the incurable, passionate romantic, Katie the gentle, sensitive, emotional one. Dee (short for Dorothy), the pragmatic, rational, practical one who at the ripe age of eighteen made the declaration that "she refused to be likened to a whiny teenager who wore ruby slippers, associated with three social misfits and carried around a yippy mutt named Toto."

Katie envisioned the countless antics through their school years, their weddings, and being godmothers to each other's children. They had raised their families together in the same neighborhood. Dee and Moira had been her salvation when Danny died. In fact, it had been Dee who was finally able to slap Katie out of mourning and into reality. But even the closest friendships had limitations. While Dee and Moira had provided her ready shoulders to cry and lean on, they could offer her no long-term solutions. They couldn't solve her money problems.

She had no training or skills, unless one considered potty training a skill, and certainly there were few job prospects for a mother with four young sons. Married within months of her high school graduation, Katie had gone from being a daughter, to being a wife, to being a mother and had never considered the possibility that someday those distinctions would not be enough.

Again, the concerns of the present crept into her thoughts and with them, her stomach roiled and churned. Katie needed a mental distraction to dilute the burning bile of panic that percolated inside her. She forced herself to concentrate on the unfamiliar, yet beautiful scenery.

On the brisk morning that heralded the fourth and final day of the journey, Katie noted that spring had made its appearance early. The temperature was crisp, yet the sun's radiance and warmth affirmed that winter had bowed to defeat. The trees had not yet leafed out, but eager buds had popped, ripe and ready, waiting to burst open with their summertime greenery.

Along the tree-lined road she spotted a small clearing with a bit of a roadside park. With relief, she noted it came complete with a picnic table and outhouse. As she steered the car and led the trailer carefully onto the shoulder, the gravel crunched under the weight of the tires. With the car in park, she pulled on the emergency brake. The sudden intermission from the steady hum of the highway grabbed the attention of the malcontent sharing the front seat with her.

Brendan had staked out his territory in the first mile since leaving Boston. Not to be dissuaded by the limited confines of the sedan, he had intentionally placed as much physical distance as possible between himself and his mother. He slumped against the passenger door, face partially hidden by the brim of his Red Sox ball cap and behind the pages of the latest *Superman* comic book.

She was certain that he must have memorized every word by now, and was merely using it as a ruse to avoid conversation. If he wanted to be left alone, then so be it. She was tired of having all her efforts greeted with monosyllabic grunts at best and his grumbled complaints at worst. Well, if it provided him a subterfuge for his anger and frustration, then it was twenty-five cents well spent.

Brendan broke his apparent oath of silence from his throne beside her. "Why are we stopping here? The squirrels finally shut-up and fell asleep. Now they're gonna wake up and go at it all over again."

As she turned off the ignition, Katie bit back the harsh words and sighed deeply. "Don't take that tone with me, young man. At the moment, you may not like me very much, but I'm still your mother and deserve some respect. And please don't say shut-up. It's rude."

She wanted to avoid another tiresome lecture and changed her direction. "I'm sorry we have to stop, but I really need to take a short break and use the bathroom ... and I need to empty the mayonnaise jars."

Brendan scrunched up his face in disgust and complained, "That's so sick. I can't believe I'm stuck riding around in this car for a gazillion miles with two jars of pee."

Katie winced at the *P* word and searched for an ounce of patience and understanding. "Brendan, I know that this move is scary and frightening for you ..."

Brendan argued, "I'm not scared."

"Okay. Wrong choice of words. Perhaps angry and upset are better. I'm angry and upset, too. And *I am* scared. I know that this move has been the hardest on you. Uprooting you from the neighborhood, your school and your friends ..."

Brendan interrupted her with emphasis. "And just when baseball season was gonna start."

She conceded the point and continued, "... just before baseball season started, carting us a thousand miles away from home, to a strange town, a strange house and strange people. It was not an easy decision for me to make.

"I know how difficult this must be for you to accept, but we talked this over a hundred times and I decided that it was the only choice we had. There weren't any other options."

Katie flinched at the words *choice* and *options*. By definition, there had been no choice, no options. Only submission.

She had worked all the numbers. Even with the Social Security check, the mortgage payments and taxes gobbled up her meager savings and her nest egg had dwindled to almost nothing. No matter how many times she added up the columns, the totals grew no closer. It was either sell the house or lose it and any equity it had accumulated. The only money that remained untouched was Danny's life insurance death benefit and the equity the house had earned. She and Danny had solemnly promised each other that if the boys wanted to go to college, that money was designated for that purpose and that purpose alone. Katie would starve before she would touch one penny of either.

Her tone softened as the twins stirred in the back seat. "Almost all of our savings are gone. We don't have enough money coming in. We couldn't survive from hand to mouth forever. In a few months we would have lost the house as well. Do you know how lucky we are to have a home to go to? Free and clear? No mortgage payments. Not everyone is as fortunate as we are that we have that to fall back on. I don't expect you to like it right off, but I do expect you to try. I need your understanding and acceptance most of all."

Tears stung at Katie's eyes as she fought desperately not to let them spill. Brendan had seen enough of her tears over the past year and a half. Unfortunately, he was old enough to recognize their financially desperate situation but too young to be able to do anything about it. He was a thirteen-year-old boy, feeling it necessary to be grown up when he wasn't grown up at all. He should have been happily rolling along, chasing fly balls ... and girls ... and the dreams that every young teenage boy had the right to dream.

"We had the money from my paper route and mowing lawns and shoveling snow."

Katie's heart warmed immediately with his generosity and naiveté. "Don't think I didn't appreciate your sacrifice. It was a big help. It just wasn't enough to cover all the bills."

"You could'a got a job."

Immediately Katie's stomach turned as if she had swallowed a quart of curdled milk. Of course she had considered that. Dee had introduced that possibility months ago. But hearing it from Brendan, the statement stung like an accusation.

"We're not having this discussion again, Bren. I would have scrubbed floors or cleaned toilets to put food on the table. Only four small problems. Who would take care of you boys? You've lost your father and I refuse to have you grow up without a mother as well. I've made the decision and right or wrong we're all going to have to live with it. I try to think that things always work out for the best. We'll simply have to try to see the positive in this, too."

Katie's bladder forced her to change the subject and avoid an argument that was pointless. "I'll only be a few minutes, just long enough to stretch a bit. You can slip out of the car for a while too," she added.

Angry and defeated, Brendan only grunted and turned back to his comic book.

Katie exited the car as quietly as she could, retrieved the mayonnaise jars from the floor of the back seat. She stole a quick look at her three, peaceful, sleeping angels and thought to herself how unbelievably deceptive appearances could be.

After relieving herself and emptying the jars, she strolled back to the park. With arms spread wide she stretched her back and neck until her face turned upwards to the sky. The newborn spring sun penetrated her sweater and thin cotton housedress. It felt warm and comforting and she thought that she could stand there forever, letting the rays sink deep, washing through to every weary muscle and aching bone. If only it could seep into her mind and soul.

She tried to envision the home waiting for them, beckoning them to begin again within its snug walls. Crisp white curtains on every door and a yard that would allow the boys room to play, and for her, a small flower garden. Her vision depicted a cozy cottage on a quiet lake, its chimney cheerily puffing and smoke curling from its depths instead of dollar signs.

While the vision still danced in her mind, Katie made up her mind. No more sniveling breakdowns. No more holding her breath waiting for life to throw her another curve ball. No more wasting her energy wishing for things that could never be.

Being an immobilized bystander no longer appealed to her. With resolve and determination she made up her mind that the Katie of the present no longer existed and the Katie of the past was lost forever. Self-reproach and self-recrimination were pointless. Beyond that, they were destructive because after a while one starts to believe them. She couldn't change the circumstances of her past; she couldn't erase the realities of the present. Those were the facts. However, she did have the opportunity to affect the future.

For the first time in months, no matter how inept or precarious, she would be the one in control, the one making the decisions; she was finally acting instead of reacting. She would no longer allow herself to entertain the possibility of failure. She would *make* this their fresh start, their new beginning. She automatically made the sign of the Cross and mouthed a silent prayer that she would somehow find a way to make everything right.

Her thoughts were interrupted as Brendan hollered from the open car window. "Mom, Tommy woke up and now he's going to wake up the twins. Can we p-e-l-e-a-s-e get going?"

Katie muttered, "Well, if Tommy doesn't wake them up, your shouting certainly will."

She signaled that she was coming. Katie delayed a few seconds and tried to capture as much of the clear, sweet, spring air as she could. Perhaps she could absorb enough of nature's nectar of rebirth to re-ignite her soul. Maybe this glorious spring day was a sign from above that everything would work out.

03 &0

As she measured their inch-by-inch progress on the map, Katie calculated that they had little more than a half-hour to go. She consulted the road map spread out between her and Brendan and verified that she was indeed on course and relieved that they were approaching their last few miles.

Katie wanted to arrive before dark and noted the shadows lengthening as the sun began its steady descent to her west. She was immediately excited and at the same time a bit anxious. Relieved to finally see the end of their long journey but scared witless of the unknown.

Brendan suddenly spun around and growled at Casey through clenched teeth, "Quit kicking the back of my seat, you little jerk, or I'll let you have it!"

"I ain't kickin' your dumb seat. Colin is."

"Liar. Am not."

"You am too."

"I ain't even sittin' in back of him. You are."

Brendan growled again, "Great. Then I'll let both of you have it."

Katie intervened, "No one is going to let anyone have it. Casey or Colin or both of you, quit kicking the back of the seat. The next one that does will spend the rest of the trip in the trunk."

"How come Bren gets to sit in the front seat all the time?" Casey questioned.

Katie responded, "Because he's the oldest."

"I'm gonna get sick," Casey warned.

"Idle threat. You don't get carsick," Katie dismissed him.

"I'm gonna barf all over," he persisted.

Bren turned and swatted at him. "You better not, Moron."

Katie ignored Brendan's comment. "You tried that two days ago, Casey. It didn't work then and it won't work today."

Annoyed and rebuffed, Casey landed one solid kick at the back of the seat.

"We're bored. There's nothin' to do back here," he complained.

"Color with your crayons or look at one of your picture books," Katie suggested.

"We done all that an' it's boring. How come Bren gots a comic book an' we got these old, crummy color books?"

"Brendan can read and you can't, that's why."

For what Katie figured was the thousandth time, Casey whined, "How much further do we gotta go?"

Colin added, "Yeah, are we pretty near there, yet?"

Katie thought that patience was a virtue wasted on youth. Happy for the first time in four days, she was thrilled to announce, "We are almost there, only a few more miles." She added quickly, "Let's play a guessing game. I'll ask the questions and you can take turns answering. That will make the time pass more quickly."

Casey excitedly called out, "Me first!"

"You always think you kin go first," argued Colin, "jus' 'cuz you wuz borned first."

"Casey, let's let Colin go first this time." Katie settled the dispute. "How many states have we traveled through to get to Eden Croft?"

Colin was stumped. So were Casey and Tommy. Brendan knew, but he wasn't about to play the dumb game.

Allowing them a full thirty seconds to respond, Katie finally said, "We have passed through Massachusetts. ..."

Casey jumped in, "That's where Boston is. Massatusetts."

Katie kept them on track. "That's right. And after Massachusetts came New York ... then Pennsylvania ... Ohio ... and finally ..."

All three chimed, "Michigan!"

"Now, it's Casey's turn. What state is Eden Croft in?"

After a moment of arguing that the question was way too easy, Casey proudly announced, "Michigan!"

"Now, Tommy. What shape is Michigan?"

His little freckled face reflected that he was thinking very hard, then, with recognition, he beamed and cried, "Jus' like a mitten!"

"Two mittens," Katie corrected him. "Take your left hands and hold them up. Now take your right hands and lay them sideways over your left. That is what Michigan is shaped like."

The little boys did as their mom had instructed and studied their hands.

"Mommy," Tommy asked, "Does Michigan have snow like Boston? And is there an ocean?"

Disgusted by the whole stupid game, Brendan barked, "You guys are all stupid. Michigan isn't anything like Boston. It doesn't have an ocean, 'cuz it's in the middle of nowhere. And it doesn't have the Red Sox, 'cuz it's got the crummy Tigers. And it doesn't have any of the guys like Kevin or Brian or Tony, 'cuz it's only got hicks."

"What's a hick?" Casey asked.

Before Katie could answer, Brendan snatched the opportunity. "A hick is a backward yokel that lives in a shack and wears raggedy clothes and howls at the moon like a werewolf. They eat possum and skunks and rats and anything else that moves. They mostly like juicy little squirrels like you and when they catch 'em, they skin 'em alive then eat 'em raw."

Shock and fear so real it was palpable descended on the gullible occupants of the backseat.

In an effort to suppress the murderous thoughts that crossed her mind, Katie counted to ten, then for good measure, backward to one again.

Finally, she intervened and nearly shouted, "That's enough, Brendan, They're not hicks at all, just normal people like us who eat the same food we eat, wear the same clothes we wear and do not skin and eat little boys raw, or anything else for that matter."

Brendan snapped back, "Doesn't matter. It's not gonna be like Boston and I'm never gonna like it."

"Bren, you're only partly right. No, it doesn't have the Sox or Fenway Park, or the old neighborhood or any of your old friends. And it doesn't have an ocean. So, let's concentrate on what it does have, like lots of lakes, and we'll be living right on one of those lakes. And isn't a lake almost like an ocean, only smaller?"

Katie tried to sound enthusiastic. "Michigan even has lakes so big you can't see from one side to the other, just like the ocean. And it has seasons like we had in Boston. They get lots of snow in the winter for sledding and building snowmen. Their summers are warm and since we'll be living right on the lake you'll be able to fish and swim all summer long. In the fall, we'll rake leaves and you can make leaf forts. Our yard will be so much bigger than our yard on Delancey Street. You'll have plenty of room to play without worrying about Mrs. Sweeney getting mad at you when your balls landed in her vegetable garden."

Her enthusiasm was contagious.

Tommy piped in, "I'm gonna pretend it's just like Boston."

Katie smiled as she looked in the rear view mirror. Leave it to Tommy to try to see the best in everything. His rosy disposition could charm the pants off anyone, even cranky old Mrs. Sweeney who was never charmed by anyone or anything.

"Michigan's sure got a lotta trees," Colin noted.

"A lot of trees and a lot of hicks," Brendan mumbled.

Katie noticed that this stretch of scenery was quite pretty. She couldn't remember ever seeing quite so many evergreens and pines before. She watched as stand after stand of the beautifully deep green trees passed by. There must have been acres and acres of them covering the hilly landscape, interrupted only by an occasional farm or orchard.

These weren't scrawny, wind-blown, or sparse like the loblolly pines along the Cape coast, but verdant and dense with thick, heavily needled branches. Their lush arms formed a canopy, sheltering and protecting a nursery beneath where a tiny forest of soft, green, lacy ferns was springing to life. Katie enjoyed the fragrance that permeated the car through the open window, clean, almost pungent.

A quick flurry of anticipation tickled her tummy as she noted increasing signs of civilization. On her left, she noticed there were more mailboxes and driveways, though she couldn't see any houses. The drives disappeared into the darkness of pines and hardwoods that obviously hid the houses.

If town center was on the northwest shore of the lake, she concluded that the lake must be off to their left, though she couldn't catch a glimpse of that, either. Off to the right of the road was a huge meadow that yawned and stretched until it butted against yet another stand of magnificent evergreens.

She craned her neck at the next crossing and read the sign that assured her she was indeed on Lakefield Road. She studied her hand-written note secured to the dashboard by St. Christopher and with a quickening in her chest, realized how close they must be. Around the next curve in the road, she read the road sign that pointed to her left. *Eden Croft 3 miles.*

She had memorized the directions, from reading them over and over again, "… the fifth mailbox after the sign …" She slowed the car down to a near creep, not wanting to miss the drive.

"Could you please help me out?" She asked Brendan. "We need to find the mailbox that reads *Donovan*. It should be the fifth one we come to."

Brendan, sensing the excitement in her voice, realized how close they actually were. Anxiously, he turned his attention to her side of the road. He counted to himself, "Two … three … four …" and cried out almost simultaneously with Katie, "five! There it is Mom!"

Over a thousand miles, five states and four long, exhaustive days, there it was. Their ray of hope, their safety net, their future, resting on a plain white mailbox, seemingly in the middle of nowhere, with a crisply painted sign, nearly hidden by a cluster of cedars. In dark green lettering, it read DONOVAN.

Katie gingerly turned the car and trailer loaded with their precious possessions and guided them onto the macadam drive. She fought the itch to press the pedal to the floor and bring a hurried conclusion to this mysterious, nerve-racking migration. But composure, not impulsiveness was required at the moment. To risk a disastrous accident at this point was foolhardy. Still, she noted that her palms were sweaty, her knuckles white, and the steering wheel sticky wet in her grasp. She nervously let out a wisp of air and thought, *I wasn't this nervous on my wedding night.*

As she inched the car down the winding drive, she became impatient that she couldn't see the house or the lake. Dappled sunlight danced on the hood of the car as the rays occasionally broke through the tunnel of branches that spread out from the trees. Finally, after what seemed a small eternity, the car emerged from a tree-shrouded bend. Katie gently pressed on the brake pedal. She looked sideways at Brendan, mirroring his look of shock. She swallowed back the butterflies that fluttered in her throat.

In awe, craning his head out the window, Casey announced, "If this is where hicks live, hicks ain't *nothin'* like us!"

Five pairs of eyes widened as five chins dropped with mouths agape. Casey's observation was a monumental understatement. Never, with all the foresight and planning, had Katie been prepared for this. All her newfound strength, determination, will and resolve seemed to drain completely from her in one mass exodus.

The quaint cottage she had envisioned only hours before was accurate in only one small detail and the picture dissolved from her thoughts. There wouldn't be dollar signs but twenty-dollar bills that would float skyward from its chimneys. All four of them.

She automatically made the sign of the Cross with a numb right hand. More of a plea than a prayer, she muttered, "Holy Mary, Mother of God … Aunt Katherine, what have you gotten me into?"

chapter two

Katie thought it wasn't as large as the compounds in Hyannis or on the Cape but that was being petty. Any slight differences in size were insignificant and moot. By any comparison, it was immense.

The two stories of white clapboard seemed to spread out in all directions under the green gabled roof. It had steep Victorian eaves and two large bay windows that stretched from first floor to roof. Second floor turrets worthy of Rapunzel capped them. The front of the house actually faced the lake, while the rear faced the drive.

Like mighty bookends, on either ends of the house stood four, sturdy, enormous limestone chimneys. Beveled or leaded glass graced every window. Gingerbread trim gave it the appearance of a huge, frosted wedding cake. An ornately carved, pair of double oak doors, complete with oval, top-to-bottom beveled glass greeted one as the main entry. The entire package was tied up neatly in a deep, wrap-around porch that circled the entire house.

The house was built on a small bluff, with a broad, sweeping lawn that terraced down and ended at the wide, sugary-sand beach. Just like a lacy Victorian valentine, a snowy white gazebo, trimmed with delicate curlicues and graceful moldings crowned a small grassy knoll. Katie decided that someone had made a wise decision, for the view from the house to the water's edge and beyond to the lake, was spectacular.

In contrast to the house and gazebo, the lake was a deep cobalt blue under the clear spring sky with lacy peaks of whitecaps dancing across the surface. The remaining sunlight shimmered on the water's surface like a scattering of a million diamonds. The steady sound of the waves beat against the shoreline, carrying with them the distinct scent of the lake. The opposite shoreline, several miles across, was just visible as its greenery jutted upward atop high sand dunes. Katie couldn't have known that only two weeks before, the last scattered patches of ice still floated on the lake like the gray remnants of a crazy quilt.

The house belonged to another place, another time. Yet, to Katie, it instantly felt like a place that she could call home, and from the first moment she saw it, knew it would be impossible to keep. That realization would make leaving it behind all the more heartbreaking.

While Tommy and the twins explored the property like sailors too long at sea, Katie and Brendan stood at the water's edge. Even disgruntled Brendan thought that maybe the move's sole purpose wasn't to make him as miserable as possible.

"So, Brendan, what do you think of it?" Katie's voice held a wary edge.

"I guess it's okay."

"Okay? Okay is the best you can do?"

He replied, "The lakes kind'a neat."

"It is neat."

"The house is sort'a big."

Katie nearly choked, "Sort'a? It's enormous. We'll never be able to manage it, Bren."

"What d'ya mean?"

Katie sighed deeply. "I mean it's enormous. I can't help thinking how expensive it must be to keep up. I barely had the money to pay the utilities and taxes on our small home in Boston. There is no way I could manage this place. We don't have that kind of money. It would be impossible."

Brendan turned his gaze from the lake to his mom. "Do you mean we aren't staying? Are we going back to Boston?"

She laid a hand on his shoulder. "Oh, Bren. I hate to say it, but, yes, I guess that means we'll have to go back to Boston. What else can we do?"

He shrugged her hand off. "Then why'd we leave at all? Why'd you make us come all this ways? We don't even have a home in Boston no more. You sold it."

"I know I did, you don't have to remind me. It seems that you and Mrs. Sullivan were right. The whole idea of moving here was ridiculous. I should have listened to you."

"Dad would'a listened to me. He wouldn't a done nothin' this dumb. He'd a figured something out. Dad would'a let us stay in Boston." Brendan's words were filled with venom and they cut deep.

"Well, your dad isn't here. I am. So I guess you're stuck with me."

Brendan started to walk away, "I'm gonna go sit in the car."

"We're not starting back, *now!*" she exclaimed.

He whined, "Why not? If we can't stay here then I say we leave right now."

"I need a few days, some time to try and figure things out. I need to meet with the lawyer and decide what we're going to do next."

As Brendan walked away he called back to her, "Don't bother. Whatever you come up with will end up being a big, fat mess."

03 80

The first two days absolutely flew by in a frenzy of tasks and chores. Katie busied herself with the necessities of settling in, for however short that tenuous stay would be. What had initially started as numbing disbelief had translated into deep dread; what held promise of her salvation had turned into a fiasco.

The first few moments that disgruntled Brendan had reluctantly showed subtle signs that he might eventually adjust to the move had disappeared. Silence had replaced any further conversation. For two days he and Katie hadn't exchanged more than a handful of words. The thought of how she had failed them, once again, that the move had been one big, disastrous mistake, nagged her every waking moment and haunted her restless sleep. But, first things first and Katie felt the need to stay as busy as possible.

Mr. Mulholland, Aunt Katherine's attorney, had been absolutely right. Through correspondence, he had assured her that the house was completely self-contained, from kitchenware, to furnishings, to lawn tools. White, sheer curtains adorned the windows and the linen closets were fully stocked with towels, table linens, bedding and thick, downy quilts.

None of the furnishings were new, but Katie could tell quality when she saw it. Items had obviously been carefully selected for both durability and comfort. The entire house was warm, inviting and spoke of a lived-in hominess.

There were floral chintz fabrics in the bedrooms, sunroom and upstairs sitting room. A huge living room and smaller parlor, both with fireplaces and filled with well-placed furniture, invited intimacy and echoed with the sounds and memories of generations of family gatherings. Canvas white and nautical blue slipcovers swaddled overstuffed sofas and chairs transforming them into welcoming cradles that begged one to snuggle in.

The kitchen and dining room were light and airy with carved, ornate, mellowed oak trim. Scatter rugs and carpets lay over rich hardwood floors that shone with preservation and care. The house had stood up to the test of time and its character had not only lasted, but had grown richer with age. The whole effect was anything but modern or sophisticated and Katie immediately fell in love with it.

Fourteen rooms total. The boys had counted. Exploring the house had been an adventure, a treasure hunt, each door opened onto a new discovery. Each massive room boasted ten-foot tall ceilings. All four fireplaces, one upstairs and three down, were framed with carved oak mantels and moldings.

Along with the living room, dining room and kitchen, a back entranceway, front foyer, sunroom and a small bath composed the first floor. An open oak staircase, wide enough to accommodate three persons walking abreast, led to the second floor. Tommy, Casey and Colin immediately claimed the banister as their own, private, indoor slide.

Upstairs were five bedrooms, two bathrooms and a sitting room off the master bedroom. The boys would no longer have to be cramped into one bedroom.

Though the house was completely furnished, marketing and stocking the pantry were still a priority. The few food provisions Katie had packed for the journey had run out and while their external necessities were supplied, she needed to provide for their nutritional needs. She left the boys in Brendan's care and made her first visit to town.

When Katie first saw it, she felt as if she had come home. Eden Croft was small and quaint and reminded her of the rural towns that dotted the New England landscape so familiar to her. Traffic flowed in a one-way direction on either side of a long village green that bisected the downtown. The dozen or so blocks were a mixture of businesses and residential dwellings.

Black, wrought iron benches and tall, clear, globed, coach lights were scattered about the green and the eye-catching centerpiece, a large, white gazebo stood proudly in front of the courthouse. Atop its cupola, the silhouette of a copper weather vane contrasted against the backdrop of blue skies. Katie could imagine the summertime concerts and celebrations that would take place under its silvery, cedar shake roof.

Shops and businesses lined one side of the boulevard and very large, period, well preserved homes the other. Crabapple and cherry trees hinted at their new sprouts of blossoms and foliage. There were majestic, mature trees everywhere. Katie noted grandfather elm, maple, oak, sycamore and ash that in summer would cover almost everything with their soothing shade. She could almost feel the coolness that would envelop the entire town when the trees leafed out completely from spring's warmth.

A fairly good-sized marina with weathered piers and docks stood in a natural cove at the far end of Main Street, but only a few fishing boats and a single sailboat were moored. Snowy-white and smoky-gray seagulls, the ever-present denizens wherever water meets land, swooped and screeched in their determined effort to feed or roost. Katie could almost visualize the lively activity when summer was in full swing.

She drove slowly and explored the town like a nosy tourist. The residential section expanded beyond the town proper and wound its way for several blocks around the near end of the lake. The homes extended along a cobweb of small lanes that stretched away from the lakefront.

Interested in seeing more, she followed one of the curved, hilly lanes. A few blocks later, the lane dead-ended at a park-like setting. Four and five story limestone buildings were set at quadrangles around a tree lined, grassy expanse. Like the spokes on a wheel, the lawn was traversed by brick walkways and converged at the center where an ivy-covered, stone bell tower stretched towards the sky. With carved letters, a crisp white sign announced that she had entered the campus of Blair College.

The entire area buzzed with young men and women. Some were alone, but most were in companionable groups of three or four laughing and chatting. All had arms laden with heavy books. For a brief moment, she envied their youth and carefree hubris, burdened with nothing more pressing than completing assignments, getting to class on time and what to wear to the sorority dance on Saturday night. She envied the fact that they were standing on the brink of exciting futures with limitless possibilities. Not all that much younger than Katie in years, yet worlds away from her in circumstance.

After Katie had completed her driving tour, she noted that she had counted five churches, a hospital, three schools, three banks, five pubs, six restaurants, four gas stations, one department store and with the exception of the church steeples, not a single building taller than four stories.

It certainly wasn't Boston.

Having found the grocer's and meat market she completed her shopping. She arranged for milk, cream and butter deliveries from White's Dairy and registered her new, but temporary address at the post office.

A short, stout, balding man named Foster with an ample spare inner tube circling his middle welcomed her to town. He was fussy and fidgety with quick bird-like movements that belied his plump build. In fact, he reminded her of a sparrow busily tending its nest, yet twisting its head, wary of every movement and possible danger.

"Been to Michigan before?"

"No, actually, this is the first time I've ever been farther than a hundred miles from Boston," Katie explained.

"It's a mighty big step for such a little lady. Got family or friends here?"

"No one, now. My Aunt Katherine and Uncle Sean Donovan lived here until they died. They willed the property to me."

Foster looked at the information on the address card. "So, you're taking over the Donovan place? Pretty high-end real estate." He sucked air through the space between his two front teeth. "And aren't you the lucky one. You've got some pretty interesting neighbors. Have you met 'em yet?"

Katie admitted that she hadn't. "Not yet. I've been too busy unpacking and getting settled. There hasn't been much time for visiting."

"Just you and your husband?" He noticed the wedding band on her left hand.

Katie shook her head. "No husband. Just my four sons and myself."

Intrigued, Foster's face lit up like a light bulb and he ogled Katie up and down. "Separated? Divorced?"

"No. Widowed."

Foster felt somewhat cheated. "War widow?"

"My husband was killed in a car accident almost two years ago."

"I wasn't in the war myself. Not that I didn't want to serve, you understand. They gave me a 4F. Trick knee." He slapped his hand against his left thigh. "But I did my duty here on the home front managing the ration stamps. There wasn't a single case of hoarding or cheating while I was on duty.

"I was block warden and made sure every house in the neighborhood bided the curfew and blackouts regulations. Roosevelt sure sold us down the river on that one. Far as I'm concerned, Old Blood and Guts Patton was right. Should'a listened to him and let our boys keep right on going until they marched into Moscow. Could'a dropped another couple of *A* bombs on the Reds, too. Then we wouldn't have these Ruskies to worry about."

"Actually, I think the war went on more than long enough for those that had to fight in it."

"You aren't one of those Commie sympathizers are you?"

"Politics really don't interest me. I happen to think our boys earned the right to come home," Katie said.

Foster ignored the remark. "All the way from Boston. Eden Croft'll be quite a change for you. It's not as fancy and exciting as a big city. But, I think you'll learn soon enough that we've got our own brand of excitement here. And you smack dab between two of the most interesting people in the county." He nodded his head. "Yeah, I guess you'll find things can get pretty interesting. I could tell you more than a story or two."

He leaned across the counter and confided, "Being postmaster, I have first hand access to all the scoop about the residents and happenings going on. Not much happens in Eden Croft that Foster Pritchard doesn't know about. If you've got the time, I've got the tales." He winked a beady brown eye at Katie.

Katie suddenly felt very uncomfortable. "That's okay. As I said, I still have a lot to do today. I'm sorry to cut short our chat but I really do have several more errands to take care of. Thank you for your help."

Foster was disappointed. "Sure. No problem. Best be on your way, then. Don't forget what I said. Need to know anything at all just stop in and see me."

Katie politely nodded him good day. She was fairly certain that the local lines of gossip were already buzzing about her before she was ten feet out the door.

The next stop was the local Catholic School where the boys would be enrolled to start school on Monday. They had already missed a week of school with the move and she was anxious to get them back into the classroom before they fell too far behind in their studies.

Ms. Bernice MacCauley, the school secretary, greeted Katie. She looked at her watch and noted the time.

"You are ten minutes late, Mrs. O'Neill. I expected you at eleven."

"Yes, I know and I apologize. I was so caught up touring your lovely little town that I lost track of the time."

Katie's smile met with a stern reprimand. "Perhaps it would have been wiser to have reserved your expedition until after this appointment."

Katie was stunned. "Of course, if this is a bad time, I could come back when it is more convenient. But, I am an anxious to get the boys enrolled in school."

"Rescheduling won't be necessary. Since you are here now, shall we proceed? Sister Mary Therese extends her apologies to you. Her presence was required at an important diocesan meeting that presented itself unexpectedly. She left last night for Grand Rapids and won't be returning until tomorrow. She left the orientation to me. I have all the paperwork prepared and trust this meeting should not take more than a few minutes."

Miss MacCauley was waif thin, stood tall and military erect with a no nonsense way about her. She also must have shopped with the same no nonsense attitude toward fashion. Dressed in a grim, muddy gray dress and brown brogues, unadorned by nothing more than her functional silver wristwatch, she oozed disciplined function rather than fashionable form.

Her wiry hair, the same shade and texture as steel wool, was combed back severely, wound tight and setting neatly on the crown of her head like a Brillo pad. It appeared to be more of a punishment than a style. She must have frightened it into obedience.

As claimed, Miss MacCauley had all the enrollment forms and paperwork competently and thoroughly completed. Katie didn't even feel the need to read any of it as a pair of brown eagle eyes dared her to find even one letter amiss. She was convinced that there was no way on earth that Miss MacCauley would ever be accused of being derelict or erroneous where her paperwork was concerned.

With economy and quiet efficiency she gave Katie an abbreviated tour of the school and grounds. Katie had the distinct feeling that being a tour guide fell far beneath her. While she possessed excellent clerical talents, she was terribly lacking in public relations. Making it very clear that she had already wasted enough of her precious time, she abruptly dismissed Katie like a troublesome five-year-old and pointed one bony finger toward the rectory.

Katie did precisely as Miss MacCauley had instructed and obedient as a first grader, Katie made her way to the rectory.

That, too, like many of the homes she had seen lining Main Street, was solidly built, well-preserved, carved out of the last century, very large and very grand. She rang the bell and waited only a moment before the massive door, its metal hinges complaining slightly, opened to reveal a pixie-sized priest with happy blue eyes and a face that matched.

"You must be Mrs. O'Neill! Welcome my child. I'm Father Michael Davey. Come in. Come in. We'll be having our nice little chat in the study." The pastor welcomed her with warmth and friendliness and much to her surprise an Irish accent.

Without allowing Katie more than a quick second to reply, "Good morning, Father," he whisked her into the hallway and on tiny feet, scurried along through a wide doorway that led to the study. Father Davey indicated a chair for Katie and settled himself behind a walnut desk the size of a small automobile. It only served to make the wee priest seem even more diminutive. He looked like a child playing grown-up at daddy's desk.

Father Davey's private study was lined on two walls with floor to ceiling bookshelves of the same dark walnut as the wide baseboards and crown moldings. On one of the opposite walls, two wide, gold and mother-of-pearl framed portraits hung. One was a portrait of St. Patrick, the other of his Holiness Pope Leo XII. Above them hung a beautiful, gold filigree crucifix of the dying Christ. Anywhere else, the intricate metalwork would have been ostentatious and overdone, but the mood of the room emitted enough confidence to handle it.

A well-worn Aubusson rug covered the floor, nearly wall-to-wall. Two tall sets of windows were framed with heavy, burgundy velvet curtains and restricted the amount of natural light that might brighten the dark room.

If the room was lacking in brightness and cheer, Father Davey more than made up for with his affability and lightheartedness. He was an older priest with a generous mat of wavy hair, white and soft as eider down. His complexion was fair, but with ruddy cheeks. He was so short and slight that his long black cassock nearly swallowed him. As any conscientious shepherd, years of caring and sharing the worries and woes of his flock had left their mark on his face. His quick wit, sense of humor, and ready laughter had also left their stamp in bright blue eyes that smiled easily.

"I apologize that there are no tea and cakes. "'Tis Mrs. Callahan's marketing day. I am completely out of my element in the kitchen. And I'm not at all eager to suffer the wrath of Mrs. Callahan for messing up her kitchen. She is fiercely protective of her territory and the kitchen is unmistakably her bailiwick."

Katie learned that Father Davey had been born in *County Wicklow, Ireland*, had immigrated to America with his parents as a young lad, was orphaned soon after and entered the seminary two years later. He had been at St. Anthony's nearly all of his thirty-five years in the priesthood.

Katie never attempted to interrupt or interject while he carried on his narrative. Being raised in a thoroughly Catholic home, in heaven and on earth a priest was situated in a position not very far from the right hand of God. They were treated with quiet respect and awed reverence.

"I think you'll feel very welcome and at home here. For nearly two generations I've baptized and buried them, confirmed and married them, held their hands when they were sick and wiped their tears through joy and sorrow. I gave them absolution for their sins, advice when they asked for it and many a time when they didn't.

"I can tell you these are good people. They've welcomed me into their homes and into their hearts and I love them as I would my own family. Come to think of it, for more years than I care to recall, they have been my family.

"But enough about me. I think I detect a bit of the Irish in your voice, Lassie."

Katie straightened her skirt and replied, "I haven't had anyone comment on that in a long time. Back in Boston, in our neighborhood, a bit of the brogue is hardly noticed." She crossed her gloved hands trying to decide where to start. "Originally a Dubliner, I came to America with my ma and da when I was five years old. It seems that I haven't completely lost my accent. I attended St. Dennis' School in Boston for all of my twelve years."

The humorous truth of that particular fact coaxed a knowing smile from the old priest. "Ah, the determined and disciplined blessed Sisters of Mercy. 'Tis no wonder you still carry a bit of the brogue. Have you met dear Sister Mary Therese, yet? Seen our little school? We are all rather proud of it," he boasted.

"No to your first question and yes to the second. Sister Mary Therese is out of town, today. But her secretary was nice enough to show me around." Katie figured that was only a little white lie and certainly an excusable transgression.

"Ah! So you've met Miss MacCauley. Or as the students secretly call her, 'Old BM.' Not altogether kind, but I'm afraid accurate."

Katie and Father Davey both smiled in agreement.

"She really was very efficient and gracious to interrupt her busy day and show me around." Katie, feeling a bit guilty, quickly came to her defense.

"Efficient *and* gracious. Mrs. O'Neill, you too, have a way with the blarney. A might Draconian is perhaps closer to the truth. But, she is conscientious and hard working and she does run a tight ship over there."

"What I saw of the school I could see why you are so proud of it. And I fell in love with Eden Croft the moment I saw it. It has so many beautiful old homes."

Though he made a rapt and empathetic listener, Father Davey was also an enthusiastic and fascinating narrator. Like anyone whose vocation requires keen and copious verbal skills, Father Davey could talk a leg off a chair.

"In the last century, entrepreneurs were drawn to the area by the thousands of acres of virgin timber. With the lumber barons, came millions of dollars that built the towns and fattened bankrolls. Those wealthy enough built the first mansions. There is even a small college here, established by one of the more philanthropic kings of commerce from that era, Jonathan Blair. Thus the name of the college, the county and almost everything else of any worth for miles around."

He continued, leaning back in his leather nest, "Though the lumber era died, around the turn of the century big money from Detroit, Grand Rapids and Chicago found its way north as the wealthy and privileged built lavish summer residences around the lake for their families."

Father Davey was comfortable to be around, warm and jovial and spoke from the heart with typical Irish blarney and mischief sparkled in his clear blue eyes. So entertained, for a few brief moments, Katie was able to enjoy a brief hiatus from her worries.

As he talked, the old priest was perceptive enough to note the look of animation and interest that replaced the anguish on Katie's face. But, eventually, he had used up most of his stories and anecdotes and gradually wound its way back to Katie. With some subtle nudging, he pressed Katie about her plans.

Katie chose her words carefully. "When Danny died, I felt as if my world had ended. In these past months, I've become so tired of facing each day with dread and each night with loneliness. Tired of wondering if anything will ever be all right again. Have you ever felt so completely tired, Father? Not physically tired, but spiritually, deep inside tired?"

Father Davey nodded, "Aye, more times than I care to admit."

"I'm so tired of living in near panic, holding my breath, waiting for it all to come crumbling down. My financial situation had grown more desperate by the week. Then, came the letter from the attorney.

"Mr. Mulholland wrote me that my Aunt Katherine had died and bequeathed her home to me. It seemed like a miracle. It was a miracle. God had heard my prayers and answered them. Owning the property free and clear, without a mortgage payment, I felt I could stretch the Social Security benefits far enough to cover our living expenses."

"How well did you know your Aunt Katherine and Uncle Sean?" Father Davey asked.

"Not well at all. I haven't seen them in twenty-five years and can barely remember them. Aunt Katherine and my ma were sisters, separated by eighteen years. I suppose my ma's birth came as a bit of a surprise. When my grandma and grandda died, my ma was only six, so Aunt Katherine and Uncle Sean raised her as their own. That is until she married. That is when things become vague. Apparently, they had a falling out with my ma and da and never reconciled.

"My folks never talked about it, rarely mentioned Aunt Katherine and Uncle Sean. That's why the letter from the attorney seemed like a miracle from Above." Katie paused for a moment. "Then, as quickly as my miracle materialized it evaporated.

"There is no possible way that my income could support a property of that size." Katie willed her voice not to break. "I had no idea what the exact circumstances of the inheritance were. The house and property are beautiful and leaving it will be difficult. But, keeping a roof over our heads and food on the table need to be my main concerns. I have to keep my priorities in order. I am not a wealthy woman, Father, and my financial situation makes keeping the property impossible. Unfortunately, as you can see, our stay here will only be temporary."

Katie felt emotionally drained and was tired of the whole mess and it only hurt worse to dwell on it.

Father Davey noted that the revelation had suddenly clouded her bright green eyes. "Surely, there is something that could be done. Some arrangements could be made that would allow you to keep the property," he offered. "You've come such a long way. 'Twould be a shame that everything you have sacrificed should all be wasted."

Dee's words of practicality pricked her consciousness and made her feel all the more defeated.

"I think you buried your common sense along with Danny. Don't make any hasty decisions. Stay here, in Boston. Work things out. At least here you know what you're dealing with. There are too many unanswered questions for you to risk everything by trotting off to Michigan."

"I have never worked at any job other than homemaking. What could possibly be here for me, Father? Especially in a town where I know absolutely no one."

"That's not completely true. You know me," Father Davey teased her, "And Miss MacCauley. 'Tis a good place to start. Many people have started with a lot less. You know that where our Blessed Father closes a door he always opens a window. Perhaps you haven't looked hard enough for that window."

"Thank you for the vote of confidence, Father." Katie forced a tiny smile. "But I think it would be best for me and the boys to go back to Boston. As soon as the boys finish their school year and arrangements can be made, we'll be returning to Boston." Her voice was tainted with regret and surrender, her face a mask of disappointment and resignation.

Father Davey felt a sense of poignancy. He took an immediate liking to Katie. As he appraised the young woman sitting before him, he sensed a genuine goodness and purity of spirit in Katie. There was a basic honesty and sincerity there. He knew she had courage and spunk. Any single woman with enough gumption to transplant herself and her four children across five states had to be blessed with a lion's share of pluck. He could see it in her eyes and Father Davey always placed great stock in what you could see in one's eyes.

Before saying good-bye, he assured Katie that he would make the necessary arrangements to find a place for Brendan in the altar boy rotation for Mass. Providing he kept up with his Catechism, Tommy could make his First Communion with the second grade class that May.

Giving Katie his blessing, he offered his help and counsel at anytime.

Even as Katie walked down the steps of the rectory, the old priest felt a deep concern in his heart for the hardships she had faced so early in her young life and the hardships that he knew she had yet to face. He also couldn't, for the life of himself, image how that delightful creature could possibly be related, in any way, to Katherine Donovan.

Οϐ   ϨϽ

With all of the necessary errands in town taken care of, Katie turned her full attention loose on the house. She would put off any major cleaning until after things were more settled.

While attacking the dust on the living room mantle, her eyes fell on the large framed print that hung prominently above the fireplace. For the first few days she had seen it but had been too busy to pay it much attention.

As she took the time to study it, on closer inspection she realized that it wasn't a print at all, but an actual oil painting of a small girl of four or five. She was bent over, throwing what appeared to be pieces of bread, into a pool or pond. Four, fuzzy ducklings were feeding on the crumbs. The child had long, curly, auburn hair, loosely tied with a long, lavender ribbon. The spirals of curls were flowing wild and free as if being blown by a soft summer breeze. She wore a simple powder blue dress, but no socks or shoes, her plump, bare feet touching the water's edge.

The painting was beautiful, the pastel colors soft and fragile and Katie was struck by the feeling that it had been painted with great affection. Katie felt something vaguely familiar and gnawingly intimate, yet elusive about it. It was signed in the lower right corner, simply with the letter *K*.

Katie felt a picture needed to draw the viewer in, to be the language that translates emotion from the artist to the audience. It should arouse interest, pique curiosity, tell a story. A story without an ending … leaving the ending up to the imagination. In essence, it should never be completely finished, but constantly evolving and redefining itself. It should say, "See me differently today than you did yesterday ... and still differently tomorrow." Katie was no art expert, but the painting had those qualities.

She reached out and gently brushed her fingers over the girl's hair, as if she could smooth it back into place. Briefly, she contemplated who the little girl was, and even more importantly, who had painted it. Still intrigued by the painting, she broke from her musings and returned to her chores.

Linens, stale and musty, stored too long, were washed and line-dried before putting them into use. Though they wouldn't be staying for more than a few months, Katie felt the need to make them feel somewhat at home. She needed to surround them with familiar objects.

Family photographs were carefully unpacked and selectively placed on the fireplace mantels and end tables. Their wedding portrait and Danny's army photograph were placed prominently on the living room mantel. Her few, favorite, precious pieces of china and bric-a-brac were unpacked and lovingly and protectively placed in the china cabinet.

Packing had been done frugally and with great care, limited by the confines of the small trailer she had bought to carry their belongings. She had brought along only the essentials and things that she couldn't bear to part with. Everything else had been sold to stipend the move.

It had been an emotionally draining chore, sifting through a lifetime of precious memories, wrapped up in countless objects. Katie had had to divine what could be discarded, what could be replaced and what couldn't. She had felt as if her whole life had been ripped apart, leaving behind a trail of little pieces of herself. Like the trail of crumbs Hansel and Gretel had dropped to guide them home again. Yet, as the pieces were gobbled up, her path home would disappear, leaving her hopelessly lost.

Then, seeking consolation in the only way possible, she told herself, *"they are just things, Katie, just things. You'll always have the memories."*

She hoped to ease the pain of homesickness and allowed the boys to bring a few of their own valued possessions, things that would make them feel as if they were keeping little bits of their past. Things that would make them feel somewhat anchored and less displaced. But, in deference to the limited space, they were restricted to one box each. Katie had not invaded their privacy or tried to influence them, rather, she left the decision-making entirely up to them. She had resisted the urge to sneak even a peek at what items they had selected. She considered them private and personal.

chapter three

The weekend disappeared in a frenzy of activity and Monday morning arrived, in spirit, mirroring all the bleakness of the dismal, cloudy, putty-gray sky outside. Though an unseasonably early spring had prematurely melted all the heaps of snow, the unpredictability of March in Northern Michigan roared like a lion. The calendar may have heralded the official end of winter but a cold front, blowing in from Canada, had chased away the brief days of warmth that had welcomed them.

Hoping it would improve their moods, Katie cooked a hearty breakfast of scrambled eggs, bacon, toast and jam; all the boys' favorites.

Her strategy hadn't worked. Facing a strange school with strange classmates had put Brendan in a foul mood that was contagious and pleasant as chicken pox. He was morose and pouting and not the least bit interested in "making any new friends" or "fitting right in" as his Mom had insisted he would. He seemed more interested in chasing the cold, uneaten, scrambled eggs around his plate.

The twins were lagging sluggishly behind and Katie surrendered herself to the fact that you simply cannot rush six-year-olds.

"Is everyone anxious to start their first day at a brand new school?" She asked enthusiastically.

"I am," Tommy answered with equal enthusiasm.

Katie smiled. "It's always exciting to start something new."

"Bren says we ain't gonna like it," Colin added.

"Well, starting something new can be a little strange, but in a few days you'll feel right at home. Once you've made some new friends it won't seem strange at all."

Bren grunted his disagreement.

"Bren says they ain't gonna like us, neither." Colin's voice was muffled as he took a swig of orange juice.

"Well, in case you haven't noticed before, Bren doesn't know everything. Colin, those eggs aren't going to find their way to your mouth on their own." Katie noticed his eggs remained untouched and she tried to speed up the process.

"I ain't eatin' 'em. Casey spit in 'em." He crossed his arms across his chest.

"Did not."

"Did so."

"Tattle-tale, tattle-tale, hanging on a bull's tail," Casey sang.

"I ain't no tattle-tale."

"Are so, you big baby."

"I ain't no baby."

Katie threw her dishtowel on the counter and shook her index finger at Casey. "Casey Michael O'Neill. If I find out that you've been spitting again, you'll be finding out what a bar of soap tastes like."

"I didn't spit in his eggs. I jus' told him I wuz gonna. He wouldn't let me in the bathroom."

"If I find you even threatening to spit, you'll get the same punishment, young man. Colin, eat your eggs."

"I can't eat 'em even if I think he spit in 'em." Colin pushed his plate away.

"I guess I can't argue with that logic. Don't eat them, then. Eat your toast and bacon and drink your milk."

The school bus was due to pick them up at the end of the drive and deposit them at the Eden Croft Elementary School then they would make the short walk to St. Anthony's. All Katie had to do was get them out the door in time. But, Tommy, as usual, was the only one cooperating. Finally, with a flurry of jackets and caps, notebooks and lunch pails, she ushered them out the back door with only minutes to spare.

Enjoying the immediate quiet as all chaos disappeared instantly with the exiting of the troops, Katie poured her first enjoyable cup of tea of the day. She had one welcomed hour of bliss before she needed to tidy the kitchen and herself to make her appointment with Mr. Mulholland at ten o'clock.

Though the morning was dismal, blustery and cold, she felt the need to step outside for a few minutes and enjoy the peace and quiet. She wrapped herself in a thick, wool sweater over her bathrobe and carried her tea outside.

Mimicking the circumstances of her life, the fickle spring weather she had enjoyed the first few days had abandoned her. The sky and lake were a seamless, steel gray. It was almost impossible to detect where one ended and the other began. The wind had whipped the soft whitecaps up into icy cold waves that beat frantically at the shoreline.

Though not cold enough to snow, Katie felt the bitter wind bite sharply against her face and gust under the hem of her robe. Despite her mood, her floundering future and the dismal, dreary day, she felt invigorated by its harshness and electrified by its intensity. Perhaps it was her birthright, her proud heritage, her roots buried deep in Irish soil.

The land of her birth was a series of islands that the earth had forced
upward from its briny depths. Her ancestral roots were buried deep into the
rocky, unforgiving soil of the land. As the waters of the womb nurture a baby,
the Celts were drawn to the water. Even miles inland, the land they inhabited
was dotted with hundreds of lakes and crisscrossed with an abundance of rivers
and streams.

Katie loved the water, always had. Whether salt-water or fresh, she shared
an indestructible, mutual and everlasting bond with it. She found something
constant and eternal about its movement. It instilled in her a sense of permanence. It had been following in the same motion and pattern for thousands of
years before and would still be there for thousands of years into the future. The
same as it was at this very moment, as if frozen in time. It could change shape
and form with each season, yet still remain the same.

A seagull shrieked overhead and interrupted her reverie. All of the doubts
and fears that had plagued her for so long came rushing back. She missed the
pace and chores of the past few days. Activity and work kept the ghosts at bay.
Idleness opened her mind to self-delusion and doubt.

She finally conceded that the meeting that morning would clearly settle
the impracticality and impossibility of her staying on under the circumstances.

Katie ran back into the house, cleared the table, washed the dishes and
tidied the kitchen. She raced upstairs, bathed and dried and donned her navy
blue wool suit, the best she owned. It was several years old but well made and
wore its years well.

With impatience, she brushed her unruly hair trying to tame it into a twist
with hairpins. The springy curls that rendered it completely unmanageable exasperated her. Danny had always liked the natural look of it, but Katie always
teased him that that was merely a polite way of calling it "wild."

After quickly applying some lipstick, her only concession to make-up, she
straightened the seams in her stockings, slipped into her shoes, pulled on her
gloves and tweed wool coat, grabbed her handbag and ran out the door, slamming it behind her like one of the twins.

೮೫ ಔ

The attorney's office was located in town center on one of the side streets
adjacent to the courthouse. Katie took the stairs to the third floor, found the
door that identified his office, drew in a deep breath and went inside. She
closed the door behind her without a sound.

Inside, the office provided a large waiting area with several chairs and a
coffee table that displayed an array of magazines. Unfamiliar with protocol,
Katie didn't announce herself, but quietly settled in one of the chairs and glanced
over the magazines. Every one of them was about sailing and the date on their

covers reflected not the present year but a past one. She soon discovered that she could resist the urge to read them. *So much for current topics*, she mused.

On the far side of the room, a middle-aged woman sat in profile behind a mahogany desk. Obviously Mr. Mulholland's secretary, she was busily tapping the keys on a typewriter. Under different circumstances Katie would have enjoyed the friendly tapping of the keys. It was a comforting sound, like that of corn popping in the kettle.

Not wanting to disturb the woman at work, Katie sat silently and studied her. She was of average height and weight and, like a pianist at the keyboard, sat ramrod straight in her chair. Her fingers flew over the keys as light as air. She wore a white cardigan sweater over a black and white patterned dress with a large, bibbed, white collar. Her hair was swept up in a loose bun with a pencil poking through, like a knitting needle in a ball of yarn.

Several framed photographs were scattered across the desk and Katie could see that some of them were of children of various ages. An enormous black coffee mug sat within easy reach and the woman turned to it to lift it for a drink. She immediately noticed Katie and stood.

Meeting Katie's eyes, she smiled warmly and spoke. "Heaven's sake! I'm sorry. I didn't hear you come in. How long have you been waiting?"

"Not long at all. I just arrived," Katie assured her.

Katie was ill equipped and inexperienced with any matter of a business or legal nature. Like a fish out of water, she rose and walked across the room. If the secretary had been an eight-year-old with a runny nose Katie would have stepped up to the plate like a pro. As it was, Brendan's description immediately leapt into her consciousness, aptly shouting *"HICK?" Who was the hick now?* Just as quickly, she tried to dismiss it from her mind.

As she approached the secretary's desk, she said a silent prayer that her voice wouldn't betray her hesitancy and discomfort.

"I have a ten o'clock appointment with Mr. Mulholland."

The secretary stopped her from speaking further. "Of course. You must be Mrs. O'Neill. Land sakes, is it ten o'clock already? I've completely lost track of the time."

Offering her hand, she continued, "I'm Violet, Violet Marden, Matt's ... er ... Mr. Mulholland's secretary. But, most people call me Vi. Welcome to Eden Croft, Mrs. O'Neill. I hope the move hasn't been too difficult. Things settling in nicely for you?"

Katie noted Violet was the antithesis of Miss MacCauley.

"Yes. Thank you for asking. It took us a few days to get things organized, not that things are ever completely organized with four boys. But we'll figure it all out."

Katie added the last with far more confidence than she felt.

"If I can help you with anything let me know. I mean like schools, where to shop, when to hit the big sales, finding a doctor, a dentist, those kinds of things. I can do my best to steer you in the right direction. But you have probably already discovered the choices are fairly limited in a town this size. Eden Croft isn't at all like Boston, I'd venture." The secretary smiled.

Katie found it uncanny that the very same phrase had passed through her mind the first day she saw the town and her musings reflected in her smile.

"It is a beautiful little town. But you're right. It isn't at all like Boston.

"Thank you for offering your help, but I already have the boys enrolled in St. Anthony's. As far as the others things are concerned, I'm afraid there's been a terrible misunderstanding. That's what I'm here to straighten out. After I meet with Mr. Mulholland, I think our stay here won't be all that long."

A questioning expression clouded Vi's face. She was unsure exactly what Matt had told Mrs. O'Neill and what arrangements he had made that could have been so obviously misunderstood.

At a loss for anything more to say, she asked Katie to have a seat, excused herself and exited through the door that led to what Katie assumed was the lawyer's private office.

Katie lowered herself to the nearest chair and sat stiffly, crossed her ankles and tried to muster up her courage as well as deciding exactly how she would translate into words the absolute impossibility of taking on a house as large and expensive as Aunt Katherine's. Mr. Mulholland had made the most ludicrous of all assumptions. If he thought Katie came from money, boy had he made a gigantic leap in the wrong direction. What had Aunt Katherine told him about her?

There had been a few letters and long distance telephone calls from Mr. Mulholland. Perhaps she had been so caught up by the grand possibility that her prayers had been answered that she failed to consider all the specifics. Brendan and Dee were right. This whole thing had been a big, fat mistake. She could see Dee shaking her head at the folly. She should have listened to them instead of Moira who had painted it as some fabulous, exciting, romantic adventure. It wasn't Moira who would have to slink back to Boston a failure with her tail between her legs. Katie wondered how could she have been so stupid?

Her thoughts somersaulted. Mentally, she counted off the pertinent points. Number One. She had uprooted her family. Number Two. Dragged them half way across the country. Number Three. Selling practically everything she had ever owned, including her home (Number Four), to make this ridiculous trip. And just when she thought nothing could possibly get any worse, somehow it managed to do exactly that. Numbers Five … Six … Seven … Eight … and on … and on.

She seesawed between anger toward Mr. Mulholland for not making the situation completely clear and anger at herself for not asking any of the right questions. He was the experienced lawyer. He knew all the details. Why hadn't he been more conscientious and forthright? The more she thought, the angrier she became. She suddenly realized that anger was wonderful. It was fantastic and it beat the devil out of being scared and afraid. She could always go back to being scared and afraid later.

She could feel the flush radiating up her cheeks. They always reddened when she was embarrassed or something had really gotten her dander up. The anger gave birth to determination and fortified with resolution, she concocted a plan. The plan would turn Aunt Katherine's behemoth bequest into a workable solution that would hopefully get her out of this jam.

The door opened suddenly and startled her. Well, now she was as ready for him as she ever would be. She was glad she had had the opportunity to sit and stew. It had allowed her enough time to harness the courage, as well as the indignation, to tell him exactly what type of quagmire he had led her into and how she proposed to get herself out of it.

Vi stepped back from the open door and told Katie that Mr. Mulholland would see her now. Vi silently closed the door after Katie. She shook her head quickly trying to clear her thoughts and returned to her desk. She hesitated for a moment before she resumed her typing.

The lawyer's office was unmistakably masculine. Dark cherry paneling, rich with age, covered all of the walls. Dominating the room was a desk of warm teak wood that appeared as large as Katie's whole kitchen in Boston had been. A black telephone, gold pen and pencil set and a single brass lamp were the only other items occupying its uncluttered surface. The floor was carpeted, wall-to-wall, with a forest green rug, thick and plush. Katie noted that the whole office emanated elegant masculinity. Even the scents were manly, a mélange of aged wood and bay rum.

The man sitting behind the desk, in a well worn, maroon leather chair, set down the papers he had been reading and stood to greet her.

Mr. Mulholland was not at all what Katie had expected. He appeared younger, probably only a bit older than she and she admitted to herself, much more handsome than she had imagined. She was immediately shocked and embarrassed by the thought.

Tall in stature, he wore a plaid flannel shirt under a beige fisherman's knit sweater. His shirt was unbuttoned at the neck and cuff. The sleeves were pushed up to the elbow. The fact that he wore neither suit nor tie surprised her. She expected an attorney to be impeccably and severely dressed in a dark serge three-piece suit complete with gold watch and fob, an immaculate white shirt and regimental tie. She thought he would be sober, serious, intimidating and reeking of lawyerly propriety. Instead, an easy smile greeted her.

He ran his fingers through tousled blond hair, wiped them on his tan corduroy trousers, reached across the expanse of the desk and extended a hand to her. Before Katie had the chance to accept his handshake, an unruly lock of curly hair flopped right back on his forehead.

"Mrs. O'Neill, Matthew Mulholland, attorney-at-law, fourth in a long line of Mulhollands-at-law, reluctant pillar of the community, confirmed bachelor, a terrible golfer, fair second baseman and a terrific sailor. In fact, I hail from a long line of distinguished seamen. Or at least that's what I've been told. But, I'm sure there are at least one or two rogues scandalously buried in my past who probably looted and pillaged their way all across the Seven Seas. Oh ... and I make a mean Irish stew."

He winked with one of his clear aquamarine eyes and gestured for her to sit in one of the two wing-backed chairs that faced his desk.

Katie suddenly found it difficult to maintain her anger and newly honed resolve. Her entire battle plan was set a-kilter by the man's relaxed attitude. In fact, she was shocked by his calm and easy manner. Words abruptly vanished from her mind and she seemed unable to find her tongue. She numbly did as he proffered and sat down.

"I apologize for not coming out and seeing you situated before our meeting today, but I've been tied up with some very important and pressing business.

"That statement is for your benefit so that I exude an air of confidence and trust, as taught to me by my late, great and ever so industrious and stuffy grandfather, God rest his soul. On the other hand, being taught honesty by my late, great, ever so precious and dear grandmother, in truth, I was taking delivery of a new sailboat. A thirty-two foot sloop. Ordered it last year. She's a beauty of a boat. Just launched her."

Again, he employed the same, easy and conspiratorial wink that Katie was finding very disarming.

"Also, my apology for rambling on, Mrs. O'Neill. As you have probably already figured out, I'm not unlike most lawyers. I have been blessed, or cursed, whichever you prefer, with the gift of gab. Likewise, we lawyers also labor under the misconception that everyone is as anxious as we are to hear us talk. However, unlike most lawyers, I am willing to admit it."

Now he felt he was finally getting somewhere. A hint of a smile tugged at the corners of Mrs. O'Neill's mouth. And a lovely mouth it was. In fact, he found the entire face very attractive. It wasn't an obviously, glamorous, cover-girl beauty, but possessed a rather delicate and fair gracefulness.

She wore no make-up, save a bit of pink lipstick, and he was glad of it. Make-up would have been lost and unnatural on that peaches and cream complexion. And those eyes! The greenest eyes he had ever seen. Two sparkling emeralds brilliantly shone under dark chestnut lashes that were such a deep shade as to be nearly black. Matthew conceded to himself that it was going to be extremely difficult to keep his mind on business. All in all, Mrs. O'Neill was very easy on the eyes.

He forced himself to stay on track and launched into the business at hand. "Your Aunt Katherine was, may I say, a unique woman. She spoke when something needed saying and pretty much shot from the hip. So, applying her austere and critical philosophy towards tact and subtlety, I will lay the cards brutally on the table."

He shook his head as if he could hardly believe the characteristics of the person he was about to describe.

"She knew exactly what she wanted and wouldn't rest until he she got it with no regard for any body that stood in her way. She had the tenacity of a bulldog, the stubbornness of a mule and took no prisoners. Katherine Donovan was the type of person who felt the need to control everything and everyone in her path. She also had no use for anything or anyone that didn't serve a purpose. And she had no use for lawyers. But recognizing that we are at times a necessary evil, she decided that an Irish lawyer couldn't be any worse than any other.

"That being said, let's discuss the legalities of her will."

Katie realized she hadn't uttered a word and not wanting to sit there like a dunce, was finally able to find her voice.

"I'm afraid that I've just come a very long way for nothing, Mr. Mulholland. Aunt Katherine and Uncle Sean may have had some degree of wealth but I can assure you that I do not. I don't know what I may have done or said to give you the idea that I'm in a financial situation to even begin to be able to afford the house and grounds that Aunt Katherine left me. As a matter of fact, things are exactly the opposite."

Katie didn't want to lose her momentum and continued. "I made the move out here, and I must add, at no small expense or trouble, because I thought the house you wrote to me about was exactly that, a house, not a mansion. Our entire home in Boston could fit in the living room.

"Without mortgage payments and with Social Security benefits I felt I could afford a modest home. But, Mr. Mulholland, with a property that immense, there is no way I could manage the upkeep. And the taxes. I can't even begin to imagine what the taxes would be on a place like that. Just heating the place must cost a fortune." Katie felt she was really on a roll now.

"Since we're already here and the boys' school year will be over in three months, we'll stay on until then. But then I'm afraid we'll have to sell Aunt Katherine's place. I would imagine that a property of that size could bring in a fairly large sum. With the money from the sale we should be able to re-establish ourselves in Boston with enough left over for a nice little nest egg."

Katie felt fairly confident that the plan was a solid one.

Matthew smiled mischievously. "I can see you, too, have been blessed with the gift of gab, Mrs. O'Neill."

Katie blushed, embarrassed by his comment.

"And I can also see that you embarrass easily."

Katie's face reddened even more with his second observation.

"I must explain the entire intent of her will. There is a specific condition of the will that I'm afraid is completely binding and irrevocable.

"In legal terms, the house, properties and estate are bequeathed to you in their entirety. It is here that Katherine's wishes were very emphatic and nonnegotiable. Unless you maintain residency in the house, you forfeit all rights and claims. The entire estate and remainder of her inheritance would then be bequeathed to Blair College where she and Sean taught for many years."

Katie suddenly felt as if the earth had disappeared from under her. Her throat tightened as her stomach wrenched and churned. She fought back the swell of fear and tried to swallow. Her mind was numb. Even as she felt the tears building, she willed herself not to cry. She would not cry in front of this man.

Hoping that a mental diversion would quell the tears, she muttered, "I wonder what a cashier gets paid at the A&P."

Mr. Mulholland didn't hear what she said. "Excuse, me?"

She dismissed the remark with a wave of her hand, "Never mind. It's unimportant."

Katie forced herself to say something concrete. "Mr. Mulholland, my whole life has been turned upside-down. I have sold the only home my boys have ever known as well as nearly everything I have ever owned. We have left behind any friends or attachments we had. The boys have been asked to sacrifice their past for a future that right now seems rather tenuous and ludicrous.

"By nature, Mr. Mulholland, I'm not a pessimistic person, but right now I'm finding it impossible to see anything positive about the situation I'm in." Even as she spoke, Katie didn't recognize her voice. It sounded confused and defeated.

The Irish lilt crept into her voice and she stared directly into his eyes. "In my words, this is how I see it. This is an all-or-nothing situation. I have to live in this monstrosity of a house I can't afford. I can't sell it, or risk losing everything, which brings me right back around to the fact that I can't afford it to begin with. Please, not in legal gibberish, but in plain English, you tell me, exactly what am I going to do?"

Matthew smiled impishly and Katie felt that he was mocking her.

"I will explain in it to you. *In plain English*. If you'll give me a chance."

He smiled again and that smile was really beginning to annoy her.

He steepled his fingers and rested his elbows on the desktop. "Your Aunt Katherine did stipulate," he corrected himself, "excuse me, desired that you live in the house. That is clearly stated. Your Uncle Sean inherited the property that had been in his family for three generations. After Sean passed, Katherine wanted it to stay in the family. Logically, as their closest living relative, after her death, she wanted it passed to you. In the event of your death, she hoped it would then pass to your sons.

"Katherine was nothing if not foresighted. She also has made financial arrangements in the form of a trust, or fund that can be drawn on to help maintain the property as well as pay taxes. Katherine and Sean Donovan were not wealthy, but the estate isn't insubstantial. They had earned respectable incomes, lived sensibly all their lives and planned well for their retirement years. Those plans however, did not take into account the eventuality of raising four children. The fund is not inexhaustible, but with sensible spending, should be able to meet any costs that arise. With the remaining estate, there are funds to provide you with a reasonable monthly allowance for several years. After that, you may need to find employment."

He paused a moment to let that sink in.

"So, in answer to your question, that is exactly what I think you should do."

Matthew watched as confusion, surprise and relief washed over her face. Her entire body seemed to respond.

In that brief moment a transformation took place. It was as if a massive yoke had been lifted from her shoulders and Katie very nearly burst from excitement. She didn't care if domineering Aunt Katherine was controlling and manipulative, even from the grave. This meant she wouldn't have to fret and worry about every dime she spent, not knowing where the money to replace each and every dime would come from.

"Live sensibly!" She almost laughed out loud. "The past several months I have become an expert at living excruciatingly sensibly. Even with cutting spending to the bare bones, the expenses have gnawed away hungrily at my meager savings. Living sensibly will be a giant step upward.

"I'm at a complete loss, Mr. Mulholland. I'm not sure how one is supposed to respond to such wondrous news." She again, fumbled for words. "I have no idea what to say. You must think that I'm a blathering idiot. But at the moment, I don't care one little bit."

"Quite the contrary. I would never consider you any kind of idiot. So, Mrs. O'Neill, before you float out of here on could nine, we need to proceed with some necessary signatures and other legal nonsense."

He rose from his chair, walked to the door, opened it and called to his secretary. "Vi, you want to come in here and witness some signatures for us? And please bring in some coffee fixings."

After they had dispensed with the paperwork, all necessary documents signed, witnessed and dated, Matthew explained that subject to her approval, he would be making the banking arrangements for her, including a household account for living expenses. An escrow account could be drawn upon to take care of taxes, maintenance and insurance.

With the meeting concluded, he clasped his hands behind his head, leaned back in his chair, looked into those emerald green eyes, smiled liked the proverbial cat that ate the canary and said, "Now, with all that business out of the way, let me tell you about your tenant."

chapter four

Katie had not even known that the guesthouse existed.

Even if she had, she would have thought it belonged to the neighboring property. It was situated on the far west border of the property, on the other side of a high, dense wall of yews. She had thought that her property ended at that natural fence. Once she learned of its existence, upon closer inspection, she found a worn path almost totally obscured by the hedge. The path cut through the hedge.

Katie was surprised that one of the boys hadn't discovered it in their first few days of exploration. How it had escaped detection was anyone's guess. She was grateful, for the sake of the old gentleman, that the path had eluded them. She was also grateful that the dense hedge would continue to guarantee him some privacy.

Mr. Mulholland had explained that the gentleman living in the cottage was a professor at the college and head of the horticulture department. In fact, that is how he had come to know her Aunt Katherine and Uncle Sean. In exchange for tenancy in the cottage, he tended the grounds.

The arrangement had suited everyone perfectly. No money had ever exchanged hands. Katherine had made provisions in her will for that arrangement to continue. Not at all comfortable with being anyone's landlord, Katie decided she would simply think of him as a neighbor.

 og 80

The following day Katie decided to make the introductory call on her neighbor. She considered that the old gentleman may be accustomed to his privacy and may not welcome the noise and activity of children. She timed her visit carefully. With the boys at school, they wouldn't be assaulted by their relentless interruptions.

Katie carried a freshly baked plate of peanut butter cookies, slipped through the hedge and approached the guest cottage. Compared to the main house it was almost elfin in size. Not unlike Snow White's dwarfish discovery in the deep forest. It, too, wore a coat of white on clapboard but was less ornate than its formidable neighbor.

Dark green shutters ensconced each multi-paned window. English ivy had crept upward, nearly concealing the fieldstone chimney. There were window boxes beneath each window and Irish moss outlined the curved, stone walkway. It led to the front door that was painted the same dark green as the shutters. In the door, at head height, there was one small, diamond-paned, leaded glass window.

Katie walked to the door and knocked. After a moment without a response, she knocked again. Still she received no response. The urge to stand on tiptoes and sneak a peek inside tempted her. But, the two concrete lions that flanked the door like watchful sentries, warned her to exercise discretionary restraint. Instead, spotting a small brass bell hanging from a wrought iron pole, she pulled on the leather cord attached to it. It clanked cheerfully, but garnered no response from inside or outside the cottage.

Katie considered the possibility that she would find him working outside and purveyed the surrounding grounds. They were immaculately manicured and beautifully landscaped, surprisingly more so than the main house. Rich, fertile beds were raked and free of debris. Mounds of groundcover, periwinkle, pachysandra and ivy sculptured the edges of the lush, green grass. The lawn disappeared into a grove of blue spruce trees that circled the perimeter, creating an arboreal fence around the entire yard.

Nested in a bed of euonymus was a copper sundial oxidized green from age and the elements. There was writing on it and Katie walked closer to read it. In graceful lettering, the inscription read,

There is a Time to Every Season

Scattered about in the rich, dark earth, spring bulbs had poked through their pale, young shoots. The warming spring sun would force them to burst into colorful tulips, jonquils, hyacinths and daffodils. Already, there were blooming crocuses and snowdrops, the first harbingers of spring. Stonecrop and Irish moss grew intermittently between rocks and limestone. Arches and trellises supported clematis, wisteria, jasmine and climbing roses waiting for the summer sun to coax them from their winter sleep. Katie imagined how it would look, vital and vibrant with the freshness of growth and the splendor of color, reaffirming nature's need to continue its perpetual cycle of life, just as the inscription intimated "... *a time to every season ... a time to sow ... a time to be born ...*"

Failing to find the gentleman on the grounds, she circled around to the back of the cottage. Like twins of the cottage, there was a small garage and shed of white clapboard, but no sign of life. Then she spotted the greenhouse.

It was almost as large as the cottage with panes of glass forming the roof and all four sides. A metal chimney extended up through the roof and wisps of gray smoke curled upward. Though condensation had formed on the windows, through them she was able to see verdant green, leafy growth accentuated by occasional hints of color.

Katie ventured over and cautiously entered through the open door. Unlike the biting chill outside, a warm, moist heat welcomed her. As she looked inside, Katie couldn't believe the vision that lay before her eyes.

Three rows of wide wooden tables ran the entire length of the structure, front to back. Covering nearly every inch of surface were hundreds of plants in a prism of color. There were hues from ivory white, to blushing pink, to sunny yellow, to crimson red and every shade in between. She identified irises and lilies, coleus and violets, creeping phlox and alyssum, amaryllis and begonias. Having exhausted her meager botanical knowledge, there were dozens more that Katie couldn't identify, all in varying stages, from dormancy to bloom. A wonderful loamy, earthy scent mixed with the floral fragrances and created a potpourri of delight.

Katie's postage stamp sized yard on Delancey Street had permitted her but a miniscule fraction of earth in which to plant flowers. Though she treasured her tiny garden, it had been a poor relation to this display. Katie, only a fledgling gardener, felt as if she had stepped into paradise.

Not only was she assaulted by color and scent, there was the thrill of so many different textures. Lush and dense, grassy and spiky, smooth and supple, fuzzy and furry, she wanted to touch and feel each and every one. Beads of condensation and moisture from the humidity dotted the foliage like thousands of crystal ladybugs. The source of the moist heat was a wrought iron, potbelly stove set at the very back of the greenhouse. It cheerfully and dutifully massaged the plants with needed warmth.

Terra cotta pots spilled onto the stony paths and laid lackadaisically like discarded fez hats. There were trays of moss and seed pots and pea stone everywhere. Burlap bags of peat, vermiculite and potting soil were stacked against the table legs. Wire baskets lined with dried heath and tufts of coconut grass suspended from the beams like fertile wombs waiting to be filled. Like an abandoned deck of cards, seed packets were strewn on top of a small cleared work pace. Trowels, rakes, spades, work gloves, twine and chicken wire hung from nails pounded into the wooden support beams.

Letting out a whistle, Katie murmured, "Someone takes his gardening very seriously, indeed."

So engrossed and bewitched by the magical spell cast by the greenhouse, Katie was startled by a voice behind her and almost dropped the plate of cookies.

"I see that you have found your way to my private Garden of Eden."

Katie would never forget those first few words so softly spoken by Dr. Abraham Franke.

Katie always felt that most people fell into one of two categories. One was the type that was easy to figure out; they were exactly what they appeared to be. There was no mystery about them. They were neither oracular nor cryptic. They were either someone you felt comfortable with or someone with whom you immediately knew you would never feel a closeness or connection.

The second were enigmas. They carefully and discreetly hid their depths and vulnerability under layers of protective armor. For their own private and personal reasons, they felt that distance and reservation would create a separate, safe and impregnable world. Katie soon learned that Dr. Abraham Franke was from the latter.

When she first saw his face she thought him older than his sixty odd years. His salt and pepper hair, more salt than pepper, was uncombed, thinning and beginning to recede from his brow. Though his slight carriage was almost pain-fully erect, as if he was a scarecrow held up by a wooden pole, when he walked it was not with affirmation or purpose. Rather, he walked furtively with a hesi-tancy that gave the impression he was unsure or burdened by a far too heavy load.

His features were unremarkable, neither homely nor handsome, but there was a balance, an evenness, a steadiness about them. Not only did his carriage and movements seemed to be forced and deliberate. Years of living had etched their way across his face and his expression possessed a hollowness that spoke of pain, loneliness and need.

Katie recognized those emotions immediately. In the past year-and-a half, she had seen them often enough in the mirror. Not a glimmer of animation sparked his eyes. Half-moon shadows darkened his lower lids. Deep creases were carved at the sides of his mouth and hinted at long-ago smiles. Yet, it wasn't an unkind face. In fact, Katie felt she saw an elusive gentleness in those sad, dark eyes.

Their first conversation was stinted and uncomfortable. Dr. Franke, with a thick accent, hadn't been rude or dismissive, just perfunctory and wary. By its conclusion, Katie's social skills were exhausted. Still, she may have been de-pleted but far from discouraged and defeated. She was intrigued by Dr. Franke and felt an inexplicable attraction to him.

When she excused herself to return to her morning chores, she made a silent vow that if anyone could peel away the heavy curtain he had drawn around himself, she could. Da had always said she possessed a magical quality that naturally drew people to her like bees to honey. She had the ability to make people feel safe and comfortable. That Katie could strike up a friendship with the Devil, himself.

chapter five

Sensitive to Dr. Franke's need for privacy, Katie gave him a hiatus and didn't call on him again for a few days. Instead, she concentrated on the O'Neill side of the yews.

Now that she knew their stay would be permanent, the house and lake, the town and all their surroundings took on new meaning for Katie. Initially, she had viewed them as pleasant, but temporary. She hadn't allowed herself to feel an attachment and affection. Now, she felt as though she could embrace them without risk or trepidation. For the first time in months she felt safe. Her newfound sense of security rejuvenated her soul and exhilarated her spirit. She faced each new day with enthusiasm and was anxious to plant their roots as deep and as quickly as possible.

As was true of most mothers and housewives, Katie's social life revolved around her children, home and hearth. She joined the PTA and Ladies' Altar Society and signed up to be a room mother at school in the twin's class. Katie, the consummate extrovert, cheerfully greeted as many townspeople as possible on her weekly errands and somehow managed to find her way to the mailbox everyday just as Ernie Leszko was driving up for his mail delivery.

She introduced herself to fellow parishioners at Mass and resumed her Thursday night Novenas. Katie, bubbling with personality and affability, was quickly becoming the latest addition to many Christmas card lists. Exclamations and exciting news bubbled from the pages of her letters to Dee and Moira.

And, of course there was the lawyer. Matthew Mulholland paid weekly visits to his newest client. There were always documents to sign and a myriad of decisions to be made about a lot of legal mumbo-jumbo that made little sense to her. On occasion, the boys would be home from school when Matthew made one of his house calls. Tommy would retreat into his timid mode and needed gentle prodding to feel comfortable around Mr. Mulholland. With sensitivity, Matthew acknowledged Tommy's shyness and backed off. Since he had no children of his own, Katie had been surprised by Matthew's perceptiveness.

The twins, too intrepid to be timid, immediately took to him. That didn't surprise Katie in the least. Matthew Mulholland appeared to be no more than an over-grown kid. Brendan, wary at first, was soon won over by Matthew's easy charm and affable personality. Many times, the business calls turned into recess at the O'Neill's.

Katie had tried to work up the nerve to ask Matthew to dinner as a thank you for his help as well as the attention he paid the boys. She had no idea why she was so hesitant. It wasn't her nature to be cautious and reserved around people. Yet, she didn't want to appear to be assuming or forward. Perhaps she was afraid he might misconstrue her motives. Bothered and befuddled by her dilemma, she tried to dismiss her procrastination as unimportant. The right time would happen when it happened.

Katie was giddy as she busied herself with housework and discovered the personality of their new home, flaws and idiosyncrasies included. One of the upstairs bathtub faucets leaked and to stop the toilet from running incessantly, she had to wiggle the handle after each flush. The washing machine had to be coaxed from rinse to final spin and the refrigerator made sporadic clinks and clanks at odd hours of the night. Of course, there were strange creaks and squeaks that emanated with no definable source, peculiarities expected in any home. As inquisitive as the boys, she discovered treasures and surprises hidden in the attic and every closet and bureau drawer. Each day was a new adventure.

As Katie's fondness for their new home grew, she couldn't fight the feeling that she was still an intruder. At times she thought of herself as nothing more than a temporary guest. She harbored a strong sense that the house and every-thing in it still belonged to Aunt Katherine and as much as Katie longed to know her, only her ghost lingered, intangible and elusive. Even though they shared the same bloodline, Katie slept in the same bed, walked in her footsteps, breathed the air she breathed, Aunt Katherine still eluded her grasp and re-mained a mystery. Like trying to view a person through a hazy mist, it was impossible to make out their form and clear image of their features.

Katie felt that perhaps by immersing herself into Aunt Katherine's world, she would assimilate some knowledge of who she was. Katie could be as patient as necessary. She consoled herself that she had all the time in the world to let Aunt Katherine reveal herself how and when she was ready.

Katie likened herself to a blade of grass emerging from its winter solstice. How wonderful it must feel when the sun burns its way through thick March clouds, melts away the last crystals of snow and the first rays of warmth breath life into the blades of grass. Katie was ready to burst open with the exuberance of life too explosive to contain.

The change in their mother was contagious and translated itself to the boys. Katie hadn't been worried about Tommy and the twins. Small children were as pliable as putty. As long as the twins had room to run and each other they would be happy living in a cave. Tommy posed no concern, either. He would adapt and make the best of any situation. As long as the family was intact, Tommy would be content.

Brendan had caused her the most concern. He was at a vulnerable age when any move outside his comfort zone could be disastrous. He was a powder keg with a short fuse and had an attitude that would bring Santa Claus to his knees. Yet, Katie noticed that he too, seemed to be adjusting. He no longer walked around miserably with his shoulders hunched and his ball cap rim tugged low to conceal his face in shadows.

He talked about school and joining the baseball team. He unpacked the few items he had brought from his old bedroom and had scattered them around his room. Three pitching trophies, a bobble-head statue of Ted Williams, his missal and rosary, His Davy Crockett bank and locked toolbox containing his most treasured items had been placed on his dresser and windowsill. Out of reach of grubby little hands, his bat and mitt were tucked safely on the top shelf of his closet. Katie knew Brendan would be all right when she secretly viewed him from the hallway. He had a rare look of satisfaction as he nailed two Sox pennants to his bedroom wall.

α β

As soon as the inside was settled to her satisfaction, Katie turned herself loose on the outside. With the arrival of warmer weather she was itching to get outside and start the yard work. The boys had left for school and her morning chores were finished. She threw a heavy sweater over her housedress and disappeared into the garage to scare up some gardening tools.

The garage disappointed her. Her search hadn't been successful turning up a single shovel or rake. In fact, the place was immaculate and free from any of the usual tools and contraptions that littered most garages. Their garage in Boston had been so chucked full with maintenance paraphernalia, toys and useless junk that the car had been evicted to the driveway. Perhaps the garage attic would be more promising but she doubted it. Those were the kind of tools that were kept handy.

Then she thought of Dr. Franke. Certainly he would have the yard tools she needed. She recalled the greenhouse and knew she had seen plenty of tools and equipment. That would be an easier solution than stumbling around in the dark, spider-webbed attic.

It had been nearly a week since their first meeting. Surely he wouldn't consider her a presumptuous pest if she approached him to borrow some tools. He may not even be home, but Katie dismissed the possibility and headed in the direction of the guest cottage.

Not only was Dr. Franke home, she found him outside painting the door of the greenhouse.

Hands clasped behind her back, bent at the waist and standing on the balls of her feet, she greeted him softly so as not to startle him. "Good morning, Dr. Franke."

He hadn't been startled. In fact, he acted as if he hadn't heard her. Katie was unnerved by his silence. Just as she was about to repeat the greeting, he slowly returned his brush to the paint can and turned in her direction. His expression wasn't one of annoyance. In fact it seemed empty and passive.

"Good morning, Mrs. O'Neill," was all he said, slowly, timidly and without emotion.

"Isn't the sunshine wonderful?" she asked. "I thought I would take advantage of it to get some yard work done. But, there don't seem to be any gardening tools in the garage."

She paused a second to give him a chance to respond. She only met more silence. Silence could be pregnant with meaning. Only Katie couldn't be sure what the silence meant.

"If it wouldn't be too much trouble, I wondered if I might borrow a few from you?" she questioned.

After an eternal moment he finally answered. "Certainly. I am accustomed to doing all the lawn care and gardening. It had not occurred to me that those circumstances would change."

Katie immediately backed off. Angry with herself for sounding accusatory, she stammered, "No it wasn't … I mean … you weren't … you had no way of knowing that I would want them. It was such a nice day and I thought I might do a little yard work. Get some fresh air and be productive all at the same time."

Dr. Franke said nothing. The only sign Katie had that he was alive was the fact that he stood upright.

"Dr. Franke. I've never been a landlord before and to be honest, I'm a bit uneasy with it. Of course, I want things to remain as they've been. The last thing I want to do is disrupt your routine. Let's dispense with the whole landlord-tenant thing and just think of each other as neighbors. Think of me as a pesky neighbor here to borrow some of your lawn tools."

She risked a smile and he seemed to relax slightly.

After several seconds he asked, "What items would you like?"

"Just a rake and shovel." She added, "If you're not using them."

"I had no intentions of using them this morning."

At first Katie thought he might be merely accommodating her, then he continued his explanation. "I have no classes until the afternoon and hoped to get this painting finished before then."

The wind gusted and played with the idle strands of hair on his forehead.

For an instant, it reminded her of the way the wind played with Tommy's hair. In fact, Dr. Franke's entire presence put her mind of Tommy, timid, reticent and shy.

"Then I won't hold you up any longer," Katie said.

He slowly disappeared around the corner of the greenhouse. Katie wondered if he would disappear from the earth completely. But, he returned a minute later pushing a green wheelbarrow laden with a rake, trowel, spade and shovel.

"It looks as though you expect me to get quite a bit of work done," Katie laughed. "A wheelbarrow would be great, Dr. Franke."

"I thought it might be helpful. If it would not be too much trouble, I would be appreciative if any leaves or grass you rake could be returned to me. I believe very strongly in organic gardening and have a compost pile that is useful for providing nutrients to the soil naturally."

"No problem. I'll be glad to," she assured him. "Well, I'll let you get back to your chore and I'll get started on my own. I'll return all this when I'm finished."

Katie grabbed the two handles of the wheelbarrow and started home. Before she had gone ten feet, he said, "If I am not home you may park it next to the greenhouse. Do not worry about putting things away. I will take care of them."

Katie offered him a warm, "Good-bye, Dr. Franke."

He called a barely audible, "Good day, Mrs. O'Neill." But, his eyes didn't leave the tiny figure until the hedge engulfed her.

CZ   ED

Nearly another week passed before Katie and Dr. Franke had their next encounter. From her sitting room window she spotted him raking the remainder of last years' leaves from the side yard and felt it was as good a time as any to expand their relationship. His remoteness was puzzling. Whether it was a ruse or a plague, Katie wasn't sure. Either way it was unsettling.

She quickly threw on a pair of ancient, denim, bib overalls and tied her unruly hair with a handkerchief.

Dressed for dirty work, she approached him and offered her help. "Could you use an extra pair of hands, Dr. Franke?"

"This is not as enjoyable as it looks, Mrs. O'Neill."

He shocked her. The remark seemed droll and Katie wasn't sure if it he was joking or serious.

"Hard work suits me," she told him. "And I don't think I can mess up your gardens too much by raking leaves."

He gave a pensive thought to her offer and Katie thought he was building up to a refusal. He surprised her a second time. "If you would like to continue raking, I will dispose of this load and commandeer another rake."

Katie tucked a tress of curls that had escaped from her kerchief and reached for the rake. Dr. Franke surprised her a third time. He removed the yellow felt work gloves from his hands and handed them to Katie. Brown eyes dared her green eyes to meet his gaze and for a handful of seconds they did.

"If you continue to engage in yard work, you must learn to wear gloves, Mrs. O'Neill."

With a soft smile, she accepted his offer. "I'll wear these on one condition. You have to stop calling me Mrs. O'Neill. Katie works just fine."

"And Abraham works just fine for me."

Thus began the second journey for Katie that spring.

ෆ ฝ

For the first two weeks of their tenuous relationship, Katie was careful not to overstep the boundaries that were clearly important to Abraham. Even though she was eager and anxious to have him share his extensive knowledge of horticulture and expertise with her, she had to tread very carefully and curb her enthusiasm. There was more than a physical boundary of hedges and shrubbery that separated their two worlds. Far more impenetrable was the wall of isolation he had protectively constructed, the detachment he maintained.

Being alone was not the same thing as being lonely and Abraham was both. Katie knew that being alone was a physical condition and not necessarily an unpleasant one. There was a great deal of pleasure that could be derived from peace and solitude. Being lonely was an affliction of the heart. Loneliness was a state of personal desolation, either from nature or mankind. It was unhealthy and unnatural. Katie had been proof of that and she saw the same signs in Abraham.

At times, Katie sensed it; felt it more than saw it. Maybe it was because she had encountered the same sense of loneliness, the total, consuming realization of separateness. She could detect the subtleties that revealed a spiritless soul and the absolutes of aloneness.

She was perceptive enough to recognize that if they were to develop a friendship, it would have to evolve carefully, slowly, at a pace that he was comfortable with. Katie didn't want to crush it before it bloomed. Much like the plants and shrubbery he painstakingly tended, Abraham couldn't be forced or hurried, but allowed to emerge and evolve at his own pace, in his own time.

For Katie, gardening became the common ground in which to plant the seeds of friendship. As they worked together, she gently drew him into her life and approached him cautiously and with gentleness. She knew that familiarity is accomplished by subtlety, not force.

The formula worked. Hour after hour, day-by-day, baby-steps-by-baby-steps, Abraham began to, if not enjoy, at least become familiar with Katie's presence in his life. He respected her desire to learn and appreciated the interest she showed. Never rude or abrupt, he was always polite and pleasant and showed great patience and consideration.

She found the heavily German-accented, but perfect English he spoke, sweet and endearing. He always spoke with a softness and gentleness, yet carefully, as if he was consciously weighing every thought and word so as not to reveal too much about himself. His trepidation and sensitivity endeared him to her even more.

Katie had rapidly come to enjoy, anticipate and rely on their little putterings. She thought of herself as his budding protégé. He introduced her to the names, needs and characteristics of the plants that they lovingly toiled over. Katie all but gave up trying to master the Latin names of the Althaeas rosea, the Euphorbia marginata or the leontopodium something or other. She much preferred their common, familiar, whimsical names, such as hollyhock, coral bell or snow-on-the-mountain. Abraham and Katie discovered their common ground, that they loved them not for their botanical significance, but for their gentle beauty and subtle scents.

So, it was that first spring that the two of them could be found, when schedules and weather permitted, Dr. Abraham Franke and his little shadow working knee-to-knee and shoulder-to-shoulder, she barefoot, in her rolled up, worn overalls and floppy, straw hat, he in his black trousers, green Wellingtons and moth-eaten gray sweater, raking and digging, planting and transplanting, fertilizing and feeding.

Surprisingly, although he obviously valued his privacy and solitude, Katie noted that he never showed impatience or annoyance with the intrusion of the boys when they invaded his quiet peaceful world.

He immediately seemed to form a bond with Brendan, though Lord only knew why. Katie, herself was beginning to become annoyed with the unpredictability of his moods and had all but given up trying. In a matter of seconds, Brendan could leap frog from one extreme to the next. One moment helpful and considerate, the next, cool, cranky, self-absorbed and totally unapproachable. But, Abraham appeared not to be the least bit affected by Brendan's precarious disposition and often, the two worked well together, sharing the heavier chores and tasks of the unending demands of yard work and maintenance.

Perhaps, she reasoned, it was because Abraham was a grown up, not a pesky little brother. For the first time in a very long time, Brendan was exposed to an adult male instead of three pint-sized boys. Whatever the dynamics, she hoped, that each in their way, they would be good for each other.

In a totally different way, Abraham and Tommy had forged a mutual attachment. They were like two gentle spirits and like all the lost, injured and abandoned creatures that Tommy continuously brought home to be adopted, nurtured, mended and nursed back to health, he wanted to fix what was broken in Abraham. He wanted to minister and tend to Abraham's wounded soul as he would a baby rabbit mauled and mistreated by one of Mrs. Sweeney's cats or a baby bird that had fallen from the safety of its nest.

In return, Abraham allowed Tommy to prod and pamper him. He succumbed completely to the physical ministrations, never raising a hint of an objection when Tommy affixed a Curad over a blister or drowned a scuffed knuckle in Bactine. He would always gratefully accept a tepid glass of water, drinking it down as if it was icy-cold and he had just crossed the Mojave Desert.

Tommy would trail behind with his little red wagon, a miniature version of Abraham and his wheelbarrow, offering, at the very least, companionship. Though Tommy's interventions were often more a hindrance than help, Abraham didn't see it that way. He saw them as outward expressions of a generous heart.

The twins were another matter. Abraham appeared quite out of his depth when it came to their inexhaustible energy and the explosion of noise and activity that frequently invaded his quiet world. Suffering in silence, he would forbear with stoicism the annoyance and disquietude he felt when they would stalk him from the cover of brush or shrub.

On more than one occasion, Katie had to sternly point out that it was "impolite to stalk Dr. Franke even if they were Davy Crockett and Daniel Boone."

As she reasoned with them, Katie explained that he wasn't used to having little boys around and that they needed to respect that. Sometimes, ignoring her warnings, they would persist. Katie would have to resort to her ace in the hole, the sure-fire threat that always worked, "NO DESSERT."

Eventually, the twins adjusted their behavior and when not lying in wait, ready to ambush him, the remainder of the time, they treated him with complete indifference. Since he served no further purpose and his presence didn't directly affect them, they were unconcerned with the comings and goings of Dr. Franke who in their terms was "prob'ly at least a hundred years old."

C

Dreary March disappeared and was relegated to the past with other unremarkable and un-notable periods of time. Fulfillment of the promise that April showers give way to the sunnier days of May seemed imminent. The little path that led through the hedge of yews became well traveled. For both Abraham and the O'Neill's, the curious became commonplace and the strange became prosaic. As strangers became acquainted, the unfamiliar became the familiar and friendship began to grow.

After a weekend of heavy rains that began on Friday night and didn't disappear until late Sunday afternoon, the driveway's low spots were drowned in a chain of deep puddles. As if finally being released from under house arrest, Tommy and the twins were outside searching for an outlet in which to pour their pent up energy. Wearing their black, rubber galoshes they were performing an Eden Lake production of *Singing in the Rain*. Gene Kelly would have been appalled.

As most brilliant ideas, a lightening bolt struck Casey. The lake was way too cold, but the puddles weren't. Only a few necessary items were missing. He shared his brainstorm with his brothers and they scampered over to Dr. Franke's.

He, too, was outside taking advantage of the clearing skies when besieged by three, eager, soppy O'Neill children.

Tommy, being the most comfortable with Dr. Franke, was elected spokesperson. "Dr. Frank. We wanna build some boats. 'Cept we don't got any way to build 'em. Can you help us?" His soft features were splattered with muddy water.

Abraham was perplexed by the request. He had no knowledge of sailing vessels and even less about building them. "I would be happy to help you, only I have no materials and know nothing of boat building."

Tommy and Colin were immediately deflated and disappointment joined the freckles and mud on their faces. Casey would not be so easily discouraged.

"It's easy. All we need is some hunks of wood, nails an' string. We'll help you," Casey instructed as if the roles were reversed and Dr. Franke was the six-year-old.

Abraham tried to envision the finished products and the steps required to arrive there. His contemplation was taking far too long for the twins.

"We promise we won't make a mess or nothin`," Colin coaxed Dr. Franke.

All three, spattered faces stared at him with eager eyes, Tommy's the deep green of his mother's and the twin's as blue as bell flowers.

Abraham discovered that he couldn't resist. "Very well. I believe the items needed may be found in the greenhouse."

He propped his spade against the shed and led them to the greenhouse. Only Tommy and Brendan had ever been inside. The twins had been too disinterested in Dr. Franke to care.

When they entered, Casey's surprise translated into naive impudence. "Man alive! Dr. Franke what a mess!" He turned a three-sixty. "Mommy`d have a cow if our bedrooms got this messy. You gotta lotta neat stuff in here. What'cha got all that dirt an' junk for?"

"All of this *stuff* is necessary for gardening. This is where I grow all the plants until they are strong enough to be transplanted outside."

Colin, spotted a bucket of tiny white balls and asked, "What's this stuff? Looks like snow. How kin ya have snow if it ain't winter?"

"That is vermiculite," Abraham answered matter-of-factly.

Casey asked the obvious, his face a question mark, "What'cha do with it?"

Abraham struggled to find the right words. His vocabulary hadn't needed to bend to a child's in many years. *How does one explain vermiculite to a small boy?*

"It is mixed with the soil and helps it to breathe. Just as you must breathe, so must the plants."

Unimpressed with the vermiculite issue, Casey moved on and pointed to the trays of soil. "An' this dirt. What'cha got it for?"

"Those are the beds where I plant the seeds. Soon, all of them will have tiny, green sprouts growing from the soil."

Colin asked, "How come ya gotta have so much dirt. What'cha need so much dirt for?"

"It is not only dirt. Some of it is peat, some of it is mulch and some of it is potting soil. Different types of dirt and soil are needed for different types of plants."

Abraham, a born teacher, welcomed their inquisitiveness but was nervous as their energetic bodies bobbed around like corks on water. He was acutely aware that their exuberance and lack of physical restraint would spell disaster for his delicate seedlings.

Casey and Colin fired "how comes," "what's" and "why's" until Abraham was frustrated and mentally exhausted. He finally managed to turn their attention back in the direction of boat building. He sought out three sections of one-by-fours that had been cut for garden stakes. Each one of them had one end cut in a *V* so that they could be easily tamped into the soil.

"Will these be acceptable for boats?" he asked the boys.

Colin exclaimed, "Yeah! Those'r keen!"

Satisfied that he had supplied acceptable vessels, Abraham dug a handful of two-penny nails from the coffee can on the workbench. He removed a small ball peen hammer from its perch on a shelf and prepared to hammer the first nail.

Casey immediately complained, "We gotta pound our own nails. They won't be *our* boats if we don't make 'em ourselfs." With a forceful nudge of his shoulder, he wiggled next to Dr. Franke, virtually pushing Colin out of the way.

Colin wasn't about to be usurped and jammed himself against Dr. Franke's other side. "I get to go first this time, Casey. You always go first."

"Do not."

"Do so."

"Hunh unh."

"Uh huh."

Colin started to wrestle the hammer from Casey's grip. "Get your own hammer. I got this one."

Tommy stood back and patiently waited his turn. He'd been around the twins long enough that he was beyond getting embarrassed and he had no interest in getting caught in the middle.

Abraham intervened and removed the hammer from both their fists. "Since Tommy is being so patient and acting like a gentleman, I will let him be first."

"That's cuz he's your favorite," Casey accused and stuck his tongue out at Tommy.

"Put that tongue back where it came from. I have no favorites. I am simply rewarding good manners and proper behavior. If your manners do not improve there will be no boat building for anyone." He was very stern. It was the closest Abraham had come to raising his voice in over a decade.

His tone worked. Casey and Colin settled down.

After all three had nailed several nails around the perimeter of the wood, Abraham took a ball of twine and demonstrated how they should apply it. Tying one end to the prow, he stretched the twine from nail to nail, circling the nail head once. When he had traced the entire perimeter and returned to the first nail, he tied a snug knot and cut the twine, leaving six feet of excess for propulsion.

When the boats were completed, Abraham put the materials away. Several minutes passed as each boy admired his boat as if it were a shiny, new yacht. Abraham eventually shooed them out the door and pointed them in the direction of home.

Tommy tugged on Abraham's sleeve. "Ya gotta come watch us," he insisted. "Ya helped us build 'em. Ya gotta watch 'em float."

Colin agreed. "Yeah, Dr. Franke. See which one of 'ems fastest."

Casey was so busy admiring his craft that he couldn't have cared less if Dr. Franke came or not. But, Tommy and Colin did and with persistent cajoling, Abraham finally gave in.

The trio sloshed and slopped across Abraham's yard, through the hedge and across Katie's saturated grass. As the boys zigzagged a path across the lawn, Abraham took note that not a single puddle escaped their attention as the boys splashed through every one. Like a dog shaking after a bath, the leaves and branches showered down on them in thousands of droplets.

When they arrived at the launching site in the driveway, their hair was drippy wet and their shirts splattered dark with moisture. Even Abraham looked like he had been sprayed with a garden hose.

Casey eagerly launched his boat first in the biggest puddle he could find. Colin and Casey soon followed. The maiden voyages were a success. The *Casey*, the *Colin* and the *Tommy* all cruised successfully if not gracefully. The boys ran back and forth, pulling their crafts behind, sometimes so fast that the boats became airborne, other times lazy and slow, creating miniature ripples in their wakes. Peels of laughter and as many nautical terms as their limited vocabularies could muster filled the air.

Katie was removing an apple pie from the oven when she was drawn to the kitchen window by the commotion. With a mitted hand, she drew back the edge of the curtain to broaden her view. Initially confused, her brow scrunched in bewilderment. She couldn't figure out when, where and how the crude boats had materialized.

Then she spotted Abraham leaning against the maple tree next to the drive, his arms crossed and his wispy hair plastered to his head like wet ashes. She studied the solitary figure and her questions were immediately answered. Abraham was usually sober as a monk. Yet, she saw something extraordinary and provocative settle across his features. She saw something she had never seen before in Abraham. She saw satisfaction.

Brendan wandered into the kitchen thirsty for a glass of milk and noticed his mom's attention riveted at the window. His curiosity got the best of him and he joined her at the window. Katie, immediately aware of his presence, turned to look at him. He towered over her and it seemed as if he had sprouted six inches overnight. Her mother's heart wondered how it had happened without her realizing it.

"What are the little morons doing now?" he asked.

"Something that I remember you doing not so many years ago."

"The little goof balls," he sneered. "I never did anything that dumb in my whole life."

Katie suppressed a chuckle. "That dumb and a lot dumber."

"No way," he insisted. "Sometimes I can't believe I'm related to those jerks."

"I hate to burst the balloon of sophistication and selective memory that you have miraculously developed, Bren. But you did the exact same thing as they are doing right now and enjoyed it just as much."

Brendan decided he didn't have to stand there and be accused of all kinds of stupid things that he knew he never did. It was just his mom in one of her moods again. He took one last look at the little dweebs and sputtered, "Dufuses."

Forgetting about his thirst, he evacuated the kitchen before his mom said any more dumb stuff.

 C3   80

If Abraham ever looked forward to anything with anticipation, it was spring. It was a time of change and rebirth. A time when things long buried under the solitary repose of winter would renew, grow and flourish. And nowhere else was that more evident than in his quiet world of gardening. It was his world, alone and apart. It was a world where the sights and sounds of a haunted past would be borne away on the wisps of the wind.

Abraham knew every inch of the soil as well as he knew the wrinkles in his hands. He also knew that the covenant of spring was finally fulfilled when winter ceded its grip. But, that spring Abraham sensed that something was different. Nothing obvious, merely an impression he had of a subtle, fleeting glimmer, like a glint of sunshine on a nugget of gold, half-buried, half-uncovered in a stream bed. It was a peculiar, unsettling sensation of something being slightly off kilter. He thought it was an odd feeling, but not an unpleasant one. It was a strangely fascinating, though elusive sensation that he could not quite identify. Yet, it felt as real to him as the rich soil between his fingers.

⋈ ⋈

Early one Sunday morning, just after sunrise, before the sun's rays had warmed the night dew from the grass, an alarming level of screams and shouts drew Abraham through the hedge. Normally, a disturbance of that magnitude was not the least uncommon coming from the O'Neill's. But due to the unusually early hour, he was simultaneously intrigued and concerned.

Three little boys, still dressed in pajamas, scampered about the lawn in the gray, early light of morning. Each carried a wicker basket. They squealed and hollered and searched the lawn for what appeared to be colored eggs. Each time they located one of the vibrant ovals, it was added to their baskets and peals of laughter filled the air.

Excited, high-pitched voices exclaimed, "The Easter Bunny came! The Easter Bunny came!"

Up until that morning, Abraham had to admit, that he had never seen anything quite like it. Of course, he had heard about the American custom of celebrating Easter but had never witnessed it. It was one of the most delightful exhibitions he had ever seen.

In robe and slippers, Katie sat on the porch steps sipping a cup of tea and calmly, enjoyed the activity. Totally engrossed and occupied by the drama, she never noticed Abraham.

As dramatic as the lawn frenzy was, Abraham found that his gaze was drawn to Katie and he observed her with quiet fascination. The damp air curled her hair into a chestnut halo that almost glowed. He noted her gentle smile. In their hours together, he could not remember a time when a smile did not brighten her face and fill it with life. But, it was more than a physical, angelic luminance that attracted him. Katie was the most genuinely joyful person he had ever known. There was something very special and grand about her that radiated from within. Her spirit was gentle but strong. At times, she almost made him want to feel and care again.

Those were sentiments he had buried a long time ago. Feelings he thought could never be resurrected and he had thought that was where he wanted them to stay. He began to question his guarded solicitude. It was a skill he had honed sharply and effectively. Now, he was no longer certain and that doubt was both stirring and frightening.

What was it that he expected? He challenged himself. *What was it about Katie that frightened him? What was it he did not want from that special young woman?* Perhaps the more frightening question was *what did he want?*

He left the O'Neill's to their celebration and more confused than ever, he turned and disappeared back into his own world.

chapter six

It was Monday morning and Katie was busy packing lunchboxes.

For once, the boys had all managed to arrive at the breakfast table on time and together.

Casey questioned, through a mouthful of pancakes and syrup, "Mommy, what's a macaroni slapper?"

Brendan nearly snorted milk out of his noise, trying to stifle a fit of laughter.

"Don't talk with your mouth full. I have no idea what you're talking about," Katie answered.

"A macaroni slapper. I heard it on the bus."

Brendan intercepted, wiping milk from his chin. "It's not a macaroni slapper, you little goof ball. It's a mackerel snapper."

"Some of the kids on the bus call us that," Colin joined in.

"And fish sticks, too," Tommy added with a furrowed brow.

Katie dried her hands on her apron and sat down at the table. She looked into their questioning eyes. "Does it bother you when they call you that?"

"Yeah, 'cuz some a the other kids laugh at us." Tommy's voice reflected his pain.

"We're Catholic and Catholics don't eat meat on Fridays. We call it abstinence. Since we don't eat meat, we have to think of different things to eat, like fish. A mackerel is a kind of fish that some people eat on Fridays."

The expression on the boys' faces revealed that Katie's explanation hadn't answered the question. She drew a breath then continued. "Some people who aren't Catholic don't understand that. Sometimes when people don't understand things, it makes them afraid. They think that if they make fun of it and call other people names it will make them feel better and less scared. You know we've talked about how calling other people names might hurt their feelings."

"But what am I supposed to do when they call me a name?" Casey asked.

"Just ignore them. Most people will get tired of teasing someone who just ignores them. It doesn't make it fun anymore." Katie knew that was far easier to do in theory than reality. "Try to remember what I've always said …"

Casey cut in. "Sticks an' stones may break our bones, but names will never hurt us." He rocked his head back and forth.

Brendan rolled his eyes and Katie warned him with one raised eyebrow. That signal, told him she meant business.

"Now, finish your breakfasts, or you'll all be late for the bus. Colin, wipe the milk mustache off your lip. And use your napkin instead of your sleeve."

They all wiped their faces with their napkins, gathered their belongings, put on their jackets and Katie kissed and hugged each one good-bye.

Brendan moaned as his turn came. "Mom, I'm too old for that."

He tried to duck out the door. Katie caught him. "You'll never be too old for that."

She managed a hurried hug and stolen kiss.

As they all ran off down the drive, she called after them, "Have a good day, my little mackerel snappers."

CȜ ȣ

Tommy, Casey and Colin all adjusted to their new school and classmates. Every night, the dinner-table-entertainment included shared stories about the many adventures and misadventure that involved their playmates and filled their school days.

Rotating the privilege, Katie allowed them to have friends over. The invitations were reciprocated and the mom's often alternated and shuttled the boys back-and-forth to one another's house. Katie's social circle was growing mommy by mommy.

As Katie had predicted, Brendan fit it in well and was readily admitted into the cruelly pragmatic and oftentimes, arbitrary, selective and closed fraternity of male adolescents. His good looks and natural athletic abilities helped insure his immediate acceptance into their teenage brotherhood. He quickly struck up a friendship with four other boys from school and Katie affectionately referred to them as the Five Musketeers.

At first, matching the correct name to the correct Musketeer proved a challenge. It wasn't that Katie had a problem with names, but the boys complicated the process by calling each other nicknames. So, Katie decided it was much simpler to call them by their given names.

Steven Brisbois, or Breeze, as he preferred to be called, was moderate in both physical and personality characteristics. His willowy body was of average height, hair a neutral brown and features balanced. He was the most easy-going of the five. Like the waves, he would ebb and flow with the prevailing wind. Whenever an argument arose among the group, he applied the wisdom of Solomon and played the role of arbitrator.

Arthur Stueben, called Stump, was built like a pile driver, solid and compact. He was the comedian and rascal of the group. He laughed easily and never took anyone or anything too seriously. Fair skinned with strawberry blonde hair, the abundant smattering of freckles across his nose and cheeks rivaled that of the twins. He had an impish grin and a glint in his eyes and Katie considered them ever-present reminders that he was a bag of mischief looking for a place to happen.

Walter Polaski was affectionately known as Puke. Katie didn't even want to know the origin of that moniker. Walter moved at his own pace, which had three speeds, slow, slower and standstill. He was notoriously late for everything. Except mealtime. Convinced that he must have at least one hollow leg, she had never seen any male, boy or adult, who possessed a stronger proclivity and preoccupation with food. He could out eat everybody and looked the part. Soft, round and cuddly, he reminded Katie of a roguish *Winnie the Pooh*.

Vincent Mizzano, simply called Vinnie, shared the strongest bond with Brendan. They both had dark hair and eyes, were handsome, trim and athletic. They were the two stars of the baseball team, Brendan the pitcher, Vincent the catcher. They sat next to each other in school and shared the same altar boy rotations. Mature and earnest for their age, on the puberty scale, they were eons ahead of the other boys. Unlike Bren, Vincent was an only child, but like Bren, Vincent had lost a parent. His mother had died of complications shortly after giving birth. Maybe that commonality is what drew them together, the pain of growing up in a wounded home.

It became a common sight to see Vincent and Brendan walking home from baseball practice or a game, bats resting on their shoulders, mitts dangling from the end of the bats, immersed in the dialogue of two teenage buddies.

Of all the new mommies Katie had met, her favorite was Angie Brisbois, Steven's mom. She was as comfortable as an old slipper and she and Katie struck up a quick and easy friendship. Besides her sense of humor, Angie's physical appearance brought a smile to Katie's face. There wasn't anything petite about Angie Brisbois. She was built like a freight train and had a voice and laugh to match. Ironically, she wore her dark brown hair in a pixie cut. The cropped hair-do made her look as if as an afterthought, her pea-sized head had been screwed on her broad shoulders. Every time the Brisbois' station wagon pulled up, Katie prepared herself for a few minutes of hilarious banter.

One Tuesday, Vincent and Steven had come over after school and had eaten dinner with Brendan. Angie and Mr. Mizzano were due to pick them up at any moment. Typically, late, Angie arrived at seven-thirty and caught Katie on the side porch watering some potted begonias.

"Maybe that's what I'm doing wrong with my pitiful pansies. I never thought to water them." Angie's voice boomed at Katie without a "hello" or "hi-ya."

"Water and a little attention and you can convince anything to grow." Katie smiled at her.

"The only thing I manage to grow is crabgrass and my backside. How much would you charge to come over to my place and rescue me from some of the weeds I call flowers?"

Katie promised, "For you, Angie, I would do it for nothing."

Angie leaned one beefy elbow on the porch railing. "On second thought, forget it. It would only leave Fred with my weight to tease me about. Every time I come home from the nursery with another victim he tells me that I might as well save myself a lot of time and go toss my money in the lake."

"Have time for a cup of tea?"

Angie's laughter rolled from her chest like thunder. "You know better than to even ask, Katie. As usual, I'm running two days behind. You could set your watch by me. That way you'd always know what time it was an hour ago."

"You're not late, Angie. Just perpetually unhurried."

"Leave it to you to be diplomatic, too. You're gorgeous, have a shape most females would kill for and are so sweet sugar wouldn't melt in your mouth." Angie shook her head.

"Don't forget my green thumb." Katie wiggled her digit like a nervous hitchhiker.

"You're so disgustingly perfect I feel obligated to hate you. Haven't figured out a way to do it yet. But, I'm working on it."

"You like me because Steven eats half his meals here. I save you grocery money so you can waste it on plants." Katie's dimples deepened as she smiled.

"Speaking of my first-born. Shoo Steve and Vinnie out here. I got a cake in the oven at home. Fred hasn't figured out how to open and close the oven door. The cake could start on fire and burn to a crisp before it would occur to him that maybe the black smoke billowing from the kitchen warranted investigation."

"I can save you some time there. Vincent said his dad was picking him up," Katie tried to force out the sentences amid her laughter.

"Uh ... no. I'm taking Vinnie home. Frank Mizzano is slightly *indisposed* at the moment." Angie rolled her eyes.

"He's sick?" Katie asked with concern.

Angie looked around to make certain there were no little ears or eyes around. Assured they were alone, she raised her hand to her mouth, tossed her head back and pretended to be tipping a bottle.

"He drinks?" Katie nearly squealed.

"Like a fish."

"He comes here selling vegetables and I never noticed." Katie suddenly felt very sorry for Vincent. "I had no idea."

"What do you do all day, Katie? Polish you halo? You mean you never heard anyone refer to him as 'Fermenting Frank'?"

Katie scolded her. "Really, Angie. That's a terrible thing to say. No I haven't. And even if I did, I wouldn't have believed it."

"Well, Miss Congeniality, you'd better believe it. Fred says he saw Frank's truck parked at the Rest-A-While on his way home from work. And it was still sitting there when I drove over here. That means only one thing. He's on the sauce and will not be picking Vinnie up."

"I see Mr. Mizzano twice a week when he stops by to sell produce. He always seems fine to me. A bit quiet and abrupt but I assumed that was just his nature." Katie tried to recall any signs that she may have missed and drew a blank.

"The Frank Mizzano you see today is not the man he once was," Angie explained. "Before Corrine died he was as good as they come, a loving husband and steady provider. It took Corrine a long time and a half dozen miscarriages to carry a pregnancy to term. Frank was thrilled when it looked like they were finally going to have a baby. When Corinne died, only days after Vinnie was born, I think a huge part of Frank died with her."

Katie's brow lined with concern. "But Frank must have been conscientious enough to care for Vincent. Babies are a lot of work. How did he manage?"

"After Corrine died, Frank's mother came to live with him to help with Vinnie. For a few years it looked as if Frank had weathered the storm. But about eight years ago, Mrs. Mizzano passed away and that was when Frank found the bottle and Vinnie lost a father. Since then, he's never been the Frank Mizzano that married Corrine."

Katie was shocked. "And he's been drinking heavily for all these years?"

"You could say off and on. He's a binge drinker. Lays off the booze for weeks then goes on a real toot."

"That must be horrible for Vincent."

"Don't cut Vinnie short. He can handle himself. He's probably got more recipes for curing a hangover than anybody. And in spite of the drinking, down deep inside, Vinnie loves his dad and I figure Frank loves Vinnie. In his own way."

"Vincent could spend the night here."

"No way, Katie. Vinnie has his pride. He'd die before he'd swallow it and embarrass himself and his dad and let you make a big deal out of it. He's almost fourteen-years-old. He'll be all right. Nothing he hasn't dealt with before."

After they had rounded up the boys, Katie slammed the passenger door after Vincent and Steven were settled in the front seat. Angie started the car, put it in reverse and started to creep down the drive. She hollered out the window, "I owe you one, Katie. You've fed them the last three times. The next one's on me." She waved her left arm, the chicken fat of her underarm flapped through the window. Katie and Brendan watched them disappear in the trees.

Katie turned to Brendan. "Make sure all your homework is done. I'll be up in a few minutes."

After Brendan went inside and the kitchen door slapped shut behind him, Katie stared off at the darkening yard. As the last of the daylight dwindled to a blue-gray, she thought about Vincent and Mr. Mizzano. She finally realized that perhaps the death of a father wasn't the worst thing that could happen to a boy.

chapter seven

April was escorted out by May and the O'Neill household settled into a comfortable routine. Katie welcomed the routine. It meant that their lives had settled into predictability, which Katie equated with stability.

Orvis Skrippy, the milkman came on Mondays and Thursdays; Marie Dreffs, the egg lady, on Wednesdays. Mr. Mizzano continued to come by like clockwork, twice a week, and delivered fruits and vegetables from his truck. Katie couldn't fight the urge to try and detect the signs that would tell her whether or not he had been drinking. Maybe it was wishful thinking, but she didn't think he acted oddly or differently and she was sure she couldn't smell alcohol on his breath. She hoped for Vincent and Mr. Mizzano that his last binge would truly be the last.

Mondays were laundry day; Tuesdays Katie ironed and mended. Wednesdays were devoted to cleaning the upstairs, Thursdays she marketed and ran errands and Fridays she cleaned the main floor. The boys always knew it was Friday. The last day of the school week was confirmed when Katie headed them off at the back door by calling, "Use the front door, I just waxed the kitchen floor."

Katie continued her daily rendezvous at the mailbox with Erwin Leszko. Besides his cheerful personality, Katie enjoyed the arrival of letters from Dee and Moira and news and happenings from other friends back east. It was refreshing to actually look forward to the daily arrival of the mail, no longer afraid to face dunning statements and overdue notices from creditors.

Saturdays were sacred because they were reserved for gardening.

Abraham had tutored her well. Katie loved to get outside and feel the dirt between her fingers. She even enjoyed the tedious task of weeding. Anything to do with gardening was a labor of love. She had learned to recognize and appreciate even the subtlest of changes. There was something constant about the garden, something solid and dependable, yet exciting about it.

As prophesized, April showers did bring May flowers. And the rain-soaked, precarious, sometimes cool, sometimes warm days of the month of April bowed to the arrival of May. With its warmer, sunnier days, May brought with it her first rewards.

The spring bulbs began to give way to the early summer bloomers. The annuals were firmly established and beginning to show off a palette of colors that would last well into the fall. Katie thought of them as the meat and potatoes—the old reliables. They didn't need to be thinned, or dug up in the fall. They didn't need to be mulched and protected through the winter months. Sturdy and dependable, they weren't temperamental or fragile. While the perennials came and went, the annuals would continue to bloom and share their beauty until the first hard frost of autumn ended the growing season.

Katie and Abraham's efforts were beginning to yield a profit. Tulips of every color, from fiery red to blushing pink, sunny yellow daffodils, buttercups and jonquils, pastel purple and gold irises, vibrant orange, coral and mustard narcissus and delicate spring starflowers, even the white, subtle snowdrops and calla lilies, all took turns dotting the beds with every hue and color imaginable. Mother Nature was throwing a birthday party and the blooms were her balloons.

Each day, Katie reveled in their varied colors and lights scents and couldn't wait to peek outside to see what new treasure had unfolded overnight. Her favorites, though, were the lilies-of the-valley. Maybe it was because they had been her mother's favorites, or maybe it was their wonderful fragrance, or maybe it was because they blossomed for such a short time that made them all the more precious.

Even the grassy green of the lawn deepened in color. The dull, pale brown of winter disappeared and April showers and the sun's increased intensity had warmed it into a healthy, Irish green. The fleeting, sweet, scents from the flowering cherry, crabapple and lilac trees had peaked and performed their brief dance. They had begun to fade as the delicate, waning blossoms showered the air with pastel snowflakes.

May, the month of Mary. The month chosen to honor the Blessed Virgin who represented the sanctity of motherhood and the fertility of spring. Mary, the most privileged of all women, was chosen to bear the Son of God and within her chaste womb she carried the baby that would be called Jesus.

Katie felt a special bond with Mary. Of course, she was her patron saint. But beyond that, Mary was a mother and knew the joys and sorrows of that vocation. Katie prayed often to Mary and asked for her intercession. She prayed the rosary, a special devotion to Mary, daily and offered it up for special intentions.

The thoughts of May and Blessed Mary carried Katie back to her schoolgirl days when every May was welcomed with a special celebration. All of the girls donned their best dresses. With wreaths of flowers woven in their hair and carrying sprigs of hand picked flowers, they would make a procession into church.

Joining them were the boys in starched white shirts and navy blue trousers. Together, they would form two lines leading from the school, up the church steps and into the church, all the way up to the Communion rail.

Each year, one girl was chosen to place a crown of flowers on the statue of the Blessed Virgin Mary. Katie had never been lucky enough to be selected, but it hadn't mattered. She was happy to simply be a part of it all.

She could still hear the hymn joyously sung by that chorus of sweet, youthful voices.

O, Mary, we crown thee
With blossoms, today,
Queen of the Angels,
Queen of the May.

Humming the music and recalling the words silently in her mind, after all the years Katie could still remember every word.

Katie, still humming the tune, hung laundry on the clothesline in her usual attire, a cotton housedress and barefoot. When indoors, or the outside elements permitted, she loved going barefoot. It made her feel carefree, gave her a sense of impulsive spontaneity. Besides, she loved the feel of cool grass, or smooth clean floors, sun warmed sand, or snugly carpets against them. She loved to stand at the lake's edge and let the waves of water squish the sand between her toes.

The day was warm and breezy, perfect for line drying and Katie loved to watch the clothes as they billowed in the wind. They always seemed cleaner, brighter and fresher when warmed by the sun's rays. She felt there was no scent more wonderful than that of laundry, wind blown and sun kissed.

As she hung the last of the towels, she heard a car pull up the drive. She wondered who could be paying a visit this early in the day. Matthew Mulholland often dropped by, but never without calling first. Still … ?

Katie half-hoped it would be Matt and smoothed the folds of her housedress. Her fingers danced quickly through her hair, and tried to coax the wild strands of curls back into her braid. As usual, it wasn't cooperative. She walked around the house and stepped out inquisitively from the side yard.

If Katie was disappointed it wasn't Matthew Mulholland, it didn't show. Had she been wearing shoes, she would have jumped out of them as her auditory senses were blasted with an ear-splitting assault. A long, loud, horn blast belched from the biggest, shiniest, gaudiest, chromed, candy-apple red convertible she had ever seen. It was Detroit's version of the Queen Mary.

A woman, of indeterminable age, swept out of the Cadillac and clip-clopped her way across the macadam, red high heels smacking the pavement. She un-wound a pink chiffon scarf from her head and uncovered a lacquered mass of tangerine curls pasted to the top of her forehead. The rest of her hair was swept up in a bouffant confection of swirls. Never in her life could Katie remember seeing hair that color.

In one hand, the visitor carried a huge pink straw purse covered in big, artificial daisies. In the other hand she carried a bouquet of snapdragons, carnations and larkspur that she immediately thrust at Katie.

"What on earth are y'all doin' out in this sunshine without a bonnet on yawr head?" She scolded Katie in a slow, smoky, southern drawl.

"With that fair Irish skin of yawrs, yawr gonna freckle up an' burn in no time, Sug. Let's get y'all an` those flowers inside 'fore y'all wilt. Ma name's Lottie Devereaux. I'm yawr next dawr neighbor."

Katie followed the woman inside like a child of Hamlin being led by the Pied Piper. Lottie tossed her purse on the table and began opening and closing cupboard doors until she found what she was looking for. In one fluid motion, she extricated a tall crystal vase, filled it with water and taking the bouquet from Katie, proceeded to arrange the flowers in the vase.

"Don't mind me makin' maself ta home. Ain't never been one ta stand on ceremony." That was as close as Lottie ever came to apologizing for her behavior.

All Katie could manage was a dumbfounded, bewildered grin.

"After I get maself settled in ta ma place, I'll welcome ya proper like. Jus' got back last night. Can't cotton ta these long Michigan winters. Without a so long or adios, I usually take off 'round February an' head on down south ta Nawlans.

"I usually go on down there fawr tha Mardi Gras celebrashun. What a hoo-ha that is, I tell ya what! Raise some Cain, see ma kin, an' let tha Gulf air chase tha winter chill outta ma bones. Usually don't come back 'til I'm convinced tha snow's stopped blowin'."

"Been livin' up north here, sorta permanent like, ever since Rollie, that is Regis LaFontaine Devereaux, husband number four, God rest his soul, brought me up north here ta live … 'bout ten … twelve years ago. I was born an' raised down in bayou country an' even after all these years, I still ain't used ta yawr northern climate. Guess there's too much Mississippi mud runnin' through ma veins."

Katie found she had to concentrate on every syllable to understand or follow the conversation. So enthralled by the woman's accent and flourish, Katie almost forgot herself. Like a startled chipmunk, she scrambled for the teapot.

As she fussed with collecting the china, she apologized, "Excuse my manners, I'm Katie O'Neill. Mary Katherine, to be exact. But for as long as I can remember, everyone's called me Katie. May I offer you some tea?" She began to prepare the pot.

Lottie waved a blood red nail-polished hand at her. "Don't be puttin' yawrself ta no trouble on ma account, Sug, but I sure could go fawr a glass a iced tea. Been inta town pickin' up some groceries an' essentials an' I'm drier'n a popcorn fart. Oh, speakin' a groceries, I almost forgot."

She dipped into the depths of her purse, rummaged through the contents, in an unhurried, but determined fashion. She raised her eyes toward the ceiling and concentrated as her fingers dug through the debris. Finally, she triumphantly pulled up two fruit jars, dark with jam.

"Voila! Brought these all tha way from Lewzianna. No store bought jam these are, but pure, sweet blackberry preserves. Berries picked right from ma Uncle Zwilly's blackberry bushes an' then straight ta ma Aunt Effie Lee's cannin' jars. Nothin' sweeter or finer y'all ever have pass through yawr lips, Sug."

Katie thanked her for the flowers and the jam, served her iced tea, complete with lemon and sugar. Katie almost choked as Lottie tossed four, heaping spoonfuls of sugar into her tea.

"Got me a bit of a sweet tooth, I do." She winked at Katie and with dancing, dark chocolate eyes leaned in close and added, "Mosta tha men in ma life liked their women with a few well placed curves. Like ma Granddaddy Pope used ta say, 'Can't bide no woman without a fair-share of meat on her bones, gotta have somethin' there ta hold on ta.' 'Course, I can see I got a ways ta go ta put some a Granddaddy Pope's advice ta work on y'all. Yawr nothin' but a rack a bones, not 'nough there ta hang a coonskin on.

"Gets mighty breezy up here, comin' off tha lake an' all. Y'all are likely ta blow away, ya ain't careful, Sug." She stopped talking just long enough to take a long draw of her iced tea. "Yawr a right pretty thing. Musta come by it on yawr daddy's side, 'cuz y'all sure don't take after yawr Aunt Katherine. Had a face like she'd been weaned on a pickle. Now there was a woman needed handlin' with kid gloves. Had a tongue that could clip a hedge, I tell ya what."

She wagged a single finger at Katie. "Let me tell ya, had ta give that one wide berth. She was all take an' no give an' made it clear, right off, that it was her way or tha highway an' was so ornery an' uptight y'all couldn't a have pulled a needle outta her ass. Stubborn as a mule in August heat.

"'Course, it ain't Christian to be judgin' nobody by yawr own half bushel. I reckon she had her good side an' all, even if ya had ta look long an' hard fawr it. Ya gotta give her her due, though. An' it seems her stubbornness paid off. Looks like she finally got her way after all. Was hell bent on havin' y'all come live here after yawr loss, an' sure 'nough here ya are. That woman had one heck of a long reach, all tha way from tha here-after."

Katie took advantage of the brief pause as the woman took another drink of tea. "I didn't know my Aunt Katherine all that well. Even though she was my godmother, I hadn't seen her since I was five or six. She and my folks had a parting of the ways and had cut off all contact years ago."

Katie noticed that Lottie listened intently. Maybe she knew something of the history. Maybe Aunt Katherine and Uncle Sean had talked to her about it. Lottie may be able to fill in some of the blanks.

Eager to find out, she continued, "Aunt Katherine and Uncle Sean immigrated to America first, then my ma and da followed with me. They stayed close until something happened between them and that was the end of it. My folks never told me what happened, but whenever they spoke of Aunt Katherine it was always with anger and bitterness.

"I'm never sure if I actually remember her as she was or as my folks wanted her to be. I do remember that Uncle Sean always had peppermint candies in his vest pocket. It's funny what memories our minds choose to save. Anyway, seeing as you were neighbors, I wonder if Aunt Katherine ever told you what happened between them? Did she ever talk to you about it?"

Lottie didn't give it more than a second's thought and snorted. "Ha! Y'all sure didn't know her very well. She'd a rather swallowed poison than discuss anythin' as delicate as feelins an' emoshuns. Yawr Aunt Katherine never talked much 'bout anythin' with me. But, knowin' her, I reckon tha biggest slice a tha pie a blame was likely hers. Mos' folks find it easier ta make a meal outta good sense than ta make a meal outta pride. It's highly likely neither of 'em could remember tha gist of it, after all them years. Sometimes things jus' have a way a snowballin' all outta control. That's tha trouble with mos' feudin.' After it's all over, it's mighty hard ta remember what set it off in tha first place."

Like two clucks in a henhouse, gathered around the kitchen table, Lottie and Katie passed the next hour. Lottie did most of the talking, and Katie, most of the listening. Lottie glanced quickly at the kitchen clock and realized that she still had groceries to put away and unpacking to do. She thanked Katie for her hospitality and promised her "that real soon they'd have a proper chin wag."

Katie made a spur of the moment decision. She asked Lottie to celebrate Tommy's First Communion Day with them the upcoming Sunday. Mass in the morning, then dinner in the afternoon. It would be a kind of a welcoming, neighbor-to-neighbor get together. No gifts, though. They would be happy simply to share the day with her.

Lottie didn't hesitate for a moment. "That's thoughtful a ya, Sug. Haven't stepped foot in a church in a coon's age. Interestin' thought though. Mos' likely tha Lord would be sorta knocked witless seein' me sittin' in one a His pews."

Katie was shocked that anyone could go for a "coon's age" without going to church. "You mean you never go regularly or you never go at all? Weren't you raised on it?"

"Hell, yes, Sug. I was born an' raised in tha Bible Belt. I jus' ain't never had much use fawr organized religion. Seems ta me that mos' preachers got one hand on tha Bible an' tha other in tha collecshun plate. Them an' their congregashuns are too busy tellin' ya what ya should an' shouldn't be doin' when they oughtta be showin' ya.

"Had ma fill a Baptist preachers an' pious, Sabbath Day Christians that left their charity an' decency on tha church steps. I still got ma faith, but I'm happy ta do all ma prayin' private like, whenever tha mood strikes me. Hafta turn ya down on tha church thing, but, I'd be tickled pissless ta join y'all fawr dinner."

Katie nearly choked on an ice cube.

Katie saw Lottie to her car. Lottie settled in the driver's seat and slipped the car into reverse. She called out to Katie, "Don't worry 'bout dessert, Sug. I'll bring a coupla pecan pies."

As abruptly and ceremoniously as she had arrived, Lottie fishtailed down the driveway and disappeared in a squeal of tires.

Katie was simultaneously astonished and enthralled by her new neighbor. She felt an immediate fondness for Loretta Tarpy Bobbitt McSweyne Devereaux, a.k.a Lottie, who whirled into one's life like a gust of warm, southern air.

Somewhere out of the distant past, Katie recalled her ma's words and they echoed in her memory. *"A real lady doesn't use foul language, drink hard liquor or paint their nails."*

Katie suddenly questioned that childhood teaching. Lottie had already broken two out of three of her ma's rules and Katie strongly suspected she probably broke the third, regularly. And in Katie's eyes, Lottie was a real lady.

She relived the last hour's conversation with amusement and shook her head in good-natured disbelief as she put away the tea fixings and got on with her housework.

chapter eight

Saturday morning found the O'Neill house busy as a beehive.

Katie doled out the chores according to the level of difficulty. Brendan's assignments included washing the outside windows and mowing the lawn. Tommy was responsible for making sure the house and yard were free from toys and clutter. Although the twins were most helpful by staying out of everyone's way, they were none-the-less appointed the task of tidying up their room and picking flowers for the table decoration.

Katie, a compulsive list-maker, checked off the jobs one by one as they were completed. By afternoon, she was satisfied that the "done" list was growing, while the "to do" list was dwindling.

The table was covered with her best, freshly pressed, Irish linen tablecloth. Her ma had hand embroidered the edges with pink tulips and green ivy. She carefully set the table with Aunt Katherine's Dalton china and Waterford crystal. Newly polished silverware and pink, linen napkins, carefully folded, adorned each place setting.

It was Katie's first real chance to entertain in their new home and she wanted everything to be perfect. After she arranged the carnations, daisies and last of the spring tulips in a crystal vase she stood back and admired her table setting. The flowers, recently picked by the twins showed only minimal battle scars.

She was pleased with the result. The table looked elegant, yet festive. Katie had decided against candles. The last time she had used candlesticks, they had narrowly escaped a near disaster with the twins. She was confident that Casey and Colin were capable of creating enough unpredictable mishaps at least she could avoid the predictable ones.

Katie had finally gotten around to inviting Matthew Mulholland. She had been reticent about the invitation. She didn't want to appear forward and didn't want the casual invitation to be misconstrued as anything more. Her patience paid off and the First Communion celebration presented the perfect opportunity. Matthew Mulholland had seemed pleased, almost excited, by the invitation and eagerly accepted. And of course Lottie, though not coming to church, would be coming for dinner.

Abraham was another story. Katie felt that he had seemed rebuffed by the invitation, reserved and reticent, as if he were struggling with some sort of inner turmoil. He offered no excuse, nor explanation. Instead, he had deferred and promised Katie he would let her know. She had not pressed him further. It was now Saturday and he still hadn't responded.

Most of the meal preparations would have to wait until morning, but Katie was able to complete some the day before. She washed and rinsed the produce; cut, chopped, diced, marinated and seasoned. She baked two loaves of soda bread, one white and one brown. For her last culinary effort of the day, she baked Tommy his favorite dessert, lemon layer cake covered in cream cheese frosting and sprinkled with coconut.

Their Sunday clothes were laundered, ironed, polished and laid out for the following morning. Katie knew from experience that the morning would be hectic enough and she wanted to minimize the last minute confusion.

The only gifts Tommy received were a black beaded rosary, scapular of the Sacred Heart, statue of his patron saint and a black leather First Communion prayer book. In deference to tradition, the family presented them to him at the kitchen table for dinner that night. He opened each package carefully and deliberately and handled each item with respect and gentleness.

His eyes lit up with awe as he summed his thoughts into one brief comment. "Now I have my very own prayer book and rosary. I can pray grown-up just like Bren and Daddy."

For one fleeting moment, Katie's eyes welled with tears. She fought back the ache of sadness and regret. It all seemed so unfair. Danny should have been there with them to share in these precious, simple moments that marked the milestones in his son's lives.

How long would it be before their young minds would be unable to remember their father? Would they forget his laughter, his face and the sound of his voice? They were all so young, the twins, hardly more than toddlers, when their father was stolen from them. How long would it be before his love and warmth would be completely erased away by time, like the steady, lapping waves wash away the sand?

As quickly as the feelings came, she suppressed them. This was a time for joy and celebration, not sorrow and heartache. She would not permit it to be overshadowed by the futility of wants and wishes of things that could never be.

While she dried the twins after their bath, Katie could hear Brendan and Tommy murmuring as they completed last minute quizzing from the *Baltimore Catechism*. Tommy had insisted on it, just in case he was called on to answer a question in church, tomorrow. He wanted to be absolutely sure he had it all memorized, to the letter.

"How many Persons are there in God?"

"There are three Persons in one God. The Father, the Son and the Holy Ghost."

Bren continued the interrogation. "How many Sacraments are there? And name them."

Tommy had to think that one over. His memory working overtime, he started to count them off on his fingers. "There are seven Sacraments. Baptism. Penance. Holy Eucharist. Confirmation. Matrimony. Holy Orders ..." there he paused for a moment before answering in jubilation, "Escenucshun!"

Bren corrected him, "Extreme Unction."

And so continued the interrogation until Brendan finally surrendered. "Tommy, we've been over this a million times. You know it inside out and backwards. I'm tired of going over it. Go take your bath. And don't worry. You probably won't get called on by Father Davey, anyway."

A calm and quiet descended upon the house after Katie had them all tucked in for the night. She had sat with the younger ones as they said their bedtime prayers. They knelt beside their beds, chubby fingers folded in prayer, heads bowed. They began with the sign of the Cross, "In the name of the Father and the Son and the Holy Ghost ...

Now I lay me down to sleep.
I pray the Lord my soul to keep.
If I should die before I wake
I pray the Lord, my soul to take.

They always waited for their mom to finish with her own little Irish blessing. She had been saying it each night, since they were born, just as her ma had done. "May God grant you always a sunbeam to warm you ... a moonbeam to charm you ... a sheltering angel, so nothing can harm you."

Together, they would close with the sign of the Cross and "Amen."

After goodnight hugs and kisses Katie said her goodnights to Brendan. While picking up a stray piece of clothing here and there and picking invisible pieces of lint from his church clothes, she spoke to him in a soft and calming voice.

"I want you to know how much it meant to me to hear you with Tommy, tonight. And though you two don't realize it right now, it will mean a great deal to you both in years to come."

Defensively he answered, "It's no big deal, Mom."

She learned over and kissed his cheek. "Bren, that's exactly my point. It's the little things that are a big deal."

With that said, she turned off his light and called back, "Love you. And don't forget your prayers."

Brendan watched her leave his room until all he could see was her silhouette backlit by the hallway light. After she was gone, in a near whisper he added, "Love you, too, Mom."

It was well past nine and Katie spent a few quiet minutes in the gazebo and sipped from her last cup of tea of the day. She loved the gazebo and had claimed it as her sanctuary. It was a clear night and she could see the stars twinkling far off, like diamonds cast carelessly across a sea of black velvet. The lake was moderately calm, but she could hear the waves gently roll to the beach.

Katie was awed to live in the midst of such beauty. The gentle breeze played lightly with the leaves and carried in its arms the subtle scents and fragrances of the pines, the hedges, the plantings and the lake. Each scent was definable and unique, and still they all mingled and melded into a delicate ballet. The breeze billowed her nightgown and robe and caressed her skin with smooth, silky fingers.

The spring peepers were exceptionally loud that night. Like an invading army, they peeped and chirped in a dissonant battle, each trying to outdo the other. Sometimes, Katie thought she liked the touch, the sounds and scents more than the sights. She found it intriguing to clear hear mind of all thoughts and images in order to absorb the subtleties; concentrate on the tenuous and fleeting sensations.

That was where she felt the closest to God. When she felt she could talk to Him and pray for Him to heal her broken heart. That was where she drew from His strength, peace and comfort. As she stared at the stars in the heavens, she asked Him to guide her, to direct her, to help her raise her boys with wisdom and understanding. That He, in His infinite wisdom and boundless love lead her in the direction she was meant to go, to let her know that she was never truly alone. Just as He had quenched her anger, comforted her grief, lifted her sorrow and tamed her fears. As He had led her to this new chapter in her life she needed Him to help her through the uncertainties of trying to be both a mother and a father. This was where she could almost feel Him reach down and gently hold her in His comforting arms.

Katie imagined it was a "night made for fairies and leprechauns," as her ma would have said. It had a magical, enchanting quality. Danny would have called it a "night made for mischief and shenanigans." The thought almost made her giggle with a lightness of heart. How good it felt to simply sit there and surrender to the peace and tranquility of those memories.

She heard soft footsteps behind the gazebo and thought that one of the boys had woken and undoubtedly wanted a drink or some other fabricated necessity that would delay bedtime. She was surprised to see Abraham approach the gazebo.

"I hope this interruption is not an unwelcome intrusion on your private time."

She reassured him and replied, "Not at all, Abraham. I was just wool gathering. Please, join me and enjoy this beautiful evening. It's so peaceful and pleasant, made even more pleasant by good company."

She smiled softly at him. "I could go into the house and brew some more tea, if you'd like."

Abraham quickly said, "No. Please. I only wanted to have a few words with you."

He planned his words carefully and began. "I feel the need to explain to you, or at least offer a partial explanation as to why I reacted so ungraciously to your invitation to Tommy's First Communion." He paused a moment.

Feeling his uneasiness, Katie soothed him. "Really, Abraham, you don't have to make any apologies to me. I don't require an explanation."

"You may not feel it is required. However, I do."

"I certainly never intended the invitation to make you feel uncomfortable. I'm sure you have your reasons. Don't feel you have to justify them to me. And certainly, Tommy would understand."

Abraham ignored the exculpation she offered. "Because Tommy would understand without question, is precisely why I feel the need to explain. He deserves at least that much.

"You know, Tommy is very special to me. He has a gentle and unselfish nature that is not often found in one so young. It is no secret that I have become very fond of him. To be included in his special day is a true honor but one I find very difficult to accept without reservations. I feel it is only right that I try to explain my hesitancy to you."

He stared out at the lake, as if drawing the strength from it to find the right words. A bridal train of moonlight glimmered on its soft waves and illuminated the surface of the lake.

"I am Jewish, as you may have already learned. For those who are not, to be Jewish is complicated and not easily explained or understood. It is not only our nationality, our ethnicity, it is not only a religion, a language, it is our way of life. It is as much a part of us as our heart or lungs; from the moment we draw our first breath until we breathe our last. It dictates what and when we eat, what we wear, who and how we marry, how and where we pray, how we mourn and bury our dead. It is our history, our beliefs, our heritage and woven inseparably into the fabric of our lives.

"Even beyond that, it defines who and what we are. Some are born French, Italian, Swedish or Russian. There are choices as to what religion you wish to encompass to express your beliefs, Buddhism, Catholicism, Orthodoxy or Protestantism. You are Irish, you are Christian, you are Catholic. We … we are singularly Jewish. For us, there is only Judaism.

"Several years ago, for reasons that are private and personal, I denounced the faith that my ancestors had embraced, a faith that had withstood thousands of years. I denounced their God … the God who had turned his back on me. The God of my boyhood no longer exists. The God of my people is dead to me. I cannot embrace Judaism, its God or its teachings. I have not stepped foot in a synagogue in many years, nor have I observed any of its traditions, practices or rites. I can't extricate myself from the Jewish blood that runs in my veins but I can sever the bonds that tie me to its heartless God.

"Though Judaism and the God it venerates are dead for me, it is not my intention to criticize or condemn your God or your faith in that God. I have no right to question your religious traditions. So, for Tommy's sake, I am pleased to accept your kind dinner invitation and am greatly honored that you have included me in his celebration. I am pleased to accept your dinner invitation but it is impossible for me to attend the church ceremony."

Abraham's voice wasn't petulant or raised in anger. In fact, he spoke calmly and softly, just above a whisper. Katie found that much more disturbing. He spoke quietly, deliberately, without emotion. It was obvious to Katie that Abraham felt more than aloneness. He felt abandonment.

There was such finality and despondency in his tone that Katie was frightened for him. His words were cold and empty and his manner chilled her. Abraham suddenly seemed like a stranger, as if some alien being had taken possession of his soul; his words were directed toward some invisible presence.

She wanted to ask questions, to know what hurt had rendered him so implacable. What event or circumstances had broken his spirit? What had happened that caused him to denounce, to turn his back on his God and the only way of life he had ever known? What unspeakable thing had brought him to this place, where he could point such unforgiving blame?

Katie wanted to help him with words of wisdom and comfort, to share and ease his pain. She wanted to offer him comfort and compassion, but did not. There was something unreachable about Abraham that night. Something had pulled him completely out of touch. She knew that whatever consolation she tried to offer would not be welcomed. She knew that any words of comfort would be futile and fall on deaf ears.

chapter nine

Katie had beaten the sun up.

Tommy's First Communion Day dawned with the promise of a balmy, pleasant day and welcomed her before the sun had broken above the horizon. Huge, fluffy cotton ball clouds moved lazily across the gray blue sky of dawn. They were the puffy-kind-of clouds that, with imagination took on whimsical shapes.

As most days, there was a breeze off the lake, but that day it was soft and gentle. The birds and squirrels flitted and frolicked, peeped and chattered, busily carrying on their unending activities of survival. Likewise, inside the O'Neill house, there was also a flurry of activity. The O'Neill's survival skills were being tested. Seriously.

Sunday mornings were characteristically hectic, getting everyone moving, fed, dressed and out the door in time for eleven o'clock Mass, usually with only minutes to spare. Katie's organizational abilities were being stretched to the maximum.

They had to be at church by ten-fifteen. Brendan was serving Mass and needed to be there early to dress and prepare the altar. Sister Diane had been explicit in her instructions. Tommy needed to be dropped off at his classroom for last minute preparation and instructions. And of course, she wanted to be there early enough to find an open pew near the front of the church.

By nine o'clock, she had completed her kitchen chores. As she went down her list, she assessed each item. She had peeled and sectioned the potatoes and set them in water on the stove. The fresh asparagus was washed and cut the day before, placed in a covered casserole, and only needed to be warmed shortly before serving. She finished the deviled eggs, Tommy's favorite, placed them on a serving plate and stored them in the refrigerator until dinnertime. The salad would be tossed and dressed later. The roast had been seasoned and marinated overnight. Katie had almost choked when Mr. Kessler told her how much the bill was. Almost the entire weekly allotment she had budgeted for meat. But, as she carefully counted out the money, she justified it to herself that this was a very special occasion.

She reassured herself that everything was in order, tidied the kitchen and turned her attention toward getting everyone dressed. She had delayed dressing

Casey and Colin until the last minute, otherwise they would be mussed and dirtied by the time the rest of them were ready. Brendan was dressed and helping Tommy with his new white shirt, navy trousers and black bowtie.

Katie brushed her hair and, running short on time, decided against either braid or a twist. Instead, she wore it unrestrained and framing her face. Katie would have been the last person to admit it, but the look fit her perfectly. It accentuated her rosy, fair complexion and delicate features. Not being one to fuss and primp, she causally applied her lipstick. She wore a simple gray mohair dress with a full skirt, wide black patent leather belt and shoes.

She quickly dressed the twins in their Sunday clothes and tied their dress black oxfords. She noted that they must have been on the verge of another growth spurt. The pant legs were again beginning to creep up. Katie sighed. They would definitely need new trousers very soon. Lengthening them was no longer an option. She wouldn't be able to squeeze even another eighth of an inch out of them. Having been handed down first from Brendan then from Tommy, the knees were shiny from wear; the fabric had become painfully thin.

New shoes for all the boys last month, as well as shirts and dungarees for Tommy and Brendan. She was going to have to see about adjusting her clothing budget. The four weeds she was raising under her roof were raising Cain with her budget.

Using a little dab of spit to control their cowlicks, she combed their curly blond hair and hoped her efforts would last long enough to get them all to church. Satisfied that they passed muster, she scooted them off to find Tommy and Brendan and get loaded into the car.

Katie was not a hat person. Regardless of the style, she thought she looked ridiculous in them. Even when she tried on whatever concoction the latest fashions had to offer, she felt like a little girl trying to play dress-up. When going to church, which dictated that she cover her head, she wore only a simple tam or beret, soft felt in the warm months and wool in the cooler months.

Taking one final, hurried look at herself in the mirror, she settled the beret into place. She grabbed her white gloves, handbag and Missal, took one last look at the clock, and ran out of the house at ten-o-five exactly.

 C3 80

The altar candles were lit for High Mass.

Brendan and Vincent Mizzano, dressed in red cassocks with white lacey tunics, were finishing the altar preparations for Mass. Brendan looked so handsome, with his father's dark hair and good looks. He was tall for his age and Katie had noticed the last few months how his body was filling out. He was leaving behind the lanky awkwardness of youth and developing the lean muscles of a man. His shoulders were broadening and his waist was slimming.

The change had not only been physical, but emotional, as well. In a matter of a few months, Katie had fallen from the lofty perch of a mom who knew absolutely everything to the basement level of being the dumbest female on the planet. If that was what puberty and adolescence was all about she couldn't wait for the other three to reach that age.

She and Brendan had been through a lot together. For almost the entire first five years of his life it had been only the two of them. Then, the past year and a half of seeing each other through Danny's death and the long nightmare that followed. How quickly the time had passed. It seemed only a short time ago that she was rocking her firstborn to sleep, cradled in her arms. She had lovingly caressed his fine baby skin and stroked his black, downy curls, naively thinking that it would always be that way; that his need for her would be as total and endless as time. Her mother's heart longed for him to need her now, in the same ways, just as he had needed her then.

At times, he was still her little Bren, helpful, sweet and caring. And now, more often than not, he was quiet, moody and belligerent. He was not only growing up but in many ways was growing away from her, and a huge, chasm had opened between them. She tried to stretch her reach across, but always seemed to fall short. Katie prayed to the Blessed Virgin to share her guidance and motherly wisdom.

Though the church was completely full that morning, Katie relished the calm and peace that she experienced inside its walls. It was a beautiful church. The altar and Communion rails were pink and white marble. Gold paint and flocked fleur-de-lis wallpaper covered the walls; interrupted only by tall, arched, stained glass windows. On the back wall of the apse was a twenty-foot mosaic of Jesus crucified to the Cross.

Ornate chandeliers, like magnificent, gold earrings, hung from the arched ceilings. Time had turned the oak pews a rich whiskey. The kneelers were covered in burgundy velvet, as were the celebrant's chairs on the altar. To the left of the apse, several steps led to the elevated white marble pulpit. The front of the nave was flanked by life-size statues of the Blessed Virgin Mary to the left and St. Joseph to the right. Heavy oak carvings hung along the sides of the nave that depicted the twelve Stations of Christ's passion and death.

The scent of burning votive candles was ever present in the church, as was the lingering, sweet, cloying redolence of incense. Mingled with the scent of candles and incense were the subtle fragrances of the floral sprays of gladiolas, white chrysanthemum and palms arranged in huge brass urns, placed strategically in front of the altar. Sunshine streaked through the windows and created prisms of muted color that tinted every surface they touched. Tiny particles of dust, captured in the rays, danced about in the colored sunbeams.

Katie applied the divide and conquer strategy. She placed the twins, one on each side of her, and hoped that their good behavior would last throughout the High Mass. As she finished the last of her prayers, she looked up to see Matthew Mulholland quietly genuflect and slip into the pew next to them. She and the twins scooted over to make room for him. He sat back and cast a wink and a smile at her. Without the wink, Katie returned his smile.

As the organist and choir began the entrance hymn, the congregation rose to greet the entry procession. Brendan and Vincent led, one carrying the Crucifix high, the other carrying the Psalter. Behind them, came Father Davey dressed in a green, silk moiré chasuble and white stole. Perched on his snowy white head was a black, four-cornered biretta. In his hands he carried the purificator and the chalice cover with veil and pall. Following Father Davey, marched the First Communicants.

Two rows of second graders, arranged by height from the shortest to the tallest, the girls on the left and the boys on the right, paraded by. As Tommy, the boys were all identically dressed. The girls had donned flounced, virginal white Communion dresses and veils. Eden Croft must have been cleaned out of every yard of white tulle, lace, satin, taffeta and organza, as well as every last silk flower, petticoat and pair of white patent leather shoes. Each child carried a prayer book and rosary.

Heads slightly bowed, one by one, they solemnly walked toward the apse. Occasionally a small face would turn up to cast a beaming, partially toothless smile toward his or her parents. Katie, as every proud parent, glowed with love and pride as she watched Tommy march past. She felt truly blessed that that sweet, gentle, angelic face had actually sprung from her womb. She nearly wept from pleasure and joy. She spoke to Danny, privately with her thoughts, "*I know you are looking down on him, today, Danny, just as happy and proud as I am.*"

Sister Diane guided her flock into the reserved front pews.

Father Davey began the ordinary of the Mass. "In Nominee Patris, et Fili, et Spiritus Sancti. Amen."

He didn't give a sermon from the pulpit that day. Instead, Father Davey walked down from the apse and talked directly to the children. He randomly asked questions of several of the children and each answered correctly and enthusiastically. When Bobby Travis stood up to give his answer he shouted it out so loudly that it brought stifled laughter from the congregation.

Father Davey joked, "Well, Robert, I'm sure that answer was heard by God the Father, God the Son and God the Holy Ghost … as well as all the Angels, St. Peter, and the whole Communion of Saints."

Demonstrating the wonderful rapport he had with the children, he talked to them briefly about what a special day it was in their Catholic lives. From that day forward they could share completely and totally in the miracle that is the celebration of the Mass. Now, they too, could invite Jesus into their bodies and into their souls through the sacred Host. He wanted them to remember later that day, should they receive presents and gifts in honor of their First Communion, that the greatest gift would be the gift from Jesus ... the gift of Himself.

After the Consecration, it was time for the children to receive the Sacrament of Holy Eucharist for their very first time. As the choir sang "Panis Angelicas," they all exited their pews in the same fashion as they had entered them. They knelt at the Communion rail, hands steepled in prayer, thumbs crossed, symbolizing the Crucifix. Father Davey brought the consecrated host to each one of them, as they raised their heads, extended their tongues, received the host and made the sign of the Cross.

When it was Tommy's turn, Brendan held the paten under his chin. The closeness and bond that they shared was very evident in that simple act, that quiet exchange between two brothers. Brendan looked down on his younger brother with a look of such warmth and love, that Katie felt deep in her heart that they would share this priceless moment with each other, forever. Tommy and Brendan had always been especially close and Katie knew that if they had to choose a favorite brother, they would pick one another. The twins had each other. The natural order of things simply provided for the other two.

As the ceremony ended, the Communicants stood and filed to their seats. Katie couldn't believe her eyes. Peeking out from under Tommy's trousers weren't his new, brightly polished, black dress shoes, but his old tattered, well-worn, dirty, black P.F. Flyers.

Katie almost gasped out loud. What would all the other mothers think?

She didn't know whom she was angrier with, Brendan for being so irresponsible, or herself for not performing a final inspection. She was glad Brendan was far out of reach, for both their sakes. As it was, her anger would have time to abate before he was near enough to strangle.

CZ ED

Matt arrived first.

He knocked on the back door and Katie walked over to let him in. He was dressed casually in a white oxford shirt and gray wool trousers. He handed Katie a bottle of wine in one hand and a small nosegay of violets in the other.

"The wine is for the cook and the flowers are for the hostess. You surprised me in church this morning. Not surprised that you were there ... but surprised that you weren't barefoot."

He glanced down at her stockings and shoeless feet.

Katie burned red with embarrassment.

"Every time I've seen you, outside of my office, that is, which doesn't count, you've been barefoot. I was beginning to wonder if you owned a pair of shoes or if you were afflicted with some sort of medical condition that precluded you wearing them. And here you are, on such an auspicious occasion, barefoot again."

After recovering, she teased back. "I'm not barefoot, I'm wearing nylon stockings."

"Splitting hairs," Matt said.

"And while we're casting accusations, I have yet to see you, even once, in or out of your office, appropriately attired for a lawyer. I'm beginning to wonder if you own even one respectable suit."

"I confess. You've caught me." He raised his hands in mock surrender. "I'm totally unrespectable."

Just then, Casey and Colin tumbled into the kitchen.

"It's Mr. Mulholland!"

Casey accused him, "You ain't been here forever."

"Yeah. Forever," aped Colin.

"Has it really been that long? Forever?" Matthew teased them. "Here I only thought it was five days."

In a clamor of voices, tugging, coaxing and begging, a staccato-barrage of questions and orders were fired at Matt.

"Knock, knock."

"Who's there?" Matt played along.

"Ben."

"Ben, who?"

"Ben waitin' for you to get here so we could play some ball!"

"Will you come play catch with us?"

"We'll get the baseball an' bat."

"You can pitch us some balls."

"Are you staying 'til supper?"

"You can't leave 'til you play with us."

As Matt untangled himself from the boys, Katie scolded them, "Leave Mr. Mulholland alone for half a second and let him catch his breath. He's our guest, today. He doesn't have to earn his meal by babysitting you two."

Casey argued, "We ain't babies, Mommy."

Colin countered, "Yeah, we ain't babies. 'Sides, Mr. Mulholland likes playin' with us, don't you."

They both looked up at him, looking as serious and sincere as two little con artists could.

Matt couldn't resist. "Don't be batting those innocent eyes at me. I've managed to resist being conned by better than the likes of you two. But I'd be lying to you if I said I didn't fancy some baseball right about now."

He faked an elaborate exit, with arms and legs flapping in every direction. "Let's see if we can round up those other two hooligans and make this a real game."

Glad to have all *five* of the children out from under foot, Katie bounced from refrigerator to stove to dining room table making sure that nothing cooled off, burned or melted. As she was warming the cream and butter for the chive champ, Lottie knocked and announced her arrival through the screen door.

Katie hollered a "Hello, come on in."

Carrying a pie in each hand, Lottie used an elbow to open the door and hip to bang it shut.

She was dressed in sinfully tight, red toreador pants and a gold lame blouse. Rouge, powder, mascara, lipstick and other cosmetics had been applied, none too sparingly. Her hair was piled high in a mass of apricot swirls, sprayed and adorned with rhinestone combs. Three-inch long red and gold rhinestone earrings swayed from her ears. Her fingernails and toenails were painted a glossy deep red. A black, patent leather handbag was tucked under one arm. She had no less than a half dozen jeweled bracelets on her arms and two sparkling gemstone rings on each hand, one the size of a walnut. Katie wasn't sure if the rings were real or not but suspected they were genuine.

She tottered on spiked, backless, gold shoes and Katie wasn't sure how Lottie managed to defy gravity.

Lottie announced, "Two pecan pies delivered as promised."

Katie wiped her hands on her apron, took the pies and set them on the counter.

"Oh, Lottie they look delicious. I hope you didn't go to too much trouble."

"Not a t'all, Sug. Whipped 'em up in no time. I like ta cook when there's someone ta cook fawr."

"You look like you've dressed for a fancy soirée at the Copley not a humble Sunday dinner at the O'Neill's." Katie's dimples marked her smile.

"I believe no Southern lady should ever be found outside her boudoir lessen she's been properly powdered, rouged, sprayed, coifed, scented, cosmetized an' accessorized."

"Help yourself to some iced tea, it's in the refrigerator," Katie directed, as she whirled around the kitchen taking care of the last minute details. Cooking was the easy part. The hard part was making sure that everything was ready to be served at the same time.

"Slow things down jus' a notch, Sug, yawr busier than a three-legged cat tryin' ta bury shit on a marble floor. Yawr liable ta blow a gasket. I'll give ya a hand. Jus' say hop an' I'll ask how far."

Abraham arrived just in time for them all to sit down together. The meal started with the usual grace. Tommy was elected to lead the prayer, as he occupied the seat of honor.

"Bless us, oh Lord, and these Thy gifts, which we are about to receive, from Thy bounty, through Christ, our Lord. Amen."

Katie ended the prayer with a traditional Irish blessing. "May joy and peace surround you; contentment latch your door. Happiness be with you now, and bless you evermore."

Matt stood and offered a toast. "To Tommy. A happy, generous nature, a friendly spirit, too, these are the gifts St. Patrick, has surely given you. And may every day bring a generous part of all things in life that keep joy in your heart. Slaintsa."

The tribute was genuinely spoken from the heart. How perfectly those few words characterized Tommy. It was a side of Matthew that Katie had not seen before. What other character secrets was he hiding behind his rapscallion act? Katie decided, at that very moment, that there was a great deal more to learn about the dubious Matthew Mulholland.

Katie's meal turned out beautifully. The roast was moist and juicy, medium on the outside, rare on the inside. The chive champ mashed perfectly with fresh cream and butter. The asparagus tender and the salad fresh. Tommy was especially pleased with the deviled eggs and lemon cake. The only down side were the pecan pies. To say they were awful bordered on understatement to the point of an out-and-out lie. Too much molasses and too little experience had resulted in a fiasco. The filling spread across their dessert plates like lava oozing from Mount Etna.

Where the adults were too polite, Casey spit a mouthful of the mush back on the plate. He sputtered, "This pie tastes like barf!"

Katie was appalled. "Casey! Watch your language and your manners! That is no way to behave at the dinner table in front of our guests!"

Lottie was unruffled. In her easy going nonchalance, simply said, "I only claimed that I like ta cook, I didn't say I was any good at it."

Everyone seemed to have a good time. The conversation never lagged as Lottie entertained them with her lively narratives, wild adventures and colorful expressions. Katie had only raised an eyebrow a few times, warning Lottie of venturing into too delicate an area for the boys to hear.

Matt was his characteristically teasing and lighthearted self. Katie suspected a few cases of hero worship were developing. Tommy, the twins, even Brendan seemed to have fallen under his spell.

The boys didn't appear to be bored. On the contrary, they seemed to enjoy being included in the adult chatter. The afternoon disappeared in a cacophony of laughter, teasing, banter and friendly discussions.

Katie couldn't decide about Abraham. At times he seemed to be enjoying himself. At other times, he was withdrawn and quiet. She definitely detected an undercurrent of uneasiness between Abraham and Lottie, though. Not really ambivalence, but more of an apprehension. Lottie appeared nonplused by it. But, there was no doubt that Abraham was uneasy around her.

Everyone ignored Katie's instructions and brought Tommy a gift.

Matt gave him ten, shiny, brand new silver dollars. Tommy's eyes lit up and widened to almost the size of the coins.

Casey was equally impressed as he asked, "What'cha gonna spend that much money on? You sure kin buy an awful lot of candy with ten whole dollars."

Katie quickly set the record straight. "Silver dollars are very special. They're not for spending. They're for saving. The entire *ten whole dollars* will be kept safely in his piggy bank."

The boys moaned that that was no fun. Matt shared their dampened enthusiasm. "Sometimes moms can be way too sensible. They just don't understand us guys, do they?"

Lottie presented him with a pocketknife attached to a rabbit's foot. The one for good-luck and the other, according to Lottie, "'Cuz Granddaddy Pope always said every boy should have one fawr whittlin' an' other necessities."

Tommy beamed with pride that Miss Lottie thought he was grown up enough to have a pocketknife.

Abraham presented him with a potted shamrock plant. He instructed him how to care for it. Abraham told Tommy that he understood that the shamrock was very dear to anyone who was Irish. A look of cognizance passed between the two, as if they both knew how special the gift was.

Katie was proud that Tommy remembered his manners. Without any coaxing or gentle reminders, he thanked everyone for the gifts.

As all pleasant days have a way of doing, the time passed all too quickly. Daylight disappeared into the cool blue of twilight. Matt and Abraham had left. Tommy, Casey and Colin were already in bed exhausted from the day's activity. Brendan was in his room finishing his homework. Lottie stayed to help clear the table, wash and dry the dishes and finish the last of the clean up. She and Katie retired to the peace of the gazebo, neither quite ready to call it a night. Katie had brewed a pot of Earl Gray for herself and pitcher of iced tea for Lottie.

At first, they relived the events of the day. Then they talked lazily, about little or nothing. Eventually, they simply sat in silence, enjoying the cool, calm night.

After a bit, it was Katie who broke the silence. "Tell me if I'm out of line, but did I sense something strained between you and Abraham. He seemed to be uncomfortable around you. Not anything obvious, just a nuance, a hint at something."

Lottie dismissed the notion. "Since Eve tempted Adam, there ain't been a man born between booties an' boots that Lottie Devereaux couldn't figure out an' know how ta handle."

Katie suspected that Lottie's declaration was absolutely accurate.

"Oh, Abraham an' I get along well 'nough. 'Though he is a might standoff-ish where I'm concerned. We're kinda like two possums swingin' from tha same tree. He don't much mind me, s'long as I don't get too close ta his branch."

Katie smiled at the analogy.

"I'm kinda like that bright, shiny new harmonica he's been seein' in tha window of tha Five an' Dime. Then he wakes up one mornin' an' by Jove, there it is. Only now he doesn't have tha slightest idea what ta do with it. I don't think Abraham quite knows what ta make a me. Kinda like I might scare him a little. I could work tha ol' Lottie magic on him with ma two pinkie fingers tied behind ma back. If I wanted ta. I jus' ain't never wanted ta."

That last statement piqued Katie's curiosity. "How come?" She asked.

"How come *what*? How come I never worked ma magic on him or how come I never wanted ta?"

"How come you never wanted to?"

"Even I have ma standards. Abraham Franke jus' never interested me, that's all. He ain't ma type."

"Do you know much about him? I mean things like where he came from, how he ended up in Eden Croft? Was he ever married? Does he have any family?"

"Abraham's past is a mystery, I tell ya what. I only know bits an' pieces. He tends ta be contented bein' a loner. Has no friends or kin that I know 'bout. 'Cept fawr yawr Aunt Katherine an' Uncle Sean. 'Course me, now I don't think it's natural goin' through life alone."

Twirling one of the rocks on her ring finger, Lottie continued. "Seems ta me I heard somethin' happened to him in WW Two. Musta been somethin' powerful bad, 'cuz it sure crawled under his skin an'' it's been festerin' there ever since. Now, yawr Aunt Katherine, she probably knew more than a thing er two. They got pretty close over tha years, 'specially near tha end. But she never broke his confidences with me."

"Lottie, sometimes I ache with wanting to bring some happiness, some sunshine into his life. He just seems so broken and alone. I keep thinking if he would open up a little and let someone in to share some of his pain. I know what it's like to feel isolated and lost and I can see that in Abraham."

"Well now, that's tha motherin' in ya. But sometimes a mother has ta know when ta be a mother an' when ta let go. Sooner er later, everyone's gotta learn ta fly an' find their own way in this world."

Lottie turned to face Katie, even though it was too dark to see her features. "An' speakin a unattached men. What about that Matthew Mulholland? You two got somethin' goin' on behind ma back, Sug? I hope ta tell ya, that's one man I wouldn't throw outta ma bed fawr eatin' crackers."

Katie chuckled out loud. "Lottie, you are one for the ages. Haven't you had enough men in your life?"

"Sug, there ain't no such thin' as '*nough* men. 'Sides, it wuzn't ma bed I was referrin' ta. It was yawrs."

Katie thought that was the most absurd idea she had ever heard from Lottie. "What are you talking about? He was Aunt Katherine's lawyer, and now he's my lawyer by default. We're nothing more than friends."

"Well, I kin tell ya, he's ma lawyer, too, handled all ma legal affairs, since Rollie died, an' that man ain't never looked at me tha way he looks at y'all, I tell ya what! It's written all over his face that he's got a bit more than lawyerin' an' friendship on his mind where y'all are concerned. I kin recognize when a randy rooster is a struttin' himself 'round tha ol' hen house. Seen it maself, all right. First hand. Been on tha receivin' end a that often 'nough."

Katie was grateful for the darkness of the gazebo. She blushed from neck to scalp.

"As my Granddaddy Pope would'a said, 'he's knee-slappin', ass-over-apple cart' crazy 'bout ya. He's jus' bidin' his time 'til he makes his first move."

Katie figured that two could play that game. "And as my Granddaddy Hynes would have said, 'Don't you be reading something into something that isn't there.' I'm not the least bit interested in Matt Mulholland."

Katie couldn't help but silently acknowledge that at the corner of her thoughts, the possibility was somewhat intriguing. Just as quickly as the notion surfaced, Katie's practicality swept it under the rug. It was too ridiculous to contemplate.

"Did you ever consider that maybe there's a good reason why he's unat-tached, like maybe he wants it that way? I'm a widow with four sons, for Pete's sake. Neither of those qualities makes me particularly irresistible to a man as committed to bachelorhood, as Matt Mulholland seems to be. The last person in the world he'd be interested in is me, and for sure, the last thing in the world I would do is become interested in him."

Lottie wouldn't be dissuaded and preceded without skipping a beat. "It's too dark ta see tha expreshun on yawr face, but I'd give ma Uncle Lucius's left arm ta see it, right now. An' that's somethin', 'cuz Uncle Lucius, he only had but

his left arm. Be careful Sug, don't ever say what ya wouldn't do, 'cuz y'all probably do everythin' ya said ya wouldn't, an' a thousand things ya never thought a
doin'."

"I'm not sure I followed one word of that advice, but at any rate, it's too
ridiculous to even warrant a discussion. And I'm too mellow and too tired to
argue the point with you, right now. "

Katie stifled a yawn. "I hate to cut short your fantasizing about my nonex-
istent love life, but I think I'm going to turn in. Unlike you, a lady of leisure, I
have to get up early in the morning with the boys."

"Y'all know what they say, Sug, if it's too hot in tha kitchen, get out. Seems
ta me y'all are gettin' a might bit too defensive. Leaves me with a suspishus taste
in ma mouth. I'm gonna make one a ma famous predikshuns. Famous 'cuz I
make 'em an' famous 'cuz they always come true. One a these days y'all are
gonna find yawr tit in a wringer where that man is concerned an' yawr gonna
cum runnin' ta Lottie ta tell ya how ta get it out."

With that, Lottie waved her jeweled fingers at Katie and purred, "Well, I'm
off like a prom dress. See y'all later, Sug. An' jus' s'posin' I am right, which I
always am, y'all are too stubborn an' too scared ta admit it."

She wasn't ten feet from the gazebo when she turned around and drawled,
"Oh, an' jus' in case y'all didn't think 'bout it before, here's a little somethin' ta
tuck under yawr pillow, tonight. What are y'all gonna do when he does make
his move?"

⊰ ⊱

Within a few weeks, Katie fell in love with Lottie's easy manner and southern charm. She welcomed the laughter and vivaciousness that oozed from Lottie
like sweet, maple syrup. Lottie was animated and candid, without a reserved
bone in her body. While she appeared harsh, boisterous and coarse on the outside, she was tender, sensitive and caring where it mattered the most.

Lottie's mannerism, language, stories and experiences were entertaining,
stimulating and restorative. She was fresh, trendy, outrageous and Katie, who
felt her life was so mundane, predictable, so ordinary, enjoyed Lottie like an
exciting, exotic novel.

The affection was reciprocated. Lottie liked Katie right off. And that was
an unusual experience for Lottie who had always found it easier to get along
with men than women. Lottie was attracted to Katie's naive charm, non-judg-
mental attitude and easy laughter. She came to admire, cherish and value the
simplicity, the innocence and goodness that were Katie. Yet she knew not to
mistake that for weakness, or fragility, or lack of substance. Instead, she soon
came to rely on Katie's gentle strengths and unique individuality.

A more unlikely twosome was nearly impossible to imagine; Katie, once wedded, once bedded and once widowed. And there was Lottie, who, in her own words, "Never slept with a man I didn't marry, an' never married a man I hadn't slept with. Married 'em fawr times an' buried 'em fawr times."

Yet, with the dawning of each new season, summer, fall, winter and again spring, the friendship between Katie O'Neill and Lottie Devereaux, from two distant and enormously different worlds, germinated, budded, blossomed and grew.

chapter ten

The fourth week of every month was Hot Dog Wednesday.

There were two room mothers for each class. They took turns, every other month, working the Hot Dog sale. As a room mother for the twins' class, it was Katie's turn to work May's Hot Dog Wednesday. It was her first ever and she felt as anxious as a diva on opening night.

Normally, the students of St. Anthony's carried their lunches and ate in their classrooms. But, as a special treat, once a month they would march over to the parish hall for a lunch of hot dogs, potato chips, dessert and chocolate milk. Hot dogs were twenty-five cents each and milk a nickel. The potato chips, donated by the A&P, were free. The students had to place their milk orders the day before so Orvis Skrippy knew how many cartons to deliver from White's Dairy. Each room mother had to bring a dessert for her assigned room. Katie had baked double fudge brownies.

Katie arrived at the church hall at ten o'clock dressed in a sherbet lime, cotton, shirtwaist dress. She hadn't known what to wear and wanted to make a good impression. She had called Angie Brisbois the night before for advice.

Angie assured Katie that it didn't matter what she wore. "We're on K.P. duty with Queen Celia McBride and Lady Charlotte Hamilton. The two cattiest females in Eden Forge. No matter what you wear they'll peck it to pieces."

Katie had met them both before, briefly, at the Altar Society meeting. Celia McBride, wife of the president of Blair National Bank, the Chamber of Commerce, and the Country Club, was co-incidentally president of the Altar Society and the PTA. Katie laughed that politics must run in the family.

Charlotte Hamilton was married to Dr. Benjamin Hamilton, D.D.S., one of two dentists in town. A notch down the political hierarchy, Charlotte was only vice-president of the two organizations.

In spite of Angie's warning, Katie was enjoying her first Hot Dog Wednesday. She had been looking forward to it. It was an opportunity for her to meet other mothers and enjoy a few hours socializing.

Angie had been right about Celia and Charlotte. When Katie greeted them with a "Good morning, Charlotte. Hello Celia. As assigned, I'm present and accounted for," Charlotte was the first to respond with a nod and a "Ka-tie" with the same distaste she would have said "Dog-turd."

Celia was no warmer though her vocabulary was a bit broader. She graced Katie with an "It is Katie? Isn't it? I'm so terrible with names." Icicles hung from every word.

With frigid appraisal, they looked Katie up and down and used their most practiced disapproving sneers to make her feel inadequate and small. Celia's eyes were a mean gray, cold as slate, and Charlotte's gold eyes so pale they were almost colorless. Then, as if Katie were invisible, they abruptly turned their backs and left Katie standing with her mouth opened mid-sentence, as if she were too insignificant to waste their time.

Katie thought, *So much for socializing.*

Liz Coughlin tossed Katie an apron and a reassuring wink. "This is what the peons wear. Tie it on and join us."

Katie and Liz were filling the steamers for the hotdogs and buns. Katie couldn't help over-hearing a conversation between Celia and Charlotte who were sequestered at the opposite end of the kitchen. Their voices were lowered, but not enough. When Katie heard Matt Mulholland's name her ears perked up.

"Did you see the last tramp he brought to the Country Club Valentine's Dance?" Celia half-whispered and wrapped her red lips around her cigarette. Exhaling a cloud of spoke she added, "All peroxide and push-up bra."

Charlotte snickered. "And about pushed herself right up and out of that sluttish chunk of fabric she called a gown. I have tea towels with more fabric than that dress."

Katie blushed crimson. She didn't know if she should feel jealous or embarrassed. Either way, the topic of conversation made her uncomfortable.

Liz elbowed Katie and whispered into her ear, "That's the pot calling the kettle black. Or should I say, blonde? Celia should know a bleach job when she sees one. Her hair hasn't been its mousy brown since eighth grade."

"Where did he find her, anyway?' Celia asked.

"Don't have a clue. Probably some hoochy-coochy club in Chicago. All I know is that she wasn't local," Charlotte responded. "Who's his latest flavor of the week?"

"I haven't seen him with anyone lately," Celia mused. "No one has. I can tell you. I wouldn't think twice about leaving Harvey if Matt Mulholland ever made me an offer."

Charlotte gasped, "Celia! I can't believe you said that."

"Don't play all sweet and innocent with me, Charlotte. I know you'd throw good old Benny aside faster than that," she snapped her fingers, "if Matt asked you to help him break in a new mattress."

"Like the *Catch of the County* would give either of them a second glance," Liz whispered again. "Matt Mulholland could have his pick of any fair maiden from here to Chicago. Women with fewer stretch marks and capped teeth than either of those two."

Even across the kitchen, the cigarette smoke and stench from the half bottle of perfume each of them must have doused on reached Katie. The combined effects of the smoke, Charlotte and Celia's cloying perfume and the subject of their discussion caused Katie to feel nauseous. And Liz's comment about stretch marks crawled into her stomach and twisted and turned like a worm.

Liz started a sneezing marathon; her eyes red and teary and her nose started to run. Between sneezes she muttered, "Darn them with their perfume and cigarette smoke." She wiped her nose with a Kleenex from her apron pocket. "They know I'm allergic. I ought to waltz over there and blast them with a healthy sneeze and spray all over their designer dresses."

Katie and Liz had finished with the steamers and were carrying trays with bowls of chips, bottles of catsup, mustard and relish to distribute among the tables. Horace Chaffee, the school custodian, had arranged the banquet tables and chairs according to classroom. Angie Brisbois and Rose DiMarco were setting places with paper plates and napkins. The mothers worked their way down the rows of tables, Katie and Liz on one side, Angie and Rose on the other.

It was Katie who posed the obvious question. In a hushed voice, she asked, "Do Celia and Charlotte actually work or do they just supervise?"

Angie laughed all the way from her toes. "Work? And risk breaking a nail? Not on your life."

"Then why do they even bother to show up?" Katie the Naive asked.

Rose DiMarco answered, "They show up with the sole purpose of making make us poor serfs feel more inferior."

Angie offered Katie a brief biography. "Celia McBride, nee Gardyszewski, married up about five tax brackets ..."

Liz interjected, "Had to get married! Their first-born brat was conceived in the rumble seat of Harvey's roadster and arrived seven months later. *Premature.*" Liz rolled her brown eyes skyward. "How many eight-and-a-half pound, fully developed preemies have you seen?"

"And spends most of every day and her husband's paycheck trying to make the rest of us forget her humble beginnings." Angie continued, "Charlotte, hoping that some of Celia's glitter will rub off on her, follows her around like a puppy looking for a teat to suck on."

Katie was shocked by the gossip but lapped it up like cream to a cat.

"Celia keeps Charlotte around as her cohort and confidante," Liz added.

"I told you it didn't matter what you wore, Katie," Angie said. "Queen Bee and Lady Fingers there would dress with the sole purpose of making you look like you shopped at the Goodwill. Who the hell wears pearls to a Hot Dog Sale?"

Liz and Rose answered her in unison, "Celia and Charlotte."

Angie fussed with her flowered blouse, big as a tablecloth, wiggled her rotund bottom in her black peddle-pushers and said, "And I wore this outfit especially for them. I thought it might just drive them both crazy. Give them something to talk about at their next bridge club. Too bad I forgot my tiara and necklace."

"They do appear to be a bit overdressed for hot dogs and potato chips," Katie admitted.

"They're just showing off their latest purchases. Of course they wouldn't be caught dead in an off-the-rack number from Woodbury's. They have to shop at Hudson's in Detroit. La-de-dah. Their noses are so high in the air I'm surprised they don't get nose bleeds." Angie mimicked them and raised the tip of her nose with her index finger.

The ladies continued their serpentine course, winding around the tables. The aroma of steamed hotdogs drifted from the kitchen. Rose remarked, "Smells like the wienies are cooking." She inhaled long and deep. "Beats the heck out of the stink of Evening in Paris."

Again, Angie's chest heaved with laughter.

Katie wondered, "They must have some redeeming qualities. How else were they elected officers of the PTA and Altar Society?"

Rose answered, repositioning her thick glasses, "Bullying. Pure and simple. Half the women are afraid to cross them."

"Actually," Liz clarified, "No one else wants the jobs. Too much work, too much politics and too many headaches. So, we just go on letting them think they earned the coveted titles."

"Reverse psychology," Angie added.

"Come on," Katie persisted as lines of curiosity striped her forehead. "They can't be that bad. Maybe they only act that way because no one's taken the time to try and get to know them."

Rose guffawed, "Katie, are you for real or is this just an act? Nobody's that sweet."

Angie assured them, "Oh, she's for real all right. No one can accuse Katie O'Neill of being insincere. Sweet as syrup every time I see her. Disgusting isn't she?"

Katie blushed pink from embarrassment. "I think they're both rather attractive. Pretty, even. In a way." Katie stumbled over her words.

"Pretty, if you think mannequins are pretty," Angie dismissed the compliment. "You're pretty, Katie. They're fabricated. And don't let the packages fool you. They'd consider anyone that looks like you a threat. Just watch yourself around them. We've all known them since we were in diapers. They would chew you up and spit you out and not give it a second's thought. Never trust a woman that can diet successfully."

Liz shook her head. "My advice to you, Katie, is treat those two like you would a pair of rattlesnakes. They're as phony as used car salesmen. One will plaster a smile on her face and bat her Maybelline eyelashes at you while the other slips a knife in your back."

An abrupt announcement from the main entrance of the church hall grabbed everyone's attention.

"Better late than never. Got stuck in the bathtub and it took me an hour to get back out. Did I time it right? Is all the work finished?" Winded, red-faced and very pregnant, Connie Kirby shuffled her bloated body inside. Waddled was more accurate. Her swollen belly pushed so far forward that she appeared to be listing backward and ready to topple over. Katie's midsection experienced sympathy pains. Connie looked like she was eleven months pregnant.

Charlotte and Celia looked at her as if she were buck-naked.

"My God, Connie! You're positively grotesque!" Charlotte nearly shouted. "You're as big as a barn!"

Coming from anyone else it would have been humorous. Coming from Charlotte it was an insult.

"You've completely outgrown your maternity clothes. And what in heaven's name are you wearing on your feet? Are those *house slippers*?" Charlotte shrieked as if Connie had sanitary napkins strapped to her soles.

Angie looked at Connie's feet, placed her palm against her bosom and teased, "Connie. Those shoes are to die for. Did they have them in a ten wide? I'd love to pick up a pair."

Connie tried to visualize the scruffy mules on her feet. It was hopeless. She hadn't been able to see her feet for two months.

"Leave me alone, Angie. I'm not in the mood." Her freckled cheeks puffed and she exhaled a sigh. "These were the only things I could get into. My feet are so swollen it was these or a pair of Ward's galoshes."

Connie plopped down in the nearest chair and tossed her purse on the banquet table. She didn't sit as much as slouched, her swollen legs sprawled in front. She patted her carrot curls into place, trying to undo some of the damage the wind had done. "Lord, I must look like an elephant seal. I feel like I've been pregnant forever. If this baby doesn't come pretty soon I may well be."

Angie walked over to Connie. "For God's sakes. Go home Connie. We can handle this. You're not going to be much good to us, anyway."

"No way I'm leaving, now. It took me the better part of two hours to get here. It'll take me the rest of the morning to recoup enough energy to make the trip back home. Besides, if I go home I might have to make some effort to clean the house. Seeing it only makes me feel guilty. If I'm here I don't have to look at it."

"Then you're working the cash box. At least that way you could get off your feet and sit down."

If Connie had had the energy she would have split and run. Charlotte and Celia usually worked the pay station. As if no one else could be trusted to handle the millions of dollars the hotdog sales brought in. There was no way that Connie was going to be subjected to those two the entire time.

"Don't make a fuss over me. We've all been in this condition before. I'll be fine. Just humor me and let me grumble and complain a while. After I catch my breath you can prop me against the serving counter like a beached whale. If I'm lucky, maybe all this activity will stir things up and I'll go into labor."

Katie grabbed a folding chair. "At least prop your feet up on this, Connie."

"That would require me to bend at the waist," she laughed. "In case you haven't noticed, I no longer have one."

Katie had empathy pains. She had carried the twins through the hot summer months and vividly recalled the distended tummy and swollen feet. "I'll say a rosary for you that the baby comes soon."

"Ward's been driving me down bumpy roads and I've drunk enough seltzer to float a hot air balloon. I even resorted to a soapsuds enema. Nothing I've tried seems to be working. If you think prayers will help, be my guest."

Angie added with certainty, "They'll help, I guarantee it. Katie has an unbelievable pipeline directly to the Man upstairs." She pointed a finger upward. "Her prayers are so reliable you can pick the date and time. Asked her to pray that Fred's mother wouldn't make her annual month long visit from Topeka and sure as taxes she developed a nasty case of gout and had to cancel."

Katie defended herself. "I didn't pray for your mother-in-law to become ill. It was just a coincidence."

Angie smiled. "The Lord works in mysterious ways. Who am I to argue with His methods?"

It was an ingenious assembly line. After years of experience, the ladies had it down to a smooth operation. Charlotte and Celia worked the high finance. They took the money and wrote down on each student's slip how many chocolate milks and hotdogs they had paid for. As fast as the steamers warmed the buns and cooked the hotdogs, Angie, Connie and Rose stuffed the buns with wieners and wrapped them in squares of waxed paper. The finished products were placed on the serving counter where Liz and Katie served them to the youngsters, filling the orders according to the receipts. In deference to her condition, Connie slouched on a chair and supervised. That was the best concession the ladies could make for her.

Three mothers usually manned the serving line, but the crew was down by one. Lorraine Driscoll was knocked out of commission by a migraine. Katie and Liz would have to pick up the slack.

With only ten minutes until the lunch bell rang, the ladies were enjoying their last few moments of peace and quiet.

"It's a boy, Connie." Liz proclaimed through a wheeze.

"No it's not," Rose argued as convincingly as if her theory was based on scientific fact. "It's a girl. You're carrying it all out front. Boys carry wider."

Angie stated critically, "You can't go by that. I carried Steve all out front and Mary Frances wide. Babies decide how they want to be carried. Next thing, you'll be dangling a needle over her belly or consulting a palm reader to figure out the sex."

Katie was confused. "What's that about a needle? I never heard that one before."

Angie, wrapping hotdogs as quickly as her stubby fingers could work, explained. "You thread a needle and dangle it over the woman's stomach. If it spins clockwise, it's a boy. If it spins counter-clockwise, it's a girl. How's that for modern medical technology?"

Rose argued, again, "You've got it backwards. Clockwise, it's a girl. Counter-clockwise, a boy."

Everyone had an opinion.

"No, Rose. I think Angie had it right." Liz mentally searched her wealth of scientific knowledge. "My cousin Velma, in Milwaukee, swears by the needle and thread. She's had six kids and hasn't been wrong yet."

"Out front. Wide. Clockwise. Counter-clockwise. Boy or girl or both. I don't care what it is and don't really want to know. The suspense is what gets me through the labor. I just want it out of me and with all its parts, whatever they are, in all the right places." Connie was tired of all the discussion about her swollen, grotesque belly.

"My philosophy is to keep them in the oven for as long as possible, Connie. They're a whole lot easier to take care of in there. One colicky baby and you'll wish it was right back where it came from," Angie affirmed from experience.

The lunch bell squawked and within sixty seconds the diners stampeded into the hall like a herd of hungry hippos.

For the younger boys, it was always exciting to have their mom's work the school functions. It made them feel special, select, even privileged. To children, school is a social environment and to see their moms in that atypical location was a strange and exciting sensation. It cast their moms in a whole new light.

Tommy and the twins were no different.

The twins announced with pride to their classmates, "That's my Mommy."

Tommy, with less exuberance but no less pride, flashed Katie a beaming smile.

But then, something happens with puberty. Mom is no longer a source of unexpected pride. She suddenly undergoes a mutation and becomes an alien being to be avoided. Especially when they materialize in forbidden territory. School was one of the few places that a teenager could escape to without parental interference. It was sacred ground and protected at all costs. Instead of a source of pride, Mom at school was embarrassing. They were not welcomed, encouraged or acknowledged. And there was always the ever-present danger that Mom would say or do something really dumb.

Brendan and Steve tried to pretend that they hadn't seen their moms. When that tactic failed, they attempted to shrink so small that they might pass unnoticed.

Katie sensed Brendan's annoyance and resisted the urge to "run out and hug and kiss him in front of everybody" as Brendan had forecasted when he found out she would be working the hotdog sale. She proved him wrong and risked a discreet, quick smile.

Steve was less fortunate. Angie, in her booming voice, greeted her son. "Steven Frederick Brisbois! If you drink three chocolate milks you'll be broke out in pimples for a month."

Steven Frederick Brisbois turned three shades of red. So much for maternal sensitivity.

When the diners were finished and the last of the lunch crowd disappeared out the door, Charlotte and Celia evaporated along with the children and left the entire cleanup for the bourgeoisie.

Connie missed most of the cleanup, as well. She employed a different tactic to escape the chores. She didn't go into labor, but five minutes after the last child left the hall she announced, "You can skip your rosary, Katie. My water just broke."

Like a bloated bladder that had sprung a leak, she stood in her mules as amniotic fluid trickled down her legs and formed a huge puddle on the parish hall floor.

chapter eleven

The school year ended with its final days in June.

To the boys, it had arrived at a snail's pace.

Days when the weather was clear and warm the O'Neill's activities were usually on, in or near the water. They had fallen madly in love with the lake.

The boys, like their mother, took naturally to the water. Casey, Colin and Tommy were learning to swim like little guppies. Katie would often tease them that soon they would be growing gills and fins. All of them were turning a toasty brown from spending so much time under the summer sun. Except for the twins. They were the fairest. Instead, the sun only managed to coax a layer of freckles across their noses and cheeks.

Saturday nights brought an extra treat. Katie would pop a huge batch of popcorn dripping with butter and allowed the boys a slightly later bedtime. They would play a board game. Each week, with a democratic rotation, the boys would take turns selecting the game.

The little boys would pick either Sorry or Cootie. Thank goodness they had outgrown Candyland and Uncle Wiggily. Katie didn't think she could stand to play either one of them one more time. Brendan, of course, would grudgingly pick Monopoly. He had recently begun a full-blown campaign, complete with arguments, debates and reasons why they needed to buy a television.

He punctuated the end of every argument with, "Everybody I know has one, except us."

His mom had heard all the arguments a hundred times, but she stubbornly and repeatedly rebuffed him. "Right, now, we just don't have that kind of money for such a frivolous and expensive purchase."

Sundays followed their own routine. They were treated as family day. Sunday morning Mass followed by an early dinner left the remainder of the day free for leisure. If the weather forced them inside, they would play board games, read or listen to a baseball game on the radio. On the rarest occasions, for a special treat, Katie would take them to a picture show at the Strand Theater in town.

As the school year ended, the Musketeers became inseparable. When not doing chores at home or at a family function, the five could be found either on the baseball field, swimming, fishing or merely hanging out.

For some unclear, mystical reason, known only to them, the boys seemed to migrate to the O'Neill house. Katie never minded. In fact, she enjoyed having them around. They were as well mannered and behaved as could be expected of teenage boys. She grew fond of their constant banter.

Frequently, her kitchen table, normally set for five, would be stretched to accommodate at least an extra body or two. She would permit an occasional sleepover that always included a deviation from normal bedtime. She allowed them to stay up later for a lakeside campfire, or a real bonus, let them sleep outside in an old canvas tent Brendan had discovered in the attic of the garage.

The younger boys always complained that they couldn't participate. And when the twins had their first overnight guest, C.J Coughlin, Liz's son, Katie almost had a revolt on her hands.

"You always let Bren and his buddies sleep out in the tent. How come we can't?"

Katie responded with the all too familiar reply, "Bren is older. When you're that old, then you can do what the older boys do."

In the meantime, they would have to settle for building indoor tents. By the time she announced bedtime and lights out, C.J. and the twins had transformed the living room into a wall-to-wall encampment fit for the Union Army.

Like two-legged arachnids, they strung a web of clothesline from every doorknob, chair leg, window latch and drawer pull. Then they raided Katie's linen closet for every blanket, sheet and quilt they could scavenge and secured them with a gross of clothespins. They draped end tables, sofas, chairs, coffee table, every piece of furniture into series of warrens and tunnels.

C.J. Coughlin was very high maintenance. Like his mother, he was allergic to an entire basic food group and half of another. Katie had to analyze every drop of liquid or crumb of food before she served it to him. Among the long list of can't haves were eggs, wheat germ, barley, peanuts, eggs, strawberries, cow's milk and coconut. Add to the nutritional no-nos, he had to avoid environmental allergens such as bees, ten kinds of pollen, smoke, dog dander, goose down and cat hair.

Katie wasn't sure if he was a hypochondriac in training or if the allergies were real. It didn't matter. She couldn't risk it and had to take his condition seriously. If his digestive and immune systems were fragile, you couldn't tell by looking at him. He was hefty, round and his afflictions didn't affect his horsepower. He kept right up with the twins with all pistons operating.

Tommy had school friends, but being shy, he rarely accepted a sleepover invitation. In truth, he wasn't sure he could go all night without getting homesick. Rather than risk embarrassment, he simply declined. He seemed contented to play with the twins or spend time with Abraham. It wasn't until two weeks after the school's summer recess that he finally asked his best friend, Douglas Kirby, to spend the night. Because it was the first time Tommy had asked, Katie nodded her permission immediately.

As if he were hosting a celebrity, Tommy tidied his room without being told. Where the twins' room could have been declared a disaster zone, Tommy wanted his room to be immaculate. He had spent the greater part of the afternoon choosing which games they would play and asked his mom if they could have popcorn before bed. Katie said that she'd pop them enough to feed their whole class.

During supper, Tommy's patience was running thin. He asked Katie every few minutes what time it was.

"It's five minutes later than the last time you asked," Katie smiled at him. "When the big hand is on the twelve and the little hand is on the six is when his mom said they would drop him off. That's only a half hour away."

Half an hour in grown-up time translated to an eternity in kid-time.

"And Casey and Colin. When Doug arrives, I want you to leave Tommy and him alone. He is Tommy's guest and they don't want you bothering them all night. Brendan, you can entertain the twins for one night."

The twins pouted and Brendan grunted and focused his attention on his meal. It had been one of his less communicative days.

Finally, the big hand was on the twelve and the little hand on the six and as if they had synchronized their clocks, Ward Kirby drove up the drive. Tommy bolted out the kitchen door without giving Mr. Kirby a chance to shift into park.

Ward carried Doug's overnight bag to the back door and handed it to Katie. Katie hefted the bag that must have weighed a ton.

"What's he got in here? Lead?" Katie asked as she set the suitcase down.

"You'd think he was staying a month instead of one night. Connie, the mother hen. I think she packed everything but his fish bowl." Ward scratched his thick, wiry, brown hair as if he were digging for buried treasure. "If you run short of anything, check his bag, what you need is probably in there."

"How are Connie and the baby doing?" Katie hadn't seen them since she dropped off a spaghetti dinner, garlic bread and a lemon meringue pie their first week home from the hospital.

"Connie's pretty much back on her feet. That is when she's not passed out from exhaustion. First we couldn't wait for the baby to be born. Now, I wish we could send it back where it came from so we could get a decent night's sleep." He rubbed his eyes drawing attention to the dark sacs that hung from his lower lids.

"And the baby?"

"He's doing great. All eleven pounds twelve ounces of him. Connie calls him Little Joe. There's nothing little about him including his lungs. Doc Hughes says the bigger the baby the better they sleep.

"He sleeps, that's for sure. The only problem is he has his days and nights mixed up and figures the rest of the house ought to adjust to his schedule. Which would be fine if he were the only kid we had and I didn't have a job that required me to be awake and in an upright position. We're walking around like zombies. I've resorted to stuffing cotton balls in my ears so I can get some sleep."

"Well, consider yourselves minus one child for the next twenty-four hours."

Ward looked so miserable and pitiful Katie had to bite her tongue to keep from giggling. "I'll bring him home tomorrow night after supper. Is there anything else I can do for you?"

"Unless you can breast feed an eleven-pound baby or calculate homeowners insurance premiums, probably not." He sounded as tired as he looked.

"Sorry, Ward. Tell Connie I'll stop over on Thursday and help her with the kids and housework. At least I can give her a little break and maybe she can sneak in a few solid hours of sleep."

"That's great, Katie. I'm sure she'd love it. Oh, something I almost forgot. You may want to curtail the liquids before bed. Doug hasn't exactly mastered the art of knowing how much he can hold during the night. If you don't want an accident, cut him off at a half glass."

"Thanks for the warning. Bren had the same problem until he was nine."

Ward turned and trudged down the steps so slowly, Katie wasn't sure he was going to make it. His feet shuffled as if they were made of pig iron.

Before he was gone a minute, Katie remembered the stew and hollered to him, hoping he hadn't left yet, "Wait a second, Ward."

As she hurried to the refrigerator, she tripped over Doug's suitcase and nearly fell flat. She muttered, "Son-of-a-biscuit."

Katie retrieved the pot from the refrigerator and the cake and rolls from the counter. Juggling them like a circus performer, she ran down the steps and out to the car. Ward's forehead rested against the steering wheel.

"I made extra stew tonight and a chocolate cake." She handed them through the open window and Ward placed them on the seat and floor beside him.

"And there are a dozen poppy seed rolls in the bag. Tell Connie I'll collect the pot and cake pan on Thursday."

Ward mumbled. "Thanks a lot. This'll beat grilled cheese sandwiches and canned soup. They're the only two things I can cook. I'm a walking advertisement for Campbell's tomato soup."

"My boys would live on grilled cheese sandwiches if I'd let them."

"Then send 'em over to my place. I'm getting to be a pro."

"Are you sure it's safe for you to drive home?" Katie asked with concern.

"I'll be all right," he assured her. "Promise I won't fall asleep until I'm turning into our driveway."

Katie allowed Tommy and Doug an evening swim and let them have the run of the house. They played Marco Polo in the lake and poison tag with the twins. At eight o'clock she shooed the twins inside for bed. She let Tommy and Doug play for an extra half hour before she called them in for the night.

Katie liked Douglas Kirby. He was a miniature version of Connie. He had orange, curly hair like a pumpkin with a perm and a million freckles. His disposition was as calm as Tommy's but a little less shy. He was well mannered, well behaved and he and Tommy got along well.

"Do we gotta go to bed right now?" Tommy asked, disappointed.

"No. I'll let you stay up until nine-thirty. Then it's lights out. Okay?"

"Wow! Nine-thirty!" Doug exclaimed. "My mom never lets me stay up that late." He looked at Tommy, eyes wide as saucers. Tommy was so shocked he was speechless.

"This is a special occasion. I'm sure your mom would agree that nine-thirty is okay."

Tommy and Doug scampered up the stairs before Katie could change her mind. From the top of the staircase, Tommy called down, "Don't forget the popcorn, Mommy."

"I'm right on it," she called back.

At nine forty-five Katie went upstairs to tuck Tommy and Doug in for the night. They had been having such a good time that she stretched bedtime an extra fifteen minutes. They brushed their teeth and said their prayers. She heeded Ward's warning and made sure Doug made one last trip to the toilet.

"Who won the Cootie game?"

"Nobody," Tommy stated. "We changed our minds and played find the thimble."

Katie raised an eyebrow. "And where will I find my thimble?"

Tommy pointed, "It's on the dresser."

After prayers, she tucked the quilt around them. "So, Doug, tell me what you think of that new baby brother."

Doug shrugged. "He cries a lot."

"That's what he's supposed to do. New babies eat and sleep and cry."

"And pee an' poop their diapers," Doug added.

"You're right. I forgot babies do a lot of that, too." Katie staved off a grin.

"He's kinda boring. Jus' lays there an' cries an' don't play or nothing. You can't play with him 'cuz he's got a soft spot in his head."

"Don't worry. Before you know it he'll be chasing after his big brother and getting into your stuff and making a real pest of himself."

Katie gave each boy a kiss on the forehead and they smelled of sun, lake, buttered popcorn and the freshness of youth. Before turning out the light she asked, "Doug, do you need a nightlight left on?"

"I ain't a baby, Mrs. O'Neill. I ain't afraid of the dark."

"Sleep tight. Don't let the bedbugs bite."

Katie left the bedroom door slightly ajar and the hall light on just in case.

○₃ ○

Katie's bedroom door crept open and a sliver of light washed over her face. She almost sensed it before it actually reached her and her eyes drowsed open. She checked the bedside clock. It read two forty-five.

Tommy tiptoed over to her bedside. Katie sat up in bed and asked, "Is something wrong? Are you sick?" He never woke during the night unless he was ill. She reached up and placed her palm against his forehead checking to see if he had a temperature. His skin felt cool and dry.

Tommy shook his head, "It ain't me. It's Doug."

"Is Douglas sick?"

In an itty-bitty voice, Tommy said, "He ain't sick. But we got some big troubles. I think he went Number One in bed. It's all wet and so are me and Doug."

Katie slipped her legs and feet over the side of the bed and reached for her bathrobe.

"Take off your pajamas and put on a pair of dry ones. I'll take care of Douglas."

Doug was sitting up in bed in a matted nest of sheets stained dark with urine.

"Douglas, I hear you may have had an accident."

He nodded slowly, on the verge of tears. His eyes were lowered in shame, his chin puckered and lower lip quivered.

Katie sat next to him on the bed and soothed him, "It's okay. Everyone has accidents. I'll strip off these old, wet sheets and put on some clean one's. Everything will be all right. No harm's done."

"My jammies are wet."

"You can put on a pair of Tommy's."

"I wanna go home." He spoke so quietly that if Katie hadn't been sitting next to him she wouldn't have heard him.

"You don't have to. This is no problem. I'm not mad."

"I don't wanna stay," he persisted. He was wet and embarrassed and probably a bit homesick. He wanted to go home.

Katie didn't want to push him over the edge. "Okay. We'll get you home. Put your play clothes on. I'll be right back. And then I'll take you home."

Katie almost got to the bedroom door when he asked, "You ain't gonna tell nobody, are you?"

"I have to tell your mom and dad."

"I mean you don't gotta tell Bren or Casey and Colin, do you?"

Katie smiled and reassured him, "Of course not. I promise I won't tell them a thing. It will be yours and Tommy's and my secret." She gestured with her fingers as if she were locking her lips.

Katie woke Brendan to tell him that Douglas wanted to go home. Brendan would have to sit watch until she returned. She instructed Brendan to let Tommy sleep in her bed then telephoned the Kirby's to let them know what had happened.

"I'll come pick him up," Ward offered in a voice heavy with exhaustion.

"No, I'm already up. I'll drive him home. No need waking everyone up at your house," Katie insisted.

"Don't worry about that over here. We've been up for hours. In fact, I can't remember if we've even been to sleep, yet." Ward yawned into the phone. Katie could hear the familiar, middle-of-the-night wail of a baby in the background.

"I'll be there in a few minutes," Katie promised.

"I'll leave the porch light on."

Katie didn't bother to dress. Instead, in nightie, robe and slippers she packed Douglas up and dragged his leaden suitcase to the car. Before she was two miles down the road, he had fallen asleep, his head resting on her arm.

ᘓ ᘔ

By the time summer was in full swing, the ranks of the boys of Lakefield Road had tripled in size. The O'Neill homestead was nearly always alive with the chaos, tumult, noise and energetic activity of boys being boys. Katie's clothesline was in constant use, laden with wet swim trunks and towels. There was a steady stream of Kool-Aid to quench thirsts and her cookie jar was under relentless siege. Matt accused her of having a secret, deep-seeded ambition to be the "Old Lady who lived in a shoe." Lottie joked that she was "happier than a pig in slop, tha more younguns she had 'round her."

Abraham continued to keep a polite distance. While her own boys maintained their respective relationships with him, the Musketeers avoided him like the plague. On occasion, Katie would overhear them making cruel remarks which she knew had to stem from gossip that was undoubtedly passed along by some careless, thoughtless adult. She made it abundantly clear that she would not tolerate them repeating that kind of malicious gossip in her house.

On a regular basis, often, twice a week, Katie invited Lottie and Abraham to join them for dinner. It appeared that the uneasiness Abraham demonstrated around Lottie had begun to ebb a little. He seemed less nervous, less intimidated and conversations between the two less stinted. Katie hoped it was genuine and not just her imagination, for she firmly believed that things that were meant to be, happened in their own good time.

It was a Sunday evening. The day had been raining, off and on. Lottie had left, following after dinner conversation. The boys were in their rooms playing before bedtime. The day had been unusually chilly and Katie had built a fire in the living room fireplace to chase the chilly dampness out of the air. She and Abraham were comfortably settled in the plush overstuffed furniture, enjoying the crackling fire. The scent of burning apple wood and cinnamon tea filled the room.

Their house in Boston had not had a fireplace and Katie couldn't believe that she hadn't missed it. Now, she couldn't imagine living without one. Since moving to Eden Croft, on cooler days and nights (sixty degrees was her official line of demarcation), it had become a treasured ritual for her to have a fire burning and crackling away cheerfully.

She looked forward to the quiet times when she and Abraham would have the opportunity to chat. Katie enjoyed the opportunity to have a conversation that exceeded a vocabulary of one-syllable words and didn't require her to be constantly correcting improper grammar.

On that evening, Abraham and Katie had been chatting away like two old women, the discussion included topics about anything and everything that drifted into their minds. Katie broached a subject that she had wanted to bring up with Abraham, but the right time hadn't presented itself, until then.

She walked over to the mantle and asked, "This painting, Abraham, I've been wondering about it since we first moved in. I asked Lottie. She didn't know anything about it, but said that you could probably shed some light on it. I know that you were quite close to Uncle Sean and Aunt Katherine. Perhaps you could tell me something of its origins."

Abraham placed his teacup on its saucer and looked up, first at the picture, then turned his gaze to Katie.

"I strongly suspect that you may have your own suspicions about the artist as well as the subject. That portrait was painted as part of a series titled, 'The Godchild.' The artist was your Aunt Katherine.

"That collection of pieces was both a commercial and critical success. She even had a very successful showing at a gallery in Chicago. As a result, all of the pieces were eventually sold. With this one exception. Even though it was considered the premier piece of the series, Katherine refused to sell it at any price. Instead, she brought it back here and it has hung over that mantle ever since."

Both Katie and Abraham studied the piece and it moved them in two, distinctly different ways.

Abraham asked, "Beautiful, isn't she? Katherine painted that, many years ago. It was inspired by her memories of a tiny, sweet, captivating child that she loved deeply and had always filled a special place in her heart. It is a reflection of cherished memories of a time and place and a little girl that were both very precious and very lost to her. That little girl was you."

His words were soft and melodious. They seemed to come from some place far away. It was as if he were feeling the same emotions, the same regret, the same tenderness, the same longing, as Katherine must have felt.

"She had spent so many of her last years away from you and your mother in a precarious state of mourning and loss. Somehow, seeking forgiveness and redemption, she searched for the path back. In her lifetime, Katherine never found it."

His recollections and words brought tears to Katie's eyes. Looking into Abraham's own soulful eyes was almost more than she could bear. Instead, she turned her gaze back to the painting.

Abraham reminisced, "Katherine was a remarkable woman, a brilliant artist and teacher. She was one of the strongest, most generous and most independent person I have ever had the pleasure of knowing. Perhaps too strong, too independent. Your Uncle Sean told me once that Katherine had disapproved of your parent's marriage and threatened your mother that she would have to choose between her and your father. The choice your mother made is obvious.

"After Katherine and Sean and your parents immigrated, though they tried to mend their differences. However, relations between them became very strained. Apparently, Katherine never completely accepted your father and the marriage and when you were still a child, they had a dreadful argument. Despite being your godmother, Katherine severed all ties. That is when she and Sean moved to Eden Croft. Katherine spent the rest of her life ruing that decision. She was consumed by a constant struggle between self-righteousness and self-reproach. The result was a person of deep regrets and unhappiness."

"After my ma and died, why didn't Aunt Katherine make an effort to contact me?" Katie asked.

"We humans can be self-destructive. Too often, we allow certainty to undermine conciliation. More than that, I believe Katherine was afraid you would not give her absolution.

"She loved you and your mother very deeply. She just never felt that she could undo the damage she had done. Though Sean loved her as much as life itself, he was never able to help her find the inner peace that eluded her for so many years. He was never able to teach her that we can only find inner peace by making peace with ourselves."

"It all seems so unfair," Katie spoke softly. "Everyone deserves a second chance. Aunt Katherine was never given one."

"That is where you are wrong, Katie. You are her second chance. That is why it was so important to her that you brought your sons here to live, to make her home your home. It was the only way she could see to make reparations. Where she could never find the words she finally found a way to say what was in her heart."

Katie wiped at the tears that were slowly running down her cheeks. The emotional tidal wave left in its wake a need for her to reciprocate the love of a woman for whom she had almost no memories or recollection. She searched the deepest recesses of her mind for just a semblance of recognition.

Finally she spoke. "You have helped me to understand why the terms of her will were so specific. Why she was so insistent that the boys and I live here. I wished I could have known her as you did, instead of through the tainted eyes of my parent's hurt and bitterness. She was always this unseen, mythical ogre that I had conjured up based on the stories I had been told.

"And now, when she's gone, just when it all should have been too late for me, when she would have been completely lost to me, you have shared with me a piece of my heritage, a side of my Godmother that few people had a chance to see. A facet of her that remained hidden for so long, that would have been buried along with her, forever. Thank you, for giving me that gift, Abraham."

Abraham noticed that Katie's tone wasn't filled with harshness or regret. Instead, she spoke with gentleness. Where he expected to see sadness and sorrow, her face reflected joy and contentment. Her reactions surprised him.

Katie thought back on her years of growing up with so few close relatives. Unlike so many of her childhood friends, she hadn't any uncles, aunts or cousins. Her grandparents had all passed away years before. The only aunt and uncle she did have were virtual strangers to her.

"It's a strange feeling to know that you have had such an impact on another's life that until this moment, was someone I had never really known. How could I have meant so much to someone that I barely knew existed? How could I have summoned up so much love from her without ever having given her any measure of love in return?"

Abraham thought for a minute then answered with the only truth he knew. "That is the untenable nature of true love. It happens without invitation and provocation. It endures time and adversity and asks nothing in return."

chapter twelve

June was nearly over.

Matt had stopped out to see Katie on several occasions, always preceded by a phone call and always on some fabricated premise that he needed her signature or to discuss some contrived legal matter.

He had become very adept at invention and deception. It was totally out of character for him to feel the need to legitimize his visits by inventing fictitious paperwork or to discuss a legal matter with her. He was becoming very annoyed with himself and embarrassed by the need for subterfuge. None of it made any sense.

Where women were concerned, his life read like a little black book, an alphabetical prospectus of beauty pageant contestants. At any time or any place he could be found escorting a beautiful lady. And like any lothario worth his weight, he could simultaneously flirt with extraconubial bliss while eluding the dreaded *M* word.

Since meeting Katie, he hadn't had one single date. That was way out of character for him. In the past, a monogamous relationship had never held any charms for him. But from the moment she had first walked into his office, he hadn't had the slightest interest in any other female.

What was wrong with him? Why was this woman any different from any other? Fun. Smart. Quick sense of humor. Captivating. Nice enough looking. Oh, hell. Who was he kidding? She was a knockout. And sexy as silk.

He reassured himself that he wasn't violating some outdated, archaic, Victorian standard of a socially acceptable period of mourning. She had been widowed nearly two years. Women no longer needed to confine themselves to wearing black crepe and bolt themselves behind closed doors, avoiding any form of social contact for a prescribed period of time.

Besides, it wasn't like he was interested in anything more than an innocent date or two. It wasn't like he was committing some moral impropriety. With at least half a dozen eager and very noisy chaperones lurking about nothing sensational or lurid was likely to come up on the agenda. There was nothing like spilled milk or a skinned knee to set a romantic mood. Hey, he liked kids as well as the next guy, but everyone was entitled to a little privacy and R&R.

He had a plan. It was a plan that definitely did not include five or six juvenile escorts. His plan was brilliant and would ensure them a few private hours, alone, without endless interference from her brood.

It was a gray, humid, gloomy Wednesday afternoon when he finally made up his mind that he was going to pay Katie a visit that was not precipitated by some contrived legal concern. Bolstered by his new resolve, he was going to put a stop to the charade, once and for all.

The Fourth of July was coming up. He wanted to invite Katie to join him for a sail … maybe a picnic … nothing fancy. They might even be able to stretch it out until after dark and watch the town's firework celebration from the boat.

He could just imagine those emerald green eyes dancing, twinkling, illuminated by the brilliant explosion of spark and color. There was no doubt in his mind which of the two would sparkle the brightest. It would be no contest. The only things that sparkled more than emeralds were diamonds. And diamonds weren't nearly as intriguing.

Armed by courage and the vision of Katie's eyes gave him the impetus needed. Like a maniac on a mission, he left the office early, headed out of town and turned onto Lakefield Road.

Casey sat on the back steps when Matt casually strolled up to the house, hands in his pant's pockets. Casey's chin was rested on his hands and he looked like the bastard at the family reunion.

Matt couldn't be sure if it was Casey or Colin. He still had a devil of a time telling them apart.

He sat down next to him on the step and nudged him. "Hey, buddy!" *Buddy was safe.*

Normally, the kid, whichever one, would have greeted him with one of their droll knock-knock jokes, but *Buddy* remained mute.

"What? No knock-knock joke for me?"

"Nope."

Relieved, Matt thought, *Thank goodness for that. There was a God, after all.*

"How come?"

"Don't feel like it."

"If you tried taking a step, you'd trip over that lower lip. Why the long face?"

"Bein' punished."

Well, that statement provided him with a wealth of information.

"What for?" *Come on squirt. Give a guy a break, would ya? I hope a few more details will be forthcoming.* Matt made a silent plea.

"Me an' Colin got inta big trouble."

So, this one's Casey. Brilliant deduction, counselor.

"Well, where is your partner in crime?"

"Up in our room."

"He look half as bad as you do?"

"Nope. It was my idea."

Matt almost laughed. *No surprises there.*

"That's where you made your first mistake, Buddy. Always plead the Fifth."

"Huh?"

"That means that if it's going to get you into trouble, don't say anything. Never admit it was you."

"Don't matter. Most a the trouble we get into *is* me."

"So, based on your prior convictions, you're charged with the felony and Colin gets aiding and abetting."

Casey looked up at Matt, confused. "What?"

"Never mind. Lawyer talk. By the way, what's your sentence?"

Casey looked confused again.

"What's the punishment?"

"Gotta sit an' think 'bout what we done."

"If you need to hire a good lawyer, I come cheap. Since you and I are pretty good buddies, I'll even cut you a deal." Matt could hardly maintain a sober face. "Is your mom home?"

"Yeah. But she's pretty mad right now. She cussed at us. She said a bad word. I wouldn't go in if I wuz you."

Cussed? This was getting better by the minute. "I'll take my chances. By the way, what did you two do that you gotta sit and think about?"

"Throwin' eggs."

It was Matt's turn to be confused.

"Bren's in big trouble, too."

"What did he do?"

"We were his 'sponsibility."

"I'll give you some free advice. It's the same advice I'd give to any criminal. Don't do the crime if you can't do the time."

As he got up, Matt patted Casey on the shoulder and said, "I'll try talking to the judge. Throw you on the mercy of the court. Maybe I can get you a lighter sentence. See if she'll let you off with time served."

Katie was putting the mop, cleaning supplies and pail away in the closet. She had her hair tied up haphazardly in a kerchief. The humidity had curled her hair even more than usual and more of it had escaped the kerchief than not. She was hot and sweaty and dirty. Her faced flushed from exertion. Her temper had not completely cooled down when Matt standing in the doorway, tongue-in-cheek, with a cocky, mischievous gleam in his eyes, startled her.

Matt noticed her legs bare to mid-thigh and thought she had never looked more delicious. The look on his face was an exact replica of Rhett eyeing Scarlett from the base of the staircase.

Half angry and half embarrassed, Katie untangled her housedress, which she had hiked up and tucked in her belt for cleaning. Of all days, he picked this one, to show up unannounced.

"While the rest of the world is sweltering and suffering in this oppressive heat, some of us actually dressed up, may I point out, in a three-piece-suit and necktie. And here you are casually and comfortably dressed, leisurely lolling around, cool as a cucumber."

Katie gave him a warning look. "You may want to curb your sarcasm. I'm in no mood for it. I've just finished spending the greater part of this afternoon washing and scrubbing, as you describe 'in this oppressive heat.' I'm tired, steamed, drenched from sweat and dangerously near the boiling point. I feel as if I've spent three hours in a Turkish bath. Between my exasperation and exhaustion, you'll find I'm not my usual charming and irresistible self.

"And to add fuel to the fire, I've had to suppress the urge to physically abuse three out of four of my children. If I'm that close to harming my own flesh and blood, imagine how easily I could turn on someone who isn't. Consider yourself forewarned."

Matt threw up his hands. "You have unfairly judged me. Never, have I seen you look more ravishing. And speaking of judging, Casey tells me you sinned … said a bad word … cussed. He is also told me a wild and wicked tale of your abuse. About cruel and unusual punishment. Before I throw them on the mercy of the court, what terrible and unforgivable crimes were perpetrated by your own flesh and blood?"

Weakening from his drollness, Katie offered him a chair and surrendered. "This could take a while. While I get us some lemonade, do you want the condensed version, or the complete unabridged edition?

"By all means, the whole undiluted narrative of *The Egg and I.*"

Katie groaned.

"Sorry, I couldn't resist the temptation."

It took Katie the better part of two glasses of lemonade, to tell the tale.

Having left Brendan in charge, she had made a quick trip into town to deliver a meatloaf and as a member of the Altar Society, to help set up the church hall for the Hennig funeral luncheon. Tommy was at Abraham's, helping him in the greenhouse. Meanwhile, Marie Dreffs dropped off her usual weekly order of three-dozen eggs, as she did every Wednesday.

Brendan's nose was slightly out of joint because his previously made plans with the guys were being delayed by an unreasonable request to watch the rug rats for a couple of hours. He had gone down to the dock to pout and ruefully ponder what an unfair and wicked mother he had. In a snit, he failed to put the eggs away in the refrigerator.

The exact sequence of the next chain of events was slightly clouded as Casey and Colin tearfully argued over two distinctly opposite versions. Katie pieced the puzzle together.

The twins must have had a heyday. As soon as she opened the car door, she could hear their squeals of laughter, interspersed with their verbal simulation of bullets flying and bombs whistling to earth and exploding. They proceeded to throw enough ammunition at the enemy, namely each other, in the form of three-dozen, raw eggs. The assault rivaled MacArthur's retaking of the Philippines. While the kitchen walls, ceiling, cupboards, tables and chairs, counters and windows bore the brunt of the attack, the twins were sufficiently spattered with shell fragments and drippy, runny, egg whites and yolks.

Katie hoped that they had thoroughly enjoyed themselves. While the siege may have been short-lived, the repercussions would not be. The appropriation of guilt was leveled on the culprits. After they had spent ample time thinking about their escapade, and allowing Katie's temper time to cool off, they would be responsible for setting and clearing the table before and after meals for two weeks. They would also have to forfeit two weeks allowance to reimburse her the cost of the eggs.

Brendan served the first part of his sentence bathing the twins and cleaning up the bathroom, which had also been ravaged in the process. Being grounded for a week constituted the remainder of his sentence. And just for good measure, he too, had to forfeit two weeks allowance.

Matt couldn't resist, and risking her wrath, laughed at the recitation. His reaction was infectious. Soon, Katie was giggling and laughing right along with him. Though he had seen her easy smile a hundred times, for the first time, Matt actually heard her laugh out loud. It was magical. She had the giggly, merry laughter of little girl, contagious and uncontrollable; tinkling like soft wind chimes in a gentle breeze.

When she laughed, her eyes sparkled and her cheeks dimpled. He found he was as captivated by her laughter as he was by her words. In spite of being mussed, hot, dirty and sweaty, even on her worst day, she was more beautiful than any other woman he had ever seen … on their best days.

"Thus ends my story of another exciting and exotic day in the life of Mary Katherine O'Neill."

"Far be it from me to undermine the unconditional love of a mother for her children, but based on their past histories and now this most recent escapade, I must say those two suffer from a double dose of original sin."

"Today, you'll get no argument from me."

Katie changed the subject. "And what sudden business brings you out here? It must be terribly important. You usually telephone first."

So caught up in their conversation, Matt had completely forgotten his mission.

"Sorry. I just came out here on an impulse. No business concerns. No legal matter to discuss. Instead, I have a proposition for you."

He was suddenly uncharacteristically unsure of the tack he wanted to take and was dangerously close to being tongue-tied. He stammered and forged on. "The ... a ... Fourth of July is next week, and I wanted to ... sort of ... bounce an idea off you."

All of the moisture had drained from his mouth to his palms and armpits. He swallowed back a full-blown case of nerves. Fighting for control, he stumbled forward. "I've bored you often enough with my rhetoric about my passion for sailing ... and I'm sure you've already figured out that I'd rather be on the water than anywhere else. But, like most things in life it could always be improved upon."

He began to ramble and lose his composure. The timing was miserable, but he started this. Now he had to finish it. Then an encouraging thought filled his mind. Maybe his timing wasn't as shitty as he first thought. Coming on the cusp of her brood's latest escapade might prove fortuitous. She might well be ready to spend an entire day free of them and their incorrigible behavior.

"I know that the twins are in the dog house ... and due to his dereliction of duty, Brendan is likewise in the soup ... well, this may not be the right time to bring this up, but I was thinking ..."

Katie's eyes lit up and she interrupted and saved him the need to continue stumbling over every other word. "Matt what a generous and thoughtful idea. The boys would love it! This is such a coincidence! I was going to ask you to join us for the holiday. We were planning to have a picnic, spend the day on the beach. Later, we were going to have a campfire, sparklers and all, and watch the fireworks on the lake.

"Offering to take the boys sailing would be such a wonderful surprise. Of course, I'll let them suffer and stew for a few well-deserved days before I tell them. They'll be so excited! Brendan will think he died and went to heaven."

Matt sat there with a stunned, stupid grin on his face, while his whole fantastic, amazing, incredible day with Katie deflated before his eyes and landed in a discarded heap.

Katie jumped up from the table, rejuvenated by the idea. Immediately, her mind filled with plans, as she anticipated her menu, marketing and preparations. She couldn't wait to get started. It was going to be a wonderful day!

Still anesthetized from the unexpected shock of his whole plan gone awry, Matt's car drove itself home. He trudged up the steps to his back door and in a clouded stupor, he shook his head and mumbled, "Congratulations, Matt, you suave, sophisticated, silver-tongued devil. That all went exactly as planned."

෬ ෨

The steamy, thick, stifling weather that held Eden Croft in its clammy grasp for over a week ended that night.

As was her reward, at the end of a long day Katie retreated to the sanctuary of the gazebo. Hopefully seeking some relief from the triple digit temperatures and with hair still damp from her bath, she slipped out into the night, the air still and oppressive with humidity. She felt as if she could actually reach out, grasp it and wring the moisture from it. Even with the sun down, the thermometer loomed near ninety and with the humidity rivaling that of the Amazon, it felt like a hundred-and-ninety.

Throwing modesty aside, in deference to the temperature, Katie wore only a light, sleeveless, cotton nightie. As she sat thinking of how seldom the lake air was still, she prayed for a whisper of a breeze. Occasionally a streak of heat lightening would dance and spark in the distance, electrifying the black sky over the lake. The night creatures were unnaturally quiet, they too, conserving their energy, as if waiting with bated breath, anticipating that something untamed, some turbulent force of nature was building, growing, imminent.

Katie drew a great deal of satisfaction from her motherly responsibilities and household duties. Yet, she still looked forward to her quiet time. If motherhood was her vocation, then the peace and solitude of these nights were her sustenance. Mothering was a full-time job. But, even mommies needed to recharge their batteries. When the demands of the day left no room for thought or contemplation, she sought them out in her gazebo.

Sometimes she felt like a squirrel, busily foraging and storing her cache and treasures throughout the day. She would horde them until, under the cover of darkness and in the tranquil moments of the twilight, she would search them out, uncover them and reflect and feast on them.

Her thoughts and contemplations were her own. She didn't have to share them, rationalize or justify them. They could be as nonsensical and frivolous as her imagination wanted or as profound and philosophical as her intellect allowed. Often times, she welcomed the company of Lottie or Abraham. At other times, like that night, she was most comfortable being by herself, with her own thoughts.

At almost the exact instant that Katie felt that the weather would never break, a gentle breeze began to stir and then build steadily in intensity. Katie stood and with arms stretched out, let the warm air and wind entwine around her, brushing soft cotton against skin, soothing wind against skin. Her loose, unbraided hair tossed carelessly in the wind.

Soon the rumblings of distant thunder started and the sky was illuminated by streaks of lightening like witches bony, misshapen fingers clawing at the clouds. The air became scented with the hint of rain, at first subtle, then heavy and urgent.

Suddenly, it was as if the heavens broke open. At first, nickel-sized drops struck sporadically here and there. Then carried on the wings of the wind, the rain exploded, as warm pellets began striking everywhere. They chattered across the dock, plunked on the lake, and pit-a-patted a wild, rhythmic drumming on the roof of the gazebo. It was like a calypso beat resonating from a steel drum.

All around her, Katie could feel the stale muggy air becoming cleansed and refreshed by the rain's restorative powers. Like lifting a heavy velvet curtain, the stuffy, dank air was chased away by the cool, rain-moistened scent of balsam, cedar and fir. As if electrified by the lightening, encouraged and spurred on by the thunder, exhilarated by the wind she laughed in the face of a good soaking. Like a night nymph, Katie made a boisterous, uninhibited, very un-lady-like dance toward the house, splashing and slopping her way across the flooded lawn.

She was sopping wet long before she ever reached the porch.

After shedding her soaked nightie and changing into a dry one, she towel-dried her hair and slipped between the clean, dry sheets. The humidity had all but disappeared from the linens leaving them fresh and cool to the touch. She said her usual prayers and one decade of the rosary.

Before she fell to sleep, Katie would always have what she called a "mind chat" with Danny. This was the time when she missed him the most. Driven by the need to share their life with him, she would mentally relive the everyday events and occurrences. As she lay alone in bed, she could almost feel his presence next to her. She would stretch one arm across the empty bed and gently stroke the sheets, wishing, hoping and craving the touch, the warmth and closeness of his body, instead of the cold, stark emptiness.

If she closed her eyes she could imagine every scent and nuance of him. Old Spice, the only after shave he ever used, clung to her memory, unforgettable. Sometimes the longing and loneliness, the need for intimacy would be so powerful, she would have to fight back the tears. But not that night. It was as if the rain had washed over her, too, taking with it any sadness or melancholy. That night, feeling the finest of gossamer threads connecting her heart to his, her soul to his, her body to his, she slept peacefully.

chapter thirteen

The telephone rang as Katie was getting ready to leave for her day of errands and marketing.

It was Fred Brisbois, Steven's father. After he and Katie exchanged amenities, he got to the point.

"Steven's birthday is in a few days. As a special surprise, I told him he could invite his four friends to join us for the Tiger game on Saturday, my treat. Now, Steven tells me that Brendan is grounded and can't go. I'm not trying to interfere or undermine your discipline. Trust me, I believe that rules are rules. But, since I already have the tickets, I was hoping maybe you might consider letting Brendan go, just this once. They're playing the Red Sox."

Katie found herself in a quandary. She paused a moment and rolled it over in her mind before responding.

"Fred, I appreciate your calling me. Brendan hadn't told me about the outing." She stalled, trying to organize her thoughts.

"I didn't tell Steven until last night. When he told me about Brendan's situation, it presented me with a bit of a predicament. I didn't want to put too much pressure on you so I haven't even told Steven I was calling."

Katie didn't want to make a rash decision and asked, "Can I think things over for a bit, maybe give you a call this afternoon? Unless that will be too late to give Steven time to invite someone else?"

"That's fine. I'll be at the office the rest of the day, you can reach me here." He gave Katie the number.

"Thanks again, for telephoning me. It means a lot to me that you care enough about Brendan to put yourself in this position."

"Hey, you've got a great kid there. And quite a baseball enthusiast. Even if he is a Red Sox fan. I'm a parent, too. I'll understand, whichever way you decide. Sometimes this parenting thing isn't all it's cracked up to be."

"I'll ring you after lunch, Fred," Katie promised.

They said their goodbyes and hung up.

"Well, this certainly hangs the rag on the bush," Katie muttered to herself.

Her mind told her that she should let the punishment stand, ball game or no ball game. But her heart told her otherwise. Perhaps she had been too hard on Bren. It did seem as though he was always called on to help with the boys. Most of the time he had one or the other or all three wanting to tag along. Maybe she needed to give him a little more time to himself, without having to be the big brother all the time. She began to doubt and second-guess herself.

"No, Fred, sometimes this parenting thing isn't all it's cracked up to be."

Eventually, Katie decided that she would rescind the punishment, or at least amend it a bit. The forfeiture of his allowance would stand. She told Brendan in exchange for being grounded he would have to be her indentured servant for the week. She could use help with the housework, gardening and the car did need washing and waxing. She made it perfectly clear that because this was a special circumstance, for this once, she would give in.

She hadn't seen him happier or more excited in a long time. He gladly agreed to the terms of the contract. He worked like a ditch-digger on a deadline. Katie could have asked him to disassemble the gazebo, move it to the other side of the lawn, reassemble it and he would have enthusiastically agreed to it.

⋯ ⋯

Saturday morning Brendan was up at the crack of dawn. Washed, groomed, dressed and fed an hour early. He even cleared the dishes and tidied the breakfast fixings.

Brendan was outside, pacing like an expectant father, waiting for Mr. Brisbois to pick him up. Katie stepped out on the back porch and said to him, teasingly, "You aren't at all anxious, are you?"

"You don't think they forgot me, do you? What time is it? Should I call Breeze? Do you think something happened?" He questioned, worried.

"Calm down. You're going to explode. They're not even due for a few minutes."

She slipped off his ball cap, ran her fingers through his dark curls, straightening his already perfectly combed hair and replaced the cap. She reached into her robe pocket and pulled out a ten-dollar bill. She took his hand and pressed the money into it. Brendan looked first at the money, then up at his mom, stunned.

"Mom, this is a whole ten dollars. Way more than my allowance. It's an awful lot of money. Can we afford it?"

Katie smiled at his concern. "It's my treat. Your dad always used to say that it makes a man feel important to have a little extra money in his pocket. And for Heaven's sake, you don't have to worry about the money. That's my job. Buy the Musketeers a hot dog. Buy yourself a souvenir. I don't want to see you come home with one penny."

Just then, the Brisbois station wagon pulled up. Katie resisted the urge to hug and kiss him goodbye in front of the guys.

Surprising her, Brendan turned and brushed a hurried kiss on her cheek, and said, "Luv ya, Mom. You're the keenest."

He literally floated down the steps and Katie called a reminder to him, "Watch your manners and remember to thank Mr. Brisbois. Have fun!"

As the car pulled away, she waved and hollered, "Go Red Sox!"

cg   &

After lunch that afternoon, Katie took three slightly disgruntled little boys to the library. It wasn't fair, Bren got to do a lot of fun stuff and they didn't get to do anything. The trip to the library wasn't Fenway Park or even Tiger Stadium, but, being the closest they were going to get, it seemed to placate them. As added enticement, she let Tommy invite Douglas and the twins asked C.J. Suddenly, the library looked almost as good as the ballpark. Katie hoped C.J. wasn't allergic to library paste.

A trip to the library was always a special treat. The boys had inherited Katie's love of books. It was like a silent paradise with all those books under one roof. Even the smell of aged leather, glue and paper was inviting, nostalgic, comforting in its familiarity. Within the covers of each book, an entire universe lay hidden. Thrilling worlds created of fact, fiction and fantasy.

The boys headed straight for the children's section. The shelves were low, no taller than four feet, making their contents accessible to little arms and hands. Immediately, the boys embarked on their search, looking for just the right books. As Katie scanned the titles, she spotted several that were familiar from her own childhood.

There were miniature, circular oak tables with chairs the perfect size for little people. Each boy found his place and began paging through the books they had selected. Katie let them browse and didn't hurry them in making their choices. She sat next to them, like *Alice in Wonderland*, feeling very large in the ridiculously tiny chair. She watched over them so that they handled each book with care, turning the pages correctly.

Checkout time was especially thrilling. Each one had his own library card that made him feel very grown up. Casey picked a *Curious George* adventure, and Colin chose *The Tales of Peter Rabbit*. Douglas and C.J. each selected a *Bobsy Twins* episode. Tommy, as Katie could have predicted, decided on his favorite, *Timothy Turtle*. Katie could have recited the familiar tale to him with her eyes shut.

"Are you sure you want *Timothy Turtle*, again? We've read it a hundred times. You must know the story by heart."

Tommy answered logically, as if the answer was obvious, "That's 'cuz it's my favorite."

Taking turns, they all reached above the tall counter, deposited their selections and presented their library cards. Mrs. Howard, the librarian, took the books, stamped the cards, and placed them in the envelope glued to the inside back cover of each book. She slid them back to the boys and smiled.

"Great choices, Boys. These are some of my favorites. I'm sure that you know to treat them with care, no torn pages or dirty smudges. Remember, these are your responsibility. They're due back in four weeks. Have fun reading."

After the library excursion, Katie surprised them with a visit to Hastings' Drug Store. Proud as peacocks, and feeling very cool, they sat at the counter on chrome stools with padded, shiny, red vinyl seats. They twisted, and turned and spun round and round like the Tilt-A-Whirl at a carnival.

Katie finally had enough. "This isn't a playground. Where are your manners? Now behave yourselves and quit that spinning around. I want you to sit quietly, like little gentlemen."

The fountain was paradise. Polished, stainless steel refrigerators and coolers held a cornucopia of delectable dairy delights and soft drink concoctions. The menu included malted milks, ice cream shakes, floats and cones, sundaes, banana splits, strawberry, cherry and chocolate sodas and phosphates. More than one or two tummy aches had resulted from sitting at that gray linoleum counter.

That day, Bud Hastings, the star quarterback of the high school football team, worked the fountain for his father. Dressed in a white shirt, white apron and white paper hat, he was tall, broad shouldered and the heartthrob of Eden High. According to any female between the ages of fifteen and fifty, was just too dreamy and to die for.

He served the boys their thick, rich, chocolate malteds in tall, clear, stemmed glasses with long, paper straws. Katie had an ice-cold cherry-cola. C.J., who was allergic to milk, had a chocolate fizz. Bud teased and joked with the boys. To first and second graders a seventeen-year-old captain of the football player was like a god. They developed an immediate case of the ga-gas and hung on his every word. He was just about the swellest football player in the whole school and they could hardly believe that such an important guy would pay them any attention. Noisily slurping every last drop of their malteds, they couldn't wait to tell Brendan about it.

ꙅ ꙅ

The boys were tucked in bed and asleep. After their baths and bedtime prayers Katie had read to each of them from their books. The twins nodded off before she had gotten to page ten. And she had nearly fallen asleep from boredom reading *Timothy Turtle* to Tommy. She laid out their clothes for church and settled in the gazebo with a pot of tea, to wait for Brendan to come home.

It was a cool moonless night, with a slight breeze. Night creatures, feeling bold and safe, under the cover of darkness, began to entertain her with their usual symphony. Frogs croaked their mating calls. As if on cue, the crickets chirped their own musical Morse code. Occasionally, the reed section would join in with an owl's hoot or a loon's call. And all the while, the lake kept beat with its constant, rolling rhythm. Fireflies, with their fluorescent green winking and blinking, were like tiny fairies, dancing to the serenade among the trees and shrubbery. That night, the scents of jasmine, viburnum, cedar and balsam were heavy in the air.

Shortly before eleven, a car pulled up, its lights illuminating the yard through the trees. There was a quick beep, followed by the slamming of a car door.

Seeing the house was dark, Brendan headed out to the gazebo, knowing exactly where to find his mom. He bounced up the steps and plopped down next Katie on the wicker settee. "Mom, I had the best day!" He was nearly breathless.

"Well, if you can catch your breath, tell me all about it. Don't leave out one detail."

Brendan broke into an animated account. "The seats were great, two rows up, down the third base line, right in back of the Sox dugout. I got to see Piersall, Goodman and Kell, even Ted Williams. Parnell pitched for the Sox and Garver for the Tigers. Got to see Boone and Kuenn from Detroit. They're swell players, too. Breeze's dad bought the hot dogs, but I bought the sodas."

Non-stop he continued, his excitement never wavering as the diatribe continued. Katie didn't count them, but it seemed that every sentence contained at least three positive adjectives.

"After the game, we went to a real restaurant, called White Castle. We had hamburgs and fries and chocolate shakes. Breeze's dad paid for everything, but I did offer, Mom. The whole day was super swell. Puke only got sick once in the car. We had to stop and pull over so he could catch a good barf."

Katie laughed. *So that's where the nickname came from.* "You could have left out that detail. So, sounds like you had a pretty big day. Did you remember your manners and thank Mr. Brisbois?"

"Yeah, Mom," he said rolling his eyes. "I remembered my manners and I thanked him, like about a thousand times."

"Did you get a souvenir?"

"Oh, yeah, almost forgot. I got Tommy a Sox baseball cap and the twins each a souvenir button."

"Bren that was an unselfish and generous thing to do. You know, they were all pretty depressed that you got to go and they didn't. They'll be thrilled. But, didn't you get anything for yourself?" she asked.

"Yeah, I got a game program and a collection of pictures of all the Sox. It even has their records and stats. I'm gonna hang them on the wall in my room."

The excited dialogue between mother and son continued. For Katie it was wonderful. It felt as if she finally had her smiling, happy contented Brendan back. How she missed the times when he was younger, when he would situate himself on her lap and jabber on and on about all things significant in his tiny, little world. She realized that time, life and change keep moving on and with them, they carry along small boys and turns them into men. No amount of determination or wishes of a mother's heart could freeze time.

Suddenly, that provocative truth struck her with the reality that, if given the chance, she would never choose to hold them back. That wasn't a mother's purpose. Her role was to guide … help … to facilitate that journey. To nurture was not to grasp and stifle but to support and sustain. It was a natural, driving force of nature for everything to strive to thrive and flourish, to reach its potential, to stand on its own, to grow up and out and eventually to grow away. Even little boys.

It had been a long day for Brendan. Soon, his excitement gave way to exhaustion as his words became inflexed with a series of yawns. They exchanged a goodnight hug and kiss and Katie shooed him off to bed. As he jumped off the step of the gazebo, he turned abruptly and said, "Thanks for everything, Mom. It was a swell day."

As he started running across the lawn, Katie called to him, "You forgot."

He hollered back, "Forgot what?"

"You didn't tell me who won the game."

"The Tigers."

Katie voiced her disappointment, "I'm sorry, Bren."

"Don't be, Mom. I'm not."

☙ ❧

Independence Day, as if it anticipated the significance of the holiday, dawned bright, sunny and warm. The sky was a clear, sapphire blue and cloudless. Matt picked the boys up early in the morning and drove them to the marina to board his boat. Katie took advantage of the quiet of an empty house to prepare for the picnic.

Besides inviting Matt, Lottie and Abraham, she also asked the Musketeers and Douglas to join them later for the afternoon picnic and celebration. Since Katie wasn't serving Airedale or Angora for dinner, the twins invited C.J. As recompense for the Tiger game, she had also asked the Brisbois. But, as they had already made previous plans, they declined but made her promise to give them a rain check.

Cold fried chicken and potato salad would be the main course. Since the day was warm, she prepared a fruit salad, replete with fresh strawberries. For dessert, Katie had baked two cherry and two apple pies and made orange Jell-O for C.J. Parker rolls, fresh baked that morning, were cooling in the kitchen that still held the delicious aroma of yeast and rising dough. The sweet corn was shucked and ready to boil. A tart batch of fresh squeezed lemonade and iced tea would serve as the refreshments.

Abraham and Brendan had constructed a picnic table of four, twelve foot long wood planks, commandeered from the garage, supported by three strategically placed saw horses. Katie had covered them with the only thing she could find big enough. She had perused the contents of the linen closet and took two, snowy white sheets that would serve as a tablecloth. To add some color, she picked two big bouquets of hydrangeas and ferns, set them in vases and placed them on either ends of the table. Miniature paper flags from the Five and Dime had been tucked in amongst the cuttings. In honor of the occasion, napkins of patriotic bright red and royal blue were at each place setting. Every chair from the kitchen and dining room had been brought outside and spaced around the makeshift table. As Katie stepped back to admire the effect, she was satisfied that everything was ready and waiting.

&#x03cg; ʀ

Abraham, Lottie and Katie were relaxing in the gazebo, enjoying the afternoon. Throughout the day, Katie noticed something unusual about Abraham and Lottie. There were four unoccupied chairs to choose from and Lottie had sashayed over to the settee and settled next to him. As intriguing as Lottie's seat selection was, even more interesting was Abraham's reaction. Katie would have expected him to bolt like a frightened fawn. Instead, he remained composed. It also appeared to Katie that more than a physical hurdle had been crossed.

The unusual mood between the two of them was more evident in Abraham than Lottie. Normally, he would revert further into his shell when Lottie was around. But, that afternoon he seemed less disturbed by her presence. Though certainly not a warm exchange, their conversation didn't exclude one another. Rather than Lottie thrusting and lunging and Abraham parrying and retreating, they actually engaged one another in conversation. It was far cry from romance, but Katie could always hope.

By mid-afternoon, four excited, exhilarated, flushed and wind-blown boys came flying across the yard. Following was a haggard, frazzled, much the worse for the wear Matt, clumsily wrestling with a heavy, galvanized metal cooler.

Katie couldn't resist. "Are you a Greek bearing gifts?"

Matt dropped the cooler with a thud and barked back, "I am most certainly not a Greek. Right now I feel more like a Montana cowboy that has been thrown consecutively from four bucking broncos. The cooler is filled with enough orange soda and grape Ne-Hi to drown your tribe of ruffians. Lord knows I wasn't successful drowning them in the lake.

"Those boys have more energy than a power plant. It was like trying to keep a swarm of bees inside a canning jar, without the lid. I should get down on my knees and thank the Lord that I'm still on my feet. But I'm afraid if I kneel down, I won't have the energy to ever get up, again."

Abraham and Lottie sat back quietly, thoroughly entertained by their verbal sparring.

Katie pushed Matt further. "Captain Bly sailed for many years on the high seas, taking much greater risks, facing countless dangers and confronting greater challenges than four little boys. Are you conceding that he was a far superior sailor?"

"Captain Bly was a neophyte compared to me. After today, I could sail rings around him. And may I remind you that his long, illustrious nautical career ended with a mere mutiny, while I had to deal with your pack of pirates. Most of the time I didn't know who was the captain and who was the crew. Brendan was the only one who showed me any mercy. If this is going to become an annual event, I am convinced I need to buy a bigger boat." He slumped down and sat on the edge of the cooler.

Katie mocked him. "I can see that whining and complaining has certainly sapped the strength from you. While you were calmly enjoying a leisurely sail, without a care in the world, I've been slaving over a hot stove. Prepare to be resuscitated with a wonderful meal complete with the recuperative powers of ice cold, fresh lemonade."

"My dear Katie, what I need to drink right now, I know for a fact can't be squeezed from any lemon. As for the meal, you had better be one heck of a cook. I can't be bribed that easily. The way I feel right now, there may not be anyone, anywhere, in anytime past, present or to come, who could ever be that good a cook."

The feast was over. Platters, plates and bowls were empty and tummies full. The only food left, virtually untouched, was Lottie's pan of homemade corn bread.

Experience had taught them to tread carefully when facing anything home-made from Lottie's kitchen. Even Stump the human eating machine, passed on the cornbread. Matt, who clearly should have known better, took a healthy bite. Everyone watched with anticipation as he played the guinea pig. The look on his face validated what they all expected. It was inedible. It tasted like some-one had injected a Titan's dose of lard into a pile of sand.

The boys couldn't hold out any longer. They all burst into a fit of laughter.

Matt looked sheepishly around the table. Finally, he managed to force the greasy, grainy concoction down his throat. After washing away any lingering taste or residual grains of grit with a big swig of lemonade, he eventually recovered enough to utter a sentence.

"If the way to a man's heart is through his stomach, how did you ever manage four husbands, Lottie?"

"Fixin' vittles was not ma forte. Tha men I married were much more interested in what talents I had in tha bedroom than tha kitchen," Lottie cooed back.

The boys rollicked, romped, held wheelbarrow and three-legged races and swam away the rest of the afternoon. The adults had retired to the lawn chairs and lazily digested the meal.

Matt complimented Lottie. "Miss Lottie, you look captivating and bewitching, as usual. Interesting new hair color you've got there. Exactly what color do you call it?" Matt thought she changed hair color more than most people changed the oil in their cars.

Adjusting the blueberry scarf she had tied around a curly ponytail, she said, "Eleanor at tha 'Color, Cut, an' Curl' calls it scandalous scarlet. She says it sets off ma deep brown eyes. I thought it went nicely with ma Fourth of July frock. Don't y'all think I look kinda patriotic? Like tha good ol' Stars an' Stripes."

It was an apt statement. She had on a skirt with red and white stripes, like a circus tent, and a royal blue halter-top encrusted with glittery silver stars. Earrings festooned with red, white and blue rhinestones, arranged in the shape of the flag, sparkled from her earlobes. They matched the design on her sandals.

"I have always taken great pleasure in anticipating what interesting fashion trend you will be sporting. And I must say, you have never disappointed me," Matt said.

"A Southern woman is nothin' if she don't know how to keep up with tha current style a la mode. Ma sense a style is ma trademark." She batted her heavily mascaraed eyes coquettishly. "An' since we're discussin' trademarks, how's Eden Croft's mos' eligible bachelor? Tell us Matt, how is yawr love life? Got anyone special danglin' on tha line? Somebody I might know?"

She avoided looking at Katie, who was sporting her own trademark, one raised, warning eyebrow. As far as Katie was concerned, Lottie was treading on thin ice, like waving a red flag in front of an angry bull. Thankfully, the innuendo went right over Matt's head.

"Recently, I've managed to escape the clutches of one or two beauties. Haven't met the woman yet who has grown a mast and prow that can cut through water like a hot knife through butter. The only female I'm interested in has a mainsail and a jib and can tack on a dime."

"If that don't sound like a manure salesman with a mouthful a samples. I've never known ya not ta be dippin' yawr oars in an' outta tha water on a regular basis. Maybe ya been fishin' in tha wrong pond, lately."

Katie decided to shift the subject before things went any farther. "Abraham, tell us about the new landscaping project you've been working on for the college. You told me you had almost completed all the preliminary plans for the changes."

As the sun set, Abraham and Matt lit a campfire down by the lake. The boys joined them while Katie and Lottie did the last of the kitchen clean up.

Katie gloated, "Well, I guess that particular can of worms you tried to open was a failure. You're insinuation was far too subtle. It was completely lost on Matt."

"Jus' 'cuz he's playin' coy, don't mean he kin fool me, Sug. He kin talk nineteen ta tha dozen, if he wants. An' I kin see right through him. That man is bass ackwards crazy over y'all. I seen that look in his eyes. Y'all ain't ever gonna convince me otherwise."

"You've been reading too many of your romance novels. Matt is no more interested in me than I am in him."

"Interestin' choice a words. That's ma point exactly. Y'all kin deny it all ya want, but mark ma words, there's a powerful lot a sparks flyin' between ya two."

"I'm not wasting another moments breath on this ridiculous fantasy of yours. There never has been, isn't now and never will be anything between Matt and me but friendship."

"Hey, Sug, whatever blows up yawr dress."

A huge boom followed by a rapid succession of sharp bangs startled both of them. Katie, shocked by the barrage, jumped a foot into the air and nearly dropped the dishes she was putting away. "Saints alive! What in Heaven's name was that?"

Just then there was a second bang, immediately followed by a long barrage of sharp pops exploding. The distinct odor of sulfur and gunpowder drifted through the kitchen window.

"Sounds ta me like Matt is providin' some fireworks a his own. With er without ya, Sug."

Katie raced out the back door. "Doesn't he know how dangerous those things can be? I'll give him a healthy sample of my own fireworks."

Lottie ran out after her. "This is one Fourth a July display I'm not 'bout ta miss."

Katie's temper didn't flare often, but when it did it could flare with a vengeance. Especially when something threatened the safety of her children. Like a mother bear when her cubs are in danger, Katie, all one hundred pounds of her, posed a formidable offense. She quickly scanned her memory to see if gunpowder was on the list of C.J.'s allergies.

She spared no words scolding Matt. What was wrong with him? Didn't he know better? Didn't he know the boys were too young to be around explosives? Not to mention the noise that would certainly disturb anyone within five miles. She expected foolish behavior from kids, but Matt was supposed to be an adult. He was as irresponsible as any of the boys. She shuddered to think what thoughtless danger he had put them in on his sailboat. She considered herself lucky that they all hadn't drowned.

Matt tried to defend himself against the bombardment. They were only a few firecrackers and bottle rockets, just some innocent cherry bombs. Well, maybe an M-80 or two. Besides, it wasn't as if he wasn't supervising. He didn't let the little guys anywhere near, and certainly didn't let any of them light the things. After all, everybody did it. It was the Fourth of July for Christ's sake.

But, it was no use. Katie put a quick end to those shenanigans. She had plenty of sparklers to go around. The older boys groaned and pleaded, but Katie stood her ground. "What if your folks found out about this? No one is going to loose a finger or an eye while I'm on duty. The sparklers will just have to do."

The fireworks over the lake started promptly at dark. A chorus of "oohs" and "aahs" followed each illumination. They lasted longer and were much more dramatic than Katie had expected. In Boston, the celebration would go on for more than two hours. She had assumed that Eden Croft, being such a small town, couldn't come close to that. But, the display continued for well over an hour, ending in a finale that was just as spectacular as the one's of her past. Seeing the explosions over the lake only added to the beauty as the rainbow of colors danced and reflected across the surface of the water, like a bridal train of sparkling gemstones.

It had been a long day for everyone. Lottie trotted off home. Abraham, Matt and the Musketeers put out the campfire. Abraham thanked Katie for the wonderful day and bid his goodnight. Matt offered to take C.J., Douglas and the Musketeers. It only made sense, since he had to drive himself home, anyway. He assured Katie it was no problem, even if she had thrown a damper on his pyrotechnics.

Katie tucked three exhausted sleepyheads into bed. Casey and Colin were so tired they fell immediately to sleep the moment their heads hit their pillows. She sat next to Tommy on the edge of his bed as he said his bedtime prayer. He told Katie that this was the bestest day ever.

"Did you wear the life vests like I told you?"

"Mr. Mulholland made us wear 'em tha whole time."

Thank God for that, Katie thought

"I really like Mr. Mulholland. He's funny. He even let us tinkle over the side of the boat. He told us a lot 'bout the sailboat, but I don't remember most of it. He told us stories about the Indians who lived here, way before the white man came. He told us about the Canada goose. He says that they get married forever. They raise their babies just like people do. But, if one of them dies or gets killed, the other one never gets married, again. It goes through the rest of its life all alone."

Katie smiled softly, "And what else does Mr. Mulholland say?"

Tommy giggled. "That you want to shoo them off if they land in your yard, 'cuz they go Number Two all over it."

Katie brushed a sun-blushed cheek with her lip and lifted the Red Sox cap from his head and set it on the bedpost. He had worn it twenty-four seven since Brendan had given it to him. After whispering a goodnight, she turned off the light and padded off to Brendan's room. He was already in bed. Pinned on the walls, above his head, were the recently purchased pictures of the Red Sox, fanned out, forming a half circle around his favorite legend, Ted Williams. In Brendan's opinion, he was the greatest baseball player that ever was.

"How did you like sailing, today? Mr. Mulholland said you were a natural."

"It was swell, Mom. He taught me all kinds of things about sailing and the right names for the different stuff on the boat. Says that sometime he'll take just me, 'cause the rug rats kept getting in the way. Says it'll be cold day in hell before he takes them sailing, again. He says he'll even teach me how to steer the boat, all on my own."

"Sounds to me like you've been bit by the sailing bug."

"Mom, it was so neat. When do you think Mr. Mulholland will ask me to go again?"

Katie laughed. "Don't expect an invitation tomorrow, Bren."

Bren insisted, "But he promised he'd take me."

"I'm sure he did. But, sometimes people make promises that they can't keep right away. Just don't get your hopes up too high. I don't want you to be disappointed. Mr. Mulholland has legal clients and he does have a life of his own, you know. All I'm saying is be patient."

"I can't wait until I get a boat of my own."

"Whoa. Slow down a bit, Captain. That possibility is a long way off. The money tree in our front yard hasn't grown that large. A sailboat is not going to magically fall from the sky. I think you had better settle for being first mate for a while."

Bren folded his arms under his head and looked up at the ceiling. "A guy can always dream, can't he, Mom?"

As she turned out the light, Katie replied, "You're right, Bren. A guy can always dream."

chapter fourteen

The dog days of summer had arrived.

August, with its simmering, sizzling temperatures, was nearly half over. The katydids were busy with their humming, droning, lonesome songs, a sure sign of rising mercury, record-breaking humidity and stagnant air. It was as if all the oxygen had been sucked out of the air. In the oppressing heat, even the birds and squirrels seemed to know it was too hot. They were unusually quiet.

Dragonflies, nature's tiny helicopters, sailed just above the surface of the lake. Looking out over the lake, there was a gauzy haze, as if one could actually visualize the heavy, steamy, still air. An occasional gull would hover, sloop low, then settle on the water, as if it, too, was seeking the cooler temperatures of the water.

Desperate for the hint of a cooling breeze, Katie sat on the dock, bare feet dangling in the water. She had on khaki walking shorts and a white, sleeveless, cotton blouse. Trying to stay cool, she had tied her hair up in a kerchief, off her neck. A heavily southern-accented curse drew her attention toward the yard.

"What tha hell is this? Shit! Sug, what tha hell? Some dawg left a pile a poop on yawr lawn, an' I jus' stepped in it. Got dawg shit on ma favorite pair a sandals."

Lottie hopped across the dock, teetering on one wooden sandal like a one-legged pirate. She dangled the other from her finger like it carried the bubonic plague. Her Shalimar arrived ten seconds before she did.

She was dressed in a Hawaiian print halter top with bare midriff that strained against her generous bosoms. Short shorts, almost immodestly short, showed a great deal of bare leg. A huge straw hat, as big around as a car tire bounced on her head. Black, rhinestone studded sunglasses, shaped like a harlequin mask, perched on her nose. In spite of the heat, she wore a pink beaded necklace, two inch round plastic daisy earrings and plastic bracelets, one every color of the rainbow. She knelt down next to Katie, took the soiled sandal and leaned over. Agitating and rinsing it in the water, she managed to get most of the dog doo off.

"Welcome to the O'Neill menagerie. What you have just stumbled into is some of the droppings from our latest acquisition. As if I don't have enough mouths to feed and bodies to clean up after. Tommy is convinced we now need a puppy to make more messes. He found a stray last week, no collar or identification tags, and started feeding it. We ran an advertisement in the paper but nobody claimed him. Well, one thing led to another, and we are now the proud owners of a not completely house-trained puppy named Chance, of questionable lineage and legitimacy, who is treading on thin ice with me.

"I told Tommy the dog gets three chances, incidentally, the name by which he is now known. After that, any more accidents in the house and he is headed for the pound. That warning was issued at least ten accidents ago. Once I saw him with Tommy and the other boys, I knew he was here to stay."

As she inspected her soaked sandal for residual poop, Lottie drawled, "Oh, heck, Sug, a dawg ain't nothin' ta take care of. Ya jus' feed 'em, water 'em, an' shoo 'em outside when they get under foot. Why, every boy needs a dawg ta grow up with. 'Course, ya gotta train them boys ta clean up after it."

"Where have you been the past few weeks?" Katie asked.

"Went ta Chicago. Had maself a real shoppin' spree in tha big city."

"You left without saying good-bye," Katie scolded her. "We didn't know if you had been kidnapped or were lying dead in some ditch."

"Like I told ya before, I ain't never liked good-byes."

Katie patted the dock, "Pull up a plank and sit down." Katie looked her up and down. "Tell me about your big shopping trip? Is that ensemble a recent purchase?"

Lottie sat down and carelessly flipped her hand, dismissing the question. "Naw, this ol' thing. It's older'n ma grandma's girdle. Got back late last night."

"Do anything interesting in the big city?"

"Mos'ly I jus' tried ta make as big a dent in ma widow's endowment as a person kin do in a month, I tell you what! As far as ma other activities go, Sug, I never kiss an' tell."

She reached into her enormous straw bag and pulled out a lace-perfumed hankie. She dabbed at her neck and cleavage. "Luv a duck, if it ain't hotter 'n hell's hinges out here."

Wrinkling her nose at Katie, she questioned, sharply, "Y'all losin' weight? Yawr so thin, ya look ta me like you'd have ta jump up an' down in tha rain ta get wet. Y'all oughta start takin' better care a yawrself an' ya better have some lotion on, Sug. Though y'all could use a bit more color in those cheeks, this here sun ain't none too good fawr a lady's delicate skin. As my Grandma Lizzie Pope used ta say, 'If the Lord would'a wanted ya brown, He'd a started ya out that way.'"

"I've only been out here a little while. I was hoping to catch a breeze."

Brendan was on the far edge of the property raking weeds that had washed up on the beach. Lottie waved and hollered to him. He looked up, forlorn and with a limp unenthusiastic wave, signaled back.

"What bee buzzed up his butt?" Lottie asked, fanning herself with her hanky. "Some girl been wavin' her undies in front a his face?"

"For Heaven's sake, Lottie. I swear, sometimes you talk like you were raised in a locker room." Katie shook her head. "No. It's not a girl. You're never going to believe this one."

"Nothin' that happens over here is ever beyond believin.'"

"After Matt took him sailing, the first thing Bren started talking about was getting a boat of his own. No sooner were the words out of his mouth and I had to tell him that a boat wasn't going to miraculously fall from the sky. No sooner were those words out of my mouth and Abraham introduces Bren to an ancient day- sailer that was stored overhead in his garage. Who says miracles don't fall from heaven?

"Ever since he made the discovery, he's been a boy possessed and won't rest until he gets it on the water. It's been stored for God knows how long. Matt checked it out and it needs a lot of work before it comes close to being seawor-thy. It's going to need a new sail and rigging that I'm sure will cost an arm and a leg. And I don't know how, if ever, I'll ever be able to afford them. Matt told him before he even thinks about taking it out alone that he needs to learn a lot about sailing. It's not like a dinghy, where you just hop in and start rowing."

Katie paused a moment before continuing.

"Brendan is driving Abraham and Matt crazy to work with him every spare minute. Abraham's been tied up with his college landscaping project and Matt has his law practice and a life of his own. Their time is so limited and I'd hoped Bren would lose interest but everyday he seems more determined than ever. He's been in a mood for a week because neither one of them has had the time to help him.

"I told him to rake the beach and that I don't want to see him until he can see the rose in the vase instead of the dust on the table. So what you see before you now, is a long-suffering, frustrated lost soul. Honestly, Lottie, sometimes I'm at a complete loss how to handle him. It's as if I can't do anything right where he's concerned. I feel like everything I do is the wrong thing." She stared at Brendan, discouraged.

"Don't be beatin' yawrself up, too much, Sug. Y'all are a good mama. Whatever yawr doin' with those younguns, ya oughta bottle it an' sell it."

Katie wished she could believe her. "I'm not so sure about that. Danny had had so little time to teach him the lessons of growing up and becoming a man. Now Brendan has to learn them on his own. I can cook and clean, do laundry, shop, mend torn knees and darn holes in socks. But a boy needs a father. Someone they can look up to, admire, emulate. Someone they can share guy stuff with. I can't be or do any of those things."

"Yawr overlookin' tha obvious, Sug."

"Don't get me wrong, Abraham's great with him, tolerant and patient. And Brendan is very fond of him, too. They get along well. But it's not the same thing."

With a twinkle in her eye and mischief in her voice, she said, "Maybe it ain't Abraham I'm referrin' ta."

Katie was determined to steer them away from the direction they were headed. "Lottie, I'm warning you. Don't even think about going down that path with me, again. That book is closed."

"Maybe y'all oughtta think 'bout openin' up that book."

"Lottie, for the last time, please don't try to play matchmaker where Matt and I are concerned. For Heaven's sake, I'm still in love with Danny. I don't know if I'll ever get over losing him."

"I ain't sayin' yawr not er ya shouldn't. One ain't got nothin' ta do with tha other, Sug. Ya think jus' 'cuz Danny's gone yawr not entitled ta ever have those feelins again. Why, I loved each one a ma husbands, each one in a different way, but I loved 'em jus' tha same."

Katie thought about the story Matt had told Tommy. The story about the Canada goose. "I'm not you, Lottie."

For the first time, Katie saw a look of hurt settle on Lottie's face.

"Lottie, I'm sorry. I didn't mean that to sound critical or condescending. We're not the same in that respect. There's nothing wrong with you. If anyone's flawed, it's me. I'm not sure that I'm capable of loving more than one man that much. Sometimes, when I think that maybe I'm ready to put the past behind me, a voice starts nagging in the back of my mind … that in some way, I'm being disloyal … unfaithful. That it would somehow diminish or lessen what I felt for Danny."

"It ain't got nothin' ta do with loyalty er faithfulness. If tha situation was reversed, wouldn't ya want Danny ta have whatever kind of happiness he could find? Don't ya think that he'd want tha same fawr you? Ya got a long life ahead of ya. I find it mighty hard ta believe that he'd want ya ta go through it alone."

Everything Lottie said made complete sense. Katie had no trouble telling it to her mind. It was her heart that wasn't listening.

"Even if what you say were true, Lottie, I'm not about to get involved with a man with an ulterior motive, a convenient way to provide a father for the boys. Besides, Matt, or anyone else, for that matter, isn't their father. It wouldn't be the same thing."

Lottie patted her on the leg, reassuringly. "'Course it ain't, Sug. That ain't never gonna be. Sometimes a bodies got ta move on, settle on tha next best thing. As fawr Brendan, with er without Matt, er anyone else, he'll find his way. He's smack dab in tha middle of a tough age."

"That's a gross understatement. I wish I could crawl inside his head to see what's going on in there."

Lottie harrumphed. "Lookin' inta his head ain't gonna tell ya nothin.' What's goin' on inside a him ain't got nothin' ta do with his brain. He's got an ol' fashun case of a hopper full a hormones. Ain't nobody, momma er daddy, kin help him through that, Sug. They hafta work that out fawr themselves. God gives every bird its food, but He don't drop it inta tha nest."

Lottie never ceased to amaze her. "Tell me, Lottie. You've never had any children. How did you get to be so wise when it comes to children?"

"Y'all don't hafta get burnt ta know a fire's hot an' y'all don't hafta be a momma er daddy ta know what it takes ta grow up. Ya jus' gotta have lived a little, an' believe me, Sug, I've done my lion's share a that."

"You know, I've never heard the whole sordid story. You've only tempted me with bits and pieces. Tell me about your childhood, your growing up. How Lottie Devereaux found her way from a Mississippi bijou, to Eden Croft, Michigan. That's about as big a jump as anyone can make."

Lottie grinned, dropped her chin and peered over the top of her sunglasses. "Now that's a story that requires sittin' in tha shade an' sippin' somethin' a whole lot stronger than iced tea, Sug."

Lottie Devereaux was born Coral Mae Tarpy to Wenonah Tarpy (who preferred the shortened version-Nona said it was less bijou, classier and suited her better), in a tiny cabin in a town that was no more than a dusty intersection where two country roads crossed. It was a backwoods community where folks used to say you could straddle the state line, one foot in Mississippi, the other in Louisiana. The legitimacy of her birth was in question, but her mama always claimed that she had married her daddy before Coral Mae was born, though he didn't stick around longer than a month afterward.

Nona was not a woman of strong moral fiber. Whoever Coral Mae's daddy was, he was followed by a long and steady procession of *uncles*. For *kin*, they sure didn't stick around long. Two times after Coral Mae was born, Nona found herself in the family way. And each time, she paid a visit and twenty-five dollars to a local *midwife* to fix the problem. Swamp Sadie must have botched the job the second time because Nona never got pregnant again.

Coral Mae grew up dirt poor, but so did pretty much everyone else on the bijou. It was the depression and money was scarce as snow in Shoal. They were so poor that they had to eat cereal with a fork, so the others could share the milk. Nona had a job of sorts. Off and on. Mostly off. She waited tables down at Big Tiny's Shrimp Shack. Granddaddy and Grandma Pope wanted Coral Mae to come live with them, but Nona wouldn't hear of it.

By the time Cora Mae had reached five, her mama didn't cotton to being called mama, anymore. First off, it only served as an unwelcome, contrary reminder that she was old enough to have a child that age. And second off, unlike every other mortal, she had convinced herself that she was never going to get a day older than twenty-five.

Anyway, about the time Coral Mae turned eleven, her *Aunt Flow* came to visit for the first time. The rest of puberty followed quickly and soon Coral Mae developed the buxom curves of a woman. It also wasn't long and Nona started to notice that the uncles started to notice Coral Mae. The competition didn't make her none too happy. Often enough, in a jealous rage, Nona would accuse Coral Mae of flirting and baiting them, sashaying her behind right in front of their noses. For the longest time, Coral Mae had no idea what Nona was talking about. But, just before her fourteenth birthday, she figured out why Nona was so jealous.

Uncle Euchas, who had been living with them for a couple of months, started sniffing around Coral Mae like cat after nip. At first, behind his back, then right to his face.

Coral Mae called him Uncle Useless, for the obvious reasons. One day, when Nona was gone, he cornered her in the bedroom. He stunk of sweat and cheap booze. He tongue stabbed her, pawed her bosoms and groped her privates. It wasn't that she minded losing her virginity, but when the time came, it was damn well going to be her idea. She was the one who was going to say when and with whom and she sure as heck minded losing it to that pig.

She fought like a cornered hellcat, but Useless was too big and nearly had his way with her. Nona came home just in time. After a screeching tirade that lasted for a whole day, Nona laid most of the blame on Coral Mae for tempting Euchas. What was the poor man expected to do? Finally, Coral Mae was sent packing to live with her Granddaddy and Grandma. For once in her miserable life, Nona did the right thing, even if it was for all the wrong reasons.

It was the first time in her young life, that Coral Mae was truly happy. Oh, they were still dirt poor, but respectable poor. There was a big difference in being poor and being poor white trash. If they didn't grow it, catch it or kill it, they didn't eat. Grandma Pope could stretch a meal and a penny further than anybody. She lived by the philosophy that you use it up, wear it out or go without.

The reason she never learned much about cooking wasn't because her grandma didn't try. Grandma Pope was known to be the best cook around. It was because Coral Mae much preferred being outside with her Granddaddy.

She loved everything about him. The way he walked, whittled and whistled. The way his whiskers would tickle her face when she hugged him. The way he told stories, rocked on the porch, fished, hunted, tracked and trapped, even the way he scratched his butt and spit his chew. Wherever Granddaddy Pope was, that's where Coral Mae wanted to be.

Unfortunately, real life rarely imitates fairytales and Coral Mae was not destined to live happily ever after. In a short four years, she buried both her Granddaddy and Grandma. But they would always be the happiest four years of her life.

The first thing she decided was that Coral Mae Skrippy had to go.

With Grandma and Granddaddy Pope gone, there was no way in hell's half acre she was moving back in with Nona. She had to find herself a new life and Bufford Bobbitt, affectionately nicknamed Billy Bob, was as a good a place to start as any.

She had never had any trouble attracting men. She was pretty as a picture and built like a brick outhouse. Billy Bob had always had a heck of a crush on her and was as good looking as a movie star. But, she was no way going to repeat Nona's mistakes. Billy Bob could have her, but not for temporary and not for free. They were going to do it legal and proper like, with a wedding ring and license. So, she figured as long as she was getting hitched and changing her last name she was going to go for broke.

She always liked the name Loretta. One of the fancy ladies at Miss Deautrieve's establishment was called that and she liked the name right off. So, from her wedding day on she was known as Loretta.

Billy Bob and Loretta Bobbitt set up housekeeping. She never exactly knew for sure where Billy Bob got his money, but he always seemed to have more of it then most. If it was something illegal, she really didn't want to know and told herself she really didn't care.

Two years later, the honeymoon was over. Billie Bob had promised her that they would always have enough money, as the saying goes "the Lord willing and the creek don't rise." Well, the Lord apparently wasn't willing and the creek surely did rise. The easy stream of money suddenly jumped the levee and found a different way to flow. Billie Bob was gone for days at a time and when he did come home, he was nervous as a nun in a whorehouse. As it turned out, outside the bedroom, Billie Bob was as useless as an ashtray on a motorcycle. Soon enough, time proved he had more looks than sense. Three months before their third wedding anniversary, Billie Bob was found face down in a cypress swamp, knifed in the back.

So, Loretta was a widow, penniless and homeless. She didn't have a pot to pee in or a window to throw it out. Looking on the good side, though, she was free, white and twenty-one. Packing up all her belongings in two suitcases, she hitched a ride to New Orleans and never looked back. And never saw Nona Skrippy, again.

Billie Bob had left her high and dry but he had taught her two valuable lessons. The first lesson he taught her in the bedroom. The second lesson that it was as easy to fall for a rich man as a poor man. Within a year Loretta would apply both those lessons.

She married Donald (Dooley) McSweyn, a wild, hard drinking, hard living Irishman, who just happened to be filthy rich and also just happened to be twice her age. This began what Lottie would call her McSweyn years. Dooley had a brother, younger by two years, John (Buck) McSweyn, who was just as wild and just as rich. Neither brother had ever married and they had been as close as pages in a book their whole lives. So, when Lottie married Dooley, she ended up getting two McSweyn's for the price of one.

Though they lived hard and fast, the McSweyn brothers were still gentlemen when it came to a lady. Never, at any time did Buck ever step out of line with Lottie. The three of them would party all night. Sleep all day. They traveled together, gambling, boozing and raised hell from one end of the country to another. Dooley lavished her with jewels, furs and closets full of clothes. What he didn't buy for her, Buck did. The three were inseparable. So, when Dooley's heart gave out and he dropped over dead in a speakeasy, it was natural for Buck to step in and fill his shoes. Six months after they buried Dooley, Lottie and Buck got married.

Buck and Lottie had a good marriage, but things were never quite the same after Dooley died. They buried a lot of their zest and gusto with Dooley. They both missed him terribly and longed for old times. Five years later, Buck joined his brother in side-by-side graves. Some said it was his lifestyle that killed Buck, just like his brother. But Lottie knew better. Buck had simply died from a broken heart.

After years of living high off the hog, poor was something Loretta never intended to be again and the McSweyn family money she inherited would keep her for life. Without money worries, she didn't need to rush into anything and took her time playing the field. Just for kicks, Lottie tried going it single for a time. But, it was no good. It wasn't only the sex, though that was a big part of it. By nature, Lottie needed to have a man. She needed the companionship, the attention, the coddling. She needed to be pampered by a man. Some people just aren't meant to be alone. Lottie was one of them.

It was a few months before the war broke out. Lottie was catching a train from New York back to New Orleans. She had just spent five days and nearly five thousand dollars on some of the latest fashions. Laden with an over night bag, pocket book and make-up case, she was wiggling her way down the narrow aisle, heading to the sleeper car. The train jerked and rocked suddenly. Lottie lost her balance and fell right into the lap of Regis LaFontaine Devereaux. It was a much steeper fall for Regis. He fell immediately, head-over-heals in love with Lottie. After a whirlwind courtship of three weeks the two of them married. The other half of the pattern also continued. Rollie had turned twenty-six-years-old the year Lottie was born.

Lottie finished off a pitcher of very dry martinis, shaken not stirred and polished off an entire jar of onion-stuffed green olives. Katie never had a drink stronger than wine and stuck to her iced tea.

"So Sug, as tha sayin' goes, tha rest is history. After Rollie an' me got hitched, we spent most a tha year travelin' 'bout er at his family plantashun house outside Nawlans. Tha summers, though, those were sacred ta Rollie. His mamma was a Northerner an' ta escape tha hot Lewzianna summers she always took tha train an' her baby boy north ta spend tha summer in Eden Croft. So, jus' as he did when he was growin' up, he brought me here our first summer an' I been comin' back ever since. When he died a few years back, comin' back here jus' seemed like tha natural thing ta do. Like a homin' pigeon, I reckon.

"Now, I spend most a ma time here. Ever so often, I do get tha bug ta fly away, so that's jus' what I do. Whichever way tha wind blows, that's tha way I go. Sometimes I jus' pack up ma bags, hop a train or gas up ma Caddy an' head off, not sure where I might end up."

Katie was fascinated. How different their two backgrounds were. Katie had never before considered herself especially fortunate or that she had led a charmed life. She too, been raised during some of those lean years when jobs were scarce and money was often tight. But, as humble as her beginnings had been, she had never gone to bed unclothed, unclean, unfed or most importantly, unloved.

Yet, Lottie, who had been taught the lessons of life, harshly, cruelly, and at such a tender age, had been all but robbed of the innocence of childhood, had not a bitter or spiteful bone in her body. Instead, she had grown into a loving and lovable, caring, compassionate and generous woman. On the outside she was wild, loud, gaudy and flashy. But inside, under the layers of cockiness and bawdiness, underneath all the bravado beat a sensitive and discerning heart. Lottie possessed a newly discovered quality that Katie admired, perhaps more than any other.

Lottie Devereaux was a survivor.

chapter fifteen

"I'll pick you up first thing in the morning. Bring along a sweater, it gets cold out on the water late in the day."

Matt had finally managed to maneuver Katie into a day of sailing on the lake. He couldn't believe that he had let most of the summer slip by. But, after the debacle of his first attempt, he had been left shell-shocked and gun-shy.

Born privileged, attending the best schools, high school sports hero, he was the golden-haired boy. Besides his Adonis-like good looks, he was all charm and guile where the ladies were concerned. It was an unusual predicament Matt found himself in. Instead of being the pursued he had become the pursuer. He wasn't sure he liked the role reversal. He ached to see more of Katie, to be around her; thought about her every moment that he wasn't.

Most of the women he had dated shared his outlook of fun with no strings attached. When he did encounter a vulnerable one who wanted and needed more, he walked away before anyone got hurt. He carefully steered clear of commitment and had never met anyone who he had more than a casual interest in. Never had he even come close to uttering those famous three words. Never had he experienced that kind of provocation. Then again, he had never dealt with Katie O'Neill.

The day before their sail, Matt had dedicated most of his time washing, polishing and buffing the boat. He polished the brass until it shined like his grandmother's silver tea set and he could see his reflection in the teakwood. He wanted everything to be absolutely perfect. Leaving nothing to chance, the plan included a wicker basket stocked with wine, fruit, bread and cheese, and chicken salad sandwiches with the crusts cut off. The only detail he had no control over was the weather. He uttered a threat to the gods of the elements that tomorrow had better bring atmospheric conditions of a cloudless sky, warm temperatures and ideal winds. Comfortable that he had anticipated every eventuality, leaving nothing to circumstance, he headed home.

Sleep did not come easily. He tossed and turned like a teenager facing his first high school dance. *This is ridiculous*, he thought, *just close your eyes, count sheep, or goats or whatever.* But the only image his mind could picture were a pair of sparkling, emerald green eyes.

Katie had faced a bedtime battle of her own. Brendan had complained all day that not only was he not invited for the sail, but also that Mr. Mulholland would be spending the day on the lake instead of working with him on his boat. To add salt to the wound, he was stuck baby-sitting all day and probably half the night. The only saving point was that his mom had agreed that he could have his friends over for the afternoon.

He had grumbled and moaned to Katie right up to bedtime. Worn out from defending herself all day, Katie was going over her last instructions with Brendan. "You can have Cheerios and juice for breakfast and peanut butter and jelly sandwiches for lunch. For dinner, there is a chicken casserole in the refrigerator. All you have to do is reheat it in the oven, at three hundred and fifty degrees for forty-five minutes. There were plenty of cookies and Kool-Aid for snacks. Mrs. Stueben is picking the Musketeers up at four."

Brendan rolled over in bed and faced the wall.

"Bren, are you listening to me? This is important stuff."

He grunted, "Yeah, yeah … peanut-butter and jelly, oven three hundred … for an hour …"

"I said three-hundred-and-fifty for forty-five minutes. The instructions are all written down. When you're done, be sure you turn off the oven. Bedtime for the boys is eight o'clock sharp. If you have any problems, call Miss Lottie or Dr. Franke. And it wouldn't kill you to do the dishes and make sure the house is half-way picked up."

She bent over and kissed him. "Please, don't neglect your brothers. Don't let them go in the water past their waists and they can't even go near the water without life jackets on." As she turned off the light, she added, "And please, try not to fight with them. Remember, you're in charge. I'm depending on you."

og ഒ

Matt and Katie must have sailed every one of the ten thousand acres of Eden Lake.

The gods had indeed smiled on Matt. There was a stiff breeze all day that made perfect sailing conditions. Katie was impressed. Matt handled the boat like he had been born to it. Even his eyes attested to the fact that Mother Nature had no other choice but to give him them the same blue-green color of the sea. His golden hair was wind blown, his cheeks flushed, a permanent smile of pleasure and joy on his face. It really was his element. His love for sailing had not been exaggerated. The passion reflected in his aqua eyes.

She was taken on a twenty-five-cent tour of the lake. Matt pointed out various landmarks, structures, homes and cottages that were scattered along the shoreline, like tiny Monopoly houses. So and so lived there, and that used to be the Governor's summer home, that was Christmas Point and over there was the O'Reilly place, draped in mystery and scandal.

On the east end of the lake, was the Mulholland compound. It had become Matt's permanent home. Even at that distance, Katie could appreciate its massive size and the extensive property. It was more of an estate than a single dwelling, with a palatial main house, surrounded by smaller cottages. Even those were much larger than their house in Boston had been. She laughed to herself that as impressive as Aunt Katherine's place was it was only small potatoes compared to the Mulholland's.

Matt explained the terms *snow birds* and *fudgies*. The locals used those vernaculars to describe the summer residents and tourists that had invaded their shores. *Snowbirds* lived in Eden Croft in the summer from Memorial Day to Labor Day and then flew south to Florida for the rest of the year. *Fudgies* referred to the tourists in honor of the tons of fudge they would consume from the fudge shops that dotted northern Michigan resort towns. Most locals never touched the stuff.

Matt introduced her to some of the intricacies of sailing. Katie helped him as he raised and lowered the mainsail and jib, using the appropriate ropes and pulleys. Matt taught her about tacking or coming about. She learned to duck when the boom abruptly swung across the boat, as they came about. Terms like fore and aft, port and starboard, hold, keel and rudder easily rolled off his tongue as he introduced her to the language of sailing.

Katie was a quick learner and Matt was amazed at how much she had absorbed in such a short time. He was equally enthralled by how at ease she seemed to be on the water. Her chestnut curls blew about her face and she seemed totally unconcerned about being mussed or wind blown. She was perched on the deck, sitting back on her arms, shapely legs stretched out and chin raised with her face to the sun and wind. The sight of her took his breath away. He knew every freckle on her nose, and how deep her dimples were when she smiled. He could anticipate the slight upturn of her chin when she laughed. Her eyes mesmerized him as they glittered playfully, her face animated when she spoke. Matt didn't realize it until that very moment, watching her when she was totally relaxed and unaware of his stare, that he was quickly and hopelessly falling in love.

They anchored in Scott's Bay, a calm cove on the north shore of the lake, and took a swim off the stern. Matt watched as she gracefully dove into the water. She hadn't grown a mast, but she could cut through water like a hot knife through butter. She swam effortlessly, and would stop at times to simply float, motionless on the surface.

Famished from the full day of sailing and swimming, Matt set up the basket lunch on the topside of the cabin while Katie toweled off and changed from her wet suit into dry clothes. She emerged from below wearing a navy blue turtleneck sweater and white Capri's. With her still damp hair and sun kissed face, Matt wouldn't take his eyes off her. Afraid that if he did the magical moment would evaporate.

Invigorated by the day of fresh air, the simple meal was wonderful and both Katie and Matt ate heartily. They had settled themselves on the deck to finish off the strawberries and wine. Kate felt the exhilaration of the day and the warmth of the wine deep inside. She wasn't anywhere near tipsy, but heady from the day's activity and the gentle rocking of the boat as the water lapped rhythmically against the hull. She was beginning to feel very relaxed and very mellow.

"Interesting name for a boat, *Scattering*." Katie mused lazily. "It's hard for me to believe that anyone, Irishman or not, born and raised anywhere but Ireland, would have any idea what that means."

Matt adjusted himself, turned toward Katie on one elbow. "Born and raised by died in the wool Irish, none-the-less. When I was a small lad, about seven or eight, my Grandfather Donnelly took me abroad. I spent a whole summer with him on the fair Isle of Eire.

"What I remember most was the Puck Fair in *Killorglin*. Normally, my grandfather was very conventional, very stern and very, very proper. But, for that one week, I saw a side of him that I'd never seen before. He shed his pompous airs like a snakeskin. We celebrated those three days, Gathering Day, Fair Day and Scattering Day, shoulder to shoulder and side by side with the locals. He laughed, and drank, and sang like he'd been doing it all his life. The last day, Scattering interestingly enough named, seemed to go on for days and days, as we partied through more pubs and saloons than I could count. When I think of my grandfather, that is how I want to remember him best, on Scattering Day, a sentimental old Irishman." Matt took on a winsome, far-off look as he retold the story.

"So, that is how the vessel came by its name. Outside of my family, you're probably the only one who understands the significance of the name."

Katie smiled. "Why, Matt, I didn't know you had such a soft and sentimental nature ... though, I always suspected as much. You don't immediately strike a person as being a romantic but out here you look positively dreamy."

"You mean my suave and flippant manner didn't fool you. I try not to let on what a thoughtful, caring and sincere person I am. It would destroy, forever, the image I have carefully and painstakingly tried to create."

She ventured further. "What else don't I know about Matt Mulholland that lurks behind that mirthful mask?"

"Truthfully, my past is surprisingly boring." He cocked his head and looked over at Katie, who gave him a mock disbelieving look. "I know, I know, I give the impression that I have lived an exciting, scandalous and decadent life. That, too, is part of the charade. Are you sure you are quite prepared to have all your illusions about me shattered in one day?"

"I'll risk it."

"I was born Matthew Maclain Mulholland. Don't laugh, but my nickname used to be M&M. Born with a silver spoon in my mouth to Gwenyth Quinn Donnelly and Michael Kiley Mulholland. I am sure my family's wealth was built upon ill-gotten gains and the backs of oppressed tenant farmers. Anyway, my grandparents came here and multiplied their already substantial coffers to the point where they had more money than God.

"In spite of my parents' all-but-arranged marriage, they fell madly in love and had a wonderful life together. That was until it was interrupted by my arrival. I have a sister, Margaret, married and living in Chicago, who has made me an uncle four times and still counting. My baby brother, Ryan, is still in law school at Northwestern. Unlike me, he is responsible, reliable, brilliant and the favored son. We grew up in an area north of Chicago called Lake Forest, but spent our summers here, on Eden Lake.

"Being shamefully spoiled and precocious, I went to prep school in the East, and much to the surprise of my parents, deans and professors, managed to graduate from the University of Michigan. The war gave me a temporary hiatus from law school and I spent the next four years bobbing around the Pacific in a tin can of a destroyer."

"Boston has a huge shipyard and naval base. What was the name of your ship?" Katie's question was filled with interest.

"The U.S.S. Stanton DD416. Commissioned at the Boston Navy Yard on March 16, 1942. I was in and out of Boston for shakedown cruises until May 23rd when we sailed for the Pacific."

Katie's face beamed. "You were only a few miles from where I lived in Boston. I used to take Brendan there for walks so he could see all the ships coming and going. It was an impressive sight."

Matt teased, "So close and we never knew it."

Katie encouraged him to continue.

"The war came and went. Coming home victorious and modestly deco-rated, I finished my education and graduated from Law School. Being the rebel of the family and rarely ever doing what was expected of me, I did not join the well-established and very elite family firm of Mulholland, Mulholland & Donnelly. Instead, I came back here, hung my shingle and have continued in the fine Mulholland tradition of practicing law. Living off my substantial trust fund, I'm still the spoiled rich kid I always was, but to stay respectable, I do represent an occasional client now and then."

He took a brief moment to refill the wine glasses.

"See. Very boring stuff. Hardly the script that would make a lavish Hollywood extravaganza."

So, it wasn't a Dickensian tale. Nor was it on the scale of a Homer epic. But Katie found it engaging. It seemed that things had always come easily for Matt. And he was smug, droll, coy, somewhat arrogant, immodest and insufferably conceited. That was what Katie found so amusing. In spite of himself, you couldn't help but like him. He was like a self-centered, egotistical, spoiled little boy, who thought there was nothing more engaging than his capriciousness. But, he had a way of pulling it off. She could only imagine the trail of broken hearts he had left in his wake, carelessly cast off and wantonly abandoned.

Katie stood and started to clean up the paper plates and napkin and other items that constituted the remains of their meal.

Matt scolded her. "Leave that for me. You just sit back and enjoy the last waning moments of that glorious sunset."

She ignored him. "Force of habit."

Katie noticed that his narrative was very cursory and superficial. As if he purposely avoided anything too personal or intimate. She wondered. "Tell me, though, how did such a charming, handsome, witty, obscenely wealthy person such as yourself manage to avoid the shackles of matrimony. You were blatantly obvious in omitting that from your autobiographical sketch." Katie's dimples deepened as she smiled, mischievously.

"It is reputed to be very poor form to talk to a beautiful woman about the indiscretions and loves of one's past. That would be both discourteous and unwise. It would be foolish and ill-advised of me to disclose my tactics to a possible conquest."

"I promise, I won't be insulted or frightened off. And you and I both know that a widow with four ruffians, as you so insensitively called them, doesn't draw a very likely picture of one of your potential conquests. Seriously, there must have been one or two romances that nearly led you to the altar."

They were facing each other now, dangerously close, in the small cockpit.

"After Sue Ellen McCaffrey broke my heart when I was ten-years-old, I guess it was always a case of the wrong girl at the right time, or the right girl at the wrong time ..." His voice trailed off as his thoughts became lost in her eyes, her delicate features, and her wild chestnut mane. The melons, pinks and blues of the glorious sunset washed her face in pastel hues.

The boat lurched and Katie found herself suddenly leaning into Matt for support. He gently wrapped his arms around her, lowered his head and kissed her.

It was a long, tender, at first undemanding kiss. Then he pressed harder and it deepened from a greater need to caress, to touch, to taste, to devour that beautiful face and full lips. Her lips were yielding and velvety soft. His tongue explored and probed her mouth, eliciting the same response from her. She tasted sweetly of wine and strawberries. Matt felt the rush of adrenaline from his stomach all the way to his toes, his heart throbbed against his chest and his groin ached. He felt his need, hunger, desire build and burn. He could feel his heat melt into hers.

Katie was lost entirely in the moment. She was at first frightened and scared witless. Then passion, longing, stirring too long at rest, possessed her body and forced out any reason, logic or sane thought. Ecstasy followed quickly on the heels of surprise. A tidal wave of desire washed over her, as she surrendered to it, responding to his urgency. At first, she let his tongue probe her mouth, then, driven by need, wantonly and tentatively, followed his lead.

She could feel his heart pound against her and echo her own frantic heartbeat. Unable to keep up the pace, she thought each beat would be her last. His embrace held her tight against him and molded her body to his until she could feel every contour of his firm body. Her skin felt his heat, as if it were being touched by fire. She never wanted it to end. There was nothing as exciting, stirring, sensual as a first kiss and her rising desire willed it to go on and on until she ached for more.

Taking every ounce of restraint, he had to force himself to pull away. He didn't want to rush her or force her. Katie was delicate and vulnerable. She needed to be handled deftly, carefully and tenderly.

When he did draw his lips away, she was light-headed, breathless, her legs trembled and shaky. He still held her, but not as tightly. Questioningly, inquisitively she searched his smoldering eyes, like a frightened deer.

"I've wanted to do that since the first time I saw you in my office, he said. "You were so determined, so resolute, so firm and so completely and irresistibly vulnerable. You have no idea the amount of willpower and restraint I've had to use to keep my hands off you since the first moment we met."

Suddenly, Katie's passion dissolved and she was overcome with panic and dread. She was shocked and ashamed by her reaction. Where was this whole thing going? Where had she wanted it to go? Had she completely lost her senses? What was he going to think of her? What was she thinking? Well, obviously she wasn't thinking at all. She berated herself for letting it happen. For enjoying it. For wishing it hadn't ended and desperately wanting more.

As he saw apprehension and panic spread over her face, he completely mistook its meaning.

"How stupid of me! Forgive me for not thinking properly. There's not a lot of blood flowing to my brain right now. All my talk about tactics and conquests. I don't want you to get the wrong idea. Don't think this is just a flirta-tion. I'm not scoring a victory here, adding another notch to my belt. This isn't some casual fling for me. I've never come close to feeling this way about any woman, ever. Katie O'Neill, I'm falling ..."

Katie simultaneously felt regret and self-reproach, and wasn't exactly sure how to fix the mess she had made of things. She took her finger and gently touched it against his lips, stopping him from saying anything they would both regret. Her sorry for him having said it and him sorry for having her hear it. She stepped back slightly, hoping a physical distance would make what she had to say easier.

"Matt, you know you mean a great deal to me. I have come to rely on you both as my lawyer and as my friend."

Matt cringed at the sound of the dreaded *F* word no man ever wanted to hear from any woman he was in love with.

"It's not that I didn't enjoy that." She thought, *God, I'm ashamed to admit how much I enjoyed it.* "Or that I haven't enjoyed today. It was the happiest and most contented I've been in a long time. But, you really don't know me; know who I am, down deep inside. And, for the first time in my life, I've started to look at who I am. I have gone from being a daughter, to being a wife, to being a mother, to being a widow. No breaks, no pauses in between. Romantically, I've only been with one man in my life and I married him. In some ways, I've been a widow what seems like an eternity, and in other ways, the ways that really count, it seems as if it was only yesterday."

She had been successful holding his gaze this long; she figured she would continue. *Please, let me find the words.* The last thing in the world she wanted to do was hurt him.

"Right now, I don't know what I feel about myself, beyond being a mother. I don't know what I feel about you right now, beyond friendship. I don't know what I feel about ever having those kinds of feelings about a man, ever again. If we are ever meant to have that kind of a relationship, I want it to come fresh from want, not desperate from need. I want it to be right. We both want it to be right. But for now, I need time to sort those things out."

She broke the tension with a gentle smile. "A wise man once told my boys the story about the Canada goose. About the special bond that forms between the male and female. That once it selects its mate, it does so for a lifetime. That if its mate should be killed, become lost, or should die, it never mates again. Maybe I'm a little bit like that. At this point, the answer is, I simply don't know. Can we continue to go on, just being friends for a while?"

"My own words coming back to haunt me. The man who told that story was not wise at all but an absolute fool."

Trying to lighten the mood, she joked, "I'm not touching that statement with a ten-foot pole. Besides, don't you think I have my hands full enough without having to juggle a romance with someone who's as challenging and unpredictable as you?"

Matt took her in his arms and held her there for a few moments, his chin resting on her head. Finally he spoke. "I guess this time it's a case of the right girl at the wrong time. None of that matters a wit to me, you know. But since it's all so damned important to you, it's important to me. I've waited my whole life for you to come along. I guess I can wait a little longer. Let me warn you, though. Just because you stopped me from saying it, doesn't make it any less real. Not hearing it doesn't make it go away. You and I both know that something unmistakable, something inevitable just happened between us. Trying to deny us it is like trying to deny our need to breathe.

"And you're wrong, Katie O'Neill, I do know you. I do know you a great deal better than you know yourself."

Casey and the twins were playing tag on the beach. Brendan and the Musketeers had finished a swim and were laid out on the dock like drowsy seals, soaking up the afternoon rays when the teasing started.

"So, Sox. Your Mom and Mr. M got a thing going?" Stump asked.

Brendan was confused by the question. "What d'ya mean?" he demanded.

"What d'ya think I mean. The two of them ... alone ... on his boat ... nobody around that can see 'em. What d'ya think they're doing? Holding hands? They're probably playing tonsil tennis right now. You know what they say, 'sin or swim'!"

The unbelievable, disgusting, sick thought pierced Brendan's brain. "Quit talking about my mom that way," he shot back.

"Ya mean you don't know what's goin' on between 'em?"

Stump baited him,

"Pinocchio had a wooden dick.

He diddled girls with his ten-inch stick.

When Pinocchio died

Shocked, the mortician cried,

'Sawdust's all that is left of his prick'."

Brendan warned him, "Go pound salt, Stump."

"Heck, they don't call him 'Matt the Masher' for nothing. Geez, he's crossed home plate more than Stan the Man. Wonder what they're doing right this minute?" He pressed the point.

"I'm warning ya. Cut it out!" Bren was really getting pissed off.

"Hey, ya think maybe their playing house yet? Maybe he'll even end up being your dad."

Vinnie didn't like what Stump was saying. He liked Mrs. O'Neill. Besides, you didn't talk about another guy's mom that way. He figured things had gone far enough. "Sox is right, man," he intervened. "Cut it out."

Brendan was embarrassed and his embarrassment was making him angrier by the minute.

"I told you to shut-up. Shove it up your ass, pecker head," Brendan lashed out.

The shouting match had reached Tommy and the twins and the ass-word made their ears perk up.

Casey threatened Bren, "Aaaw. I'm telling Mommy you swored."

"Tell her, you little mongrel and I'll kick *your* ass!" Brendan shouted back.

For the first time in his six years, Casey was rendered speechless.

Stump and Brendan shouted back and forth.

"Homo!"

"Ass-wipe!"

"Prick!"

"Shit head!"

"'Course if he was your daddy you could sail with him all the time and you wouldn't have to fix up that busted down old boat with Dr. *Frankenstein*. But then he'd be too busy messing with your mom to have any time for you." Stump put his lips together and made a smooching sound.

Brendan jumped up and shoved Stump, hard, knocking him off the dock and into the water.

"You dick wad. I'll make you take it back. I'll paddle your ass all the way up the river, if you don't take it back." He spat out the threat. Every muscle in his body was taut with fury.

Finally, Breeze broke in. "Come on, guys. Sox, he was just kidding. Didn't mean anything by it. If he knew what he was talking about he'd be dangerous. Stump, this time you went too far. You can be such a prick licker sometimes."

Puke joined in and shoved Breeze in the water and broke the tension. Vinnie followed suit and Puke landed in a huge splat, soaking everybody. Then Vinnie dove in the water after them.

Brendan stood on the dock, fists clenched in anger. He was mad at Stump, but madder at his mom. Why did she have to go with Mr. Mulholland? Maybe he didn't care at all about him. Maybe he was just hanging around so he could see his mom. Didn't she know how stupid it looked? She was his mom, for crying out loud. Mom's didn't do stuff like that. What if Stump was right? What if they were making out and stuff? How could she embarrass him like this? Worse, how could she do it to Dad?

He was suddenly ashamed.

Vinnie, with Stump in a headlock said, "Come on Sox. I'll hold him while you punch him in the nuts."

But, it would be a long time before Brendan cooled off.

ভ ৪০

As soon as Katie got home, she checked on the little ones. They were a bit dirty, but sleeping peacefully. Under the door to his room, Katie could see the light was still on in Brendan's room. She took a deep breath and steeled herself for the maelstrom she was sure would follow. Hopefully, he had forgiven her for being stuck with the little ones all day. If he was lying on his stomach, knees bent, feet kicking back and forth, reading a comic book, he was in a good mood. As she knocked and opened the door, he was slouched against the headboard, on his back, scowling, angrily flipping the pages of *Treasure Island*. She knew luck wasn't with her that night. He tossed the book aside and glared at her.

"Gettin' home pretty late, aren't you?"

"It's only ten, Bren."

"How do you sail a boat when it's pitch black outside, anyway?"

Katie looked out the bedroom window. "It's just dark now. By the time we got back to the marina ..."

"Or didn't you two notice? Guess you two were too busy. Couldn't stop making out and stuff."

Katie stared at him in disbelief. "What are you talking about, Bren?"

"You and Mr. Mulholland, on his boat ... all alone ... all day. The guys all making fun of you. Saying things. Do you know how sick it is to think of you swapping spit and ..."

His mom cut him off. "It's important to your future and physical well-being that you don't finish that sentence. Mr. Mulholland I are simply friends, nothing more, and nothing happened on that boat that I have to be ashamed of."

That wasn't entirely true, but Katie was too disquieted to care.

"What about Dad? Don't you love him anymore? Don't you even care about him? I wished he was here, instead, that you woulda ..."

"Don't you dare drag your dad into this. He's dead, Brendan. He died almost two years ago leaving me alone to raise four boys, one of which is being very selfish and very disrespectful right now. One that he would be very disappointed in. It was okay for Mr. Mulholland to take you sailing and spend countless hours helping you work on your sailboat when he could have been doing other things, things that are important to him. He was good enough and generous enough to cater to your whims, as long as it suited you."

Katie had to remind herself to lower her voice. She didn't want to wake up Tommy and the twins. "Listen to me, young man. If you want to be treated like a grown up, you had better start acting like one, instead of behaving like a spoiled, ungrateful brat. It's time you started thinking of someone other than yourself. It's also time you start thinking *for* yourself and not let your friends do your thinking for you.

"Not that I have to explain myself to you or justify my actions, but I will decide who I see and when I see them. And if I ever do decide to start dating someone you will find it in your best interest to show me respect and consideration. I have never laid a hand on you in anger your entire life but I'm dangerously close to introducing you to the business end of a wooden spoon. If you know what's good for you, I suggest you turn out the light, go to sleep and wake up in an entirely different mood. You're not too big for a good old-fashioned spanking."

With that, Katie spun around and left the room. No goodnight, no kiss, no hug. Brendan who couldn't remember ever seeing his mom that mad did exactly as she had suggested. He turned off the lights and went to sleep.

Katie pounded the pillows and tossed and turned until the covers were a tangled mess. It was useless. She was too upset and too angry to sleep.

Like peering through a kaleidoscope, the day tumbled through her memory, the events, scrambled and disjointed. It was as if nothing connected or made any sense. Between her argument with Brendan and her feelings of guilt, regret, confusion and turmoil over the incident with Matt, she was hopelessly and desperately in need of some advice.

Knowing that the state she was in would make sleep impossible, she threw on her robe, slipped on her scuffs and padded he way out of the house and across the yard. Luckily, there were still lights on at Lottie's. She tapped gently on the screen door. She could hear Frank Sinatra playing on the record player.

Lottie hollered, "Hope y'all ain't come lookin' for a roll in tha hay, 'cuz this barn is shut up fawr tha night."

"Lottie, it's only me. I know it's late, but may I come in?" Katie pleaded.

"Sure, Sug, meet ya in tha kitchen."

Katie went in and paced the floor. A minute later, Lottie waddled in on her heels; toes spread apart by balls of cotton toenails polished a glossy fuchsia. She was covered neck to toe in a flowing, geometric patterned, silk caftan. Her hair was pin curled and covered with a huge pink lace cap, drawn up on the top in a huge pompon. Black slime had crusted on her face leaving her eyes, nose and mouth uncovered. She looked like Al Jolson made up for a minstrel show.

"What brings y'all over here at this time a night? House burn down er somethin'? Those younguns finally drive ya out? Don't mind me, ma life isn't always as glamorous as it looks. As tha years march on, a woman's gotta spend a little extra time on maintenance. Tonight I was overdue fawr an oil change an' a lube job."

Everything came crashing down on Katie. She started sobbing and blubbering to the point Lottie couldn't understand a word she was saying.

"Hold everythin' right there, Sug. Can't make head ner tails of what yawr tryin' ta convey. Give me a second ta get this here beauty pack offa ma face. I'll fix ya a nice tall cool one. Y'all look like ya could use it. An if'n ya can't use it, I kin. Shush, now. Get yawrself out on ma lanai. I'll be there in a jiff."

Katie slumped into a patio chair. Within minutes, Lottie joined her outside, sans mudpack.

"I made y'all a toddy fawr tha body. Now, tell Lottie what's got yawr undies bundled."

Katie shook her head, refusing the temptation. "Thanks, Lottie, but I think I've already had enough to drink, today."

"Sug, this ain't none a that sissy wine yawr so fond of. That stuff's useless as fartin' inta windstorm. Yawr on tha verge of a good ol' fashioned cryin' jag. Y'all need a good stiff drink fawr fortificashun. Miz O'Neill, I want ya ta make tha acquaintance of Mistuh Rob Roy."

With that, Lottie poured them both a tall, cool one and settled in, anxious to digest every juicy detail. And here she had thought she was going to face a long, lonely night with just herself, her martini shaker, her beauty treatments and Old Blue Eyes.

After Katie had sobbed through the entire story, from the beginning of her day, right through her fight with Brendan, Lottie sat back and let out a slow, sultry whistle.

"That's it? That's all you can do? That's the best advice you can give me of your famous homespun wisdom and experience? My nerves are shot. I'm half drunk. My life is in a shambles. Matt, not to mention Brendan, will probably never speak to me again and your best advice is to whistle?" Katie punctuated the last question with a hiccup.

"Well, if this ain't tha last button on Gabe's coat! Let me jus' get ma bearins here a bit, gotta digest things first. Ya want me ta tell ya what ya want ta hear er ya want me ta tell ya tha way it is? First off, though, I gotta correct ya, Sug, y'all ain't half drunk. Yawr nearly all tha way ta bein' one hundred percent plowed."

Lottie handed her a hankie. Katie blew her nose, not altogether ladylike. She attempted to hand the hankie back to Lottie, who rolled her eyes, curled her upper lip, and muttered, "Y'all kin keep that one, Sug. I got plenty more."

Her voice quivering, Katie continued. "I threatened Brendan, Lottie. He was so belligerent and nasty. I threatened him ... with violence. I spoke mean, harsh words. Things I can't take back." Katie took in a good sniff of air, followed by another hiccup.

"Hell, that ain't nothin' new. Tha battle between parent an' pup has been goin' on since Adam spanked Abel. Did ya ever think that maybe that boy had it comin'? Seems ta me he said some spiteful things, too. Ma opinion is ya needed ta shake him up a bit. Besides, nothin' knocks tha sass outta a boy like a trip behind tha woodpile. Kids are like a bed spring, Sug, no matter how many times they been sat on, jumped on er slept on, they always manage ta bounce right back."

"Some of what Brendan said may be true. Have I betrayed Danny? Am I being disloyal, unfaithful to him? God, I feel so scared ... so guilty."

Lottie put a comforting arm around her shoulder. "Sug, yawr husband died, not you. What's ta feel guilty about. Those feelins are natural. It was tha good Lord that made ya that way, in tha first place. Don't seem likely fawr Him ta condemn ya ta hell fawr havin' feelins. Yawr makin' a mountain outta a molehill. Why don't y'all jus' sit back an' see where it all takes ya an' enjoy tha ride?"

"There is no place for it all to take me. That's exactly what I'm talking about. My behavior has ruined everything. What about the muck I've made of things with Matt? You warned, me, Lottie, but I was too willful and too stubborn to listen."

"Don't worry none, Sug. I won't scold ya with a lotta I told ya so's."

As if Lottie hadn't said a word, Katie rambled on, "Now, I've ruined everything ... especially our friendship."

"I s'pect Matt's a big 'nough boy. He'll survive. Although I ain't so sure he's ever come 'crossed anythin' as powerful as Hurricane Katie. Don't ya be too hard on tha guy. Ya can't fault tha man for trollin' his bait. Yawr available ... he's available. Seems kinda natural fawr him ta come testin' yawr waters."

A new horror surfaced as Katie, in a panic, asked, "How will I ever face him? You know how things are. Once you've crossed that line, you can never go back. I don't know how I'm ever going to look Matt in the eyes again."

Lottie chuckled at that one. "I strongly suspect those eyes of yawrs are what got ya inta this mess ta begin with."

"I promise, Lottie," raising her left hand as if she were taking a solemn oath, "I swear I never gave him any reason to believe that we were anything more than friends. I've never given him the slightest bit of encouragement to expect anything more."

In spite of the fact that Katie swore her oath with the wrong hand, Lottie believed her sincerity and didn't doubt for a moment that Katie firmly believed she was telling the truth. Due to her inebriated state Katie had no idea which was left ... which was right, or which was up ... down ... or cross-way and Lottie cut her a little slack.

"Oh Sug. Wake up and smell the coffee. Didn't yawr mamma teach ya anythin' useful concernin' men? There's nothin' more attractive ta a man, than a woman who's not interested."

"One kiss and I melt like a teen-ager. Seriously, Lottie, I can't explain it. I don't know what possessed me ... what came over me." Katie's words reflected a state somewhere between confusion and hysteria.

"I'll be dipped an' fried! He really did git yawr juices flowin', didn't he! I think tha word yawr lookin' fawr is *horny*, Sug."

The vulgar word was like a mental slap across the face and Katie gasped with shock. "I can't believe you said that. I've never been h-h-h ..." Katie couldn't even coax the word to her lips. She fought to defend her honor. "... th-th-that word in my life!"

An accusatory "HAH" erupted from Lottie. "Yawr Danny's been gone close ta two years, now. So, it's been at least that long since ya had any. Trust me, Sug. Yawr horny."

Katie nearly died from shame. "Oh ... my ... God! If you think that about me, Matt must think the same thing."

"Tha only thing Matt's thinkin' is that yawr a normal, healthy woman with a normal, healthy sexual appetite."

"Quit calling it that!" Katie couldn't bear the thought of Matt thinking the same thing.

"Don't tell me yawr afraid of S-E-X?" Lottie teased, spelling the word out, as if it were too naughty to utter out loud. "Y'all have had fawr kids of yawr own, fawr cryin' out loud. Y'all don't expect me ta believe ya ordered 'em from tha Sears an' Roebuck. Ya had ta have done tha horizontal cha cha at least a few times. An' unless ol' Danny boy's swimmers hit a dead-on bull's eye every time, I'm mighty sure y'all practiced it a few more times n'that."

Katie defended herself. "That was different (hiccup). I was married. "It's a sin to have those kind of relations outside of marriage."

Shaking her head in disbelief, Lottie lectured, "Catholics got a mighty peculiar notion on that subject, I tell ya what!"

"It's not a Catholic notion! It's one of the Ten Commandments. 'Thou shalt not covet thy neighbor's husband.' "

"Matt ain't nobody's husband, Sug. That makes him fair game."

"Don't be so literal. It's a sin just thinking about doing that with someone you're not married to."

"Tell me if I got this right, would ya, Sug?" Lottie crossed one knee over the other and leaned back in her chair. "It's a sin *doin'* it. An' it's a sin jus' *thinkin'* 'bout doin' it. Right?"

Katie nodded emphatically.

"So ... if both of 'ems a sin ... seems ta me it'd be kinda foolish not ta go fawr broke, then. Go all tha way. Hell, I mean ... as long as yawr sinnin' ... y'all might as well make it worth tha effort. Get more bang fawr tha buck!"

Confused by that logic, the situation and no doubt the amount of alcohol she'd consumed, Katie was wearing down and muttered, "I haven't been out on a date in years. I definitely don't remember things being this complicated. We met, we dated, we fell in love, got married. Danny was the only man I had dated more than once or twice. Until today, Danny was the only man I had ever kissed. I had kissed a few boys before Danny, but those don't count." Katie was starting to slur her words. Badly.

"It sounds ta me like yawr blowin' this way outta proporshun, Sug. It wuz jus' a kiss. Not a night at tha Do-Drop-Inn. Yawr makin' way too much of it."

"And you're not taking it serious enough (hiccup)! No boys I ever knew kissed me like I was kissed today."

"Ya know what I think? I think yawr not nearly as upset 'bout tha kiss as yawr reacshun ta it."

"And Matt probably knows exactly what my reaction was. Let's face it. I'm just not going to see him, again. Ever. I'd be too humiliated."

"Ever kin be a mighty long time, Sug. I wouldn't be makin' no hasty decishuns, tonight, 'specially not with tha amount a hooch y'all got flowin' in yawr veins. Ma Granddaddy Pope always said ya had ta sleep on anythin' important, mull it over in yawr mind, kinda get used ta tha idea. Ma advice ta you, is don't be throwin' out tha baby with tha bath water. An' you sure as shingles better not be decidin' nothin' right now. Tha winters kin get mighty long, cold an' lonely here."

Lottie helped Katie up, steadying her wobbly legs. "Come on, Sug, let's get ya home an' tucked inta bed, snug as a bug. Lottie'll walk ya home."

Halfway across the lawn, Lottie mumbled, "Sure as tha Pope's Catholic, I'm gonna step in more a that dawg's shit."

chapter sixteen

With one sleepy eye opened, Katie awoke for the first time in her life with a jackhammer battering her brain. Sunshine streamed through her bedroom window and stabbed her eye. Waves of nausea and queasiness gripped her stomach as she choked back the sour urge to vomit. Her mouth was dry as a cotton ball and tasted like dirty socks. Squeezing her eyes shut, she tried to ignore the pounding and racket that assaulted her head. The whole bed was spinning like a whirligig. She thought if she could manage to place one foot on the floor she could stop the spinning.

Clattering and clanging wound its way up the stairs. *How late was it? What day was it?* She thought.

"Oh God," she whispered, forcing her brain to try to process one coherent thought, "the boys are up."

She slowly turned her head to the bedside clock. Never had she slept in so late. Pulling the covers over her head, she tried to delay the inevitable. It was no use. Suddenly gripped by a spasm of nausea, she stumbled to the bathroom and clung to the toilet, retching. Her trembling legs were barely able to lend support. Beads of perspiration peppered her forehead as she willed the whirling and spinning to stop.

Her thought processes slowly and reluctantly began to clear the fogginess that clouded her senses. *Oh, my God, I've sinned,* she thought, *I haven't been poisoned ... I'm hung over!*

Shame and disgust crept into her consciousness. The sins were really piling up. Now she had added the sin of drunkenness to the already repugnant list of lust, lechery and lewdness. Her next confession to Father Davey was going to be a bell-ringer. As another thump from downstairs registered that the boys were fending for themselves, her tally grew by two more offenses, negligence and sloth.

She braved a quick glance at herself in the bathroom mirror to see if her latest transgressions were evident on her face. A gaunt, putrid green, red-eyed monster stared back at her as vertigo forced her to sit on the edge of the bathtub for support. She was convinced she couldn't possibly be any sicker if she were at death's door.

In the hopes of reviving herself and not wanting to have the boys see her this way, she quickly bathed, washed her hair and dressed. As she brushed her teeth, she gagged back the returning, sour nausea. Her hopes of recovery were shattered. She didn't feel one iota better. With a mouthful of water, she popped two aspirin in her mouth, then, for good measure, choked down a third and then a fourth.

Eventually, she gathered up the courage and strength to gingerly venture downstairs, her lack of equilibrium forced her to grip the banister like a drowning man clings to a lifeboat.

The kitchen could have been declared a disaster zone, but gratefully, the boys had vacated and disappeared outside. Like a sailor trying to find his sea legs, she shuffled around the kitchen trying to muster up the strength to brew a pot of tea. The back door slammed shut and her head amplified the decibels to near ear-shattering levels. She pressed her shaking fingers against her ears in the hopes of preventing her head from being rent in two. An overwhelming, nauseating, perfumed odor preceded her visitor and caused Katie's stomach to roil and churn.

"So, y'all have decided ta return ta tha land a tha livin'. Sort of. Sug, y'all look like a cow's chewed ya up fawr cud an' spit ya back out. I don't think tha wreck of tha Hespes coulda looked much worse."

Katie turned, lifted her head slowly, carefully, not wanting to tempt fate, and focused two veiled, evil, blood-shot eyes on Lottie and pointed a shaky finger at the pitcher of *Lord knew what* she was carrying. "Thanks for the hospitality last night. Did you come back today to finish me off with that?"

"When it comes ta bottled spirits, Sug, if ya can't run with tha big dawgs, ya best stay home on tha porch. An speakin' a dawgs, this here is a bit a tha hair of tha dawg that bit ya. Ma personal home remedy fawr a hangover."

Katie spat back, "Thank you for the kind, understanding words of sympathy. You were the one pouring drinks down me like it was my last day on earth. Ironically, that's precisely the way I feel today … and if the Lord hasn't abandoned me completely or turned a deaf ear towards me, after my behavior of the last twenty-four hours, that is exactly what I'm praying for."

Lottie poured a tall glass of the thick, blood red concoction. "Stop feelin' so sorry fawr yawrself. It ain't becomin.' An' don't be layin' tha blame at ma feet. It wasn't ma hands liftin' tha glass ta yawr mouth. Now drink up."

Katie slowly shook her head. "There is no way I can possibly choke down one sip of that, Lottie. Unless you won't mind seeing it come right back up."

"Trust me, not only will it stay down, but this here will perk ya up in a jiffy, guaranteed."

Reluctantly, Katie forced some of it down her throat. Surprisingly, she did manage to keep it down. At first she was going to ask Lottie what was in it, then thought better of it. It was probably best not to know.

"Sorry I snapped at you, Lottie. I'm not feeling very good about myself, right now. I've managed to jeopardize any kind of friendship I may have had with Matt, probably pushing him right out of my life. Add to that the fact that I know I've treated him very badly, neither of which he deserves.

"I'm a lousy mother, who has recently made some very bad choices that may have permanently damaged the already tenuous relationship I have with my oldest son. My children have had to eat cold breakfasts, on their own, motherless, two days in a row. Last night I got so drunk, I don't even remember coming home. And due to my drunken stupor, I wake up this morning so sick I was actually relieved that my children were nowhere around to bother me. All together, a pretty pitiful picture. Danny would be thoroughly disgusted with me." On the verge of tears, Katie's lip trembled.

"Don't go getting' all weepy over this. An' before ya go sewin' a scarlet letter on yawr bosom, as far as Danny is concerned, if he was half tha man y'all have described ta me, Sug, I'm pretty sure he would forgive ya. I suspect he may even be havin' a good ol' laugh over it."

Lottie urged her to take another healthy drink of the cure.

"Mark ma words, Sug, Brendan will come around, usin' one of yawr favorite phrases, 'all in good time.' Children are supposed ta be a major pain in tha ass, that's their job. An' most of 'em are damn good at it. Even Matt, who, by tha way, ain't much more than a big ol' kid himself, will manage to survive this. Why, he'd walk through hell in gasoline underwear fawr ya. Don't ya think he'd be willin' ta give ya a little time ta work this all out. Jus' give Matt an' Brendan some space ta deal with things. Trust me, Sug, things always manage ta work themselves out."

Much to her surprise, Katie began to feel better, physically. The jackhammer that pounded her head had reduced to the level of a woodpecker's beak against an oak tree. The quivering that had plagued her hands and legs had begun to subside. She felt less like gelatin and more like Gumby. Other than possessing the thirst of the French Foreign Legion, her tummy began to calm down. She no longer had the sickly pallor of puce. Instead, she had the sickly pallor of the underbelly of a dead fish.

"I hope you're right, Lottie. The way I feel right now, things can only get better. They surely can't get much worse."

"Jus' think, Sug, as ma very favorite singer, Frank Sinatra says, 'people who don't wake up in tha mornin' hung over are feelin' tha best they're gonna feel all day.' Come on, I'll help ya tidy up this kitchen. Then ya kin send Brendan over ta ma place. Got a few odd jobs that been needin' done. It'll give him a chance ta earn a little extra pocket money."

After the kitchen was returned to its pre-disaster state, Lottie flew out the back door and gave one last instruction to Katie. "Water, Sug. Drinks lots a water."

The screen door slammed shut and Katie nearly jumped out of her skin.

Brendan showed up at Lottie's about an hour later, sullen, sheepish and with as much enthusiasm as a condemned man walking to the gallows. Lottie thought he looked like a cross between a whipped dog and one of Uncle Zwilly's sway-backed old mules.

In spite of his less than spirited mood, he worked hard. He cleaned out the gutters, raked weeds off the beach and washed and waxed Lottie's most prized possession, her Caddy, until it shone like a polished apple. After he had put all the tools and cleaning supplies away in the garage, she met him on the lanai and paid him generously. She hadn't heard him utter more than five words the whole day, responding mostly, with nods or gestures and an occasional grunt.

Letting him stew in his own juices, Lottie allowed most of the afternoon to pass before she broached the subject. "Who peed in yawr corn flakes, this mornin'?" Y'all are lookin' like yawr momma's feelin.' Could it be 'cuz you an' her had a little row?"

Brendan gave Lottie a martyr's sigh.

"I heard that y'all had quite a few interestin' things ta say ta her. Also heard that maybe ya were a bit rough on her."

"I apologized this morning. Said I was sorry."

"Sorry don't feed tha kitty, Bren. She's still yawr momma an' deserves yawr respect."

Brendan, with head bent, hands in his dungaree's pockets, chased a stone around with the toe of his tennis shoe.

"The guys were all making fun of her … and Mr. Mulholland … and me … it was sick and creepy. And all the time I thought he liked me. That he liked being around me."

"Me. Me. Me. In three sentences ya used *me* three times. No wonder yawr lookin' sadder 'n a whipped puppy. Feelin' a bit sorry fawr yawrself? Feelin' sorry fawr yawrself kin be mighty tiring' on a body. There's a few other people around that ya might want ta consider what they're feelin' while yawr at it."

"I don't care about her. It's all her fault. What she did is wrong. She isn't right. I am. I'm right about this."

"Bein' sure ain't always tha same as bein' right. An' bein' right all tha time kin put a mighty heavy burden on yawr shoulders, too. Pitiful an' right, both. Now I kin understand why y'all are lookin' so miserable.

Her sarcasm was wasted on Brendan. "It's not fair. I been so stupid think-ing he cared about me. I wish he'd go away ... I never want to see him again. I wish they'd both just go away ..." His voice trailed off. Saying it aloud only made it more real. True. Worse.

Lottie shook her head and warned him, "Be careful what ya wish fawr, Bren. Sometimes, it jus' might come true. An' sometimes ya end up findin' out it wasn't what ya really wanted."

Tired of staring at the top of his head, Lottie reached up and lifted his chin until their eyes met. "I know y'all are hurtin' over this. Change kin be a scary thing."

Brendan shrugged, as an uncomfortable silent moment passed between them.

"Not every child is necessarily blessed with a momma that loves 'em as much as yawr momma loves you. 'Course, y'all not knowin' any better, may have a mind ta take it fawr granted. Now, ya take me. Had a momma didn't pay me much mind, 'cept makin' sure I stayed outta her way. She most likely woulda sold me if tha right offer woulda come along.

"But not yawr momma. Ya know she loves ya more than y'all probably deserve, sometimes. That's tha wondrous thing 'bout her love, it's there whether ya know it er not an' it's there whether ya deserve it er not. Y'all don't have ta earn it, it's just there."

Brendan remained mute and Lottie wondered if he was hearing anything she said. *Kids. Can't live with 'em. Can't shoot 'em.*

"I'm 'bout ta break one of ma rules. Don't much believe in handin' out advice, unless I'm asked fawr it. Ain't nothin' more tiresome than a person that thinks they know all 'bout how other people oughtta be livin' their lives, but I'm gonna make an excepshun in this case.

"I know, in some respects, life's dealt ya a pretty rotten hand, losin' yawr daddy, an' all. Like ya said, some things in life jus' ain't fair. But, when tha world hands ya lemons, squeeze 'em on yawr fish. I tend ta measure a man by how tall he stands when tha crops've failed not when tha crops a good one. Life don't test ya a bit, ya don't learn ta 'preciate tha things ya got instead a cryin' 'bout what ya don't. Life don't throw ya a few curve balls ya don't learn ta watch tha pitches. "

Lottie wiped a smudge of dirt from his forehead.

"But what about my dad? Doesn't she love him anymore?"

Lottie thought that over for a minute. "Sure, she does, Bren. But yawr daddy's gone. Only tha good Lord knows why He took 'em, but He took 'em. Yawr daddy's dead, but yawr momma, tha Lord intends fawr her ta go on livin.'

"Sometimes it's mighty hard for a child to see their momma an' daddy as real people. Mos'ly y'all don't see 'em as bein' anythin' else than yawr ma an' pa.

Ya know how ya don't like bein' 'round yawr little brothers all tha time. Ya like bein' 'round yawr friends an' Dr. Franke an' Mr. Mulholland. That's 'cuz yawr growin' up an' sometimes ya need ta be 'round older folks. Yawr momma has tha same need.

"I hate ta burst yawr bubble, Bren, but washin', an' cleanin' an' lookin' after y'all ain't necessarily 'nough fawr her. Sure, she loves ya boys, but sometimes she needs ta be 'round grown-ups, folks her own age, doin' grown up things. That's tha way it is when yawr an adult. I expect yawr old 'nough ta understand that.

"Yawr momma an' Mr. Mulholland are jus' friends. An' if yawr half as grown up as I think you are, y'all can see that. Whether it ever comes ta somethin' more, then I hope yawr also grown up 'nough ta deal with that, too. Yawr momma would walk over hot coals barefoot fawr ya. Tha last thin' on earth she'd do is cause ya any hurt. Don't ya think she deserves tha same from y'all?"

Brendan didn't answer out loud. He searched Miss Lottie's eyes for answers and understanding. Finally, he gave her a little nod; she winked and smiled in return.

"Hey, kiddo, bein' a grown up kin be kinda tricky. But, will ya promise me that y'all at least give it some thought? Tha least ya kin do is give it a try."

Grudgingly, like a drunk taking an oath of sobriety, he nodded his promise.

"Now, after all this deep, grown-up thinkin' I think y'all an' I have earned tha right ta have a little un-grown up fun."

Brendan followed her as she walked around the house and lead him to her Cadillac. Brendan went around to get in the passenger side, when Lottie stopped him and tossed him the keys. "No, Bren, I'm not drivin', y'all are. But, it'll have ta be our little secret. Don't be sharin' this with yawr momma. She'd have a connipshun fit if she was ta find out. Now climb in behind tha wheel an' let's see what this baby can really do."

Shocked, not believing what he had heard, but not wanting to risk that Miss Lottie would change her mind, Brendan piled into the driver's seat.

Five minutes later, the shiny red Cadillac, with top down, radio cranked up to ear-splitting amplification, was weaving down Lakefield Road, Lottie singing along in the passenger seat chiffon scarf blowing in the wind. And Brendan, wishing the guys could see him, nervously gripped the wheel and beamed from ear to ear.

chapter seventeen

Different people measured the passing of time in different ways. Abraham was driven by a gardener's time clock. His calendar revolved around the various stages of the growing season; the planting and fertilizing in the spring, the watering and weeding in summer and the putting it all to rest in autumn. Winter would force him into the greenhouse, where he would prepare to begin the cycle all over, again. It was as if he saw the entire world through the revolution of time in his gardens.

For Matt, it was much simpler. He viewed the passage of time through a much narrower scope. There was the pre-sailing period, the sailing period and the post-sailing period. Even within the confines of the sailing period, the days were marked by good sailing days or poor sailing days. If he wasn't on the water, he was either preparing to be, wanting to be or merely biding his time until he could be.

The rules of logic and dimensional concepts that governed others, never applied to Lottie. She had no concept of time. She wasn't constrained by anything as simple, mundane or sensible as a calendar, season or clock. She never measured anything by conventional methods. Instead, she appeared to be attuned to inward urges, controlled by some sort of mystical, invisible, driving force of nature that was peculiar to her and her alone. When and where these urges would surface was completely unpredictable by orthodox standards. And just as indefinable.

Outwardly, her metamorphosis was evidenced by a chameleon-like characteristic of changing hair color or styles at will. Another outward sign that substantiated those impelling, biological, forces of nature was her predilection to instinctively take-off on some irresistible adventure. She could disappear for a few days, a few weeks or a few months. She would often joke "that if bein' a hobo wuz a bit more luxurious an' accommodatin' ta physical comforts, she would be tha best damn hobo that ever lived."

The passage of time, for Katie, was marked by holidays, special occasions and celebrations that fell within each three hundred and sixty-five days. By significance, she classified them into two categories.

159

She applied the same concept as the Church did for masses based on the amount of pomp, preparation and importance that surrounded them. Valentine's Day, St. Patrick's Day, Easter, the Fourth of July, Thanksgiving, the scattered birthdays and of course Christmas were the high celebrations. They required the most thought, preparation and time. How much shopping needed to be done, decorations, costumes to be made, gifts to purchase and wrap, special foods and time were all carefully anticipated, planned and executed. The low holidays were New Year's Day and Memorial Day. Since Katie's ma and da had died, Mother's and Father's Day had lost their significance. As for herself, every day she spent with the boys was her Mother's Day.

The lowest of them all was Labor Day. It had a nostalgic, bittersweet feel to it. Though Katie loved the autumn, she always felt a distinct sadness to see the summer's end. Saying good-by to the long, balmy, sunny-warm, carefree days always left her feeling melancholy. But, it brought rewards of its own. To Katie's elation, and of course, to the boy's dismay, it heralded the start of another school year. Though she thoroughly enjoyed summer's free time with the boys, by September she was ready for the return to a routine. Anticipating eight blessed hours of peace and quiet a day made her positively ecstatic.

She tried to ease the pain of the back-to-school-blues for the boys and planned an end of the summer picnic. She planned it for Sunday, giving her Monday to get things settled for school to start on Tuesday. Casey and Colin asked C.J. and Brendan could have the guys over to enjoy one of the last, fleeting, warm days of summer. Since Tommy and Doug had become joined at the hip, Doug was invited too.

Though she hadn't heard from Matt in nearly two weeks, she broke the gnawing silence that had risen between them and marked the days since they had gone sailing. She called and invited him to join them.

For Katie, the conversation seemed stinted and forced; gnawing silences stretched out between sentences. The discomfiture appeared one-sided. Unlike Katie, Matt had sounded perfectly relaxed and comfortable on the phone. His complacency only served to further pique her uneasiness. Exasperated that he sounded so normal and she felt so un-normal, she tried to sound calm and unruffled and was certain she had failed miserably. She felt betrayed by her voice and tone as she tried to bite back the hesitancy and uneasiness. Eventually, Matt declined, having made plans to spend the holiday with his family in Chicago. Katie was surprised to find that she was definitely disappointed that he wasn't coming. She was also surprised that she actually missed seeing him ... very much.

In the past, Katie had never given much thought to her sexuality. She had no idea what men thought about it, but it was a topic rarely explored by women.

It wasn't that she was a prude or didn't enjoy sexual relations. In fact, she and Danny had enjoyed a very satisfying and active sex life. On their wedding night, they were both virgins and had shared the thrill of awakening sexuality, exploration, experimentation and eventual ripening of their lovemaking. Together, with tenderness and passion, they brought each other to sexual maturity and satisfaction.

But, since that fated afternoon with Matt and the subsequent discussion with Lottie, Katie had thought a great deal about passion … and sex … and sexual relations … and Matt.

A lot.

And her face burned crimson every time.

Katie placed the majority of the blame on Lottie's fixation on sex. From the very beginning, Lottie had been the one to start feeding her fantasies. And like a sex-starved strumpet, Katie had allowed herself to be sucked right in. Bothered and befuddled by the whole sticky mess, Katie made up her mind that she was simply going to stop thinking about it. She would put an end to anymore silly fantasizing … sexual … or otherwise. Matt wasn't coming. He most likely never would, again, and that was the end of it. She tried to console herself with the empty rationalization that it was probably all for the best.

೦೩ ೞ

No one had told Mother Nature that Sunday was the beginning of September. Katie noted the milky blue sky of a hot and humid day and was glad she had planned to cook hot-dogs and hamburgers on the barbecue grill. She would have dreaded adding fuel to the fire by having the oven turned on half the day and heating up the kitchen anymore that it already was. Besides, the boys would be happier with hot-dogs, hamburgers and potato chips, than they would be with a roast or chicken. Bowls of vanilla ice cream with chocolate syrup would be perfect for dessert. C.J. could enjoy his wiener and hamburger naked and instead of ice cream, fresh melon from Mr. Mizzano's garden.

Under the shady branches of the huge maple tree, Katie spread a blanket and the boys had picnicked there off paper plates. Though afternoon was quickly turning into evening, the heat of the day still hovered in the air. The boys, all except Vinnie, were playing Marco Polo in the lake. Chance, who labored under the misconception that he was people, too, was right in the middle of the action. He leapt and bounded in and out of the water in inexhaustible puppy fashion. C.J. didn't seem the least bit bothered by Chance and Katie wondered how many of his allergies were real and how many were imagined.

Katie spotted Vinnie sitting alone cross-legged on the dock; his shoulders slumped. With a twig, he was tracing imaginary figures on the bleached wood of the dock when Katie walked up to him.

"Why aren't you in the water cooling off with the rest of the Musketeers, Vincent?"

"Don't feel much like it, right now, Mrs. O'Neill."

"You must be awfully hot, sitting here in the sun with all those clothes on." He shook his head. "Naw, I'm fine."

"I haven't seen you swim all day. Come to think of it, I haven't even seen you put your swimming trunks on. Are you feeling okay? Maybe you're coming down with something?"

She squatted next to him and felt his forehead for a fever. It was the first time that day that she had looked closely at him. She noticed that there was an ugly bruise on his cheek and around his left eye. Vinnie tried to avoid looking at her and turned his head toward the lake. That was when she spotted the bruises on his arms.

She reached and gently tried to turn his head to face her. The game of Marco Polo came to an abrupt halt as the boys all stopped frolicking and stood in the water. Instantly the air became eerily quiet. She lifted the tail of his T-shirt. Katie was stunned. There were a half-dozen more bruises on his back.

"Vinnie. What's happened here?"

Avoiding her eyes, he answered, "I just fell."

"Have you been in a fight?"

Vinnie didn't respond. His silence answered her question and she stood up.

"Brendan, I want to see you up at the house, right now."

Vinnie panicked. "It ain't nothin', Mrs. O'Neill, got some bruises from messin' around with the guys. It's no big deal."

"Brendan Daniel, I said up to the house. Now!"

Not knowing exactly what to do, Brendan hesitantly waded out of the lake and followed his mom. When they were well out of range of being overheard, Katie questioned him. "Tell me exactly what's going on here. Right now. Have you boys been fighting?"

"No. Just messin` around." He was as convincing as one of the twins trying to talk themselves out of a jam.

"Would you care to elaborate on messing around?"

"It was an accident," he stammered.

"What? An accident mountain climbing? Those marks on his back were no accident."

Brendan stood silent. He stared, head down, at the ground, not wanting to look at his mom. It was obvious to Katie that he knew what had happened, so she pressed further.

"The answer isn't in the grass, Brendan."

"I can't tell. I promised Vinnie."

"Well, Brendan Daniel O'Neill, I'm making a promise to *you*. You tell me what this is all about, or I promise you, you'll be grounded until you're eighteen. I'm dead serious. What happened to Vinnie? I want the truth and I want it this instant."

Brendan simply stood there for what seemed like hours, arms akimbo, trying to decide whether to lie or whether to tell the truth. Finally, he lifted his head and looked straight at his mom. "It wasn't me, Mom. It wasn't any of us guys. He's embarrassed, doesn't want nobody to know."

He paused, looking for the courage to tell her.

"It's his dad."

At first, Katie didn't know what to say. The ugliness and disgust of what Brendan had said knocked all thought and comprehension from her head. Finally, the odious, repulsive impact struck her … deep. As the reality sunk in, she felt a sour, sickening nausea claw its way into her stomach. Then, the shock, the pity, the panic turned into a deep, burning, all-consuming anger. She was outraged. How could a father do that to his son? That beautiful, precious boy, how could any father do such a thing?

"His father beats him?" Katie couldn't believe the words even as she said them.

"He gets drunk. When he gets drunk anything can happen, Mom. I've seen him."

It was like the floodwaters of truth, too long held back, broke free and gushed forth, unstoppable. "When he comes home drunk he yells at Vinnie. This time he was so drunk, when Vinnie tried to help him out of the truck and into the house they both fell down the steps. That's where he got the bruises. Then he threw a beer bottle across the room and it caught Vinnie in the face. He didn't really mean to hit him with it. But it was bad, Mom. Real bad.

"Sometimes when he comes home like that, he falls asleep, but a lot of the time he doesn't. Sometimes he hollers when Vinnie didn't even do nothing! Says really mean things to him … blames him for his mom dying … that Vinnie should have died instead of his mom. That he's brought him nothing but trouble … that Vinnie's not good for anything except messin' up his life.

"Vinnie doesn't do nothing wrong, Mom … he doesn't even yell back … he just takes it." His voice trailed off to a deafening silence. Brendan couldn't remember his dad ever yelling at hitting him like that. Not once.

Katie closed her eyes on the horrific picture Brendan painted and she gently put her arm around her son. "Shush, Bren. I've heard enough."

Her gaze settled upon the lone figure sitting on the dock, shoulders hunched, head hung, rejected and defeated. His body and soul still those of a boy, but with the weight of a man crushing them.

"There's no one on earth who could ever do anything to deserve that abuse. I want you to understand me completely that no child could ever deserve that kind of treatment from a parent. There is no excuse, no reason, no justification. Not alcohol, not anger, not temper, not discipline."

First Lottie, and now Vincent. Katie thought, what monsters spewed forth those kinds of demons that could so heartlessly abuse the precious children entrusted to their care? Why did some children have to suffer the loss of their innocence at such tender ages?

In the next thirty seconds, Katie made up her mind. "I'm glad you told me, Bren. Regardless of whatever promises you made to Vincent you needed to tell me this. You're his best friend. You did what you had to do. Believe me, you did the right thing.

"Right now, I want you to go back down there and pretend that this conversation never happened. Mr. Polaski will be picking the other boys up, soon. Mrs. Coughlin is coming to get C.J. and Doug. I want Vincent to stay here. You watch your brothers for me for a while. I won't be gone long."

"Don't do nothing`, Mom. Don't say nothing to Vinnie. He gets real embarrassed. Please don't tell anyone else. I promised." He was pleading desperately, but in spite of his pleas, Katie knew what she had to do.

"I promise I won't ever mention a word of this to Vinnie. Don't you worry, I won't tell anyone, though Lord knows it's about time somebody did. I can't stand by and let this continue to go on. Trust me, I know exactly what needs to be done. Something that should have been done a long time ago."

Vincent and his father lived outside town, off Lakefield, on an unpaved side road. The house was a small frame structure that Katie always thought could do with a fresh coat of paint and some TLC. Well, now she knew that what it needed couldn't be fixed with nails, hammer or paintbrush. Now that she knew what had gone on inside, behind closed doors, it appeared even seedier and more broken than before. The word neglect was the only word that came to her mind. The whole place looked miserably neglected.

She pulled onto the dirt driveway, stirring up whirlwinds of dust and parked behind Mr. Mizzano's vegetable truck. Apparently, the only thing that Mr. Mizzano cared about was the vegetable garden. It was bursting with end of the season produce. Rows of plants were separated by rich, black, fertile soil. The tomato plants were pregnant with large, fleshy, red-ripe tomatoes so juicy you would need a lifeguard nearby while you ate them.

Zucchini, squash and pumpkins, of orange, green and yellow were ripened, plump and ready to be picked. Snap bean, pea and pepper plants were lush and heavy with fruitage. A respectable size orchard stretched out, in back of the house, with healthy apple, cherry, peach and pear trees. All the trees had been picked clean of fruit, except for the apple trees. Like red Christmas ornaments, big, fat, juicy apples tugged at the branches, heavy and ripe, waiting to be harvested.

Katie climbed the crumbling steps and knocked on the warped screen door. The only sound she heard was the drone of a radio. After thirty seconds, she fisted her hand and readied herself to pound harder when a gruff voice called from the dark interior.

"Hold your horses. I'm coming."

Nearly a minute passed before Frank Mizzano's face materialized at the door and he peered down on her. Only the torn, rusted screen separated them. He was surprised to see Mrs. O'Neill at the door. Usually she would drop Vinnie off in the drive and leave. This wasn't a good sign.

"I would like to come in, if you have a minute, Mr. Mizzano?" She questioned.

"Evenin' Mrs. O'Neill," he said as he squinted his right eye suspiciously. "Something happen to my boy? He get himself into some trouble at your place?"

"Something did happen to Vincent. Something that I need to discuss with you," she replied.

As he pushed open the door to let her in he muttered, "Don't mind the mess, I wasn't expecting company. If that boy's gotten into any trouble, I'll see to it he gets what's coming to him."

With the outside temperature pushing ninety, the inside must have been one hundred. It was insufferably stuffy and hot. The house stunk of stale smoke, stale beer and stale indifference. Frank Mizzano didn't smell any better. He was dressed in a dingy, white, sleeveless undershirt with crescent-moons of sweat around the neck and armholes, dirty, worn dungarees and bare feet. His face didn't appear to have seen soap, water and if the stubble was any indication, a razor in several days.

He was a large man with a generous spare tire that bulged over the belt that strained under his weight. A small, metal fan with chipped green paint oscillated next to him, cooling nothing, but ineffectively moving the stagnant air. But, giving housekeeping tips was not in the forefront of Katie's mind. Finally, she spoke to him as sausage fat fingers casually lifted a beer bottle to his lips.

"Thanks, Mr. Mizzano for offering, but I prefer to stand. What I have to say, won't take long," Katie stated sarcastically.

"Like I told ya. If he's done something wrong, I guarantee ya, he'll be punished."

Taking a deep breath, Katie dove in for the kill. "That's exactly what I've come to talk to you about. I would say he's been punished enough, already."

His upper lip curled and he snarled, "What the hell ya talking about?"

Katie's voice shook in her throat. "I've seen the aftermath of one of your binges. It's not a sight I'm likely to forget for a long time. I've come to tell you just one thing. If I ever hear of any harm coming to that boy …"

"That kid come crying to you about his old man? He's been whining to ya like a spoiled brat? Telling ya lies about me?"

"The *truth* didn't come from Vincent. He's kept quiet about your dirty little secret."

"I don't know what ya heard, but a man's got a right to drink when and where and how much he wants."

"I saw the bruises. I know what happened last night."

"The sissy can't go crying to you every time his old man has a drink or two. All Vinnie needs to do is grow up. Act like a man." Frank's words were filled with contempt.

"That's exactly the point, isn't it? He isn't a man and certainly no match for you. He's a frightened, scared boy, who's lost his mother … and now …"

Frank Mizzano moved more quickly than a man his size should have been able to; he stood and towered menacingly over Katie. His eyes were hot and angry; his body stiff and his mouth a tight, thin line. Her pulse leapt and her breath caught in her throat.

"Don't you dare bring up his ma to me. You don't know nothing about it." His sour, warm, beer and smoke-tinted breath hit her in the face.

As if moths the size of bats pulsated inside her stomach, she ignored them and stood her ground. From somewhere far off, as if listening to someone else speaking in the distance, she heard the words forming. Yet she recognized the voice and knew that the words were her own.

"I dare because I do know something about it. That some days, the hurt and loss are so great you feel as if it will tear you in two. That some days, just thinking about them is more than your breaking heart can bear." Suddenly, Katie's pretense of calm was gone and anger exploded in her. "You aren't the only one who's been hurt. You suffered the loss of your wife but Vincent has suffered the loss of his mother. Now, he is scared that he's lost his father, too."

Frank's anger was so real he could hear the blood roaring in his ears. Face purple-red from rage, he hissed, "Look, ya ain't got no right to tell me what I should or shouldn't do. I thought ya were different. But you're like all the rest of the do-gooders in this town. You're a meddlin' busy body. Now, ya get your nosy ass the hell out of my house."

Katie thought his bellowing would shake the paint off the walls but she stood strong. She was out-sized and out-manned. Like Judith facing the mighty Holofernes armed with only courage and determination, she steeled her will, her face set with firmness of purpose. She would not back down.

"Don't you even try to intimidate me like you've intimidated your son. You're a bully and a coward and I'm not leaving here until I've finished what I came to say.

"Your wife died and in her place, she left a precious piece of herself behind. Someone you two created together, someone for you to love in her stead. Vincent is the one hope you have of keeping her memory alive, to affirm that she was real. That for those few, brief years she was allowed on this earth, she lived and loved and was loved. And what do you do with that treasure she's entrusted to you? You neglect or abuse him until you've made a mockery of everything that love is.

"Vincent loves you, in spite of it all. God only knows why, but he does. Apparently, even a bad father is better than no father at all. That boy needs his father not some broken down excuse of man too mired down in his own misery and self-pity to appreciate and return that love."

He snapped back at her, "Don't ya tell me I don't love my son. Who told ya to come nosing around butting into my affairs? Ya got no right to tell me how to raise him."

"I have every right." Katie was fueled by fury, but managed to maintain her composure. "When your sick sense of mourning, your selfishness, your bitterness spills over into abuse, abuse of your own child, then it does become my business. Physically, you've caused him unconscionable pain. God only knows what kind of pain you've caused him emotionally.

"Are you on some personal mission to destroy his spirit, like you've let bitterness destroy yours? In some convoluted, warped, twisted logic, you blame him for what happened to your wife. Lord, forgive you, for laying that kind of burden on that boy, because He's the only one that will. I can't. I'm not feeling very Christian, right now."

For a few frightening seconds, Katie thought Frank Mizzano was going to strike her. She fought back the fear. Her physical safety wasn't what mattered. Her single concern was for Vincent.

"I don't know what you have to do to fix what's wrong inside of you but you'd better fix it. Go to mass, go to confession, go see Dr. Hughes, go see Father Davey, quit drinking, crawl out from beneath that rock of cowardice you've found to hide under. I don't care how you do it, just do it. And mark my words, if I ever hear even a whisper that you've stumbled home drunk and taken it out on that boy, I promise you, I'll see to it that next time it'll be Sheriff Guzy who comes knocking on your door."

In spite of legs that were rapidly turning to gelatin, Katie spun around and started for the door. Without turning back, she said calmly and firmly, "Vincent will be staying with me for the next two days. I'll bring him back Monday night, in time to get ready for the start of school on Tuesday. That should give you enough time to think things over and start making a few changes in your life.

"And in case you don't know where to start, you might begin by cleaning up this place and taking a bath."

First, Katie slammed the screen door behind her then she slammed the car door angrier than she could ever remember being. She took two deep cleansing breaths and counted to twenty before she dared to put the car into drive and take her anger out on the gas pedal.

Frank Mizzano stood where Katie had left him. He watched her back out of the driveway and the car disappear in a cloud of dust.

Up until now, he had liked Mrs. O'Neill. She seemed like a nice lady and Vinnie always talked about her like she was something special. But he had faced hypocrites like her before. High and mighty. Nice to your face then as soon as your back was turned they changed. He knew what the women in town thought of him and he had stopped caring a long time ago. He hadn't thought Mrs. O'Neill was like them. Goes to show how wrong you can be. What did any of them know? They didn't know what it was like to be Frank Mizzano. Know what it felt like to have a part of your insides cut out. Being a widow-lady Mrs. O'Neill should have known. But she didn't know, either.

As hard as he tried to fight it, Katie's words kept hammering at his brain. Kept repeating over and over until he thought he would go crazy.

He grabbed a full bottle of beer, uncapped it and drew long and hard. Maybe the beer would wash the sound of her voice from his head. He didn't plan on getting plastered only drunk enough that the alcohol would dull his senses. All he needed was a few more beers and then he would be too numb to feel anything.

After he guzzled the first bottle he reached for another but Mrs. O'Neill's words only grew louder, more persistent.

Last night. She had been talking about last night and Frank couldn't even remember what had happened. He looked at the unopened bottle and studied it. From deep inside his gut an ache rose until he felt it twist his stomach. Revulsion formed a fist and stuck in his throat and threatened to choke him. As he looked at the bottle, something snapped inside him. He raised the bottle and as if he could smash all the ugliness from his life, he heaved it across the room and watched as it exploded into a million pieces.

After Katie had put the little ones to bed, she went to Brendan's room. She found the two boys sprawled out on the bed sorting through Brendan's collection of baseball cards. A discarded checkerboard and Sorry game lay scattered on the floor.

Neither boy said a word but two pair of anxious eyes followed her as she walked over to the bureau. She opened one of the drawers and pulled out two clean pair of pajamas and tossed them on the bed. Leaving the room, she started to close the door behind her. She paused, turned around and looked Vincent squarely in the eyes.

With a warm smile, soft and calm voice, she reassured him. "Vincent, your dad was more than happy to give his permission for you to spend tomorrow with us. I'll take you home tomorrow night.

"After you two get washed and dressed for bed, there are two pieces of apple pie on the kitchen table with your names on them. And don't stay up too late. Good night and don't forget to brush your teeth and say your prayers."

Katie never mentioned a word to Vincent or Brendan of what had happened between her and Frank Mizzano that late summer afternoon.

෪ ෩

It was Labor Day, a holiday, but Frank Mizzano figured a priest was pretty much on call everyday. Even a holiday.

Unable to lie in bed another minute, Frank crawled out of bed. He hadn't slept most of the night, staring at the ceiling. Only the clock on the dresser was visible, its fluorescent hands crawled so slowly that he thought time had stood still. When the pale, gray light of dawn traced the outline on the window shade he was relieved. It finally brought an end to the endless night.

His mind had somersaulted most of the night. Not from booze but from turmoil. Mrs. O'Neill's words had followed him to bed and haunted him making sleep impossible. It was more than her words. Something about Mrs. O'Neill that he hadn't been able to grasp until well into the endless night. Then, as sudden as lightening, it flashed from his pre-conscious into the ugly mess of his consciousness. It was Corrine. Mrs. O'Neill reminded him of Corrine.

It wasn't a physical likeness. Though, they were both petite and delicate and had a face that could light up a room just by smiling, Corrine was dark where Mrs. O'Neill was fair.

Everything was warm and dark and comforting about Corrine, her black hair, her olive skin and her eyes deep and rich as blackberry wine. Frank had never seen eyes that color before or since. It had been so long since he allowed himself to remember Corrine with joy and love. Instead, he had let the smoldering pain and anger cloud his memories of her beautiful image.

Corrine and Mrs. O'Neill were tiny and fragile, yet strong in a way that had nothing to do with physical size. Just like Mrs. O'Neill, Corrine wouldn't have taken any crap from him. She would have tried to knock some sense into him with more than an encouraging word. Corrine never would have stood idly by and watch him slowly destroy himself … and Vinnie.

Corrine and Mrs. O'Neill shared something else. Concern for Vinnie. Even with Corrine's body tortured by fever and infection, her last thoughts and words were of himself and Vincent, *"You'll have to love the baby for both of us."*

Frank Mizzano had betrayed that trust.

The things Mrs. O'Neill said showed how much she cared about Vinnie. Corrine would have liked that; she would have liked Mrs. O'Neill. But, if Corrine had lived, everything would have turned out differently.

Frank drank a half-gallon of orange juice and took a long, steamy shower, shaved and combed his hair. Frank despised the face that stared back at him. He despised it because he could see in those eyes, a blackened soul. He prayed for the first time in years. He prayed that it wasn't too late for that soul.

There was one thing that Mrs. O'Neill was wrong about. Frank did love Vinnie. His love for Vinnie was more important than his vow that he would never love again.

Dressed in the best clothes he owned, a plaid shirt and khaki work pants, he left the house before he lost his nerve.

It wasn't even eight o'clock when Frank Mizzano pulled the truck in front of the rectory. Slowly, but deliberately he trudged up the stairs. An adrenaline ball the size of his fist clutched his guts. Hat in hand, he mentally squared his shoulders and rang the bell. A minute later, Father Davey opened the door in his robe and slippers and would have dropped his coffee mug if his thirty-five years as a priest hadn't conditioned him beyond surprise.

Father Davey led Frank to his study. Disappearing for a few minutes, the old priest returned with a mug of coffee for each of them. Instead of sitting behind his desk, Father indicated for Frank to sit down in one of the visitor's chairs and settled himself in the other.

Frank played with his homburg until Father Davey thought he would wear out the brim. Finally, he spoke. "Start at the beginning, Frank. 'Tis usually the best place."

For half an hour, Frank dominated the conversation telling Father Davey about the events that led up to and his eventual visit from Mrs. O'Neill. Father never interrupted and listened intently. Frank's face was grim and his voice flat in defeat and regret. He felt the sharp, cold pain of emptiness inside.

"The scariest thing about it was that I couldn't even remember what had happened the night before. What I had done to Vinnie. I could have hurt him so bad and not even remember doing it. So ... it kind of got me thinking ... what Mrs. O'Neill said about Vinnie ... and Corrine ... and everything .."

When Frank mentioned Corrine, Father Davey recalled the gentle, sweet lady and the tragedy of her death so soon after the birth of Vincent. It was a tragedy of the past that haunted the present.

When Frank had finished, Father Davey thought about what he had said. "The Lord's interventions come in interesting packages, don't they? Mrs. O'Neill. 'Tis something isn't she? She has a true spirit of kindness and indulgence. But only to a point." Father Davey's voice was crowded with emotion and respect.

Frank avoided Father Davey's eyes. "I've been such a son-of-a-bitch. Excuse the expression, Father."

"I've heard far worse, Frank."

"Vinnie looks so much like Corrine it breaks my heart. Whenever I look at him, instead of seeing that in him, I see a constant reminder of what I've lost. I've blamed him for her death and worse. I've committed the worse sin a man can. I've hated that she had to die because of him. What kind of evil, miserable person has those kind of feelings?"

"The kind of flawed, confused and weak type of human being most of us are when we have lost the way our Heavenly Father has laid out for us. We don't often like the path He has chosen for our lives to follow. 'Tis when we try to forge our own way that we get ourselves into all kinds of trouble." Father Davey answered with clear blue eyes of affirmation.

"I've wasted so many years. I been wallowing in regret, self-pity and a bottle so long, I don't know how else to act. I'm scared, Father. Not only for me. But for Vinnie." His eyes scalded with unshed tears.

"I call it spiritual sacrifice, Frank. 'Tis a change you have to make on your own. Well, not really alone. You and our Heavenly Father. You have to make the effort to surrender your spirit to Him so that He may empty the sadness from your soul and fill it with His peace. There is no power on earth that can do it for you."

Father Davey gave Frank the opportunity to respond and when he didn't, he continued. "You are an alcoholic, Frank." As he said it, the color bleached from Frank Mizzano's face.

"'Tis no way to say it kindly. The sooner you face it, the sooner the healing can start. There's an AA meeting every Thursday night at Holy Cross. The Program works, Frank. One of the few that does. If you're really serious about this, you should go."

Frank heard the pendulum on the clock tick-tock the seconds. His heart beat in triple time to the cadence. "I couldn't do that, Father. I'd be too ashamed. Everyone would find out." A cloud of embarrassment washed over Frank's face.

Laughter bubbled from Father Davey. "Got news, Frank. Everyone in this town already has an opinion on that. The shame is in not doing something about. Anybody can drink. Not everyone can stop."

"I can do it on my own. I've done it before."

The mirth left Father Davey's face. "Not too successfully, Frank. Booze isn't the symptom. 'Tis the disease. If you have a headache, you take aspirin. But when a brain tumor is what's causing the headaches, they keep right on coming back as the tumor grows larger and larger. You need to cut it out, fix what's wrong, not simply treat the symptoms."

Frank refused to look up; his head flopped forward on his chest.

"I'll pose a question to you. 'Tis a simple one with a simple answer. Is Vincent worth it to you? Yes or No? There is nothing else that matters here."

Frank waited so long to answer that Father Davey thought he had stopped breathing. Finally, he lifted his eyes. "Of course, he's worth it. I love Vinnie."

"Sometimes, loving isn't enough."

"I'll do anything I have to get him back."

"Then 'tis decided. Thursday night. Eight o'clock. I'll go with you so you don't loose heart. Do we have a date?"

Frank's eyes met the priest's and he nodded slowly.

Father Davey slapped his palms on his knees. "Before you go, I want to hear your confession. I've never heard one in my pajamas before. If I like it, I may start a new trend."

"I'm not sure I remember how to make a good confession."

"Not to worry, Frank. I'll talk you through it and we'll go from there."

Frank flashed a weak smile.

"One day at a time, Frank. One day at a time. 'Tis a phrase you're going to be hearing a lot of. 'Tis also a wonderful philosophy. One day at a time. 'Tis how we should all approach life."

After Father Davey heard Frank's confession and gave him absolution, he suggested they finish off the pot of coffee. "You a smoker, Frank?"

Confused, he answered, "Yes. Father."

"Good. I could use one. Get used to smoking and drinking coffee, Frank. I hear recovering alcoholics smoke a lot of cigarettes and drink a heap of coffee."

chapter eighteen

As she sat in the principal's office, Katie's memory jerked her back to St. Dennis' where she had spent her twelve years as a student. She had been a model pupil, well behaved, taking her conduct and studies seriously. But even she had, on rare occasion for some minor infraction, been summoned to Sister Ignatius' office. Though no longer a disobedient student, all the dread and fears came rushing back to her as she waited uneasily for the scolding and reprimands to begin.

Sister Mary Therese's office was much the same as she remembered Sister Ignatius' to be, as she suspected every principal's office in every school, in every parish must be, stark, functional and parochial. The sturdy, honey-colored oak desk held all the typical articles, pens and pencils, random folders, papers and textbooks, all the essentials, neatly stacked.

The room was furnished with two gunmetal gray file cabinets, a credenza, and three, identical, slat-back oak chairs, one behind the desk, the other two facing the desk. Katie occupied one of them. There was the requisite statue of the parish patron saint, St. Anthony. A large Regulator clock, hung above the credenza with its pendulum ceaselessly, ticking away the minutes. With the exception of the clock, there were only two other decorations on the walls. Above the large window was a large oak crucifix and on the opposite wall hung a picture of the Blessed Virgin Mary.

The door opened, startling Katie and Sister Mary Therese whisked into the room.

"Good morning, Mrs. O'Neill."

"Good morning, Sister."

The nun was tall and generously built with a shelf of bosom jutting out, too large to be camouflaged by the bib and layers of habit. She made the sign of the Cross as she passed under the crucifix and settled herself into her chair. Her black wooden rosary beads chattered against the desk.

First, she adjusted her frameless spectacles then rearranged the papers on her desk and opened the folder in front of her.

Katie studied her face. Black veil and white wimple framed a full face with rosy cheeks and skin as soft, clear and unblemished as Katie had ever seen. Pale eyebrows showed the early stages of graying. She folded her hands on the desktop and a wide, gold band, identical to the one on Katie's hand, gleamed on the ring finger of the nun's left hand. A large ebony crucifix hung from her neck and rested on her chest. Her gray eyes lifted from the paper and she smiled at Katie.

"Thank you for taking the time to come on such short notice. I usually don't take these minor infractions too seriously, but I feel the sooner we address the situation, the sooner we can rectify it."

Katie swallowed nervously. All her hopes that this meeting would not involve some misdemeanor on the part of one of the boys were immediately lost. She folded and unfolded her gloved hands.

"I take it that you didn't call me here to report that Brendan has had a vocational calling to the priesthood," she said.

Katie cringed at her pitiful attempt to bring some humor to the situation. Sister Mary Therese responded with a robust laugh, her ample bosom shook, the crucifix bounced up and down.

"No. To my knowledge, Brendan has not shown an interest in entering the seminary. Right now, neither Casey nor Colin is showing any signs of being candidates for the sacrament of Holy Orders, either.

"As you know, their first grade teacher, Sister Thomas Aquinas has had to take a leave of absence due to the sudden illness of her mother. We expect that she will be gone through most of the semester. In her absence, we have had to call into service, from retirement in the Dominican Mother House in Grand Rapids, one of our older sisters."

Sister Mary Therese paused a moment, organized her thoughts, and then continued. "Poor Sister Benedetta, bless her soul, is the sweetest dearest person. She has spent her whole adult life in the service of the Lord. She was a wonderful teacher in her day, adored children and for fifty some years, was dedicated to the education of hundreds of boys and girls. I emphasize this, because I am afraid that her once sharp and astute mind is ... how should I word this? Well, dulled some. She may at times become a bit forgetful and confused. Anyway, boys will be boys, and I'm afraid that Casey and Colin have definitely exercised the applicability of that cliché. You know how children can sense weakness or vulnerability and will prey on those flaws."

Katie nodded. Anticipating the worst, she pleaded, "Oh, please don't tell me they've mistreated or taken advantage of Sister Benedetta."

The nun shook her head and forged ahead cautiously, searching for the right words. "Well, not exactly mistreating her. More a matter of taking advantage of the situation. Those two boys look so much alike that even I have trouble telling them apart. So, you can see how someone older, less sharp, less observant may not be able to make that distinction.

"It seems that they have concocted a scheme where they have repeatedly changed places with each other, literally. I have discovered that they switch seats, swap work assignments and trade responses in class. You can understand how very upsetting and disturbing that behavior can be.

"Needless to say, Sister Benedetta is so confused and befuddled, she doesn't know which papers belong to which boy, which child is responding and she is at a complete loss trying to distinguish one from the other. In desperation, she finally resorted to pinning nametags on them. But of course, that only made matters worse. They simply switched the nametags.

"She is completely bewildered by the ruse. Their antics are beginning to upset the entire classroom. The other students are following their lead and are beginning to taunt her with pranks of their own. Yesterday, they finally pushed her into a near frenzy. While the other children were outside for recess, Casey snuck back in and hid in the storage closet, next to Sister's desk. She was correcting papers. He cracked the door a pinch and lowered his voice, pretending to be God. Well suffice it to say, the poor thing carried on a five-minute conversation with God, before I happened by and put an end to the sacrilegious performance. Poor Sister Benedetta was so upset that she nearly needed to be sedated."

Katie gasped and her face reddened with embarrassment. If shame were fatal, she would have died, right on the spot.

"Sister, I am so sorry for their behavior. Just when I start thinking that I have anticipated every possible scheme where those two are concerned they surprise me and invent brand new ones. A friend of mine once said that they suffer from a double dose of original sin. I'm afraid I must admit that he's right."

Again, Sister responded with deep laughter. "I've handled the situation here at school. They are being punished with extra assignments and cleaning the chalkboards and erasers. Now that the cat is of out of the bag, so to speak, I believe we'll see a change in their attitude, as well as their behavior. However, I did think it prudent to inform you of their escapades."

"Believe me, Sister, I'm very grateful that you called me. Rest assured, their behavior of the past few weeks will not go unpunished and will definitely not be repeated."

The principal relaxed her posture and sat back in her chair, interlaced her fingers and rested her hands in her lap. She looked Katie and her expression softened.

"I've dealt with children for many years, Mrs. O'Neill. Some brought more joy to my life than others. I have seen more creative mischief than a hundred parents have seen. But, these two rascals of yours come dangerously close to winning the grand prize. You have a couple of real scalawags on your hands. I'll share a secret with you. In my private thoughts, I refer to them as Tom Sawyer and Huckleberry Finn. In spite of their tendency toward tomfoolery, they are two of the happiest, most likable, well-adjusted boys I've seen. Just between you, me and the fence post, when I'm rocking away in my retiring years, remembering this latest antic will probably bring me a great deal of entertainment."

03   80

Katie's day continued its downward spiral. The call from Sister Mary Therese had put her in a mood. In the hopes of turning the day around and salvaging some of it, as long as Katie was in town, she decided she would take advantage of the opportunity and pick up a few items at the market. Halfway down the second aisle, she realized things weren't going to improve. Her shopping cart had a defective front wheel that wobbled and stuck in a sideways position every time she turned a corner.

As Katie fought with the stubborn contraption to turn into paper products, Angie Brisbois hollered from the frozen food section, "I thought I was the only one who ever got that cart. No wonder I lucked out today. You've got it."

"Hi, Angie. This is how my day is determined to be. Frustrating and aggravating."

"You're dressed up pretty fancy for marketing," Angie remarked.

Katie wore a two-piece, green, boucle suit, black heels and green wool tam.

"What's the problem?" Angie maneuvered her cart along side Katie's.

"A call from Sister Mary Therese. The twins." Katie answered and rolled her eyes.

"Should I ask?"

"Unh uh."

Just then, Liz Coughlin spotted them and made a beeline. "Hi Angie. Katie. God am I glad I ran into you, Katie. I'm dying to know what happened between you and Frank Mizzano. After Labor Day weekend, C.J. rambled on in bits and pieces, but I couldn't figure out exactly what had happened. Then Gertie …"

Angie's gossip antennas started to spark. "Frank and Katie! What? I haven't heard anything." She nudged Katie, shopping cart to shopping cart.

Katie gave them both a warning glance. "Nothing happened. I don't know what you're talking about."

"I heard something happened to Vincent and you went over to see Frank." Liz's brown eyes gleamed with curiosity.

"You'd better double-check your sources, Liz." Katie was determined to keep Vincent's and Brendan's confidences.

"Come on, Katie," Angie coaxed, "you're holding something back." She gave her another urgent push with the cart.

"I am not," Katie insisted.

Liz persisted. "And now Frank's going to the AA meetings."

"I always understood that one of those *A*'s stands for *Anonymous*," Katie replied.

Liz laughed. "When someone sees Frank's vegetable truck parked outside Holy Cross on meeting night, it doesn't take a brain surgeon to figure out why he's there. Anyway, I got it first hand from Gertie who got it first hand from Evelyn at the beauty parlor who got it first hand from ......"

"For heaven's sake, Liz. That's like fourth or fifth hand. Hardly reliable. Nothing happened. So drop it. Both of you." Katie's voice took on a tone of finality that the discussion about Frank Mizzano was over.

Angie switched gears faster than an Indy driver. "Speaking of the Color, Cut n' Curl, what's this I heard about Lottie Devereaux and Dr. Franke? You live between her Abraham, Katie. What's going on between those two?"

Katie was legitimately on the dark. "Lottie and Abraham? Nothing that I know of."

"Gertie says ... ..." Angie began.

"Here we go with Gertie, again. That woman gets around more than flu." Katie's aggravation intensified.

"... ... that the two of them were at the last summer concert in the park. Together," Angie related the information as if it were a national secret.

"So what if they were? I'm not saying they were. But even if it were true, what's the harm?" Katie asked.

"We're not saying there's any harm. That's not the point." Angie explained. "What's interesting is that it involves the two of *them*. Dr. Frank*enstein* and the intriguing Madame X."

Katie scolded her. "Angie, I'm ashamed of you. Now I know where the Musketeers get their cruel comments. I think you had better be careful who's listening when you throw around off-hand remarks. People can get hurt. Badly."

"Oh come on, Katie," cajoled Liz. "The people in this town have Lottie Devereaux painted as Mata Hari, the Queen of Sheba and Greta Garbo all rolled into one. And Abraham Franke is secretive, dark and mysterious. The two of them together is very Alfred Hitchcock."

Katie's face suddenly flushed with anger. "I'm disappointed in both of you. If you knew either one of them you'd know they were both kind, generous people who wouldn't raise a hand or word against another human being. Any happiness or comfort they find in each other's company is well deserved. They are dear friends of mine and I won't stand here and listen to you malign them when you know nothing beyond cruel gossip and idle speculation."

Katie left her shopping cart right where it was stalled and stormed away.

After the dressing down that Katie gave them, Angie and Liz exchanged a sheepish look. Like two juveniles trying to push the blame elsewhere, they scolded each other.

"Why did you have to bring up Frank Mizzano?" Angie accused Liz.

"You brought up Lottie Devereaux and Abraham Franke and were just as bitchy as I was and probably more anxious to hear the scoop. Don't pile all the blame into my cart," Liz warned.

"I might as well fill it with blame. There's plenty of room. With your precious C.J. allergic to everything under the sun I don't know why you even bother to market."

With that remark, Angie turned in a huff and left Liz standing there with her gaping mouth as empty as her cart.

☙ ❧

Setting the dinner table was the responsibility of the twins. It was a simple task that they couldn't mess up and Katie felt it was important for them to share in the household chores.

That evening, thinking that their task was completed, they raced through the kitchen to play outdoors until called for dinner. As they ran by their mom, Katie grabbed each by the shirt collar and stopped them in their tracks. Between the visit with Sister Mary Therese and her encounter with Liz and Angie Katie was not in a good mood. And she had all afternoon to plot her strategy.

"Wait a minute, you two. You boys did a nice job, setting the table, but you'll need to add two extra places."

"Mr. Mulholland and Dr. Franke coming to dinner? Miss Lottie?" Colin asked.

"No, we're having extra special guests for dinner tonight." She beamed at them, gritting her teeth, eager to drop the bomb. "I thought it would be nice if we invited Sister Mary Therese and your substitute teacher, Sister Benedetta."

Casey and Colin stood still as statues. They exchanged identical looks of panic. Katie thought to herself that even in a crisis, they responded like mirror images of each other.

It was Casey who recovered the quickest. "How come?"

"I just thought it would be a nice idea. Why, is something wrong? You don't look too happy about the idea."

Colin, failing to come up with anything to say, jabbed Casey with his elbow and urged him to take the lead.

"They can't, Mommy." The gears in Casey's mind were spinning, frantically looking for a plausible excuse. "They gotta eat in the convent. It's a rule. Gotta eat with the rest of the nuns. They can't eat nowhere's else, like reg'lar people." He stopped only long enough to add an essential codicil. "Otherwise, they commit a sin."

Katie looked perplexed. "That's odd. I never heard of that particular sin."

"That's 'cuz it's only a sin for nuns." Casey was finally getting his bearings. As his confidence built, he became bolder with each lie. "Reg'lar people, like us don't know about it."

"If regular people like us don't know about it, then how did you find out about it?" Katie baited them to dig their hole a little deeper.

Colin, bolstered by Casey's creativity, jumped in. "We learned it from one of the older kids ... mmmm ... I think it was Puke ... yeah, it was Puke all right." His head bobbed up and down like a marionette on a string.

"I don't understand this. Sister Mary Therese seemed especially excited about the invitation. She said she couldn't wait to have a nice little talk with me. Why would she want to commit a sin like that?" Katie asked.

Casey quipped, "Prob'ly doesn't care if she sins."

Colin offered his own explanation, "Maybe she just forgot about it." An unbelievably convincing look of innocence masked his face as he shrugged his shoulders, elbows bent, palms turned up.

Katie was having way too much fun with this. "Maybe I'd better call and tell them not to come, remind them of the rule. I wouldn't want them to commit a sin on our account. Saturday's not a school day. Maybe Saturday would be better. Is it a sin for them on Saturdays?"

"That's a way worse sin. They gotta stay in the convent an' pray all day." It was the best Colin could do.

"All day, you say?" Katie asked.

"Yup. Nuns jus' teach an' pray. Everything else is a big fat sin," Casey explained.

Katie arched her right eyebrow. Casey and Colin both knew what that meant.

"Casey Michael and Colin Brian O'Neill! I think this nonsense has gone on long enough. The Sisters aren't coming to dinner. Sister Mary Therese called me to school this morning to discuss your behavior towards Sister Benedetta.

"What you have been doing to that poor nun has been very, very wrong. It was mean and cruel and hurt her feelings. Only bullies tease and make fun of people who can't defend themselves. I hope I haven't raised you two to be bullies. That nonsense stops right now. There will not be any reason for me to be called to school, again about you two, from this point on, for any repeat behavior like that. Do you understand? Have I made myself perfectly clear?"

They both slowly nodded.

"And on top of it, the lying. Both of you stood right there, looked me in the eye and lied. If you two were *Pinocchio*, your noses would be a foot long, by now.

"There are two types of people I don't have any use for, thieves and liars. You two are halfway there, already. I'm ashamed of you both. Besides your shameful behavior at school, now you lie like fishermen. You both know that it's a sin to lie, don't you? That lying hurts you, other people, it hurts me and it hurts Jesus."

The two sinners stood side-by-side, shoulders slumped, heads lowered in shame.

"Do you know what happens to little boys that lie?" Katie asked them both.

Finally Colin answered. "They go straight to hell."

"No, they don't go straight to hell. Although that may be where they belong. They tell enough lies and pretty soon no one ever believes them again. People start to think that if they told so many lies, how could they know when they were telling the truth?"

Katie sat down at the table, so she could talk to them, face to face, on their level. She proceeded to tell them the story of the little shepherd boy who cried "wolf."

"Worse than that people stop believing you, when you lie, other people stop trusting you. And once you lose people's trust it is very hard to earn it back, again."

She doled out their punishments. The first. No playing outside, before or after dinner, for one week. They would have to go straight to their room and play quietly, thinking about what they had done. Secondly, their mom would help them write letters of apology to both Sister Benedetta and Sister Mary Therese. Finally, they would forfeit two weeks allowance, putting it in the poor box at church.

"Mommy," Colin asked, "Are we bad? Bren says we're bad."

She looked at the co-conspirators and her heart was filled with a combination of affection and overpowering exasperation. "Contrary to what Bren says and your most recent behavior, no, *you* aren't bad. I'm not sure that six-year-olds are ever bad. But some of the things you do, like your behavior toward Sister Benedetta, are bad *things*. What is most important is that you learn a lesson from them."

She gave them each a swift swat on the behind. "Now, run off to your room until I call you for dinner."

Katie watched as they scampered off. What a pair! Now, she could understand fully the true meaning of fairies. They were angels that had fallen to earth, not altogether good enough to stay in heaven, but not quite bad enough for the fires of hell, either. And she was blessed with the privilege of raising two of them!

chapter nineteen

Katie thought autumn to be the best of all the seasons.

She loved the intense brilliant colors of fall. Outside, nature was hosting a huge, grand, dress ball. All of the trees were showing off, donned in their full, flowing gowns of magnificent colors, each brighter, more vibrant than the next. It was as if they knew it was their final performance, their last chance to regale the world with their spectacular, lavish displays of color. Before nature stole it all away with winter's stark dormancy. Before nature replaced the crimson and russet, the melon and tangerine, the gold and saffron with winter's lifeless, chalky, achromatic white.

Even the gardens had burst forth with their last valiant efforts to display their finery. Finally, the asters, chrysanthemums, dahlias, gladiolas and hollyhocks all gave birth to their long-awaited rich, colorful blooms.

Autumn was invigorating with its cooler days and chilly nights. Even though Katie loved the fall, she also felt it was a wistful, nostalgic, sentimental time of year. Melancholy and bittersweet, because she so enjoyed it and at the same time regretted it. It ended the glorious, sunny-bright summers and ushered in the long, cold, dark winters.

With the end of summer, Abraham taught Katie about the demands of gardening in the autumn. Spent summer perennials and shrubs needed to be cut back, clipped and pruned; bulbs needed to be dug up, separated, some replanted and some stored in the greenhouse. Used up annuals were dug up and discarded to the compost pile.

They stitched burlap jackets around the vulnerable shrubs to discourage hungry rabbits and deer from feasting on their bark and tender shoots and protecting their delicate branches from winter's heavy ice and snow. Mulch had to be spread to cover and insulate some plantings from frost and frigid temperatures. And of course, as the leaves dropped, beds needed to be raked. There was no immediate gratification to fall gardening. Rewards for all the work, time and toil would have to wait through the long winter months. For Katie, fall gardening wasn't nearly as much fun, but Abraham taught her it was unavoidable and necessary.

It was the last of September. Katie and Lottie were sitting on Lottie's lanai, enjoying one of the few warm evenings that remained before autumn chased them away with its nippy night air. The early Indian summer night was brightened by a harvest moon. Full and bright, low in the sky, it shone clear in a cloudless sky. So clear, that staring at it, they could almost imagine visualizing the features of the legendary Man in the Moon.

The night smelled of autumn. It was an indefinable scent, different from summer. It held the anticipation of change that hinted at the end of hot, sun-warmed days and balmy nights. It was a unique scent, almost more of a sense, subtle, indescribable, and elusive but real, all the same.

"So, Sug, tha Eden Croft gossip grapevine is jus' a hummin' 'bout tha latest news. Seems a hundred-pound, five-foot-two, little ball a fire matched wits with a two-hundred-pound, six-foot-tall, sorry excuse fawr a human bein'."

Katie still hadn't discussed her confrontation with Frank Mizzano with anyone. "It still amazes me how everyone seems to be an expert witness on the subject. I only recall Frank and myself present at this major event."

"In a town this size, Sug, ya can't keep nothin' a secret fawr very long. An' those same reliable sources tell me that someone stuck their hand inta a real hornet's nest. That someone paid a not so sociable call on Fermented Frank Mizzano."

"It's nothing to joke about, Lottie. If you had seen what had happened to Vincent. I want to cry every time I think about the kind of hell that boy has been living in. The drinking was bad enough, but the neglect and abuse. Where were all your reliable sources when that poor boy had to suffer the consequences of Frank's drunken behavior? Someone in this town had to know what was going on. Why didn't someone try to stop it? How could people turn a blind eye to it for so long? Doesn't anybody care what was happening to Vincent? *That* secret seemed to be one that this town had no trouble keeping."

"Sorry, Sug. I don't mean ta be belittlin' tha seriousness of tha situashun. Sometimes it's a case a seein' what ya wanna see, an' what ya don't wanna see stays invisible. Hell, tha whole town knew 'bout his drinkin' an' bad temper. Got in more 'n his share of barroom brawls. But I'm not too sure anybody had any idea how bad things were fawr tha boy. 'Course, people can act mighty peculiar 'bout noses bein' poked inta their business. People think they gotta right ta decide how ta raise their own yunguns. Since humans figured out how ta breed, a whole lotta little folks been raised by lousy mas an' pas."

Katie shook her head and questioned, "How can you defend them? Of all people, you should understand cruelty. Maybe if someone had poked a nose into Wenonah's business things would have turned out differently for you. If the folks in this town had any idea, they had a duty, a moral obligation. Common decency should have forced them to do something about it."

"That's exactly what I'm sayin.' Sug, ya jus' can't go stormin' inta somebody's house an' take their kids. Ya can't go 'round accusin' somebody 'cuz a yawr suspishuns. Suspectin' an' provin' ain't tha same thin'."

"The bruises I saw were more than a suspicion. Well, it's still very hard for me to believe that in a town this size, Frank could keep something like that hidden. The people in Eden Croft are very selective about what they keep secret."

Lottie dismissed the inconsistency with a shrug and forged ahead with the more interesting part of the discussion.

"Anyhow, tha talk is that there's been a vacant bar stool in tha Rest-A-While Tavern ever since a certain concerned citizen paid Frank a visit. He ain't been back since. They're thinkin' a rentin' his favorite stool out permanent. An' Floyd De Shone says he ain't sold him a pint a whiskey since, either. Seems Ol' Frank Mizzano's become a new charter member of the AA. He's dried up like a raisin. All tha gals down at tha Color, Cut an' Curl say he's been sober ever since Hurricane Katie struck. Y'all must ta put tha fear a God inta him. Don't know what ya said ta him, Sug, but I'd a sure like ta have been a fly on tha wall ta witness that confrontashun."

"I guess you could say that I threatened him. Maybe not very Christian of me but it sounds like maybe he re-evaluated his life. Anyway, I'm not talking about it anymore. Let the gossipmongers beat it to death. I made a promise to Brendan, and I guess, in a way, a promise to Vincent. I intend to keep that promise."

"Sug, sometimes y'all jus` plum knock all tha pleasure outta tha most interestin' discushuns."

Katie changed the subject. "Here's a discussion for you. Tell me all about this monumental date you had with Abraham. I spent most of the afternoon with him. And he was typically Abraham, close-mouthed as usual. It was like trying to squeeze blood out of a turnip. I finally gave up on him. Now, I'm dying to hear every intimate detail. Don't leave out a single thing."

"Yawr practically salivatin', Sug. It'd serve ya right if I wuz ta pull one a yawr tricks an' clam right up. But since it wasn't even a real date, I guess I kin fill ya in."

Katie looked at her, skeptically. "What do you mean not a real date? He took you out for dinner, didn't he? I know you didn't cook him dinner last night, because he's still alive. Where'd he take you for dinner? Don't tell me you ate at Collier's? Pretty fancy digs."

"We took a little drive ta Clearwater, ate at a restaurant there ta avoid jus' this kind a gossip from gettin' started."

"Dinner … out of town … sounds more and more like a date to me. What else did you two do?"

"Went ta tha picture show, there. An' I'm gettin' tired a repeatin' myself, I'm tellin' ya, it wasn't a date. Jus' two friends out fawr a change a scenery."

"Whoa, the movies, too." Katie counted on her fingers. "A drive in the country ... dinner ... a movie. I hope to tell you, Lottie, you two were definitely on a date." She giggled, mischievously.

"Yawr a worse gossip than Gertie Hoffmeyer down at tha A&P. Tha Hedda Hopper of Eden Croft, I tell ya what. Tha day that Lottie Devereaux needs ta settle fawr a date with an ol', broken down, stick-in-tha-mud like Abraham Franke is tha day I hang up ma girdle an' garter belt fawr good."

"Oh, come on, Lottie, you get him out of those ratty old gardening clothes of his, dress him up, use a little spit and polish and Abraham could be quite nice looking. Rather distinguished, I might add."

"Well ... I guess tha whole evenin' was a might better than a poke in tha eye with a hot stick ... still ... I ..." Lottie stumbled a bit, looking for the right words.

"Well, cut off my legs and call me shorty ..." Katie stopped herself. "Lord, I've been around you way too much. I'm beginning to talk like you. I'm just so shocked, I couldn't help myself. Lottie, never, in all the time I've known you, through all the gab sessions we've had, under the influence or not, have I ever seen you at a loss for words. This is truly a momentous occasion ... it's high time ..."

Suddenly, Katie realized what time it must be. She had completely forgotten about bedtime for the boys. She jumped up and pointed her index finger at Lottie. "Hold it right, there, Lottie. Don't you dare go anywhere. Don't you move a muscle. I've got to run home and get the boys settled into bed. I'll be back before you can say 'Jiminy Cricket'. Jeez Louise, you really are starting to rub off on me."

Katie mumbled to herself as she ran off toward the house, "Darn, just when the conversation was really getting interesting!"

A few minutes later, Lottie was sipping her martini grateful for the interruption from Katie's interrogation when she was startled by an angry shout.

"Where is she, Lottie? Where in the hell is she?"

Lottie jumped and sloshed her drink down the front of her blouse.

"Christ's creepers! Yawr crazier than an outhouse rat! You'd like ta scared me ta death! Caused me ta spill half a ma martini on ma brand new, fifty-dollar silk blouse."

Matt stood on the edge of the lanai. "I'll buy you a new silk blouse. Damn, I'll buy you ten!" he shouted.

"Have ya taken leave a yawr senses?"

"I'm in complete control of my goddamn senses. She's the one that isn't. You'd better tell me where the hell she is. I've never been angrier in my life than I am with her, right now."

"If tha her an' tha she y'all been referrin' ta is Katie, she ain't here." Lottie tried to defuse him.

"Dammit. I want to know where the hell that willful, stubborn, crazy woman is. I stopped at her house and Brendan told me she was over here. She probably ran for cover when she heard me coming. I'd like to wring her pretty little neck. If you don't get her out here, I'm going in after her and I won't be held responsible for any damages your furniture may suffer."

Matt was paced angrily, trying to burn off some of his anger.

"Now ain't ya'll been like two ships passin' in tha night. If y'all would stop jumpin' 'round like a fart in a mitten I'll tell ya. She went on home a few minutes ago, prob'ly jus' after ya left there ta come over here." Lottie chuckled through a sip of her martini. "Y'all kinda remind me of an Abbott an' Costello movie.

"'Course, it took ya long 'nough ta finally pay her a visit. Yawr slower than tha second comin' a Christ, I tell ya what. She tells me she ain't seen or heard from ya in weeks. Now, when ya finally do show up, ya come rantin' an' ravin' like a lunatic. If y'all don't settle down, yawr gonna go off half-cocked, creatin' a real clusterfuck an' spoil what could be a real heartwarmin' reunion."

Still pacing and still just as angry, Matt shouted back at her, "The only thing that's gone off half-cocked is *her*. And you … you're supposed to be her best friend. Why the hell didn't you stop her? I wouldn't have expected her to listen to me, but you, what the hell was wrong with you? Jesus H. Christ, I'm so damn mad I could spit nickels."

Matt struck his fist down on the glass tabletop, threatening to crack it right down the muddle. "Goddammit! I swear, if she were here right now … I'm so pissed off at her, I could strangle her with my bare hands …"

His tirade was cut short.

"What, in the name of Heaven is going on, here? I could hear you shouting and cursing half the way to my house. Who do you want to strangle with your bare hands? It wouldn't be me, would it? Brendan said you stopped by the house, looking for me."

Matt spun around. "What in the name of Christ were you thinking of? It's painfully clear you weren't thinking at all. Do you have any idea what that drunken son-of-a-bitch could have done to you?"

Katie advanced into the line of fire and stood nearly on top of him. "I would appreciate it if you would stop cursing and screaming at me. I think you'll find most people are much more willing to listen when they're not being bullied and sworn at. And who died and left you in charge of the universe? Who gave you the right to become my keeper? Telling me what I can and can't do?" She steeled herself with chin raised defiantly, hands on her hips.

Matt asked, "Lottie, would you mind giving us some privacy while I try to talk some sense into this lunatic?" He never took his eyes off Katie.

"Don't you dare give him the satisfaction, Lottie. If he thinks he can threaten us, order us around, he's got another think coming. Who's being a brute now? You stay right where you are, Lottie. I don't need any privacy to tell him exactly what I think of his less than gentleman-like behavior."

Lottie stood, took her pitcher of martinis and started for the door. "I'm a whole lot smarter than allowin' maself ta get caught in tha middle a this row. An' as much as I enjoy bein' entertained by tha lightenin' an' sparks out here, I think I'll jus' take ma martini inside an' use my imaginashun ta conjure up ma own endin' ta this friendly tete a tete.

"Call it woman's intuishun, but I got a hunch that 'they lived happily ever after' may not be a fittin' endin'. There ain't gonna be a program on ma brand new Crosley televishun set that's gonna be near as entertainin' as this." She lifted her martini glass in a toast. "Here's ta tha finish. May tha best, stubborn jackass win."

When Lottie left, Matt resisted the urge to grab Katie by the shoulders and shake some sense into her. "Do you have any idea how dangerous that cretin can be when he's been drinking? He's like a powder keg on a short fuse. Sober, Frank can be mean. Drunk, he can be plain dangerous. He's been in more bar fights than a marine. What ever took possession of your senses? What made you think you should go over there … alone? It scares me to death when I think of what could have happened to you."

"And it scared me to death thinking of what it must have been like for Vincent living with that same unstable man. I couldn't stand idly by and let it continue to go on. I had to do something. So, I did. Besides, nothing horrible happened. He didn't touch a hair on my head. And as long as we're pointing critical fingers, if you knew what behavior he was capable of, why didn't you step in and do something?"

"Me? How is any of this my fault?"

"If you knew he stumbled home drunk half the time, neglected his own son, why didn't you do something to protect Vincent? To help that boy?"

"Because I never knew what when on in that house. A lot of people drink. A lot of people are drunks. And a lot of them raise children. Vincent wasn't starving or running around naked. He had food on the table and a roof over his head."

"So if someone throws verbal insults and beer bottles in a drunken stupor as long as there's food in the refrigerator it's okay with everybody!"

"Katie, you're preaching to the choir. I'm telling you that no one knew what was happening *inside* the Mizzano house. Sometimes Sheriff Guzy would throw the bastard into the slammer for drunk and disorderly ... or a bar brawl. I never thought it was anything more than that. I never had any idea things were that bad for Vincent. If I had, I would have kicked Frank's ass up to his head a long time ago. You had no business confronting him on your own. Why didn't you call me? I would have gone over there and tried knocking some sense into his Neanderthal-thick skull."

"Oh, that would have been a more effective solution. Letting cooler heads prevail." Katie's words dripped with sarcasm. "You men, you think that every crisis can be settled with fists. Control violence with violence. Having both of you end up in the hospital would have really helped Vincent. And, it never occurred to me, that calling you was an option. What makes you think that I would have considered calling you? That you are my knight in shining armor? You've been avoiding me for weeks. Not a word."

Matt defended himself. "It's been exactly six weeks, three days and twenty-two hours. Forgive me, I've lost track of the minutes and seconds. Me? Avoiding you? Don't make me out to be the bad guy in all this. You were the one who proclaimed the need for some distance, to quote you, 'some time to sort things out.'"

Katie shouted back, "You certainly blew that way out of proportion. I asked for some time, not an eternity. And what about Brendan? He wonders why you haven't come around to see him? You're the one who got him all fired up about sailing. Now he feels like you only used him to get closer to ... he's confused enough by our friendship ... or relationship ... or whatever you want to call it."

Matt's voice began to soften. "Look, I'm sorry. I'm sorry I've behaved like a heartbroken school kid. You're right. I have been avoiding you. You know, I'm not used to having my ego bruised and my declarations of affection so casually rebuffed. Am I allowed one mistake? Well, two, actually. I'm sorry if I've hurt Brendan. I didn't mean for any of this to spill over onto him. I promise I'll make it up to him."

The tension between them started to abate.

"Matt, I really have missed you. I've missed having you around. I've missed the companionship. I've missed our time together. I never meant for you to drop completely out of my life. Can we find some kind of neutral ground? Halfway between a love affair and killing each other? Since I last saw you, I've run the gambit from confusion, to uncertainty, to regret. I'm not sure if it's possible, but I guess I want everything to go back to the way it was. Can we at least try? See where it all takes us?"

Matt took his arms and wrapped them around the tiny creature that had completely captured his heart. "If you can forgive a selfish and insensitive jerk, I promise you, I'll stop acting like a complete ass. On one condition. You'll have to promise me that you'll stop acting like your indestructible. No more valiant crusades against foes twice your size."

Katie placed her hands on Matt's shoulders and brushed his cheek with a light kiss. "It's a deal. Sealed with a kiss. We can start right now. How about walking a lady home?"

ᓂ ᔡ

"Mom! Phone call! Long distance! Person-to-person!" Bren hollered to the upstairs bathroom where Katie was taking her evening bath.

Long distance, person-to-person telephone calls were as rare and expensive as telegrams. The third thing they had in common was that they usually carried bad news.

"Darn! Long distance! I wonder who died?" Katie exclaimed to herself as she stepped out of the tub, threw on her robe and dripped all the way down the stairs.

Brendan was neither impressed nor concerned about a long distance telephone call. He tossed the receiver at Katie like a discarded a banana peel. Throwing an accusatory glance at Bren, she bobbled the hand piece.

"Yes? Speaking. Yes, Operator, I'll hold for her." Katie was so excited she nearly wet herself.

When the call was put through, Katie squealed into the phone, "Dee! I can't believe it's you!"

"Well, believe it. Moira's here, too. We're sharing the receiver." Moira yelled into the angled mouthpiece, "Hello, Katie!"

"Hello, Moira! Geez, you two! Who died?"

"What do you mean, who died?" Dee asked.

"Who died and left you the money to pay for this telephone call?"

"Nobody died and left us any money. We don't have any rich old aunts, like you," Moira answered.

"That's not funny and Aunt Katherine was far from rich."

"We pooled what was left over from our grocery money. Been saving for a month. So stop wasting our nickels and tell us how you've been," Dee ordered.

"Fine. Everything is fine."

"You better come up with something better than fine. Fine is for letters," Dee told her.

"Great. Wonderful. Stupendous. The boys are great and so am I. I have to beat the suitors off with a stick."

Moira squealed into the phone, "Really! Katie, are you seeing someone? Tell me all about him? Everything. Don't leave out a single detail. Is it that rich lawyer you wrote us about?"

"Can it, Moira. If you'd give Katie a chance to talk maybe we'd learn something."

"Yes. It's the lawyer. But, right now, we're no more than friends. I'm taking my time and so is he. We're not starry-eyed teenagers."

"Good for you, Katie. Don't go diving into the pool before you know there's water in it."

"Don't listen to Dee, Katie. Listen to me. You're not getting any younger. Tell me, has he pledged his undying love to you. Please tell me you haven't scared him off by rebuffing his advances. Don't destroy my romantic fantasies of him making passionate love to you by a moonlit lake, nothing covering you but his gorgeous, hot body and a blanket of stars."

"Stop that! Be careful how you talk over the telephone. Someone could overhear this."

"Yeah, Katie. That's the highlight of every operator's life to wait for an obscene telephone call from Dee Sullivan and Moira Monahan to Katie O'Neill," Dee teased.

"It would take me two weeks to explain everything. And you'd be bored to tears. Tell me about Boston. Dee, how are Mike and the kids?"

"We're still married. The kids are driving both of us crazy. Seven Sullivan's living under one roof is more than two decent people like Mike and I should have to put up with. When his mother moved in that should have nailed the last brad in our coffin. Mike and I are either too shell-shocked or too stupid to run away."

"Details, Dee."

"Okay, here are the details. Mother Sullivan and I haven't spoken a civil word to one another in a week. Tony needs braces, so those will eat up Mike's raise this year. Maggie finally got her period and is in the throes of puberty. So one week out of the month we all walk on eggshells. Patrick fell off his bicycle and broke his collarbone trying to set a new speed record. Rosy can't seem to master *Dick and Jane*. And Brian turned the bathroom walls into a Crayola masterpiece. How are those details?"

"Sorry I asked. What about the neighborhood?"

"Here's a real shocker for you. Myrtle O'Malley was thrown out as treasurer of the PTA. There's some talk about improprieties and missing funds. It's the talk of the neighborhood. Guess whose lap they dumped that mess into? Since Mike's an accountant they figured I must have soaked up some of his expertise. So, he's been trying to help me balance the books."

Dee continued, "The Flattery boys are in trouble, again. They used Mrs. Sweeney's cat for target practice and shot out its left eye with their BB guns. Now, poor Clancy is short one eye to go along with his missing back leg. That cat has more than *nine* lives. That's the bad news, but here's the good news. The Bishop just announced that Father Ganlon is being elevated to Monsignor. St. Dennis' finally has a Monsignor as pastor and it's about ten years past due."

"That's wonderful. I always loved Father Ganlon. He deserves the promotion. Moira. How are things with you?"

"Fabulous. Jerry and I are still like two kids on their honeymoon."

Dee choked out, "Gag me while you're at it."

"Jerry was just voted in as Grand Knight of the Knights of Columbus."

"We're all invited to the Vatican with them when Jerry has his private audience with the Pope," Dee joked.

Moira ignored the jab and continued. "I'm redecorating the kitchen in turquoise and peach. The fabric for the curtains is a calico print and I just finished sewing them. Jerry is hanging them this weekend.

"The children are doing fabulous. Mary Elizabeth has the lead in the autumn play. They're doing *I Remember Mama*. She is just so beautiful, Katie. You wouldn't believe how grown up she is. A little lady and so talented! She's going to break more than a few hearts at St. Dennis', believe me. But, she still has a terrible crush on Brendan. She asks about him every time I receive one of your letters. Tony and Kevin are both great. Tony's life still evolves around baseball and Kevin is bound and determined to follow in his footsteps. They drive Mary Elizabeth crazy every chance they get."

"Enough from Shangri-La, Moira. That's about all the blarney I can stand. See what you left me with, Katie? I'm stuck here in Boston with her and nobody to give me any relief."

"I love your letters, but they don't compare to hearing your voices. It's like we're sixteen again, sitting on Dee's porch swing."

"Talking about school and boys and the homecoming dance," Moira added.

Katie reminisced, "Dee, do you remember when Ralph Zeek asked you to the dance and your mom made you go because she didn't think anyone else would ask you."

"God, Ralph the geek Zeek. Ears that stuck out like Dumbo, glasses thick as a petrie dish, handsome as Jimmy Durante and a pencil protector in his shirt pocket. What a catch he was."

Moira joined in the memory, "He weighed about ninety pounds and was six inches shorter than you. And gave you a huge chrysanthemum corsage that covered half your chest."

"I'd forgotten the corsage. But I haven't forgotten the dance. Poor Ralph didn't know that Dean Flattery and Warren Seaver had spiked the punch and he drank like a gallon of it. He was so drunk he tripped on his own feet and spilled punch all over your new outfit." Katie laughed. "I wonder what ever happened to him?"

"He probably married one of his lab experiments, conceived his offspring in a test tube and has a dozen little runts running around just like him. What ever made you think of him?" Dee asked.

"I don't know. He simply popped into my head. I guess talking to you two has stirred up a lot of old memories."

"Now, you sound like Moira. Don't go getting all-maudlin on me. We didn't call to get all weepy and sappy."

Moira argued, "I love weepy and sappy."

"I received all the school pictures in your last letters. Moira you're right. Mary Elizabeth is beautiful. As soon as I get the boys' pictures back from school I'll send them along. When am I going to see the two of you in person? I'd love to have you come out and spend a week or two."

"That sounds like another one of Moira's fantasies that's never going to happen. Who would take care of Mike and the tribe while I'm off an a carefree holiday?"

"Mother Sullivan could fill in for a few days. She raised nine children of her own. Your five would be like a vacation for her."

"And give her more ammunition to use against me? I've never been her first choice of a wife for Mike and a mother to her grandchildren. Criticizing me seems to be her sole ambition in life. I think it's what keeps her alive. A little adventure like that and I'd forever be her wayward daughter-in-law. She'd slander me to the whole neighborhood that I'm a lousy wife and an unfit mother."

"So make it a family vacation. You could all come out. There's plenty of room."

"Well, when I find the pot of gold at the end of the rainbow, we just might take you up on your offer."

"Since Dee has about a million excuses, how about you, Moira? Next summer? You could take the train out. Jerry and the kids would love the lake. Brendan would get to see Tony," Katie tempted her.

"Oh, gosh, Katie. That sounds wonderful. I'll talk it over with Jerry."

"Promise me that you'll both think about it. The boys would love to see all the kids again. Brendan really misses Tony. And Mary Elizabeth, of course. The door of hospitality is always open."

Dee wound up the call. "I hate to always be the one to throw the damper on things, but we had better wind this up or it will take us another month to pay for the rest of this call. Give our love to the boys, Katie."

"I will. And mine to Mike and the kids and Mother Sullivan."

Moira's voice broke. "Dozens of hugs and tons of kisses, Katie. I love you. And miss you."

"Bye, Moira. I miss you."

"Bye Katie. Don't do anything I wouldn't do," Dee ordered.

"Bye Dee. Miss you, too."

Moira had one last sentiment. "Blow a kiss to Matt for me."

"Bye yourself. Love both of you bunches."

The line disconnected. Katie replaced the receiver and realized that tears were flowing down her cheeks. She sat on the sofa and clutched a toss pillow to her breast. She visualized her two oldest friends and her heart ached for them. Thinking of Dee and Moira and what they had meant to each other through the years rekindled a flood of memories. They had giggled their way through childhood and dreamed together through their teens. They had become so close they could finish each other's sentences. Katie considered friends the most precious treasures a person could have, more precious than a good marriage or perfect children.

Tommy had wandered into the room and stood next to his mom when he saw she was crying. "What's the matter, Mommy?" he asked. "Did something bad happen?"

"Nothing's wrong, Tommy." Katie could barely force the words past the lump in her throat. "Nothing bad happened."

"Then how come you're crying? Are you sad?"

Katie wrapped him in her arms and gave him a squeeze. "Nothing is wrong. Sometimes mommies cry when they're sad and sometimes when they're happy."

"Are you sad or happy."

"Right, now Mommie's a little of both."

chapter twenty

It was Lottie's birthday. The specifics of which she never shared a lot of details.

Katie tried to do the math. "If you were in your teens before the Depression hit. 1927 … minus sixteen … give or take a year … that puts your birthday somewhere around …"

"Never you mind, Sug. Let's jus' say yawr 'rithmetic's close 'nough."

Abraham planned cake, ice cream and cocktails at his place to celebrate the event. Matt was due to pick Katie up at seven and they were going to walk over to Abraham's together. Colin woke up sick that morning and Katie had tried unsuccessfully to reach Matt all day to cancel. When Matt arrived, Katie answered the door in a housedress and black galoshes. A rubber plunger hung from one hand. Matt wouldn't have cared if she wore greasy coveralls and combat boots, but it wasn't an outfit he expected Katie to wear to Lottie's birthday celebration.

"I tried telephoning you all day but couldn't reach you," Katie explained.

"I took Scattering out for her last sail of the season. Then Toby Grisham and I spent the rest of the day at the marina putting her in dry dock. I was only home long enough to shower and shave." Matt's face was rosy and wind burnt.

"Colin's sick. He must have caught a bug because he's been vomiting and had diarrhea all day. Now, he's running a temperature. The toilet is plugged. Either he used a whole roll of toilet tissue or Casey launched some object down the upstairs toilet to explore the plumbing." Katie waved the plunger. "I just spent an hour plunging."

Matt took an evasive step backward. He nearly gagged. "Now that is one of my top ten most favorite fantasies."

Katie smirked. "Don't worry. I won't conscript you. I got it unplugged. Now I have to mop up the mess. I'm going to have to cancel on Lottie's party, though. Why don't you go on without me? Make my apologies to Lottie and Abraham."

Matt thought it over. "No. I'll just go home and pout about the long winter months ahead and Scattering sitting up on blocks all cold and lonely. Besides, three's a crowd."

"Lottie and Abraham will be disappointed if neither of us shows up. You should go," Katie tried to convince him.

"I think Lottie and Abraham will be perfectly happy to celebrate with only the two of them," Matt replied.

Katie's eyes lit up. "Do you really think so? Do you think there's more than friendship developing between them?"

Matt threw up his palms. "How would I know? Abraham doesn't exactly wear his emotions on his sleeve. He's harder to read than the small print on a contract. You and Lottie are thick as thieves. What's she say?"

"Every time I bring up the subject she gets all huffy and tells me to butt out and mind my own business. Those aren't exactly her words. Out of decency I've paraphrased."

"Me thinks she dost protest too much?"

"Do you really think so, Matt? I hadn't thought of that. You're right! It's so obvious now."

"Hey! Hold on a second, Cupid. Put your arrows back in the quiver and don't be buying a new dress for the wedding, yet. I'm only saying that maybe they'll enjoy the evening more without feeling like they have to entertain me. I probably won't be missed. I think they're learning to enjoy each other's company. That's a far cry from wedding bells."

Katie was deflated. "Still, why don't you at least stop by before you go home and give Lottie a birthday hug and kiss?"

"That'll work," Matt agreed. "And I think I'd better vacate the premises before you throw a pair of rubber gloves on me and put me to work."

He gave Katie a quick kiss not wanting to risk contact with the plunger.

"I'll call you tomorrow. Tell Colin I hope he's feeling better and that only the good die young." Matt turned to leave.

"You're living proof of that." Katie couldn't resist. "Give Lottie and Abraham my love."

CB ED

It was one of the last, bright days of autumn and Katie and Abraham were taking advantage of the crisp fall weather. It had rained so hard and steadily for the past five days, that Katie had contemplated the possibility that they might all float away. But, finally, the sun broke through and the skies over Eden Lake were the color of bluebells. Both the air and the lake were calm but there was a definite nip in the air.

After being kept restlessly indoors by the rain, the boys were outside burning their pent up energy. Brendan, Tommy and the Musketeers were fishing off the end of the dock, although messing around off the end of the dock probably was a more accurate description. Katie was sure that sooner or later one of them would end up falling into the chilly waters. It would be the last day before they would have to bring the dock in for the winter. Chance, who shadowed Tommy wherever he went, sat faithfully and vigilantly along-side him, the sun glistening off his shiny chestnut coat.

The twins buzzed around the yard like gnats. They were playing *Flash Gordon*, complete with towels, secured with safety pins for capes, black galoshes for space boots and water pistols for ray guns. For space helmets, Casey had tied an aluminum colander to his head and Colin wore his mother's white bathing cap.

Katie and Abraham were working in one of the flowerbeds. Studying the rich, black soil for the last time before winter, Katie remarked, "Abraham. I finally understand what you have tried to teach me about the garden and working with nature. You can't truly understand life until you've felt the earth between your fingers. In the smallest and simplest things of nature I find something new and wonderful."

On his knees next to Katie, he stopped working and leaned back on his heels. "It is a gift to understand and appreciate it as you do. Not everyone feels that. Certainly, a great many of my students do not."

Katie laughed. "Their loss, Abraham."

"Do you know what I think you should do? I think that you should take one of my classes. Now that the fall term is in session and the boys have retuned to their classrooms, you could easily fit one into your schedule."

Katie thought about it for a moment. "Oh, Abraham." She shook her head. "I couldn't. I wouldn't have the nerve. I haven't been in a classroom in fifteen years. School is for the young. Besides. I don't know that I could afford it. College must be very expensive."

"It would cost you nothing." Abraham tried to persuade her.

"That is very generous of you, Abraham, but I couldn't ask you to allow me to go for free when all the others have to pay."

"It is called auditing, Katie. You attend a few sessions of the class to decide if it is a subject you would be interested in. There is no obligation involved. Auditing is available to anyone," Abraham explained

"But I'd be like a fish out of water. I'd feel too out of place."

"It will hurt nothing to think it over. Give it some thought and if you change your mind I will make the arrangements."

"I'll think about it. That's all I'll promise. Is there some sort of deadline for this auditing? Would I have to make up my mind right away? There must be rules about that sort of thing."

Abraham came as close to a smile as Katie had ever seen. "I am head of the department," Abraham stated. "I may do anything I want."

When the bed was finished, Katie decided it was time for a break. With smudged faces and muddy hands, they escaped to Abraham's cottage to clean up and enjoy a steaming cup of tea. She had only been in the cottage a few times, and only then, for a brief moment or two. Abraham could be painfully private.

Besides the small vestibule, the cottage consisted of two rooms and a bath. The kitchen-dining-living areas all flowed together, each area designated by the positioning of furniture. The bedroom was the only other room. The furniture was typically cottage style, warm woods in the dining area and overstuffed upholstery in the living area. Honey-pine end tables and braided rugs pulled the whole look together.

While the tea was brewing, Abraham coaxed a welcomed fire to life in the fireplace. Katie sat in an easy chair next to it, to warm her chills away. She surveyed the living room.

It was small, warm and cozy. Mellowed, knotty pine tongue-and-groove covered all the walls. Smooth river rocks of random shapes and colors formed the fireplace and chimney. Bookshelves, on either side of the fireplace, were filled with volumes. Katie read their worn leather spines. She recognized many of the classics, Stevenson, Hawthorne, Melville and Austen. There were random texts on botany and gardening. Some of the titles were in a language foreign and indecipherable. Katie assumed they were German, Abraham's native language.

Though the room was comfortable and inviting, Katie noticed that there were no photographs, pictures or any personal objects. Not a knick-knack, keepsake or memento anywhere. The only item of distinction was an oil painting. It was a beautiful study in warm, muted tones. It had a haunting quality that evoked a sense of solitude, isolation and aloneness, yet still conveyed the feeling of peace.

The subject of the painting was a man in worn sweater, gray hatless head and trousers and knee-high Wellington's, tending a bed of flowers. His face was in profile, but Katie was sure who the subject was. She was just as certain of the artist. The style, form and technique were unmistakable. She didn't need the affirmation, but in the lower right hand corner of the painting was the familiar signature, a sweeping *K*.

Reading her thoughts, Abraham interrupted her musing. "She painted that without my permission. At first, when I saw it, I was angry with her for the intrusion. Then, after seeing it through her eyes, I came to appreciate the vision and perception she possessed.

"For her, painting was a compelling need to translate to canvas those perceptions and visions. Katherine had a magnificent gift for introspection. Her true genius was her ability to see beyond the physical, to see into the soul, the spirituality, the essence of the person. Through the strokes of her brush, she told the story of what she saw. A biographical revelation, a symphony, not with words or notes but with her brush and paints.

"Besides her friendship, her gift to me was that painting. She promised that it would never be shown publicly and until today, you and Loretta are the only other persons who have ever seen it. Ironically, it was the last painting she would do."

Abraham's eyes misted. His passionate recollections were filled with admiration and obvious affection for Aunt Katherine. Katie was somewhat saddened by the thought that time and circumstance had robbed her of the opportunity to know Aunt Katherine as Abraham had.

"I can only imagine the closeness you shared with Aunt Katherine. Until you shared with me your insight, I never knew her. You have revealed a beautiful and poignant side to her that few others saw. I now know what an exceptional person she must have been. I'm grateful to you. You've brought her back to life for me."

Abraham poured the tea and reached to hand Katie a cup. His sweater sleeve pulled up and revealed the upper part of his wrist. Katie noticed, for the first time, a series of numbers tattooed in his skin. She was intrigued.

Pointing to his wrist, she questioned him. "Abraham, what do those numbers mean?"

Abraham's face registered anguish, and at the same time anger, as her question aroused the smoldering embers of emotions to flame and burn. Time seemed to stop and Katie began to think that Abraham was not going to respond. Then his quiet voice broke the tension.

"They are the mark of treachery. They are burned into my flash to serve as a permanent reminder of people, a time and a life that are dead to me. That existence has been violated, annihilated, erased. This mark is all that remains … the only proof that any of it ever existed."

Katie was shocked by the utter desolation and hatred that filled his words. It was a frightening, unsettling side of him that she had never seen before.

"I have never heard you speak one word about your past. It is as if you were suddenly transported here, without a past, without a history. And never have I heard you speak with such contempt and despair."

Abraham stared thoughtfully into the fire, as if he were searching the flames for a response. It had been a long time since he had shared his past secrets with anyone. Katherine and Sean Donovan were the only people he had ever allowed into his private world of bitterness, loathing and pain. He settled into the chair opposite Katie. Suddenly he realized a feeling of trust in her. Katie had the ability to elicit confidences. It was because she had asked nothing of him, hadn't pried, that Abraham began his story.

Zora and Abraham Franke had married later in life. Both had been born into well-to-do Jewish families. Abraham had attended university and was a professor of horticulture at Ruprecht-Karls-Universitat in *Heidelberg* where he met, courted and married Zora. After numerous miscarriages, it was several years later when Zora was able to successfully carry a child to term. After a long and difficult labor and delivery, a son, Daniel Isaac Franke was born, robust and healthy. Due to the strains of pregnancy and the ravages her body suffered from a stressful labor and difficult birth, the doctors advised against any more children.

The proud parents were undaunted by the knowledge that no more children were to follow. The Lord had blessed them with Daniel, and that was blessing enough. He was a beautiful, bright, active child with a warm and easy disposition. The doting parents had focused all their parental affection, attention and love, lavishing them on their one, bright, shining star.

In many ways, Daniel was a great deal like Tommy. Not in physical appearance. Daniel had been as dark as Tommy was fair. But, they were very much alike in spirit. Perhaps that was why Abraham had developed such closeness with Tommy. He saw in Tommy all the wondrous innocence and beautiful goodness he had seen in Daniel.

So, totally engrossed and contented, wrapped up their perfect world, they were unconcerned and unaware of the cloud of doom that was taking shape on the horizon.

At first, there were small, subtle changes. Many, as did Abraham, discarded them as simply rumor. Gradually, the threat grew until it reached its greedy claws, endangering the fragile safety of their world. Then, the monster grew bolder. Like a serpent, it had slithered in silently, undetected, until its venom finally spewed forth in carnage.

Abraham and Zora had ignored the early warning signs. While many German-Jews were emigrating from *Germany*, being forced out by the anti-Semitism that was being touted by the Nazi regime, they remained, with the naive hopes that the tide would turn before it had the chance to wash away the foundation of their existence. Stubbornly, Abraham still refused to be driven from their homeland.

In November of 1938, they still failed to recognize the signs that would be the beginning of the end. The "night of the broken glass" served as a signal to most German Jews that leaving their homeland was inevitable. That night, all synagogues in *Germany* were set on fire, windows of Jewish shops were smashed and thousands of Jews arrested. Still not convinced of the dangers, the

Franke family remained in *Germany*, unknowingly to face an uncertain fate. Near the end of the decade, the Third Reich had introduced into the vocabulary of *Germany*, the evil term "Aryanization," complete with its poison and prejudice.

By the fall of 1941, all German Jews were marked with a yellow Star of David, to identify them as non-Aryan. Two weeks into November, the Franke's were paid a midnight visit by the Gestapo. Rousted from their beds, the emigration that Abraham and Zora had refused to take part in, the Nazi's forced upon them. However, this emigration would not be to the safety of an unoccupied country.

It was known as the "final solution." A monster by the name of Hermann Goering ordered a final solution to the Jewish question. That order would give birth to one of the most horrific, fiendish, demonic acts that man has ever conceived against his fellow man.

Zora and young Daniel were separated from Abraham. It would be more than four, tormenting years before Abraham would learn of their fate. For all those years, and every moment of every day for the rest of his life, he was condemned to be haunted by the last memory of their confused and desperate faces. Faces frozen in fear, eyes reflecting terror, looking to him for strength and salvation, while he stood by passively, inert, weak, betraying their confidence and trust.

Abraham was transported by train to a detention camp in *Buchenwald* near *Weimar, Germany*. There, he was marked, tattooed, stripped of his identity, his worth reduced to numbers. One of the camp's junior officers learned of Abraham's education and field of study and devised a brilliant plan. He was convinced that his plan would reflect favorably on him to his superiors, bringing him recognition, perhaps a promotion, maybe even a field command.

Polluting the beautiful countryside near *Berchtesgarden*, the Nazi party had designed and constructed a fabulous, palatial residence in the Bavarian Alps. They presented the surprise birthday present to their leader, Adolph Hitler. It was a name that brought such hatred and bitterness, that Abraham was barely able to utter the words. The wolf's den, ironically, would be profanely misnamed the *Eagle's Nest*. It was here that Commandant Herkimer suggested to his superiors that Abraham be used to design, oversee and manage the landscape and gardens around the residence. Guaranteeing Abraham that his wife and child would not be harmed they insured his cooperation.

Abraham guffawed with mockery. All of their efforts had been in vain. In the three years Abraham spent at the Kelsteinhaus, he saw the deranged madman, the villain, the butcher, only once, surrounded, insulated, protected by his henchmen. Ironically, Hitler would never be able to enjoy the beautiful surroundings. Their great, invincible, omnipotent Fuhrer was afraid of heights. That was the only satisfaction Abraham had drawn from his unholy pact with the Nazis, and his stupid, naive belief that his cooperation was providing protection for his family.

Liberation for Abraham came on April 15, 1945. With the Allied occupation of *Germany*, Abraham was finally released.

Post-war Europe, especially *Germany*, was in ruin. The displaced tried in vain to pick up the pieces of their shattered lives. The Franke family wealth and properties had been confiscated, destroyed or lost. Penniless and desperate, Abraham began the paramount task of locating Zora and Daniel. It wasn't until the end of 1945, with the help of government agencies and friends that Abraham learned of their fate. It wasn't until then that Abraham, along with the entire world, would begin to comprehend the unimaginable, to believe the unbelievable. How could human beings develop such a hatred for their fellow man to conceive, authorize and justify such atrocities and horrors?

Zora and Daniel had been herded, like cattle, onto a train and transported to a Jewish ghetto in *Poland*. When learning of the carnage of the "final solution," it was inconceivable to Abraham that they survived as long as they did. Many died of sickness and starvation before ever reaching the concentration camps. From the ghetto they were taken to the death camp, *Belzec*, where they, along with 600,000 other Jews were gassed. Innocent souls, who had committed no crimes, no wrongs, had broken no laws, except that of being born Jews. They were exterminated, stamped out, eradicated, squashed, like so much inconsequential, insignificant, worthless fodder. Daniel died before seeing his seventh birthday.

Then, Abraham became suddenly silent. It was eerie and unsettling. Like the hush that comes over a courtroom after the judge passes the death sentence.

Katie wiped the tears from her cheeks. "Abraham, I don't know what to say."

He assured her with eyes of stone, an unreadable expression on his face, "There is nothing to say. Do you see the ultimate irony, the ultimate slap in the face, my ultimate shame?"

He paused a second, his face transformed into a mask of torment. "That while I toiled for the butchers, the Nazis, day after day, doing their bidding, trying to plant beauty where only ugliness and evil could grow, that while I prayed to a God that was deaf and prostituted myself to buy salvation for my wife and child, they were already beyond saving.

"That night ... the night they took them away ... when they looked to me for protection, I should have resisted, fought like a tiger, even killed to keep them safe. Instead, I chose to do nothing ... absolutely nothing ..." Any more words died on his lips.

"But, you couldn't have known. You thought it would be best for them if you cooperated. It's very likely that they would have killed them on the spot if you had offered any resistance."

Abraham sighed deeply; his eyes wet with unshed tears. "What difference did it make? It all turned out the same, did it not? All I was able to ensure was that instead of a swift, merciful end, they would have to endure months of starvation, suffer beatings and unimaginable abuse and a horrifying death. No remains to bury. Not a stone to mark their resting place."

"That's not fair, Abraham. You had no other choice. You did what you thought you had to do. You share no blame for something that you were powerless to prevent."

"You know what is not fair? The cruelest reality of all? I did have a choice. I had time, opportunity and the means to get them to safety. I was too stubborn, too stupid, too blind to see what was happening all around me. Many fled to safety, but not arrogant, proud Abraham Franke. I refused to be driven from my homeland. My passiveness, obstinance and ignorance signed their death warrants. That last night that I saw them, they looked to me for an answer. Their eyes turned to me, filled with hope for me to do something … anything. They looked to me for assurance and protection. I had a responsibility, an obligation to keep them safe. Instead, like sheep being led to the slaughter, I chose to do nothing. I believed that surrender and cooperation would keep them from harm. I allowed it to happen. I betrayed their trust. I failed them and I failed myself."

Katie felt as if her heart would break. "Blame is a cancer, Abraham, especially when it's misplaced, turned inward. It can spread silently, eating away at all the good. Don't let it consume you. There is too much good in you."

"There is much blame to go around. How can a God that I believed in all my life to be a loving, a merciful, a compassionate God, how could He allow that kind of evil to simply wipe away all those souls, as if they never existed?"

"He is the same loving God I believe in. It's not God's fault. He didn't create the evil. Man did. He gives us the freedom, the free will to make the world a good place, or a bad place. Based on those choices, we choose to accept Him and eventually share a place in heaven with Him, or we choose to reject Him, suffering an eternity without Him. Pray to Him, Abraham. Find a place in your heart that still has room for Him." Katie was afraid that to Abraham it was a hollow argument.

"There is no such place."

"If you turn your back on God, on His teachings, on His promises, you turn your back on Zora and Daniel. You're condemning their souls, their memories to a death that is final, a death that holds no promise for a resurrection or rebirth, redemption or eternal life. Don't condemn them. Don't erase the importance of their existence. Don't tarnish those precious lives that touched your life, brought you love, happiness and fulfillment. Some people live their whole lifetimes and never find even a moment of that."

"At one time I did believe, I prayed. Why did He not answer my prayers? I have asked God why them? Why could He not have taken me? I would have died a thousand times to barter for their lives. Why could it not have been me?"

She searched her heart and mind for an answer. "I don't know why some good people die young while some bad people are allowed to live. I don't know why some of us are forced to endure unbelievable pain and suffering while others manage to escape it. But, I do know three things for certain.

"We have to live the lives we were meant to live. God gives us the gifts of His grace and strength to endure whatever wrongs the world throws at us. And I know deep within my heart that Zora and Daniel are at peace with God in heaven, looking down on you, right now, waiting for the day when God calls you home to join them. We have to have faith in Him. We can't barter and trade. Faith must be total and absolute.

"I know that Catholicism and Judaism are very different in their beliefs. But, will you let me share a bit of a quote from a famous Christian Teacher?"

Abraham reluctantly nodded, almost imperceptibly.

"They are called the Beatitudes. I can't remember them all, word for word, but they go something like this.

Blessed are the meek, for they shall inherit the earth.
Blessed are they who mourn, for they shall be comforted.
Blessed are they who hunger and thirst for justice, for they shall be
satisfied.
Blessed are the merciful, for they shall obtain mercy.
Blessed are the clean of heart, for they shall see God.
Blessed are they who are persecuted for justice's sake, for theirs is the
kingdom of heaven.

Katie stood and took Abraham by the hand and sat on the edge of his armchair.

"If we have to make a choice, choosing to feel loss and anguish is better than choosing to feel nothing at all. Let those feelings run their course and then get on with living.

"I think that your Zora and Daniel were much the same as my Daniel. They possessed a purity of spirit and heart bringing only joy and happiness to the lives that they touched. Both earth *and* heaven are richer places for them having lived. That *we* are better persons for having known them."

chapter twenty-one

"Would it be too much trouble for you to come over? Right, now? I have a bit of an emergency. Abraham is at the college and Brendan is at Vincent's. It was either call you or the fire department."

Reacting to the concern in Katie's voice, Matt broke nearly every land speed record and traffic law in existence and rounded each corner on two wheels, stripping a minimum of one inch of rubber off his tires and leaving it on the pavement. If he could have sprouted wings and flown, he wouldn't have arrived at Katie's a second sooner.

The twins had managed to climb to the highest reaches of the sycamore tree that would support their weight. They were stranded, perched precariously twenty feet in the air and too frightened to reverse direction and climb back down.

When he arrived, Matt found Katie in a near panic and Tommy on the verge of tears. They stood at the base of the tree, staring up into the sky at the two little monkeys who were by that point stripped of all bravado and crying hysterically.

Matt reluctantly admitted to himself that the two weren't aliens hatched from pods. They were actually human. Both boys, for the first time that Matt had ever seen them, actually appeared daunted and shaken.

"How in the heck did they climb up that far?" Matt asked.

Katie, without breaking from her skyward gaze, nearly cried, "I don't have the faintest idea. They got the notion in their heads to build a tree house. And I guess one thing led to another. It doesn't matter how or why they got there. Please, just get them down!"

At that precise moment a hammer suddenly spiraled from the heavens and crashed to earth, missing Matt's cranium by mere inches. As he realized that he had narrowly escaped a fatal concussion by the slimmest of margins and at the hands of those two monsters, he contemplated retrieving the hammer and returning the favor.

Almost too ashamed to admit such a thought, Matt briefly considered a less felonious attack … leaving them stranded there. It would serve them right. Matt had to hide his euphoria at the prospect of them spending the rest of their lives far removed from human contact. At least the rest of the world would remain a safer place. But, eventually his villainous side lost the battle to his super-ego and good prevailed over evil.

After carefully planning his strategy, it took Matt a few minutes, via a long extension ladder, to scale within a few feet of the boys. With coaxing, prodding and coercion, was finally able to extricate them from their perches. All the while, as if watching a high-wire act at the circus, Katie and Tommy watched the exercise that seemed to be unfolding in slow motion.

After an eternity of minutes, the two chimpanzees were finally lowered to the safety of ground level and delivered to their mother's waiting arms. Katie inspected them, like a scientist examining organisms under a microscope, to be sure that they were indeed intact and unharmed.

Matt, convinced it would only be a matter of time before he regretted his heroics, stood back silently, giving Katie a few moments to determine if they passed inspection. He was convinced that her efforts were unnecessary and considered the two to be completely indestructible. Matt couldn't immediately think of a single thing on earth that could possibly pose a threat to them. In fact, bemused, he felt the exact opposite to be the case. With those two around, nothing animal, mineral or vegetable was ever completely safe from harm.

And right on cue, with the sensitivity of a slug and the gratitude of a goon, Casey quipped, "Knock, knock."

Matt thought of a profane response, but humored him. "Who's there?"

"Tack."

"Tack, who?"

"Tack ya long 'nough to get us down."

Eventually, Katie relaxed enough to throw her arms around Matt and with a grateful hug, thanked him. Finally, when he was sure that Katie was sure they were none the worse for the wear, he spoke. "If that's the thanks I can count on for helping get these guys out of a jam, I hope they manage to get into a lot more of them."

"Don't encourage them. Believe me, they don't need it. Sometimes they're not safe, for a short second, out of eyesight," Katie laughed.

"Oh, I'm not completely convinced they were in any real danger. The thought even crossed my mind that they may have set this whole thing up, just to jeopardize my health and safety. If I ever find out that that was the case, I warn you two that I'll carry you right back up that ladder and leave you there until the vultures start circling to pick your carcasses. Have you two monkey's learned your lesson? No more climbing trees and scaring your mom half to death."

Simultaneously, he ruffled the hair on both their heads and said, "Now, run along, before I change my mind and haul you right back up that tree. I want a word with your mom."

Within seconds the twins had completely recovered, the death-defying feat all but erased from their short-term memories. As all three boys tore off for parts unknown, Katie and Matt strolled down to the shore.

It was a damp, cool autumn day. The sun, hidden behind a wall of gray clouds, hadn't shown its face all day and Katie, suddenly feeling the chill, buried her hands in the sleeves of her sweater.

"Thank you so much, for coming so quickly. I was worried to death that they'd fall before you got here."

"They weren't in any real danger. The branches were sturdy enough. They were more scared than anything. It may have done them a world of good to be on the receiving end for a change. But, for some reason I'm very doubtful that it will leave a lasting impression on either of them."

"You think you know them so well, do you?" Katie baited him.

"I've been exposed to them often enough to be considered a fairly reliable source."

"How would you like me to show my appreciation for your heroic deeds by asking you to join us for dinner, tonight? That is, if you could tolerate being exposed to the twins for another hour or two." Katie's dimples deepened as she smiled at Matt.

"Since, I'm the one being rewarded here, joining you for dinner could be considered ample repayment for risking life and limb, but I have one addendum to the agreement that I am compelled to insist upon. Dinner with you, yes. Dinner with the twins, a definite no."

Katie shook her head, "Sorry, it's a package deal. You get all of us or none of us."

Matt played his trump card. "I'm afraid I have you at a distinct disadvantage, for a change. You're the thanker and I'm the thankee. That means I'm the one that's being repaid and I insist on the repayment being on my terms. You and me. Dinner at my house. Saturday night. No problems finding a babysitter. I happen to know you have a built-in model. No sore throats or temperatures. No minor catastrophes with the plumbing or major catastrophes with the twins. No excuses."

Katie pretended to contemplate the proposal. "It appears that I have no choice. An actual dinner invitation. A dinner that I won't have to prepare or clean up after. Terms accepted. It's a deal." She offered Matt her hand to seal the contract. Instead, Matt leaned in and kissed her softly on the mouth. That was it. No lingering looks, no warm embrace, no prolonged goodbye, only a single chaste kiss.

He simply turned and walked away, leaving Katie in a state of complete bewilderment.

ك ل

Every other Friday night was card club. Because Charlie and Birdie White were childless, the girls usually met at their house. But Charlie was repainting their living room and Liz Coughlin said the smell of fresh paint made her sick. So, tradition was broken and Katie offered to hold card club at her house.

"Am I the last one here?" Birdie asked as she removed her coat and laid it on the sofa with the others. "I can't believe Angie beat me here." She joined the girls at the dining room table.

"The only reason Angie arrived on time is because she thought Katie said eight instead of seven," Liz explained.

"Slow and steady wins the race," Angie replied.

Connie rolled the dice and said, " Little Joe hasn't mastered the concept of slow and steady, yet. Let's get this game going. I have less than four hours until he starts screaming that he wants his midnight snack. I rolled odd."

Katie dipped into the punch bowl. "I think we can give Birdie a moment to get a cup of punch."

All the girls took turns rolling the dice until they had two teams, one odds and the other evens.

Rose shuffled the decks and dealt the cards.

"How's the living room coming?" Katie asked Birdie as she arranged the cards in her hand.

"Charlie promised me it would be finished in a week. That was one week ago and it still looks the same." Birdie reached into her handbag and pulled out her cigarette case.

"Don't you dare light up, Bernadine White. You know I'm allergic," Liz warned her.

"For crying-out-loud, Liz. One lousy cigarette isn't going to put you in the hospital. I've always thought that a little cigarette smoke would probably do you a world of good," Birdie threw back at Liz.

"Quit arguing, you two. Have *one lousy* cigarette, Birdie, then put them away. And Liz, you can hold your breath for five minutes. What's your bid, Katie?" Angie asked as she adjusted the straps of her brassiere.

"Four spades."

"Five diamonds," Angie raised the bid.

Birdie took her reading glasses that hung around her neck on a chain and situated them on the end of her nose. She arranged and studied her cards for a small eternity.

"How long do we have to wait for your bid, Birdie? That was five minutes of my life I'm never going to get back," Connie chided.

"If I can't see my cards, I can't bid. What was Katie's bid?" she asked.

"Have you lost your mind as well as your eyesight? Would you like a pencil and paper so you can keep track? Katie bid four spades. Angie, five diamonds," Connie spat at her.

"Birdie's not the only one losing her memory," Angie said. "Today I sat down on the toilet and forget if I had to pee or poop."

"Lists," Katie instructed. "You have to make lists."

"Six spades." Birdie's cigarette bobbed up and down in her lips.

"Pass," Liz couldn't top a bid of six anything.

"That's a lot of help, Liz," Connie snapped. "How are we supposed to know what you have if you don't bid?"

"I don't *have* anything. That's why I PASSED!"

Rose declared, "Seven spades."

Connie marked the score pad. "Seven spades it is, then."

Rose won the bid, so she played her first card.

"Charlie says, 'Thank you' for holding card club. He's thrilled he gets to watch his Friday night programs without distractions."

"What color are you painting the living room, " Katie asked.

"Off white."

"Off white?" Rose asked. "All the beautiful colors available and you pick off white?"

Angie laughed. "Surrounded by cows and milk all day, I can't believe you're painting it white!"

"It's neutral. Goes with anything. Speaking of no distractions. Where's the tribe," Birdie asked.

"Next door at Lottie's. They're spending the night."

"Loretta Devereaux and four young boys. Now there's an unlikely picture of domesticity," Angie played her card. "Aren't you worried she might corrupt them?"

"With a television set and as much ice cream as they can eat, I doubt if there'll be much time for corruption, " Katie remarked.

"I think I could like that woman," Birdie offered. "Seems to me she's got a lot of guts and doesn't give a flying fig about what other people think."

"It's easy to be cavalier when you can buy and sell anyone in town," Liz commented as she waved away a cloud of smoke.

Birdie wasn't discouraged and blew a smoke ring. "Money doesn't build character. Courage does."

Rose played trump and took the trick. "That's our seven tricks. The rest is gravy. I knew I underbid." She reeled in the trick. "What was wrong with your station wagon, Angie? Saw it at Schwartzkoph's Garage last week?" Rose asked and continued to play.

"Not exactly sure and when it comes to auto mechanics, Fred doesn't know a monkey wrench from a monkey's butt. So, I took it in to Gus and seventy-eight dollars later the chunk-a-chunk and thump-thump sounds I kept hearing are gone."

Rose took the next trick and kept the lead. "Louie says that when a car starts to nickel and dime you to death, it's time to trade it in."

The evens won the first hand. Birdie shuffled and dealt the cards.

"Pass," Liz couldn't open the bid the next hand.

"If you pass one more time I'm going to light up one of Birdie's cigarettes," Connie threatened.

Rose opened, "Six hearts."

"Seven no trump," Connie raised her.

Katie bid, "Eight hearts."

"You all can't have hearts," Angie reasoned. "I'll call your bluff. Nine hearts."

Birdie passed. "You have it with nine hearts. Play carefully, Angie. I smell a euchre."

Angie led the hand and took the first trick.

"Katie, I just love this house. But, I sure wouldn't want to pay the heating bill. It must be sky high," Rose surveyed the room.

"That has me worried a bit. I haven't gone through a winter, yet."

"What are these, Katie? They're delicious," Liz asked taking another bite of the confection Katie had laid out for snacking.

"Meringue Macaroon Clouds. One of my ma's specialties."

Angie chewed hers and rolled her eyes. "God, these are good. They taste rich enough to shorten my life expectancy."

"I'd love the recipe. I'm trying to figure out what's in them," Liz said.

"They're a snap to make. Just four ingredients. Egg whites, sugar, coconut and vanilla."

Angie quizzed Liz, "Aren't you allergic to eggs, Liz?"

"The yolk. Not the whites."

"Can you cut the chatter? I'm trying to concentrate," Connie snapped as they lost the next two tricks.

"Rose, that sweater is beautiful. That shade of pink looks great on you," Katie commented. "Is it new?"

"Bought it last year at Woodbury's end of the season sale. Now that the weather is turning colder, this is the first chance I've had to wear it."

"Is it cashmere?"

"Poor man's cashmere. It's mohair."

"Triple stamps at the A&P today," Birdie announced. "I'm only one book short of a new mix master I've had my eye on."

"Triple stamps!" Liz exclaimed. "I didn't know anything about it."

"It was advertised in the Sentinel," Birdie informed her.

Liz complained, "I can't believe I missed it. I've been so busy this week, who has time to read?"

"Angie does. What are you up to, now Angie? Three novels a week," Birdie teased. "Maybe we'd better start calling you for news bulletins. Read anything good lately?"

"I just finished a steamy one. *Lady Chatterley's Lover.* I've had to keep it hidden from Fred. I read it under the covers with a flashlight. Thank God he sleeps like a bear in hibernation and snores like a buzz saw so he can't hear me turn the pages."

"How steamy is it?" Liz nearly whispered, her eyes wide with curiosity.

"So torrid it would steam up your glasses, Liz."

Connie complained, "Are we going to play cards or have Angie thrill us with another book review?"

Birdie trumped the trick and took the lead. "The best way to do this is quick and clean. Like tearing a Band-Aid off your crotch. Do it one swift motion." She swept all the rest of the tricks. "I believe we just set you, Ladies. The name of the game is Euchre."

Connie barked at her, "Sand-bagger."

"You dug your own grave bidding up. All I had to do was pass."

"If I had known that I was playing without any partners, I would have passed, too."

"I never wanted hearts in the first place," Liz added. "I wanted clubs."

"So why didn't you bid clubs?" Connie accused her.

Rose snickered as she tallied the euchre, "Divide and conquer."

"It's only a card game, Connie. What's got you in such a mood, tonight?" Birdie asked. "You've been snipping and snapping all evening."

Connie immediately dropped her head and tears spilled from her eyes.

Katie jumped up and went to her side. "Come on over here and sit on the sofa." Katie moved the coats and patted a spot for Connie to sit down. All the other girls immediately lost interest in cards and joined them.

"You this upset over a euchre?" Angie attempted some levity. The only response she received was the evil eye from Birdie.

"How about one of my Pall Malls?" Birdie asked.

Rose offered, "Do you want a cup of punch?"

"No, I don't want a cup of punch."

Liz waved a cookie under her nose, "A Meringue Macaroon Cloud?"

Connie finally blurted it out. "I don't want a cup of punch or a macaroon or a cigarette. And I don't give a rip about the euchre. I want my goddamn period."

Katie drew Connie into her arms and let her cry until she was cried out. No one said a word until Katie finally asked, "How late are you?"

"Over a week," Connie's voice shook.

Angie stroked Connie's red curls. "A week's not very late, Honey. My period's late more than it's on time."

Connie sniffled, "That's small consolation, Angie. You're late for everything."

All the girls laughed. It broke the tension.

"How can you be pregnant? You're still nursing. You can't get pregnant when you're nursing," Birdie paused. "Can you?"

Angie rolled her eyes. "That statement would only come from a woman who's never had kids. Birdie, stick to breeding dairy cattle. You know less about human reproduction than any woman I know. Half the people running around were conceived when their mothers were nursing."

"Then I think we can assume from the state you're in that pregnancy *is* a possibility?" Birdie asked unfettered.

"What kind of dumb question is that?" Liz elbowed Birdie.

"Well, I was just asking. It could be her change, you know. Some women go through it earlier than others. Contrary to Angie's opinion, I do know about menopause."

"It's not my change. And yeah, pregnancy is a possibility." Connie paused for a moment to wipe her nose. "I thought we were being so careful. I monitored my cycle on the calendar. I'm usually regular as rain. Somehow, I must have miscalculated."

Katie reassured her. "Connie, it may be nothing. You might simply be late."

"That's what's got me so worried. I'm never late."

"Have you talked to Ward about it? What does he say?" Katie took another direction.

"Lord, no! I haven't worked up the nerve to tell him. We were kind of hoping Little Joe would be the last. I'm pretty sure I know what Ward's reaction is going to be. We just paid off Dr. Hughes' bill for Joey. He's not even four months old, yet. Ward's not ... I'm not ready for another baby this soon. Maybe not ever."

"Just go home and tell Ward. What's he going to do? Divorce you?" Birdie asked.

All five ladies stared steel at Birdie.

"That's easy for you to say, Birdie. You have a quiet, sane existence to go home to with no kids under foot and no other worry than when Charlie's going to finish painting your living room. You don't have to go home to a husband that won't understand, five kids under the age of ten, and a baby that nurses around the clock all crammed into a puny, three bedroom house that you out-grew three kids ago."

Connie hadn't meant to attack Birdie and she immediately regretted her words.

"Well, if you are pregnant, and I'm not saying you are. But, if you are, you didn't get that way all by yourself. Ward had better *learn* to understand. He played a less than minor role in this little drama," Angie said.

Rose added, "You know how men are. They think with the organ between their legs instead of the one between their ears. They figure getting us pregnant is their responsibility and not getting us pregnant is ours."

Katie tightened her arm around Connie and gave her a squeeze. "We're not going to know if there's actually anything to worry about, tonight. We won't know that for a few weeks. But, we do know that if you aren't pregnant, we'll look back on this evening and laugh about how badly we euchred you. And if you are pregnant, we'll get through that, too.

"There isn't a woman alive who wasn't scared about another pregnancy. That it was too soon, or that she had enough babies, or that she couldn't afford another. There also isn't a woman alive who would ever consider sending back one of her children.

"So, this is what we're going to do. You are going to stay right here and do what ever you need to do to get through this tonight and we are going to sit here with you while you do it. Talk if you want. Cry if you have any tears left. I have a couple bottles of wine and some cooking sherry. We'll all get tipsy if you want. If it takes half the night, we'll figure this all out together."

"I have to be home by twelve to nurse Little Joe."

"Okay, Cinderella," Katie said, "We've got until midnight."

chapter twenty-two

The Halloween pumpkins were hollowed out and carved.

Frank Mizzano had delivered four huge pumpkins free of charge, one for each of the boys. He and Katie hadn't spoken about them. He had simply dropped them off one day, without a word. At first, she had thought it a strange thing to do. But, the more she thought about it, the more she started to view it as a kind of atonement or peace offering. That maybe, it was his way, the only way he had of making amends.

Their conversations had been limited to polite exchanges when he would stop to sell fall produce. Neither Katie nor Frank Mizzano had mentioned Labor Day. However, Katie sensed something about his manner had changed. He smiled more, shyly but deliberately and he appeared happier, less tense and more talkative. His physical appearance had improved as well. He was always clean-shaven, his hair washed and combed and his clothes worn, but unsoiled. Brendan had told Katie that as far as Vinnie knew, his dad hadn't had a drink since school started.

Katie continued to include Frank Mizzano and Vincent in her nightly rosary intentions.

The side porch was covered in pumpkin seeds and piles of orange, stringy pulp and scrapings from stripping and cleaning them out. Brendan carved a jack-o-lantern that winked with a lop-sided grin. The twins wanted theirs to be more traditional, one smiling with a single-toothed grin, the other frowning menacingly. Tommy, who wanted to do his own carving, had created an interesting piece. It most closely resembled a Martian with three eyes.

As she did every year, Katie baked her special Halloween barm brack and planned an early dinner of hearty Irish stew and oatmeal bread, allowing the boys time to dress in their costumes.

Tommy was a pirate. He wore a patch over one eye, a charcoal beard, a cardboard sword and a bandanna tied to cover his hair. Lottie had contributed to the ensemble one gold hoop earring that he clipped to his earlobe. He looked as authentic as any of the crew on the Jolly Roger, with one small exception. Though it was totally out of character, he insisted on wearing his Sox baseball cap.

Casey chose the Davy Crockett look, complete with coonskin cap, wooden musket, buckskin shirt and pants fashioned from a burlap sack. Colin was a pint-size version of Emmett Kelly, with painted clown face, an ancient, black bowler hat, vest and an oversized, red and white polka-dot necktie. Katie donated three old pillowcases from the linen closet. There was still enough life left in them to hold strong under the weight of the pile of candy that the night's begging would produce.

Brendan had proclaimed that as a teenager, he was too old to go trick-or-treating and that after he took the little boys on their rounds, he and the guys were going to hang around for a while. Katie knew what that meant and warned him against any Halloween mischief.

By dusk, she scooted them out the door, giving Brendan instructions that he needed to have them home by seven-thirty. She frisked his pockets for contraband soap and candles and was relieved to find them empty. Katie lit the jack-o-lanterns and placed them outside to welcome ghosts and goblins to her own back door. She and a dispirited Chance, down-in-the mouth about being left behind, remained at home to pass out the candy.

At seven-thirty, Davy, Emmett, and Blackbeard returned with sacks bulging full of tummy aches. Because tomorrow was a holy day of obligation, All Souls' Day, there was no school. Katie let them stay up a bit past their normal bedtime since they would be able to sleep in until it was time to get up and ready for Mass.

Casey and Tommy took hurried baths, eager to sort their candy. Colin complained about the delay. He required extra scrubbing to remove the charcoal from his face. Finally, the three misers were sprawled out on the living room rug, tallying their booty like Ebenezer Scrooge counting his money.

There was a system to the entire operation. Candy was lined up according to size, type and popularity. Some were more valuable than others. Candy bars and Mallow Cups were the most rare and coveted followed closely by popcorn balls. Next came the smaller pieces of packaged penny candy like saltwater taffy, Mary Jane's, candy corn and Smarties. Finally came bubble gum and suckers. The dregs were apples, cookies and bags of popcorn. Pencils and pennies were so undesirable they didn't even warrant comment, however quarters were extremely rare and precious.

With the sorting and counting complete, the trading began. It was like Monday morning opening at the New York Stock Exchange with bartering, haggling, bidding and counter-bidding.

Colin, who disliked Black Jacks, traded them to Tommy, who wasn't especially fond of Hershey kisses. Casey preferred Baby Ruth's to Butterfingers. And so, the swap meet continued until everyone was reasonably satisfied. Chance watched the whole exhibition with feigned interest, one ear cocked in confusion, wondering what the proceedings were all about. From his vantage point in front of the fire, his only concern was why no one was offering him any treats from their stash.

But, all good things must come to an end and Katie ordered them to pick it all up and head off to bed. After all their meticulous sorting, counting, trading and categorizing, the candy was scooped up, put back into the sacks until tomorrow, when the painstaking process would start all over again. Three excited, but exhausted trick-or-treaters trotted up to bed, with their sacks of goodies slung over their backs like a trio of Santas.

While Tommy and the twins were saying their goodnight prayers, hauls stowed under their beds, the night was still young for the Musketeers. Armed with stolen contraband the Halloween festivities were just beginning.

It was a night made for mischief and mild for the last day of October. The full moon played a game of peek-a-boo from behind an occasional cloudbank. One could almost conjure up the silhouette of a witch on broomstick, riding across the sky, her shrieking and cackling carried on the night air. Pitch tree branches, leafless, like bony hag's fingers, swayed in the wind with lifelike movement.

Meanwhile, the Musketeers were up to no good. Armed with stolen rolls of toilet paper supplied by Stump, eggs taken from Puke's mom's refrigerator, two bars of soap and four candles contributed by Breeze, they soaped, papered, waxed and egged their way around the south end of the lake. Mixed in, for good measure, they smashed the occasional pumpkin that was too tempting to resist. But, they were just getting warmed up. With four precious M-80s and five cherry bombs that Vinnie had saved from last Fourth of July, they managed to blow five mailboxes to smithereens.

Walking Brendan home they approached Abraham's mailbox. Stump asked Vinnie if they had any explosives left.

Brendan tried to discourage them. "Don't do nothing to Dr. Franke's. Leave the old guy alone."

Stump accepted the challenge. "Hey, Sox. You afraid of spooky old Dr. Frankenstein?"

He staggered stiff legged, with arms outstretched, voice deep and menacing, mimicking the famous monster. "Are you scared of the monster's revenge? That he'll break into your room, as the clock chimes midnight and strangle you in your sleep and crush your spine to powder?"

The rest of the guys started to join in the teasing. Brendan was trying his best to dissuade them. Apprehension and foreboding were forming a weighty ball of dough inside his stomach.

"Come on, guys, leave him alone. He never hurt anybody. He's just a poor old guy. Besides, what if he finds out? My ma'll have my hide?"

"It doesn't matter, anyway, guys." Vinnie unwittingly came to Brendan's rescue. "I'm all out of cherry bombs and M-80s. We used the last ones on Erickson's mailbox. All we got left is four eggs, a bar of soap and half a candle."

Brendan breathed a sigh of relief.

But, Stump had a back-up plan. "I got a way better idea, anyway. Come on guys, follow me."

He started down the drive to the guest cottage. "They'll be talking about this Halloween for the next fifty years. Sox, if you're too chicken shit to come, go on home to your mommy, like a good little boy."

Brendan ignored his inner voice and the warning signs, flashing like beacons in the night. After a long minute he finally caved.

Five pairs of Chucky Taylor's silently made their way towards the greenhouse.

Ϙ ⁊

The air was filled with the strong scent of burning leaves and carried thick, gray clouds of smoke. After Mass, Katie and Brendan were raking and burning the last of the season's leaves that had covered the yard in a crunchy, nut-brown carpet. Tommy, Casey and Colin were building leaf houses and forts, hoarding, scavenging and scattering, leaves. For every step of progress Katie and Brendan took forward, they took two steps backward. Brendan, who had remained quiet and reserved all morning, had become frustrated and angry. He grumbled and complained that they would never finish. Katie, as usual, remained tolerant and let the little boys have their fun.

As an autumn treat, she had cored apples, filled the holes with cinnamon and sugar, sealed them with butter and wrapped them in aluminum foil to slowly bake in the smoldering embers of the burn piles. Later, they would search for the buried treasures in the ashes and enjoy the seasonal treat. Tasty and warm, she would unwrap the apples and serve them with vanilla ice cream. Her mouth watered, just thinking about it.

The activity was brought to an abrupt halt. Sheriff Guzy pulled up to the garage and parked his patrol car. He unfolded himself from the car and placed a visored hat on his head. Hoisting his brown leather belt laden with law enforcement paraphernalia, he sauntered over.

The only way to describe him was king-size. The snuff-colored, khaki uniform stretched over his six-foot-four broad frame. The taut, muscled body of his youth had remained dense, but gravity and time had softened and rearranged it. The once iron-hard, flat stomach had seen too many slices of banana-cream pie at Hannah's Hamburger Hut and too much inactivity behind a desk or riding in his patrol car. Fingers as big around as bratwurst, curled and rested on his belt. Heavy, pewter eyebrows arched above his pale blue eyes like fuzzy caterpillars. He resembled a sober W. C. Fields. But his facial characteristics were the result of genetics rather than generous doses of ethanol.

His arrival elicited three different reactions. The younger boys were awed and dazzled. Too excited for words, they stood frozen, thoroughly entranced by the gleaming, cherry-topped, black and white cruiser. Likewise, they stared at the official uniform, complete with gun and holster, handcuffs and glistening, gold badge. A rare state for them, they were rendered speechless.

Brendan was rendered speechless and motionless, too, but not from awe. He spotted the *Sox* ball cap tucked under the Sheriff's arm. The cold dread of fear snaked up his spine, gripped his stomach and squeezing the color from his face. The flee or fight syndrome raced through his insides creating spasms of panic. It was no contest. Fleeing or fighting would have been futile. His feet and arms felt like hardened cement, incapable of motion.

Katie, confused, quickly did a mental search, trying to comprehend what emergency or tragedy would warrant a personal visit from the sheriff. Like a blast of frigid arctic air, the realization and one dubious word assaulted her physically, mentally and emotionally. HALLOWEEN!

 C8 80

Brendan spent the remainder of the day in exile in his room, branded, ostracized and dinnerless. He was certain that he would die an old man, never seeing the guys again, never having his mom talk to him, again. He would have preferred that she yelled and hollered. Her silence was the real torture. It hung over him, ominous and threatening. Casey and Colin were uncharacteristically perceptive. Sensing Katie's mood, they had wisely played quietly and without incident until bedtime.

Sheriff Guzy related that the trail of destruction had been easy to follow. All the way down Lakefield Road until it led to Dr. Franke's place and abruptly ended there. If there had been any question as to 'who did it' was answered when his initial investigation turned up a red and black *Sox* baseball cap in Dr. Franke's shrubbery. The Sheriff's interrogation of Brendan had been unsuccessful in turning up any other suspects. Brendan remained close-mouthed about naming any accomplices. Sheriff Guzy knew they existed and had a darn good idea who they were, but without proof, Brendan would have to shoulder the blame alone.

Katie had remained cool and distant, all day. More than once, she had to resist the compelling urge to commit homicide and for the first time in her life she understood how some species could actually eat their young. She recognized her murderous tendencies throughout the day and before confronting

Brendan decided to wait until the felonious feelings passed. She was certain that she had experienced every negative emotion known to man, in descending order, shock, doubt, shame, disappointment and finally a boiling, searing anger. She persuaded herself to wait until her emotional thermometer had dropped thirty degrees. By eight o'clock, convinced that it had, she mounted the stairs to face the imprisoned. Brendan nearly disproved Newton's laws of gravity when his mom entered the room. He must have jumped three feet into the air.

At first, Katie paced back and forth, hoping the repetition would conjure up the magical words. After what Brendan thought was an eternity, she finally spoke.

"I keep turning one question over and over in my mind. How could you be a party to such a destructive and cruel act? Breaking windows in the greenhouse was bad enough, but destroying the plants. The plants that you know are precious to him. It was a vicious, mean, cowardly thing to do. Never have I been so disappointed in you. You've really let me down, this time. I would have thought you had more regard for Dr. Franke. He has been nothing but kind and giving to you. Is that how you chose to repay him? Destroying what he loves most? I want you to know how ashamed and disappointed I am. I gave you more credit than that."

Brendan remained silent, head hung, nervously picking at the tufts of yarn tied to the quilted squares of his coverlet. Katie glared at him and nearly bore a hole into his brain.

"Just when Miss Lottie had convinced me that you needed to be treated more like an adult, you go and pull a stunt like this. What you did was at the very least un-Christian. It was mean and hurtful."

Katie shook her head, still not quite believing that the whole ugly mess had happened. "As far as I'm concerned, Sheriff Guzy was far more lenient than you deserve. Don't make the mistake of assuming that I feel anywhere near as generous. I don't share the same view as he does that repairing the damage and bearing the financial burden to replace the windows and plants is punishment enough. What about the damage you did to Dr. Frank? People can't be fixed that easily. Replacing some putty and panes of glass doesn't begin to repair the pain and hurt you've caused him. You betrayed his friendship and his trust. You can't win that back by buying new plants and shrubs."

Katie sat down on the edge of the bed. Brendan forced himself to look up at her.

"You were raised to respect the property of others. What possessed you to disregard all that your dad and I have taught you?"

Finally, Brendan managed a response. "We didn't mean for all that to happen. When we threw the eggs and soaped the windows, some of 'em broke ... and then ..."

Katie latched onto the pronoun *we*. "Now you're willing to admit that it wasn't only you. Why didn't you tell Sheriff Guzy the truth?"

"'Cuz a guy doesn't rat out his friends."

Katie sighed heavily. "Under different circumstances that might be admirable. These are not the right circumstances. Your loyalty is misplaced and wasted. Sheriff Guzy and I both knew you were protecting someone. We also know most likely who. He plans on having a talk with everyone's parents."

"It wasn't any of my idea. I tried to talk the guys out of it. They wouldn't listen."

"And you call them your friends? True friends wouldn't have put you in that position. They would have respected your feelings for Dr. Franke. You are lucky that Steven, Walter and Arthur come from good homes and that Vincent needs your friendship or I would pull the plug and forbid you to see them outside of school."

At first, Bren panicked at the thought of never being able to hang out with his buddies. Then he realized that at that moment Vinnie, Stump, Breeze and Puke were the last people he wanted to see.

"We never meant it to go so far. One thing just led to another. I didn't even do anything, mostly stood back and watched."

"Even if that were true, Brendan, you know perfectly well that the sin of omission makes you equally guilty. It's exactly the same. And equally serious. And if the guys all decided to jump off a bridge, I suppose you'd jump right in after them?

"We've talked about this before. About standing on your own and not letting others decide things for you. There are two kinds of people in this world, Brendan. There are leaders and there are followers. You'd better decide which type of person you want to be. A leader who is strong in his convictions, confident in his decisions or a follower, always being led around by the nose, being told when, where, how and why by someone else. Seems like a pretty obvious choice to me."

"The guys only picked on him because he acts so weird all the time. Why doesn't he act normal, like other people?"

For a fleeting moment, Katie thought of sharing the circumstances of life that had brought Abraham to the guesthouse, but decided not to.

"How Dr. Franke acts or doesn't act isn't the issue here. Judging others is a very unfair and foolish habit to develop. Have you heard the expression, 'don't judge a person until you've walked a mile in his moccasins'? Do you know what that means?"

Brendan shook his head and shrugged.

"It means that we should be very careful to form opinions, good or bad, about others, until we learn about them and what experiences they've had. You need to look at people from the inside, not the outside."

"I know what we did was real bad. I knew it the whole time it was happening. I just didn't do anything to stop it."

"And that, Brendan, is what separates the men from the boys, the difference between behaving like a child, or behaving like an adult. That is the difference between being a leader and being a follower."

Brendan digested that for a minute. "I get a weird filling in my stomach, like I'm gonna puke every time I think about what we did."

"That weird feeling you're experiencing is called your conscience."

"I don't like it. How long will it last?"

"That's how a good conscience works. It'll only make you feel bad as long as you're supposed to."

"Mom, I'm scared. How am I going to face Dr. Franke? How will he ever like me or trust me again. He'll be so mad, I'm not sure I ever want to see him again."

Katie arched one eyebrow. "Oh, Bren, you sound a lot like the thief who wasn't nearly as sorry he had stolen as he was about getting caught.

"His trust? I can't help you there. I'm afraid that's something you'll have to earn back. Every path has its puddles. Sometimes the road to forgiveness can be long and lonely. Consider it part of the punishment. It'll build character. That, my son, is a bridge you'll have to cross on your own. But, I'll be standing on this side of the bridge, cheering you on.

"As far as Dr. Franke being mad, give him some time. I think you'll find that time has a way of healing the worst wounds. If you really make an effort, it'll work itself out, all in good time."

"Are you still mad at me? Do you still love me?"

Katie gave him a quick peck on the cheek and mussed his black curls. "Now, get some sleep. You've got a busy day tomorrow starting those repairs.

"And yes … very much … to both your questions."

CƷ ꝝ

At school the next day, before the morning bell rang announced first hour class, Brendan was at his locker putting his cap and coat away and getting out his textbooks. Breeze, Stump, Puke and Vinnie came up to him and stood there, hands in their pants' pockets, books tucked under their arms. For a long minute, Brendan ignored them. Then without looking at any of them he spoke to the open locker. "Don't worry. I didn't squeal on you."

Vinnie answered, "We know. Sheriff Guzy told us. He came to all our houses to talk to our parents."

Breeze added, "We knew you wouldn't rat on us. Stump's the one that spilled his guts."

Stump defended himself, "I had to. My ma said she wouldn't feed me 'til I told the truth."

"Did Sheriff Guzy pull his gun on you? Did he handcuff you?" Puke asked.

Stump rolled his eyes. "You moron. This ain't Dragnet. We didn't *kill* anybody."

Puke responded, "I wuz just thinkin' ..."

"Do us all favor, Puke. Don't think," Stump quipped.

"Did you get into much trouble, Sox?" Breeze asked.

Bren refused to respond and made an elaborate show of rearranging the stuff in his locker.

"My ma and dad still ain't quit yellin' at me. What'd your ma say?" Puke persisted.

Bren still refused to answer.

Breeze leaned against the locker next to Bren's. "Come on, Sox. Talk to us."

"Don't call me Sox," he said in a half-whisper.

"You gotta talk to us sooner or later."

Bren slammed his locker shut and the sharp report of metal against metal vibrated through the hall. "I don't gotta do nothing! I covered your asses, now you can all drop dead!"

"We don't care about our asses and we ain't gonna drop dead. We wanna talk to you," Vinnie tried to reason with him.

"Well, I don't give a crap what you want. I got nothing` to say to any of you."

Vinnie pleaded, placing his hand on Bren's shoulder, "Bren. Look, man, I'm sorry. We're all sorry. What more do you want us to say? It was a dumb and stupid thing to do. We should've listened to you."

Bren shrugged Vinnie's hand off. "Don't touch me, neither."

"We all feel like shit about you getting' caught and everything. What do you want us to say?" Breeze pressed further.

"You don't gotta say nothing and I don't really give a crap about how you feel."

"We know you didn't want to do it." Stump spoke.

Bren snapped, "It doesn't matter. I did it and what I wanted or didn't want doesn't matter shit."

"Breeze offered, "Look, we know you tried to take the wrap for us and we're sorry."

Bren looked at the ceiling then lowered his stare and focused on the wall across the hall. "You guys just don't get it. It's got nothing to do with me taking the blame. It's got nothing to do with whose idea it was or who did it."

"Then why you so pissed at us?" Stump asked.

Bren had to remind himself not to scream, as he spat through clenched teeth. "Why's this got to be about any of you? It ain't about you. I ain't pissed at you. Even if I gave a rat's ass about any of you, it's got nothing to do with you. It's got to do with Dr. Franke and me. Just him and me. Nobody else. I don't expect you to understand that. You didn't the other night and you don't today. So you can all just drop dead and leave me alone."

"There must be something we can do?" Breeze pleaded.

"I told you. You can all just leave me alone."

"Come on, Bren. What can we do to make it up to you?" Vinnie asked.

"Don't you guys see? Don't you get it? Don't you get it that there ain't nothing you can do and there ain't nothing I can do! It's too late."

Bren swung around and headed to his first class.

chapter twenty-three

Brendan and Abraham were in the midst of re-glazing and replacing the broken windows. Abraham had to repair the integrity of the greenhouse before the cold weather arrived and threatened any more of the plants inside. The crunch of tire on stone announced the arrival of a vehicle. He and Brendan stopped their work long enough to see who it was.

The Brisbois' station wagon came to a stop in front of Abraham's garage. Four boys piled out. Without saying a word, Vinnie, Stump, Puke and Breeze removed shovels, rakes, potted plants and bags of soil from inside the car's tailgate. Mr. Brisbois hollered that he would be back to pick them up at dark, threw the car into reverse and backed out.

The Musketeers transported the tools, plants and bags of dirt over to the greenhouse. Standing with his hands on his hips, Vinnie stated, "Tell us what you want done first, Dr. Franke."

The Musketeers didn't apologize and Abraham didn't ask for one. They exchanged looks, the Musketeers' soulful yet determined, Abraham's perplexed. For the longest time, no one spoke. Then, as if common purpose dissolved dissonance and bridged chasms, they began a fervent exchange. At first, speaking only what was necessary, then the idle chatter between workmates filled in the uncomfortable silences. The work progressed in proportion and efficiency to the boys' understanding and learning curve. As Abraham explained and demonstrated and the boys absorbed and learned, their roles began to evolve. Abraham became the instructor and the Musketeers his disciples.

Brendan and Abraham's relationship did survive in the aftermath of Halloween night.

For the first few days a strained tension hovered over them, as if they had declared an uncomfortable cease-fire. But as the two worked side by side with the Musketeers to repair the damages to the greenhouse and the plants, Abraham buried the stabbing pain of betrayal. He was convinced that he knew Brendan well enough, that down deep inside, under the recklessness and immaturity of youth, he possessed an inherent goodness and honesty.

Forgiveness for the other Musketeers soon followed. Brendan was stunned by Dr. Frank's ready forgiveness. While the two of them finished repairing the last of the seedbeds in the greenhouse, Brendan asked him about it.

"How come you forgave us, Dr. Franke?"

Abraham thought it over. "Tossing a pebble onto a lake is not a solitary act. The ripples created by that pebble spread out, in ever increasing circles, growing larger and larger. So, Brendan, I had a decision to make. I could let those ripples spread anger, resentment, or I could let them spread forgiveness."

"Aren't you still mad at us?"

"No. I wanted to be. However, your mother has taught me that one must be willing to forgive without compromise. Forgiveness must be total and complete. Otherwise, one is a fraud, deceiving no one but himself. It is a hard lesson to learn. One that I am just beginning to learn myself."

"So, you're saying I should forgive the guys, too?"

"That is a question only you can answer, Brendan. Somehow, I already know what your answer will be."

Brendan's expiation did not go unnoticed by Katie. From a distance, Katie observed his interaction with Abraham. Through the physically and emotionally strenuous reparations she saw a transformation take shape. The incident and repercussions of Brendan's actions had a profound effect on him. At first, she couldn't quite put her finger on it. Then, the revelation was so obvious she was astounded that she hadn't immediately recognized it.

Brendan had grown.

Not in stature, but in character.

Discovering that change in Brendan, she discovered something else. Missteps, misunderstandings and mistakes as well as change, growth and maturity are what constitute the process of life.

Brendan was growing up and it was evident that he was beginning to grow away from her. Becoming a person independent of her. And suddenly, that fact wasn't scary anymore. Instead, it was exciting; it was satisfying and held the thrilling rewards of promise and possibility. What in nature doesn't plant a seed and want to watch it flourish and grow? To nurture was to encourage new things to grow separate and apart until they were able to stand on their own. The oldest of her children was taking his first steps away from her and that truth was that that was exactly as it should be.

And Brendan didn't disappoint Abraham. He forgave Vinnie, Stump, Puke and Breeze.

chapter twenty-four

Next to Christmas, Thanksgiving was Katie's favorite holiday. Despite the many hours she spent in the kitchen with preparation, she loved every hectic, chaotic, festive moment. It was an American tradition that she embraced. This year it was even more exciting. It would be their first Thanksgiving in Eden Croft and she anticipated it with the exuberance of a child.

Katie was up and going by five a.m. She needed to be. The parade started at nine o'clock and she had a table to set, desserts to make and a bird to stuff and get in the oven. Her Thanksgiving table would welcome newfound friends. Exhilarated and inspired, she positively danced through her tasks, humming merrily.

Bundled in flannel and wool, Katie and the boys stood at the curb like Lapland mummies as they watched the parade. Though the day was bitter and gray, spirits were high and their enthusiasm unaffected by the dismal skies. With siren squealing, Sheriff Guzy led the parade as it approached Main Street. The Mayor and his wife, Trump and Izzy Baskins, were the Grand Marshals, riding in a shiny, tan, Buick convertible. A color guard from the VFW post marched next with flags held high.

A total of eighteen floats all sponsored by local businesses and civic groups chugged by mobilized by everything from horses to farm tractors to pickup trucks and sleek automobiles. All the county's resident royalty were represented. The Apple, Cherry and Homecoming Queens, Miss Blair County and the Snow Princess all shivered in their thrones, evening gowns, sashes and rabbit stoles useless against the frigid wind. Cub Scouts, Brownies, Boy Scouts, Girl Scouts, Rotarians, Elks, and any other organization that could assemble ambulatory members marched by, interspersed among the floats. Peppy, acrobatic cheerleaders with pompons and megaphones bounced and somersaulted. Their energy and enthusiasm were contagious.

But, the most thrilling of all, were the marching bands. Katie loved the bands. The Eden Croft Lumberjacks came first in their bright blue and gold uniforms. A drum major and majorette led them. In precision formation they marched and played their seasonal renditions of "Jingle Bells" and "Hark the Herald Angels Sing" and the essential patriotic standby, "Stars and Stripes Forever."

As an added treat that year, Clearwater had been invited to send their pride and joy, the Cavaliers' Drum and Bugle Choir. In orange satin capes, black pants and heads covered by black felt diggers with orange plumes, they formed eight perfect rows of musicians. Ten flag bearers dipped and waved their orange and black silk banners, cutting the air with skill and precision. Awed by the colors and performance, the boys could feel the percussion of every drum beat in their chests. Their faces frozen in perpetual grins while mittened hands applauded every display and performance.

The parade planners saved the best for last. The musical piece d'resistance was the Blair College Screaming Eagles. Ahead of the major body, sequined majorettes twirled and spun their batons like magicians. Row after perfect row, the band followed, one-hundred-twenty strong, in striking silver and crimson uniforms and patent leather high hats. They were strategically placed to herald the arrival of the guest of honor, ending their repertoire with a jubilant "Here Comes Santa Claus".

Katie could feel the boys' excitement. Except for Brendan. He would have eaten liver before he would have admitted that he was enjoying himself. He was too cool and way too old to be impressed by any of it.

The arrival of Mr. and Mrs. Santa Claus marked the end of the parade. The denizens of the North Pole sat in a ruby red sleigh atop a snowy white wonderland created by the employees of the Blair National Bank. The float was a confection of yards of cotton batting, pounds of silver glitter, thousands of strands of tinsel and a mini-forest of white-flocked pine trees. The scene was completed by an accompaniment of the requisite hardworking and trusty elves (members of the college Drama Society), all dressed out in green velvet costumes as they handed candy canes and peppermint sticks to eager admirers.

The Clauses, resplendent in scarlet velvet and milky rabbit fur, lived up to their reputation. Every child from the age of one to eighty-one thrilled at the arrival of the guests of honor. Santa's "Ho Ho Hos" and "Merry Christmases" rumbled from his corpulent belly and the sleigh bells rang metallic and clear of seasonal cheer. Mrs. Claus' eyes sparkled from behind rimless spectacles. They waved and smiled, first to one side and then the other, as if they were greeting each and everyone personally. The little boys were knocked speechless. Any doubters, who had come to the parade that day, left believers.

CB &O

Katie slapped Matt's hand and reprimanded him. "If you keep opening up the oven door that bird will never be done. Don't you know that a watched teakettle never boils? And I'm never going to get this dinner on the table with you—here in the kitchen—getting in my way. You're worse than Chance. Every time I turn around, I trip over you."

"It is a long standing Mulholland Thanksgiving tradition that the men sneak a peek at the turkey every five minutes, get under foot as much as possible and the women complain about both the entire time."

"Then maybe you should think about spending next Thanksgiving with the Mulhollands. The O'Neill tradition maintains that the womenfolk rule in the kitchen. This is my kitchen and I am the mistress of my domain."

"May I remind you that Thanksgiving is an American institution' and I am an American born and raised, while you are a mere immigrant. I'm exercising my territorial rights of primacy. First in time, first in line. I have the inherent right to first claims where the fruits of bounty are concerned."

"Well, if you insist on opening that oven every five minutes, you'll be laying claim to an undercooked turkey and uncooked stuffing."

"It's all your fault. Dinner smells so delicious, the aroma is getting my digestive juices flowing."

"Don't waste any of your blarney on me. Flattery will get you nowhere."

"You sure could use some manners when it comes to making a guest feel welcome."

Katie choked back, "Ha! A guest. You stopped being a guest about ten dinners ago. You're more of a pest than a guest. Now, make yourself scarce. Go join the rest of the men in the living room where you belong. It sounds to me like they've got a lively game of Monopoly going."

Matt reached into his trouser pockets and pulled the linings inside out. "Can't. The greedy landlords wiped me out. Heartlessly, threw me out in the street, bankrupt. You're raising some mighty unscrupulous, entrepreneurs. Abraham will be lucky if he still maintains possession of his cottage, and Frank even a quarter of an acre of his land, by the time those five vultures are done picking apart what remains of their carcasses."

He reached into the relish tray and stole a short fistful of black olives. He managed to pop them into his mouth before Katie swatted him with a wooden spoon.

"Stop snitching. You'll spoil your appetite. You're worse than having another boy around here. You possess absolutely no patience."

She raised her one eyebrow. Matt recognized the warning. Through a mouthful of olives he surrendered.

"All right, all right. I'm leaving. There's no need to resort to violence."

He mumbled as he left the kitchen, "I'll never learn. That is one single-minded, stubborn female."

Lottie virtually blew in the back door on a gust of icy wind. "Lord, but it's colder'n a witch's tit in a brass bra, I tell ya what! Ain't snowin' yet, but not fawr lack a tryin'. Those clouds are 'bout nine an' a half months pregnant an' jus' a waitin' ta bust open."

Lottie twirled into the kitchen and slapped down a dish of what Katie could only guess, were candied yams. Taking off her long, mink coat, underneath Lottie was dressed to the nine's.

She wore a scarlet, scooped-neck, cashmere sweater that scooped dangerously low, revealing her generous cleavage. Black, stretch toreador pants fit her like a second skin and she added three inches to her elfin height with black, sling-back heels. Ruby and gold jewelry hung from her ears, neck and wrists. She unwound a serpentine-long chiffon scarf from her head, revealing coal black hair, coifed and molded like Cleopatra.

Katie clapped her hands. "Love the new hair-do, Lottie."

Lottie stroked the glossy strands. "Ya do, huh? I ain't so sure 'bout it. Could be a bit tame fawr ma taste."

Katie cocked her head to one side and re-evaluated. "Yes. I do. I really do. It becomes you."

Lottie shrugged her shoulders. "What tha heck. Guess I'll try it fawr a while." Giving the situation no more than a second's consideration, she dismissed it, grabbed an apron from the drawer and tied it on. "What kin I do ta help?" Lottie asked.

Katie almost snapped back at her, "Nothing! Don't touch anything! I have it all under control."

Shock registered on Lottie's face. "Well, 'scuse me fawr askin'."

"I appreciate the offer," Katie's voice softened as she tried to undo the damage, "but you already brought a dish. That's help enough."

"So what am I s'posed ta do? Jus' stand here an' itch ma ass while ya do all tha work?"

Katie scrambled quickly, running a mental list of what assignment she could give Lottie that wouldn't result in something inedible. She zeroed in on the relish tray. Even Lottie couldn't ruin that.

"Why don't you finish arranging the relishes? The rest of the things are in the refrigerator—pickles, celery, carrots, green olives and spiced apples. You'll find them."

Lottie retrieved the items and sat down at the table. "Sug. Y'all been dietin' er somethin'?" She scoped Katie up and down, "Ya look like ya lost some weight."

Katie wiped her hands on a dishtowel. "No, I don't think so? I sure haven't been dieting. Weight's never been a problem for me."

Lottie clicked her tongue. "Puttin' weight on may not be a problem fawr ya, but keepin' it on sure is. Them clothes are hangin' on ya like a flour sack."

Katie did a quick assessment. Lottie was right. Her black sweater and slacks were a bit loose. She just never paid any attention to it. "Guess I have lost a pound or two. It's no big deal. I'll be able to eat more turkey and stuffing and pumpkin pie." She pushed it aside without further thought and changed the subject. "Didn't see you at the parade this morning. You missed a good one. It was wonderful. The Mayor and his wife were the Grand Marshals."

"Wuz he shakin' hands an' kissin' babies?" Lottie asked.

"No. He was riding in a convertible."

"Wuz she sober?"

"I would think so! It was nine o'clock in the morning!"

"Well, that explains it. Musta been too early in tha day fawr her ta have her tootful. Is she still fat an' ugly?"

"Be kind. This is Thanksgiving. She's not fat at all, just plump."

Lottie was unimpressed. "Still ugly."

"Retract your claws, Lottie. They looked very nice and were the picture of propriety and sobriety. Can I assume from your comments that you don't agree with Trump's politics?"

"I vote fawr tha man not his politics. Politics ain't got a thin' ta do with it. Trump Baskins is like mos' politicians an' prostitutes. Jus' lookin' for another way ta screw ya, take yawr money an' get away with it."

"Lottie, I'm surprised at you. Not every politician is crooked."

"I don't like either of 'em, pure an' simple. They think their farts don't stink. Hell, Izzy and Trump Baskins got more skeletons buried than Forest Lawn. They jus' buried theirs deeper than mos' folks. He'd lie ta ya outta both sides a his mouth at tha same time. An' she waddles inta tha beauty parlor without an appointment an' expects Evelyn ta drop what she's doin' an' wait on her hand an' foot. Both of 'em have forgotten that they wipe from front ta back jus' like tha rest of us."

Katie redirected the conversation. "But, the bands! And their uniforms! They were really terrific. They played beautifully and certainly put me in the holiday mood. You could use a bit of that Christmas spirit to put you in the holiday mood." Katie warbled cheerfully.

"If I get me an itch ta hear "Rudolph the Red-Nosed Reindeer" I got a Burl Ives record ta put me in tha mood."

Katie shook her head and rolled her eyes heavenward. She wasn't going to let Lottie dampen her good humor. "Well, bah-humbug to you, too, Lottie Scrooge. You missed Mr. and Mrs. Santa Claus. The beautiful floats. Reindeer and elves. Made me feel like a child again. I enjoyed it as much as the boys."

Lottie popped a pickle in her mouth and munched, "Sug, unless Charleton Heston an' Kirk Douglas were marchin' in that parade buck-ass-necked, there ain't no way I woulda froze off ma giggly-weeds outside taday."

Like Matt, everyone's digestive juices were flowing as the house filled with the delicious aroma of roast turkey, sage stuffing, cinnamon and nutmeg spices and fresh baked bread. By six o'clock, the meal was ready and Katie presented the twenty-two pound, golden, luscious, juicy bird to the hungry crew.

The dining room table, stretched to its maximum, almost groaned from the weight of the Thanksgiving feast. Katie always cooked as if she were preparing an army to go off to war. There was the relish tray, coleslaw and oyster soup for the first course. Side dishes of mashed potatoes with giblet gravy, tart cranberry-orange relish, and like the guests at the first Thanksgiving, Frank Mizzano contributed six beautiful acorn squash to the feast. The glazed carrots, rye bread and chestnut stuffing were passed around. Lottie's candied yams were also passed around untouched, with record-breaking speed.

Matt carved the moist, tender turkey. He declared that the drumsticks were presented to whomever had been extra good the past year. He laid the first on Tommy's plate, winked and placed the second on his own plate. Casey and Colin called the wishbone. Katie outdid herself with dessert. She had baked a porter cake, blackberry-apple and pumpkin pies. By the end of the meal, waistbands had tightened in direct proportions to the amount of food consumed.

The celebrants had a lot to be grateful for that Thanksgiving. Each one, going around the table, had to share one thing that they were thankful for. Katie started, blessing the special friends that had honored them by their presence at the table, Abraham, Lottie, Matt, Frank Mizzano and Vincent. Katie had gone way out on a limb when she invited Frank and Vincent. The branch could have snapped and left her dangling in the air. But, Frank had seemed pleased and accepted the invitation without pause.

Brendan was grateful for all the help he had received from Dr. Franke and Mr. Mulholland making the sailboat seaworthy. Lottie was thankful that they weren't crotch deep in snow, yet. Tommy thanked the Lord and his Mommy for letting him keep Chance, even if he still had accidents on the floor. Casey was glad that he finally got all his spelling words right. Colin was happy to have Sister Thomas Aquinas back and Sister Benedetta gone. Vincent thanked Mrs. O'Neill for having them over for Thanksgiving dinner.

When the progression made its way to Frank Mizzano, he held his breath for a moment and then verbalized his thanks. "I'm thankful to Mrs. O'Neill for inviting us here today … and … for … other things. To the school for giving me a full-time janitor's job. And to Father Davey and my sponsor at AA, Hugh Vauld, for keeping me sober for eighty-seven and a half days."

Matt was thankful that there were only five months left until the lake would thaw and he could launch Scattering.

Finally, it was Abraham's turn. Katie lifted her eyes to gaze upon the man who had become her dearest friend. Abraham paused a moment before he began.

"I am pleased and honored to be sharing this meal with so many wonderful people and good friends."

Katie, who knew more secrets about Abraham than anyone else, was the only one aware that he had avoided the words grateful or thankful. The omission weighed upon her heart like a stone. She reconciled herself to the fact that, for now, she would have to settle for the satisfaction that he had accepted them into his life. For now that would have to be enough.

With eyes fighting back tears, she softly added, "Amen."

The warm glow of cheery light filled the muntoned, windowpanes, painted by nature's delicate hand with crystals of frosty, lacy-white strokes. The O'Neill home was immersed in the comfort and companionship as friends shared the holiday. The merrymakers continued the feast and festivities in a clamor of activity, uproarious laughter and conversation, snug and cozy inside. Outside, darkness completed its descent all along Lakefield Road and the firstborn snowflakes of the season were silently, steadily falling, covering everything with a soft, downy white quilt.

chapter twenty-five

Lottie, driven by invisible demons, was itching for another of her famous precipitous expeditions. She dreaded facing the gloomy, gray, slushy days as November passed into December. She had taken a fancy to the thought of taking the train out of Grand Rapids and visiting friends in Natchez. While she was there, of course driven by her other equally insatiable appetite, that for spending money, she could do her Christmas shopping.

Katie seized the opportunity to drive her to catch the train and do some Christmas shopping of her own in Grand Rapids. Woodbury's Department Store in Eden Croft was sufficient for routine, day to day purchases, but is was sorely lacking in toys and other extravagances that put the excitement into Christmas. Katie was used to shopping in Boston, where she had endless choices and selections, limited only by time and purse strings.

That Christmas, Katie vowed, was going to be the best one ever.

Katie had a deep and passionate love affair with the season, complete with its traditions, trappings, merriment and chaos. After the holidays of the last two years, she felt the need to make up for lost time. They had been especially difficult times for her and the boys. The first had been overshadowed with mourning and the still fresh wounds from the loss of Danny. His absence darkened the entire season, transforming it from one of celebration and jubilation to one of loneliness and pain.

By the second Christmas, not only did they have to deal with another season without Danny, Katie had also been overcome with the hardship of living without the luxury of a steady paycheck. Even though she had scrimped and saved, counted every spare dime to be able to have something special under the tree for each one, even though she had struggled with tree trimming and decorations, even though she had cooked and baked and fussed, nothing had seemed like Christmas, at all.

For the boys, she had forced herself to go through all the motions. But in spite of all her efforts, the tinsel hadn't been as shiny, the lights hadn't been as bright, the icicles hadn't sparkled, the packages had been fewer and less intriguing, the delicacies she had created had been flat and tasteless. Even the manger, with the infant Jesus, hadn't seemed to radiate the same awe and wonderment of years past. But, this year would be different. Katie planned the holiday right down to the tiniest sprig of holly.

The idea of shopping in Grand Rapids, a place she had never heard of before moving to Michigan, thrilled Katie to her bones. She was so excited by the prospect of exploring the shops in a new city that she thought the day would never arrive. She planned to shop from dawn to dusk. All the arrangements had been made. Abraham had graciously rearranged his schedule and lectures that day enabling him to come over in the morning to see the boys off to school and return, again, after school to see to their dinner and homework. Katie had baked her famous sticky buns for their breakfast. By now, the boys were beginning to groan about Thanksgiving leftovers, "Again"? So for dinner, she had prepared homemade chicken noodle soup, salad, yellow buck and a pineapple upside-down cake for dessert.

The meal would be easy for Abraham to reheat and serve and the boys would be responsible for clean up and dishes. Their clothes were all laid out for school and lunch boxes packed. Katie had hoped to be home before the boys went to bed, but she prepared them in case she ran late.

Rivaling the conscientiousness of Santa Claus, she made her list and checked it twice and then checked it a third time. If all went as well as expected, she planned to reward herself with a quiet, leisurely, not too expensive lunch at a nice restaurant. She couldn't remember the last time she had done that!

Setting the alarm clock had been an unnecessary precaution. She hardly slept the night before. The Monday after Thanksgiving she had woken an hour before it was set to go off, washed, bathed and combed her hair in record time, humming merrily the whole time. She slipped into her black mohair sweater, gray wool skirt and black flats. She was too excited to waste even a second's glance at herself in the mirror. After hurriedly gulping down toast and a cup of tea, she capped her head with her jaunty black wool tam, threw on her gray tweed coat and black gloves, zipped up her rubber galoshes, snatched her purse and all but flew out the back door on Mercury's wings.

Lottie chewed her up one side and down the other for knocking on her door "before anybody livin' in a civilized society had a right ta be up!"

Still miffed about Katie's excited and early arrival, Lottie had scolded her half the way to Grand Rapids, but the tirade hadn't dampened Katie's spirits. After dropping Lottie off at the train station, her well-planned day began.

Grand Rapids greeted her dressed-up in its finest holiday costumes and decorations. Colorful, electrified poinsettias, blinking bells and Christmas trees hung from every lamppost and tinsel and colored lights were strung across every intersection and anything that would stand still. Store and shop window's displays sported animated, wintry woodland and North Pole scenes complete with prancing reindeer, bouncing bunnies and raccoons and sledding hedgehogs, while penguins whirled and twirled across a make-believe frozen pond. Gaily clothed, red cheeked, busy elves peeked out from the windows of gingerbread houses and Santa's workshop. Every doorway enticed shoppers with red bows; sprays of holly, candy canes, draped garland and shiny ornaments adorned Christmas trees in all the store windows. Traditional Christmas music escaped from opened doors as customers, arms laden with packages, hustled and bustled in and out.

The festive atmosphere elevated her holiday spirits higher and bolstered by the electrified mood, Katie had been able to complete nearly all of her shopping and still worked in a restful unhurried lunch at a quaint little cafe. The few items left on her gift list could be easily purchased at Woodbury's. Even Old Man Winter cooperated. It had been cold, blustery and sunless all day, but the heavy clouds held, and the roads stayed clear and dry, both occurrences an apparent novelty for late November in Michigan.

It was later than Katie had originally planned when she turned onto Lakefield Road. But, even though the boys would be asleep, it still wasn't all that late. She hoped the day had been uneventful for Abraham. No matter how skilled her planning had been, the boys were like ticking time bombs, capable of going off at any second, blasting any stratagem or schedule to smithereens. Well, she always had a back-up plan, Brendan. There was no way, even for the twins, to hold both Abraham and Brendan hostage.

Her rendition of "White Christmas," that she had been singing nearly the entire way from Grand Rapids, died upon her lips. As she pulled up to the garage, Katie's self-reassurance quickly dissolved. The house was lit up like a church. It was well past the boy's bedtime; they couldn't possibly still be up. She blinked away the vision of walking into the living room and finding both Abraham and Brendan gagged and bound to chairs, while two savages, complete with war paint, danced and circled their captives.

She quietly entered through the kitchen door, pulled off her gloves, boots and hat and set them, along with her purse, on the kitchen table. The house was quiet, enough. No Indian war hoops, no muffled screams of hostages. As she was beginning to relax, Brendan came running into the kitchen. His face was flushed, a look of panic in his eyes.

"Brendan, it's way past your bedtime. What are you still doing up? You have school tomorrow, young man."

"Mom, you got to come upstairs, quick. Tommy got sick at school today, Dr. Franke had to come and get him. He's up in his room. He's real sick. We didn't know what to do."

Katie put her arm around his shoulder, trying to calm him. "It's okay,

Bren. Kids get sick all the time. You boys are always coming down with one thing or another. I'll go up and check on him, now. It's probably no more than a cold or flu, maybe his tonsils. Remember how sick you used to get before you had your tonsils out? Don't get yourself so upset over this."

She calmly slipped off her coat and went upstairs. When she walked into Tommy's room, Abraham was sitting in a chair next to the bedside holding one, tiny, limp hand in his. Chance was in his usual place, lying at the foot of the bed. Taking one look at Tommy she knew it wasn't a simple cold or flu or even tonsils. His eyes were closed, face crimson, hair wet from perspiration. Abraham had placed a wet washcloth on his forehead. Katie knelt down beside him, feeling his cheeks with the back of her hand.

She lifted the covers and his pajama top to look at his chest. Pressing them back into place she asked Abraham, "How long has he been this warm?"

Abraham shook his head, his face gaunt and drawn in anguish. At that moment he looked and felt far older than his years.

"He did not get this sick until around six o'clock. Up until then he just complained that he felt ill and ached all over. He refused any dinner or drink, not even a sip of juice or water. He has been restless, half-asleep and half-conscious like this, since eight. The only thing I could think to do was to try and keep him cool with compresses. I remember … I seem to remember Zora doing that when … when Daniel had a fever."

Katie patted his hand, understanding the pain that the memory elicited. "You did the right thing, Abraham. Have you taken his temperature?"

All Abraham could manage was a slight shake of his head.

"You stay here with him. I'll go get the thermometer."

Returning to Tommy's bed, she snapped the thermometer, shook down the mercury and tucked it under his armpit. After the requisite three minutes, Katie verified what she already suspected; it read one hundred and four degrees.

"I'm going downstairs for just a minute to telephone Dr. Hughes. I'll be right back. Tommy will be fine," she added with far more surety than she felt. "Dr. Hughes will be here shortly. It will only feel like an eternity. It always seems that way, waiting for the doctor to come."

Waiting for the doctor did seem like an eternity. And it seemed like a second eternity waiting for him to complete his examination and give them his diagnosis. Abraham and Chance paced outside the bedroom, each one looking more somber than the other. Brendan sat on the top step of the staircase, repeatedly pounding a baseball into his mitt. As if on autopilot, like a robot, he must have repeated the motion a thousand times. Thankfully, the twins were sleeping undisturbed in their room. The house was deathly quiet. The silence broken only by the steady, rhythmic sound of baseball slapped against leather.

Finally, the door opened and Dr. Hughes came out, alone, carrying his black leather satchel. Abraham and Brendan looked at him with frantic, questioning anxious eyes. Abraham held his breath and anticipated the worst. He didn't know if he had the strength to lose another loved one.

"Don't you two look so fatal, the boy has rheumatic fever not small pox. With rest, a mother's care and God's blessing, he'll be good as new. Right now, my main concern is that he doesn't spread it to anyone else."

Abraham quickly offered, "I can take the boys to the guest cottage. They can stay there with me as long as necessary."

Dr. Hughes rubbed his weary eyes.

"I think I have a better idea. Rather than upsetting the whole household as well as spreading the germs to everyone else, it may be wiser to have Katie and Tommy move into your place. Keep them isolated. That way we'll have a better chance of keeping the virus contained. It usually runs its course in ten to fourteen days. Do you think you two bachelors can manage those twins on your own for that long?"

Abraham and Brendan both nodded. Abraham assured him they would do whatever was required.

After Dr. Hughes left, Brendan and Abraham went to the cottage to pack clothes, toiletries, texts and papers, all the essential items that Abraham would need for the next two weeks. Then they readied the cottage for Tommy and Katie.

Shortly before midnight the small entourage made its way to the guesthouse. Katie carried a cardboard box filled with the few things she anticipated needing. Anything missed or forgotten could be delivered as needed. Abraham carried Tommy, swaddled in a quilt. Katie hadn't wanted to increase Abraham's exposure to the fever, but her protests were summarily dismissed. He wouldn't trust the precious cargo to anyone else. Trailing behind was Chance. Wherever Tommy went, Chance tagged along. He wasn't about to be left behind. Katie didn't have the heart to send him home. Besides, she thought his companionship would be good for Tommy.

Abraham didn't leave the threshold of the cottage until he was certain that Katie and Tommy were comfortably settled in. At last, the green door closed on him. With a sad and heavy heart, tears of fear and dismay stinging his eyes, feeling desperately lost and afraid, for the first time in eight years, Abraham Franke prayed.

CB BO

The first five days were the hardest and most trying on everyone. Ministering to Tommy, Katie had hardly slept a wink. It was a continuous, round the clock effort. To reduce the dangerously high fever, she continuously bathed his flaccid, limp, feverish body in tepid water. The best she could manage was preventing it from going any higher. Tommy had slept restlessly and listlessly, occasionally mumbling and had to struggle to stay awake longer than a few minutes at a time. She applied glycerin with Q-tip swabs to his parched, cracked lips to keep them moistened. Ice chips, Jell-O water and Popsicles were the only fluids or nutrition she could coax him to swallow. Getting him to swallow the medicine Dr. Hughes had prescribed and baby aspirin every four hours was a monumental task.

Over and over, like a mantra, Katie sang Irish lullabies and read his favorite stories. She didn't know for sure if he comprehended any of it but the repetition and familiarity helped soothe her worries. Each day she recited the rosary offering it up for Tommy's recovery. Chance hardly left the bedside. It was as if his canine instincts sensed that something was terribly wrong. Katie couldn't explain it but she was convinced that he somehow knew.

Abraham stopped by every morning and evening. He used the excuse that he was the self-proclaimed errand boy, but in reality, he hoped for news of improvement. One evening, he brought along the shamrock plant he had given Tommy and his beloved baseball cap. He thought they might help cheer him up.

He would answer Katie's many questions about the boys. How were they managing? Were they keeping up with their schoolwork? Was everyone eating properly? How was the laundry getting done? He tried to alleviate her worries that the household was managing nicely. Angie, Connie, Rose, Birdie and Liz rotated bringing meals and helping with laundry and housework. Each one took three days and they divvied up the household chores and marketing.

The boys weren't allowed to go into the cottage, but each night, before bed, they paid a visit to the little cottage and from the threshold, Katie would blow them goodnight kisses.

Brendan had risen to the occasion. Abraham reported to Katie that he had become quite the zealous taskmaster. He was like a shepherd with a little flock. He herded the twins off to school in the morning, home again in the afternoon and off to bed at night. He made sure that homework was completed and that they were reasonably clean and tidy for school. He nagged after them to pick up their messes and complete their chores. He settled their disagreements and spats. The twins had threatened mutiny, on more than one occasion, that "he wasn't the boss," but Brendan squashed their protests with sometimes vulgar, but apparently effective threats. Though Abraham questioned his tactics, he could not argue with the results.

Dr. Hughes made a house call each evening to check on Tommy's progress. He reassured Katie that the fever was good as long as it didn't rise higher. The fever would help his body fight the germs. Hospitalization wouldn't be neces-

sary as long as he kept taking fluids and the symptoms didn't worsen. Katie had
gasped at the mere mention of a hospital. Both of her parents had been hospitalized and it was there that they had both died. Dr. Hughes reassured her, that
in this case, he was confident that Tommy would make a full recovery.

He was not as confident about Katie. Her face was pallid and drawn, her
lips colorless. Dark crescent-moons had formed under her eyes. Even her eyes
had lost much of their sparkle. Dr. Hughes was sure she had lost weight as her
already slender frame grew painfully thinner. He felt her forehead, hoping he
wouldn't find her feverish, but her skin was cool.

He scolded her, "I'm more worried about you than I am about your patient. Mrs. O'Neill. It won't do Tommy, or anyone else, any good if you catch
the fever, too. Taking one look at you, it doesn't require a doctor to figure out
that you're not taking proper care of yourself. When was the last time you slept
or ate a decent meal?"

"Missing a meal or two isn't doing me any harm. I'm sure I'll be fine."

Dr. Hughes admonished her, "Let me be the judge of what's harmful and
what's fine, Mrs. O'Neill."

"It's just that I'm afraid to leave his side. And I need to keep bathing him,
to help control the fever … and the ice chips …"

Dr. Hughes interrupted. "It's more likely you'll bathe the skin right off
him. Here is my prescription, for both of you. Bathe him every three hours, not
constantly. Ice chips and fluids when he rouses. Aspirin and penicillin every
four hours. When he sleeps, you sleep. For you, young lady, orange juice three
times a day and at least two proper meals a day. Step outside for a breath of
fresh air. It will do you and him a world of good."

Katie managed a strained smile and nodded her head. Dr. Hughes grabbed
his bag, hat and coat. He wagged an accusing finger at her, before he left. "Rest,
food and some fresh air for you. Doctor's orders. If you don't follow them, I'll
throw both of you into the hospital."

ᘓ   ᘔ

The cloud of worry that had hung over them for twelve days lifted as
Tommy's fever finally broke and he showed rapid improvement. By the end of
two weeks Dr. Hughes was satisfied the risk of the contagion had passed and
the separation and quarantine ended. Katie and Tommy moved out of the cottage and the household settled back into its routine.

As Dr. Hughes predicted, Tommy made a full recovery. He had lost weight
and was weak for a while, but gained back his weight and spunk quickly. At his
final check-up he was declared sound and fit, again, with no residual after effects. Listening intently with his stethoscope, he couldn't detect any discernible
heart murmur and Dr. Hughes gave him a lollipop and a clean bill of health.

Katie's recovery was not happening as quickly. Not only had the pallor not improved, she appeared even more washed and anemic. She was plagued with fatigue and listlessness. She had to force herself out of bed in the morning and fell into bed at night, worn and weary. Routine, daily tasks that were usually performed automatically and vigorously suddenly became overwhelming and exhausting. She hadn't even been able to make the drive to pick Lottie up at the train station, as promised. Instead, she had to prevail upon Abraham to make the trip. Giving into pressure from Abraham and Matt, she promised Dr. Hughes that right after the holidays she would schedule an appointment. It was past due, anyway. She hadn't had a thorough examination since the twins were born.

☙ ❧

The memory of the days of tension and fear were soon washed away by the needs of the present. With the passage of time, they became less clear and significant and like all of life's trials and tribulations, once they were endured, they joined the ranks of the past, not to be forgotten, but simply laid to rest.

The adversity and hardship of Tommy's illness tested the character of everyone as well as the relationships. During the days of the forced isolation and quarantine, an interesting transformation had taken place. Abraham discovered something about himself and about the special family that had miraculously found their way into his life.

He was convinced that fate ruled the universe and some of the most important things in life happen as a matter of chance. If chance was the parent of circumstance, then in this case, its offspring came in the shape of a transformation. The most amazing aspect of the transformation was Abraham's realization that he had come to understand need. Human need. That Katie and her sons needed him as much as he had come to need them. That they had become as important to him as life itself. In spite of his effort to remain autonomous, they had silently crept into his life until suddenly, he needed them. He needed them to remain a part of his world and he needed to become a part of theirs. He no longer wanted to be alone.

What a fool he had been. His self-imposed retreat from humanity had been wasteful. Absorbed with bitterness and hatred he had squandered time and wasted far too many years. All of it had been so senseless and useless. His self-pity and self-reproach could never bring Zora and Daniel back. As their images crept into his mind, the heartache of that vision mingled with the panic he had felt when he saw Tommy so dangerously ill. In his mind, that sweet face and that of his Daniel's melded together as one.

Abraham struggled with internal turmoil. He had existed alone for so long. Would he know how not to be alone? Was he being given a second chance? He had no power to change the past, but he did have the power to guide his future. Was he willing to risk caring that much, again, to be that vulnerable, again?

The questions alluded to something absolute and portentous and the startling truth shocked his soul. He hadn't been afraid of finding love again. He had been afraid of losing it.

chapter twenty-six

The camel, donkey and lamb weren't cooperating at all, threatening to level the palm trees, inn, stable and manger, destroying *Bethlehem* domino style.

Already de-crowned and nearly defrocked, the Magi were engaged in the first stages of a full-blown fisticuffs because Wise Man Number One had stepped on the robes of Wise Man Number Two and Wise Man Number Three, not wanting to be excluded, jumped right in.

Like a meteor, the star in the east had fallen to earth. Mary and Joseph were anxiously poised, like racehorses at the starting gate, ready to grab the baby Jesus and head for Egypt. Two shepherds had been forced off the stage and a disgruntled and disgusted Angel of the Lord had thrown down her halo and wings and stormed offstage. She had completely given up trying to bring tidings of great joy. Only the baby Jesus stayed in character, due entirely to the fact that the role was filled by a Tiny Tears doll. Katie spotted Tommy and the twins in the chorus of Bethlehemites and smiled and waved to them.

The production was being played out before a packed house, the school auditorium filled to capacity, overflowing with faculty, parents, family, friends and Father Davey and the Sisters. Incapable of stifling their laughter any longer, laughter spread across the auditorium like a wave over water.

Katie laughed so hard her sides and cheeks ached. Even Abraham, who already held a skeptical view regarding the birth of Christ and who was usually serious as sin, couldn't help himself and was infected by the laughter. Matt's assignment had been to take pictures and capture the moments on film. But he was shaking so much from laughter that he finally gave up trying to steady his camera.

Poor Sister Aloysius stood backstage, hiding behind the curtain, on the verge of tears, convinced that God had abandoned her in her hour of need. She watched as her carefully planned, rehearsed and directed Nativity play turned into a low-budget version of the *Little Rascals* meet *Ben Hur*. Sister Mary Therese feared for the safety of the youngsters and the health and sanity of Sister Aloysius. She pulled the curtains closed and brought a decidedly timely and final conclusion to what would be forever after referred to as the "Christmas Calamity of St. Anthony's."

Since the disastrous pageant had to be aborted, a gaping space of time needed to be filled. Sister Mary Therese made an executive decision and an impromptu group sing-along unfolded. They closed the holiday program accompanied by Sister Francis De Salles on the piano. The entire cast and audience joined together with a selection of favorite Christmas hymns. It wasn't a performance anywhere close to the Mormon Tabernacle Choir, but it was festive, all the same.

As they devoured banana splits the size of the Grand Teton's at the fountain at Hastings', Matt's treat, they relived, rehashed and repeated their fits of laughter over the performance. Katie, Matt and Abraham simultaneously came to the same conclusion. The one shocking circumstance was the fact that not one of the contributing causes of the disaster could be directly or indirectly, however remote the possibility, linked to, or in any way associated, with either one of the twins.

CR   BO

The school year of 1953 ended three days before Christmas. It was amazing to every adult that any teacher anywhere could be successful in holding the interest of their students the last few days before the holiday break. Keeping all of that energy and emotion under control must have been am impossible endeavor. The O'Neill boys of Lakefield Road were no exception. On the last day of school, they arrived home from the bus giddy with the excitement of the season as well as the thrill of no more school until after the New Year.

The gift giving had already begun. All the older students were given a silver chain bearing a medal of the Sacred Heart, the younger students, a holy card depicting the birth of Christ and a stand-up, three-dimensional, cutout scene of the Nativity complete with a glittered star over the manger. Casey and Colin scurried upstairs to their room to seek out the perfect spot to display theirs. Tommy wanted to share his and displayed it prominently on the living room mantle where everyone could enjoy it. The Advent wreath candles were well burned and the Advent calendar had only three more windows to be opened until the long-awaited night that would herald the arrival of both Santa Claus and the Baby Jesus.

Since Matt would be spending Christmas Eve and Christmas Day with his family, Katie decided to have their get-together on the twenty-third. Two large balsam wreaths with bright red bows, hung on the double entrance doors. The house on Lakefield Road was filled with the pungent fragrance of cedar, balsam and spruce boughs. Poinsettias, wreaths and garlands of bayberry, ivy and holly from Abraham's greenhouse, adorned every archway, staircase, vacant tabletop and unoccupied surface. One healthy sprig of mistletoe hung from the arched beam leading to the foyer.

The center of attention, of course, was the twelve-foot tall Douglas fir that Matt had helped Brendan cut and set it up in the oriel overlooking the lake. It had been a monumental task that Matt pointed out would most likely result in bilateral hernias for both of them. As they wrestled and dragged the tree through the entry, they left an eight-foot-wide trail of needles through the living room.

The tree listed precariously to one side and Katie had begged and pleaded with them that it would never remain standing. Tired and exasperated, Matt solved the problem once and for all. As Katie gasped in horror, he nailed two spikes through the base and right into the wooden floor.

When Katie pulled out the tangled jumble of light cords, Matt took one look at them, groaned, and sent Colin to the punch bowl for another cup of mead. There was no way he was going to tackle that mess without potable fortification.

Eventually, the tree decorating was completed. It was trimmed in heirloom ornaments that Katie had carefully protected through the years. Added to her own collection, she had found a treasure trove of beautiful glass bulbs stored away in the attic. There were three glass birds with real white feather tails that clipped to the branches. Some of the ornaments were as delicate as spun sugar, some simple and some as ornate as Faberge eggs. Letting the boys hang the less treasured bulbs, Katie reserved the most delicate and fragile for hanging, herself. The most prized ornament was a four-inch-tall glass figurine of Santa Claus. Each year, in rotation, the boys would take a turn hanging it. This year, it was Brendan's turn, but he said that he would give his turn to Tommy. He didn't elaborate why, but his mother knew.

For more than two weeks, Katie had popped dozens of batches of popcorn that she had fed onto thread, alternately with cranberries, creating yards of garland that draped the tree. Atop the tinseled, garlanded, icicled, ornamented, pop corned and cranberried tree was the finishing touch, a snowy white angel, hands folded in prayer.

With fingers crossed hopefully, they all stood back to watch the official lighting. Matt sifted through the noodle swamp of electric and extension cords to find the plug and pushed it into the socket. Everyone, with simultaneous precision, breathed a sigh of relief and wonderment. Every light lit and created a halo of soft light that cast a warm glow over the entire room. No one spoke the words, but everyone knew that it really was the most beautiful Christmas tree in the world.

Before opening gifts, they had a light meal of cold roast beef, pickled herring, cheese, fruit and rye bread. An assortment of cookies, cakes and confections that Katie had baked and prepared for the holidays were displayed temptingly on white, lacy doilies carefully arranged on a huge silver tray. Sweet meringues, scones with raspberry jam, oatcakes, plum cake, gingerbread and molasses cookies, butterfly buns and iced queen and fairy cakes laid tempting and tantalizing.

Finally, she could hold the boys at bay not one minute longer. Katie mused that patience wasn't a characteristic of the young. Once turned loose on the gaily-wrapped packages, the twins virtually dove into the gifts Matt had placed under the tree, tearing away the paper that concealed the loot. The twins squealed with delight at complete cowboy outfits with shearling vests, silver spurs, red cowboy hats, fringed chaps and holsters with cap guns. Just to irk their mother, Matt had filled two shoeboxes bursting with rolls and rolls of caps.

The twins, in unison, shouted, "REAL CAPS!"

Katie gave Matt a raised eyebrow and lectured him, "You certainly have a preoccupation with explosives. What is so intriguing about gunpowder? Why does it hold such a fascination for you? If you had your way, my children would eventually blow this house into kingdom come. I promise you that you and I will have a serious discussion about the gunpowder issue, later."

He winked at Katie. "Guess I just like seeing how close I can get to anything that might explode without getting burned."

Katie ignored the innuendo riding the crest of that remark.

Trying to appear very grown up, Brendan took his time opening his package. Inside he found six shiny brass fittings and cleats for the sailboat. Never imagining that he would ever be able to afford real brass, they may as well have been made of solid gold. His eyes and mouth formed three perfectly matched circles of surprise.

"Wow ... brass! Thanks, Mr. Mulholland. These are swell. I promise I'll keep 'em polished and shined like new."

"Any proper sailboat deserves proper fittings. It wouldn't do to have anything second rate on a first rate boat."

Matt reached behind the sofa and pulled out a large wooden box. The tag on the box read, "To the O'Neill Boys."

He announced, "One last gift for the whole gang."

They unlatched the metal clasp and lifted the lid. The inside was packed with a virtual treasure chest of games, dominoes, checkers, chess, Chinese checkers, Parcheesi, Pick-up-sticks, Backgammon, Yahtzee and four decks of cards, including Crazy Eights and Old Maid.

Matt teased them. "I'm getting sick and tired of having my pants beat off me in Monopoly by you four cut-throats. Now, you're going to have to face me on my own playing field. I'm accurately known in these parts as the undisputed champion of Chinese checkers. So, gentlemen, prepare to meet your match and hold onto *your* pants."

Tommy sat patiently on the floor. He noticed that there wasn't a present under the tree with his name on the tag. Not wanting to appear greedy or selfish, he said nothing. But his mind raced trying to figure out a plausible explanation.

"Oh, holy smokes!" Matt jumped off the sofa. "Tommy, I almost forgot, Tommy."

After a minute, he returned from the kitchen carrying a large, plain, unwrapped, brown cardboard box and carefully set it down in front of Tommy.

"Sorry for the plain packaging, but I couldn't chance wrapping it."

Tommy couldn't have cared less. He slowly undid the top flaps and peered inside. His expression was pure amazement. Carefully reaching in, he extracted a large, round fishbowl. Inside, among marbles, pebbles moss and small pool of water, perched on a stone was a tiny, painted turtle, no larger than a fifty-cent-piece. The O'Neill menagerie grew by one more species.

Tommy carried it over to coffee table and gingerly set it down. He was nearly speechless, but words weren't needed. The look of utter joy beamed from his freckled face. He walked over to Matt and placed a soft, gentle peck on his cheek. He whispered into his ear, shyly, a simple but genuine, "Thank you, Mr. Mulholland."

Matt replied in kind, "You're welcome, Tommy."

Brendan broke the spell of the moment. "Now maybe you won't be dragging home every busted up animal you find."

Matt asked, "What are you going to name him?"

Katie and the boys exchanged knowing glances and paused for a few seconds. Not because they were contemplating the questions, but because they shared the same thought that the answer was all too obvious. Collectively, they replied, all at the same time, "Timothy, of course."

Katie and the boys surprised Matt with an antique ship's bell that Katie had found in a small shop in Grand Rapids. It was brass and polished to a high gloss. They had it engraved in Gaelic letters with the name Scattering. Matt told them it was the finest ship's bell he had ever seen. And to him, coming from them, it always would be.

Saving the best for last, Matt handed Katie a small square, gold foil wrapped box tied with a green velvet ribbon. She carefully untied the bow and removed the top. Nestled in white tissue paper was an oval, ivory porcelain music box edged in gold. A circle of delicate, tiny green shamrocks adorned the lid. She lifted the lid. Clear, soft, tinkling notes played Katie's most cherished Irish tune. Losing herself completely in the moment, her memory recalled the words. She softly hummed along with the notes of "When Irish Eyes are Smiling".

Matt watched, as Katie's own smiling, sparkling, Irish green eyes misted over. Her face reflected the sweet radiance of an angel.

In a near whisper, she thanked him. "How beautiful ... how perfectly beautiful. That song takes me back to the dearest memory I have of my childhood. It is as if I can still hear my ma and da singing it to me, right now, just as they used to do when I was a wee one. It was at those times that I think they were the most homesick for Ireland. And I used to sing it to my boys when they were babes. There are times when I still do. How could you have ever known?"

"Let's just say that I know old St. Nick, personally. He owed me a favor."

Casey, with wide eyes, asked, "You really know Santa Claus?"

"You bet, Pardner. And let me warn you that because I know him so well, he sometimes asks me how certain little boys have been behaving, kind of like a spy. He asks if they've been naughty or nice. So, you'd better watch your step around me. If I give him a good report, you'll find a special gift under the tree this year. But, if I give him a bad report ... well, you might just find rocks in your socks."

Casey and Colin and Tommy shared looks of awe, wonder and perhaps a little fear. Brendan sat back, laughing, enjoying their reactions. "And if you two guys don't stay out of my stuff, I'll ask Mr. Mulholland to pass it on to Santa for me, too."

On cue, the grandfather clock struck nine o'clock, as if its chimes were omens, foretelling of impending doom, warning all little boys that Santa had eyes and ears everywhere. Unless they wanted to face disaster on Christmas morning, they had better mind their mothers. Likewise, on cue, Katie announced that she had let them stay up an hour later than usual and it was now time to toddle off to bed. They heeded Matt's warning and went without a struggle.

All the lights were turned off, but the soft light from flickering candles and the twinkling lights from the Christmas tree provided a soothing aura. Katie was physically exhausted but blissfully serene and happy. She and Matt snuggled into the soft cushions of the sofa. If either had asked of the other, "A penny for your thoughts," Katie would have answered that this Christmas was turning out to be just as magical as she hoped it would be. She would have said that just two years ago she had felt that her life had all but ended. Yet, here she was, experiencing a new, wonderful, exciting journey of possibilities. Maybe Lottie was right; maybe she could find true happiness again. Maybe it could happen twice for her.

And Matt would have responded that never, in his wildest dreams, had he ever thought that he could ever be so completely happy, that a Christmas could be this special, that a woman this special would have completely stolen his heart and left in its place a splendor of its own. As impossible and wonderful as it was, this was exactly where he wanted to be, where he felt he could be, where he wanted to be for the rest of his life.

Yet, each with their own kaleidoscope of thoughts, neither asked and neither answered. Instead, as peace and solitude settled over the house, at the same time it settled over the two of them. And it was there that they sat, content and satisfied with the simple joy of being in each other's company.

Katie nestled under an afghan and her head rested on Matt's shoulder until almost midnight. Speaking little, settled in front of the fireplace, they preferred to let the peace, tranquility and quiet, the crackling of the fire be their conversation.

chapter twenty-seven

After all the weeks of frantic preparations, the big night had finally arrived. By Christmas Eve, as the famed poem goes, "the stockings were hung by the chimney with care." More or less.

Before going to bed, the boys pounded four nails into the living room mantle and their stockings dangled in front of the fire. They were nothing fancy, simply plain, white, work socks that had belonged to their dad. Along with their lists, the boys left a glass of milk and a plate of cookies for Santa and a bundle of carrots for the reindeer. It had become a tradition for Katie to read "The Night Before Christmas" before her four excited boys scampered off to bed, anxious and certain that they would never be able to fall asleep. Their Mom had given them strict orders that six o'clock was the official acceptable hour for waking her up Christmas morning and not a minute sooner.

As they lay in bed, the twins chattered and fantasized about what surprises Santa had in store for them. Casey wanted Tinker Toys, army men and a truck. Colin was sure he would find Lincoln Logs, a teddy bear and paints under the tree.

"I betcha Bren doesn't get nothin' but a lump a coal. He doesn't even believe in Santa," Colin remarked.

"Sometimes Bren kin be such a big poo-poo face." Casey laughed.

"You better take it back. Mommy doesn't like us to use potty words," Colin warned him.

"Mommy can't hear us." Casey braved.

"No, but Santa's helpers kin. Remember what Mr. Mulholland said? Do you think Mr. Mulholland really knows Santa Claus? That he's a spy?" Colin asked.

Casey thought a minute before answering. "Prob'ly. He said so. He's a grownup an' grown-ups hafta tell the truth."

"I been extra good. 'Specially the last two days." Colin tried to sound convincing.

"I'm gonna stay awake all night so I can hear the reindeer on the roof," Casey proudly announced.

Colin added, "Me too. I wanna hear Santa come down the chimney an' land slap dab in the fireplace."

Within minutes of their proclamations, too tired to hold their eyes open, they both fell asleep.

Exhausted from the day, Katie pressed her tired body a bit further, making the dozen trips up and down the stairs, carrying packages from her closet and placing them under the tree. Winded and depleted, she finally snuggled under a quilt and had a cup of tea in front of the dying embers.

Katie loved Christmas Eve, maybe even more than Christmas Day. The anticipation, excitement and expectation made it a magical night. Tomorrow, it would all be over so quickly that it was almost anti-climatic. But, Christmas Eve crackled with excitation and promise; Katie savored the thrill of anticipation. Much like the mystery and wonderment of imagining what is inside an intriguing package, it was always more provocative to fantasize than to actually uncover the contents. The fascination of wondering was more thrilling than the discovery. Much like reading a good book, Katie wanted to prolong the anticipation as long as possible before it all ended with the final chapter. Christmas Eve was her time to relish in that expectation.

She could hear the moan of the wind beating the snow against the windows, making the warmth inside all the cozier. As she sat, she quietly savored the moment. Katie imagined the boys' reactions as they opened each of the gaily-wrapped gifts addressed to them from Santa Claus. With the addition of the customary pajamas and slippers, she had pretty much filled their wish lists. As she mentally clicked off every item, she was certain that it would be a wonderful Christmas. The only wish not granted were canvas sails for Brendan's sailboat. She had priced them, and disappointed, Katie had to eliminate them from his list. The cost was way beyond her budget. Maybe next year, she thought. He would just have to be patient. All things in good time.

ψ ω

Eden Croft awoke Christmas morning snowbound. Over night, three feet of snow had fallen with gusting winds causing drifts up to five feet. Santa must have had a rough night of it flying in that blizzard.

Outside was a winter wonderland. The Snow Queen had covered everything with mounds of purest white, like blankets of cotton batting and heaps of marshmallows. Then, as if she had taken a huge wooden spoon, dollops of whipped cream covered each evergreen bough until they were stooped and bent from the weight of the snow. For a finishing touch to her confectionary delight, she had sprinkled it all with fairy dust, glinting and sparkling, like millions of diamonds.

By morning the clouds had cleared and the sky was a brilliant blue, the air smelt crisp and fresh. Going to church that Christmas morning to celebrate the birth of the Christ Child was out of the question. Unless on snowshoes or with a horse and sleigh, no one was going anywhere.

After three false starts, one every fifteen minutes, starting at five o'clock, Katie had finally given up shooing the boys back to their rooms and dragged herself out of bed at five forty-five. The boys raced downstairs whooping and hollering that "Santa Came," as Katie padded slowly behind them yawning, still as tired as when she went to bed.

That year, it was Colin's turn to place the baby Jesus in the manger. They knelt before the stable and prayed together, wishing the newborn Savior a happy birthday. After checking to see that Santa had found their lists, the cookies, milk and carrots, they smiled with satisfaction when they discovered the glass empty, only crumbs on the plate, the carrots vanished and their lists no where in sight. They always attacked the stockings first, filled with oranges, nuts, a silver dollar and a special little treat. That year it was yo-yos.

With four rear-ends sticking up in the air, their heads all but buried in the pile of presents, the four boys tore through their presents in record time, in a fury of wrapping paper, ribbons, tags and boxes. Katie laughed that her carefully boxed, wrapped and tied packages, the task consuming hours of her time, were reduced to a heap of scrap in a matter of minutes.

Chance had landed in doggy heaven. He pranced and danced; tail wagging, tangling and untangling ribbons and chewing up paper and bows. He explored and sniffed discarded boxes like a bloodhound. While all around him, squeals of delight and laughter echoed through the house that hadn't heard the youthful joy and exuberance of Christmas morning, in many, many years. The room looked like someone had taken a huge eggbeater and whipped through a paper factory.

Like the calm after the storm, the dust settled from the tornado that had annihilated the pile of gifts from Santa and the boys presented Katie with their gifts.

The twins had made potholders in class, decorated with buttons and yarn. Tommy had made a candle inside a baby-food jar, with simulated stained glass from multi-colored tissue paper and a healthy coat of glitter. Abraham had helped Brendan build a birdhouse that he painted blue, his Mom's favorite color. They would be added to her cache of hand-made ashtrays, pinecone and popcorn ornaments, yarn dolls, and all the other handcrafted gifts that they had given to her over the years. Each one was imperfect, amateurish, gaudy and all the more precious to her because they were.

Making a fuss over each one, she tearfully thanked them, one by one, and told them that the best gifts are gifts that are handmade ... because they came from the heart.

Cઙ ℘

Lottie and Abraham joined them later that day for Christmas dinner and gift exchanges. It was lucky that they lived within walking distance; the snow-fall would have made driving impossible. As it was, Lottie grumbled and whined about "wadin' through more'n 'nough snow ta bury an Eskimo."

Katie greeted her at the back door and lavished her with compliments about her Christmas outfit. Lottie had pulled out all stops with her Christmas finery. Like one of Santa's elves she wore bottle green, shantung silk slacks with matching silk sweater, trimmed in white fur at the neck and sleeves. Bright red, green and gold jewelry was lavishly worn, throwing understatement to the wind. Two glittery, jeweled poinsettia barrettes were clipped in her hair. Katie was certain that somewhere in her ancestral background there must have been one or two gypsies. Unzipping her black, rubber boots, she slipped her feet out to reveal a pair of gold brocade Turkish slippers covered in one-inch rhinestones.

Lottie returned the compliment with a shocked look. "What in tha world have ya done ta yawrself, Sug? Ya look like ya been pulled backwards through a knothole. Ya got circles under yawr eyes darker'n ma mascara. Oooh, doggies! I go away fawr a few weeks, an' y'all go ta hell in a hand basket, I tell ya what!"

As her eyes poured over Katie with 20/20 critical acuity, the five-second assessment registered on her face with furrowed brow, wrinkled nose and curled upper lip. She shook her head with dismay. "Ya gotta let me set ya up a date with Max Factor. He'll help me take some a tha color from under yawr eyes an' put some back inta yawr cheeks. Y'all would be surprised what miracles a little make-up can do."

Lottie was right. Katie's navy blue, wool sweater and skirt hung on her frame, like a little girl playing dress-up in her mother's clothes. A look of complete exhaustion covered her face like a mask. The natural rosiness that perpetually blushed her cheeks and lips was gone, leaving her looking pale and wan.

"Thanks for the handful of compliments. You look nice, too."

"I didn't think it wuz possible but I think yawr skinnier than tha last time I saw ya. Ya been sick er somethin'? Ya didn't catch tha fever, too, did ya?"

"No, thank Goodness, none of us did. I've lost a little weight, that's all. Taking care of Tommy, I guess I neglected myself a bit."

Lottie just shook her head. Long, dangling earrings swaying back and forth. "A bit! Why ya can't weigh more'n ninety pounds, drippin' wet. How ya keepin' those clothes on? Elmer's glue? I've seen alley cats that weigh more'n you."

Katie dismissed Lottie's overly dramatic concern. Lottie's had the tendency to put a climatic twist on everything. She had become accustomed to Lottie's theatrical reaction to most things and though they were endearing, they were likewise greatly exaggerated. Katie seldom took them seriously.

"There's nothing wrong with me that a little tincture of time won't cure. Now, put on an apron. Make yourself useful and lend me a hand. I want to hear all about your trip."

Katie outdid herself on the meal. She made an old-fashioned Irish Christmas feast. There was succulent leg of lamb with mint jelly, wild potato and herb soup, celery in cream, peas, chomp chive, yellow buck, barm brack and Christmas cake. She topped the meal off with caraway seed cake and *Ballymore* fudge, for dessert.

She had decorated the table simply, with an ivory lace tablecloth; red linen napkins with ivory porcelain napkin rings and crystal candlesticks circled with rings of holly held white candles. A garland of cedar boughs hung on the chandelier above the table.

With full tummies, and following K.P. duty, they all sat around the Christmas tree for the gift opening with Lottie and Abraham. The boys couldn't believe their good fortune. Not one, not two, but three Christmases of gift giving and getting! Nothing like that had ever happened back in Boston!

Katie wanted to have the adults go first, but Lottie dismissed that idea. "Let tha yunguns go first, ya ol` spoil-sport. They've waited long 'nough. Besides, I kin hardly wait, maself, ta see 'em tear inta tha loot."

Abraham decided that he would give them his gifts first. Being raised in Judaism, he had never experienced the Christian holiday. Since his boyhood days, Abraham had always loved books and the world of wonder and knowledge that they held within their pages. He read them, collected them and cherished them. It only seemed natural that he should give them. Because he wasn't sure at what level the twins were reading, he gave each a coloring book and a big box of sixty-four Crayola crayons. Brendan received a book on the *Skills of Sailing* and Tommy was presented with his very own copy of *Timothy Turtle*. Abraham couldn't have chosen his gifts with any more thought or care. The boys were each thrilled and Katie was impressed by Abraham's solicitude and astuteness. His selections reflected the thought, time and effort he had put forth to find the perfect gift.

Lottie was a bit more frivolous and extravagant with her shopping. She bought each of the younger boys a pair of ice skates, hockey sticks and pucks, and directed them outside, where, on the back porch were three, shiny new racing sleds. The boys were out of the house in thirty seconds to ogle and drool over them.

She handed Brendan his gift. It was a large, heavy box, gaily wrapped in blue foil paper and tied with an elaborate silver bow. Inside, Brendan could hardly believe his eyes. There was an authentic, honest-to-goodness, brand new, hand-sewn canvas sail and rigging. He didn't know whether to laugh or cry or jump up and down, so he settled on a big thank-you, including a hug and a kiss for Miss Lottie.

Eager to begin enjoying their new presents, the boys vacated the living room, leaving the adults to quietly enjoy opening their gifts. Katie jumped at the opportunity.

"Lottie, you went way overboard, no pun intended. The skates would have been more than enough. And the sailing gear! You'll have them spoiled and expecting a repeat next year. You shouldn't have spent so much on them."

Lottie dismissed the idea with a flick of her wrist. "Never y'all mind. What good is ma money sittin' in tha bank, jus' accumulatin' more? Money is like manure, Sug. It's not worth a thing unless it's spread 'round encouragin' 'young thins ta grow."

"And which one of your infamous relatives are responsible for that saying?" Katie asked.

"Are ya insinuatin' that ma words of wisdom are all jus' so much back-woods, folksy prattling'? I'll have ya know, even us hicks from tha sticks kin read an' write. Listen Miss Fancy Pants, that was a direct quote from Mr. Thornton Wilder, one of America's mos' famous playwrights." Lottie proudly defended herself

Abraham and Katie were both impressed.

Katie, toyed with her and said, "Please accept my sincerest apology for spurning your cracker barrel philosophy. I'm truly amazed. There doesn't seem to be any limit to your depths. You have certainly been hiding them well under that down-home, country facade."

"My deepest apologies, also, Madame." Abraham performed an exagger-ated bow of supplication. "Since you have our undivided and complete atten-tion, please, enlighten us further. Could you share with us one or more of the illustrious works penned by your famous Mr. Wilder?"

Lottie threw a pillow at him. "Sit down, ya ol' coot. Struttin' 'round like a cat contemplatin' a mouse. Y'all think I don't know when I'm bein' mocked. Ya two'll be sorry as Samson fawr yawr scoffin'. Don't think I don't have ma own ways of getting' even."

They eventually called a truce and opened their gifts. Abraham kept with a literary theme and gave Katie a collection of Irish verse and Lottie a book on the great homes of the South. To each, inside the front cover, he had written a special inscription.

"To Loretta: Nowhere, can the beauty, the charm, the warmth of the Old South be found more abundantly than in your heart."

To Katie he wrote, "For the fairest Irish rose. My gratitude for the gifts you have brought to my life. Joy to my spirit, laughter to my voice and faith to my soul."

Truer worlds or deeper sentiments had never been expressed more eloquently. For Abraham, who often had great difficulty openly sharing what he felt, found that by putting pen to paper, hoped he had found the way to convey how profoundly those two women had touched his life.

The biggest surprise to Abraham had been Loretta and his attraction to her. Initially, she seemed hard and crass. But, under the ostentatious layers of eccentricity, worldliness and tough exterior she had an unbelievable loving spirit of kindness and generosity.

Lottie gave Abraham a hand knit, fisherman's sweater. "I'm gettin' mighty tired of seein' ya in that worn out ol' moth-eaten' sweater yawr so all fired fond a wearin'. Thought I'd spruce ya up a bit. I'd a preferred ta buy ya a fancy, bright, argyle patterned one I spotted, but I knew ya wouldn't be caught dead in anythin' that fashunable."

"Your instincts were correct. The sweater is beautifully crafted and it is much more suited to my taste. Thank you, Loretta."

Katie opened a long, red velvet case. She gasped at the single strand of natural, perfectly matched, ivory-white pearls. "Oh, Lottie," she exclaimed, "They're absolutely breathtaking. Far too grand and expensive. We agreed to keep things simple."

"Hell's bells, it's ma money, an' nobody tells me how ta spend it. 'Sides, I've probably eaten more'n they cost at yawr dinner table. I saw those an' they spoke right ta me. They're elegant an' classy, jus' like you, Sug."

"They are elegant, far too elegant for me. When will I ever wear them?"

"Ya wear 'em whenever ya feel like. Fine jewelry is meant ta be worn. Makes a lady feel special. Ma Grandma Pope used ta say that special stuff was meant ta be used. Doesn't do nobody any good havin' 'em sittin' in tha drawer."

Katie did as she was told and hooked the gold clasp. She gently stroked the smooth orbs. Lottie was right. They did make her feel special.

Lottie was, in her own words, "happier than a preacher on Sunday," when she opened her gift from Katie and the boys.

"A genuine, alligator handbag! Sug, y'all do have class. This jus' shouts out good breedin'. Ain't I gonna looked cultured an' sophisticated when I visit Nawlans this Mardi Gras. Might even buy maself a pair of matchin' high-heeled shoes an' a new dress ta go with it. Like what those fancy bowtiques in Naw Yawk call an ensemble."

Katie was a little nervous as Abraham unwrapped his package. She prayed that she hadn't overstepped her bounds. She hoped he wouldn't be upset or offended. Her prayers were answered. As he lifted the object from it's bed of tissue paper, his eyes told her that not only was he not offended, but was deeply moved.

In his trembling hands he reverently held a gleaming silver Menorah. How long it had been since he had last gazed upon one. It was the symbol of Hanukkah, the festival of lights, the festival of celebration, commemorating the rededication of the Temple of Jerusalem, nearly twenty-two centuries ago. For eight days, beginning on the twenty-fifth day of Kislev, the Menorah would be lit and simple gifts exchanged. Though it wasn't the most revered or sacred or significant of the Jewish holy days, it had always been his favorite.

As he held it, the traditions, the reverence, the memories, all came flooding back. It represented a past that he thought had been forever lost. A buried past that he had only recently started to uncover and awaken. Ironically, it represented a symbol of his own rededication, of his own spiritual rebirth. His heart ached for the lost years, the presence of God in his life.

His eyes glistened with tears and memories from his past.

"Katie. I do not know how to say thank you. Any words I could express would seem inadequate."

Katie rose and walked over to Abraham. She bent down and softly laid a kiss upon his cheek. "That expression was more than adequate."

Abraham looked at Katie and then at the painting that hung over the mantle. Both put him in mind of Katherine.

"Your Christmas and my Hannukah. So different in meaning, yet both so precious to children. Children are what the two celebrations are about. It would have made your Aunt Katherine and Uncle Sean so happy to have seen this house bursting with love and the joy of children. Katherine knew. She knew all along that it was perfect and right that you move here from Boston and fill these room with your beautiful children. She had missed out on so much of your childhood and all of the boys'. This was Katherine's way of finally being a part of your lives and you a part of hers. Thank you, Katie, for granting her last wish."

At that moment, Katie made a wonderful discovery. Aunt Katherine had finally revealed herself and Katie could see her as clearly as if she standing with them in that room. The past years of separation never existed. Katie no longer felt like an intruder. She felt that she had come home.

Abraham discovered something as real and profound as Katie had. Holding the precious Menorah in his hands, he discovered that forgiveness was possible, forgiveness for God and forgiveness for himself.

chapter twenty-eight

Lottie insisted upon welcoming in the New Year with a gathering at her house. She decided on a wingding of a celebration with Katie, Abraham and Matt. After the cornbread experience, Matt nearly declined the invitation until he was assured that Lottie would be doing none of the cooking. Instead, she had decided to take the wise course and had the meal catered by Collier's, the best restaurant in Eden Croft.

Initially, she had selected enough dishes to provide a seven-course meal for a party of at least fifty. Katie had taken her under her wing and, with guidance and expertise, had convinced her of a more sensible, streamlined selection.

Shortly after six o'clock, Lottie accepted delivery of three platters of some of the tastiest dishes northern Michigan had to offer. An array of appetizers, including their specialties, stuffed mushrooms and mussels in garlic butter would be served for starters, followed by a variety of cheeses, liver pate, garlic toast and crackers. A mixed platter of smoked whitefish, salmon, crab cakes and beef medallions would serve as the main course. The buffet would conclude with chocolate éclairs and slices of New York style cheesecake dripping with fresh raspberry sauce. All Lottie had to do was keep the warm dishes warm and the cold dishes cold. Lottie had placed four bottles of champagne in the refrigerator to chill.

Certain that she had the situation well in hand, Lottie escaped to her bath and bedroom to put the finishing touches on her personal toilet. She had spent the greater part of the morning and afternoon at the Color, Cut an' Curl for what she called the "full treatment." For the paltry sum of twenty-five dollars, including a generous tip, Lottie was pampered, primped and preened with a manicure, pedicure, lip waxing, shampoo and style. She had a full two hours to apply the finishing touches with make-up and dress.

Lottie had been saving a hot little silver brocade number for just the right occasion and this was just the right occasion. The cowl-neck dipped low enough to peak a man's interest, but was high enough to keep them guessing. Tight pants, probably one size too small, hugged every dip, bend and curve. Two diamond and silver barrettes clipped back her hair revealing spangled crystal earrings dangling from each earlobe. With silver eye shadow and wearing silver high-heeled mules, a silver silk scarf tied at the neck, and more silver jewelry than a sultan's wife, Lottie looked like a pin-up girl for a Las Vegas chorus line. For the finishing touch, Lottie generously spritzed herself from an atomizer of Chanel #5. As she viewed the overall effect in her full length mirror, Lottie whistled and exclaimed, "Professor Franke, y'all better hang on ta yawr socks, 'cuz this outfit is gonna knock yawr shoes right off."

Katie was never fond of New Year's Eve. It was melancholic and wistful to ponder and contemplate, to let go, to bid farewell to the old year. Danny and she were never interested in going out and painting the town red. They had preferred to ring in the New Year with a quiet evening at home. Instead of going to a dinner club, they would sit and reminisce, play some Mills Brothers or Bing Crosby records on the Victrola and slowly dance away the evening.

All day long she dreaded going to Lottie's and nearly called her a dozen times to cancel. Katie hadn't felt at all well for a while. She was exhausted all the time and every bone in her body ached, making the simplest of tasks a painful effort. Getting bathed and dressed for the evening had been a monumental chore. And Lottie was right. She had lost more weight, but with a non-existent appetite, she had to force herself to eat.

What was wrong with her? These were the holidays and she loved them. She should have been flying high with excitement instead of feeling like a wet mop.

Maybe that was it. All the seasonal hubbub and activity, the frantic pace had finally caught up with her. Maybe going out would be good for her, being surrounded by good friends and good cheer might help to lift her spirits. It wasn't like she was being dragged out for a wild night at the Copacabana. Besides, she couldn't bear the thought of reneging on the invitation and disappointing Lottie.

A few minutes after eight o'clock, giving Brendan his final instructions, Katie had put on her coat, gloves and galoshes and was ready to walk over to Lottie's.

A disgruntled Bren and Vinnie were drowning their sorrows in chocolate milk. Breeze had invited them to celebrate New Year's at his house. But, Bren was stuck at home baby-sitting the rug rats and Vinnie felt an obligation to not let Bren suffer alone.

"How come I gotta be the stinking babysitter all the time?" Bren whined into his glass.

"Because we're a team around here. I cook, do the dishes and laundry, shop and market, make the beds, clean up after all of you and drive you around like a chauffeur. And you baby-sit." Katie winked at him. "You and Vincent can stay up as late as you want. Just try to keep it sensible. The boys have already had their baths. I want Tommy and the twins in bed by eight. Don't forget to wake them up just before midnight. I promised them they could go outside and ring in the New Year banging pots and pans. But, then I want them to go back to bed right afterwards. No exceptions."

"Breeze is having a party with records and sodas and all kinds of food. What do we do if we get hungry?" Brendan asked. He had recently become an eating machine, intent on eating her out of house and home.

"There are cold cuts and cheese in the refrigerator, bread and potato chips in the pantry. You can make yourselves sandwiches. There's ice cream in the freezer and I mixed up an extra pitcher of chocolate milk specially for tonight."

"How late you gonna be?"

"Probably shortly after midnight. If you have any problems Miss Lottie's number is on the notepad next to the telephone."

"I know the number by heart, Mom."

"Nevertheless, I wrote it down. Remember, now, no teasing or fighting with the little ones. Make sure you all pick up after yourselves. I'd appreciate it if you'd keep the house this side of a disaster zone."

Matt had offered to pick her up and they could drive to Lottie's together, but Katie said she would rather walk; the crisp night air would be refreshing and cathartic. Besides, it really wasn't all that far. She wished Brendan and Vinnie a Happy New Year, gave all the boys a New Year's hug and kisses and headed out the door.

If the Donovan/O'Neill house was a reflection of a quieter, nostalgic, more traditional time, then the Devereaux house would best be described as hip, trendy and vogue. Shortly after Lottie and Regis were married, he turned her loose with complete freedom and an unlimited purse to redecorate and renovate the house. Lottie went crazy and after fourteen months, three decorators, four contractors and a wad of money that would choke a hippo, she had created a swank, sleek, contemporary look that could have graced the cover of the latest *Better Homes and Gardens*.

The rambling, single story, ranch of sand-colored brick, Tennessee stone and sculptured concrete sat atop a sandy bluff. Walls of glass wrapped around three sides of the house providing an uninterrupted, panoramic view of the lake. Glass brick flanked either side of the huge double front doors. Blond ash wood was carried throughout the house, from kitchen cabinets, to moldings, to window trims, including built-in closets, wardrobes, bureaus and china cabinets. Katie would have described the interior colors as black, pink, gray and white, but Lottie corrected her, on more than one occasion that the color scheme was silver, ebony, salmon and putty.

Every appliance in the kitchen gleamed in ebony porcelain and chrome. The countertops and floor were salmon linoleum with tiny splashes of putty and ebony, like a painter had taken a wet brush and spattered the entire surface. A round, fluorescent ceiling light and additional lights concealed under the cabinets, lighted the room. Twelve matching chairs surrounded a Danish modern, Formica-topped, blonde dining room table. Above the table hung a ceiling light that consisted of three separate globes hanging from individual half-inch chrome tubes.

But Lottie's pride and joy was the living room, carpeted, wall-to-wall in plush putty carpet. An eight-piece, low slung, white sectional, upholstered in looped nylon intertwined with silver threads circled the living room. Four salmon upholstered side chairs completed the suite. At least two dozen, silk, decorative toss pillows, of every geometric shape, were strategically placed about on the furniture. A sculpted, bleached ash coffee table sat in the center of the room, like an oversized artist's palette.

Above the mantle of the massive, ebony marble fireplace hung a huge sunburst wrought iron and chrome clock. Four cubist style paintings, chosen for color rather than content, hung on the putty walls. Katie couldn't quite figure out how anyone would know which way to hang them. Upside-down, sideways, or right side up, they still would have been just as indefinable. Her observation hit the bull's eye. As a matter of fact, initially the workmen had hung the arrangement up side down.

The decorateur, a fussy little fop called simply, Xavier (pronounced Haveyare, but for Lottie it always came out Exavyawr) made his final inspection, nearly suffered a fatal coronary when, upon discovering the error, screeched in horror, "Ey carumba! Holy sheet! Dunt jou peoples know notheeng about art? Jews have thees hanging all focked up!"

Ashtrays as big as flying saucers and other objets d'art sat on every horizontal surface. Overlooking the whole room were Lottie's favorites pieces, two eighteen inch tall, porcelain, Japanese geishas that stood side-by-side on the mantle. An RCA Victor high-fi sat next to her Crosley console television set. Four-foot long antennas stuck up like chrome chopsticks. In keeping with the spirit of the season, setting in the living room was a nine-foot tall, aluminum Christmas tree, sans any ornamentation other than a few well-placed pink and silver orbs. The silver tree changed from red to blue to yellow to green, as the electric color wheel hummed and rotated. Katie had never seen anything quite like it, but it was definitely Lottie.

"Sug, ya look positively smashin'."

Lottie placed a lipstick smeared kiss on her cheek. Katie, in spite of her weight loss and paleness and feeling like a wet mop, did look smashing. Her Kelly green sweater set with pearl buttons set off the emerald green of her eyes and her curly, auburn tresses. She wore her black wool slacks and black flats hidden under her galoshes. Wearing her hair combed long and free, the only accessories she wore were a green velvet headband and, much to Lottie's pleasure, the single strand of pearls. Soft pink lipstick and the brisk walk over had brought a bit of color to her face.

Katie quickly rejected the remark. "Next to you, I look like the poor relation. We could pose you atop your Christmas tree, like a sparkling, twinkling star. I saw Matt's car in the driveway. Is Abraham here, yet? Sorry I'm late. I had hoped to make it over earlier, to help you get everything set, but I was running a bit behind."

Katie forced a weak, apologetic smile.

"Yawr not late, jus' fashunable. A lady's expected ta make a grand entrance. Tha men folk only got here a few minutes, ago."

Pulling a bottle of champagne from the refrigerator, she ordered Katie, "Grab those glasses, Sug, an' let's get this shin dig launched."

Abraham was uncharacteristically dressed for the occasion. He wore a dark gray wool suit, crisp white shirt, black patterned tie and shiny black oxfords. He almost looked out of place without his Wellingtons, which Katie had begun to think were permanently attached appendages. He had even taken the time to place a precisely folded white linen handkerchief in his breast pocket. Katie noted the effort he had made, and told him so. Lottie must be having a very positive influence on his grooming habits.

Matt hadn't chosen his attire with the same amount of care or formality. He was dressed, typically, in tan corduroy trousers, plaid shirt, and natural fisherman knit sweater. But, that was Matt, casual and comfortable. Meeting with clients and court appearances forced him to suffer the constraints of a monkey suit often enough. In his leisure time, he was sure as heck not going to wear a suit and tie, voluntarily.

Lottie had planned the celebration right down to purchasing noisemakers, confetti and streamers to be thrown, tossed and tooted at midnight. Included in her party favors, were two silver, glittered, cardboard tiaras for the ladies and shiny, fuchsia-glittered derbies for the men. Tiny, white, elastic bands stretched under their chins and held the silly chapeaux precariously on their heads. They looked positively ridiculous.

When they first put them on, Katie and Lottie had laughed hysterically for five minutes. In response to the ridicule, Matt and Abraham threatened to take them off, complaining that it was emasculating to be subjected to such humiliation and mockery for wearing the goofy things. But after coercion, coaxing and threatening that unless they wore them, all food or drink would be withheld, they conceded.

The appetizers were served first, and then the foursome played pinochle and a few lively games of charades. The rest of the buffet served as a late supper, winding down to a couple of hours of quiet conversation. All the while, Old Blue Eyes, Lottie's favorite, crooned in the background.

Katie had eaten like a sparrow and hoped Lottie wouldn't notice. She didn't want her hurt after agonizing over and carefully selecting the menu with so much thought. But, other than lacking an appetite and feeling like a sodden dishrag, Katie really did enjoy the evening.

Relaxing in front of the fireplace, they were enjoying the radiant warmth and apple wood scent of the fire. Matt and Abraham were happily puffing away on expensive Cuban cigars that Lottie had purchased specially for the evening. They had polished off a pitcher of martinis and three bottles of champagne. Lottie reserved the last for the highlight of the evening, the New Year's toast at midnight. Katie had limited herself over the evening and slowly nursed only two small glasses of champagne.

"How 'bout a little dancin' music? Seems like it's been ten years since I've cut a rug."

Abraham didn't make the slightest effort to leave the comfort of his chair. But, Lottie, who was never one to stand on ceremony, wouldn't be dissuaded. She didn't care who did the asking and who did the accepting. She grabbed him by the hand and hoisted him out of his chair.

Lottie teased, "Abraham, it's likely been much closer ta a hundred years fawr y'all. Yawr steppin' on ma feet more'n I do. It'd go a lot more smoothly if only one of us wuz ta lead an' one of us wuz ta follow. Now, I might be goin' out on a limb here, but usually tha privilege of leadin' belongs ta tha man an' tha followin's usually done by tha woman. An' not that I'm complainin', but yawr holdin' me like I got leprosy er somethin.' Get a decent grip, I promise I won't bite."

They danced awkwardly and clumsily for a few minutes, before Abraham started to relax.

"Now this is more like it," Lottie nuzzled Abraham's neck. "See, ya ain't too far gone fawr dancin'."

Katie and Matt joined them, moving much more smoothly and rhythmically. They swayed gently to the music. Soon, the romantic lyrics and the physical closeness fueled their passion and cloaked them from the rest of the world. They were only aware of each other and their shared intimacy. It had seemed like a lifetime ago, since last summer, when they had held each other for the first time. They could each recall what their lips felt like, what the kiss felt like. What that kiss did to them.

Katie felt wonderful to be dancing again, being held by a man, this man. Laying her head against his chest, she could smell the subtle scent of his aftershave, through the fabric of his clothes. It was musky and masculine. His body was firm, taut and muscular. Warm touching warm, she pressed against him with the desire to melt and flow into the warmth and contours of his body. There was a familiar comfort and safety in his arms. The calming warmth of his closeness and touch spread through her. Her fantasies took her on an imaginary journey to a place where she would feel forever safe, rejuvenated, whole again.

Holding her close, Matt could discern every line and curve of her body. The swell of her small, firm breasts pressed against him, he could feel the flutter of her heart. She felt frail and fragile, vulnerable, like she could be crushed as easily as if she were made of paper mache. Her hair carried the scent of lilacs in a late winter snow, flowery and fresh. How could anything so small, so petite, so delicate have the power to arouse such intense such passion. He yearned to take possession of her, mind, body and soul. As he craved the air to breathe, he craved her. The need to protect and care for her spread over him until he was aware of nothing beyond the desire to love her as a man needs to love a woman.

Lottie excitedly announced it was almost the New Year. "Come on Fred an' Ginger. It's almost midnight. Matt, ya get tha confetti an' noisemakers. Abraham, ya get tha streamers. Sug, ya get tha glasses an' I'll get tha bubbly." Like a drill sergeant giving orders to his recruits, Lottie was flying. "We're gonna ring in 1954 Devereaux style."

Matt and Katie's magical, enchanted spell was broken. Shattered like a bell jar, the fragile pieces of glass splintered into a million pieces around their feet. In a reluctant, valiant effort they tried to emerge from the haze and cloud of intimacy that had taken possession of their bodies and their senses. With smoky eyes, they captured each other's look, sharing the same thoughts, the same wants, the same needs. Like suddenly being shaken, awakened from a wonderful dream, they weren't ready to let go of it. They wanted to recapture it and cling to it forever.

chapter twenty-nine

"Dr. Hughes will be with you in just a few minutes. We're running a little behind today. He was late getting to the office. Delivered a healthy baby girl to the Lawrence's early this morning." Bonnie Beckett, Dr. Hughes' office nurse, explained while she weighed Katie and made the notation in her chart.

Next she checked Katie's blood pressure, took her temperature, and counted her heart rate and respirations.

The nurse was tall, slender and quite striking. Probably close to the same age as Katie. She had big brown eyes, full lips, a dark complexion, a wide smile and an interestingly exotic beauty. Her cinnamon colored hair was cut short and styled with clipped bangs that framed her heart-shaped face attractively and was topped by a white cap that looked like an over-size, upside-down, pleated, pastry cup. Even through her stark white nurse's uniform and stockings Katie could tell that she had a good figure and shapely legs.

"Have you had any other symptoms, besides the weight loss, Mrs. O'Neill?" Bonnie held her pen at the ready, waiting to make additional notes in the record.

Katie thought the question over a minute before she answered. "Maybe ... just feeling awfully tired all the time. It seems like I can't get enough sleep, lately. Even after a full night's rest, I still wake up tired and worn out. Most of the time, it's like I have no energy. That's not at all like me."

Bonnie questioned her further, "How about your periods? Are they regular?"

"Pretty normal, I guess, I don't pay them a lot of attention. I have noticed that my flow has been heavier and I've been having a lot of spotting between periods, a little cramping, but nothing serious. You think maybe it's my iron? That would explain why I feel so rundown. I probably only need a prescription for some iron pills."

Katie was fairly confident that her diagnosis was right on the money. She felt foolish for not thinking of it before, she could have saved herself a lot of worry and Dr. Hughes his precious time. Bonnie didn't offer an opinion and Katie could read nothing in her expression.

"Dr. Hughes will want to do a full examination, anyway. There's a gown on the table for you. Please take off all your clothes, brassiere and panties, too, and you can slip that on."

263

She smiled and left the room, closing the door behind her. Katie did as instructed, undressed and donned the *stylish* patient gown. She sat uncomfortably, immodestly and chilled in the chair. She always wondered why doctor's examination rooms weren't kept warmer, considering that most of the people occupying them had to strip down to nothing.

Looking around the room, she satisfied her suspicions that it held all the requisite gear, contraptions, furnishings and equipment, like every other examination room she had ever been in. Venetian blinds on the windows, medicine cabinet, sink, wastebasket, scale, blood pressure gizmo, tongue depressors, thermometers, cotton balls, rubber gloves and gooseneck floor lamp. And sitting proudly and menacingly in the center, the black leather examination table with Katie's favorite accessories and the bane of every woman's existence. The infamous stirrups perched on either side, sitting shiny as a new dime and just as icy cold. It even smelled of a doctor's office, a mixture of soap, medicine, alcohol and disinfectant.

Katie was startled as the door opened and Dr. Hughes came in, followed by his nurse. For a brief minute or two, he scanned the notes that Bonnie had made in her chart, then settled on rolling stool and crossed his legs.

"Sorry to keep you waiting, Mrs. O'Neill. Nancy Lawrence picked the middle of the night and half the morning to deliver her baby. Her first, a girl, and like most females I know, she sure as heck took her sweet time making her big entrance."

He smiled warmly at Katie. "How's Tommy been doing? Things were looking pretty good at his last check-up."

"Looking at him, you'd never guess how sick he'd been. I want to thank you for all you did. Without you, things may not have turned out the way they did. It could have been a far worse time for all of us if you hadn't been there."

The warm smile immediately disappeared from his face. "And, you took your sweet time making this appointment. Seems to me I recall, long before the holidays that I wanted to see you in this office for a check-up."

Katie was now feeling immodest, uncomfortable, cold, embarrassed *and* berated.

"Doctor, I feel so foolish wasting your time, like this. I'm sure that it's a simple matter of being run down. Like I was telling Bonnie, all I probably need is a prescription for some iron supplements."

"And what medical school did you attend back east? Harvard or Yale?"

Bonnie, stationed discreetly near the door, had to give him credit. That was a new one.

"Okay, besides fatigue and some unusual menstruation patterns, cramping and of course the anemia you've so expertly diagnosed, what other symptoms do you not want to tell me about?"

Katie back-pedaled. "I wouldn't call it unusual, just some spotting, a few cramps. Nothing serious."

Dr. Hughes was not one to coat the truth with Pepto Bismol. He had the appearance of a beardless Santa Claus, including the extra padding around the middle, and one could easily be misled. But, he was no pushover. When it came to the relationship between himself and his patients, he expected complete frankness and candor.

"Listen, Mrs. O'Neill … Katie. I won't tolerate any of your Irish malarkey, here. Don't waste my time and your money with editorializing or amateur diagnosing. I need you to be honest, straightforward and accurate with me. We need to find out what's going on with you, diagnose it and then hopefully, fix it."

As he pulled the stethoscope out of the pocket of his long white coat, he continued, "Now, scoot yourself onto the table. Let's start with the heart and lungs then we'll take a peek down below. How long has it been since your last vaginal examination?"

After the thorough examination, Dr. Hughes excused himself and Bonnie from the room, and told Katie she could put her clothes back on, he would be back in a few minutes to discuss his findings.

As she tried to forget the whole uncomfortable, humiliating affair, Katie dressed quickly. She knew that the pelvic examination was necessary, but even after three pregnancies and four deliveries, the feelings of discomfort and degradation never lessened. After giving birth four times, it was nearly impossible to maintain even a shred of modesty or dignity.

Dr. Hughes returned, alone, fifteen minutes later. Finding his stool again, he sat down, replaced his gold fountain pen in its pocket and looked straight into his patient's green eyes. Any good doctor included an overall assessment of a patient's appearance to be an integral part of any conscientious physical examination. Dr. Hughes was no exception. Katie was skeleton thin. Her flawless skin was nearly transparent with pallor and a sallow tone. She looked gaunt and tired with shadows around her eyes. Still, he thought, in spite of it all, she was a very beautiful woman.

Delaying the inevitable wouldn't make it any easier, so he began. "There are some things I found that are very disturbing. Your lymph glands are tender, swollen and I palpated some irregularities. You've had recent, unexplained weight loss. Vaginal bleeding and pain. In and of themselves, individually, the symptoms are not necessarily significant. But when you combine them all, including what I saw in the pelvic examination … well it causes me some concern."

Katie wasn't at all sure she was hearing him correctly. Usually Dr. Hughes was painfully direct, now he was uncharacteristically vague and enigmatic. His subterfuge and evasiveness scared her.

"Dr. Hughes, you asked me to be direct and honest with you, now I'm asking the same consideration in return. What are you trying to tell me?"

Seeing the distress and doubt reflected in her eyes, he took her hands in his, and continued. "I'm a simple, small town, but I'm also a very good one. Good enough to recognize when a patient requires expertise and the benefits of modern medicine that they won't get from me or in Eden Croft. All in all, I don't like what I'm seeing here.

"While you were dressing, I took the liberty to call a colleague of mine in Chicago. Dr. Malcolm Vertage and I went to medical school together. He's very well known and respected in the field of women's diseases. Besides teaching at Northwestern University, he has a very exclusive and limited private practice. I just spoke with him on the phone and he has agreed to see you."

It was absurd, Katie thought, *I can't go to Chicago.*

"I appreciate what you've done, but Chicago? I have four boys at home. I can't go gallivanting off to Chicago. It's out of the question."

Dr. Hughes spoke succinctly. "This isn't a matter of choices, here. This is a matter of getting you to the best doctor in one of the best hospitals as possible, as quickly as possible. The best decision you can make right now, for you and your boys, is to follow my advice."

Squeezing his hand she asked, "Exactly what do you think is wrong with me?"

He tried to be reassuring, but was finding it impossible. "Speculation is not going to get us anywhere. Suffice it to say that your pelvic examination didn't look good to me. I could run a battery of tests that would give us more information but I know that Dr. Vertage will want to order all his own. It would be a waste of time and money for those tests to be done twice."

A sudden panic gripped Katie. "The costs ... what about the costs? It all sounds so expensive. How will I ever be able to afford them?"

"As a favor to me, for now, Dr. Vertage said that he will see you without charge. Hospitals can be expensive, and there will be some hospital costs, but payment arrangements could always be worked out. I want to remind you, Katie, you can't afford to be frugal. It could be your life we're talking about, here, not a new Easter bonnet."

There, he said it. It was glaringly, painfully and unavoidably out in the open. Katie again questioned if her mind misinterpreted what her ears heard. She was thirty-four years old, not sixty-four. Up until the last few months she had felt fine. There was no way that any of this was happening. It was only a terrifyingly horrible nightmare from which she could not awaken.

Well, she'd prove him wrong. She'd follow his recommendation. She'd go see his world-famous colleague. Let him run all his tests. And when they found out it was all one big mistake … she'd show them a thing or two about Mary Katherine O'Neill.

Denial was a wonderful thing. It empowered one with a sense of security. It allowed one to erase from consciousness all the ugly, scary, raw truth of reality. Denial kept the demons at bay and Katie wrapped it around her like a layer of insulation.

"Miss Beckett is making all the arrangements and will be in soon to give you all the directions and necessary information. You're expected to check-in Sunday afternoon. Dr. Vertage will see you first thing Monday morning."

Well that was impossible, Katie thought.

"You've got to be kidding, Doctor. That's three days away. I can't take care of all the details at home in that short time. I'll need at least two weeks. I promise by the end of the month."

With emphasis, Dr. Hughes ordered, "This isn't deciding which day to do the ironing or wax the floors, Katie. I said this Sunday and I meant it. And that isn't up for debate."

"Okay. You win. They can have me for a couple of days, but not one day longer. I have to be back in time for Valentine's Day. I need to help the boys decorate their Valentine boxes for school."

CB BO

On Friday afternoon, Lottie, Abraham, and Katie had one humdinger of an argument. Their first ever.

"There is no way I'm going to let you miss your trip to New Orleans on my account. You always go to Mardi Gras." Katie argued with Lottie.

"Bein' Lottie Devereaux means I don't always hafta do anythin'. There is no way I'm gonna leave while yawr in tha hospital. When frogs do fracshuns, I tell ya what. 'Sides, Nawlans ain't goin' nowhere. Mardi Gras'll be there next year."

"I'm not going to be in the hospital, like I was sick. It's just so they can run some tests. Dr. Hughes isn't concerned and neither am I. He's sure that all I need is some time and rest. I'm a little anemic, but that's all. A simple female problem."

Abraham wasn't convinced. "Then why send you all the way to Chicago for something as simple as that? Why is he unable to run the same tests, here?"

"As much as we all love Eden Croft, it's far from being a medical Mecca. Some of the tests that are involved, they don't have the capability to do here. And he knows that this Dr. Vertage will want to run all his own tests. Besides, he says he'll feel better with a second opinion."

Katie intentionally avoided telling them any details, for two reasons. First, she didn't want to burden anyone with any unnecessary fretting or worrying. She had always felt uncomfortable being the center of attention. Instead, she preferred to inconspicuously meld into the background. She loathed having anyone fuss over her. Secondly, she hadn't even allowed herself to completely grasp the cold, numbing possibilities. She had, so far, successfully kept them hidden in the recesses of her mind. Maybe if she didn't acknowledge them, didn't validate them, avoided the words, they wouldn't become real.

"I didn't jus' fall off tha tomato truck, Sug. Ya might be sellin', but I'm sure not buyin' any a this." Lottie gave her a dubious look.

"But sure as tha sun don't rise in tha west, arguin' over this isn't gettin' us nowhere. Once I set ma mind on somethin', I kin be jus' as stubborn as y'all. Why I was decidin' mos' thins fawr maself since before Pontius was a pilot. I'm stayin' ta take care a tha yunguns, an that, you kin both take ta tha bank."

Abraham shared Katie's skepticism and tried reasoning with her. "Loretta, you have never been around youngsters. Caring for them is a full time endeavor. What makes you think that you are equipped to handle their needs and demands?"

Katie agreed. "You won't find the answers in any of those movie magazines or romantic, dime store novels you're so fond of. There's getting them up and ready for school, to bed on time, packing their lunches, seeing to their homework, baths, laundry, picking up after them. You can't even clean your own house, for Pete's sake."

"It's not that I *can't* clean ma own house. I jus' *choose* not ta. Why do it yawself, when ya kin hire it done?" Lottie defended herself.

But Abraham was persistent. "The whole idea is preposterous, Loretta. I have taken care of them before, when Tommy was ill. I am well acquainted with the routine. It only stands to reason that I am the logical choice to fill in while Katie is away."

"Listenin ta y'all, ya'd think I didn't know which end of 'em ta feed an' which end of 'em ta wipe. Land 'o Goshen, they're still people, jus' smaller models."

"I'm glad you mentioned feeding them. Cooking and finding your way around a kitchen isn't your strong suit," Katie added and Abraham nodded in agreement.

"Didn't y'all ever hear of a little creashun called tha T.V. dinner? Jus' open tha box, peel back tha foil, toss it inta tha oven at three hundred an' seventy-five degrees, an' voila, a complete meal in minutes. It's a wonderful invenshun."

Abraham and Katie both moaned, their heads in their hands. It was then that Lottie was struck with the perfect solution.

"Here's tha compromise. I'll come over in tha mornin', get 'em ready fawr school an' be here when tha bus drops 'em off. I think I kin manage ta stumble through that. Then, Abraham kin relieve me fawr dinner, homework, bedtime an' spend tha night."

Thinking it over for a few minutes, Katie and Abraham finally, reluctantly relented. Though the plan was only slightly flawed, they agreed it was doable. They both came to the same conclusion that Lottie couldn't do too much damage in that small window of opportunity.

Satisfied that the discussion was over and she had won a moral victory, Lottie ventured one last question. "An' when Matt calls, what in tha Sam Hill are we s'posed ta tell him?"

Katie was adamant that Matt wasn't to be told. She would be home in a couple of days and she would tell him then. After the fact. There was no need for him to get all upset and protective and insist on driving her to Chicago. Katie was rarely sick, but when she was she suffered in silence and wanted no fuss made. This was no big deal and she didn't want squeamish Matt Mulholland anywhere near her in the hospital. If he didn't know then it was one less issue Katie would have to deal with.

Katie had told the same half-truths to the boys that she had told Lottie and Abraham. She wasn't going to have their lives disrupted anymore than was absolutely necessary. One other issue that Katie had stood firm on, despite begging pleading, and coercion from Lottie, she emphatically refused to be driven to catch the train from Grand Rapids. She would drive herself, and leave the car in the car park. It would only be for a couple of days. That way, if her return were sooner than expected, she would have the car waiting for her.

So, in the dark, early, lonely, Sunday morning hours, Katie left long before dawn had broken the eastern horizon, taking nothing but her handbag and small overnight case. She prayed silently and asked the Lord to watch over her four little sons, to protect them, to keep them from harm until she came back. As she fought back the tears, she knew that the next couple of days were going to be the longest days of her life.

C3 &0

Katie exited Union Station and was immediately assaulted by noise. She suddenly realized how accustomed she had become to the peace and quiet of country living. Chicago, like Boston was busy and congested, with constant, perpetual, unavoidable noise. The relentless sounds of vehicles, the elevated trains, buses and taxis, horns honking, people engaged in the fervor and activities of talking, laughing, shouting and living. The noise of chatter and radios escaped from buildings as doors quickly swung open and closed. Katie immediately decided she didn't miss it at all. She had unknowingly become attached to the serene sounds of nature.

Instead of the sparkling, pure white, fluffy drifts of snow that covered the world of Eden Croft, she looked about at the dirty, muddy, icy heaps that no longer bore any resemblance to virginal snow. Even her sense of smell revolted. These were not the pleasant, clean fragrances of lake, trees, flowers, grass and pristine air. She inhaled the offensive odors of smoke, exhaust, fuel, heat, coal, asphalt and refuse. She was immediately overcome with the deep ache of homesickness.

Steady, intense, biting cold winds swept from the icy lakefront down the canyons of skyscrapers. There was no way she could endure the elements for the three-mile walk to the hospital. She was too overwhelmed and far too tired to try and figure out the elevated trains or bus schedules. Instead, she bit the bullet of expense and hailed a taxicab. Traveling north and east, fifteen minutes later, she was deposited on the concrete steps of the main entrance of Divine Child Hospital.

The Sisters of Charity had established the hospital in 1864 and had continued to administer and staff it. It was ten stories of red brick and stone, slate roofs, Victorian spires and ornate, wrought iron grillwork. It was shaped like a huge *H* with four wings spreading out from the main building. Above three sets of glass doors that served as the front entrance, was a five-foot tall, concrete statue of the child Jesus, dressed in splendor and crowned in glory. He held a globe of the world in His left hand and two fingers of His right hand were held up in peace.

Katie hesitantly and reluctantly climbed the steps and approached the far right door. Struggling and pulling forcibly against the strength of the wind, she was barely able to escape through the opening before the wind slammed them shut behind her.

Sister Elizabeth Clare had tucked her latest patient into bed for the night, making her as comfortable as possible under the circumstances. She was such a tiny, mere wisp of a girl. The nun, whose chubby body betrayed her love for food, couldn't imagine what fuel the little thing was running on. Only picked at her dinner tray and barely touched any of it. She didn't appear to have an extra ounce of flesh on her bones. She took note that Mrs. O'Neill was nervously rubbing the beads of her rosary, turning the crucifix over and over.

"Would you like me to stay and say the rosary with you? I'm scheduled to go off duty, soon, but I wouldn't mind staying on longer."

Katie smiled at the nun. Her compassion had helped Katie through the first frightening hours of panic. She had chattered constantly. As Lottie would have said, "she could talk a leg off a chair." She fussed about, in her royal blue, floor length habit. The white, starched contraption that covered her head wasn't a hat or veil at all, but instead an elaborate conglomeration of geometric angles.

The headgear flopped about with her movements, like the bent and contorted, out-stretched wings of a seagull. Katie wondered if a strong wind off Lake Michigan would lift her airborne.

The nun's chatter and ministrations had created a welcomed diversion for Katie. It kept her mind occupied. She would miss her presence, her company, when Sister left for the night. But Katie didn't feel like she wanted to have an audience when she prayed.

"Thank you for offering, but I think I'd like to be alone for a while. I've been going since four o'clock this morning ... traveling ... checking in. It really has been a long day."

Sister Elizabeth Clare patted Katie's shoulder and fluffed the pillow. "Of course, you must be exhausted. A sound night's sleep will do you good. Dr. Vertage will be in bright and early tomorrow morning. You know, you're already quite a celebrity around these hallowed halls. It isn't often that he graces us with his presence or his patients. He is a very famous and sought after doctor, a virtual demigod in the field of gynecology. Divine Child isn't his usual hospital of choice, but I have seen his work on rare occasions, when his Catholic patients insist on coming here. Pure brilliance and talent. Though I think his bedside manner could be improved upon. Believe me, Mrs. O'Neill, you really are in the very best of hands." She smiled, pointed to the crucifix above the bed and added, "Both pairs."

The nun filled Katie's pitcher with fresh water and turned off all lights in the room except a small night light next to the bed. She wished Mrs. O'Neill a goodnight, offered her blessing, and as she made her way into the corridor, quietly closed the door. Katie rested her head back on the pillow.

She hated hospitals. Except for having babies, and that didn't count, people who came to hospitals never left, except to be taken to the funeral parlor. It was to the hospital where she had twice brought her loved ones, her da and ma, and it was where they had both died. She didn't want to be here. She wanted to be home.

Strange sounds echoed in the corridor. Her nose and stomach recoiled at the strong antiseptic odors. Her skin felt chafed by the stiff, coarse sheets. Everything here was strange and threatening. It was as if she had been transported to another dimension, a displaced person. Katie willed herself not to cry, squeezed the rosary to her chest, and sought the only presence that was familiar to her, she prayed.

chapter thirty

Having one strange man look at her private parts, was one thing, but Katie was definitely not going to let all seven of them have a peek.

Dr. Malcolm Vertage was indeed a formidable man, in stature, character and reputation. Whenever or wherever he saw patients, an entourage of eager young medical students, interns and residents trailed in his considerable wake. Katie didn't care how prominent and important he was. When the show got started, she was going to have only one person in the viewing audience. She didn't care who it was, Dr. Vertage, or someone else, she didn't care, let them pick. Choose numbers, hold a lottery, sell raffle tickets, but when the curtain went up, there would be only one winner.

Dr. Vertage was built like a tackle on the front line. He was big, tough and forceful. He also had an ego to match. His large head was shaved clean as a baby's behind. Piercing, keen blue eyes that saw everything, missed nothing and could have stared down Wyatt Earp at the showdown at the O.K. Corral, scrutinized from under bushy white eyebrows. Under an immaculate, crisp white coat, he wore a three-piece gray suit, starched white shirt and maroon and black tie. He was a tough taskmaster, a demanding professor and brilliant doctor. He never expected anything less than perfection from his underlings, just as he never expected anything less than perfection from himself.

He lived and breathed for the practice of medicine, his days consumed by the need to excel. Except for a scant three to four hours to sleep, he could be found, day or night, at the hospital, in surgery or poised at the dais, lecturing. There was never a scheduled day or weekend off. He never vacationed and his rare absences occurred only when he would grace some international symposium or conference with his presence and expertise. His obsessive dedication had destroyed two marriages and was rapidly in the process of ruining a third. The hospital grapevine wondered when he found the time to marry, let alone time for romance and courtship.

When he first approached Katie it was from a safe distance as if he were insulating himself from the intimacy of personal contact. An air of intolerance, arrogance and pomposity oozed from him. Katie was immediately put off by his manner and instantly formed a strong dislike for the man. Apparently, one didn't need to be cordial, or even civil when you were a demigod. He talked around her, about her and through her, but not once did he talk to her. Instructing the nurse to prepare the patient for examination, he abruptly turned his attention to a scrutinizing analysis of the chart.

She startled everyone present, including Dr. Vertage and herself, when Katie asked if she might have a minute alone with the doctor. After a few uncomfortable seconds of complete silence, he nodded and dismissed everyone from the room.

"Mrs. O'Neill. I am a very busy man, as are the staff and, though they register decidedly low on the food chain, so are my students," he scolded her. "We have an established protocol, one that has worked exceedingly well. One that I have developed specifically that equates to optimum return on the expenditure of time. In a word, it insures that none of anyone's valuable time is wasted. I haven't the time for theatrics or dramatics. Whatever you may have to say to me could as easily have been said without deviating from that protocol and creating an emotional upheaval."

Katie, for the second time, in less than a week, couldn't believe her ears. Of all the nerve. Who did this pompous ass think he was and more importantly, who did he think she was? Some poor, inconsequential charity case that he had been pressed upon and coerced into seeing?

Her green eyes flashed and her face flushed with anger. "Dr. Vertage. I came here on the recommendation of a dear, sweet, kind and very capable doctor who wanted me to see the best. At the moment, I value his opinion a whole lot more than yours. You don't have to like me and I sure don't have to like you. But I do need to respect you and all I ask in return is that you respect me.

"I'm sure you have seen hundreds, maybe thousands of female bodies, but you have never seen this one. I'm scared, frightened and feeling very lost and alone right now. The relationship between a doctor and patient is one that I view as very sacred and private. And as sure as the Pope's Catholic, I will not be displayed like a piece of meat in front of a herd of probing eyes. Now, if you and I can't come to an agreement on that, I'll quietly pack my bag and return to Eden Croft and you can return to your ivory tower. Equate *that*, Dr. Vertage."

His response nearly caused the walls to vibrate, the paint to crack and the plaster to crumble. He laughed deeply, robustly, heartily, as his entire body shook.

"Well I'll be damned! You have a great deal of spunk stored up in that puny, little body of yours. I haven't had anyone stand up to me in more years than I care to count. Not since my first wife decided to divorce me. I had forgotten what it feels like. It's good for the soul to be put in one's place, every now and then. When Nelson called me about you, he warned me that you were something special. I completely misunderstood his meaning. You, young lady, are indeed something very special."

After a thorough, and very *private* examination, Dr. Vertage swore Katie to secrecy. "As I have graciously granted your request, Mrs. O'Neill, now I am asking you to return the favor. I want your promise that you'll not breathe a word of this to anyone. My carefully constructed and guarded reputation wouldn't remain intact if rumors spread about the almighty, omnipotent Dr. Malcolm Vertage getting his comeuppance from a hundred pound spitfire."

The co-conspirators sealed their pact with a handshake.

                                    ☙ ❧

Valentine's Day came and went. The three days that Katie had originally agreed upon stretched into ten. She had counted every floor tile, one hundred ninety-six … every slat in the Venetian blinds, ninety-eight … the number of cracks in the ceiling and walls, six … and the number of tubes on the metal headboard and footboard … sixteen. The room, she estimated, measured four-teen-feet square. There must have been a sale on white and olive drab paint when the room was decorated. They were the only two colors in the room. Jesus' left elbow was missing a small piece of plaster of Paris and the paint was flaked on the top of the crucifix. Dr. Emerson, whoever he was, won the popularity contest by being paged a total of fifty-seven times. And Sister Elizabeth Clare worked twelve hour shifts, everyday, from seven a.m. to seven p.m.

For a week and a half, Katie was examined, probed, explored, x-rayed and biopsied. She had been quizzed, queried and questioned. Dr. Vertage knew every inch of her intimately. They had drawn enough blood from her veins to float a battleship. She had been weighed ten times and had her temperature read thirty-six times. Blood pressure and pulse taken, her respiration's counted every four hours, around the clock, totaling fifty-eight times. The food was lousy, the temperature in the room either too warm or too cold and the sheets rough and coarse. The radiator rattled and the mattress and pillow were de-signed for function rather than form. But, Katie never questioned, complained or argued. She wasn't there for the hospital's cuisine or decor. It wasn't a resort where she expected to be pampered and catered to. She endured it all, simply as a means to an end.

And through it all, watching the minutes tick away slowly, counting the hours, through every waking moment and into her dreams, through every painful test, examination, biopsy and blood draw, she hadn't shed one tear, but had clung to the promise that when it was all over, she would return to her home and her four boys on Lakefield Road.

And back home on Lakefield Road, Lottie had experienced her own baptism by fire.

The first and second days had gone fairly well. No serious disasters, only medium to rare. But, by the third day, Lottie figured it had all been beginner's luck.

She had started out the calamitous day behind the eight ball when she over slept. And of course, Abraham had to pick that day to have an early faculty meeting at the college, so left the house before the boys were scheduled to get up. Then Chance, who had chewed up and swallowed God-only-knew-what the night before, had barfed it back up in a disgusting, slimy, gelatinous mess on the floor which greeted Lottie before she had had even a single cup of coffee. Choking and gagging through the entire ordeal, she had finally gotten it all mopped up. The upstairs toilet had plugged and overflowed when Casey or Colin, she never did find out which one, had tried to flush down a platoon of plastic army men.

The toast burned, the oatmeal was lumpy and stuck to the pan, they ran out of milk and the can of frozen orange juice was still frozen solid. The boys whined and bellyached that they couldn't eat one more peanut butter and jelly sandwich for lunch. In her own tactful, gentle, and diplomatic way Lottie told them, "Tough! People in hell want water, too, but they don't get it."

Of course, they missed the bus and Lottie had to drive them to school in her nightgown, robe and slippers, with pin curlers in her hair. Halfway back home, after dropping them off, she discovered Brendan had left his notebook on the car seat, which contained his homework for his first class.

Miss MacCauley nearly choked on a paperclip when Lottie came traipsing into the office in pink fluffy mules, a purple silk nightgown with marabou trim, raspberry chenille robe under her full-length mink coat. A pink hair net covered her hair that held enough metal to transmit UHF waves to radio-free Europe.

As the day progressed, things hadn't improved. By early afternoon she had received a scathing telephone call from Sister Mary Therese regarding the twins. At recess, they had invented an interesting, new version of keep-away. The rules of the game were quite simple. The boys snatched the woolen hats from the girl's heads and tossed them high in the air, repeatedly, and against the school's brick walls until they stuck to the brick's prickly surface. The keep-away lasted until gravity or a well-aimed snowball managed to release them. Sister made it perfectly clear that she expected no repeated incidents and that there would be no further episodes.

Out of respect for the old bat, Lottie held her tongue until the conversation ended. As she hung up the telephone, she shared her thoughts with Chance.

"Hey, she don't need ta be droppin' her troubles on ma doorstep. From eight ta three, they're her problem, not mine."

After the boys came home from school and the plumber had left, Lottie chased them outside so she could finish cleaning the bathroom. It was for their safety as well as her sanity. The twins had been testing their boundaries. Their level of cooperation could have been summed up with three, simple, two word phrases, "don't wanna, don't hafta" and "ain't gonna." Miss Lottie threatened them with a couple phrases of her own, "If ya don't wanna, fine. Ya don't hafta. But the next time one of ya sasses me, I'm *gonna hafta* wash out yawr mouths with a bar a Ivory soap."

While the boys were outside playing, Abraham had come home and found the twins with their tally whackers out, peeing in the snow, trying to write their names. Why their appendages hadn't frozen and fallen off was anyone's guess.

As a result, she and Abraham had shared a heated exchange. For the second time that day, Lottie was being reprimanded, like a snotty nosed little kid. Abraham accused her of being negligent in her duties and, fed up with the events of the day, she told him he could stick his negligence "where tha sun don't shine."

By eight o'clock that night, for the first time since she was five years old, exhausted and frazzled, Lottie crawled between the sheets of her bed and immediately fell soundly and peacefully asleep.

Abraham, on the other hand had passed with flying colors. Since he normally didn't arrive home before six, it took a bit of planning and rearranging his schedule. Rather than staying in his office completing paperwork, he brought it home and was able to have dinner on the table by five. He enjoyed preparing dinner. It was considerably more rewarding cooking for a group, then for one, solitary diner.

On Monday, he heated up a kettle of giblet soup with dumplings that Katie had made ahead of time. Tuesday's supper was fried chicken, corn, mashed potatoes with gravy, and a huge platter of spaghetti and meatballs, garlic toast and a tossed salad on Wednesday.

By six-thirty every evening, the kitchen was tidy, the dishes were done, and five studious males were seated around the dining room table, reading, correcting papers or completing assignments. Helping with homework came naturally to Abraham. He was the consummate teacher. He considered it a privilege, a great pleasure and very satisfying to be a part of the development of fine, inquisitive, young minds.

After their baths and tooth brushings and dressed in flannel pajamas, by eight o'clock sharp, Abraham tucked Tommy, Casey and Colin into bed. They had said their prayers and Abraham read them each one, last story. As the grandfather clock struck nine o'clock, Brendan's official time for lights out, a calm and quiet spread over the O'Neill house.

Taking care of the physical needs of the boys was the simple part. What Abraham found most disturbing and challenging was coping with their emotional needs. Tommy and the twins were relatively easy; they seemed satisfied with the vague explanations and reassurances about their mom's absence. They were easily placated by the promise that she was doing fine and would be home very soon.

Brendan was not so easily dissuaded. He had grilled Abraham and Lottie incessantly, driven by an instinct that told him something was very wrong. He recognized their trepidation and uneasiness each time he asked a question, and he knew that they too, shared his concerns and worries. The three of them huddled, like stranded castaways tossing about in a lifeboat, lost at sea, bound together by a rope woven from strands of doubt, deception and desperation.

CG ᛉᛜ

Thursday, Abraham had no late afternoon classes or meetings and arrived at Katie's by two o'clock. The kitchen table was cluttered with enough sheets of red construction and tissue paper to wallpaper a room. Scattered about its surface were lacy, paper doilies, scissors, yards of red ribbon and yarn, packages of sequins, bottles of glue, paste and glitter, rolls of aluminum foil, strips of silver and red lace, and four empty shoeboxes that Lottie had scavenged from her closet. Seated at the table was Lottie, tongue poking out from the side of her mouth with concentration. She was cutting out dozens of hearts of various sizes, from the sheets of construction paper.

Patches of flour and cocoa were caked on her face. Her hair was tied up with a red handkerchief. Usually heavily sprayed into place, strands of black hair stuck out, porcupine style. Dried egg, batter and greasy spots of butter and shortening stained her cashmere sweater. Chance was having an afternoon snack as he eagerly licked up spills and droppings off the linoleum floor. Every surface and countertop was covered with flour, sugar, cocoa, batter and debris; the sink was filled with a pile of dirty dishes, bowls, pan and utensils.

"What is all this?" Abraham asked, entertained by Lottie's face, contorted with concentrated effort.

"These here are goin' ta turn inta three a tha grandest, fanciest, mos' ornate Valentine boxes ever created. Don't tell me ya forgot? Tha boys been talkin' 'bout nothin' else tha last coupla days."

"I have not forgotten. It is merely surprising to find you engaged in any activity that does not require the modern conveniences and stimulation of television or radio. What happened to this kitchen? Please do not tell me that you have been cooking."

Detecting an unpleasant odor, he sniffed the air. "Loretta, what is that smell? Is something burning?"

She jumped from the chair, sending bits of paper flying in every direction. She grabbed a pair of oven mitts and retrieved two muffin tins from the oven billowing with smoke, their contents charred beyond recognition. She immediately tossed them into the garbage. Like the claws of a lobster, she waved the mitts, clearing the air of black smoke.

"Luv a duck! This is tha third bunch I've wrecked. Been slavin' over this oven like a smithy half tha day an` all I have ta show fawr it is a waste basket full a burnt cupcakes."

Disappointed and deflated, she plopped back down in the chair. "I wanted ta surprise tha boys. So's they could take 'em ta school tomorrow fawr their Valentine's Day party. I followed tha damn recipe ta tha last teaspoon. Now, what am I gonna do?"

"You are going to stop feeling sorry for yourself, get out of that chair and clean up this mess. Then you and I are going to make another batch and when they have finished cooling, we are going to frost them. Come on, now, there is no time for pouting. We have just enough time to finish them before the boys come home."

Rejuvenated by the plan, she wiped her hands on her apron and joined him enthusiastically. "Okay, Abraham. Let's you an' me show Betty Crocker how it's done."

By four o'clock, when the boys crashed in the back door, sitting proudly on the counter top were four dozen devil's food cake cupcakes with tepees of cream cheese frosting, expertly decorated with cinnamon candy hearts and sprinkled with red sugar.

That evening, Lottie and the little boys cut, glued and pasted, glittered, wrapped and decorated their Valentine boxes. She tried to let them do as much of the decorating as possible, using their own imaginations. At several points, Colin, had asked her help. With time running out he had needed to improvise and was discouraged that he had been unsuccessful in creating the perfect look.

Lottie encouraged him. "Let's apply tha rule that ain't failed me, yet. It's called tha it'll do rule. It ain't perfect, but it'll do."

಄ ಜ

On Friday night, Sister Elizabeth Clare permitted Katie a long distance, person-to-person telephone call to the boys. After two missed attempts to reach them at home or at Abraham's, she was finally successful reaching them at Lottie's. In celebration for having survived the week, Lottie had planned a sleepover at her house that included extra-special entertainment. They were going to stuff themselves on sweets, stay up way past their bedtimes and watch programs on her television set. Lottie had bought every snack food known to man, potato chips, Hostess Twinkies and Banana Splits, three gallons of ice cream, vanilla, chocolate and strawberry, Oreos and Lorna Doones and a whole case of soda pop.

Katie's heart ached from missing them, but it was heavenly to hear their voices filled with laughter and excitement. It was the best medicine for Katie to know that they seemed so happy and well cared for in her absence. Katie made sure not to abuse the generosity of Sister Elizabeth Clare.

Each of the boys was allowed two precious minutes on the telephone. Chattering like magpies, they filled her in on the past week. The twins prattled on about the television shows they were going to see, "Wild Bill", "Adventures of Kit Carson", "Cisco Kid", "Howdy Doody" and the bestest one of all, "Superman". For them, the week had been one great, exciting adventure.

Tommy missed her a whole bunch and wanted to know when she was coming home. He had made a Valentine just for her and was saving it until she got home. Chance missed her, too. Dr. Franke was a good cook, but not as good as Mom and Miss Lottie made the ickiest lunches. She and Dr. Franke argued a lot, like the twins, but he could tell that they really liked each other. Katie thought to herself, *out of the mouths of babes.*

Brendan sounded distant and reserved, leaving long, empty pauses in the conversation. Katie had to practically drag every response out of him. How was school going? What was he studying? Was he getting enough to eat? What were the Musketeers up to? Did he remember to serve mass last Sunday? Finally, Brendan ended the call, telling her he was going to miss the start of the television show. It left Katie with a cold, void, empty feeling.

As Katie replaced the receiver, tears glistened on her cheeks and stained the collar of her robe. She kept repeating over and over to herself, *Only four more days, four more days, boys, and I'll be home. I will be in your dreams as you will be in mine.*

chapter thirty-one

He dreaded making rounds that morning. It was the one aspect of his occupation that, no matter how many times he performed it in the past, it still remained the most terrifying. He found it easier to tackle the most challenging cases, to perform the most delicate and intricate surgeries, to heal patients where others had failed and deemed incurable. Maybe that was the reason he had developed such a cold, crusty, impenetrable outer core, to protect himself from the hurt and pain of the reality that he, was solely responsible for the disillusionment of hope. He had to shatter the dreams of tomorrow and snuff the flame of faith.

With Mrs. O'Neill, Dr. Vertage had let his guard down. In the time he had spent with the patient, she had completely disarmed him. He had allowed this diminutive, delicate, beautiful, sweet creature to touch his heart. It wasn't a conscious effort, but he hadn't been unable to resist the purity of spirit, the quiet determination, the enduring charm, the hidden strengths of Mrs. Mary Katherine O'Neill.

Katie had risen very early, showered and dressed and impatiently awaited his visit, anxious to get to the train and then home. A generalized weakness and lethargy plagued her movements, but she dismissed them, bolstered by the anticipation of tucking her boys into bed before one more night passed. Despite her pallor, inside she was positively radiant with excitement.

"Well, Mrs. O'Neill, I have some good news, and I have some bad news." Dr. Vertage arrived at Katie's bedside bright and early Tuesday morning. He arrived alone, not surrounded by his usual admiring entourage.

"Katie." She corrected him when he referred to her as Mrs. O'Neill. "It's Katie. For the past ten days, you have examined and probed every square inch of me. There isn't a part of me that you don't know inside and out. You are on a first name basis with every one of my body parts. Don't you think it's about time you called me by my given name? It's Katie."

Dr. Vertage patted the tops of her knees. "Okay. It's Katie. You are bound and determined to break yet two more of my established rules. Never allow yourself to become attached to a patient and never ever should we be on a first name basis."

"Only half of a first name basis. I'll still call you Doctor. All right, *Doctor* Vertage. The good news first. My woman's intuition tells me that after I hear the bad news, the good news won't matter."

Clearing his throat, he wanted to avoid looking into her deep green eyes, but she deserved better. He jokingly began. "The good news is you have donated your last vial of blood." Then, quietly with sobriety tingeing his words, his face reflecting defeat, he continued.

Katie fell as if she was drowning in quicksand, struggling with leaden, useless limbs, being pulled deeper and deeper, fighting to keep her head above the murky sand, gasping and choking for air, until she slipped under completely and disappeared. Dr. Vertage's words sounded muffled, with a far-off, detached quality, barely audible. His lips seemed to be moving in slow motion, uttering, droning, long, drawn out, unintelligible words. A seventy-eight record being played on slow speed. Only one out of every ten words he spoke actually reached her brain for processing *"cancer ... spread ... advanced ... lymph nodes ... cervix ... uterus ... terminal."*

Katie thought she was in a caught in a vacuum that had sucked all the oxygen from the air. It was a void of nothingness. She could no longer breathe, feel or think. Though her ears ceased to hear Dr. Vertage's voice rattled inside her skull like a pinball, repeatedly assaulting her brain. Each word caused her to flinch. Katie felt as if her heart should stop beating, but still she felt it pound against her chest.

Then an eerie, strange calm consumed her, as if she were suspended, floating in space, weightless with no feeling, no sense of taste, smell, not hearing, not seeing. None of the concrete, solid realities, laws of nature of a physical world existed. Time had ceased to exist. She didn't know if she had been sitting there for a minute, an hour or a day after Dr. Vertage stopped talking. She suddenly became aware of the total, complete, haunting silence.

But whatever internal, self-protective mechanisms of avoidance, denial, survival that the mind had conjured up, it slowly began to break down, as if she were awakening from a coma, erupting from a cocoon, rousing from sleep, to the harsh glare of reality. Words began to connect the fractured sentences, filling in the gaps and spaces, translating it all into the absoluteness of truth.

Katie had no idea how much time had lapsed before she spoke. Finally, when she did manage to speak, she hardly recognized her own voice. It belonged to a stranger. "So, you're not offering me much hope, are you?"

"With cancer we just don't have many choices. Our treatment recourses are very limited. There are some treatment options, of course; I'll explain all of them to you, in detail. See where we go from there."

"Realistically, Doctor, what are my chances?"

He searched his mind for the right words that would soften the futility and finality that he knew would strike her a crushing blow.

"Even with surgery, with the treatments, as advanced as the disease is ... well ... I don't want to give you any false promises ..." He faltered.

"Then, what you are saying is that it's pretty hopeless. I *am* going to die."

He could barely look her in the eyes, let alone formulate a response. He could barely manage a slight nod.

"Tell me how much ... how much time is there?"

"With this type of cancer, based on the extensive metastases, it is often difficult to predict."

Katie repeated herself, "How much time? How much time do I have left? You're the expert. Certainly, you must have some idea?" The pitch of her voice rose with impatience and desperation.

"Not long. If I had to pin it down, I would estimate four months at the least. Eight months at the most, if you're lucky. I won't kid you, Katie, it will become very painful."

Katie squeezed her eyes shut in disbelief.

"We might be able to prolong that a bit, slow down the advancement with surgery, drugs and radiation."

"Prolong it. How long could we prolong it? How much time could we gain?"

"That is impossible to tell. Some perhaps. But the radiation and drugs are not without unpleasant side effects and inconvenience. There are areas of the body that we can't subject to radiation. You would need to stay here for weeks. It would require you to spend a great deal of the time you do have left, in treatment. A lot of patients become quite ill from the side effects. There often occurs some local damage and burning of the skin. You will experience hair loss and episodes of nausea and diarrhea."

"Prolong it. But not kill it. Are you saying that there is absolutely nothing else we can do? Can't you cut it out?"

"If we could have diagnosed it early enough, when it was still confined to your cervix, before it had spread to your lymph glands and lungs, we may have been successful in treating it with surgery. But, in your case, it is much too advanced.

"At this stage, I wouldn't advocate surgery. It would be useless. I am of the school that believes unless the surgical benefits far outweigh the disadvantages, I refuse to subject my patients to futile, senseless painful intervention. I would only recommend an operation if the vaginal bleeding becomes profuse, if you should hemorrhage."

"How long have I had this monster growing inside of me?"

"Judging from our findings, the level of progression, I would say somewhere between one and two years. The onset most likely occurred well after
your last pregnancy."

Katie had left her bed and walked like a zombie to gaze out the window at
the cold, somber, windy, winter morning. The city was coming to life, the
smoky light of dawn, just breaking. Outside, millions of people were casually
going about, happily enjoying life in their own, insulated, little worlds while
her world was disappearing. They were still a vital part of life and living, while
she was only an invisible ghost. Now, she could only be a mute observer. Viewing it all with a cool detachment, like an audience witnessing a play in which
they had no role.

All the people out there, rich or poor, young or old, it didn't matter, all
functioned in their own universes, completely unaffected by their proximity to
each other. Until a few minutes ago, she had been exactly like them. How
foolish and self-absorbed is the human species. Naively thinking that they were
immune, that mortality couldn't touch them, fooling themselves that it could
happen to someone else, but never happen to them. They were exempt.

Not a single one of them was remotely aware that she existed. They were all
oblivious to her. Deaf, dumb and blind to her and her hideous, frail, mortality.
Not a single one of them would take notice of her, standing at the window.
Right at that moment, Katie would have traded places with anyone of them. It
was a peculiar irony to envy a stranger. Like a jealous lover, she could only envy
them. Covet the futures they still had.

Katie immediately wanted reconciliation, an accounting. She demanded that
she be given a second chance, a second chance to do it all over again. Differently.

Without turning around, she spoke clearly, but softly, not to anyone in
particular, more to herself than to Dr. Vertage. "There will be no radiation …
no drugs … no surgery. I won't sacrifice the time I do have left in valiant,
hopeless, wasted efforts. I want to go home. There are things I need to take care
of. Arrangements I need to make. I want to see my boys."

With her back still to him, Dr. Vertage reassured her. "When the time
comes, you may be kept more comfortable in a hospital. We have procedures,
the means to alleviate some of the pain."

Katie was emphatic. "No. No more procedures. No more hospitals. I don't
want to face the end with people I don't know, in a strange bed, in an institution, isolated from my family and friends. When the end comes I want to be
home."

"That choice is yours. And for what it's worth, I think you may be making
the right decision. I'll be in contact with Dr. Hughes, relay my recommendations to him. He can prescribe whatever medications are necessary to control

the pain and keep you comfortable. Before you go, is there anything else I can do for you, Katie?"

With a neutral, toneless response, she said, "You can tell me where I can find the nearest Catholic Church."

It wasn't a church, but rather a modest chapel on the first floor of the hospital. Softened with dark burgundy carpet and drapes, lit only by flickering candles, it was very small. Yet, to Katie, who felt shrunken, diminished, microscopic, it was cavernous.

Twelve pews, six on each side faced a small altar at the front. There was only one other person there, kneeling in a pew, head bent in prayer. Perhaps like Katie, desperate and lost, hungry for the peace and comfort of prayer, or unlike Katie, thanking God for an answered plea. Either way, Katie and the visitor left one another with the privacy of their own thoughts.

She quietly made her way up one of the center aisle to a private alcove where a tier of devotional candles sat. Sliding a nickel into the narrow slot of the metal collection box, she lit a single candle and knelt on the plush padding of the kneeler. Beginning with the sign of the Cross, she began her prayers of supplication and for the first time in the past ten days, she surrendered to her fears and sobbed.

Ↄ ↄ

The taxicab ride was endured in total silence.

Since bidding Sister Elizabeth Clare good-by, Katie hadn't uttered a word. The sea of faces moved around her and the interior of the station dissolved in a watery expanse of shadows and shapes. The voices and sounds were bizarre gibberish she couldn't understand. She purchased her ticket and boarded the train without sharing more the one or two words with another human being. She wasn't Katie O'Neill. She wasn't flesh and blood. She was a robot. She had performed every action, sitting, standing, walking, automatically, without thought, intent or purpose beyond getting home.

She stared out the train window as objects flew by in a blur, oblivious to the stops that were made at towns along the way. If anyone boarded or departed, Katie never noticed. She was completely unaware of her surroundings except that she sat alone in her seat and was relieved no one had sat down beside her. Polite conversation would have been impossible.

She hadn't even noticed that it had started to snow. Hard. Her mind was caught in its own blinding blizzard. An avalanche of questions and what-ifs swirled around, blinding her mind's eye to any sane thought. Finally, emotionally purged and too exhausted to think anymore, Katie rested her head against the icy cold pane of the window and let the steady rocking of the train, the rhythmic clatter of metal wheel against steel rail lull her to sleep.

Katie had slept a great deal of the way. It wouldn't be long now. The last few miles, she had cleared her thoughts, wiped out any notion or idea that wasn't helpful or constructive. She had to focus on what was possible, not what was impossible. As the blackness outside passed by, mile after mile, Katie searched the invisible landscape, hoping that with the occasional, distant light that passed by, like a lighthouse beacon to a floundering ship, the smallest hint of light would penetrate the fog and show her the way.

The solution didn't come to her like a blinding, bolt out of the blue. It didn't appear suddenly bright and luminous, like turning on the lights of a theater marquee. Nor did it explode like a spiritual revelation at a revival meeting, a religious epiphany. Instead, it emerged slowly. First it was merely a glimmer, a hint, a spark, then, growing steadily, gradually, but absolutely and by the time the train pulled into Grand Rapids, the answer had fully developed and Katie knew exactly what the answer was. Katie knew exactly what she needed to do.

chapter thirty-two

Faced with the acute realization of her own mortality, the world took on a whole new appearance to Katie. Or perhaps, more accurately, it was the way in which she viewed it. There were no indistinct overlaps, no vague perceptions, no evasive illusions, no gray areas. There was only achromatic verity, the absolute clarity of black and white, of past and present. The colors and shades of possibility, of tomorrows, of the future, were no longer relevant, no longer existed.

It was a strange feeling to be faced with the cold sterility of having no future. Katie realized how much of the present was squandered away, lost, in anticipation of the future. The human folly of wasting the present in the vain effort to chase the future. Instead of absorbing that precise second in time, savoring each precious moment of a now that will never be again, humans miss it by grasping at tomorrow. All too soon, the present would become the past and all the todays would become yesterdays.

Katie, for the first time, was aware how much of her time was spent looking forward. Going to bed at night, already planning for the morning. Saving for the future. Anticipating the next season, the next holiday. Hoping tomorrow will be a better day. We'll do it later. Someday. When tomorrow comes … next month … in five years.

So, it was an entirely different person that returned to Eden Croft than the one who had left. The Katie of the past was discerning, cautious, judicious and patient. But the Katie of the present, the one who had returned, could no longer afford those luxuries. The new Katie was determined and driven by purpose. Her vision had not only been reduced in depth, but had narrowed in scope. A single-mindedness and resolve became her only concerns.

She felt no fear for herself. Pain, suffering, even her death, did not terrify her. They were nothing more than minor distractions. She was possessed by one singular thought. Taking care of the boys. She had an idea, a plan, and her mind was absorbed with only two things. How to make the plan a reality, and how to protect the boys from finding out, until she felt the time was right to tell them.

CƷ ℰↄ

Katie could have won an Oscar for her performance, the night she returned from Chicago. She claimed to be too exhausted to answer any of Lottie's and Abraham's questions and begged off that all she wanted to do was sleep. She placated them with vague answers, half-truths and untruths. She was confident that she could delay telling Matt but Lottie was another matter. She hoped that she could stall Lottie for at least a day. Talking with Abraham remained her first priority, and it was a conversation that she needed to do alone. But, first, she needed to seek the counsel of Father Davey.

The next day, for the boys, Katie could have won back-to-back Oscars with her encore performance. Then again, she had a far greater motivation and impetus than mere lauds or accolades. Like a mother bear fighting for her cubs, her act was spurred on by her desperate need to protect them and maintain as much normalcy around them as possible. The little ones wouldn't be a problem but she wasn't at all convinced that she could maintain the charade with Brendan. He was older, more aware and perceptive. And Katie had so much trouble reading him.

Katie knew that if she left early enough, hopefully she would avoid an early morning visit from Lottie. So, she left the house only minutes after the boys.

CƷ ℰↄ

At first, as Katie spoke, Father Davey listened and only responded when she asked it of him. Then, when she was ready, she asked for his validation and opinion, his support and advice. He wanted to give her so much more than a heap of empty, idealistic platitudes that would fall short of giving her the guidance, comfort and direction she needed. He could only hope that he would find all the right words.

Father Davey always felt that a priest or minister was much like a doctor in that dealing with life and death was a daily ritual. Yet, he found in some ways, it was a bit more difficult for a cleric than a physician. A man of medicine ministers to the concrete and absolutes of living and dying. Their purpose and role begins and ends with those mortal, physical parameters. But, as a man of God he not only had to minister to the mortal being, but also the unseen, the soul, the spirituality that extends beyond the physical world.

So, for Father Davey, where the physicians' roles had ended, his role as a spiritual healer must begin to sustain her. It was not easy to balance the needs of each person, the total person, spiritually as well as physically. No matter how strong one's faith remains on the notion of eternal life beyond the here and now, that this whole physical existence is merely a means to an end, all the demands of a tangible world, the everyday matters of living are still ever present and real. For Katie, those realities were her four young boys. Where Katie and the O'Neill boys were concerned, he realized they were all going to need a great deal of understanding, compassion and support, physically, emotionally and spiritually, before the long nightmare would be over.

Truthfully, Father Davey felt that Katie's plan was basically sound. It appeared that she had thought it over carefully and had complete confidence in it. He had to agree, it made good sense and considering the emotional and physical strain that she was functioning under, he was amazed that she had been able to think clearly, let alone become so sure of her conviction.

Afterward, drained and exhausted from the difficult conversation, Katie accepted Father Davey's blessing and offer of assistance anytime day or night. He also reassured her that anything he could do to facilitate things, all she had to do was ask.

As he watched her walk to her car, he couldn't help but recall the first time he had watched her leave his rectory. That day, he had had no idea of the impact that she would have on his life. It had been less than a year and yet, in reality, it was a lifetime ago. At the time, he had a strong feeling that she was a remarkable woman. He had been completely wrong. She truly was an incomparable extraordinary woman. He couldn't imagine how anyone would ever be able to fill the void that her absence would leave. Yet, under the circumstances, he felt she had made the right choice. As he silently prayed for her successor, he hoped that everyone concerned would share his optimism.

After dinner and bedtime that night, certain that the boys were all asleep, Katie telephoned Abraham and asked if she could come over. She needed to talk with him, privately. He sensed the urgency in her voice and assured her that her timing was perfect. He had just finished brewing a pot of tea.

Some of the snowdrifts were knee deep as Katie trudged her way across the yard. Bitter cold winds penetrated the layers of her wool coat and scarf and blew icy pellets against her face that stung like needle picks. Katie shivered more from the cold within her soul than the icy bite of the wind. A half-moon lit her pathway as she wound and waded her way through the hedges, heaps of snow and up to the cottage door. Outside, she could smell the burning fireplace as a steady plume of pungent smoke filled the crisp night air.

A wall of welcomed heat hit her immediately as Abraham opened the door. She stomped the snow from her galoshes, removed them and took off her coat, scarf and gloves. Standing in front of the fire, she let the radiant heat warm her. She stalled for a bit and employed an elaborate ruse of rubbing her hands in front of the flames as if she were unable to lose the chill.

Katie realized that she was only delaying the inevitable. She wasn't going to succeed in making it any easier. Abraham offered her a steaming cup of tea. Katie accepted it and sat down at the table, where Abraham joined her.

Finally, sitting on opposite sides of his kitchen table, Katie told Abraham the entire truth.

Initially, she hadn't thought that she would be able to find the words, but then, like a mountain stream fed from the spring thaw, the words tumbled forth, easily. Abraham hadn't uttered one word. Hadn't interrupted or asked one question. Instead, he let Katie tell him in her own words, in her own way.

The room became suddenly still, like a marble crypt, the only sounds were the creaking of the cottage from the groaning wind, icy snow tapping at the windowpanes and the crackling of the fire.

Though he had suspected that the trip to Chicago was more than just a routine precaution, he thought he had prepared himself for the worst outcome. Yet, Abraham discovered that he was as shocked by the news as he was by the pain that suddenly grasped his insides, all but forcing the air from his lungs.

He could barely think let alone breathe. Abraham tried to draw air into his lungs but it was as if his throat had closed up. The grief and pain and anger became so entwined they were inseparable. Up until that moment, he hadn't thought there was any room left in him for pain. That he had become anesthetized to hurt and loss. He was immune to shock. But Abraham felt as if he had been struck by lightening.

First, the jolt of electricity immobilized him. Then the sharp burn spread from deep inside, outward, to every nerve and cell. His heart was pierced, as if a spike had been hammered through it. The anguish of the twisting, throbbing, lingering pain was almost unbearable. The long ago memory of despair and devastation, when he learned of Zora's and Daniel's death, came crashing down on him, again, anew, like a ten-ton stone. *Not again. Not Katie. Not this precious creature.*

Once more he asked of a God that he wasn't sure ever listened to a prayer, ever heard a plea, was ever moved by supplication. *Why not me? Take me in her stead.*

He reached across the table and took her hands in his. Face veiled by his grief, Abraham played the role of comforter. The two pair of hands grasped, reached out for comfort and solace. Their hands so very different in appearance, both sought a mutual understanding. His were weatherworn and coarse from age, hands that had known both the rewards and the challenges of toil. And Katie's, small, soft, slight as a child's. Her hands had touched so many lives with her gentle strength.

In that singular, simple, quiet gesture, their two universes forged together. They were embarking on the same path, the common ground that kindred spirits walk.

"Oh … Katie … I am so sorry …" His voice broke. He couldn't finish.

I am so sorry. He was so ashamed of the miserably inadequate, trite phrase. Katie deserved better than that. Katie, who had such goodness in her, was entitled to so much more than that. Yet, he searched in vain to find the words that would give her the sustenance she needed. Of all the millions of combinations of letters, man had not invented a single word that could ease the horror she was facing. He realized at those times when there was so much to say, and no words to say it, saying nothing was best.

Katie couldn't bear the anguish reflected in his tone and his face. Dear, sweet, gentle Abraham. How lucky she was that their paths had crossed. How fortunate that God had brought him into her life. She made not the slightest effort to blink back the tears. She let them flow freely, unembarrassed, unashamed and completely comfortable with him seeing her at her weakest.

"It's all right, Abraham. There really isn't anything anyone can say. At this point, everything is pretty much beyond conciliation. There is nothing you could say that I haven't already exhausted in my mind."

"You know what I find so ironic? How precarious our earthly lives are. All our dreams, all our plans, all our expectations can dissolve in an instant."

"Katie, this is all so wrong ... so unjust."

"It's not really as unfair as it seems. In so many ways, life has been good to me ... generous ... and absolutely fair. I have been blessed as a daughter with two wonderful, loving parents and as a mother of four beautiful children. I have shared a great marriage and love with one man and the budding love with another. I have known the deep friendship of special people, people I have come to rely on and depend on without question. Old friends in Boston and new friends here. Friends that I can confide in, bare my soul to and know that it would be held in the gentlest hands."

The faces of all those she had come to love and call friend flashed through her mind. Dee and Moira and Angie. Lottie and Matt. Father Davey and Dr. Hughes. Katie smiled with warmth as she recounted all her good fortune. The true meaning of the word friend applied to each if them and she knew it was the highest compliment one person can pay to another.

"I would say I have been blessed beyond measure."

Katie closed her eyes for a moment and when she opened them, her direction had changed. "I have worn out all the whys in a vain attempt to rationalize ... to find a reason, an explanation. Looking for a hint of sanity in an insane situation, I came to realize what a futile waste of energy that was. The time I have left is too precious to squander on the impossible. I need to conserve and channel that energy where it can do some good."

Her voice nearly disappeared in the hushed quiet of the room, then recharged with determination, she continued. "I'm fine. Really. I don't need sympathy. I don't want condolences or reassurances. I don't have time for us to get mired down with pity and regrets. I'm running out of time, Abraham. There are things I need to do … arrangements I need to make. There is something, one thing that I do need to ask of you. But before I do, I want you to make me a promise."

"Anything, Katie. If it is within my power, you have my promise." Though his voice was hushed to a near whisper, he spoke the words with total affirmation.

"I wish I could give you more time to think this over, unfortunately, there isn't much time. But, if you have any doubts. Any reservations. No matter how slight. I want you to be completely honest with me. No heroics. No valiant efforts to come to my rescue. I don't need a knight in shining armor. What I need from you is your complete candor and truthfulness, not some misguided, misplaced noble gesture that won't be of any good to anyone."

Abraham nodded, "I give you my word."

Katie looked into his kind, sincere, serious eyes and knew deep within her soul that she had made the right decision.

"Abraham … I want you to raise the boys."

chapter thirty-three

If a pig had flown by the kitchen window at that moment, Lottie wouldn't have been any more shocked.

And before she had gained her composure after Katie told her about Dr. Vertage and the prognosis, she was hit by the second wave.

Katie had been right in her predictions. There was no way she was going to succeed in putting off Lottie. Once she had gotten a whiff of anything suspicious, she could sniff out a secret like a tick hound on a scent. And sure enough, she showed up on Katie's doorstep the following morning, about thirty seconds after the boys had left and before the school bus had shifted out of first gear. She was dressed in her robe, nightie, slippers, pin curls and hairnet, not a lick of make-up, and wearing her absurd mink coat.

Lottie wasn't known to be one for displays of emotion and tears, but as soon as Katie had finished, she took her in her arms and held her there, neither one speaking. The tears flowed like Niagara Falls.

When Lottie had finally let it all sink in, she spoke. "I knew we had us a problem, Katie. I jus' never dreamt it'd be this bad."

Through her own tears, Katie joked, "Come on, Lottie. You're really scaring me. Now, I know I'm in serious trouble. Never in all the times I've seen you … in all of our gab-sessions … in all the hours we've spent together, have I ever seen you cry or have you call me by anything other than, Sug."

They laughed together, through their tears. Katie was tired of holding it all in. Since she returned from Chicago, with the exception of her talk with Abraham, she hadn't allowed herself to shed a single tear. Crying with Lottie was cathartic. It provided a release valve. And for Lottie, it served as a reassurance that Katie's inner strengths were still in place. That she wasn't running on empty, hadn't given up, yet.

When the laughter had subsided and the tears dried up, Lottie, who always spoke her mind, spoke it. "Well, how 'bout me? I can't deny that I'm feelin' a bit hurt that y'all ain't asked me ta take 'em. They'd sure have a lot more fun with me than with Abraham."

"They don't need to be raised in a circus, Lottie. They need a real home. They need stability, someone solid they can depend on. Someone they know

292

will be there for them. No matter what. You've never been around kids longer than a few hours at a time and even then it was like a big adventure for you. But being there for the long haul? That's different. It's hard work. Non-stop. Twenty-four hours a day … seven days a week. When you get tired of it, you can't simply drop into the Color, Cut an' Curl and change it."

"Jus' 'cuz I ain't never doesn't mean I can't ever. Who says I can't?"

"I can just see you wiping snotty noses with your lace hankies and picking bubble gum out of your mink coat. By, the way, may I mention how ridiculous you look in that coat. When most women would be content and happy with terrycloth, here you are, traipsing around, wearing a ridiculous mink coat for a bathrobe."

"Yawr steerin' tha boat a bit off course ain't ya. Seems like we wuz talkin' 'bout who's right an' who's wrong ta take those boys. Ma wardrobe ain't got a thin' ta do with it."

"Your wardrobe has everything to do with it. It reflects Lottie Devereaux and who she is. It reflects your lifestyle and what's important to you. And what about your trips? It wouldn't be fair to you. You can't take off at the drop of a hat when one of the twins has the mumps or Brendan has a baseball game or Tommy has a book report due. They need a full-time parent, not a part-time playmate."

"But, I kin give 'em so much more. I could spoil 'em rotten. Heck, I got more money'n some small countries. I kin provide fawr 'em. I could give 'em anythin' an' everythin' they could ever want. Seems ta me it'd make a lot more sense. What tha heck else have I got ta do with ma millions?"

Katie rolled her eyes and smiled. "What was I ever thinking? Of course, that does make more sense. Lottie, they don't need to be raised in a department store, either. You can't simply throw money at them. Money is the least of the problems."

Katie softened her tone. "If there's one thing I've learned the past few years, Lottie, is how unimportant those things are. Wealth, material possessions, the tangibles … those things don't really matter. It's the relationships we develop, the people we surround ourselves with that are important. It's the bonds and alliances we forge, the personal connections we make that really matter."

"But, Abraham, Sug? That dried-up, cantankerous, sober ol' goat? Hell, it takes every ounce a strength I got jus' ta drag some laughter outta him. An' even then I nearly had ta strip naked, dance a jig an' whistle "Dixie." I'm workin' on him, but even Lottie's got her limits. Ya might as well send them boys off ta a monastery. Have 'em reared by a bunch a monks. Every child needs the tenderness of a momma. Tha soft touch of a woman."

"Do you remember when you told me that every boy needs a dog to grow up with? Why did you say that? Why a boy? Why not a child?"

Lottie thought a minute. "'Cuz boys are different. They have different needs than a girl."

"Exactly. If they were girls, maybe the situation would be different. But they're not. Boys have special needs growing up. When they're little, I agree with you, a woman's loving touch is important, but at some point they reach an age when a man's touch is more important. Brendan has taught me that. He needs the influence and guidance of a man. Sooner or later, Tommy and the twins are going to have those same needs. They've lost a father and Abraham has lost a son. That gives them a special commonality."

"No, Lottie. Abraham has been a parent before. He knows about the work, worry, commitment and sacrifice. This will give him a second chance … to be a father again. And the boys a second chance to have a father. He'll be good for the boys and they'll be good for him. He knows the boys and they know him. I've never known anyone more suited to be a role model and father. And I can't imagine anyone who would make me happier having them grow to be like. There isn't any point in arguing about it any more. I've made up my mind, Lottie, and Abraham has agreed."

Lottie asked the next obvious question. "When ya plannin' on tellin' 'em?"

Katie thought a minute before she answered, worry wrinkled her brow. "I don't know. Not yet. It's too soon. I want the time we have left to be as normal and carefree as possible, without it being overshadowed by fear and worry. Darkened by the truth. I won't allow their happiness to be stolen from them one day earlier than it has to be. Until then, our lives will go on as usual. And in the meantime, I'll wait for the right moment."

"Tha right moment ain't gonna jus' fall inta yawr lap. I'm not so sure yawr makin' tha right decishun there, Sug. Seems ta me that it's gonna put quite a strain on ya. Yawr gonna need them an' they're sure gonna need you. Yawr gonna hafta help em ta understand. Ta get used ta tha idea. Ya ain't bein' fair to 'em. An' I'd bet ma ridiculous mink coat that Brendan's gonna raise a royal ruckus when he finds out ya been keepin' tha truth from him."

"I have to follow my heart, Lottie. And right now, that's what it's telling me to do."

"So, when ya gonna tell Matt? He's madder'n a Moses on tha mountain at ya, right now. He jus' 'bout assaulted Abraham an' me tryin' ta find out where ya were. Pretty near drove us both crazy. He even threatened ta sue Dr. Hughes if he didn't let him know where ya were."

"I have an appointment with Matt on Monday. I'm going to need him to handle all the legal details."

"An appointment!" Lottie almost popped a pin curl.

"Ya mean ta tell me that yawr gonna spring it on him at his office? Sug, y'all are playin' with fire there. An' sure as bears shit in tha woods, yawr gonna get yawrself burnt."

"Rather cowardly on my part, I know. But, I've played it over and over, again and again in my mind, and it always ends up the same. How does one go about telling the man they've fallen in love with that you're dying?"

ڣ ۃ

Matt had been moody and brooding for days. Vi had worked for him long enough to know that something was very wrong. She strongly suspected that his behavior had something to do with Katie O'Neill.

Vi had seen a steady stream of females drift in and out of his life with no more importance than temporary dalliances. But, this one was different. He had been a changed man since her arrival in Eden Croft. A female of the species had finally conquered the finite bachelor. She didn't know if he realized it or not, but it was blatantly obvious to her, Matt had been knocked off his bachelor's throne and landed squarely into love's tenacious grasp. Vi figured it served him right. He was always so sure-footed, so cavalier, so utterly confident that the female hadn't been born yet, who could put a ring through his nose. Why settle for one, when the selection is inexhaustible. Well, the higher the throne, the harder the fall.

Love must be deaf and dumb, as well as blind. Since he first laid eyes on Katie, as far as Vi knew, he hadn't looked at, talked to, heard or even acknowledged the existence of any other female. Matt Mulholland had been bit and bit hard. Apparently, true love also defies gravity, because he had been walking around on cloud nine for months. As a matter of fact, Matt and Vi's conversations had become single-mindedly boring. Katie O'Neill was all he ever talked about. He had even started to hum and whistle. This was getting serious. He was disgustingly good-natured and walked around with an annoyingly satisfied grin plastered on his face.

That was until two weeks ago.

Now, Vi would gladly trade his sour mood for that annoying grin.

She had more than enough of his snappish, ornery, temperamental attitude toward her. She was tired of being his whipping post. He hadn't said a civil word to her in days. Totally unlike Matt, he had been antagonistic, preoccupied, short-tempered and argumentative. He snapped, shouted, complained, criticized and barked orders. Vi hadn't been able to do anything right, and knowing that he was hurting, that he couldn't help himself, she had suffered his abuse silently. Not anymore. He didn't pay her enough. Heck, nobody could pay her enough to take that kind of abuse.

Fed up with his mistreatment and malfeasance, she was going to put an end to it right now. Somebody had to do something. And she figured she was the right somebody to do it. Armed with surety, steeled with the strength of her convictions, she tugged her suit jacket into place, threw open his office door and charged into the inner sanctum unannounced.

Matt was sitting in his chair, facing the window, his back to the room.

He snapped, "I don't recall you knocking or inviting you to come in."

"Well, like it or not, I'm in all the same. You may not want my intrusion or advice, but I'm going to butt right in and give it to you, anyway. I've worked for you nearly eight years and I figure that record has earned me some privileges. I'm exercising those privileges right now.

"I don't know what's going on between you and Katie O'Neill, but its obvious that you're upset by it. Why don't you give her a call? Talking to her is the only way you're going to fix it. You're making yourself and everyone one around you miserable."

He responded in a flat monotone. "You're absolutely right, Vi. I don't want your intrusion or your advice."

She rolled her eyes and sighed. "Give her a call. Tell her you need to talk."

Matt replied with indifference, "The four least favorite words a man wants to hear from a woman and you want me to say them to her?"

"You have to talk to someone about it. She's the logical choice. You can't go on like this. *I* can't go on like this," she pleaded with him.

"You're wrong on all four counts. Should have quit while you were ahead." Matt rebuffed her.

"Don't you even try to chastise me. You're the one that's acting pig-headed, here, and you know it." She wasn't going to be dismissed that easily. "You know, sometimes you can behave like a spoiled, rotten, incorrigible brat. Just turn your back on something you don't like and that will make it all go away. Well, real life doesn't work that way. At some point you have to grow up. You can't always have everything your way when you want it. And I've got a pretty good idea that your misplaced pride and stubbornness is somewhere at the root of this."

Still as a mannequin, Matt hadn't moved a muscle. "Then your pretty good idea would be full of shit."

"Listen, I've raised two sons and one husband and that experience has taught me a lot about the precious male ego. If a conversation doesn't involve engines or sports or what's for dinner, you men don't want anything to do with it. Heaven forbid you should be forced to discuss feelings and emotions."

He snapped back at her, "Since we're not discussing car parts or baseball or tonight's dinner menu, with that wealth of experience you should know when to keep quiet."

"I don't think so!" She threw it right back at him. "My experience tells me that a good dressing down would do you a world of good."

"What part of BUTT OUT don't you understand?" he shouted. "What you think or don't think doesn't matter a goddamn to me."

She was really angry now. "Don't you dare swear at me!"

"Then don't you dare come in here, again, unless I ask you to," he ordered.

Vi was exasperated, frustrated and defeated. The conversation was going nowhere. Talking to a stonewall was a monologue not a dialogue. Well, she'd given it her best shot. If he wanted to be miserable the rest of his life then let him be. But, two could play this game and she was at the least going to claim the satisfaction of having the last word. It would serve as his punishment for the cruel insults he'd slung at her and her reward for the ill treatment she'd put up with.

"Oh, one last thing. You might want to wear a suit on Monday. You have a ten o'clock appointment with Mrs. O'Neill."

Matt flinched, almost imperceptibly.

"Close the door on your way out," he barked.

"God! Men can be such king-size jackasses!" She sputtered loud enough for him to hear then slammed the door so hard she heard a picture crash to the floor.

Her only regret was that it hadn't landed squarely on top of his head.

chapter thirty-four

Vi ushered Katie into Matt's office. She felt guilty as sin, like she was feeding a Christian to the hungry lions.

Vi had thought that his foul mood of the past two weeks couldn't get any fouler. She had been mistaken. Since she told him about Katie's appointment his black mood had gotten blacker.

Hopefully, for Katie's sake, he had purged himself of most of his vicious nastiness. Maybe the worst of his juvenile temper tantrum was already exhausted. Katie didn't look as though she could hold up under the Spanish Inquisition. In fact, she looked as though she might collapse at any moment.

With Katie still standing on the threshold to his private office, Vi quickly grabbed her coat and hat, gloves and purse and fled the scene for an early lunch. Like a rat abandoning a sinking ship. Before Mount Vesuvius erupted, she was going to be on the first boat out of Pompeii.

Matt stood behind his desk staring out the window, his arms akimbo, his back turned to Katie. He was dressed as Katie expected him to be, in well-worn corduroy trousers and a thick sweater.

Katie stood for a moment and waited for him to say something, anything. But he stood his ground with chilling indifference and icy silence.

Finally, she garnered her courage and broke the silence. "I hope you're not charging me by the minute. Based on this long interlude of silence, this meeting could become very expensive for me."

Katie's feeble attempt at humor failed completely.

Eventually, Matt replied, his voice taking on a harsh, sarcastic, foreign quality.

"So, this meeting is professional rather than of a personal nature? And here I actually thought that you might want to see me, instead of a lawyer. But, I guess I was wrong, again. Seems to me, I've been wrong about a lot of things, lately."

Katie bit back the tears triggered by his venom. He wasn't going to make this easy. He still hadn't made an effort to budge and tired of being the bad guy in this altercation, Katie pleaded with him, "How long are you going to punish me by forcing me to talk to your back?"

298

He spun around and his face bore an expression that chilled Katie to the bone. She had expected some animosity, but she hadn't prepared herself for this. His blue-green eyes, usually dancing with wide-eyed mischief, were like smoldering slits of fury.

"I didn't trust myself to look you in the eye. I was afraid of what I might do. Of what I might say. But this is better. I want to see you … face to face. That way we won't have any more misunderstandings."

The truth was he hadn't wanted to face her. Not because of what he might say or do, but because he was afraid of having her see the pain in his eyes. See how much she had hurt him. At the very least, he wanted to hold on to some measure of dignity.

"Please, Matt. You don't understand …"

He shouted at her, "You're damned right, I don't understand. I don't understand how you could disappear for weeks at a time, then come back and continue to avoid me for another week. Not a word. Not a telephone call. I don't understand how you could tell Abraham and Lottie where you were … and why … and withhold the truth from me. I don't understand that at all. I don't understand you, at all. I once said that I knew you better than you knew yourself. I was way off. I'm not sure I ever knew who you were. And I'm damned sure I don't know who you are now."

His words stung like a snakebite.

"I asked them not to say anything."

"And believe me, they followed your instructions to the letter. You have that way with people. The magic touch. That Irish charm of yours has everyone wound tightly around your little finger. To get everyone to do exactly as you want. All they would tell me is some bullshit about a doctor's appointment in Chicago. For Christ's sake, what's that supposed to mean?"

"It means exactly that. I was seeing a doctor."

It was as though he hadn't heard her response. Or he didn't care. "I actually thought that we meant something to each other. That maybe you were starting to feel some of the same things for me that I felt for you. And here I was, this big chump standing around with this stupid look on my face like some pathetic, lovesick schoolboy. I'm not only the last to get the punch line, but actually the butt of the whole, lousy joke. I'm fed up with this roller coaster ride you've got me on. I want to get off."

"I didn't think …"

"You sure as hell didn't think. You didn't think that maybe I would have offered to take you? You didn't think that maybe I would have wanted to be with you? That I was concerned and worried about you? The real truth is that you didn't think that I was important enough to tell."

"Oh, Matt. You're so wrong. I only needed some time."

He walked around the desk and nearly stood on top of her. "Time! Oh, of course. You and your precious need for time. 'Let's go slow, Matt, give me some time, some room to figure all this out.' I had forgotten how important time is to you. Time? You want time? I'll give you time. And plenty of it. How about until next month or maybe even next year? Better, yet, how about the year after that? Hell, I'm in a real generous mood, right now. How about goddamn forever."

With tears streaming down her face, Katie, in a near whisper said, "That's just it. I don't have any time. I don't have next year ... or the year after that. I may not even have six months. I'm dying."

It was as though Joe Louis had landed a solid right to his gut. Then, he felt as though he was sinking through the floor, into the earth, being dragged deeper and deeper, disappearing into a black abyss. There had to be some mistake. He had heard it wrong. Those were the only explanations. And yet he must have, because a sickening feeling of nausea and despair had invaded his stomach and had spread outward to every cell.

There must be a hell, because he was in it.

Finally, an all-consuming numbness spread, paralyzing him. His blood froze solid and clogged every vessel. Every thought and sense evaporated into nothingness until the only sensation he could feel was a deep, burning, all-consuming pain as if someone had poured alcohol on an open wound.

He fought to swallow back the bitter nausea that threatened to erupt from his insides. Slowly, he took Katie into his arms and, holding each other, she told him everything.

For a small eternity they clung to each other, drawing strength and comfort from each another. There was no cancer, no pain, no death, no ending. The only reality was the two of them and what they were sharing. For them, the physical world of time and space didn't exist. No beginning and no end. There was no yesterday, no tomorrow. Only the present.

ප ෨

"What about me? I'd love to take them. I'd enjoy having the advantage pf having them in a subjective position, for a change."

Katie was emotionally spent. Her tears had finally dried up, leaving her no other expression for her feelings but words.

"Now that would be an interesting arrangement. Who would be in charge? You or them? You're no more than an overgrown boy, yourself. It would be a case of a child raising children. Besides, you're going to want to have a life of your own, someday. Meet someone, fall in love, marry. Have children of your own. There aren't too many women out there who would want to start a marriage with a ready-made family. You'd only end up resenting the boys ... and me."

Matt shook his head. "No. Not for me. That's not in my future. This kind of feeling only happens once in a lifetime. Someone like you only happens once in a lifetime. I won't find it again. I don't want to find it again." He was emphatic.

"You only say that now, because you can't see beyond what you're feeling right now. But, believe me, in time, you will get past it and move on. It happened again for me and it will happen again, for you."

"But why Abraham? Certainly his age will make it difficult for him to keep pace with their demands. I know first hand how much energy it takes to keep up with them."

Katie smiled. "Oh, I suspect that Abraham has a few good years left in him. Abraham is the right choice. He loves them and more importantly, though Brendan and the twins haven't realized it yet, as Tommy has, they love him, too. He was robbed of being a father once. This will be good for him. This will be a second chance and new beginning for him and for them.

"When I was driving here from Boston, I wondered what the future would hold for us. I wondered what path the Lord was leading us down. What purpose did He have in mind? Now, I know. It was no accident of fate. He was bringing Abraham and us together. He was preparing us for the next chapter of our lives. His plan is all so crystal clear to me, now. Call it God's plan, call it destiny, call it a Divine decree, Abraham and the boys belong together.

"So, what I need from you is your advice and legal. expertise. Is it possible? Can we arrange for Abraham to adopt the boys?"

Matt sat on the corner of his desk and thought.

"And there are no relatives or family that could file a first claim for adoption? That's an important factor. The courts would give them priority."

"There isn't anyone. And even if there were, Abraham would still be my first, my only choice. Do you think we have a chance?"

"I suppose it's possible. But there can't be too many cases of this kind that would establish a precedent. I'm not that well versed in family law. I'm going to have to do some research. I have a college chum who specializes in that area. He practices in Detroit so he'll know Michigan's laws. I'll have to contact him as soon as possible. Get his take on it."

"Matt, I don't have the luxury of time. We have to get things moving soon."

"As quickly as possible. I'll get the adoption papers drawn up. You understand, though, the official adoption can't be granted until …" Matt couldn't bring himself to say it. Saying it only made it worse, more real.

"You were going to say, until 'after I've died'? I couldn't say it at first, either. But once you say it a few times, it's not so scary. I'm not frightened by the word, anymore. It's simply a word."

Matt couldn't believe it. He was supposed to be the strong one. He was the one who was supposed to be objective, giving her guidance and support. And yet, he felt weak and inadequate.

"Now ... what's the next step? I'm going to have to have a will."

Matt shook his head trying to chase away the incredulity and grasp onto one coherent thought. "How are you doing it, Katie? How can you be so strong? So practical and sensible? I can't even think about the next five minutes of my life without you in it. I should be your pillar of strength, the one to lean on and the one with all the answers. Instead, you're the one making the decisions with a clear head ... facing it ... dealing with it."

"It's simple. I can't afford to be rueful or speculative. I don't have time for prudence and trepidation. I've worn out all the whys. Circumstances have left no room for what ifs or maybes. There isn't time for caution or hesitation. I have four sons I need to make a future for."

After Katie left, Matt slumped into his chair drained and exhausted. She had been so calm, so strong and forthright. Where did she get her will and fortitude? Her resolution and spirit? How could she maintain such determination?

Only a few hours before, he had felt nothing for Katie but anger and indignation from the hurt she had caused him. Then, with her personal hell to deal with, what had he done? He had lashed out at her, said despicable things. Tried to wound her as much as he had been wounded. What a complete fool he had been. Now, all he could feel was anguish and agony from the pain of losing her. He didn't deserve anyone one tenth as wonderful as she was. She was the one facing death and all he could do was selfishly wonder what his life was going to be like without her.

He slammed his fist down on the desktop and wanted to smash it into a million pieces, just as his universe had been smashed. He fought an uncontrollable urge to bellow, roar and scream until his voice was hoarse and his lungs ached. He wanted to look God straight in the face and ask Him why? Why Katie? Why now? He had waited his whole life for her only to have her stolen away. He had imagined making her his wife. Dreamed of learning everything about her, knowing her as only a husband could. And finally when he thought he could have it all he'd been sucker-punched.

Maybe he was being punished for all the years of selfishly protecting his independence. If God needed to punish him for his indiscretions, his wasted life, why did He have to drag her into it? If this was personal reparation between him and God then leave Katie out of it. She wasn't a part of it.

Well, now he could have his freedom and autonomy, his indifference and detachment. He could have all of that but he couldn't have her. Maybe he didn't deserve her, but she sure as hell didn't deserve any of this. God was way off base on this one. When there were millions of other lousy, miserable sons-of-a-bitches out there, people who didn't deserve to draw another breath, why did He have to take Katie?

He felt as if he were being put to some sort of test of character. If it was a test of faith, he was failing. How was he supposed to help her die? Worse, he didn't know if he had the power to stand by and watch her disappear from his life. He wasn't sure if he had the courage to watch her die.

Matt stared out the window. Just beyond the barren treetops he could see the marina, its frozen slips empty. Soon, spring would melt the ice and dozens of crafts would be anchored there. He thought of Scattering. Soon it would be safely moored there for the sailing season. A goddamned boat. Christ, but his priorities had been all screwed up. He had placed so much importance on things that really didn't matter. Trivial things that were transient, trifling and of no importance. Beyond that, any personal relationships he had, he had taken for granted, wasted and quickly tossed aside, without conscience or consequence. Now, what mattered most to him was being stolen away. The vision of himself as life's biggest joke played out before his eyes. He wanted to heave something through the window and shatter the image of a squandered, superficial life.

Instead, he went home and finished off a fifth of Jamison's and got thoroughly drunk.

chapter thirty-five

Time. Katie had become obsessed with time. It had replaced the cancer as her enemy.

How ironic it was that her tried and true philosophy was failing her now. She had always believed in the doctrine that time could solve so many problems. That it could smooth over the bumps in the road. That differences between people would resolve with time. Time could mend fences, bond relationships and heal broken hearts. It was the great equalizer, the all-powerful cure, like Solomon, it was the wise negotiator. Now, it was her enemy.

If time was her enemy then clocks served as an ever-present reminder that the enemy was closing in. Every minute movement of the hands represented another second, another minute that was being stolen from her. She had become a miser, a Scrooge, counting every second of every day. The days shrunk into hours, the hours into minutes, the minutes into seconds. She couldn't slow it down, let alone bring it to a standstill. She jealously hoarded every moment with the boys and Katie had ceased to exist beyond that.

When the boys were at school she paced, frantic for them to return. If they were more than a few minutes past due she would work herself into a near frenzy. Their requests to go to a friend's house or invite someone over were always met with the same response, "Not today." She had even come to resent the time they spent outside, sledding, skating and building snowmen because it took them from her side. The housework had become an endless list of chores that robbed her of time with them.

Bedtime was the worst thief of all. Katie had always looked forward to the intimacy of bedtime as a special time, a time of shared stories and prayers. Now, she resented it. Bedtime had transformed itself into a cat burglar that crept in under the cover of darkness and stole precious hours from her.

But she had found a way to outsmart it. At all hours throughout the night, she would wander from bedroom to bedroom like a diligent sentinel, faithfully completing his watch. From the boys' bedsides she would hold vigil. Sometimes she would gently stroke a cheek, or touch a curl, or hold a hand, ever so softly, without disturbing them. But more often, she would be content to simply stare at them trying to memorize and absorb every feature, every freckle and characteristic. She wanted to burn their images into her mind.

Katie never rested or napped during the day and rarely slept at night. Sleep was a waste of time. Time that she didn't have. Lottie and Abraham saw the change in her, but were helpless to do anything about it. Friendly chats and get-togethers that had characterized their relationships in the past ceased to exist. She begged off card club with feeble excuses and refused repeated attempts by Matt to take her out to dinner or a movie, or even go for a walk, get her out of the house for a few hours. Creating a prison of their home, she closed the door on the outside. Maybe then, death wouldn't be able to find her.

☙ ❧

Dr. Hughes' nurse couldn't believe her eyes when she first saw Katie. What had Dr. Vertage done to her? It had only been a few weeks since he had seen her and in that short time she had become a zombie. Every ounce of color was drained from her lips and cheeks. She had dark circles around both eyes that had lost all luster and sparkle. Her gaunt frame resembled a skeleton. It appeared that it took every ounce of strength she had merely to walk from the waiting room. Bonnie thought that she would topple over at any second.

Katie's deterioration was proof of how tenuous life could be. Bonnie knew it could be stolen in an instant. Katie and she were nearly the same age, still young, and yet the disease had already stolen Katie's youth and vitality.

She escorted Katie into the consultation room.

"No need to undress," she instructed Katie. "Dr. Hughes won't be doing a full examination.

She took Katie's vital signs and weighed her.

"How have you been feeling?"

"Mostly, just tired. Otherwise, not too badly."

Bonnie thought to herself, *not too badly? She looks like death warmed over.*

"How about the bleeding, has it been very heavy?"

"Some days yes ... others no."

"Has the pain increased? Are you able to tolerate it?"

"It's not bad. Nothing I can't handle."

The nurse laid a gentle hand on her shoulder and said softly, "Dr. Hughes should be in a minute or two. If you need anything in the meantime I'll be out in the hall."

Before Dr. Hughes went in to see Katie, Bonnie took him aside.

"You'd better prepare yourself before you go in there. I don't know what that conceited, over-inflated, sorry-excuse-for-a-human-being-Dr. Vertage did to her, but I'll warn you that the person sitting on the other side of that door is not the Katie O'Neill we know."

There was no way he could ever have prepared himself. Bonnie's description had been completely accurate. As soon as he saw Katie, he knew that the cancer was spreading rapidly.

He quickly scanned the most recent entries in the chart, laid it on the counter and positioned himself on the rolling stool.

"How are you feeling?"

"Not too badly." Katie lied.

"Well, you look like crap."

"Chicago took a lot out of me. I haven't gotten my strength back yet."

"The chart says you told Bonnie that the pain and bleeding aren't significant. How are you sleeping?"

"I haven't had any trouble sleeping." Katie lied for the second time.

"How's your appetite? Are you eating?"

Katie lied for the third time. "Fine."

Dr. Hughes had about all he could take. "Listen to me, young lady. Be careful how much manure you spread. I didn't wear my hip waders, today. If you lie to me one more time I'm going to triple my fee. I charge significantly more for lies than I do for the truth. Are you familiar with calendars or didn't they have that novel idea in Boston? You should have been in here three weeks ago."

"What's the point?"

"The point is that you're my patient and I told you I wanted to see you once a week. That wasn't a request. It was an order. And if I'm going to continue to take money from you, as my patient, I expect you to obey my orders. Don't get into a battle of wills with me, because you'll lose. I didn't survive four years of college, five years of medical school, four kids of my own and thirty-six years of marriage being a pushover. Now, let's start over, shall we? How much are you sleeping? Are you resting during the day?"

"A few hours a night ... maybe. I can't nap during the day. There's a lot of housework to keep up with. There's laundry and cleaning, marketing and meals to prepare. The work doesn't stop just because I have cancer."

"You've lost another five pounds. Pounds you couldn't afford. Are you eating?"

"It's hard to eat when I don't have any appetite."

"And the bleeding. Is it light, moderate or severe?"

"Light. Sometimes moderate."

"And the pain?"

He gave Katie a warning look.

"The pain isn't anything I can't handle."

Dr. Hughes looked into Katie's eyes. "I won't tolerate any heroics or stoicism, Katie. As a doctor, I have a moral and ethical obligation. If you don't start taking care of yourself I'm going to have no other choice than to throw your scrawny behind into the hospital."

Katie's jaw clamped and her whole body stiffened. A look of panic spread across her face like a mask. "Not the hospital, Doctor. Don't put me in the hospital. You can't take me away from the boys. It'll kill me if you take that away from me." Her words were a mélange of supplication and desperation.

"If you continue on this same course, the cancer won't matter. You're killing yourself."

"I've got so little time left. I'll do anything you say. Just don't separate me from the boys," she begged.

Dr. Hughes zeroed in on the anxiety and panic in her voice. All the pieces of the puzzle finally fell into place.

"Katie, have you told the boys, yet?"

"Not yet. I keep waiting for the right time."

"You're smart enough to know that there never will be a right time. You have to make it happen. You're not doing them any favors by trying to protect them. Don't smother them, Katie. Don't stifle them. They need space and room to grow, to learn to live apart from you. Help them do that. Sooner or later, they're going to have to face it. Wouldn't you rather it was sooner, while you're still here, to help them through it. Show them how to be strong on their own. They've had a pretty good teacher, up to this point. I think they may surprise you.

"I won't kid you, Katie. This is going to get a whole lot rougher before it's over. You're going to need each other. You're going to need their understanding, their support and comfort. And they are going to need those things from you. What are they going to do when, suddenly, one morning they wake up and you're not there? You have to prepare them for when that day comes."

The words struck a note of familiarity to Katie. She recalled the words and a small smile of recognition teased at her mouth.

"Lottie told me almost the exact same thing."

"Then I'd say Lottie is one smart woman."

"That she is."

"These are my orders and you will follow them to the letter. Three meals a day. I don't care if you eat one bite or one hundred. At least sit down and make the effort. Drink the calories if you have to. When the boys sleep, you sleep. I'm writing a prescription for an iron supplement, pain medication and sleeping pills to help you get some rest at night."

Katie started to object but Dr. Hughes halted her with one raised palm. "They're there for you only if you need them. If you can fall asleep on your own, fine, otherwise I want you to use them, as well as the pain pills. That's what they're for. They can't do you any good sitting in the medicine cabinet. Rest during the day. Even if you don't sleep, at least put your feet up and relax for a few minutes. Most important of all ... make some time for yourself. And for Pete's sake, let the boys have some time for themselves."

"That's great advice if I were a lady of leisure. Tell me where I can buy some pixie dust or a magic wand that will make all the work vanish."

"I have the perfect solution. I know a lady. Does a lot of domestic work. Has some nursing skills, too, that will come in handy when you need them. And you are going to need them. She'll be perfect."

On the verge of tears, Katie asked, "And where am I going to get the money to pay her?"

Dr. Hughes thought a moment. "I'll talk to Matt Mulholland. He'll figure something out."

chapter thirty-six

Jadyne Potter was short, squat and almost as wide as she was tall. The best way to describe her was rotund. So rotund that it was hard to tell where one anatomical part ended and the next began. She had deep brown eyes, a broad nose, two rows of pearly white teeth, short salt-and-pepper, wiry hair, a bosom that a plane could land on and skin as dark as pitch.

She always wore white anklets, black brogues, cotton housedresses with a handkerchief in the pocket and three safety pins hooked to the bodice.

Widowed young, she had raised two children on her own and was no stranger to hard work. Her son, Clarence, had a wife and three daughters and was a Baptist minister in Detroit. Evangeline, her daughter, was a teacher who lived in Chicago with her husband and son. Jadyne had put both of them through college and was proud to say so. She was also God-fearing, hard working and couldn't tolerate anyone who wasn't. Jadyne knew the value of a nickel and only had two more mortgage payments to make on her house and she would own it free and clear. She didn't swear, drink liquor or smoke and considered the two worst sins to be vanity and idleness.

Jadyne moved at her own pace, slow and deliberate. Her walk was more of a waddle as the two halves of her generous bottom waggled up and down like two Virginia hams. But when she cleaned, she moved like a Texas Twister. She polished, swept, dusted, vacuumed and mopped until every surface was immaculate. From the time she arrived at seven o'clock in the morning, until she put on her hat and coat at seven o'clock in the evening, she attacked her chores like it was her mission in life to eradicate every dust bunny and wipe out every cobweb under the roof. With the exception of the lunch hour.

For exactly sixty minutes, not one minute more or one less, she put her feet up, crossed her ankles, ate her lunch (which existed of exactly the same thing everyday, a peanut butter and pickle sandwich, one hard boiled egg, four cucumber slices and one Macintosh apple) and worked on her crossword puzzles. Never the easy, medium or hard ones, unless they were expert or challenger, she wouldn't be caught wasting her time. And never, ever would she consider looking up the solution in the back. If she couldn't come up with the answers herself, then the puzzle went unfinished until she could.

Jadyne had many gifts and qualities but she shined the brightest in the kitchen. Katie was an excellent cook but even she had to admit that Jadyne was every bit as good. She may have had a different style and different recipes, but they were all delicious. Some were reflections of her heritage, sugar pies, grits and greens, chicken-fried steak, Virginia-baked ham. She could fry catfish that rivaled fresh lake perch for tastiness. The boys learned to eat sweet potato pie and fried green tomatoes.

Jadyne was no stranger to living on a budget and marketed with thrift and economy and could squeeze two dimes out of a nickel. Katie was always amazed that Jadyne could make more with less than any woman she had ever seen.

Katie fell in love with Jadyne almost immediately. Jadyne was good for her in many ways. She encouraged Katie to do as much for herself as was possible. She didn't coddle or pamper her. Except for naptime. Jadyne stood firm on that. Katie had to lie down for an hour in the morning and an hour in the afternoon. That was not up for debate and Katie knew better than to argue.

For Katie, there were good days and Jadyne called them her yellow days. The bad ones Jadyne called the blue days. The descriptions fit perfectly. On the yellow days it was hard to believe that the cancer even existed. Ever present was the pain, but in spite of it, on yellow days, Katie had energy and spunk. She was animated, invigorated and enthusiastic. Her appetite returned. Even the sparkle returned to her eyes. On the yellow days, she was almost radiant, again.

The blue days were becoming more frequent. The pain was too persistent, too intense to ignore. Every ounce of strength and endurance was sapped from her. Simple everyday activities were major undertakings. The flight of stairs seemed endless. Sleep eluded her and she would be forced to take the sleeping pills. The cursed pain pills left her groggy and were unsuccessful in completely dulling the pain. But the worst part of the blue days was that they served as a gnawing, cruel reminder of the hidden parasite that was slowly and steadily stealing her life.

Abraham and Jadyne took an immediate liking to one another. They shared a lot of the same views. There was an uncanny reciprocity between the two of them. As if they shared one mind, they mirrored each other's thoughts without the need for words. Maybe it was the commonality of their backgrounds that forged a bond between them. Both had known the pain and iniquity of prejudice. Both had known what it felt like to suffer persecutions for no reason other than what blood flowed through their veins.

The boys' reactions to Jadyne, or as they called her, Miss Jade, were interesting. They had never been exposed to many Negroes. Boston, like any big city, was segregated by ethnicity. A person could be born, marry, raise a family, grow old and die without ever leaving the neighborhood. Negroes and whites rarely had much to do with one another so the boys' experience with anyone outside of their own race was almost non-existent. Curious would best describe their first impressions. But, like all new experiences, after a while, the novelty wore off and Miss Jade simply became a comfortable, familiar part of the fabric of their lives.

Brendan was the only one of the boys who questioned Jadyne's presence in the home. At first, Katie panicked. She didn't know what to tell him without betraying the whole truth, so she settled for a half-truth. When Brendan asked her about Jadyne she replied, "Dr. Hughes thought it would be a good idea until I'm feeling better." It sounded lame, even to her, but it was the best she could come up with.

Jadyne even had an effect on Chance. For some reason, that was a complete mystery to Katie, Chance took an immediate liking to Jadyne. It couldn't have been because she showered him with attention or lavished him with affection. In fact, it was exactly the opposite. Most of the time she was either scolding him or chasing him out of the way with her broom. But, like a housefly, the more Jadyne shooed him away, the more he seemed attracted to her. Chance would follow her around in unrequited adoration.

Now Lottie and Jadyne. That was another story altogether. Katie thought the most accurate term and appropriate description was a *love - hate* relationship. Lottie loved to antagonize and Jadyne hated it. It was like trying to mix oil and water. No matter how much the mixture was agitated and shaken the oil always floated to the top and the water sank to the bottom. Lottie was the oil and Jadyne was the water. Jadyne the North Pole and Lottie the South Pole.

Jadyne had known nothing but hard work her whole life. She had scrimped and saved; earned everything she had and never received a handout in her life. She thought Lottie was shallow, lazy and indolent. A streetwalker dressed with more modesty than Lottie. Jadyne could have paid off the mortgage on her house years ago with what that woman spent on cosmetics and clothes. And four husbands. Well, that was practically obscene. Even a black widow spider doesn't kill off that many mates.

Of course to Lottie it was all a game. Jadyne was so serious, so determined and so earnest that Lottie just couldn't resist the temptation. Like a cat toying with a mouse before it closed in for the kill. When Jadyne said it was white, Lottie argued it was black. But, there was a side to both of them that was very much alike. Although they both would have swallowed poison before they would admit to it. They were both generous and wise beyond their years.

Katie wanted Jadyne to move in with them. There was certainly enough room. It seemed foolish for her to have to drive back and forth everyday. But Jadyne insisted on maintaining her independence, especially now, since her house was nearly paid for. Quiet evenings at home, listening to the Victrola or reading a good book were the only rewards that Jadyne afforded herself. But they were reward enough.

03 &O

It was late one afternoon and Jadyne was scrubbing the fixtures in the upstairs bathroom. Casey wandered in and sat on the edge of the bathtub, his feet dangled back and forth. With his head cocked, he studied Miss Jade for a while.

"Wanna hear a knock-knock joke?" He asked.

"I don't know why you're asking. You'll tell me, anyway," Jadyne asked.

"Knock, knock."

Jadyne, tired with routine, succumbed to being the straight man and responded, "Who's there?"

Casey answered, "Orange."

"Orange who?"

Casey repeated himself, "Knock, knock."

"Who's there?"

"Orange."

"Orange who?" Jadyne was growing impatient.

For a third time, Casey dangled the bait. "Knock, knock."

For the third and last time, Jadyne asked, "Who's there?"

"Orange."

"Orange who?"

He delivered the punch line laced with laughter. "Orange ya glad I didn't say knock-knock, again?"

Jadyne thought that was the worst one that Casey had come up with, yet. To defuse the possibility of any more to follow, she deviously suggested, "That was a great joke. Do you know what I think?"

Without waiting for an answer, she lured him, "I think it would be a grand idea if you went over to Miss Lottie's and surprised her with it."

"Can't."

"Why not?"

"'Cuz I already tried."

"And ..."

"And she sent me back home ta tell you."

Casey eyed Miss Jadyne suspiciously then asked, "You got somethin' wrong with you?"

Miss Jade turned and looked at him. "What do you mean?"

"I mean is somethin' wrong with you?"

"Nothing that I know of."

"Then how come you're black?"

"Because that's the way God made me. How come you're not black? Maybe there's something wrong with you?"

Casey looked at both of his hands, turned them over and looked at the other side.

"Nope. Nothin' wrong with me. Mus' be you."

"Well, there's nothing wrong with me, either."

"How come you got white teeth? You're black, so's how come you don't got black teeth?"

"Now what kind of a question is that? The color of your skin has nothing to do with the color of your teeth. Everyone has white teeth."

"How come you got such big busters?"

"Because I'm a woman. Women have larger breasts then men."

"My mommy's a woman and she don't got big busters. How come you do?"

"God made everyone a little bit different. It would be an awfully boring world if everyone looked exactly the same."

"Me an' Colin look the same."

"That's because you're twins. But even you two, you're not exactly the same. Each one of you is just a little bit different from the other. I can tell the difference."

"How?"

"The little things that are different about each of you, but I can tell."

"You got any kids?"

"Yes. I have two children."

"They black too?"

"Of course they are. They're black because black people have black babies, brown people have brown babies, yellow people have yellow babies and white people have white babies."

Casey thought for a minute. "What color is your Number One?"

That was it. Miss Jade was putting an end to that nonsense. "This guessing game is over. Run off, now. Scoot. I have a lot of chores I have to finish and I'm not getting them done with you bothering me."

Miss Jade watched him scamper off and shook her head.

"What color is my Number One? If that one doesn't test the patience of Job, no one does."

chapter thirty-seven

Lottie had been half right and half wrong. The time to tell the boys did drop into Katie's lap. Unfortunately for Katie, it was nowhere near the right time.

St. Patrick's Day had arrived. Katie was having a yellow day, or more accurately put, in keeping with the theme of the celebration, a green day.

It was Saturday, Jadyne had the week-ends off, and Lottie had been over for most of the day helping Katie to prepare the supper meal. Katie had made up her mind that since it was St. Patrick's Day supper was going to have a green theme. Outside, March seventeenth was anything but green but inside the O'Neill house everything was as green as the hills of *Kerry*. Lime gelatin with crushed pineapple, split pea soup with ham and pistachio pudding. Katie went wild and even kneaded a few drops of green food coloring into the bread dough. The result was going to be a very interesting and very Celtic version of soda bread. Lottie had teased her that if Charlie White could have coaxed it out of one his cows, they would be drinking green milk for supper.

The day, like many of the days had been since the arrival of March, was windy, damp, cold and gloomy. The heavy, low, steel gray skies hadn't seen the sun, in what Katie felt, was weeks. Large fissures of gray water had opened up on the lake and created countless mini-ponds that separated the islands of stubborn ice packs. Too dangerous for ice fishing, all of the fishing shanties had been hauled off the melting ice that had become too thin to support them.

The winter had seen record snow falls and the sleds and ice skates had been well used. Abraham had built dozens of bonfires to warm frozen hands and faces and gallons of hot cocoa were downed to warm their insides against the frigid temperatures. But now, the lake's thin ice coating was too precarious and unsafe for ice-skating, ice fishing or hockey. The snow had hardened and crystallized until its consistency was no longer conducive to making snowballs, snowmen or snow forts.

Steadily, but painfully slow, there were subtle changes that confirmed the earth was warming. Mounds of snow still covered the ground but they were shrinking and atolls of brown grass and mulched beds were starting to appear. The melting snow from the roof dripped down and formed long, spiky stalagmites of ice. Frosty the Snowman, who had already lost one arm, three lumps of coal, one from an eye and two from his mouth, had shrunk, was listing badly to one side and his carrot nose sorely needed a rhinoplasty. Dawn and dusk were becoming farther apart as the days lengthened and the nights shortened. And on the rare occasion when the sun did play peek-a-boo, it was climbing higher into the sky.

Katie hated to admit it, but she was tired of winter. With each passing day she was losing the race and time was running out. It was foolish of her to wish for the passing of time, time that she didn't have, but she couldn't help herself. The crisp, clean, pure white snows of winter had lost their charm. Like overnight guests that had abused the hospitality, they had over-stayed their welcome. She wanted spring. She missed the garden, turning the soil, sowing and planting and watching new life unfold. And though it would be her last spring, Katie longed for it.

Icy sleet, the wind blowing it in diagonal sheets, had pelted the windows, on and off all day. The weather was too miserable for outside activities and the boys were upstairs. By the racket overhead, Lottie assumed they must have been bouncing around on Pogo sticks.

Katie kneaded the bread dough while Lottie performed a task that even she couldn't mess up, washing the dirty dishes.

Lottie rinsed a pot and placed it in the rack to air dry. She studied her nails. "Ya know playin' dishwasher ta yawr Julia Child is ruinin' ma manicure."

"Tightening the laces on a pair of ice skates or unsticking a zipper would do more damage to your nails. And you wanted to raise the boys." Katie shook her head.

"I hate ta nag ya, Sug. But how long ya gonna go on without tellin' tha boys? Ya might be able ta fool tha little ones, but not Brendan. He's smarter'n that."

Katie scolded her, "Keep your voice down. I don't want them to overhear us."

Lottie laughed. "Overhear us! We could set off a bottle of TNT down here an' with tha ruckus their raisin', they wouldn't skip a beat. I'm surprised they haven't cracked tha plaster. Ya know, tha longer ya put it off, tha harder it's gonna get."

Katie paused for a minute and sat down.

"Oh, Lottie, I know you're right. Everybody's right. I know what I should do, but I just don't know how to do it. I haven't found the courage. How does one go about breaking their children's hearts?"

"Harder on them er harder on you, Sug?" Lottie asked.

Katie stared at nothing and answered, "It's the same thing, Lottie."

"Regardless, they still deserve ta hear tha truth."

"You're wrong, Lottie. Children don't want to hear the truth. They only want to be told what they want to hear. The truth hurts. Avoiding it doesn't. The future is going to be hard enough on them. I can't bring myself to destroy their present."

"Sure, it's gonna be hard. But, y'all got each other ta lean on. Y'all kin help each other through it. Jus' come right out an' say it. Tha pure truth's always worked fawr me."

"So, tonight, at the dinner table, I say, 'Boys, please pass the bread and by the way, you've lost your dad and now you're mother's dying, too. And, oh, I almost forgot one more thing, if everything works out, Abraham is adopting you.' Just like that. How does that sound? Does that truth work for you?" Katie's voice broke.

She hadn't meant it to come out so cruelly. Lottie wasn't to blame. She was only trying to help. She looked up at Lottie to apologize but Lottie was no longer paying her any attention. Her eyes were fixed, frozen as she stared across the room. As Katie turned around, she saw Brendan standing in the doorway with a look on his face that caused a huge fist to grip and twist her insides.

Katie quickly rose, crossed the room and reached out to him, "Bren ... there is so much I need to tell you ... so much you don't know."

Brendan pushed by her and tore out the back door. Katie tried to run after him.

"Bren ... I'm sorry! Please ..." But Lottie held her back.

Trying to break free of her hold, she pleaded, "Lottie, let me go! He needs me!"

But Lottie held firm. "Let him go, Sug. He doesn't need ya right now. He needs ta be alone. Sometimes ya gotta know when ta hold 'em an' when ta let 'em go. He'll come back when he's ready, when he decides he's ready."

Katie twisted again to shrug off her grip. "But he doesn't have a coat or a hat or gloves. It's sleeting ... freezing outside."

Lottie held her tighter. "I don't reckon he'll even notice."

Lottie was right. Brendan didn't notice. He was numb. But not from the cold. He was numb from hurt, from panic, from anger and fear. From betrayal and lies.

He ran as hard as he could, oblivious to the icy bullets that struck his face. They clung to his hair and matted it into frozen clumps; soaked his flannel shirt and dungarees. Drenched pant legs dripped sleet and slush in his shoes. He felt he was running in a dark, endless tunnel, the beginning swallowed up behind him and the end nowhere in sight.

Splashing, slipping, his feet pounded unsteadily through ice and slush. Several times his feet slid out from under him and he nearly stumbled to the ground. Wet limbs and branches slapped him, tore at his clothes. In spite of the frigid temperature, a cold sweat poured from his body and mingled with the sleet and plastered his clothes against his skin. Barely able to see through the tears and the sleet that were stinging his eyes, he didn't know where he was running to, or more importantly, what he was running from. He only knew he had to run.

He ran until his legs and lungs burned. He ran until his muscles turned to gelatin and wouldn't carry him one step farther, until he stumbled and crumpled into a heap in the middle of the icy meadow. In summer the meadow would be teeming with color and life. It would be alive with butterflies and bumblebees lazily flitting from flower to flower; long stems of grass and wildflowers, waving in the gentle breeze. But not that day. That day it was a cold and dead, leaden, stripped and barren; a lifeless, frozen wasteland of nothing, as still and silent as a mausoleum.

Brendan's exhaustion reduced him to a near-fugue state, a coma of physical existence only, his mind suspended in limbo. For a few frightening minutes, he didn't know who he was, where he was or why. Then, reality jolted him into the present. On his knees, he pounded and beat his fists on the ice-crusted ground until they were raw.

His mom had lied to him. Everyone had lied to him. Everything was one big fat lie. Grown ups never told the truth and they always ended up leaving you.

He needed it to be someone's fault. Then, suddenly he knew where to place the blame. As much as he willed the blame to fall on someone, he knew where it belonged. It was because of him. So many times when he was mad at her, he had wished she were dead. Wished she'd just go away. Wished he had his dad back. He hadn't really meant it, but he had thought it just the same. Miss Lottie was right. Be careful what you ask for, it just might come true. Now it was true and it was all his fault.

Maybe if he took it back, told God he never meant it. Said he was sorry and then maybe it wouldn't happen. But, deep inside, he knew that he couldn't take it back, now. It was too late. His mind was reeling as he questioned, *Why God? Why?*

None of it mattered, now. God didn't care. God took his dad and now he was taking his mom. They were gonna be dumped on Dr. Franke and everybody knew about it. Everybody except him. Nobody asked him. Nobody cared how he felt. Well, he'd show them all. He'd show them that he didn't need them. He didn't need anybody. A voice screamed in his head, "*You're all liars! I hate You, God. I hate her. I hate Dr. Franke. I hate my dad. I hate you ... I hate you ... I hate you all ...*"

Katie waited for an eternity. She waited through dinner. She waited after Lottie went home. She waited, paralyzed from worry, and watched the clock hands that seemed to have stopped. She waited until she was sure she would go insane. As the last gray shadows of the day darkened into night, Brendan did come home. Exhausted, drenched, frozen, disillusioned and defeated.

Katie didn't utter a word. Instead, she let him take the lead and give her a sign that he was ready to be consoled and comforted. Physically, they remained a room apart but held each other's eye gaze. Brendan searched her face for answers and Katie hoped to see forgiveness in his.

Eventually, he crossed the room and closed the gnawing distance between them. Katie reached out to him and he offered no resistance. She wrapped him in a warm quilt. She held him in her arms and neither one of them spoke. Katie let him draw warmth and strength from her. Her body soothed the shivering tremors that had gripped his body and his soul. Physically bound together, the two of them shut out the world. Nothing else existed. Nothing could threaten or hurt them. In that stilled moment in time, they were safe.

Later, the room lit only by the flickering flames of the fire, Katie and Brendan shared what was in their hearts.

Ψ ɓ

The following afternoon Katie told Tommy, Casey and Colin.

At first, the twins were confused and perplexed. It was as if their young minds couldn't deal with the concepts of loss and death. Those were intangibles, impalpable and unreal imagery that they couldn't quite grasp. Their conceptions were limited to what they could actually see, touch and hear. Their abbreviated memories could barely recall the loss of their dad. Only that he suddenly vanished from their lives. There were no memories of pain or perdition. Nothing else existed beyond the immediate realities of their world.

If Mommy was going away, who was going to read them bedtime stories? Or make them waffles for breakfast? Know that they needed a nightlight left on? Would Dr. Franke rub their backs when they were sick and throwing up? Couldn't they live with Miss Lottie? She was more fun and had a television set.

As long as their lives went on without disruption, the future would take care of itself.

Tommy understood with painful clarity. Yet, he was more concerned about his mom, than himself. How come Dr. Hughes couldn't make it better? If the sick was so bad, how come he couldn't see it? Did it hurt? Was she going to miss him? Was she going to see Daddy? Where was heaven? How come people had to die? Why can't I go with Mommy?

For Katie, those questions were a lot harder to answer. They dealt with questions of the heart.

"Are you scared to die, Mommy?" Tommy asked.

Katie smiled at his genuine concern. There was no carefully worded phrasing. No tactful subtlety, just straightforward honesty.

"I'm not scared to die. I know that heaven will be a beautiful place. I'll be happy to see Daddy, again. That's why heaven is so wonderful. From there, Daddy and I will be able to keep watch over you ... like a guardian angels. But, I am scared and sad to be leaving my boys. I will miss being with you, very much."

"But we won't be able to see you anymore," Tommy questioned through his tears.

Katie gathered the small ones as close to her as possible and tried to find the answer that their little minds could understand.

"No, you won't be able to see me, but you'll know I'm there just the same. It will be like a cloudy day, when we can't see the sun. We can't see it, but we know it's there, only hidden behind the clouds. Just because you won't see me, doesn't mean that I'm not there. I'll always be there, watching over you, day and night, in clouds or in sunshine.

"I love you all very much and I know how much you love me. Even though you can't see me, with that much love, I will never be gone from you. You will always feel me deep inside."

"But if I pray real hard, maybe you won't die. You always tell us that God listens to us when we pray. I'll pray to Him and then you can't die," Tommy insisted.

Katie struggled with the same enigma and had no explanation. She had always trusted prayer without question or condition, but now, that blind trust was being tested. Her faith was being split in two. Part of her wanted to believe and part of her wondered why.

"God always listens to our prayers, but we have to listen to His answers. He will answer us in His own time and in His own way. But, they may not always be the answers that we want.

"Sometimes, we don't know what is best for us. Like when you have to get shots from Miss Beckett. You don't want them because they hurt. But we make you get them because we know that the medicine is what's best for you, that it will keep you from getting sick. You trust Dr. Hughes and me to know what is best for you. We have to trust God that He knows what's best for us.

"So, God has answered my prayers and He has sent lots of people to help take care of you and keep you safe. Dr. Franke and Miss Jadyne and Miss Lottie and Mr. Mulholland. Most children only have a mommy and daddy. You are very lucky to have so many people to take care of you. And, let's not forget the most important of all, you boys will always have each other."

Katie did her best. In spite of her encouragement for them to talk to her whenever they were feeling scared or confused, sometimes the words came easily, other times they didn't. It was at those times that a gentle kiss, a caress or embrace were the only expressions that didn't fail her.

Her best efforts seemed to be wasted on Tommy and Brendan who were facing private battles of their own. Struggles that she wasn't able to help them through.

Tommy had started having nightmares. With ever increasing regularity, he would cry out in the middle of the night and when Katie tried to comfort him, he was unable to relate to her the unspeakable horrors that his frightened mind had conjured up. She couldn't make the nightmares disappear. She couldn't slay those monsters. All she could do was hold him, soothe him and try to ease his fear until the images faded.

It was impossible to read Brendan. At times he seemed unaffected, distant, reserved, almost indifferent. If his moods had been unpredictable before, now they were enigmatic. Desperately, she encouraged him to talk things out, share his thoughts, tried to divine what he was thinking and feeling. Her efforts were futile. His thoughts remained carefully guarded and he forbade anyone access. There was one outward sign that worried Katie. With the exception of baseball practice, he had been spending more and more time at home. As if he had made a declaration of disassociation, he was cutting himself apart from the rest of the world.

CB EO

Late one afternoon, while Brendan was scheduled to be at baseball practice, Katie received a disturbing telephone call from Brendan's coach, Mr. Ballor. Katie was shaken. Brendan must have had an accident. Why else would the coach be calling her?

"Has Brendan been hurt or injured?" Katie was almost afraid to ask.

"No, I don't think so. At least he wasn't the last time I saw him." Mr. Ballor replied.

Both Katie and Mr. Ballor were confused.

"What do you mean? Wasn't he at baseball practice?"

"No, he hasn't been to practice for two weeks. That's why I'm calling you."

Katie said nothing. None of it made any sense.

"Mrs. O'Neill … are you still there?"

"Yes, I'm still here. Forgive me, but this is all very confusing. That's not possible. There must be some mistake. He's been going to practice every day. Brendan loves baseball. Wild horses couldn't drag him off the field."

Katie wondered if he hadn't been at practice, then where had he been?

"He said you made him quit the team."

"Mr. Ballor. I don't have a clue what you're talking about?"

"Then you won't make him quit the team?"

"Of course, not. He eats, breathes and sleeps baseball."

"Then you'll change your mind? Let him play?"

"I never told him he *couldn't*," Katie insisted.

"Boy, that's a load off my mind. Losing him would be losing my star pitcher and the meat of my batting order. He's my clean-up hitter. Vinnie and Brendan have more talent in their pinkie fingers than most boys have in all ten. I think those two are headed for great high school careers."

"There has been a huge misunderstanding, Mr. Ballor. I'll straighten this all out with Brendan. I promise you, he *will* be at practice tomorrow."

"You've made me a happy man, Mrs. O'Neill. I've got my heart set on taking the league championship again this year. Back to back championships. That's every coach's dream. Got the space for the trophy saved on my shelf, ready and waiting for it right next to last year's."

They rang off and Katie slowly replaced the receiver. She had noticed that Brendan had been coming home from practice earlier than usual, but he had said that Coach had been cutting practices short.

Things were becoming clearer by the minute.

Brendan was lying on his bed, finishing his homework, when Katie entered his room and sat on the edge of the bed.

"I had an interesting telephone call from Mr. Ballor, today. He says that you quit the team. That you haven't been to practice in two weeks. Where have you been every afternoon?"

Brendan didn't look up. "Just hanging around."

"With who? Where?" Katie questioned.

"Nowhere special. In the park. At the marina."

"With whom?"

"Nobody. Just by myself."

"Why didn't you tell me?"

"I was gonna. Just didn't get around to it yet."

"Why did you tell the coach I made you quit? Why did you quit the team? You love baseball."

"No reason. Just felt like it, I guess."

Katie lifted his chin to face her. "Brendan, you can't quit baseball and you can't quit living."

He looked at his mom. "Why not? You have."

His perception hit her like a blast of arctic air. "And that was very wrong of me. Life isn't supposed to work that way. What I did wasn't doing anyone any good. And if you try, you'll find that you're not doing yourself or me any good either. You'll only succeed in making us both miserable."

"But baseball takes up a lotta time. Practices and games. I'd rather stay home. You might need me."

His motives were so pure and unselfish. Katie felt guilty for not recognizing the truth sooner. "When did you learn about grown-up love? When did you become so grown up? Suddenly, my little boy is mature beyond his years."

Katie sighed deeply then continued. "Oh, Bren, I appreciate what you're trying to do. When we love someone, deeply, truly, unselfishly, it's natural to want to be there for them, even at the expense of our own lives. If you were an adult, with adult responsibilities, adult commitments, it would be reasonable. But, not when you're young.

"In life, there is a time for everything. This is the time in your life when you shouldn't have to worry about anything beyond hitting the strike zone or what girl you like this week. These years will be gone soon enough. This isn't the time for you to sacrifice your youth. That's a sacrifice that I'm not willing to let you make. It's not normal … it's not healthy for you. I need you to play baseball. Be with your friends. You can't stop being a part of life because I'm sick. The world keeps right on going and you need to be a part of it.

"Do you remember how bad it was for us after Daddy died? How we thought our whole world had ended? That we had no idea how we were going to live through it? But, we did. We made it. We depended on each other and somehow we worked through it. Everything worked out. It's what Daddy would have wanted for us. And now it's what I want for you. Your future lies in your becoming all that you can be not only what you are."

"But what about you?"

"If you want to see me happy, for now, you need to be a normal teen-ager. The best thing for me is seeing you happy, involved in the things you love to do. Don't worry about me. That's my job."

She teased him, "As much as I enjoy having you moping around here I'd rather see you out on the pitcher's mound, or stealing second base or laughing with your friends. Besides, I kind of miss having the Musketeers around. The cookies in my cookie jar are starting to go stale.

"Now, do we have an understanding? No more of that foolishness for me or for you. I promised Mr. Ballor that you'd be at practice tomorrow. You wouldn't want me to break my promise. Finish your homework and lights out by nine."

She planted a kiss on his cheek and ruffled his black curls. "And don't forget to say your prayers."

chapter thirty-eight

Since Jadyne had weekends off, Lottie and Abraham would fill in and help out with the boys. It was a typical Saturday morning. Katie was resting, Brendan was at baseball practice and Tommy was where he could usually be found, with Abraham. For a special treat, Abraham had taken Tommy to help him out in the arboretum at the college. Tommy loved it there. It had a large freshwater pond and among the rocks and plants was a family of box turtles who had made it their home. Tommy had become very attached to them and Abraham let him feed them, and if he was very careful, he could take turns holding them.

Lottie was on duty that Saturday morning, reading the latest edition of *Photoplay* magazine and polishing her fingernails. When the twins and C.J. Coughlin bounded in the back door like three baby elephants, they scared her half to death, and she jumped so high, she knocked over the bottle of crimson nail polish. They were covered top to tennis shoes in mud. Even their mothers wouldn't have recognized them.

Lottie stopped. "Hold on you, three. Don't be draggin' that mud all through tha house. Jadyne'll have ma hide. Where've you three been? Y'all got more muck on ya then a trio a mud-puppies."

Casey chirped, "Been huntin' frogs in tha ditch."

Lottie jumped back. "Y'all didn't bring any in here, did ya? Or any a their legless kin?"

"Naw. We threw 'em back in the ditch," Colin answered.

"I thought I heard yawr momma say she didn't want y'all playin' up by tha road."

"We wasn't playing in the road, we was playing in the ditch," Casey argued.

"Unless tha County moved it, tha last time I looked, tha ditch was up by tha road. Tha ditch, tha road, it's all tha same ta me. I don't wanna catch y'all playin' by either one of 'em. I oughtta take y'all out an' spray ya down with tha garden hose. It's gonna take me all day ta clean up this mess y'all are makin'."

As if she were unwrapping packages of raw sewage, Lottie stripped them down to their T-shirts and underpants. C.J.'s face reddened with embarrassment.

"Don't be shy on ma account, C.J. I seen plenty a men in their Fruit of tha Looms before."

While they washed the dirt and mud off their hands and faces, Lottie picked up their clothes with a broom handle and tossed them into heap next to the washing machine. She wasn't that trusting. There could be one or two frogs, or worse, hidden away in the pockets.

"Knock, knock?" Colin asked her.

Lottie played along. "Who's there?"

"Somethin,'" Colin replied.

"Somethin' who?"

"Somethin' creepy's crawlin' up your leg," he teased.

All three of the boys bent over in laughter.

Lottie turned the tables on them. "Knock, knock?"

In unison, they said, "Who's there?"

"Justin."

"Justin who?"

"Justin time fawr a snack. When yawr done cleanin' up, how 'bout some cookies an' a glass a milk?"

"C.J. can't have no milk. He's energic to it," Casey informed Miss Lottie.

C.J. corrected him, "I'm *allergic* to milk. Can't have it or I get a stomach ache."

"How 'bout orange juice? Ya allergic ta that?" Lottie asked dubiously.

"Nope. I kin drink orange juice," C.J. answered.

Lottie removed the quart milk bottle and pitcher of orange juice from the refrigerator and poured them each a tall glass.

Casey asked, "You bake the cookies?"

"No, I didn't. Miss Jade baked 'em."

"Okay, then we'll eat 'em," Casey and Colin answered, almost simultaneously.

C.J. asked, "Do they got nuts in 'em?"

"Don't know," Miss Lottie answered. "Why?"

"'Cuz I'm allergic to peanuts. I'll get real sick an' die if I eat 'em."

"Y'all sure ain't allergic ta mud." Lottie put her hands on her hips. "Well, C.J. what else are you allergic to?"

"Nuts, eggs, coconut, peanut butter, ice cream, cheese ..."

Lottie interrupted him, "I get tha drift. Maybe I better ask ya what ya kin have? How 'bout a banana? Kin ya have a banana?"

"Yeah. I don't die from bananas."

After they had transferred enough of the mud and dirt from themselves to the sink and bathroom floor, the boys' faces and hands were reasonably clean.

They showed their faces to Miss Lottie and turned their hands over for her final inspection. She gave them a wink and swatted them on their behinds.

"I reckon y'all done a good 'nough job fawr government work."

In their underwear, they settled in the chairs and dove into the plate of goodies and C.J. peeled his banana.

Through a mouthful of chocolate chip cookie, Casey asked, "Do you got a magnifyin' glass, Miss Lottie?"

"I don't know … I guess I might. Why? What do y'all need a magnifyin' glass fawr? Somethin' wrong with yawr eyes?"

Casey responded, "No. We need it to fry ants."

"What do ya mean, fry ants? That some kinda game?"

Casey, Colin and C.J. laughed.

"It ain't a game. What kind of game could you play frying ants?" Colin questioned. It was the dumbest idea he had ever heard.

"Huey Meyer, he's one of our buddies at school. His real name is Holland, but we jus' call him Huey. He's 'posed to be in the third grade, but he got flunked. Well, he showed us how ta fry ants with a magnifyin' glass. It don't work on cloudy days, 'cuz you need the sun. And if you hold tha magnifyin' glass jus' right, it gets real hot an' fries the ants. You kin start fires with it, too. If it's a real hot day, you take the magnifyin' glass, an' if ya hold it jus' right, ya kin start a piece a paper on fire, a leaf, even a stick. I guess ya kin fry jus' about anything with it. But ya gotta hold it jus' right. It works real swell. Kin I have another cookie?" Casey delivered the narration without drawing breath.

"Yawr mouth goes like a whip-or-will's butt. Y'all know, that don't ya? No, ya can't use no magnifyin' glass ta fry ants. It'd be like givin' gin ta a rummy. An' y'all sure as heck ain't gonna use one ta start a fire. I'd be lucky if y'all didn't burn down tha whole darn house."

"Kin we go back out an' squash some bugs? We don't need a magnifying glass to squash bugs?" Colin asked.

"No, ya can't go out an' squash bugs, either. Can't y'all think a playin' a game that doesn't involve killin' somethin'? Somethin' normal kids play. How 'bout tag er kick tha can?"

"Those'r boring. How 'bout a knock-knock joke?" Casey switched from a whine to eager enthusiasm in a New York instant.

"How 'bout *not*," she clipped back.

An idea lit up Lottie's face like a light bulb. Necessity wasn't the mother of invention, diversion was. "I tell ya what. If'n ya don't tell me no more jokes, I gotta surprise fawr ya. Deal?"

The twins and C.J. excitedly agreed, "Deal!"

"Y'all go on upstairs an' put on some clean clothes. C.J., y'all kin wiggle yawr heinie inta a pair a Tommy's dungarees an' put on one a his shirts. But ya boys do it real quiet like, so's ya don't disturb yawr momma. Then tha four of us are gonna sneak on over ta ma house an' watch some televishun. We'll even be really naughty an' have ourselves chocolate ice cream sundaes, nuts an' all."

"Can't have no nuts or ice cream," C.J. reminded her.

"Then we'll skip tha ice cream fawr y'all. How 'bout a Hostess cupcake?" Lottie was getting fed up with this pantywaist. He sure didn't look as delicate as he sounded.

"Don't know for sure. I guess maybe I am."

"Did ya ever have one?"

"Nope."

"Then how d'ya know yawr allergic to it? Yawr momma ain't here, so I say we take tha chance an' find out! An' Miss Jade's not 'round, either ta kick up a fuss. An' what Miss Jade and C.J.'s momma don't know won't hurt 'em. If y'all kin keep a secret, then so kin I."

chapter thirty-nine

To the rest of the world B.C. and A.D. stood for the recognized measurement of time before and after the birth of Christ. To Katie they meant something entirely different. She had developed the concept that her life had existed in two worlds, B.C., before the cancer, and A.D., after the diagnosis.

In the past she had never minded rainy, cloudy days. Her gardens needed the rain's refreshment and nourishment and the cloudy days made her appreciate the sunny days more. But, as the days of the calendar rapidly began to disappear, her resentment of the cancer and the inclement weather grew proportionately. They represented lost days that she would miss being outside. Days that would rob her of feeling that she was still a vital part of life and all living things. It was an absurd contradiction. Part of her wanted to stop the passage of time and the irrevocable conclusion it would bring, yet, knowing it would be her last, she craved the arrival of summer.

Subject to the weather's cooperation and Katie's stamina, it had become a daily ritual for Jadyne to get Katie settled in the gazebo to spend the greater part of the day out of doors. She would pass the time reading or resting, and when the pain lessened enough, she would succumb to short catnaps.

Katie so loved it there that Jadyne would deliver her meals, however meager. Often, Jadyne would take the time out of busy routine to sit with Katie while she ate and the two would chitchat. Jadyne teased Katie that the two of them could combine their efforts and solve all the world's problems right there in the gazebo.

In other ways, the gazebo had become an extension of the house, a kind of out-of-doors family room where the boys would spend hours sitting and talking with their mom about all the day's events. Tommy and the twins would carry their favorite books to Katie and she would read to them while they nestled next to her on the settee.

Since Katie was no longer physically able to attend Brendan's baseball games, she had to settle for being an absentee spectator and viewed the games through his vivid, animated narratives. She looked forward to his eagerness to share stories about all the shenanigans and antics of the Musketeers.

With the progression of the cancer, as the symptoms increased, Katie was forced into the ambiguous role of bystander. Her body refused to allow her to participate and she had to settle for being an onlooker, an observer. And she hated it. It wasn't nearly enough. She wanted more. She wanted it all.

In spite of her illness, though the frequency of her blue days began to crush the hopes of yellower days, every ounce of energy and will was directed at maintaining as normal a lifestyle for the boys as possible. In that, God was merciful and for Brendan, Tommy and the twins, life continued to go on as usual. Countless disagreements and sibling spats still occurred with regular frequency. Meal times were maintained, homework assignments addressed each evening and the boys had their chores to complete. The humdrum routine and daily challenges, their significance diluted and absorbed by the millions of minute incidentals that constitute the substance of life, were all taken in stride. Katie took comfort that, in that area, God had answered her prayers.

ᘓ ᘔ

Katie became quite the accomplished spectator. As long as she was forced into that role, she figured she might as well make the best of it. As if perched on the highest branches of a tree, it was as if she could gaze down, unnoticed and unobserved, and absorb all the activity without directly influencing or affecting it. When not physically engaged in the happenings of life, she realized one could develop quite astute perceptive talents unfettered by personal expectations. Unencumbered by her own need for integration, she developed keen understanding and insight. Sights and sounds became more vivid as the world around her played out like a magnificent stage production. She studied each nuance of the drama as if viewing it for the first time.

As much as Katie enjoyed the time she spent with the boys, she was equally entertained by the adversarial exchange that would erupt between Jadyne and Lottie. Whenever the two shared the same physical space it was the Civil War all over, again. Outwardly, they maintained a strong aversion to one another, but Katie sensed that through all the head butting and confrontations, they harbored a mutual, unavoidable attraction. Each possessed a sharp mind, was opinionated, headstrong and wise in her way. Katie firmly believed that it was no accident that they would frequently find themselves in each other's company. Instead of simply allowing themselves to be carried downstream by the natural flow of the current, like salmon, they seemed to be driven by an instinctive need to swim upstream, fighting the current and each other, every step of the way.

ᘓ ᘔ

May had overtaken April and Tuesday was incredible. It was warm in the sun and cool in the shade as a robust wind blew off the lake and carried with it cooler air. For Katie, the balmy warmth of the day unknotted some of her pain.

The deciduous trees had leafed out completely with their latest crop of new leaves. By mid-morning, the industrious Jadyne had four loads of laundry drying on the clotheslines. The sky was an uninterrupted sea of deep, cerulean blue and the sun so warm and intense that the sheets, whipped by the breeze, were a blinding white like the billowed sails of a schooner.

Only the sounds of nature could be heard that morning. As winds danced across the waves and fluttered the leaves, they carried a shared a dialogue between the trees and the lake. Robins, orioles, wrens, bluebirds and cardinals sung their songs as they busily prepared their nests like anxious, expectant parents-to-be and readied their nurseries. Squirrels in a frantic ritual of courtship, quarreled and chattered, vying for the privilege to woo and breed.

Brendan had hung the birdhouse that he had made for his mom on the low branch of the sycamore tree that shaded the gazebo. Katie had finished reading letters from Dee and Moira and was enjoying a pair of wrens concentrated on the task of homemaking.

She noted that the wren certainly wasn't the most beautiful of God's avian creations. Unlike the vibrant red of the cardinal, or striking contrast of the black and orange oriole, or the vivid markings of the blue jay, the plain, simple, tiny house wren was a boring, unalluring, dirty brown. There were no distinctive characteristics, no proud crown or plumage; they weren't impressive in size or coloring. But, Katie loved their musical serenade. Where the Lord may have shorted them in physical beauty, He more than made up for with His gift of song. She was amazed that so tiny a creature could produce such a sweet, lovely, clear melody.

They were quite the animated little showmen. Katie studied them as they carried stick after stick, trying to thread them through the birdhouse's tiny hole. They couldn't be bothered with wasting their efforts on anything as puny as twigs. Not those two industrious builders. They struggled with sticks that were three times as long as they were and weighed almost as much. They were obviously more interested in size than function.

Katie couldn't imagine how they would ever need a nest of such enormous proportions in comparison to their Lilliputian size. Back and forth, in and out, they tirelessly kept up the pace. Several times she caught herself smiling, even giggling at their interaction, their judicious labor and teamwork, their humorous, meticulous fussing and fidgeting. For nearly two hours, Katie had shared an intimacy with them. They, the skilled, accomplished performers, and she the absorbed, beguiled, admiring audience.

Jadyne interrupted Katie's retrospective with a pot of steaming, hot tea and an afghan.

"I didn't know if you would be warm enough. With this wind kicking up like it is, I thought you might be cold. So, I brought an extra afghan and a nice, hot pot of tea. "It's your favorite," she tempted, "Earl Grey."

"Thank you, Jadyne. Actually, both are welcomed. Now that you mention it, it is getting a bit cool here in the shade. I was so intrigued by the performance of the wrens that I didn't notice, until now. A cup of tea sounds wonderful. Why don't you have a seat and join me? It's a gorgeous day. We should enjoy some of the peace and quiet."

"Don't mind if I do. I'm way ahead of schedule with my chores. I'll just be a minute while I run inside and get an extra cup."

"Would you mind grabbing my hairbrush and a rubber band? My hair needs a good brush through and a tight braid. It's a snarled mess from this wind."

Jadyne returned a few minutes later and poured them both a cup of tea. Katie tried to extend her arms high enough to brush through her tangled hair but her effort was met with a deep, stabbing pain under her right arm. She winced and Jadyne noted the reflection of pain that registered on Katie's face.

"Miss Katie? You all right?"

"Yes, I'm fine. It's nothing to get upset about. I hadn't felt that particular pain before. That's a new one, Jadyne."

"You want me to get some of your pain medicine?"

Katie shook her head. "Heaven's sake, no. I hate the way it makes me feel, drowsy and foggy until I can't even think straight. And I really don't want to tempt fate by starting another episode of offerings to the porcelain god. I'd rather put up with the pain."

Jadyne stood and took the hairbrush from Katie. "Here, give me that brush. After fifty-eight years of prying a comb through my thatch of wool, yours will be no trouble at all. And I guess I've woven at least a thousand braids for my Evangeline when she was a little one."

Jadyne smiled widely with two rows of perfect teeth shining and her deep brown eyes danced with mischief. "I just got an idea. Let's you and me have ourselves a little fun."

An hour later, Lottie pranced across the lawn as her spiked shoes slapped against her heels. She wore a haltered-top, red and white polka dot dress, with a full skirt and a red chiffon scarf cinched tightly at her waist. Red, plastic earrings shaped like half-sized hibiscus with white rhinestone centers were clipped to her earlobes. Her outfit alone would have set off a fire alarm, but it was her hair that Katie and Jadyne spotted first. It was bleached as white as the kitchen curtains and combed back in a mass of soft, shoulder-length curls.

Jadyne clucked her tongue in disapproval.

Lottie stared at Katie for a full minute. What she saw rendered her speechless.

Katie couldn't stand the suspense any longer and asked, "Well, what are you staring at? Have I suddenly grown two heads?"

"No ... tha one y'all do have is plenty. If y'all ain't a sight, Sug!" Lottie almost toppled over from laughter. "If y'all ain't a regular little pickaninny! I ain't never seen a Negro child with so many cornrows, I tell ya what."

Jadyne had braided Katie's chestnut tresses into row after row of tight braids from scalp to nape and had secured them with little rubber bands. Katie ran her fingers over her new hairstyle.

"Can we assume from your critical remarks that you don't think it's flattering? I'm hurt, Lottie."

"Flatterin' ain't exactly tha word that springs ta mind. An' if yawr feelins' are hurt, well I jus' can't help maself. I think that cancer's cut off tha circulashun ta yawr brain. Don't that hurt?"

"Not at all. And nothing could be any more painful than you subjecting yourself to second degree burns from frying your hair with bleach and peroxide. Lottie Devereaux isn't the only one who knows about style. Sorry you don't like it because this is how I'm going to wear it from now on. It will be easy to take care of, no fuss, no muss. I should have done this a long time ago."

"I hope yawr not serious, Sug ..."

Jadyne cut her off. "I'd say it looks a whole lot better than that wad of cotton batten you've got stuck to your head. It's a pure waste of good money and nothing but foolish vanity. What color is your real hair, anyway? It has to be better than that."

"This here is tha latest rage outta Hollywood. I think I look jus' like a movie star."

Jadyne scolded her. "Hollywood! Well that explains it. That den of iniquity hasn't produced nothing but sin and nobody but sinners. Sodom and Gomorra that's what it is. And we all know what happened to them. And while we're on the subject of Hollywood, I don't like those boys coming over to your place to watch that television set of yours. It's not good for them. Trash is all it is."

"Why Jadyne. I do believe y'all have gotten yawrself worked up in ta a lather over this. Yawr wound up like a preacher on tha Sabbath."

"You're darn right I am. You mark my words. This television craze that's sweeping over this country is going to bring us nothing but trouble. It will eat away at the moral fiber of our children filling their minds with nothing but nonsense. This here is the real world. We ought to be investing their time and ours into teaching them how to get along in it. Miss Katie, I can't believe that you let those boys waste their time and minds on that drivel every chance they get."

"I hardly think that watching an occasional television program could be described as 'every chance they get.' Besides, it's only a craze, something new and exciting. It won't be long and they'll soon tire of it. Like any new fad, the novelty will wear off and it will fall by the wayside. I'll bet within a couple of years few people will remember or care that television ever existed."

"I'll take that bet, Sug. I predict that televishun is gonna be bigger 'n better than radio ever thought a bein.' Ma stockbroker's even got some a ma money sunk inta it. He says that I'll triple ma money in no time. Solid as tha Rock a Gibraltar, I tell ya what."

Jadyne wasn't budging. "If I had my say, you would lose every dollar of that investment. You should be ashamed of yourself making a profit from the contamination of our children's minds. Every parent should put their foot down and stop this before it goes any further. Children can't watch television if their parents don't buy one."

"Then I strongly suspect that I won't be havin' y'all come droppin' in on me ta watch Uncle Miltie on Tuesday nights?"

"Uncle Miltie, my eye! I have no intention of wasting what time I have left on this earth watching that garbage."

"I'm afraid I don't see what all the fuss is about, Jadyne? It's no more than a little harmless entertainment," Katie interjected.

"Harmless, my hemorrhoids! The best entertainment for folks is to engage in some interesting conversation, listen to some good music and read a good book."

"Who'd a thought that somethin' that come outta a bottle at tha beauty parlor woulda touched off such stimulatin' conversashun? If I'd a had a notion it was gonna ruffle yawr feathers this much, Jadyne, I woulda done it a whole lot sooner," Lottie quipped as she patted her new curls and got up to leave.

She waved over her shoulder as she sashayed her hips with extra emphasis. "Ta-ta y'all. I'm off like a bride's dress on her weddin' night."

Jadyne sputtered, "How you two get along like you do is a mystery to me. There goes a woman with more nerve than a bad tooth."

"There goes a woman who would give you the shirt off her back," Katie mused.

"The shirt off her back? Haven't you noticed that most of her shirts don't even have a back?"

"You realize she only carries on that way because she knows how much it annoys you. The more riled up you get, the more fun she has. It's called psychology."

"You've got the psycho part right … but I think the correct term is psycho-*path*."

chapter forty

While Katie struggled with the progression of the cancer and the steady erosion of her world, Matt wrestled with demons of his own. As if losing Katie wasn't enough of a taste of hell, now he had this new incubus snapping at his heels.

He phoned Katie. "We may have a slight problem. If you feel well enough, I'll meet you at Abraham's. It will insure us more privacy. I don't want the boys overhearing any of our conversation and getting upset over it. Give me an hour and I'll meet you over there."

With that, Matt thoughtfully replaced the telephone hand piece to its cradle. He turned his desk chair and stared out the window of his office. Scattering's mast could be seen high above the other boats in the marina. It had been nearly a month since he had taken her out. But, that day his thoughts weren't about sailing.

Matt had been plagued with concern and worry for the past week but had said nothing to Katie in the hopes that, like bad weather, it would suddenly clear; that it would only be a passing storm. But, this particular squall was refusing to go away. A squall in the form of a Miss Edith Corley.

He and Katie had existed in a strange state of limbo since that devastating February morning when his whole world had been ripped from its moorings. Initially, there was the anger and frustration that the invisible monster was steadily and inevitably tearing Katie away from him. In desperation, he had tried to plead, to beg … to bargain with God. He had even made an unholy pact with the devil. He would offer his soul in exchange for her life. Now, his prayers were last ditch efforts that asked nothing more than to let her have a swift and merciful death.

Once he was actually able to admit it to himself, to say the word, then the real panic had gripped him. He didn't think he had the fortitude, the guts to watch her die. Matt despised his every shortcoming and hated that he was an emotional coward, an empathetic cripple. He didn't know how to continue in a doomed relationship. He loved Katie with his whole being, yet someday, horribly soon she was simply going to be gone and that place inside him that she filled, would be cold and empty. Without Katie he was incomplete.

Under the circumstances, the whole idea of a relationship with Katie was a sham. It was almost impossible for him to go on pretending that everything was normal. Other than a few stolen moments of ecstasy, they had virtually no past, no memories to console them. They had no future to anticipate. They only had the fleeting, fading, painful moments of the present. He was completely at a loss as to how to confront that reality. He didn't know how to love someone who was dying. Matt felt dysfunctional and inutile; he could neither influence nor affect the course of his life. Like a puppet, he felt as if an invisible puppeteer controlled his every movement. He was in control of nothing, manipulated by and at the mercy of some unseen, vindictive malefactor.

Up until then, his whole life had been lived in a counterfeit state of certainty in which he had complete control over his destiny and happiness. Now, all of the things that he had hoped and dreamed for had evaporated like a mist. And the worst betrayal of all was not being able to do a damned thing about it. All his money, all his family's influence, all his legal expertise didn't matter jack shit. He couldn't buy reparation; he couldn't connive a solution. He couldn't charm his way out of this.

And then, Katie had thrown him a lifeline. That had been his reprieve from the governor. This had been the one area where he felt purposeful and confident, the protagonist, instead of standing idly by like a stupefied moron. This had been the only thing she had asked of him, the only thing that mattered to her. Now, even this scared him to death. This too, he was letting slip away.

With this latest development, how many more disappointments, how much more heartache was she expected to endure? Everyone had physical and emotional limits. Surely, Katie had given enough. But, it didn't matter. The world kept inventing new hardships to tax her heart, soul, and body. If only he could have spared her this latest worry.

He envied Abraham and Lottie their innate ability to know exactly what needed to be said and done and then, undaunted, went about it skillfully. A thousand times Matt vowed to rise above his inadequacies and a thousand times he reneged on his promise. Every time he looked at Katie he wanted to crumble into a shriveled heap. It was a shock every time he saw her. Only three days had separated his last two visits and in only seventy-two hours he saw signs of deterioration. She looked so wounded, frail and fragile, as if she would snap in two with the slightest touch. Her skin was pallid and translucent, like rice paper. It nearly killed him to watch her fade away, layer-by-layer.

If seeing her was becoming harder and harder, conversation was nearly impossible. He never knew if there would be a next one; didn't know if each word they spoke would be their last. What day would be their last? When would they run out of tomorrows? She didn't need the added burden of his suffering, dealing with his inadequacies, his doubts, his pain as well as her own. That was the last thing she needed. But, he didn't have the slightest idea how to tell her how he felt. He despised himself for being the weak link in the chain.

Yet, through all the heartache and pain, to Matt, she was still Katie. The sun still highlighted her chestnut hair with flecks of gold. The Irish in her voice accentuated every time she became excited. When not clouded by drugs or pain, her emerald eyes still sparkled with mirth. Her dimples still deepened with every smile. She could still laugh. Her mood remained buoyant and her spirit uplifting. The cancer hadn't been able to extinguish that.

Ϗ ʅ

Matt clasped his hand, inhaled deeply and steeled himself to begin.

"All the motions and petitions had been filed with Judge Wilson Aldridge. I had every reason to be confident that things would progress without a hitch. This latest problem really erupted out of nowhere and completely blindsided me.

"I expected a thorough investigation by the County Child Welfare Agency, that's protocol. Standard operating procedure. I wasn't worried and never gave it a second thought. Abraham's background is impeccable. There was no reason to think that it wouldn't stand up to the toughest scrutiny. And experts in this area of the law reassured me that the wishes of the parent carry an enormous amount of weight with the judge."

"As well it should," Katie interjected. "Abraham loves the boys. He knows them so well. In many respects, he knows them as well as I do. Surely, those factors are the most important."

"Katie. It's not a question of who loves whom. It's a question of selecting the person that they feel is ideal. They base their assessment on a lot of factors. One's background and past are high up on that shopping list."

Matt hesitated a moment and that gave Abraham the opportunity to ask the obvious question.

"You are afraid that there is some questionable incident in my past that this Welfare Agency discovered that would interfere with the adoption? I can assure you, Matthew, there is none."

"Not exactly an incident," Matt tried to explain. He was unsure how to address the delicate matter.

Sensing his trepidation, Katie urged him to go on. "Don't make us play twenty questions, Matt. Beating around the bush isn't going to make this any less of a problem. Just let us know what it is so we can deal with it."

Matt looked first at Katie, then at Abraham. "They ... rather this Edith Corley, is raising some objections because of your background, Abraham. Namely, the fact that you are Jewish."

Katie exhaled. "Oh, is that all. That's hardly a problem at all. I'll speak to her, tell her that it doesn't raise an issue with me. Abraham knows that I want them to continue to be raised in the Catholic faith. We're in total agreement on that. It was never a question."

Abraham dropped his head. He didn't know how to explain prejudice to Katie. She didn't have the strength to take on that malignancy as well.

"They know that, Katie. It's all laid out in the terms of the adoption," Matt told her.

"Then, I guess I don't understand, Matt. If I don't see a problem, why would they? Abraham already takes them to church. Maybe they should talk with Father Davey. He could vouch for Abraham. Attest to the fact that, in every respect, their welfare and best interest are Abraham's immediate priority."

"It's not the Welfare Agency, per se, that's throwing up the roadblocks. It's the investigator, Edith Corley. She's the one raising all the questions."

"So, I'll talk to her. Make her understand."

Katie had no idea why Matt and Abraham were looking at each other with a shared expression. She felt like she was being excluded from some encrypted, secret dialogue.

"I wish one of you would tell me what's going on. I'm not a mind reader and clearly you two know something I don't."

It was Abraham who finally answered. "Katie, it is not that you are Catholic and I am Jewish. It is solely the fact that I am Jewish. This Edith Corley is anti-Semitic. She dislikes Jews."

Katie immediate felt an icy hand grip the nape of her neck. Her thoughts quickly recalled the story Abraham had told her about his past. This couldn't be happening. That kind of evil couldn't exist in the world of Eden Croft. Life's circumstances had brought her there and she had come to love everything about it, including the people. She couldn't believe that kind of ugliness had invaded this idyllic place. The thought that Abraham was being hurt by all this felt like an ice pick had been driven into her heart.

Matt continued, "I'm afraid that she is on some kind of personal mission to obstruct the adoption. I'm convinced that she has some deep-seeded animosity toward Jews in general and that she's allowing her personal prejudices to influence her recommendations. She's using them to twist the facts. This is an unusual situation, all the way around, and I'm finding it impossible to cite any legal precedents that would give us grounds to usurp her."

"Abraham, I'm so sorry. I had no idea. If I had known … I never would have placed you in this position," Katie tried to console Abraham. "But, surely the judge, the Welfare Agency are wise enough to see the bigotry, the fanaticism of a spiteful, vengeful woman. If it was so evident to you, they should be able to

see through it? How could they accept her recommendation when her prejudice is so obvious?"

"She is also raising a strong argument that is based on the circumstances of
Abraham being a single man. The domestic situation would lack the presence
of a woman. It is looked upon with far more favor to have a male and female
figure in the home.

"Traditionally, Katie, the opinion of the investigator carries a great deal of
weight. Perhaps more than yours. It isn't often that the courts overturn their
recommendations. The judge will rely very heavily on what she has to say. She
has the responsibility to ensure the future welfare of the minors involved. She
must be satisfied that the environment is the best one possible."

Katie argued, "But you just said that that is going to be impossible. That
she has developed a prejudicial dislike for Abraham. So, this evil woman is
judge, jury and executioner? It's not fair. Beyond that, it just isn't right." Katie
was nearly hysterical.

"Unfortunately, more often than not, the law is less concerned with what is
either fair or right as it is with what is legal. I am afraid that one doesn't necessarily have anything to do with the other," Matt explained.

Abraham thought for a moment before he spoke. "Matthew, now that you
have discovered who and what our antagonists are, we need your expertise and
counsel as how to best approach the situation."

"I refuse to put Abraham through some sort of witch hunt or sadistic scrutiny," Katie argued. "You have to find some other way to get around this Miss
Corley, Matt."

Matt's frustrations were evident in his face and in his voice. "There is no
way around her. She has been appointed by the State. And with that position,
she holds all the cards."

"What if we can't convince her and the judge to legalize the adoption?
What is their alternative solution?" Katie asked.

There was no easy way for Matt to say it, so he said it the best way he knew.
"There are three options open. The first, which they would consider to be in
the best interest of the boys, is highly unlikely. To find a home, the same home,
for all four of them would be very difficult. There aren't many acceptable couples
out there willing to take on a ready-made family of four. And most couples
want an infant. Older children are less desirable and not so easily placed."

"You mean send them to live with strangers? People they don't even know?
How could that ever be considered to be in their best interest?" Katie demanded.

"It would be better than the other two alternatives," Matt replied.

Katie shook her head. "I'm afraid to ask what the other two alternatives
are."

"To split them up, place them in separate homes ... or, if no homes are found ... to place them in an orphanage."

Katie must have dug deep into her physical reserves. She almost flew out of her chair and knocked it crashing backward to the floor. She nearly shrieked. "An orphanage! For God's sake, Matt! Not an orphanage! Or split them up. That would destroy them." Katie paced, arms wrapped tightly around her. "I can't believe any of this. In the name of God, how could any sane person think that either of those are reasonable alternatives? An orphanage instead of a home with someone who loves them? Who are these lunatics that are deciding the fate of *my* children? What gives them the right? How could they possibly think that they would know better than their mother what is best for them?"

Abraham rose and put a comforting arm around Katie. He could feel her body tremble through the heavy sweater. He softly lifted her chin and turned her head to face him. Katie saw through her tears only kindness and gentleness in his eyes. Slowly, a calm, reassuring smile spread across his face. Nodding his head almost imperceptibly, he broke from her gaze and looked toward Matt.

"Abraham was pragmatic. "There is no other way, Katie. Bigotry is a fact of life. Miss Corley is also a fact of life. Ultimately, I must face her. I will have to find a way to change her mind.

"Matthew, you must be our general. You need to find the chink in the armor, the legal grounds that will work to our advantage. Like any wise military leader, you must study their tactics. Find their strengths and weaknesses. You will have to be as shrewd as they are. We cannot defeat them defensively. I cannot change my past, who and what I am. Matthew, you must devise a strong offensive plan. For, eventually, it will all come down to a single factor. The burden of changing their minds rests on my shoulders. You must prepare me to go into the lion's den. As the Lord armed Daniel, you must arm me with the ammunition to defeat my lions."

chapter forty-one

Katie wasn't sure if the scream was real or part of one of the many nightmares that haunted her dreams. She hadn't thought that she was asleep but couldn't find any other explanation for it. Then, groggy but awake, she heard it again. This time she knew it was real. She sat up in the rocker and shook the haze of cobwebs from her mind. She strained to determine its source. It was coming from upstairs, from Tommy's room. As quickly as her tired body would allow, she threw off the afghan and started up the stairs. She met Brendan coming from his bedroom just as she reached the top of the staircase.

"It's Tommy," he told his mom in a voice heavy with sleep.

"He must be having a nightmare. Go back to bed. I'll see to him."

She entered Tommy's room and turned on the light switch. The bedroom was bathed in soft, pink light. Tommy was thrashing, the bed linens twisted around him. Chance was restlessly sitting on the floor next to the bed.

Katie patted the top of his head. "You're upset, too? You big softy, I'll take over from here."

She sat on the edge of the bed and quickly untangled Tommy from the covers and drew him into her arms. She gently stroked his brow, damp from perspiration, and started to soothe him awake with soft, cooing words. "It's all right, Tommy ... Mommy's here."

She situated him half way on her lap and rocked him back and forth. Tommy's breathing was shallow and rapid, as if he couldn't fill his lungs.

"Everything is okay. You're safe ... Mommy's here. Shh. Shush now. No more crying. There's nothing to be afraid of. It was all just a bad dream. Let's you and me chase all the bad dreams away."

Gradually, Tommy began to waken. He looked at his mommy through sleepy, teary eyes.

"I couldn't find you, Mommy. Something was chasing me ... I couldn't see it ... but I knew it was chasing after me and it was a bad thing. I was lost and scared and alone. It was very dark and I couldn't see where I was going. I kept calling for you but you didn't answer. I couldn't find you."

"Well, you can see me, now. I'm right here. You are safe in your own bed ... in your own room. And Chance is right here beside you. Bad dreams can't hurt us. They're not real."

"But it was real, Mommy." Tommy's voice quivered.

"Bad dreams only seem real until we wake up and find out they were only pretend. Why, when you wake up in the morning, you won't even remember the bad dream, that you were scared."

Tommy wiped his sleepy eyes. "What's it like to die?" he asked through his tears.

Katie smiled at him. "I don't know. I've never done it before."

She realized that she hadn't asked that question, herself. She thought it over before she continued.

"I'd like to think that it is much like falling into a deep sleep and waking up in a bright and wonderful world. A world where there are trees and flowers and a beautiful lake that goes on forever. There are animals and birds and angels and puffy white clouds in a clear blue sky. It's a world that we call heaven. It's the place where God lives. A place where everyone is happy and no one ever hurts or gets sick. A place where we will be with everyone who died before us. All the people we love, like your daddy."

Tommy tried to think about heaven. Only he couldn't imagine it wonderful at all. His Mommy was going to be there and he couldn't go with her. "Mommy, I don't want you to die and go to heaven." He spoke so softly it was nearly a whisper.

Katie felt her throat tighten and tears instantly filled her eyes. "I don't want to die, either, Tommy."

"Then how come you gotta?"

Please God, she silently begged, *help me find the words.*

"Because I have a very bad sickness."

"How come Dr. Hughes can't make you better?" Tommy played with Katie's wedding band, turning it round and round on her finger.

"Most of the time doctors can make us better. But, sometimes they can't. This time, Dr. Hughes doesn't have the medicine to make me better."

"How come God doesn't make you better?"

"God only makes one of us. And because there is only one of us, that makes each one of us very special. There isn't another Tommy O'Neill in the whole world. And there isn't another Mommy. God doesn't have one of me in heaven, so I guess that's why he wants me there. He wants me to come home to heaven," Katie's voice broke.

"But this is home. I want you to stay here," Tommy insisted.

"I know you do. And I want to stay here with all my heart. But we can't always have everything that we want. God wants me to come to heaven so I must listen to Him and trust Him that he knows what is best for me."

"I think I'm a little bit mad at God. I don't wanna be mad, but I can't help it."

"It's okay to be a little bit mad. Sometimes Mommy is a little bit mad at God, too."

"Why do people have to die?"

It was a fair question but Katie knew there was no fair answer. "No one is ever meant to live forever. Except in heaven. God gave us that wonderful gift. Even if our bodies die, our spirits will never die. They will live forever. It's a part of life that is very hard to understand even though we know it. Some things our minds know, even if our hearts don't. Even though you won't see me anymore with your eyes, you will always be able to see me in your memory. We won't be able to talk to each other with our voices, but we can always talk with our hearts. My dying can't take that away from us."

Slowly, Tommy's tense body started to relax and his breathing became deeper and rhythmic. Katie began a soft lullaby, calming him back to sleep.

Over in Killarney
Many years ago,
Me mither sang a song to me
In tones so sweet and low.
And I'd give the world
To hear her sing
That song to me, today.
Tu Ra Lu Ra Lu Ra
Tu Ra Lu Ra Li
Tu Ra Lu Ra Lu Ra
Hush now, don't you cry..

By the end of the second refrain, Tommy was asleep. Katie gently laid him down, head upon his pillow and tucked the covers around him. With a mother's loving touch, she trailed her fingers across his plump cheek and placed a soft kiss on his forehead. She stood by his bedside until she was sure he was peacefully asleep.

After a few moments, Katie whispered, "Sleep tight my little Tommy. And from now on, may all your dreams be happy ones. I'll be in yours as you will be in mine."

Katie wasn't aware that Brendan had been standing in the hall watching her, studying every gesture and word. Not wanting to be discovered, he silently turned and walked back to his room.

Physically drained and emotionally exhausted, Katie climbed into her bed that had suddenly taken on the proportions of Mount Everest. She noted that even the prospect of all the most fundamental and simplest human acts, the ones done automatically without thought, had become torture.

Katie was restless and unable to succumb to the sleep her body so badly needed. She tossed and turned, but every muscle in her body ached and there was no relief from the pain. The episode with Tommy had unnerved her and she was plagued with her own nightmarish thoughts. It was as if the demons had followed her into her own bed and smothered her; they gnawed and clawed at her insides.

Tommy's nightmare was a portent, an omen of what was to come. Someday, frighteningly soon, she wouldn't be there to chase away the monsters and make the bad dreams disappear. His fears of being lost and alone wouldn't disappear when the lights came on. He would have nothing to cling to but a weakening image, a fading memory. He would call out for her and his cries would be answered with the sharp sting of abandonment. She wouldn't be there for him to love him back to safety. She wouldn't be there to stop anything bad from happening ever again. Tommy would soon learn that she had deceived him. That his mommy had made a promise to him that she would never be able to keep. Katie knew that the only thing more volatile than the truth was a lie.

Pain, suffering, even her own death didn't scare her. What she feared most was leaving her children. In the past few weeks the only semblance of sanity she was able to maintain was based on knowing that Abraham would be there in her stead. It would be the last act as a mother that she could do for them. Now, even that was falling apart.

Her plan was spiraling downward toward failure, and with it, her hopes for the boys, her hopes that they would grow up together, healthy, happy and secure. She hadn't asked for a miracle. She hadn't begged for Divine intervention or a wondrous cure. All she had asked from God was to grant her this one wish, a mother's wish. All she had wanted was a loving home and future for her sons.

God knows what is best for us. He knows what we need better than we do. The absurdity of the words reverberated in her head. She pressed her hands against her ears and tried to squash the sound of her own words from her mind. Tommy had trusted her to know all the answers when all she had for him were some empty platitudes. They may be enough for adults equipped with cogitative thought, but they weren't enough for Tommy. His needs were far simpler, far more important and urgent. All he knew was that his mommy was going away forever and that fact was frightening and beyond his comprehension.

Everything she had said to him was ambiguous and Katie wasn't sure she believed any of it, herself. How can one make sense of the inconceivable? Heaven was in another sphere, another dimension, another universe. Spiritual life and eternity were concepts far removed from the understanding of a small boy.

Tommy and the boys were real, tangible, here and now. Their confusion and questions deserved sane, reasonable answers not illogical, empty clichés. They needed her not prosaims.

Katie longed for the bright light of morning. During the day, diversion was easier and she managed to suppress the nagging doubts and ugly truths. But, in the lonely hours of night, they crept from their dark corners and she couldn't escape them. Katie felt the bile rising, burning her throat. She was the deceiver, the great deluder to herself and to Tommy. She reflected back on the explanations she had just pawned off on him it made her physically sicker than any cancer. She felt like a rat in a maze in a frantic search to find the right path of escape. Instead, she kept retracing her steps over and over and found nothing but dead ends.

She wondered where God and His boundless love were in all this? How could a wise and compassionate God possibly know that this was for the best? How could He know that leaving four boys motherless was a good thing? She knew what was best for them. Their lives had sprung from her womb. Her blood filled their veins. They had been nourished at her breast.

Though she had come to accept her own death, Katie had not reconciled the boys' tenuous future with God. She was prepared to accept her absence in their future, but she would not accept that Abraham would have no role in their future as well.

When at her lowest, Katie hadn't doubted God's presence or questioned His existence. Instead, she had wondered what kind of God was He? Would He hear her pleas or had He turned a deaf ear to her prayers? Had He listened to her supplication that His will be hers or had he already decided that His volition did not parallel hers? Would He lend his strength and support to Abraham and the boys during the difficult weeks and months ahead or would He abandon them? She demanded reassurances from God, an accounting, an explanation, reconciliation from Him.

Katie knew that at her most vulnerable moments her faith was weakest. Distrust and doubt had eroded her faith. It was then that she realized that faith was easiest when life was easy, stronger when life was difficult and needed to be strongest when life is denied.

Her eyes fell upon the rosary setting in its usual place on the bedside table. Katie wanted to hurl it across the room, smash it against the wall, shatter the crystal beads into a million pieces as her dreams were shattering. But, she fought the urge. Instead, she gathered the strands into her hand and gripped them until the crucifix bit into her flesh.

As she clasped the blessed rosary, with fists clenched in fury, she pounded and beat at the pillows. She damned Dr. Vertage, damned the cancer, damned

Edith Corley, damned agencies and courts and judges, damned her weak and helpless body. Then, Katie committed the ultimate blasphemy. She damned her God.

Finally, breathless, exhausted and depleted, she cried herself to sleep.

CR BO

The following morning, Katie was awakened by a need stronger than survival. She had gone to bed vanquished but woke up with purpose.

There were going to be many times when the boys would need her and, unlike the night before, she wouldn't be there. One day, she was going to disappear from their lives. That was a fact and it wasn't going away. She needed to leave them with something real, tangible, a concrete part of her that they could draw upon in those desperate times. They needed a piece of physical proof that she had been real, had existed; that her love was infinite. Something that death couldn't erase.

Her undaunted maternal instincts led her to the answer.

Before daylight broke, her tired body experienced rejuvenation. With resolve and purpose, she made her way to the writing desk, drew out a single sheet of stationery and put pen to paper.

When her mission was complete, she folded the paper as carefully as she had folded swaddling blankets around each of her infant sons. She resisted the urge to alter or change what she had written. She wanted the words to remain untouched, as they had come to her, naturally and instinctively from her heart to her hand. Someday, she wanted the boys to read the words as if she were alive and speaking them so they would be heard as if coming from her own lips. Abraham would be the courier, but the message would be hers.

After she placed the letter in an envelope, she sealed it and addressed it to her sons. She sighed with satisfaction and leaned against the padded comfort of the chair. A soft smile of contentment spread across her face.

CR BO

Two weekly visitors that Katie had come to anticipate and need were Dr. Hughes and Father Davey. One ministered to her body, the other to her soul.

It had become increasingly more difficult for Katie to find the strength or energy to make the weekly office visits, let alone mass. So, Dr. Hughes made weekly house calls and Father Davey faithfully brought her communion and heard her confessions.

Father Davey held the strongest opinion that Katie was truly a saint on earth and as such, wasn't capable of committing transgressions like the rest of the mere mortals. But, she seemed to draw solace from the contrition, so he listened to her confessions and gave her absolution.

He looked forward to the visits as much as Katie. In spite of the shadow that hung over her, there was something tranquil, serene, something mystical about her. And Father Davey found those affectations contagious. They spread to anyone who was around her. Their relationship had exceeded that of pastor and parishioner, confessor and transgressor, to one of deep friendship.

When the weather was pleasant, he would join her in the gazebo and they would share a pot of tea. When the weather was inclement or Katie was too ill, he would find her sitting in the living room seeking the warmth of the fireplace.

As long as he could remember, Father Davey had accepted the will of God without question or doubt. He had witnessed the miracle of birth and the sorrow of death and everything wondrous or tragic that filled the in-betweens. But, Katie's situation had tested his convictions. He carried on a daily struggle to defeat the doubts that had wormed their way into his soul. How could God abandon those four young lads? How could He leave them fatherless and motherless? They would miss her beyond comprehension. He would miss her. The world would miss her; it was a far better place with her in it. The nagging thoughts kept plaguing him and he wondered if this time, God was making a mistake.

Father Davey knew that some of the most brilliant minds had ventured down the same path of doubt that he was walking. Laics and clerics, philosophers and scholars, deists and atheists had dedicated volumes, tomes, even lifetimes trying to rationalize, prove or disprove the existence of a Supreme Being. Great minds such as C.S. Lewis, Caird and Freud all delved into the questions of spirituality, religion and the validity of a God. And yet, Father Davey knew that the antiphon still remained private and personal. The validity lied within the individual soul.

Through daily prayer, he had sought the Lord's countenance. He asked for the vision and wisdom to strengthen his faith and trust, to accept that it is not man's privilege to know or even understand the ultimate intent of God's purpose. He pleaded for reassurance that he must not question the challenges sent by God, but embrace them because there is a greater purpose, a Divine plan, an infinite rationale. Father Davey prayed that God would reveal what role he needed to play in this grand design. He asked God to share with him the truths and bless him with the fortitude to serve those souls entrusted to his care.

On Thursday afternoon, Father Davey found Katie resting on the settee in the gazebo. She was on the last decade of the rosary when he approached with his satchel that contained the consecrated Host. Jadyne followed behind with a tray of hot tea and warm blueberry muffins.

"Ah. 'Tis a grand day to be enjoying the lake, Katie. I see you have invited the Blessed Virgin to join you. She can be a great comfort to you, she being a mother, herself."

"I'm afraid you haven't caught me on a very good day, Father. Jadyne calls these my blue days and I'm having one as dark blue as it gets."

"Then, 'tis a blessing that I've come today. It sounds as though you could use the nourishment of the Holy Eucharist."

Jadyne set the serving tray on the wicker side table and said, "Nourishment is the one thing she does need and the one thing things she's too stubborn to take. It's easier to get the twins to eat collard greens than it is to get her to eat anything."

Father Davey sat down. "Spiritual food 'tis often more important, Jadyne."

"Save your energy and your breath, Jadyne," Katie said. "I can't break my fast before I receive Holy Communion."

"Fast! If that isn't the most ridiculous thing I've ever heard. The Lord doesn't care if you eat or not. You Catholics! I can't begin to understand some of your cockamamie ideas. I'd like you to point out to me where the Bible says anything about fasting before you come to the Lord's Table? What difference could it possibly make to the Lord whether you eat something or not? Seems to me the bigger sin is neglecting your health."

Father Davey replied, "You're a wise woman, Jadyne. And Catholic or not, you're right as rain. There is special dispensation from fasting for those who are sick. It wouldn't make a lick of sense for the Lord to deprive you of some nourishment."

Jadyne responded sarcastically. "Well, thank you very much for giving your permission for something that only makes sense to begin with. And while you're at it, maybe you can persuade her to come back into the house. I haven't been able to convince her that it's too cool for her to be outside. It won't do anybody any good if she were to catch pneumonia. Of course, she won't listen to me. Stubborn Irish."

"Now, that's where we're at crossed purposes, Jadyne. 'Tis a wonderful day to be enjoying nature. We Irish like it crisp and clean, invigorated by a bracing wind. 'Tisn't the sun that replenishes our souls, but the clouds and mist, the water and a blustery wind blowing across the green hills and the gray sea."

Jadyne grumbled as she waddled off, "I've been taking care of white folks my whole life and now, all of a sudden, I don't know nothing about anything."

Father Davey waited until Jadyne was well out of hearing distance when he coaxed, "Not that I'd want to be admitting it to her, but she may be right. Are you sure you are warm enough here? Might not be bad idea to get you inside."

"I'm fine, really. I love sitting out here. It's as if the lake calls to me. And it's where I feel closest to God."

"We Celts do have a spiritual connection with the water. Of course, it only seems natural since the land of our birth is the isle of Erin. Are you ready for Communion?"

"Not just yet, Father. I'm more in need of your earthly ministrations, to-day, than your spiritual ones. I have a situation where I need to ask a favor of you."

"Ask anything, Katie. If the good Lord's willing, you know I could never refuse you."

It was then that Katie told him about the desperate situation Miss Corley had created.

"So. What I'm asking of you, could you have a world with Judge Aldridge? We all think it could carry a great deal of influence with him."

Father Davey thought a minute. "The good Judge and I have been known to tip a few glasses of Irish malt together at the country club. And, it wouldn't hurt to let him beat me at our next round of golf. Soften him up, so to speak. When he wins, it always puts him in a wickedly good mood. Yes. I can see where it might put him in very amicable mood. Consider it done."

"Thank you, Father. I don't want to jeopardize your friendship with him. And I hate to put you in an uncomfortable situation. But, I wouldn't ask if I wasn't completely desperate. It's all I've been able to think about the last few days."

Father Davey gripped her hand. "I don't feel compromised at all. I'm sure our friendship can survive a bit of manipulation on my part. The Judge is an honest and fair man. I'm sure his ruling will be in the best interest of the lads. Katie, my girl, stop your worrying. I can't have my favorite parishioner wasting her time fretting over this. Now, are you ready to receive the Blessed Host? Then you and I will share one of Jadyne's blueberry muffins."

Father Davey had finished saying good-bye to Jadyne when Matt walked into the yard.

"Hello, Father. How is she today?"

The old priest patted Matt's arm. "She 'tisn't having one of her better days. But, as usual, Katie's spirit rises to the occasion."

Matt had been spending every waking moment either with Katie or pour-ing over his law books preparing his case for the hearing. His nights were al-most sleepless. What was left of his days and nights he filled with worries about Katie and the adoption. He was emotionally drained and physically exhausted, hollow-eyed and weary."

"You, look as though you aren't having a very good day, either," Father Davey commented.

"If God is so merciful and loving, how can he let her suffering go on?" Matt's tone was as cold as a winter night. "What did she ever do that was so terrible that she deserves this?" Matt asked.

Father Davey's voice was soft. "Matthew. God is not punishing Katie. I know deep within my heart that when she draws her last breath her soul will shoot right past Purgatory and go straight to heaven's golden gates."

Wearily, Matt muttered, "Then why doesn't He just take her and put an end to all this?" He raked his hands through his hair.

"Because we are all instruments of God. Katie isn't here to earn her way to heaven. He isn't testing her. Katie passed His test a long time ago with flying colors. He's testing us. She's here as an example to the rest of us and through her, God is teaching us one of His greatest lessons. The inextinguishable faith and trust in God. Katie isn't questioning His will and neither should we. Let her living example be an example for you. Draw faith from her courage and trust from her strength. 'Tis in the tempering of the metal that the steel becomes strong."

"I never know if I should visit her or not. I'm not sure I'm good for her right now. At the same time, I can't stay away. The car just seems to drive itself here." Matt sounded ninety years old.

"Having the people she loves around her 'tis the best medicine."

Matt's stomach tightened. "Sometimes I think that what little strength she does have left is squandered trying to make me feel better. She tries to put on a brave front when she barely has the energy to breathe," he said.

"Matthew, my boy-o. Energy is never wasted on those we love. Regrets and contrition are for those who never learned that lesson. Listen to this old priest. You put on a happy face and go see that lovely creature. Right now, she needs a bit of sunshine that only her loved ones can give. Her lads give her one kind of love and you another."

Father Davey smiled softly at Matt, gave him his blessing and turned toward his car.

Matt approached the gazebo quietly. If Katie had managed to fall asleep, he didn't want to disturb her.

As expected, her eyes were closed.

At first, Matt felt his chest tighten with panic. He couldn't see the slightest rise and fall of her chest. He was about to call out for Father Davey and Jadyne when he saw the barest hint of movement in the hollow of her throat as she swallowed. Matt didn't know if he felt relief or regret.

With grave eyes, in the peace and solitude of the gazebo, her favorite place on earth, Matt studied her tiny form that was almost lost in the plush folds of the pillows and quilt. Her skin looked opaque, fragile and weightless as white ash. The only color on her face was the faint hint of blue-gray veins just under the layer of paper-thin skin. Nearly colorless, her lips had faded to a dusky rose. Delicate lashes of long, dark chestnut curled below her eyes.

Katie's peaceful expression reminded him of the first day he had seen her. Her radiant face with peach cheeks that dimpled when she laughed. How the light danced and sparkled in her lively, green eyes; her lips rosy with life. Her mass of flyaway curls as rich and shiny as polished teak. Matt didn't know how it could be possible, but she was more beautiful now, than she had been then. It had been more than a year ago that they had met yet Matt felt as if he had known her all his life.

At that moment, Katie's eyes flickered open. She saw the recollection in Matt's eyes and her lips curled into a gentle smile. Matt bent and laid a soft kiss on her forehead then one on her lips. She reached out with her hand and traced the outlines of Matt's eyes and mouth with a single finger. Then, so softly it was almost imperceptible, her hand danced across his cheek like the fluttery wings of a butterfly. In response, Matt stroked her cheek with his hand and they spoke to one another only with their eyes.

Finally, Katie's eyes lit up and a dimple threatened each cheek.

In a near whisper, she teased, "Matt. You look twice as bad as I feel. And you never looked more wonderful."

The sun had finally broken through the clouds and the late afternoon was warm even though a brisk wind still blew across the lake. Matt had left and Lottie and Katie were enjoying the last of the day in the protection of the gazebo.

"You know what I miss most, Lottie? Going barefoot. I miss gardening with Abraham a lot, but I miss going barefoot even more. I miss the feel of the cool, dewy grass, fluffy carpets, the warm sand and the cool water. I'm so chilled all the time that I feel like these woolen socks have grown attached to my feet. I long to take them off and wiggle my toes, experience the freedom of bare feet, again."

"So, Sug. What's stoppin' ya? Come on, let's do it. I'll even join ya. Even though tha only water I ever let touch ma body is in a warm bubble bath, if yawr willin' then so am I."

Lottie slipped off her spiked heels and wiggled her painted toes. Katie was bit by the bug and leaned over and pulled off her socks and Lottie helped her down from the gazebo. The cool, moist grass against her feet rejuvenated Katie and the two scampered down to the water's edge like recent parolees.

The heavy wind had churned up the lake and the gray water rolled onto the beach in incessant, foamy waves. At first, the water, not yet warmed by the summer's sun, lapped icily at their feet. But, in only a minute or two, their feet adjusted to the temperature and they stood ankle deep in the water, letting the sand squish between their toes. The waves splashed against the hems of their clothes. Katie was immediately overwhelmed with a sense of lightheartedness and felt like a naughty child who had escaped her parent's watchful eye. She was giddy with delight. The feeling was contagious and within seconds, the two held hands and clumsily danced in a circle. They kicked and splashed and performed an aquatic Irish jig until both were nearly drenched.

Like a bulldozer, Jadyne came roaring across the lawn, her apron and housedress flying in the wind. "Miss Katie!" She shouted. "Have you taken complete leave of your senses? Have you lost your mind?"

Katie yelled back, "Actually, for the first time in weeks, Jadyne, I'm feeling blessedly and wonderfully in complete possession of my senses."

"Get yourself out of the water before you catch your death," she scolded.

Katie laughed and called out, "Don't you think that at this stage of the game that's rather a moot point?"

Both she and Lottie bent over with laughter. Jadyne stood as close to the water's edge as she dared and held up a quilt to wrap around Katie. "Don't make me come in there to get you," she warned.

"Come on ya ol' stick in tha mud. Lighten up a bit. Yawr always serious as a heart attack," Lottie hollered.

"And you're madder than a March hare. Miss Katie, I know she hasn't got the good sense God gave her, but I gave you a bit more credit. The fun's over. Now, get yourself out of that freezing water and come on over here so I can dry you off before any more damage is done."

Lottie kicked her foot in the air and with it a healthy splash of water that hit Jadyne squarely in the face. It ran off her bushy curls like water off a duck and dripped down her shiny face soaking the front of her housedress. That was the last straw.

Complete with socks and shoes, she threw down the quilt and charged into the water. Her thick, stumpy legs pumped up and down like pistons and splashed water in every direction. In no time at all, the three were knee-deep in the lake and like water nymphs, soaked from top to toes, they dripped with water and sand and clumps of wet weeds. Hysterical laughter and a chain of cuss words carried across the lawn and up to the house.

The four boys, just home from school, stood on the porch, dumbfounded, their mouths and eyes formed perfect, wide circles of shock and disbelief.

 C3 80

Tommy and the twins were at C.J.'s birthday party. The house was uncharacteristically quiet and Katie longed for the noise and chaos. The bedroom walls were closing in on her and she craved human contact. She ventured downstairs and gripped the banister for support. Brendan was sitting on the sofa in the living room paging through an old photograph album.

"Taking a walk down memory lane?" She asked as she sat down next to him.

The maroon, leather album was spread out on his lap. The black and white, glossy photographs were secured to the ebony pages by black triangles, one at each corner.

"I was kinda bored," Brendan responded.

"Miss your little brothers?"

Brendan rolled his eyes. "I miss 'em like I'd miss a hole in the head."

"Why don't you call up one of the Musketeers? Invite them over?" Katie offered.

"Naw. Stump's grounded. Puke and Breeze got chores to do. Vinnie's hoeing weeds with his dad."

"How about the sailboat? Why aren't you working on that?"

"Don't feel like it."

"I can understand that. Sometimes it's good just to have some alone time. It's therapeutic."

Brendan turned the page of the album. "I don't even know who most of these people are."

Katie looked at the page. "When you were little, you'd drag this album out and we'd look through it for hours. At one time you knew most of them."

"Must a forgot. Who are they?" Brendan pointed at one of the snap shots.

"That's your Greatgrandma and Greatgrandda Hynes. My ma's parents. That was taken in Dublin a long time ago."

"And them?"

"My ma and da, your Grandda and Grandma Malloy. You were just a wee tot when they died." Katie smiled as the photograph brought back comforting and warm memories.

"Hey, Mom. This is the little girl in that picture." Brendan pointed at the painting above the fireplace.

"You're right. It is. I'd forgotten all about that photo. Do you know who she is?"

"I guess it's you," Brendan ventured.

"Then you would be correct. My Aunt Katherine painted it from memory. She had a pretty good memory, don't you think. It's surprising how much we can remember of those we loved. The passage of time helps us to remember only the good and quickly forget the bad. I think that's how it should be."

"These must be pictures of us."

"Those are your baby pictures. Can you pick out who's who?"

Brendan picked out the twins immediately and quickly identified himself and Tommy.

"The twins looked so much alike that we had to leave their hospital bracelets on them so your daddy could tell them apart. You were four of the most beautiful babies. But, of course, every mother thinks that."

"I remember who these guys are." Brendan tapped the page. "Uncle Casey and Uncle Colin. They died in the war."

Katie nodded. "Your dad's brothers. They were twins, too, and we named Casey and Colin after them. They were an interesting pair. Just imagine Casey and Colin as grown men and you'd have exact replicas of those two. You never knew what kind of trouble they would stir up next. It was as if they never completely grew up."

Brendan asked, "Who am I named after?"

"Your daddy's da, Grandda Brendan O'Neill. You used to call him 'Da-O.' You were only two when he died. And Tommy's named after your daddy's platoon leader in the army. Sergeant Tommy Driscoll. He saved your daddy's life in the war and died doing it. Each one of you inherited your names from very special people."

"How come?"

"How come what?"

"How come we got named after people?"

Katie sighed. "Because we loved them and I guess it was our way of keeping their memories alive. That way we'd always be able to remember them through you."

"How come we don't have any cousins? Breeze and Puke have lots of aunts and uncles and cousins."

"Unfortunately, our family is very small. I was an only child and your daddy's brothers died before they married and had children of their own. Unlike most people, we don't have any close relatives. That's why it's so important that you and your brothers stay close."

For a while, Katie and Brendan enjoyed the photographs in silence. Then Katie spoke. "I think I'm going to make you the keeper of the archives. As the oldest, it will be your responsibility to make sure that these people are never forgotten. You will have to remember who they are and introduce your bothers to them. That way they will live on forever, through your children and your grandchildren. It's a pretty big responsibility, but I think you can handle it."

Brendan turned another page and it was like he was turning back the pages of the calendar. "I wish things could be like they were. Back in Boston when Dad was still alive. Before you got sick."

Katie put her arm around Brendan. "I know you do, Bren. Me too. Sometimes I wish I could wave a magic wand and have it all be like it was. But, you know that we aren't meant to live in the past. We are constantly moving forward. And none of us lives forever. We are born, we live our lives and then we die. That's why it's so important to draw as much happiness as we can from each day. Be all that we can be. Be better persons today than we were yesterday and less than we will be tomorrow."

"I'd trade a hundred todays for only one yesterday." Brendan admitted.

"And I wouldn't trade this moment with you for a thousand yesterdays."

chapter forty-two

"I know she's in unbearable pain. She's so brave and stoic, never complains. She tries to hide it, but I can see it in her eyes. Never have I seen anyone with so little physical strength possess so much willful determination. I don't know how she keeps going."

"Is she able to ambulate at all?"

"Only with help, and then, only to use the bathroom. It won't be much longer and she won't be able to manage that. I have to bathe and feed her in bed. I use the term feed loosely. She hardly swallows a bite. Her output is barely measurable and her intake even less. Liquids are about the only thing I am able to coax down her. The pain medicine makes her so nauseated that what she does manage to swallow she usually vomits right back up."

"So, you have been able to convince her to take the medicine and sedatives I've prescribed?"

"Not without a struggle. She fights them tooth and nail. To be honest, I don't blame her. The episodes of vomiting are so violent and draining for her. And even with the medicine, the pain is so severe that she can hardly sleep. Dr. Abraham and Miss Lottie take turns sitting with her during the night. They tell me that she's lucky to get one or two peaceful hours."

"What about the acetone compresses?"

"They do help some. But the effects are so short-lived. They used to last for a few hours, but not anymore."

"How is the bleeding?"

"Not hemorrhagic, yet, but it's constant and heavy. At times so heavy that she soaks right through."

It was one of Dr. Hughes biweekly house calls. Jadyne updated him on Katie condition since his last visit. The report revealed that Katie's condition was worsening rapidly. The past three weeks had marked a sharp and steady decline. The bleeding had worsened to the point that Dr. Hughes was worried that he may need to hospitalize her. It was not only becoming less debatable, but unavoidable. Perhaps a dilatation and curettage would be helpful in slowing down the blood loss? But, Katie had remained adamant, that when the end came, she wanted to be home. This was her home, where her boys were, where her life was. When the end did come, it would be in the surroundings that she loved, surrounded by those she loved.

"She refuses the blood tests, to see what her hemoglobin levels are. She argues what's the point? What good will it do? And Doctor, to be honest, I'm beginning to share her logic. What is the use of any of it?"

"Don't tell me that she's got you convinced, too? Jadyne, you were the one person that I thought I could rely to keep a cool head. Remain objective. And now, you too, have sided with the enemy. I can't fight you, too." Dr. Hughes looked more tired and haggard than Jadyne could ever remember him being.

"We're not the enemy, Doctor. We all want the same thing. I am viewing this with objectivity. She wants to die at home. Is that so wrong?"

"There are things we can do for her in the hospital. Things that we can't do for her at home. We can help to minimize the pain, build her strength and alleviate some of her suffering. We can help her to die as mercifully as our expertise and medicine will allow. Surely you can't argue with that logic."

"And in the end it will all have been futile." Jadyne captured Dr. Hughes eyes with her own. "At one time I might have agreed with you. But not anymore. I have come to see it all through her eyes.

"She loves those boys more than life itself. Not wanting to leave them one day, one hour, one minute sooner than she has to, is what keeps her going. They are her life's blood. Not medicine, not transfusions, not surgical procedures. Forcing her to be hospitalized will kill her as surely as the cancer. Can't we at least let her die with the happiness of knowing that she endured it until the end? Let her go peacefully, knowing that she was there for them until the last second possible? That is the only certainty that she has left."

Dr. Hughes knew in his heart that what Jadyne said was the simple truth. Yet, as a doctor, a man of medicine, a healer, he had engrained in his soul the need to administer, to intervene, do something. It was not in his nature to stand by and do nothing.

The reality and futility that he had failed a patient, that he could do absolutely nothing was the greatest burden he had to bear. He was in a daily struggle with mortality and with God. And it was a battle that Dr. Hughes never ceded easily. It was not easy to let a patient die. That was a course never taught in medical school. Nor was the answer in any textbook. It was a lesson that had to be learned the hard way. He had seen both the young and the old die. And with each death, the loss had never gotten easier.

Maybe he was too old for this. Maybe it was time to call it quits. Take Mildred on a long vacation. Spend next winter in sunny Florida instead of snowy Michi-

---

gan. He mounted the steps to Katie's bedroom weighted down with hopelessness and a heavy heart. With every step, he fought the gnawing realization that all the medicine in the world wasn't doing her an ounce of good.

℃ ℰ

The twins smelled sweetly of soap and their cheeks were still flushed from the warmth of their bedtime baths. The three of them were nestled in Katie's bed, her warm, snuggly quilt wrapped about them. Katie was propped up on her pillows and had just finished reading *The Cat in the Hat*. Though the hands of the clock had marched past the twin's normal bedtime, Katie wasn't ready for the moment to end.

"The heck with bedtime," she mused. "This is much more fun than eight full hours of sleep. Sometimes, a mommy needs to forget the rules."

Casey asked, "Who will read us our bedtime stories when you're in heaven, Mommy?"

Katie hugged them closer. "I guess Brendan could do just as good a job as I do."

"Nuh-uh," Colin said, "He skips pages. 'Sides, he says we ain't nothin' but a big pain in the pants."

"Brendan says a lot of things he doesn't mean. You two must know that by now. He only teases you because he loves you. That's his way of showing it."

"Then who's gonna make fried eggies jus' the way I like 'em. Bren can't cook." Casey was nothing if not practical.

"Miss Jade will. She's a better cook than your old Mommy."

Katie tickled each one's belly. They squirmed and wriggled until she stopped.

Through peels of laughter, Casey pointed out Miss Jade's shortcomings. "She always puts butter on our samiches. We hate butter on our samiches."

"She tucks our covers in way too tight and she washed my blankie and now it don't smell right," Colin added.

"Then we'll just have to teach her how to do everything right, won't we?" Katie assured them. "You know, I couldn't do everything right in the beginning, either. It took me a while to learn how. First with Bren, then Tommy, then with Casey and you."

"How come I always gotta be last?" Colin asked.

"Because last is the most special," his mom answered with a smile.

"Why do you gotta die, Mommy?" Questioned Colin. He played with the lace on the collar of Katie's flannel nightgown.

Katie though for a moment, then answered, "Well, it seems that your guardian angels have been way to busy trying to keep track of you two and sometimes they get you mixed up. God thinks that maybe they could use some help. Because you two are so special, you need extra-special attention. This way, besides your guardian angels, you'll have Mommy and Daddy to keep an eye on you ... just to make sure that you're safe."

"How 'bout Dr. Franke? Can't he do it?" Casey wondered.

"Sure he can. He'll be keeping an eye on you down here. But, even Dr. Franke can't see everywhere, like we can from heaven."

Colin remarked, "So, God kinda knows what He's doin'? Huh, Mommy?"

Kissing the tops of their heads, Katie smiled, "Yes, Colin. I guess that God does know what He's doing."

As the blue hues of twilight replaced the last, dying rays of sunset, the three bedfellows were bathed in the soft pink of the bedroom lamp. The murmurings of their melodious conversation wafted out the window into the warm evening air.

"Knock-knock ..."

&#x03C

ʀ

Katie had been awake since three o'clock. The pain had jolted her awake from a restless sleep. It was still dark as pitch outside, the black of night filled her room and the hands of the bedside clock crept around, passing the minutes. A rhythmic tick-tock marked their sluggish progress. She dismissed the thought of taking a pain pill. They had ceased to perform the role they were designed for and were no longer worth the dreaded side effects.

She lay quietly; hoping that the cover of darkness would cloak her, hide her from the spasms of pain. She fought the undertow of agony that had become a familiar and hated enemy.

In an effort to escape the pain, Katie tried to fill her mind with more productive thoughts. Katie knew that those left behind when a loved one died must endure a natural process of healing; a procession of cleansing steps. She had experienced it when her ma and da and Danny died. In the past few months, she also realized that the dying experience a similar evolution. All the same steps, shock, denial, doubt, fear and anger, in varying order, needed to be endured. Not always delineated or clear-cut, there were no distinct boundaries where one ended and the next began. There were no timetables, no guidelines, no prescribed order. They would overlap, coincide, dissolve into one another and often time she would lose ground and regress. But, somehow, in some way, despite the odds, Katie had finally arrived at acceptance.

Katie questioned whether it was a gift or curse to be able to anticipate death from an immediate vantage point. For most people, the acknowledgement of their mortality was lost in the process of living. Whether that awareness is accidentally misplaced, a cognizant act or an unconscious effort of self-preservation, Katie decided was of little consequence. The concept of death hovers at some vague, remote, unpredictable point in the distance. She discovered that even if a person could imagine their own death, the most personal and corporeal actuality, that they would find they could only be a spectator.

Her reverie was unsuccessful in eluding the pain. Every moment was an endless assault as her tortured body shook with excruciating agony. Sleep wasn't going to return soon. She turned on the bedside lamp in the hopes of finding a moment's relief. She reclined against the mound of pillows and smoothed the surface of the quilt that hid her vanishing form.

She had looked at that quilt hundreds of times and never really seen it. Her trembling fingers traced the tiny, precise stitches that had been placed carefully by someone from the distant past. Katie wondered who that person was. Neither knew of the other's existence. Two complete strangers, separated by time and circumstance. And yet, the stitches had bound two people together, transected time and bridged their two worlds.

The quilt was a collage of varied fabrics, patterns and shapes, independent and unique, yet sewn together they formed a patchwork of harmony. The communion of all their parts created a masterpiece more beautiful than each singular piece could ever have been. As her life's quilt had been made of a thousand vignettes, brief moments, stolen glimpses that created the sum and substance of her life. They were her biography ... her footsteps ... her treasury.

Katie laid her head against the pillows, closed her eyes and let the memories wash over like baptismal waters. She wanted to savor every sight, sound, sensation and flavor, capture and hold them near.

She was five-years-old, walking hand-in-hand with her ma and da to Sunday mass. The leather soles of her new shoes crunched the finite pebbles against the sidewalk. Her childhood home filled with the aroma of fresh baked gingerbread and the taste of the spicy treat still warm from the oven.

Dee and Moira and Katie sharing the silly thrill of puppy love and the wondrous discovery of the real thing. She and Danny deliciously, passionately and totally in love. The celebration of their first wedding anniversary in a ridiculous, matchbox-sized apartment with a meal of boiled dinner and a bottle of cheap wine because they were too broke to afford a night out. Their four-year-long good-bye that started at the train station and ended when she and Brendan welcomed Danny home from the war.

Danny trying to build a sandbox, while chasing two little scamps who kept running off with his tools. Four sets of handprints pressed into the freshly laid cement in the driveway. All Brendan's firsts when Danny was in Europe, and it was only the two of them. Tommy trying to feed an injured baby bunny with an eyedropper. Casey hungrily nursing at her breast. Even as an infant he possessed an insatiable appetite for life. Colin, who insisted on removing his clothes faster than she could put them on and spent half of his toddler years running around naked. The melodious lilt of his giggles as he scampered about, unencumbered and free.

First haircuts and the last wash load of diapers. Nights too short because of midnight, two a.m. and six o'clock feedings and other nights too long as they paced the floor with a fussy, teething baby. Happy birthdays and sobering wakes. The last time she saw Delancey Street and the first time she turned onto Lakefield Road. Lottie's outrageous outfits and Miss MacCauley's ugly shoes. Abraham's serious eyes and Matt's mischievous smile. The scent of the pines, the whisper of the wind, the motion of the lake, the beauty of the gardens and the nip of a winter morning.

Katie was intrigued by the reverie. The flood of memories weren't of the profound, monumental, dramatic strides that had marked the calendar. Instead, they were the brief, intimate, personal baby steps that formed the years.

If those guileless and singular scraps of events that meshed together had created her past, then the boys would be her legacy into the future. Eventually, they would become more than brothers and sons. They would become husbands, father, uncles and grandfathers. They would be the affirmation that life was meant to go on. She wasn't saddened by the reality that she would be left behind and couldn't join them on their journey. Katie was satisfied to imagine who and what they would become. No longer tortured by missing out, she held their pasts, but they held their futures.

Katie had become an expert at letting go. She had put all of her faith in Matt and Abraham and no longer worried about the adoption and accepted that there were times when one must trust that their hopes and plans will work out. She placed complete confidence in Matt and Abraham and knew deep within her heart that God would show them the way. In that, she had to trust God, one more time.

She had surprised herself, more than it had surprised those around her, that she had made peace with God and the eventuality of her death. She was ready to take that last step from the physical of the present to the spirituality of eternity and it gave her neither pause nor fear. That thought was no longer frightening. Instead, she anticipated it as surreal, calming, almost welcomed. Katie knew that she no longer had the strength of body or will to endure the process of dying, again. For the boys' sake, as well as hers.

At one time, Katie felt that the worst horror was to leave them. She had been wrong. The worst was for them to have to watch her die, all over again. She wanted them to happily remember her simply as Mommy, not haunted by the sickly mask of some infirm stranger that bore no resemblance to who she was. Instead of a face stripped of health and vitality, but a face filled with the essence of life.

Katie was ready for it to end. Weighing her bounty, the world had been generous to her and she was ready to leave it without regret.

chapter forty-three

Eden Lake lived up to its name on the beautiful July day.

Paradise couldn't have been more sublime. The sun radiated in clear blue skies since dawn, but the breeze off the lake had cooled the hot air. Seagulls dipped and soared and rode gracefully on the invisible currents of air. Sailboats with their bright white canvases puffed with wind skimmed along the water's surface like giant origami creations.

Katie wondered if Matt was out there, one of them, on Scattering. She fantasized that she was with him, the sun warming her face and a stiff wind tangling her hair with unseen fingers. She could feel herself being hypnotized by the steady, rolling dips and rises of the boat as its bow cut through the water. There would be an occasional cold spray that would escape over the prow and mist her bare skin. Her heart filled with joy as she pictured the expression of total bliss in Matt's features, doing what he loved.

For Katie, it had been a yellow day. Nearly driven to insanity, she had escaped the confining, stifling four walls of her bedroom. Both her mind and soul needed the escape. It was the first time in two weeks that she had been outside. She felt strong enough to trace the familiar path and Brendan walked her down the staircase, across the lawn and down to the gazebo.

It was just before ten when Frank Mizzano delivered a bouquet of deep pink calla lilies to Katie. He had wanted to bring her a bushel of ripe, juicy peaches from his orchard but it was too early in the season for picking.

Frank had been gone only a few minutes when Angie stopped by and dropped off a pan of her world famous lasagna, garlic toast and a Caesar salad to Jadyne for dinner. But her biggest contribution was bringing Connie and her new baby.

"Well, here's the lady of leisure. I knew we'd find you out here, being waited on hand and foot like royalty," Angie announced as she climbed the steps of the gazebo. "You're looking chipper, today."

Katie smiled, "Liar."

"Damn," Angie cursed. "I forgot the cannelloni. I brought a full course, authentic Italian dinner and forgot the dessert."

"I've told you that you have to make lists, Angie," Katie teased her.

"Lists only work when you actually remember to make them."

When Connie saw Katie her heart ached for her. "I told Angie that this was a bad idea. Unexpected company is bad enough, but with you so sick, it's a thoughtless intrusion." Connie was reluctant to sit down and felt terrible about the imposition.

"Oh, no, Connie. You and Angie would never be unwelcome. Sit down. I can't wait to see your little peanut."

Angie settled her broad behind into one of the wicker chairs. It groaned under her weight. "I knew it was a good idea. Nothing perks a person up like seeing a brand new baby. And this one is a real keeper."

"May I hold her?" Katie asked. She sat in an upright position to create a nest of her lap.

Connie carefully handed the small bundle to Katie. "Just let me know when you're tired of holding her."

Katie accepted the baby as if it she were made of crystal and cradled her against her chest. The baby was asleep and Katie studied her perfectly formed features, her petite nose, the bowed mouth as delicate as a rosebud.

"I could never get tired of holding a baby. I'd forgotten how wonderful it feels. Angie was right. I can't think of anything that would raise my spirits as much as this. Thank you for bringing her. She is so perfect, Connie." Katie folded back the pink, flannel receiving blanket revealing a crop of strawberry blond curls. "And the red, curly hair! She has your hair and coloring."

"But, the rest of her is all Ward."

Angie argued, "Ward should be half as good looking."

"I can see a lot of Douglas in her, too," Katie remarked. She pressed her lips to the baby's forehead and breathed deeply. "There is nothing more wonderful than the sweet scent of a baby. And look at her tiny fingers. They're hardly bigger than a matchstick. It's hard to believe that anything so small can be equipped with everything they need. So precious and innocent.

"They really are miracles aren't they?"

Angie grumbled, "Then they hit puberty and the miracle is how quickly they turn into hormone saturated monsters."

"Well, puberty is a long way off for this little lady. Until then, she's a perfect angel."

The baby stirred slightly as Katie traced her finger along the baby's full, soft cheek. It felt as smooth and fuzzy as a ripe peach.

"Every time I look at her, I can't believe that I was ever upset about another pregnancy. You were so right about having a baby, Katie. She's only two weeks old and already I can't imagine life without her."

"You look great for only two weeks. Was the delivery difficult?"

"She was the easiest one. None of the others were difficult, but she was a snap. Having babies isn't my problem, Katie. Not having them is where I need help."

Angie interjected, "She practically had the baby in the parking lot of the A&P. Forty-five minutes from the time her contractions started until the little thing popped out. Never even made it to the delivery room. She had her right in the emergency department."

"How's little Joey handling it? Is he jealous of her?" Katie wondered.

"He only seems jealous when I nurse. Otherwise, he thinks she's a toy we brought home for him to play with. Ward caught him trying to drag her out of the bassinette last night."

Katie asked, "Is she a good nurser?"

"Sure is. She latched on right away and suckled like a little piglet."

"I'm tired of calling the baby *she* and *her*. But, the poor thing doesn't have a name, yet," Angie introduced the line of discussion.

Connie shot Angie a look that would bore a hole through a two-inch thick oak plank. "She's being baptized next Sunday. We'll have to decide by then."

Angie urged her. "Just come right out and ask her, Connie. The suspense is killing me. If you don't quit hemming and hawing around, she'll be starting school before she's got a name."

"Well ... actually we sort of ... have a name ... picked out. Uh ... we were kind of hoping ... that is, if you don't mind, we'd like ... Ward and I would like to name her ..." Connie stammered and couldn't finish the sentence.

Katie's gaze went from the baby to Connie. "I can't think of anything that would make me happier than having her named after me. I feel very honored, Connie." Katie smiled at Connie, then at the baby.

"See, I told you she'd say yes," Angie proclaimed. "Connie was worried that maybe you'd be upset. Because of the cancer, that it would be painful for you."

Connie scolded her, "For Pete's sake, Angie. You're as subtle as diarrhea. Could you be any less tactful?"

Katie laughed. "Then she wouldn't be Angie. I'm not upset. In fact, I'm thrilled. It's not everyone who gets to see her namesake. And what a beautiful namesake she is. I'm pleased to meet you, Mary Katherine."

Connie corrected her, "Not Mary Katherine. Just plain Katie."

It must have been a day for visitors. Father Davey arrived just before noon to share lunch with Katie. Jadyne served him a ham sandwich, a dish of potato salad and a thick slice of sweet potato pie. She teased him that it was neither the luck of the Irish nor a coincidence that he always managed to show up close to mealtime. Katie, who hadn't been able to keep down solid food for a week, sipped on a cup of beef broth.

Father Davey left after giving Katie the Sacrament of Extreme Unction. At first, she resisted, "It isn't time yet, Father."

But Father Davey was persistent. "'Tis not only the last right of absolution, but 'tis a source of spiritual strength for the sick."

So, Katie acquiesced.

CR &C

Abraham was overjoyed to see Katie snuggled in her little nest. There was something homey and comforting about her customary sojourn to the sheltering retreat and he had become accustomed to the familiar sight of her sitting there. Something in the universe seemed off kilter when the settee in the gazebo was hauntingly vacant.

Not wanting to disturb her, he climbed the stairs in soft, hushed footsteps. He was relieved to see that she wasn't asleep and a welcoming smile greeted him as an invitation to sit and join her.

Abraham was convinced that there was something eerily different about Katie. He sensed it more than saw it. The ghost-white pallor was still there; pain and exhaustion masked her face. The weight loss and weariness as real as ever; her physical vulnerability unchanged as her body bore the evidence of the silent thief that was stealing her away. Yet, there was a spiritual essence he couldn't help but feel. It was an elusive emanation he detected deep within her eyes. It was a knowing, a surety, the spark that springs forth when one suddenly discovers the key to an unsolvable mystery.

"We are of like minds, Abraham. If we can't be rooting around in the dirt together, we're happy to settle for quiet companionship and are satisfied to enjoy the gardens as spectators."

Abraham carefully tucked the edges of the quilt around her, the soft folds of the fabric hiding the tiny form that seemed to be evaporating by the hour.

"I was hoping I would not awaken you. It is very good to see you out here after so many days."

Katie's face blushed with the faintest hint of color. "And it feels just as wonderful to be outside, again. Though I do miss our little putterings, this is almost as good. Are you comfortable enough?"

She slowly blinked her eyes in amusement. Then, she realized that she actually was comfortable.

"That's a loaded question, Abraham. And, I am pleased to answer a resounding yes! Actually, I'm more comfortable than I've been in weeks. It's amusing how rapidly we learn to adjust our expectations based on the circumstances."

"Is there anything you need? Anything I may get for you?"

"Those are two more loaded questions. It seems that I am forever asking something of you. With this give and take business, it seems I'm always doing the taking and you are always doing the giving."

He brushed her cheek softly. "In friendship, there are no weights and scales. You have given me that which is immeasurable."

For Abraham, those words were more than a statement of truth. They were a summation of every tenet, every precept, a tally of every belief that Katie had shared with him and given him. She had opened herself to him completely and invited him in without asking for a single thing in return. Her candor had been unlimited, unselfish and unconditional.

"You have taught me many things about myself and forced me to look at who and what I had become. That introspection led me to uncover incredible truths about Abraham Franke. I was not afraid to form attachments, again. I was afraid of having those attachments stolen. I was not afraid of feeling, again. I was afraid of losing those I had feelings for. You honored me by caring enough, being resolute enough, being patient enough. Most importantly, you taught me that it is not a risk to need. The risk is not caring enough to need."

Katie's smile deepened the dimples in her cheeks. "It was hardly an accomplishment on my part. You simply needed a gentle nudge. The discoveries were all your own, Abraham. Besides, you were the one who once told me that the in the process of learning, the teacher learns as much as the student. I have learned volumes from you. Beyond what you have taught me, you have been my savior, my hero. And most importantly, you have been my friend."

Abraham sat back in the chair and his gaze wandered to the lake. The gardens, the lake, the house, all that surrounded him would seem strange and unnatural without her. He realized how incomplete his world would be when Katie was gone. With her would go much of the beauty and vitality of life that she had taught him to appreciate. But, her greatest gift had been that she always saw the best in him.

They remained silent for a long while, both with their private thoughts. Silences never bothered them. For them, the silences were as comfortable, as companionable as conversation. He and Katie shared an unspoken dialogue that transcended the need for words. They had become so familiar that often, words weren't necessary. And at those special, shared moments of solitude, words seemed unimportant.

Sky, lake, trees and gardens surrounded the gazebo like a shell and created a private haven. Katie and Abraham understood how personal the love of all things growing was to the other. The flowers and gardens of nature had been their shared world. And when lost in nature, it was as if their make-believe world was real, and the other, the outside one, imaginary.

Eventually, Katie pulled an envelope from under the quilt and laid it on her lap. She stroked the vellum and spoke.

"Abraham. There is one last favor I need to ask of you. Actually, it's less of a favor and more of a mission." She paused a moment, then continued, her voice soft and soothing. "Someday, after I'm gone, there will be a time when the boys are going to need to know, to understand things that they don't even realize now. Perhaps it is more of a case that there are things that *I* will need them to know. Things I want them to understand and what it has meant to me to be their mother. I need them to hear those words as if they are coming from my lips. This envelope holds a letter that I want you to give to them."

With an unsteady hand, Katie passed the precious package to Abraham. Hesitantly, he accepted it.

"Surely this is something that you would want to do yourself. Something this important, this private should pass directly between you and them."

"No, Abraham. There are things that will be far more important to them afterward. The time for them to hear them isn't now. I don't know when the time will be right. It may be days or it may be years after I'm gone. But, I know without a doubt that there will be a time. I entrusted them to you once before. Now, I'm entrusting them to you, again. I am trusting you to be the judge and the messenger when that time is right."

Through eyes that burned with tears, Abraham looked at the envelope. In Katie's graceful hand, it was addressed, *To My Boys*.

Throughout the rest of the afternoon, Dr. Hughes and Matt had visited Katie. By dinnertime, she was fatigued but content. She had passed the in-between-time of visitors watching the boys play in the lake. The Musketeers had spent most of the day engaged in their usual, lakeside antics. The older boys had been unusually tolerant of Tommy and the twins and indulged them by including them in their high jinks. A calming peace washed over Katie as she watched them. These were her only valued possessions, her legacy, her boys of Lakefield Road. At last, she languished in the restorative warmth of complete satisfaction that everything was precisely as it should be. And that inner tranquility that had eluded her for so long, cradled her heart.

Katie possessed no appetite and begged Jadyne to allow her to quietly rest in the gazebo while the boys ate supper. Jadyne had long since given up her nagging and prodding. She no longer tried to persuade her to eat. Katie had little enough strength left to breathe let alone plead her case. So, Jadyne no longer had the heart to persist.

Abraham had planted six huge containers of flowers that lined the steps of the gazebo so Katie could enjoy them from her vantage point on the settee. They were vibrant with blooming impatiens, nasturtiums, bleeding hearts and bachelor buttons. Huge tufts of asparagus ferns added cool green foliage. Jittery hummingbirds, airy butterflies, fat bumblebees and busy honeybees entertained Katie as they sought the sweet nectar. They flitted and fluttered from flower to flower, spreading microscopic grains of pollen. The bees were so heavy and drunk with pollen and flew so lazily that Katie was unsure if they would be able to make it back to their hives. They were the ever-present, ever-changing affirmation of the cycles of life.

Katie liked to imagine that she was a tiny woodland fairy living among the petals. The hummingbirds were her playmates. At will, she would hop on their back and let them carry her off to their secret, private places deep within the woods. Hidden places where thick mossy beds carpeted the cool forest floor under the protection of wildflowers, mushrooms, foliage and ferns.

Jadyne didn't like leaving Katie alone for too long, so Lottie came over to sit with her while the boys were fed.

"Abraham was here a bit ago. You just missed him."

Katie's ventured into unfamiliar territory. "Isn't it about time you told me about you and Abraham, Lottie. It's one of the last few loose ends I haven't been able to tie up."

Lottie thought for a moment. "Abraham kinda grows on a person, like a kudzu vine. 'Course, I'm more willin' than mos' ta overlook his shortcomin's. I reckon Abraham an' me are doin' all right. Ta quote y'all, Sug, we'll have ta wait an' see if time tells us that we're meant ta be more'n all right."

As Lottie reflected on Katie's philosophy, she was filled with nostalgia. "What am I ever gonna do without ya, Sug?"

"Oh, I have no doubts what so ever that you'll manage just fine. I suspect that anyone who has lived the life that you have will survive anything."

"I ain't talkin' 'bout survivin', Sug. Hell, I know I'll survive. I mean ... I ain't never had a girlfriend before. Life ain't been too generous with me where women-folk are concerned. Never had much of a momma an' no sisters. Maybe I jus' never learned how ta get along so good when it came ta women."

Lottie had a far-away look in her eyes. It seemed as if she were looking out at an instant replay of her life. "We have had a good run of it, ain't we? I reckon y'all been the sister I never got. Ya been ma friend an' that's better than a sister, I tell ya what. Kin ya get stuck with. They's kinda an accident a birth. But a friend, them ya pick."

"Friends or sisters, Lottie. What you call it doesn't matter. We couldn't have made better choices. I don't think I've ever told you how much you have meant to me. How much I have valued your friendship."

Lottie winked with one of her warm brown eyes. "Heck, Sug. Good friends don't need ta say it. They jus' know it."

"But, I need to say it, just once. I love every quirky, wise, outrageous and courageous, humorous and wonderful part of Lottie Devereaux. You've been my sounding board and confidant. My shoulder to lean and cry on. You've brought sanity to an absolutely insane situation. Nothing in my life ever felt right until I shared it with you.

"You have given me so much. There is something I want to give back to you. The pearl necklace. Like you, God wasn't too generous with female relatives for me, either. That necklace would look rather foolish around one of the boy's necks. I want you to have it."

"Oh, Sug that wuz ma gift ta you. I couldn't take it," Lottie argued.

"I won't need it where I'm going. Please. You made me so happy once, when you gave it to me. Now, make me happy by accepting it as my gift to you.

"Look, if you want, think of yourself as the caretaker. When the boys marry, you can give it to their brides to wear on their wedding days. It can be passed from one to the other. Eventually, they will have children of their own and it can be passed on to them. Just think, Lottie. You could be solely responsible for unintentionally perpetrating what could become a real O'Neill tradition. You would be the guardian of a very valuable heirloom. Besides, you have no choice. It's considered to be in very poor taste to deny a dying person their last wish."

Green eyes met brown and an understanding passed between them of unspoken thoughts and tacit sentiments.

"Seein' as how ya put it that way, I kindly accept. Ma Grandma Pope would have a conipshun fit if I wuz ta embarrass her with unobligin'ness."

Katie almost laughed. "I'm pretty sure that *unobligin'ness* isn't even a word, Lottie." It didn't matter, though. Where Lottie was concerned, Katie always made an exception. She thought back to that first spring morning when their adventure had begun. At first, it all seemed so unlikely. And now, it all seemed so right.

"Who would have ever thought ..." Katie whispered, more to herself than to Lottie.

"Who'd a ever thought what?"

Katie laughed softly. "Never mind. It's not important. I was only reminiscing."

Katie brought the conversation back to the present. "It seems to me you've left out one very important, potential female for my replacement. Jadyne."

Lottie nearly choked on her chewing gum. "Jadyne! She might fit tha physical requirements fawr bein' female, but that's where tha resemblance stops. If'n we wuz tha last two females on earth we'd get 'long like a bear an' a bobcat."

The long day and conversation were beginning to wear Katie down. She closed her eyes and laid her head back on the pillow. "If you two would stop arguing long enough, you would realize that you have a lot in common. You're both too smart for your own good and as stubborn as a *pair* of your Uncle Zwilly's mules."

"Jadyne Potter is tha most cantankerous, opinionated, sorry excuse fawr a chattin' partner I ever seen. If it don't collect dust or need sweepin' she ain't interested. An' when it comes ta discussin' anythin' interestin' I'd have better luck with a parson in a pulpit. She'd as soon take a beatin' than talk about anythin' interestin.'"

"Maybe if you'd try conversation instead of discussing your libido."

Lottie became uncomfortable with the subject. She'd eat dirt before she'd admit to any likeness between her and Jadyne and changed the subject.

"Here's a juicy bit of news I heard down at tha Color, Cut an' Curl today, Sug. Now ya know I ain't one ta condone idle gossip, but this is jus' too juicy ta pass up. It seems that Gertie Hoffmeyer saw a certain widow lady by tha name a Florence Shunk holdin' hands with ol' man Ferguson in tha park last week. Normally, I wouldn't believe half a what comes outta Gertie's mouth, but tha story was substantiated by two other more reliable sources.

"Now, some a tha girls think it's a might obscene since Flo an' Shamus is kin. 'Course me, I don't see nothin' wrong with it. They're actually second cousins once removed. An' down in Mississippi, we don't have a problem with kissin' cousins kissin'. I say, live an' let live. Ma Grandaddy Pope always said that any happiness ya kin squeeze outta life, yawr duty bound ta go after it.

"What I do find so amusin' is that Flo and Shamus are 'bout as unlikely a pair as ya ever wanna see. He's skinnier'n a flagpole an' she has a back end as wide as an axe handle. If'n Shamus an' her wuz ta do tha big nasty, he'd hafta roll her in flour an' look fawr tha wet spot."

Katie was too tired to even nod. Exhausted from her busy day of visitors, she was too weak to do much talking, so she let Lottie ramble on for both of them.

"Sug. Y'all ain't payin' attenshun ta a word I said. This here is prime informashun."

Without opening her eyes, Katie answered softly, "I'm hanging on your every word, Lottie. I'm just resting my eyes a bit. Go on with your story."

Just then Chance came bounding up the steps, hell bent for election, and knocked over the lily and one of the other flowerpots spilling dirt and uprooting the plants.

"Ya mangy ol' mutt!" Lottie scolded him. "Now look what ya done. Go on, now ... git ... git outta here. I ain't got no use fawr ya. Tha last time I wuz over ya humped ma leg like I wuz a bitch in heat. Y'all hump ma leg again an' it'll be tha las' leg ya hump. Go chase squirrels, er chipmunks, yawr tail er somethin'.'"

Lottie chased him off and sat on the bottom step to clean up some of the mess.

"Jus' what I wanna do is go scrappin' 'round in tha dirt after I jus' got a new manicure. That darn dog is lucky he's so cute otherwise I might have Sheriff Guzy pick him up as a public nuisance.

"Never could understand what y'all find so excitin' 'bout this gardenin' business, Sug. Tha closest I ever come ta gardenin' is watchin' Herb Vickrey do mine from tha comfort of ma lanai. But, I reckon whatever blows yawr sails.

"Anyway … as I wuz sayin' … I'd sure like ta be tha wallpaper on Flo's bedroom walls ta have a look at tha two a them makin' soup. Ya know what they say, tha oldest chicken makes tha best soup. On second thought, that may be one mental picture that's too disgustin' even fawr me. But, ain't love grand? Jus' goes ta show ya there ain't no age limit on it. Well, Sug. That's as good as it gets. If'n ya want a better job done, y'all better have Abraham clean it up proper."

Lottie brushed the dirt from her hands and stood to face Katie. She was still, her eyes closed as if asleep, but Lottie sensed that something was different and very, very wrong. Lottie couldn't see the faint pulse at her throat. There was no sound, not a whisper of a breath, no subtle movement. Only that of the breeze, softly playing with her auburn curls; their loose tendrils danced about her face.

In the entire time she had known her, never had Lottie seen Katie look as serene and peaceful as she looked at that moment, composed, calm, angelic, beautiful. Katie's mouth bore the merest hint of a smile; dimples almost imperceptible, skin translucent, and an aura of surreal composure lay over face like the sheerest of veils.

Lottie slowly crept up the steps and knelt down in front of Katie. She searched for the faintest signs of life, yet knew that there were none. Lottie lifted Katie's tiny, cool, limp hand and held it in her own. First, she traced the delicate lace-work of blue lines with her fingers. They were like tiny lanes and byways, threading across a map, leading everywhere and nowhere. Finally, Lottie lovingly rubbed it against her lips. A single tear escaped and slowly trickled its way down her rouged cheek.

With a soft sigh, she quietly spoke. "Oh … Katie …" Her voice broke as swallowed back the stream of tears that threatened to overflow. "… Katie, I told ya … I ain't never been any good at sayin' good-bye."

chapter forty-four

The coffin rested on its bier in the vestibule of the church. Six pallbearers, all selected by Katie, flanked the oak casket, three on each side. Dressed in dark suits and ties were Breeze, Puke, Stump and Vinnie, along with Matt and Frank Mizzano.

The mourners, as large a gathering as St. Anthony's had ever seen, hovered outside on the steps of the church under heavy, churning, roiling, gray skies waiting for the requiem Mass to begin. The steel gray clouds, weighted down with rain, held back as if they were unable to find the explication and cleansing that comes from release.

Dee and Moira had made the journey by train from Boston to Grand Rapids. Matt had arranged for Vi to pick them up at the station. Dee said she'd pawn her wedding ring if needed to afford the ticket. Mike told her that she could keep her wedding ring. He'd be happy to carry mashed potato sandwiches in his lunch pail for a year, if necessary.

Abraham, Lottie and Jadyne waited behind the four little men that stood, frozen like wooden soldiers, side-by-side, holding one another's hands. They looked straight ahead at the wooden box that would carry their mother away from them, forever. Tommy, Casey and Colin had red, puffy eyes as salty tears of loss and incomprehension stained their somber faces. Brendan stared straight ahead, like the leaden clouds outside, incapable of shedding a tear, his face frozen in a mask of impassability.

The three long days of mourning had gratefully come to an end. Abraham had protested that it was far too long, too exhausting and too cruel for the boys to endure. It was such an unbearably lengthy funeral process. Unlike his own faith that buried their dead within twenty-four hours, Catholics stretched the ritual out to three, heart wrenching days. Father Davey had explained to Abraham that it allowed those left behind the needed time to face the death and ultimate separation that would follow. It offered them the comfort and release to see their loved one for the last time.

As far as Abraham could see, it was sadistic and cruel and only served to prolong the pain. It was almost more than his heart could bear to watch those

371

four boys forced to suffer the torment of endless lines of mourners, days interminably long, only to sit and stare at the lifeless, made-up remains of their mother. Though peaceful in repose, they needed to remember her as she was, full of life, vibrant and vital. Their last vision of her should have been of the warm, feeling, sensual person that she was.

Abraham had relented out of respect for Father Davey and because it was their religious tradition. But, after seeing the toll it had taken on the boys, he was convinced that the ritual was inhumane.

Father Davey, with a gold aspergium, circled the casket and sprinkled it with holy water. Then, a snowy white, linen cloth bearing a simple Celtic cross of glistening green braid was unfolded and the pallbearers draped it over the casket.

"Come to her assistance, you Saints of God. Come forth to meet her, you angels of the Lord; receive her soul and offer it in the sight of the Most High. Eternal rest grant unto her, O Lord; let perpetual light shine upon her ..."

When the blessing of the casket was complete, one server carried the Mass book, the other the Pascal candle. Its flame flickered in the brisk wind that snaked its way in through the church doors. Father Davey robed in black chasuble, led the processional into the nave of the church. Outside, a solitary piper played Amazing Grace. Besides the pallbearers, it was the only other funeral arrangement that Katie had wanted. Lottie had spent two days tracking him down in Chicago and finally convinced him to make the trip. The mournful sound of the bagpipes hauntingly marked each step taken by the cortPge. Silent and sedate, they escorted Katie to her final mass and eternal rest.

With the heavy clouds outside, only the soft light from the chandeliers and altar candles solemnly lit the church. No bright, colored beams of sunlight shone through the stained glass windows. Brushed brass urns held huge sprays of blue delphiniums, hydrangeas and white calla lilies and were placed at the foot of the altar. They dwarfed a tiny terra cotta planter that held a small, simple cluster of shamrocks.

After the mourners filled the pews, Father Davey bowed to the altar and signaled the beginning of the proper of the mass.

"All in good time. That was her favorite expression." Father Davey began his homily not from the pulpit, but standing directly in front of the boys as they sat in the front pew.

"How many times did you lads hear your mother say that? How many times did any of us hear her express that unsophisticated, unpretentious phrase? Seems incredibly simple. No deep philosophical message or intellectual rhetoric. But, that was the nature of Mary Katherine O'Neill. Uncomplicated, guileless, endearing and enduring."

Again, looking directly at the boys, he continued. "I prayed to God that He would share with me His wisdom that I might find the words to comfort you and help you to understand all this. And all the while, I kept asking Him, Why? Why did your mother have to die and leave you four lads behind? I have trouble understanding it. How much more senseless can this be to you ... Brendan ... Tommy ... Casey ... and Colin? We grown-ups are supposed to have all the answers. How will you ever be able to understand what we adults cannot?

"Then, God spoke to me through your mother. It was like the first rays of the dawning sun that slowly but surely chase away the darkness and shed their bright light across the earth. The answers were so simple and obvious. Your mother held all the answers. They are called love, faith and trust.

"No one who is gathered in this church today, not me, not any of the great thinkers, not even the saints, possessed more faith and trust and love, than your mother. She knew ... really knew in her heart and in her mind, that God has a plan for us all. And His plan for Katie was to be His instrument. He used her every day of her life, by her example to show and teach us.

"He used her in friendship so that all of us could know the comfort and joy that comes from shared intimacy. He used her in the Sacrament of Marriage, as a mate to share love and companionship as only a husband and wife can. He used her body to create new life and bring four, precious souls into this world. And, the most important task of all, He used her as a mother to nurture, foster, protect and guide those same, four, young souls.

"So, what has her brief life on this earth taught us? What have all of us learned from Katie? That God has given us all the tools, the guidance, all His strength to handle whatever challenges this imperfect life throws our way."

Father Davey gripped the rounded top of the front pew and leaned in to look directly at the boys.

"Brendan, Tommy, Casey and Colin. 'Tis never easy to say good-bye to someone we love. And in your young lives, you have had to do that twice. First, you had to say good-bye to your father and now, your mother. It doesn't seem fair.

"But, you are four very lucky young lads. I know you can't possibly see that right now. Yet, I promise you that someday you will. Someday you will realize that God blessed you with a mother whose love knew no bounds. No one loved more selflessly or passionately than your mother. And that love is stronger than death."

Father Davey captured the eyes of each of the boys. "Your mother told me once, that at birth, when she held each one of you in her arms for the very first time, that she gave her heart to you and that is where it will always stay, with you forever. Her love is locked in your hearts forever. And though you can't see her, or hear her voice, 'tis there, deep in your hearts where you will always find her.

"When you are troubled and confused and sad, hold strong to the gifts that she gave to each of you. Her gift of sensitivity so that you will be kind to others. Her love of all things that grow so that you will appreciate the wonders of the nature. Her gentle spirit so that you will find pleasure in the simple things in life. Her easy laughter so that you will never take life too seriously. Her unselfish love so that you can give selfless love.

"You will most surely miss her, but whenever you feel lonely, or lost, or afraid, or sad, talk to her with your heart and I promise you that not only will she always hear you, but in your heart you will hear her answers.

"The hurt and the pain won't go away, soon. Not tomorrow … maybe not for a very long time. But, I do know that it will lessen … all in good time."

As Father Davey faced the casket, he reminisced, "Exactly one year, three months, two weeks, four days," glancing at his watch, he continued, "and one hour ago, Katie O'Neill walked into St. Anthony's rectory and into my life. How do I remember it so accurately, the exact moment in time? The answer is simple. No one could remain the same once she had touched your life.

"It wasn't an accident that Katie and her boys found their way to Eden Croft. It was a long journey for a wee, Irish lass. That too, was part of God's plan. And what an impact it had on all of us. Her mere presence served as a weaver's loom, working the threads of so many solitary lives into a wondrous tapestry. She brought joy, laughter, humanity, kindness and love in her own, unique way and each of us is a better person for having known her. Heaven *and* earth are richer for having been blessed with her presence.

"Anam Cara. I doubt any of you are familiar with the term. 'Tis a Gaelic phrase … a Celtic notion about relationships. Anam is Irish for soul and cara means friend. Celtic spiritual tradition teaches that the human soul hovers around the body like a vibrant halo, an aura. 'Tis believed that the potential for a special type of relationship exists before time and is aroused and awakened when two kindred spirits find each other. Anam cara is what results when two like souls meet and flow together. Once this relationship, this union, binds two people together, that bond cannot be broken by time, by space or even death. An anam cara accepts you unconditionally for who you are. In doing so, helps to give birth to your own soul and that is the legacy of Mary Katherine O'Neill.

"In saying good-bye to the physical presence of Katie, I would like to recite a poem by an Irish poet, E. Gary Brooks. It was one of Katie's cherished favorites. It embodies both her love of nature and her love of *Ireland*.

Take me home to Shamrock Hill.
The glorious place of my birth.
When the glens are green and the heather grows
'Tis the prettiest place on earth.
The wind blows free and the air is fresh
And I still hear a rippling rill.
My heart is sad, but I could be glad
Take me home to Shamrock Hill.

chapter forty-five

As Father Davey predicted, the pain of loss didn't go away soon. Each boy experienced it in different ways. The twins, who had formed their common bond in the womb and were nearly inseparable in the past, clung even more strongly to one another. They were unsure of anything other than an acute awareness that they missed their mommy. Locked in the immediate present, they needed everything familiar to go on without interruption. Beyond that, they were incapable of understanding the finality of death and why their mommy was never coming back.

Brendan's pain was temporarily appeased by the need to assume the role of surrogate parent. He seemed obsessed with being both a father and a mother to his younger brothers and rarely let them out of his sight. He never went to bed until he was sure they were asleep for the night. He woke early in the morning to get them dressed, herded them to the table for meals and tucked them into bed at night. Brendan scolded them when they misbehaved like a mother goose tending to her goslings. He refused to spend any time away from home. It was as if, overnight, he went from being a boy of fourteen to being a man of forty.

But, the saddest of the four was Tommy. He seemed the most lost, the one suffering the greatest pain. There was no comforting twin for him to hold fast to and he was too young to assume the big brother role. He was old enough to grasp the reality of the permanence of death but too young to know how to deal with it. He had nowhere to channel the pain of his grief and sense of displacement. Tommy was like a lamb separated from the ewe, scared, lonely and vulnerable, lost in a futile search to reconnect with his mommy. Brendan was unapproachable, too occupied with his sense of responsibility. So, Tommy sought refuge where he felt the safest, with Chance and Abraham.

Abraham opened his heart and soul to the boys, but especially to Tommy. He could see and feel Tommy's constant need for comfort and reassurance and responded as lovingly as he knew how. If Tommy needed to talk, Abraham listened and he made himself available day and night. Tommy shadowed Abraham's every step. The two of them worked together in the gardens. Abraham had helped him plant a bed of lilies of the valley alongside the gazebo. When Chance threatened the young shoots, Tommy shooed him away, "Stay out of the lilies, Chance. This is Mommy's garden."

Yet, as sensitive and steadfast as Abraham tried to be, Tommy's eyes, haunted with abandonment, plagued him.

Influenced by Father Davey's intercession and pending the conclusion of the investigation and submission of the official recommendation of the Child Welfare Agency, Judge Aldridge issued a temporary order that allowed the O'Neill children to remain in their home in the custody of Dr. Franke. The Judge reserved his final ruling until the official hearing and set a date for August twenty-seventh.

Tension and worry hung over the O'Neill home like a funeral shroud as they began the six-week-wait in a tenuous state of purgatory. Abraham's worry about the adoption translated to the boys. They knew that their entire future hinged on the judge, a faceless stranger they had never met. Add in the mixture of fear, grief, sadness and loss and one had all the ingredients for a full-blown tempest and the clouds were already dark and threatening.

Abraham was floundering. He felt as if he were teetering on a tightrope, his steps furtive with hesitancy, almost immobilized by uncertainty. He feared that instead of making matters easier, he was only succeeding in making them worse. If he was failing Tommy, his bigger failure was with Brendan and the twins. His relationship with them was collapsing. Whatever he said, it always managed to come out the wrong way at the wrong time. His efforts were met with challenges and animosity. Most of the time, Brendan resented his intervention, his advice, even his presence. The twins followed Brendan's example and acted up, sassed and threw temper tantrums like they were on a time clock. Yet, if they had reached out to him, Abraham hadn't the slightest idea how to reach back.

The only two constants in their lives were Lottie and Jadyne. Their presence brought a soothing calm to the household. Lottie's humor and relaxed attitude managed to bring some laughter and sunshine into their lives. And Jadyne was a solid, familiar anchor of stability. How those two women managed to succeed so effortlessly was a mystery to Abraham.

Early one morning, before the boys were awake, Abraham shared his concerns with Jadyne. "I am very much afraid that Katie overestimated my abilities. I am very fearful that this arrangement is a horrible mistake."

Jadyne kept her cool. "Dr. Franke! I'm disappointed in you. I can't believe that you're willing to admit defeat so quickly. None of us thought this was going to be easy."

"I cannot help feeling discouraged. Feeling that I am failing them in every way. It is not for me that I am concerned. It is for those boys. Everything I try to do only ends in mayhem. My ineptitude seems more apparent with each day. It is as if they are drowning and I am incapable of fighting the undertow that keeps pulling them farther away, farther under. It is not only with Casey and

Colin and Tommy that I feel so inadequate. Where Brendan is concerned, I only seem capable of driving a wedge between us. What if I am unable to learn what it is they need? How will I ever be good for them?"

"The little ones are pliable as taffy, Dr. Franke. As long as there is someone to love them, and cradle them and kiss their cuts and scrapes, they'll latch right on. It's just going to take some time. It's with older children that things get a little trickier. For older children it is much more personal. Though Brendan is older, he is more vulnerable and less trusting. He is confused and scared, unaware that he is frightened that he will lose you, too. Give him some time to discover that. Until he does, he needs understanding, not in your way or according to your time clock, but in his own way and in his own time."

Abraham didn't need to verbalize his frustrations. Jadyne saw it in his eyes. He was suffering as much as the boys with his own torments. But, if he was going to come to her for advice, then advice was what she was going to give him.

"You have the blood of great men coursing through your veins. Your heritage dates back to a strong and proud people. Hasn't the history of your people taught you anything? Moses led the Hebrews out of Egyptian bondage and then wandered around the desert for forty years looking for the Promised Land. Joshua brought down the great walls of Jericho with trumpets. David defeated the Philistine giant, Goliath, with a sling and stone. And you're ready to admit defeat at the hands of four young boys who need you more than they've ever needed anyone before?"

"I am no Moses, or Joshua or David," he answered.

"Not all great men are found in the Bible or in history books. Most of them achieve greatness in small ways, in quiet ways. Miss Katie was smart enough to see that greatness in you."

"I have asked myself many times a day what Katie would have done? What would their father have done? What would Lottie or Jadyne do? What would Zora do?"

Jadyne shook her head. "That's where you're making the biggest mistake. Have you asked yourself what would Abraham do?"

Abraham searched his mind before he responded.

"It has been too many years. I lost Daniel when he was a small boy. I have forgotten what a boys needs. I have forgotten how to be a father."

"That's not something a father ever forgets, Dr. Franke, not ever. Not the good ones. And if I were a betting woman, I'd bet that you were a good one.

"If you were a woman, I'd tell you to go have a good cry, then pick yourself up and get right back on that horse and ride it for all it's worth. But, since you're a man, my advice is a little different. What you need to do is rely on your good sense and sensibility. Look to Abraham Franke, the father. Everything you need is right there. You possess wisdom, patience, compassion and love. With that combination, you can't miss. Trust your instincts. It's why God gave them to you. And God has also given you something that no one else has. Something Miss Katie put a great deal of stock in. He has given you time."

Jadyne pushed up from the table with her thick arms and said, "The good Lord may have given you the luxury of time, but not me. I got my chores to get to. And I'd better get to fixing those boys' breakfasts. They'll be up soon enough."

⁂ ⁂

That night, Abraham was jolted awake by Tommy's cries. Quickly, he came running out of the spare bedroom and switched on the hallway light. He met Brendan coming out of his own room.

"It's Tommy. He's having a nightmare." Brendan's face was set in willful determination. "He's my brother. I'll take care of him."

Abraham's first thought was to stand firm and take control and insist that he could handle the situation. Then, an instinctual feeling caused him to pause and alter his approach. Jadyne's words of advice echoed in his mind. With a gentle smile, he quietly acknowledged Brendan's assertions.

"You are absolutely correct. He needs his big brother right now. You go to him. If you need anything, I will be reading in my room."

With that said, Abraham returned to his bed.

"Tommy ... Tommy, wake up." Brendan shook him by the shoulders, trying to jolt him from the nightmare.

"It's Bren, Tommy. Come on ... wake up."

Finally, Tommy opened his eyes and looked around the room. He was frightened and disoriented but awake. His body still trembled and his pajamas were damp from perspiration.

"Nothing's gonna hurt you. You just had another bad dream."

Tommy asked, "Where's Dr. Franke?"

"He's asleep. Why? What'd ya need him for?" Brendan was both angered and hurt by the question.

Tommy was confused. "How come you don't like him, Bren?"

"I like him some. I just don't need him."

"Sometimes I need him. I miss Mommy an' Dr. Franke says it's okay to miss her. When I really miss her, Dr. Franke makes me feel better."

"You don't need Dr. Franke. You got me."

"You know, Dr. Franke told me that he had a little boy once, a long time ago, jus' like me."

Brendan hadn't known and was surprised. "What happened to him?"

"Dr. Franke said he got killed in the war. The war Daddy was in. Bad people killed him. How come people gotta die, Bren?"

"Sooner or later, everything dies."

"But, how come Mommy had ta die?"

"'Cuz she got sick."

"I got real sick an' I didn't die. How come she did?"

"You had a different kinda sick. Mom got cancer. People die from cancer."

"How come?"

Brendan grew frustrated. "'Cuz they do, that's all."

"Dr. Franke says Mommy's in heaven where she won't be sick anymore."

"I guess so."

"Will you sing me a song? Like Mommy?"

"No, you little runt. I won't sing you a song."

"Mommy always sanged me a song. So's I could go back to sleep."

"Well, Mom isn't here, anymore," Brendan spoke with finality.

"Don't you miss her?"

"I try not to think about it."

"Are you mad at Mommy?"

"Sometimes."

"How come?"

Brendan thought for a minute before he answered. "Mostly 'cuz she left us. Left us to live with strangers."

"Dr. Franke isn't a stranger. He knows us good."

"Yeah, well you don't know half a what's going on."

"Mommy said Dr. Franke loves us."

The closed doors hadn't secured total privacy; the muffled conversations hadn't gone unheard. Brendan had overheard the whispered murmurings, the pointed discussions about the adoption proceedings. First his dad died, then his mom and now they were all going to end up in an orphanage. He had made up his mind that you couldn't count on grown-ups for anything. They all ended up breaking their promises. They all ended up leaving you.

"Yeah, well maybe he does and maybe he doesn't. Come on, take off your pajamas, they're soaking wet."

"What'll I sleep in?"

"Jus' sleep in your underpants."

"Bren?"

"What?"

"You won't die, will you?"

"Don't be a nimrod. 'Course I won't. Now go to sleep … I'm tired."

"Bren?"

"Now what?"

"Will you sleep with me?"

Brendan looked down at his little brother, his arms akimbo, and rolled the idea around in his head. Finally, he sighed. "Okay, runt, just this once. But don't you dare let me catch you tellin' the guys."

chapter forty-six

"Matt, I hate ta disturb yawr beauty sleep, but I'm thinkin' we might jus' have us a slight hiccup, here."

That was how Lottie started the story of the unexpected visit from Miss Edith Corley.

Jadyne had asked for a couple of days off. Her daughter had delivered her second child, a boy, and Jadyne wanted to be there to help when they came home from the hospital.

Matt urged Lottie not to turn this into an epic saga. Just give him the condensed version and omit the embellishments.

Lottie had come over to the house, at the ungodly hour of seven o'clock in the morning, no less, to help get the boys their breakfast. She didn't even take the time to get dressed, just came over in her nightgown, robe and slippers. She and Abraham were having their first morning cup of coffee, when guess who showed up, unannounced, mind you, at the back door? None other than the old witch herself, Edith Corley. She had taken one look at the two of them, still dressed in their nightclothes, and sort of drew her own conclusions. She flew out of there like a house afire without pause or explanation. It was then that Lottie and Abraham decided they had better telephone Matt.

"Lottie! For Christ's sake! That's not a hiccup. It's more like Mauna Loa and it's going to erupt right in our faces."

Matt raked his hand through his tousled hair and tried to clear his thoughts. He recalled the adage that disappointments, disasters and death always come in threes. The initial report from Edith Corley was the first. This latest confrontation between Lottie, Abraham and Edith was the second. Matt was afraid to contemplate what the third disaster might be.

"Dammit. What in the hell were you two thinking? You knew that Corley had you under a microscope. That she would scrutinize every breath you took. How could you be so stupid? That woman has been looking for something just like this. Something concrete to use against us and you've sure as hell given her something now and served it up on a silver platter."

"Don't be getting' yawr BVDs in a bunch. It ain't like there wuz anythin' goin' on."

"Well, of course. You're absolutely right. I don't know what I was thinking.
I'm sure old lady Corley will be in total agreement with us. She's a reasonable,
understanding compassionate person. This incident was only a simple misunderstanding. Next time she has me over for dinner, I'm sure we'll have a good
laugh over this. It must be wonderful living in that fantasy world of yours."
Matt's words dripped with sarcasm. "Put Abraham on. I need to talk to him.
Maybe one of you is still in possession of an ounce of common sense. I'll need
to see both of you at my office. Today. Hopefully, *properly* attired."

Matt had been feeling the pressure of time. The hearing was only two
weeks away and time was running out. He had searched every legal text, called
in every favor and racked his brain trying to establish a legal precedent that
would support their case. But, he had reached the conclusion that the key factor was Abraham. He would bear the burden of convincing Judge Aldridge.
Matt could cite precedents, spout legalese, plead his case, but in the end, it all
rested on Abraham's testimony.

He had scheduled one last meeting to prepare Abraham. They had repeatedly gone over all of the details until he felt comfortable that they had
covered every base. There were only two factors that remained a question
mark. Like the two sides of a scale, would the balance tip in their favor? On the
one side was Abraham. Would he hold up in court? On the other side was
Edith Corley.

At some point in time they would have to sit back, try to relax and trust in
themselves and that they had done their best and then wait. Matt had felt that
after that last meeting they had reached that point. Then Lottie dropped the
hand grenade in his lap.

೫ ೩

Lottie and Abraham arrived at Matt's office.

"How much damage could this cause?" Abraham had been afraid to ask
the question.

"I won't pretend that it hasn't caused a whole new set of problems. What
were you two thinking?"

Abraham apologized. "I am so sorry, Matthew. Unfortunately, I am afraid
that we were not thinking. It was all so innocent. We did not anticipate a
problem."

"It's not like we were sittin' there buck naked. We did have clothes on,"
Lottie tried to defend them.

"You may as well have been naked. You were in your bedclothes. There's a
big difference."

"Ma peignoir covers me from earlobes ta ankles. Mos' women have bathin'
suits more revealin' than that. Tha boys've seen me in ma nighties lotsa times."

"Quit looking through those rose-colored glasses of yours. The boys aren't Abraham. It doesn't look good."

"Is it our fault that she's got a dirty mind? Tha ol' battle ax has been a boil on ma butt since day one!"

"Well, boil or boon, she's a reality and one that we have to deal with," Matt said as sharply as he could.

"What biznuss does Evil-eye Corley have showin' up without so much as a telephone call, anyway? Seems kinda rude ta me." Lottie was furious.

"Showing up unannounced *is* her business. And as much as I dislike the woman, she was only doing her job. She is required to make spontaneous visits to observe the home environment on an impromptu basis," Matt explained sternly.

"More'n likely tryin' ta dig up some dirt on Abraham. In ma opinion, she ain't nothin' but a bitter ol' bat an' uglier than tha north end of a mule goin' south."

"If you want to put it that way, yes, she is trying to find as much dirt as she can. And your opinion doesn't count."

"How's 'bout we kidnap them yunguns? With all ma money we oughta be able ta disappear in South America er China er somewhere else where ain't nobody could find us."

Matt's patience was exhausted. He snapped at Lottie. "It scares me to think that you are probably serious. There will be no kidnapping or disappearing anywhere."

Abraham intervened. "This arguing is counterproductive. What is done is done. We cannot take it back. The question is how do we defuse this bomb?"

Matt paced back and forth behind his desk trying to burn off some steam. He finally stopped and leaned with both hands on his desk.

"I'm fairly certain that Lottie will now be called to testify. To head them off at the pass, I'm going to list her as my witness and hope to call her to the stand first. That way, it will appear that we have nothing to hide. Am I right? You two don't have anything else to hide, do you? I don't want any surprises when I put both of you on the stand."

"We have nothing to hide, Matthew," Abraham quickly responded.

"All right, we haven't got a lot of time, so let's get started."

Matt settled at his desk and prepared to take notes on his yellow legal pad. "So, Lottie, you came over to the house this morning. Why?"

"Abraham had an early meetin' at tha college an' had ta leave tha house by seven-thirty. We wuz jus' havin' a cup a coffee before he got dressed. I wuz there ta get breakfast fawr tha boys."

Matt looked up from his desk with skepticism. "*You* were going to cook breakfast?"

"Look, we all know I ain't no Sara Lee, but even I kin manage ta pour Wheaties inta a bowl."

Matt bit back a cutting remark. "And that was it? Nothing happened?"

"What are you asking, Matthew?" Abraham questioned.

"I'm only asking what I need to. Believe me, they are going to ask these same questions and they won't be nearly as delicate as I'm being. Now, I need to know if anything is going on between you two?"

Abraham and Lottie sat looking guilty as two children caught with their hands in the cookie jar. Finally, it was Abraham who spoke.

"Matthew, you have my solemn word that nothing immoral has happened between Loretta and myself."

Matt quizzed Lottie and Abraham for nearly two hours before he was satisfied that no additional information was forthcoming. But, when the two left his office, in spite of Abraham's insistence, he had a nagging feeling that they were holding something back. Something important. Something they didn't want to tell him. More often than not, his clients proved to be more of a challenge than the opposition. He only hoped and prayed that whatever it was they were hiding, it wouldn't sneak up and bite him in the ass.

As Lottie and Abraham exited the office building, it was Lottie who broached the subject. "I sure hope y'all know what yawr doin', Abraham. I'm not so sure we shouldn'ta come clean with Matt. This lyin' business jus' don't sit right with me. I got me a real bad feelin' 'bout this."

Abraham took her arm as they walked to the car.

"Technically, we did not lie. We only held back the truth. Three weeks ago, Jadyne gave me some advice. She told me to trust my instincts. Now, Loretta, I am asking you to do the same."

chapter forty-seven

As the days passed, they took with them some of the sorrow of Katie's death. Abraham began to feel that Katie had been right. Under normal circumstances, time was the great healer. It would have allowed acceptance to replace the incomprehensible and ease the pain. However, Katie couldn't have known that the passage of time couldn't help Brendan, Tommy, Casey and Colin face a precarious and uncertain future.

It tugged at Abraham's heart. Though the younger boys were somewhat insulated and protected from the whole truth, he knew that even they could sense the tension and turmoil that had a stranglehold on everyone around them. And for Brendan who was already in a fragile emotional state was forced to walk an emotional gauntlet as cognizance and hopelessness tugged at him from both sides.

Brendan felt totally alone. Miss Lottie and Miss Jade were too pre-occupied with the demands of the household. Mr. Mulholland was totally absorbed in the adoption and court hearing. And Dr. Franke had become the enemy instead of an ally. Brendan saw Abraham as just another grown-up who would end up disappointing him. He considered Abraham to be almost as frightening as the alternatives. If Brendan had known how to reach out to any of them, Miss Lottie, Miss Jade or Abraham, his supplication would have met with gentleness and open arms. But, he didn't know how, so he turned a cold shoulder and heart to them.

Brendan made no effort to reach out to the Musketeers, either. And they had no idea what he needed or how to provide it. Even Vinnie could do nothing to assuage Brendan's wounded soul. Brendan seemed resigned to the worst, and in his resignation, he wandered through each day in a perfunctory trance, walked, breathed, ate, did no more and no less than was necessary.

Frank Mizzano knew that the self-imposed isolation Brendan had immersed himself in had gone on long enough. Vinnie hadn't seen or even heard from Brendan in more than a month. Frank knew that Brendan needed his friends. He also knew that the human contact that was needed when one wais grieving was also the hardest to ask for. It was hardest to reach out when all you wanted to do was disappear from the world. If Brendan wouldn't come to Vinnie, then Vinnie needed to go to him.

Frank telephoned the O'Neill house to see if a visit from Vinnie would be all right. Abraham appreciated Frank's thoughtfulness and encouraged him to drive Vinnie over that afternoon.

It was hot outside but inside the dark garage it was cool and smelled of paint and varnish. The two boys were in Abraham's garage, looking at Brendan's sailboat. Even in the dim light, the boat was sleek and shiny, the refurbishing nearly done and ready for her maiden voyage. A voyage that Brendan knew he would never witness. He had lost all interest in the project. Any sense of accomplishment or satisfaction he had enjoyed in the past was gone. His labor of love had simply become a distraction. His beautiful boat, a culmination of weeks and months of work, would never feel him at her helm.

"You're lucky, Sox," Vinnie stated as he ran his hand over the polished brass cleats.

"Why's that?"

"You're just lucky ... that's all."

Brendan rolled his eyes and responded with a weak laugh. ""Oh yeah ... I'm real lucky. I'm never going to be able to sail her."

"I'm not talking about the sailboat. I'm talking about your mom. I mean ... at least you got to know your mom. I never knew mine."

"Big deal. What difference does it make, now?"

"It makes a big difference. You're just being too big an asshole feeling sorry for yourself to see it."

Brendan leaned back against the stern and folded his arms across his chest. "Okay, wise guy, so I'm an asshole. You tell me, why am I so friggin' lucky."

"You're lucky because you got to see her ... know what she looked like. Not just in a picture, but you got to see her for real. You got to touch her, Sox. Do you know what I'd give to touch my mom just once? Your mom was real to you. You got to talk to her about stuff, got to hear her voice instead of trying to imagine what it sounded like. I never heard my mom's voice. Not one time. You had things the way they really were instead of just the way you wanted them to be.

"I used to think that my mom woulda been like yours. I'd pretend that if my mom were alive that she'd been exactly like her. Not look like her, but *been* like her. Watching me play ball. Cooking ... making cookies and having picnics ... doing stuff like that. Even yelling at me."

Brendan thought it over. "At least you've still got your dad. I'm an orphan."

"Yeah, I do have my dad, but you've got three brothers. They're a pain in the ass, but at least you still got 'em. It's kinda like you're still a family."

"Well, we ain't gonna be a family for long."

"What'd'ya mean? Isn't Dr. Franke gonna adopt you, Sox?"

"I heard stuff."

"What stuff?" Vinnie asked

"There's this old lady that decides who gets to adopt us. She doesn't like Dr. Franke. If she doesn't like him, then we don't get adopted. They bust us up or put us in an orphanage."

For a minute, Brendan and Vinnie were quiet, each lost in their own thoughts.

"What ya gonna do if they don't let you stay with Dr. Franke?"

"There ain't a lot I can do. Besides, it doesn't matter what any of us wants, anyway."

"You could run away. Join the army."

"At fourteen? Yeah, like that's gonna happen. Besides, what about the rug rats? It's not like I could run out on them."

"If you get busted up and have to live somewhere else, then what difference would it make?"

"I guess not much."

"If you did run away, I'd do it with you, Sox."

"No way. The team needs you. Nobody can catch a fastball low and inside like you can."

"If you're gone, there's nobody can hit that inside corner."

They stood in silence for a while then Brendan spoke. "If anything happens, Vinnie ... I mean if I get sent away ... I want you to have the boat."

Vinnie had a hard time finding the words. "If you get sent away, I'll miss you, Sox."

With hopelessness in his voice, Brendan mumbled, "I'll miss you, too."

☙ ❧

Jadyne was back and the house returned to its routine under her supervision. She was pouring batter into the waffle iron when the twins came running into the kitchen. They toppled two chairs as Casey chased Colin around the kitchen table.

Abraham lifted his coffee cup from the table to avoid spillage. He greeted the twins. "Good morning. It looks as though you are full of energy bright and early this morning."

"Slow it down, you two, right now! I'll have no running in the house. That's why God made the outside. And straighten those chairs. Land Sakes! I go away for a few days and the whole house goes to Hades in a hand basket," Jadyne scolded them.

"We ran around the house when you was in Sickago," Casey taunted.

Abraham gave him a warning look and put his index fingers to his lips.

"I hate to think what went on while I was gone. Well, I'm back from Chica-go, now."

She gave Abraham the evil eye and continued, "And Dr. Franke may have let you get away with no manners, but not me. I won't have people thinking you were raised in a barn. People in a civilized society need to know how to behave. Your momma didn't raise you to act like barbarians. Now, sit down proper at the table. I've got a batch of waffles here with your names on them."

The twins drowned their waffles in maple syrup and started to dig in when Jadyne stopped them cold and grabbed their hands, forks held in mid-air. "Hold on. I haven't heard either of you thank the Lord. If your momma was looking down on you right now, wouldn't she be disappointed."

"Can Mommy really see us?" Colin asked.

"Of course she can. She can look right down at you from heaven anytime she wants. To make sure you're behaving and that we're taking good care of you."

Casey told Miss Jade, "Bren says we're orphans now. 'Cuz we don't got a mommy and daddy."

"Well, you're not orphans. You have a mommy and daddy."

"But they ain't here. They're dead," Casey argued.

"It doesn't matter that they're not here. You still have them."

Colin questioned, "Then what's an orphan?"

"An orphan is somebody that doesn't have a home or anyone to take care of them ... to love them. You have a home and Dr. Franke and me to take care of you. Say grace, now, and eat your breakfast before it gets cold."

Brendan came in as they were finishing grace and sat down in his chair. Jadyne poured him a glass of fresh squeezed orange juice.

"Glad you could make it. Where's Tommy?"

"He was still getting dressed. He'll be down in a minute. He wanted to feed Timothy."

"Well, I'm glad to see that one man in this house is taking his responsibilities seriously."

Abraham winked at the twins. "If that remark was directed at me, then it is a point well taken. You have my solemn word as a gentleman that I will never let the boys run in the house, again."

Just then, Tommy walked into the kitchen. Tears stained his cheeks as he held out one tiny hand that cupped his turtle. Slowly, one by one, Tommy searched their faces. Tommy's expression and the unmoving creature in his hand told the story. Everyone knew what had happened, but it was Abraham who found speech first.

"Come over here, Tommy. Bring Timothy over to me."

Abraham stretched out his arm invitingly. Tommy walked into it letting Abraham wrap his arm around his shoulder. Tommy managed two barely audible words.

"Timothy's dead." His voice trembled from crying.

Jadyne, who handled every crisis with the composure of a drill sergeant, was on the verge of tears, herself.

Abraham gently stroked the turtle's shell. Tommy shook his head.

"I already done that, Dr. Franke. He doesn't move 'cuz he's dead. I fed him everyday, like I was s'posed to. I changed his water, cleaned his bowl. I didn't let Chance bite him even once. I took real good care of him."

"I am sure you did, Tommy."

"Then how come he died?"

Abraham looked into Tommy's searching, questioning, desperate eyes and his heart nearly broke.

"Sometimes Tommy, no matter how much care we take, things die."

"Do ya think Timothy's gonna go to heaven like Mommy an' Daddy?"

"I know he is."

"Then I guess it's okay he died. But, I'm gonna miss him a lot."

"Of course you will. But, you will always have happy memories of him. In that way, something or someone that dies is never really gone. We keep them alive forever, in our memories. And every time you read *Timothy Turtle,* it will help you to remember your little friend."

Abraham gave Tommy a hug and wiped his tears with a napkin. "Do you want to have a funeral for him?"

"Like Mommy's?"

"In a way yes … like your mommy's."

"I don't think so. Turtles don't like dirt. They like water. When Douglas Kirby's goldfish died, he flushed it down the toilet."

"That is one way to have a funeral, I suppose. Is that what you would like to do with Timothy?"

Tommy hesitated before he answered. He wasn't completely sold on the toilet idea. "I s'pose."

"I think I may have a better idea. We have that great big lake out there. Do you think Timothy would be happier if we had a burial in the lake?"

"How can ya bury him in the lake?"

"When a sailor dies while he is far away on the ocean, they have a funeral and return his body to the water."

Tommy thought for a moment and decided it was way better. "I think you're right. I'd rather have a burial in the lake than in the toilet."

Abraham and Tommy spent the rest of the morning fashioning a coffin from an empty Quaker Oats box. They cushioned Timothy's resting place with a pillow of toilet tissue and placed a few of his favorite stones inside the coffin for weight and secured it with electrical tape and velvet ribbon.

That evening, under the magnificent pastels of a summer sunset, seven mourners gathered at the end of the dock and held the second funeral of the summer for a loved one.

As they made their way back to the house, Brendan lagged behind and stopped at the gazebo. He sat on the bottom step; shoulders slumped as if he were solely responsible for the entire universe. Abraham left Brendan alone with his private burdens and followed the others into the house.

More than an hour passed. Abraham, driven by worry and concern, stole moments of observation and watched Brendan from the oriel's window. He respected Brendan's need for privacy and distance, but Abraham couldn't help the disturbing feeling that he had let Brendan's torment go on too long. Had he left him too much time to be alone?

Abraham was a patient man, but restraint was harder when watching a child in pain. He wondered if he was being patient or was his delay to avoid failure? Did his reticence come from worry for Brendan or was he more frightened for himself? Was he afraid of not knowing the right words, or worse, saying the wrong ones?

He finally decided that Brendan's solitary bereavement was not healing him, but paralyzing him. Abraham finally decided that there was a time to remain silent and a time to speak. From the recesses of the buffet drawer, Abraham slowly withdrew the envelope where darkness had concealed it since the afternoon Katie had given it to him. Since the day she had died.

Silently, he asked Katie if this was the right time. Was this the moment she had intended, had known would arrive? With no more confidence than he had felt in any one of the days since her death, he turned the envelope over and over in his hand and hoped that the gesture would validate or nullify his decision. No revelation came. So, Abraham applied what he had learned from Katie. He choked back the doubts and made his way to the gazebo.

Abraham sat next to Brendan on the bottom step. Both sat facing the lake, side-by-side, yet a universe apart.

Finally, Abraham spoke. "When I miss your mother the most, this is where I come to be close to her. It was her special place and I imagine that I can still feel her presence here. When I am confused or worried, or simply miss her, I sit here and ask for her guidance, wisdom and company. Sometimes she is so real that I can almost hear her voice ... that I can almost reach out and touch her. When I am scared about the future, I seek comfort here, from her. She has never let me down, yet."

Brendan sat in profile and continued to stare at the lake as the last light of evening faded into night.

"The other morning, it was very early and there was a thick fog that had rolled in during the night. As I came outside, through the misty fog, I thought for a brief moment that I actually saw her sitting here, covered with an afghan, staring out at the lake just as you are doing now. Of course, it was only my imagination, but that is the most wondrous miracle of all. I can imagine and remember her anytime I want. She is never any further away than that split second that it takes me to bring her back to life in my mind.

"You know, Brendan, it is perfectly natural to feel anger that a great injustice has been done. It is normal to feel rage and fury that she was taken away from you. Let the anger run its course. But, please do not turn your anger toward her. She did not leave because she wanted to, as if she had a choice. She would have moved mountains to stay here, with her boys. We parents know our whole lives that there will come a day when we will not be there for our children. We spend every moment of every day preparing them for that day. Yet, no matter how hard we try, it is never long enough. We always want just one more day. For your mother, that day came too soon."

"I'm not mad at her. I'm mad at me," Brendan stated with anger in his voice.

"Why are you mad at yourself?"

"It's all my fault."

"What is, Brendan?"

"It's all my fault she died."

"It is no one's fault. She was just too ill." Abraham tried to soothe him.

"You don't understand. She's dead because of me. I was so mad at her. I said I hated her … that I wished she was dead. And now she is. Don't you see? It's all my fault." Brendan's voice broke. Now, everyone would know the awful truth and he felt so ashamed.

Abraham put a hand on his shoulder. "You cannot wish people dead just as you cannot wish them to be alive, again. Only God holds the power of life and death. For some unknown reason, one we are not meant to know at this time, He called your mother home to heaven. We live and die by God's plan, not ours."

"But I said I hated her."

"That is a very heavy burden you have been carrying around. Guilt is always the heaviest and the most unnecessary of punishments we inflict on ourselves. We foolish humans say a great deal of things we do not mean. Those who love us have the wisdom to recognize them. Your mother forgave you the instant those words were said. She knew you didn't mean it then. She knows you didn't mean it now."

Abraham held the envelope out and offered it to Brendan. "This is a letter your mother wrote when she knew she was dying. She gave it to me, as it would turn out, on her last day with us. She asked me to pass it on to you and your brothers when I felt it was the correct time. For you, I feel this is the time. She never read it to me and I have not broken the seal since. It is not addressed to me. It is addressed to you."

Brendan looked at the envelope for an eternity of seconds. Finally, he reached for it and read the address, *To My Boys*. He slid his finger under the flap and carefully opened it as if it were made of spun gold. His eyes and mind read the words, but Katie's voice spoke to him through his heart.

You are my boys.

You know me in ways no one else ever has. You teach me things I never thought I could learn and you opened up to me a world I never knew existed. You take me places I could only dream of. You carry me to heights of happiness and push me to the edge of exasperation. You teach me tears come from joy as well as sorrow. You touch every moment of my life and I am richer, happier, more blessed because of you.

You are the light of my soul and the energy of my spirit. You are my nourishment, the beat of my heart and the air in my lungs. I loved you from the first moment I could feel you stirring in my womb and I knew you before you took your first breath. The sun has never set on a day that I didn't feel privileged to be your mom.

You are my boys.

Brendan, my first born ... strong, determined, invincible. My rock.

Tommy ... gentle, kind, wise. My dove.

Casey ... bright, energetic, extraordinary. My star.

Colin ... carefree, creative, contented. My butterfly.

Not time, not distance, not even death can break our bond. I am never more than a heartbeat away, for I continue to live on, in all of you and through all of you. For you are my legacy. You are my future. You are my story and in some way, I hope I will be part of yours.

You are forever, my boys.

Brendan's eyes closed on the last words. Not a voluntary muscle moved. Only the involuntary rise and fall of his chest as his lungs automatically respired and expired. Abraham gave Brendan a few moments alone with his thoughts before he spoke.

"Let her words fill your soul and give you comfort. You know, dying is always the hardest on those left behind. Miss her with your whole heart. Cry a dozen times a day if you need to. It is nothing to be ashamed of. It does not make you any less a man. It makes you very human. Do not shut out the beautiful memories you have of her. I wasted too many years of my life trying to do just that."

Brendan began to sob. Quietly at first, then uncontrollably. The floodgates that had been damned up finally broke free. Abraham desperately wanted to put his arms around Brendan, but he resisted the urge. Abraham didn't want to rush him. Only Brendan could determine when he was ready to reach out. Brendan needed to make that decision for himself. And as if Katie had willed their two souls together, as if she had reached down from heaven and gently nudged her son and softened his heart, Brendan turned to Abraham and embraced him.

chapter forty-eight

Murray Chilton was tough, smart and had infinite more experience in family law and at the moment seemed to be holding all the trump cards.

Like civilized adversaries, he and Matt shook hands before they climbed the steps of the courthouse.

Since Eden Croft was the county seat, the hearing was to take place in the Blair County courthouse. Designed after a French chateau, it was stately and dignified, built from granite and ornately decorated with filigree wrought iron, copper trim, steep gables, slate roof, turrets, and cupolas. It had been constructed during the same lumbering era as many of the other structures in Eden Croft. Likewise, it had been built in the no expense spared boom days when lumber was king and money flowed freely.

Oaks, maples and ash that had set their roots down a century ago shaded the grounds and lined the wide slate walk that led from the commons to the courthouse steps. From three forty-foot tall flagpoles, proudly hung the United States, State of Michigan and Blair County flags. The hot, humid, thick August day provided no breeze and the flags hung limp, like wet dishrags.

The courthouse had, in its long history, on a few rare occasions, seen the more exciting and infamous trials of capital crimes. But, more commonly, it saw the everyday, mundane, non-sensational trials that involved misdemeanors, petty crimes and lesser felonies. The dockets were kept busy with, in descending order of frequency, probate, property disputes, small claims, traffic citations, divorces, annulments and adoptions.

Abraham had orders from Judge Aldridge to arrive an hour early so he would have the opportunity to meet with the boys privately in his chambers. No lawyers, no caseworkers, not court recorders, no potential parents, only himself and the O'Neill boys.

Lottie arrived at the house to help get the boys ready. Abraham nearly fainted from shock. Lottie had dressed in a totally un-Lottie like fashion. She had on a subdued, dove gray summer suit with three-quarter length sleeves, white linen collar and cuffs and wore a sedate gray and white straw hat with a modest nest of white tulle. She carried a pair of white gloves and her small alligator handbag that matched her conservative, alligator pumps. The only

jewelry she wore were pearl earrings and Katie's single strand, pearl necklace.
Her make-up was applied sparingly. But, the biggest shock of all was her hair,
partially hidden by her hat. For the first time in more years than Lottie cared to
count, her hair was its natural color, a soft, light brown. Eleanor had cut it
shorter and styled it in soft curls.

She warned Abraham. "Don't y'all say a word. I feel like an old maid goin'
ta a wake in sensible shoes."

"Actually, Loretta, never have I seen you look more lovely. I see you are
wearing the pearl necklace."

Lottie fingered the beads. "I figured since it wuz Katie's an' we're gonna be
needin' tha luck a' tha Irish today, it might help a bit ta have her in tha courtroom with us. 'Sides, seein' as how I could end up bein' tha star a tha show, I
hafta look respectable. An' this here dreary suit is 'bout tha only respectable
thing I could find."

Abraham gave her a hug. "Katie would be so pleased. And you would look
respectable, whatever you wore."

"Yawr jus' prejudice. Come on. Let's kick it inta high gear an' get this dog
an' pony show on tha road."

Before Deputy Emerson Crane escorted the boys into the judge's chambers, Abraham took one last minute to speak to Brendan. Abraham was shaken
when he looked at Brendan who looked so nervous that he might bolt and run
at the least provocation. He couldn't help but feel how unfair it was for one so
young to have to assume such burdensome responsibilities. Whatever the judge
decided, Abraham was as proud of Brendan as any father could be of his son.

"If the judge should not rule in our favor, it will have nothing to do with
you or what you might say in his chambers. The end result is a responsibility
that rests entirely on me. Brendan, just be as honest as you can. You will do fine
if you answer all his questions truthfully."

Abraham gave Brendan's shoulder a tight squeeze and signaled a "thumbs
up."

Judge Aldridge sat on the corner of his desk, his black robes unbuttoned
and hanging loosely. He gestured for the boys to sit down in the four leather
chairs that faced him.

The chambers were paneled in dark maple with three walls covered in
bookcases, filled floor to ceiling with legal texts. His chambers were on the
third floor of the courthouse and looked down on the commons. Setting on the
desk was a bronze statue, a green-globed library lamp, a stack of papers and a
large glass jar filled with colorful jawbreakers.

Judge Aldridge noticed the twins eyeing the candy jar.

"Does Dr. Franke let you have candy?" He asked, looking at the twins.

Casey nodded at the same time Colin shook his head.

"There seems to be contradictory opinions on that subject. Which one of you is Colin?"

Colin slowly raised his hand.

"Okay then, you must be Casey." He nodded at Casey and Casey nodded back.

"All right, Casey. Does Dr. Franke let you have candy? Tell the truth."

"Dr. Franke does. But, Miss Jadyne don't. Says it'll rot our teeth. Give us cabities. Says we can only eat it at special times like Christmas an' Easter."

"Sounds sensible to me. I think this is a pretty special occasion, don't you? And since I'm a pretty important person around here, you may each have one. But not the blue ones. Those are my favorites."

He offered the jar to the boys and each one, with the exception of Brendan, took one and responded with a "thank you."

"My name is Judge Aldridge and I've heard an awful about you four boys. I am pleased to finally meet you."

He smiled at the boys, amused. They sat like three little chipmunks; each had one fat cheek that bulged with the jawbreakers.

"You young men look very dapper in those suits and ties."

"We got 'em when Mommy got dead. Had to wear 'em for her foonrel I don't like wearin' 'em. Miss Jade said we hafta." Casey explained.

Brendan elbowed him to be quiet.

"I don't blame you, Casey. I'm not a big fan of suits and ties, either. Just like Miss Jade, my wife makes we wear them, too." Judge Aldridge spoke to the twins, first. "How do people tell you two apart?"

"Sister Benedetta had to pin our names on our shirts," Colin replied.

"I'm sure you don't wear name tags at home. How does Dr. Franke know who is who?"

The twins shrugged and Colin answered, "Don't know. He jus' does."

Judge Aldridge contemplated that for a moment. "Are you boys always this polite and well behaved?"

Casey was quick to answer. "Heck no. Only Tommy is ever this good. Mos'ly we're pretty bad. Miss Jade says I'm the worstest one. But, Colin's almost as bad. But, Miss Jade said we had to mind our manners 'cuz you was an important man."

"Except for the suit and tie thing, I'm beginning to like this Miss Jade. Tommy. May I call you Tommy or do you prefer Thomas?"

"Everybody calls me Tommy."

"I have a grandson named Tommy. But he's not as well behaved as you. Tell me, Tommy, what you like about Dr. Franke."

Tommy thought for a few seconds. "He lets me hoe weeds an' work with him in the garden. Gives me real important jobs to do. He reads me stories. An' he helped me bury Timothy in the lake instead of the toilet."

The judge's brow wrinkled with confusion. "Who's Timothy?"

"Not who. What. Timothy's my turtle. Least he was 'til he died. Dr. Franke said it was better to bury him in the lake instead of the toilet."

"I must admit that I'd have to agree with Dr. Franke on that point." Judge Aldridge looked at Brendan. "Did Dr. Franke coach you? Tell you what to say in here?"

Brendan hesitated a moment.

"Don't worry, Brendan. There are no right or wrong answers here. Just tell the truth."

"That's what Dr. Franke said, sir. To tell the truth."

"Did he tell you anything else?"

"That everything would be all right if I was honest."

The judge slid off the desk, walked around to his chair and sat down. He glanced at one of the papers on his desk and continued.

"Brendan. I want to ask you about Mrs. Devereaux."

"You mean Miss Lottie?"

"Yes … about Miss Lottie. Does she ever spend the night at your house? Sleep over?"

Brendan wasn't sure what that had to do with anything. "Yes, sir."

"How often does she spend the night?"

"She doesn't anymore. When Mom was sick, she would spend the night a lot, sitting with Mom in her room in case she needed something during the night. Dr. Franke and Miss Lottie took turns."

The judge extracted a fountain pen from his shirt pocket and made some notes on his papers.

"How do you feel about living with Dr. Franke, Brendan? Having him adopt you?"

"He cares about us. What happens to us. I'd rather live with him than anybody else."

It was the first time that Brendan had admitted it beyond his thoughts. The first time he had said it out loud. Brendan realized that it was the truth and it wasn't scary at all.

Judge Aldridge pointed at the statue sitting on his desk and asked, "Brendan, do you know what that statue is called?"

Brendan shook his head. "No, sir."

"That's a famous statue called 'Blind Justice.' She stands as a constant re-minder to us, that the law must be as fair as possible. She is blindfolded so that she is always fair and impartial in weighing what is right and what is wrong. I have her on my desk so that I never forget that. Deciding what is right and what is wrong is the most important part of my job. It is also the hardest part of my job. I have to hear both sides and then make my decision based on what I hear, not what I see or want to see.

"I want you boys to understand that no matter what happens here, today, that I will have made my decision based on not only what is just and fair, but most importantly, what I feel is in your best interest. Are you four boys willing to accept that? Whatever I decide?"

Tommy and the twins looked at Brendan and waited for his answer.

Brendan responded slowly. "Yes, sir."

"What Bren says, goes," Tommy added.

The twins nodded in agreement.

"Good. We've got that settled. That's what I like to see. Brothers that stick together."

The judge called on his intercom for Emerson to come in and take the boys.

"Gentlemen, I think you all did very well. It was my pleasure to meet you. You won't be allowed in the courtroom. That's for us grown-ups. But this nice deputy is going to take you to another room where you can wait. There are some games and puzzles there and if you are very good, he's going to take you to Hasting's for ice cream."

"Can't have no ice cream, Judge. 'Cept for dessert," Casey told him. "Miss Jade says we can't have no ice cream 'til after dinner."

"Normally, that's a darn good rule. But, I'm the boss here and everyone has to obey my rules. I say that this time you can have ice cream *before* dinner."

Lottie and Abraham were seated behind the railing, in the front row, directly in back of Matt. He was talking to them when Edith Corley and Murray Chilton entered the courtroom looking sober as a Druid priest and priestess. Each carried a briefcase as they walked up to and through the railing and settled themselves at the table on the right side of the room. They opened their briefcases, removed files and paperwork, and made an elaborate display of arranging them on the table.

Lottie performed a quick critique of Edith's toilette. She had a salt and pepper crew cut without enough length for a wave or curl. She wore a severe, black serge suit and ugly shoes and Lottie harbored a wicked wish that she would keel over from heat prostration in the suffocating heat of the room.

Lottie whispered, "She's got beady eyes an' walks like someone shoved a poker up her butt."

In spite of the tension, Abraham and Matt had to stifle a laugh.

Matt said, "I'm glad you brought your sense of humor today, Lottie. We're going to need a healthy dose of it. I hope that same poker doesn't end up our butts when this hearing is over."

Matt thought that Lottie's description was right on the money. Edith was nearly six feet tall and without an ounce of fat to spare. She also didn't have one feminine curve to her body and walked and sat military style, as if supported by a steel pipe instead of a spine. She had the kind of body that made one question if God was on a coffee break when her DNA was being formed. Her X and Y chromosomes had gotten mixed up a bit and she was female only in the strictest anatomical sense.

The courtroom was cavernous with high ceilings, white plaster walls, dark walnut trim and beams. Long, wooden benches, like church pews, lined the two sides of the center aisle that split the room in two. A large, wooden carving of the seal of Blair County hung on the wall behind the judge's chair.

Massive and imposing, the walnut judge's bench, that faced the courtroom, was raised by two steps. By its proportions and position, it dominated the room and emitted a sense of authority and finality. Four huge fans hung from the ceiling beams and slowly rotated, trying to circulate the heavy, stagnant air in the room. The fans weren't succeeding. It wasn't even nine o'clock and already the room was sizzling.

It was a closed session and twelve sequestered chairs, reserved for a jury, sat empty. Father Davey, Dr. Hughes and Jadyne, as the principals, were the only other spectators allowed in the courtroom. Abraham smiled appreciatively at each one of them. The bailiff, Stu Baskins, court stenographer, Elaine Martz, and clerk, Nancy VanHerweg, entered from a door at the front and right of the room.

They hadn't been settled in their seats for two minutes when Stu ordered everyone to rise as he announced that the Honorable Judge Wilson Aldridge would be presiding. All stood as the judge entered from his chambers. As soon as the judge was ensconced in his throne, he instructed everyone to please be seated.

Judge Aldridge reminded Lottie of Friar Tuck. He was roly-poly plump with a halo of snowy white hair circling his otherwise baldhead. Bushy, tufted eyebrows like cotton balls and chubby pink cheeks gave him a friendly, kind appearance. Wire rimmed spectacles perched on the end of his nose. He had a habit of lowering his head and peering with sharp brown eyes over the top of his glasses. Many a lawyer and convicted felon had been on the receiving end of that penetrating stare.

It was common knowledge that Judge Aldridge ran a tight courtroom. Lawyers had better show up in his courtroom on time, well prepared or not at all. He conveyed an air of quiet dignity, was strict but fair and had no tolerance for fools or foolishness. Judge Aldridge was also known to be somewhat of a non-conformist.

For a few moments, he studied the documents in front of him and the courtroom remained silent as a tomb. The only sound was a low, mechanical drone from the spinning fans. Finally, he looked up and scanned the handful of people poised in the room. He was a man of few words, but each utterance was spoken with careful purpose. He cleared his throat and spoke with a deep, resounding voice.

"Are all interested parties present?" He asked Stu, who responded, "Yes, Your Honor."

"Good. As you can see by the clock on the wall, when I set a time for a hearing, I strictly adhere to it and expect everyone else to do the same. Chalk up one point for each of you. Now, Mr. Mulholland, Mr. Chilton I want this hearing to conclude before noon. So, I expect you to keep things on track. Are you ready to proceed?"

Both stood and responded, "Yes, Your Honor."

"I have carefully studied all the documents and reviewed all the motions. What we have here, is a petition by Dr. Abraham Franke, represented by Mr. Mulholland, to adopt the four surviving minors, we all know who they are, of Mary Katherine O'Neill, deceased. There are documents showing the desire of the mother that this adoption is granted. We also have a counter petition brought by the Blair County Child Welfare Agency, represented by Mr. Chilton and Miss Corley, to block said adoption."

Judge Aldridge peered over his glasses and took aim at Murray and Edith. He cautioned, "The last wishes, will and testament of Mrs. O'Neill, as are everyone's, considered to be sacrosanct and irrevocable in my courtroom. In that light, Mr. Chilton and Miss Corley, you have embarked on an ambitious venture. The burden of proof will fall on your shoulders. You will have to present substantiated proof that Dr. Franke is not a fit candidate to adopt these four boys.

"That being said," he shifted his stare to Matt. "If I feel that there is any validity or credence to the Agency's objections, then you, Mr. Mulholland and Dr. Franke, will be required to refute and disprove the allegations to my satisfaction. The welfare of these boys is at stake. They are my only concern. I will not hesitate a second to deny this adoption if I am convinced that Dr. Franke would not be able to provide a proper home."

The judge leaned back in his chair and looked at those sitting in the gallery. "This is an extraordinary and unusual situation. And, as such, I am going to proceed in a somewhat unorthodox manner. In the spirit of expediency, all witnesses have already been sworn in. I want you to remember that. I do not want to have to remind you of that when you take the stand. You will all tell the truth, as you know it. This hearing will not be conducted as a trial. There will be no objections, except by me, no badgering of witnesses and I will not tolerate grandstanding. Counselors, it has been my experience that most lawyers like nothing more than to hear themselves talk. I firmly believe that as part of their schooling they have all been vaccinated with the needle of loquacity. But, not today and not in my courtroom. In my courtroom, more is exactly that ... more."

The comment brought a smile to everyone's face except Edith Corley. She was disgusted by the judge's cavalier attitude and lack of decorum.

"So, by twelve o'clock, these proceedings will be completed. After you have called all your witnesses, you will be allowed a brief summation and after that, I will render my decision. Mr. Chilton, call your first witness."

The lawyer stood, called Edith to the stand and began. "For the record, please give us your name."

"Edith Myrtle Corley."

"And what is your occupation?"

Judge Aldridge interrupted, "Dispense with all that, Counselor. We all know who she is and what her credentials are. Get to the meat of the matter."

"Miss Corley, would you tell us why you are challenging this adoption? What were the results of your investigation?"

"Based on my research and home visits, I feel that Dr. Franke does not represent an acceptable candidate for the adoption."

"Why is that? What brought you to that conclusion?" Chilton asked.

"Two factors. The first is his religious and cultural background. It varies greatly from that of the O'Neill children. They are of the Catholic faith and he is of the Jewish faith. The second and most compelling reason is that, as a single man, we don't feel that he could provide a healthy environment. It is most ideal to have a traditional home situation, with a married couple."

The judge intervened. "But, Miss Corley, the documents show that Dr. Franke has agreed to respect the wishes of the mother and has agreed to see to it that they continue to worship in their own faith. I have an affidavit from Father Davey that attests to that fact."

"As I said, that is not my only and certainly not my strongest objection. What concerns me most is the lifestyle of Dr. Franke. As a single man, we have great reservations about the climate in which these children will be raised. What type of behavior they would be exposed to."

Chilton questioned, "Can you be more specific?"

Edith shifted uncomfortably in her chair. "On one of my routine calls, I called on the home, without notice, as we are required to do. These spontaneous visits allow us to view the character of the home as it functions on an everyday basis, candid and unrehearsed.

"It was early one morning, approximately two weeks ago, that I found Dr. Franke and a female friend in a compromising situation."

The judge stopped his note taking and straightened in his chair.

"Could you please describe to us the compromising situation?" Chilton continued.

"Dr. Franke and a friend, Loretta Devereaux, were alone, before the children had gotten up, and were engaged in what was clearly an intimate scene. They were clad only in their pajamas."

"And what conclusion did you draw from that?"

"The only conclusion I could arrive at, that they had spent the night together, under the same roof as the children. It was inappropriate behavior and highly suggestive, especially for the eldest boy. It demonstrated extremely poor judgment and questionable moral behavior on the part of Dr. Franke."

Chilton returned to his seat and announced, "Those are all the questions I have, Your Honor."

"Mr. Mulholland, your witness," the judge said.

"Miss Corley, what religion are you?" Matt began.

"I was raised Lutheran and have been a member of Good Shepherd Church all my life."

"What do you know about Judaism?"

Edith was confused for a moment then responded. "Not much, I'm afraid. I know that *they* aren't Christian. That *they* don't believe in Jesus Christ." Her voice held a hint of contempt.

"Do you dislike Jews?"

"I have nothing against them."

"Do you dislike them because of their religious beliefs? Or do you just dislike them in general?"

"I told you. I have nothing against those people."

"*Those* people? Do you mean *those* Jews as a religion, or *those* Jews as a people?"

"It's the same thing. Those people, period."

The judge was paying close attention.

"Miss Corley, do you have a *personal* opinion of Dr. Franke?"

"I don't understand the question."

"Do you like him … dislike him? What do you think of him as a person? Is he nice? Is he friendly? Sincere? Argumentative? Ornery? Dishonest?"

"I haven't formed an opinion one way or the other about any of those things."

"In all the times you have seen him, talked to him, you've never decided if you like him or not?" Matt baited her.

"It is not relevant whether I like him or not. My job is to maintain objectivity. I deal with facts, not emotions. It is my sole responsibility to determine if I think he would make an exemplary parent based on those facts. Based on the facts discovered in my investigation, I determined that he would not."

"Okay. Let's move on to the morning that you found Dr. Franke and Mrs. Devereaux in what you call a 'compromising situation.' Were they fully clothed?"

"I already said that they were in their nightclothes, he in his pajamas and her in a nightgown."

"I mean, were they partially covered? Could you see parts of their anatomy that you can't see here, today?"

"I don't recall how covered they were."

"I'm thinking that if they had been indecently exposed, exposing private parts of their bodies, that certainly you would recall that."

"I only saw them briefly. I already told you, I can't remember specifically. Their clothing or lack of is only symbolic. It is what I drew from their intimate attire that revealed what's been going on in that house."

"Were they in the bedroom?"

"They were in the kitchen."

"Was the door unlatched?"

"I don't know … I mean … it might have been. Yes, I suppose it was."

"So, anyone could have arrived at anytime. It isn't likely that they were having a clandestine meeting. Anyone, including the boys, could have come in at anytime."

"That's my point. Those young boys could have walked in on them. It was indecent."

"Having a cup of coffee, in the kitchen, in robe and pajamas, is indecent? I guess most of us are pretty much indecent every morning."

The judge warned Matt.

"They were in their bedclothes. They seemed shocked and upset, almost guilty. God only knows what had been going on before I arrived."

"You're one hundred percent right. Only God knows … and them. Certainly, not you and not me."

"Let me see if I understand you. Your first concern is not that Dr. Franke is one of *those* people, meaning Jewish. Your main concern is that he is a single man of questionable moral character because he was seen in the company of a woman and both of them were in their pajamas. Is that correct?"

"That's what I am saying. Our guidelines are very specific. It is not a desirable environment. I stand by my recommendation."

"Thank you, Miss Corley. That will be all."

Mr. Chilton called his next witness. "Dr. Abraham Franke."

Lottie and Abraham looked at Matt confused. This wasn't right. Matt was supposed to call Abraham, not Chilton. What was going on?

"I object, Your Honor. Dr. Franke was to be my witness."

The judge shook his index finger at Matt. "Mr. Mulholland, sit down. You have forgotten my instructions. There will be no objections. I'll let him take the stand. What difference does it make who calls him? All I'm interested in is hearing what he has to say. Go on, Dr. Franke, take the stand."

Abraham was thrown off balance and slowly walked to the witness stand.

"Dr. Franke, do you agree with Miss Corley's testimony?"

"Only a portion of it and only to a point."

Chilton stopped pacing and asked, "Which portion?"

"The incident of two weeks ago when she arrived at the house and found Loretta and myself in the kitchen."

"Would you agree with her that you were indecently dressed to be in one another's company?"

"I was in my pajamas and Loretta was in a nightgown, yes. However, we both wore robes. I do not consider that indecent."

"Had Mrs. Devereaux spent the night with you?"

"Not with *me*. And not that night. When Katie had become very ill, Loretta and I would alternate sitting up with her. Sometimes Katie would require assistance during the night. We were there to provide that assistance. Loretta has not spent a night since."

"When Mrs. Devereaux took her turn spending the night, where were you?"

"I occupied the spare bedroom."

"Where is the spare bedroom located?"

"Adjacent to Katie's room."

Mr. Chilton paused to let Abraham's response hover in the air for a moment.

"You are Jewish, Dr. Franke. Is that correct?"

"I am."

"Do you practice your religion?"

"There is no synagogue in Eden Croft so I cannot go to temple. I pray and worship in private."

"So, you don't go to church regularly?"

"I take the boys to church every Sunday."

"But, you don't worship with them, isn't that right?"

"Yahweh, Abba or Father. What you call Him is not important. We all worship the same God."

"I assure you, Dr. Franke, that it is very important. Let's get back to Mrs. Devereaux."

Matt knew where Chilton was headed and he started to perspire profusely. His deodorant had suddenly stopped working.

"Is she over to the house frequently? How much time does she spend with the boys?"

"They see her daily. Most often in their own home, but she also invites them to her house. She has a television set and the O'Neill home does not. The boys have favorite programs that they enjoy watching."

"Do you think that Mrs. Devereaux sets a good example for them? Do you think she is an appropriate female figure for them to be around?"

"Loretta is a wonderful human being. The boys are very fond of her as she is of them. I can think of no one who would have a better influence on them."

"We'll see," Chilton murmured.

"Tell us, Dr. Franke, what makes you think that you can properly care for these boys? You have no experience raising children, isn't that correct?"

"I was a father once. I had a son of my own."

"How many years experience did you have raising him? Ten … fifteen … more … or less?"

"Daniel was almost six years old when I last saw him. Both he and his mother died, before his seventh birthday, in a concentration camp."

"My sympathies, Dr. Franke. But, who was primarily responsible for his care for those five years? I mean the day-to-day parenting. Who did most of it? You or the mother?"

"I had a full-time faculty position at university. As with most men, my days were spent earning a living and providing for my family. So, I suppose his mother did. But, not a day passed that …"

Murray cut him off and turned his back to him. "That will be all Dr. Franke."

Abraham's memory quickly recalled that night, many years before, when he had not put up a struggle. When he had been inert and passive. This time would be different. He would not remain silent. He would fight for those he loved. He made no effort to vacate the witness chair. Instead, his body tensed and his face was set in determination.

"That will not be all!" Abraham called out.

Chilton stopped and slowly pivoted. He looked at Judge Aldridge for a ruling. The judge remained silent.

"Ask me what is most important. Ask me what I know about *these* boys. Ask me anything about them and I will tell you." Abraham challenged everyone present.

"Brendan was born after eighteen hours of labor. He said his first word when he was ten months old. He has a scar on his left knee from falling off his bicycle when he was ten. He loves sailing and baseball. His batting average this year was four hundred and seventy-five and his earned run average was one point five. That he was willing to sacrifice playing baseball because he wanted to be home with his mother for her last few days on earth.

"Ask me about Tommy and I will tell you that he crawled at six months. That he brings home every wounded creature he finds so that he may nurse it back to health. That he has his father's eyes and his mother's gentle soul. That he likes the crusts cut off his sandwiches. How he cares for a little shamrock plant as if it were a rare orchid because it reminds him of his mother. He is the most sensitive and unselfish child I have ever known.

"And then there are the twins. Casey walked at nine months and has not slowed down since. He dislikes broccoli and peas and hides them in his napkin when he thinks no one is looking. That he will not go to sleep unless you read him two stories, cover to cover, and he knows immediately if you have skipped a page. He likes his sneakers tied in a double knot. That he manages to find more mischief than I ever thought possible. How his smile lights up a room.

"Colin lost his first tooth on May twentieth. Like his mother, his favorite color is blue. He has two freckles on his left earlobe and his hair is a bit curlier than Casey's. His favorite food is spaghetti and meatballs. That he is very ticklish on his right side. How contagious his laughter is. That when he grows up he wants to be exactly like his father, a father that he barely had a chance to know.

"You ask me why I think I should be allowed to adopt these boys? Because it was their mother's last wish. But, more importantly, it is because I have come to love each one of them as if they were my own flesh and blood. I cannot imagine my life without them. I lost one family to injustice. If it takes every ounce of strength I possess, I refuse to lose another!"

The courtroom was deathly silent. Only the monotonous whir of the fans and the steady pitter-pat of Elaine's fingers flying over the keys of her recorder broke the silence. It was as if everyone, collectively, stopped breathing. It seemed that even the walls of the room had inspired and held their breath.

There was nothing more to say, so Matt stood and declared, "I don't have any questions for Dr. Franke."

Judge Aldridge dismissed Abraham from the stand and asked Mr. Chilton if he had any more witnesses. Chilton responded, "Just one. Mrs. Devereaux."

After Chilton had jumped the gun and called Abraham, Matt expected him to do the same with Lottie. He was prepared for it. His only hope was that Chilton hadn't dug too deeply. If Lottie were portrayed in the wrong light, it would have a huge impact on the judge's decision.

Lottie gave Abraham one healthy squeeze of her hand and walked to the witness stand.

"Mrs. Devereaux, how old are you?"

Lottie smiled like a Cheshire cat. "Why, Mr. Chilton, back where I come from, a gentleman never asks that of a lady."

"Nevertheless, please answer my question."

Judge Aldridge cleared his throat. "I agree with the witness, Mr. Chilton. Elaine and Nancy let the record show that Mrs. Devereaux is of legal age."

Matt was almost disappointed by the ruling. For once, he hoped that a ruling would go against him. He had always wanted to know just how old Lottie was.

"How much time do you spend at the O'Neill home, Mrs. Devereaux?"

"A fair amount, ya could say. Katie was ma best friend."

"And since Mrs. O'Neill's death?"

"I'm there quite a bit. I miss Katie an' enjoy bein' 'round her boys."

"The morning in question, when Miss Corley arrived at the house, what were you wearing?"

"It sure weren't no pajamas. I never wear pajamas. It was a lovely, blush-rose, silk peignoir set with marabou trim ..."

"This isn't a fashion show, Mrs. Devereaux. We don't need the color and fabric content. Is it safe to say that you were in your bedclothes?"

"That would be safe ta say."

"Had you spent the night at the O'Neill's?"

"No."

"Were you engaged in any illicit activity?"

"We were havin' a cup a coffee. That ain't too illicit where I come from."

Mr. Chilton changed his tactics. "Mrs. Devereaux, you are a widow. When were you married?"

"Which time?"

"From your rather active past, I see what you mean. Okay ... let's start with the first time. When and where did you marry for the first time?"

"I wuz married in Mississippi ... let's jus' say it was a ways back."

"What happened to your husband? I'm sorry ... what happened to your *first* husband?"

"He was killed."

"In the war?"

"Nope. Knifed in tha back."

"Do you know by whom or why?"

"Never did find out *whom*. Tha authorities figured it had somethin' ta do with his business activities."

"And what kind of ... er ... business was that?"

"Don't know. He never discussed his business affairs with me, an' I never asked."

"Would it surprise you to know that he was involved in the production and distribution of illegal substances, participated in illegal games of chance and the movement of stolen goods?"

"Y'all mean bootleggin', gamblin' an' fencin'?"

"Colorfully put, but accurate. Yes, that's what I mean."

"Like I tol' ya, we didn't discuss his business. But, I wouldn't be surprised none. Billy Bob mos' likely coulda been involved in any a that an' probably worse."

"I'm afraid we'll be here all day if I question you in depth on each one of your husbands. For the sake of expediency, Mrs. Devereaux, my research shows me that you were married four times."

"Well, yawr research is wrong."

Matt squirmed in his chair. He knew how many times Lottie had been married. All the marriages were legal, properly recorded and a matter of public record in four states. This was not the time or the place for her to try and slip one past the judge. If Lottie was trying to hide one of those husbands, Matt vowed he would wring her neck and send her to the hereafter to join all four of them.

"How is that? I have documents to show that I am correct. Remember you are under oath. You may want to revise your answer."

Jadyne jumped out of her seat like a wasp had stung her on the derriere.

"Don't you call Miss Lottie a liar!" she barked at Chilton. "And you, you just sit up there on your throne and let her do it!" Jadyne pointed her finger at Judge Aldridge. Her bosom heaved up and down as her dark eyes shot bullets at the judge. "Well, I'm going to do something about it. We may lose these children, but we're not going down without a fight. I sat here and held my tongue while that prune-faced old biddy said all kinds of untrue and dirty things about Dr. Franke and Miss Lottie. Then I had to listen to this high-priced lawyer in a cheap suit sling mud at Dr. Franke's good name. Well, I'll be darned of I'm going to sit here a minute longer like a bump on a log while he calls Miss Lottie a liar! Miss Lottie may be a lot of things, but a liar isn't one of them!"

Every shocked head in the courtroom snapped to attention and turned toward Jadyne.

Lottie's face immediately transformed into a smirk. "Why, Jadyne, I had no idea how ya felt 'bout me."

Embarrassed by her spontaneous revelation, Jadyne's face became hot as an oven.

Judge Aldridge banged his gavel and demanded order. "What is your name, Madame?"

"I'm Jadyne Potter, your Honor."

"Ah, the infamous Miss Jade. It isn't that this poignant moment hasn't touched me, but we will precede without a single, further, verbal interruption. Mrs. Potter, if I hear one more word out of you, if you inhale suspiciously, if you even *look* like you might open your mouth, I'll have the bailiff eject you from these proceedings. You and Mrs. Devereaux may resume your heartwarming exchange after this hearing and outside my courtroom. Madame, please reclaim your seat!"

Jadyne resettled her bottom on the bench only slightly unnerved.

"Mr. Chilton, continue where we left off."

"I meant no disrespect, Mrs. Devereaux." Chilton threw a warning look at Jadyne. "I believe we were discussing the discrepancy between your testimony and my findings. As I was saying, I have documents that are undeniable proof and show that you have been married four times."

"I don't give a flyin' fig what yawr documents say. Yawr wrong, Mr. Chilton. Actually, I been married five times."

Lottie winked conspiratorially at the judge. Judge Aldridge had been totally engrossed with her testimony. He couldn't recall the last time he had heard such entertaining testimony from a more interesting witness.

Matt moaned in his seat and tried to hide behind a strategically placed hand. He knew Lottie and Abraham were up to something. What that something was scared him to death. And now, Lottie was actually flirting with the judge.

"*Five* times. I concede to you, Mrs. Devereaux. I guess my research *was* wrong. One of them must have slipped through the cracks. What happened to your other husbands?"

"They passed on, God bless 'em."

"So, let me check my arithmetic. You married and buried *five* husbands. Seems to me it could be dangerous to one's health exchanging wedding vows with you."

"I didn't say I buried five of 'em. I only buried fawr."

"Well, where are you hiding the fifth one?" Chilton asked smugly.

"Ain't hidin' him nowhere. He's sittin' right there."

With that statement, Lottie pointed directly at Abraham. Edith Corley, Dr. Hughes, Father Davey, Judge Aldridge and Matt almost fell out of their seats. Elaine's fingers suddenly went numb and froze mid-strike. Nancy became all thumbs as a sheaf of documents slipped from her fingers and fluttered to the floor. Stu was so stunned that he inhaled when he should have exhaled, aspirated some saliva and started a choking-chain-reaction. He coughed so hard he broke wind and there was no mistaking the source. Murray Chilton almost impaled himself with the pencil he had been toying with. Edith nearly swallowed her uvula.

It took Murray a full minute to regain his composure, Elaine to relocate her keys, Nancy to retrieve her paperwork and Stu to recover his dignity.

"When did these nuptials take place?" Mr. Chilton made a feeble attempt to smear the question with doubt.

"We jus' celebrated our one month anniversary."

Lottie's answer grabbed Matt's attention. He started to count off the days and weeks on his fingers. Judge Aldridge did the same.

Matt stood up, convinced that his mathematical calculations were correct.

"Judge, may I approach the bench?"

The judge responded, "I guess you and Mr. Chilton *both* better come on up here."

Judge Aldridge directed Elaine that they were off the record and peered over his spectacles at Matt. "Mr. Mulholland, were you aware of this latest development?"

Before Matt could answer, Murray addressed the judge in hushed tones. "Your Honor, this whole situation is a travesty. It is obvious that Mr. Mulholland had full knowledge of the situation and intentionally withheld it from the appropriate authorities, including omitting it from the legal documents submitted to this court."

"It may be obvious to you, Mr. Chilton, but I'm afraid my visual acumen is a bit cloudy. Let Mr. Mulholland answer the question. Did you have any prior knowledge of this?"

Matt pled his case. "You have my word of honor, as an officer of the court, that I am as shocked as you are. I had no prior knowledge of this."

The judge leaned back in his chair. I tend to believe you."

It wasn't often that a litigator found himself the recipient of Judge Aldridge's favor. Matt decided to take full advantage of the situation, quickly, before the opportunity passed.

"If your Honor will indulge me? It seems to me that the main objection to this adoption no longer exists. Miss Corley, herself, said that her main concern was the lifestyle and questionable moral fiber of Dr. Franke. This marriage changes everything. Number One. Dr. Franke and Mrs. Devereaux were husband and wife when this alleged immoral incident occurred. Number Two. All are in agreement that the Jewish question is a non-issue. And Number Three. This marriage insures that the home environment is a traditional one, with a male and female parent."

"Just a minute, Mr. Mulholland," Judge Aldridge spoke. "I have a couple of questions that I'd like to ask of the witness, myself."

He turned his attention to Lottie who was sitting in the witness chair proud and unruffled as a peacock. "Mrs. Devereaux?"

"Actually, now that the cat's outta tha bag, y'all kin call me Mrs. Franke."

"Mrs. Franke, did you enter into this marriage with the intent of under-mining the authority of this court? If you give me any reason to think that this marriage took place in an effort to trick me, I'll deny this adoption so fast it will make your head spin."

"Am I still under oath?"

"Yes, you are."

"That's good, 'cuz I sure wouldn't want anyone ta think I wuz lyin'. Abraham an' I got hitched 'cuz tha pure, honest-ta-goodness truth is that we love each other. An' we love those boys. It's as simple as that."

"Then why did you keep this marriage a secret?"

"We figured those yunguns got 'nough new vittles on their plates ta swal-low. We kinda thought that once things got settled down, when they wuz over tha heartbreak of losin' their momma an' this adoption business got over, then we'd break it ta 'em … gentle like."

Judge Aldridge slipped off his eyeglasses and leaned back in his chair, strain-ing the leather. He tapped an index finger against the side of his nose. More than half of his entire legal career had been spent in a judiciary capacity and he had never taken for granted the trust and responsibility that had been placed with him. He had taken an oath as a lawyer and had sworn an oath when he assumed office. He had never betrayed those pledges.

Judge Aldridge wondered if he was getting too old to play God. It was an interesting case, though. He thought about the discussion he had with the O'Neill boys about Blind Justice. In reality, justice was never blind. The faces of those four boys were vivid in his mind. He thought of his own children and grandchildren. What would he want for them? He thought of Beatrice, his wife of thirty-six years. What would she do? He contemplated retiring to his cham-bers then thought better of it. He replaced his spectacles on his nose, leaned forward and addressed the small gathering.

"Mr. Chilton, Mr. Mulholland, please be seated. Elaine, put us back on the record." He paused. "The grand lady of the law, 'Blind Justice', stands as con-stant affirmation that the law must be impartial. It must be fair. It must be righteous. One thing it does not need to be is infallible. Those of us who deal with the interpretation and execution of law know all too well, that it isn't always perfect, it isn't always infallible, because things are not always black and white.

"Miss Corley told us today, that we have to deal in facts, that we must remain objective and rational, that we can't be swayed by feelings and emotions. Unfortunately, we are also dealing with human beings, who by nature are often governed by feelings, emotions and sentiments and are anything but rational. That is our nature. Those imperfections and inconsistencies are what make us individuals and give us character. They define who we are.

"But, for the sake of the hearing, today, I must deal in facts, not emotions."

Matt felt a claw clutch his stomach. He was afraid of the next sentence. If it was possible to turn back the clock, he wanted to do it desperately, now. Reverse the morning; go back so he could do it all differently. Undo the mistakes.

Abraham, Lottie and Jadyne sensed that the worst was coming. Dr. Hughes nervously tapped his foot on the floor and Father Davey recited a silent prayer.

"The County's objections are overruled. I hereby grant the adoption of the four O'Neill children by Dr. Abraham Franke." Judge Aldridge banged his gavel.

Suddenly, the climate of the courtroom was exhilarated and crackled with elation. Jadyne hugged Dr. Hughes, Father Davey, Abraham, even Lottie. It took Matt's brain a few seconds to process the words; discern what he actually heard from what he expected to hear. And as soon as it registered, Matt made a fist and punched the air, signaling victory.

Miss Corley stood and shouted, "You can't do that! He's a Jew!"

Judge Aldridge ordered, "That will be enough, Miss Corley! Another word from you and I will cite you for contempt. Now, sit down! I've not finished speaking."

She sat down, her fists clenched in fury, but she remained silent.

"Dr. Franke. This is my courtroom and I am ultimately responsible for what transpires here. My sincerest apologies to you for that outburst and any distress the remark may have caused you. I can assure you that Miss Corley's views are not shared by nor should they be construed to reflect the views of this court.

"You wanted facts, well, here are the facts. I will file an official report to the County Child Welfare Agency strongly urging that Miss Corley be severely reprimanded for manipulating her authority for personal reasons. You, Miss Corley have been entrusted with the welfare of this state's most precious natural resources, its children. In my opinion, in this case, you have abused that trust. You should follow your own advice and not let personal biases and prejudices influence your decisions. As far as the future goes, I can only hope that you have learned a lesson in humanity.

"Mr. Chilton, you have carelessly wasted the court's time and the time of these good people with a frivolous, irresponsible petition. I will see to it that your superiors also receive a scathing report to that effect. Next time you come into my courtroom, you had better have your facts in order.

"I can't think of two people who would make better parents for those boys than Dr. and Mrs. Abraham Franke. I will see to it that all the necessary name changes appear on the documents. I will sign the final papers in my chambers, effective immediately. Mr. Mulholland, you may pick them up there later this week."

Abraham stood and asked, "Your Honor, if I may, I wish to make one last request?"

Judge Aldridge nodded for him to go ahead.

"May I ask that the boys be allowed to keep their last name? I ... we ... that is ... Loretta and I would like them to keep the name O'Neill."

"Request granted. Nancy, please make the necessary notation in the documents. Court is adjourned." He banged his gavel, gathered his papers and everyone stood, he exited to his chambers, black robes flowing behind him.

Mr. Chilton and Miss Corley straightened their paperwork and jammed it into their briefcases. As both turned and exited through the railing like a pair of whipped dogs, Lottie approached them.

In a low, conspiratorial voice she said, "Edith ... I know a very talented beauty operator who could do wonders fawr y'all. That hairdo ya got goin' there ain't at all becomin'."

chapter forty-nine

Soft, fluffy fluorettes of white cumulous clouds hung high on the horizon. The blue of the sky matched the blue of the lake. Were it not for the land jutting upward on the opposite shore, it would be difficult to know where water ended and sky began. Hanging baskets held late summer hangeroners of petunias, marigolds, alyssum and nasturtiums.

Autumn was not about to be bested by the color of the summer blooms and as any formidable foe, the new season rose to the challenge to produce a dramatic display of its own.

As the sun's arc steadily lowered to the southern skies, the subtle hints of color changes in the leaves of the sugar maples, oaks, elms and aspens heralded that autumn had arrived. The burning bushes were beginning to blush and hinted at the bright crimson that would soon follow. The berries on the mountain ash were already burnt orange, like clusters of tiny pumpkins. Among the fall bloomers were deep, vibrant asters and chrysanthemums, purple cone flowers and black-eyed-Susans, pastel gladiolas and yarrow and snow white clematis. Lush, succulent sedums had turned from pea green to warm cinnamon and the sumacs and bittersweet were heavy with trios of gold, tangerine and russet fruits.

But, nature had called a truce and summer was allowed to make one last, valiant effort to rally the troops. Though the nights had taken on cooler temperatures and the scents of autumn were unmistakable, that Saturday the sun was high and warm in the sky. A stiff, warm wind blew off the lake and Jadyne took full advantage of it to air-dry linens, comforters and quilts. There was nothing as soothing as falling to sleep enveloped in the clean fragrance of bedding fresh from the outdoors. She hoped to capture some of the freshness that would have to carry them through the closed-in months of winter.

School had resumed for the year, but that glorious Saturday, everyone was drawn to the lake. Tommy, Casey and Colin were busy as carpenter ants on the beach, building a sand castle that in effort and diligence would rival the engineering feats of the great pyramids of Egypt. Their creation could have been declared the eighth wonder of the world if they were ever allowed to complete the construction. Chance was wreaking as much havoc, as Lottie would say, "As

Sherman's march through Georgia." Almost as quickly as the boys completed a new section, Chance had razed and flattened an old one. The more they shooed him away, the more persistent he became. It was a new kind of game and one that he was enjoying immensely.

Another game of sorts was being played out in the kitchen. No seasonal truce had been called there. Lottie and Jadyne were locked in mortal combat and having their usual go-around. Like addicts, unable to resist temptation, it was their daily ritual, habitual and as predictable as the sun rising and setting. No issues were ever settled; there was never a winner or a loser. Lottie relished her role as antagonist and Jadyne felt it was her God-given duty to keep Lottie in line. Abraham had long since given up trying to fill the role of peacemaker. He only succeeded in getting himself caught in the middle and he considered that a very dangerous position to be in. He soon realized that being a silent observer was the wiser course.

"Would you please remove yourself from this kitchen? I'm not getting a thing done with you hounding my every move. If you want to have dinner some-time this decade, I have exactly fifteen minutes to get this roast in the oven."

Lottie sat on the countertop admiring her latest pedicure through the open toes of her shoes.

"Would ya call this color apricot or tangerine? Eleanor calls it deep apricot, but I think it's more of a tangerine. What'd ya think, Jadyne?"

Her only response was a gruff harrumph.

"It's a simple 'nough question. It's not like I'm askin' ya yawr opinion on how ta achieve world peace."

"Orange. It looks like plain orange to me. Are you happy now? Orange, apricot, tangerine, peach, coral or salmon. It's all the same to me."

Lottie slid down from the counter and sat at the table to secure a better vantage point. I'm glad I never learned ta cook, I tell ya what. Seems ta me it jus' makes a person cranky. It sure puts y'all in a nasty mood."

As she arranged the carrots and potatoes around the meat in the roaster, Jadyne snapped, "It isn't the cooking that does that. It's having a pest like you under foot, getting in the way and bothering me with the most foolish ques-tions. Go read one of your trashy movie star magazines."

"Are ya always so serious, Jadyne? Don't ya ever wanna jus' cut loose? Like doin' somethin' wild an' crazy? Somethin' ya ain't never done before?"

"Doing something wild and crazy with you would probably land me in the hoosegow."

"What we need ta do is somethin' fun ... somethin' crazy ... jus' fawr tha hell of it."

"It frightens me to the core thinking about what you would involve me in and call it fun. And who would see to running this house while I was out having fun with you?"

Lottie kept babbling as if Jadyne hadn't said a word. "I know. Let's spend tha day at tha Color, Cut 'n Curl. We'll have tha full treatment. Manicures, pedicures, facials, shampoos an' sets. Tha whole works. It'll be ma treat."

Jadyne laughed and shook her head. "Now that would be doing something crazy, all right. Miss Lottie, just try to imagine the look on everyone's faces when this Negro lady walks into a white folk's beauty parlor and asks to have her toenails painted by a white woman. They'd have the Klan up here before the polish was dry."

"Folks up North here, they ain't like that, Jadyne. If y'all are good 'nough ta watch after those fawr boys, fix our meals, take care a us an' this house, yawr sure as heck good 'nough ta go ta ma beauty parlor."

"You are about the craziest of God's creatures to walk upright that I have ever crossed paths with. You are certifiable, you know that? Well, I'm not. And I'm not wasting another breath arguing this nonsense with you." Jadyne took a loaf of banana bread out of the oven and slid the roaster in. "And another trip to the beauty parlor is the last place you need to go. I hate to think what other part of your body you'd manage to bring home tinted or dyed."

"Ya know, Jadyne. I think I might jus' try stickin' ta ma own hair color fawr a while." She fluffed her brown locks. "With tha yunguns an' all, maybe it's time I tried settlin' down a bit. What da y'all think?"

Jadyne sliced the warm loaf of bread. "I think it's high time. This house could stand a little less excitement. You could certainly settle down a *lot* and still have plenty of room left over for improvement. But, I'm not holding my breath. Besides, your natural color isn't exactly unattractive. I've never found a way yet to improve upon nature." Jadyne treaded carefully. That was as close as she wanted to come to paying Lottie a compliment. She'd rather eat dirt.

Lotie smiled coyly. "Why, Jadyne, do I detect tha hint of approval hidin' in there somewhere? Ya wouldn't be flatterin' me would ya?"

Jadyne guffawed and waved her off. "Don't go getting any of your fancy ideas. It wasn't meant to be a compliment. It was simply a statement of fact. Now, let me get on with my chores ... and make yourself useful. Take this plate of banana bread out to Dr. Franke and Mr. Matt. And you could start settling *down* by buttoning *up* that blouse one more notch. Didn't they teach you modesty where you grew up? It's shameful for you to be around those boys with your bosoms half hanging out."

"I jus' noticed somethin' 'bout ya, Jadyne. Y'all could talk tha teeth off'n a saw when y'all are hopped up 'bout somethin.' You'd make a helluva politician ... or a lousy librarian."

Lottie chuckled and grabbed the plate of banana bread off the table. Before she went out the door, she did as she was told and fastened the top two buttons of her blouse.

Matt and Abraham were sitting in the gazebo sipping dickleberries, coffee laced with stiff shots of Irish whiskey. They were discussing the coup that Abraham and Lottie had pulled off at the court hearing.

"Murray Chilton forgot what every law student learns in Witness Examination 101. Never ask a question you don't already know the answer to. But, I still haven't figured out why you didn't tell me about the marriage," Matt said.

"If we had told you, it would have put you in a very compromised position. You would have been torn between your duty to give that information to the authorities, or to lie and keep our secret. It would have posed a difficult and ambiguous moral dilemma for you. We did not want to place that burden on you.

"By not telling you, you could honestly state that you knew nothing of it. We were not sure if the marriage would help or hinder our case. If things were progressing favorably, we would have kept it a secret until we felt the boys could handle it, just as Loretta testified. However, if it appeared that things were going against us, Loretta thought it might serve as our 'ace in tha hole.' As she called it, it was a 'crap shoot.'"

Matt took a sip of his drink. "I'm seeing quite the devious side of you, Abraham. So, you and Lottie cooked the whole thing up."

"We had thought about discussing our plans with Katie, but by the time the idea came to us, she was already so ill. We decided it would best not to burden her with it. So, we told Jadyne. That was necessary, as we needed her to stay with the boys while we went to Grand Rapids. If we had applied for the marriage license in Blair County, it would have become part of the record, here. By going to Kent County, we were convinced that we had a better chance of keeping it hidden. So, we were married there. We had intended to marry anyway, we simply decided to do it sooner than expected."

Matt sighed deeply, the wounds of losing Katie still fresh. As if he could read Matt's mind, Abraham asked, "How are you doing, Matthew?"

The irony of the question caused a small groan to escape from his throat. "Me? Oh hell, I'm doing just great. I wake up in the morning and have to remind myself to shower and shave, to eat and drink, to go to work and come home at night. I have to remind myself to breathe in and out every few seconds. The only thing I don't have to remind myself of is that Katie is gone and it hurts like hell. Yeah. I guess you could say I'm doing goddamn wonderful."

Abraham knew all too well the kind of pain and bitterness Matthew was experiencing. He knew first hand that it could tear you apart.

"I don't know how you do it, Abraham? How you manage without her? I don't know if I'm more angry or hurt that she had to suffer. That she had to die."

Abraham didn't respond immediately. He thought about it for a moment and contemplated what Matthew seemed to need from him. Finally, he answered. "I am neither hurt nor angered. To be so, would somehow diminish and nullify the deep faith and trust, the courage Katie possessed. Throughout the long weeks of her pain and suffering, I never once saw her conviction or faith lessen or her courage falter. Seeing that, in her, how could I ask anything less of myself?

"Her faith was so strong that it overflowed onto those around her. Since the first day I met her, she besieged every barrier I erected. Not in the overt way that a marauding army forces its will on the conquered. Katie did it by example. In her quiet, subtle manner, by living it, she *made* you believe in yourself and in the power of faith and the acceptance of God's plan. She showed me that armed with that immovable trust, anything is possible."

Matt wasn't convinced. "That's all well and good, but I guess I'm more selfish than you are. She wasn't supposed to die. What does God need her for? I want her here. I need her here."

"Ah. The privilege of youth. You expect that life owes you everything, immediately and on your terms. Life is not like that. You cannot pick and choose. You must learn to accept it all, part and parcel, the bad with the good, the challenges as well as the rewards. Katie earned her reward. Do not wish to steal that from her.

"Instead, find joy in the time you had with her. Appreciate how fortunate you were to have known her. Try to imagine what your life would have been like without her in it, however, brief that time was. She was like a flame, a flickering light in the dark, her spirit bright and luminous showing the way. Think how miraculously she touched the lives of those who knew her. By her goodness, she made all of us strive to be better human beings."

Boyish laughter drifted from the excavation site on the beach and drew Matt and Abraham's attention to the comical scene. Since the O'Neill's had found their way to Eden Croft, Matt had come to see it as a familiar, lakeside portrait. For Abraham, it brought to mind another portrait, a painting done years before of an endearing little girl feeding a gathering of ducklings on a distant shore, thousands of miles away. It was a recollection from another time, in another world.

Abraham realized that fate was a strange and wonderful thing. It suddenly struck Abraham that the foundation for his adventure with Katie, as incomprehensible as it was, had began more than three decades ago, long before he had known her. When Katherine, inspired by the love for her godchild, captured that love and transported it through time and immortalized it on canvas. From the first moment Abraham had seen the painting he had fallen instantly in love with the tiny, barefooted creature in the blue dress. And Katie and Abraham's adventure, with destiny's momentum, would continue on throughout the boys' lives.

Matt's observation of the boys had a decidedly different effect on him. Their existence only served to remind him of Katie. As he watched the boys, his sense of loss sharpened and his heart longed with renewed melancholy.

"Okay. Forget about me. What about the boys? They need her. How long will they remember her before time snuffs out that flame?"

Abraham spoke with conviction. "Do not worry about those boys. They have you, and Jadyne and Loretta and myself. Katie made certain that they would be well taken care of. More importantly, do not forget that they have each other to help them through the difficult times.

"Brendan, Tommy, Casey and Colin are the most fortunate of all. They are Katie's sons. They have her blood running through their veins and they have her genetic imprint permanently embedded in every cell. They have inherited the best of her. They are the true beneficiaries of all that she was, decent and strong and wonderful. Rest assured, they will remember her. Time cannot erase what is engraved in the soul. Do not worry about those boys, Matthew. They are going to be fine. And you will learn from them that letting go is not final. It gives birth to a new beginning."

Matt squeezed his eyes shut and tried to visualize the past year, desperate to cling to the memories. He wasn't sure he was ready to face a future without Katie.

"You know, Abraham, I can't even remember the last thing I said to her. Did I tell her how much I loved her? What she meant to me? Were my words comforting and reassuring or were they senseless and stupid? For the rest of my life it's going to drive me crazy that I can't remember."

Abraham smiled. "You may not recall what you said, however, I have no doubt that you can remember verbatim the last words she spoke to you."

Matt realized that Abraham was right. He could recall every word. And not only the words, but also the tone of her voice, the expression on her face, every inflection and syllable. *Promise me one thing, Matt. Don't let my passing cause you to miss out on life's generosity. I have always admired and envied your carefree approach to life. It is what I love most about you. Your ability to laugh so easily and enjoy every moment to the fullest, without thought to consequence. You never hold back. Those are rare and wonderful gifts. Don't lose them. I care too much for you and it saddens my heart to think that I was responsible for your unhappiness. Don't mourn me too long. Get on with your life.*

The memory of her words, her voice, her beautiful smile that could brighten the cloudiest day, the emerald greens eyes that sparked with mischief were almost too painful to bear. How long would it be before those beautiful memories would bring joy to his heart instead of anguish?

"Abraham, I miss her so badly it hurts. I wake up each morning, thinking that today will be better. But I end up going to bed each night with the same dull ache in my chest, just as strong as the day before. Does it ever go away?"

Abraham looked at the flowers overflowing from the pots that he had planted for Katie. "It does not go away, but in time it changes. It reshapes itself; it evolves into something else. It becomes almost dream-like, where your spirit, your soul can still see them, hear them, touch them, sense their presence, recall the joy they brought to your life. You are able to see them in all that surrounds you. For a while, in that dream, they become real, tangible and alive again.

"I see Katie in the gazebo, in the gardens, in the greenhouse. I hear the lilt of her laughter in the wind. I can smell the scent of lilacs that followed her everywhere. I can feel the gentle touch of her hand on mine. Her chestnut curls, braided loosely or flying free. I see her footprints in the earth, everywhere she walked; her handprint on everything she touched. I see her every time I look at one of the boys. She lives on through them."

Lottie made a timely entrance carrying the plate of bread. "Brought y'all some banana nut bread, still warm from tha oven."

Matt looked at her dubiously.

"Don't worry. I didn't make it. Jadyne did. You'd think I'd a poisoned ya er somethin'."

"You almost did. As it is, I have since developed a strong aversion to corn bread. It makes me gag just to think about it," Matt said.

"In spite of yawr insults, y'all wanna stay fawr supper? Jadyne's makin' a pot roast an' blueberry pie fawr dessert."

"Since Jadyne is doing the cooking, I'd love to."

"Oh, speakin' a pots, Abraham. Yawr gonna hafta call a plumber. One a tha twins flushed somethin' down tha upstairs toilet, again. It's plugged up tighter'n Big Bertha's bloomers."

Abraham laughed. "They do have an irresistible preoccupation with the functioning of a commode."

Matt asked, "Are the new owners all moved into your house, Lottie?"

"I reckon they'll be all settled in by next month. I'm sure gonna miss ma eight-piece sectional sofa livin' room suite."

"And I would have thought you'd be more broken up about leaving your precious television set behind," Matt teased.

"Don't ya worry none 'bout that. I got it squirreled away in tha garage. As soon as tha coast is clear an' Jadyne leaves ta visit her boy, you an' Abraham are gonna move it inta tha house," Lottie crowed.

"Then I'm going to be here bright and early Jadyne's first morning back to witness her reaction. Abraham, would you care to wager a small bet how long the television remains in this house?"

"I think not, Matthew. Whichever way I placed my wager, I would still come the loser. If Jadyne prevailed, I would be sleeping out here in the gazebo and if Lottie prevailed, I would be eating my meals at Hasting's lunch counter."

Just then, Tommy jumped up from the sand and hollered, "Look! It's Brendan!"

Matt, Lottie and Abraham joined the boys on the beach. Sure enough, it was Brendan, skimming along the water's surface in his sailboat. He turned the tiller and allowed the boat to sail closer to shore. He waved to them with a smile as wide and bright as the afternoon sun.

Matt cupped his hands and shouted, "Ahoy, Captain O'Neill! She's a beauty of a boat!"

They all watched as he changed tack and the boat's course carried him away from them. Matt could tell that there was a name painted on the stern, but at that distance it was unreadable. He asked Abraham what name Brendan had decided on.

Abraham, with his eyes fixed on the small craft and the young man sailing her, replied, "He named her *Danny Boy.*"

Printed in the United States
220169BV00001B/52/P